Robert Phillimore

Commentaries upon International Law

Vol. IV

Robert Phillimore

Commentaries upon International Law
Vol. IV

Reprint of the original, first published in 1861.

1st Edition 2022 | ISBN: 978-3-37505-517-2

Verlag (Publisher): Salzwasser Verlag GmbH, Zeilweg 44, 60439 Frankfurt, Deutschland
Vertretungsberechtigt (Authorized to represent): E. Roepke, Zeilweg 44, 60439 Frankfurt, Deutschland
Druck (Print): Books on Demand GmbH, In de Tarpen 42, 22848 Norderstedt, Deutschland

COMMENTARIES

UPON

INTERNATIONAL LAW,

PRIVATE INTERNATIONAL LAW

OR

COMITY.

BY

ROBERT PHILLIMORE, D.C.L., Q.C.,

ADVOCATE TO HER MAJESTY IN HER OFFICE OF ADMIRALTY,
JUDGE OF THE CINQUE PORTS.

"Plaisante justice qu'une rivière ou une montagne borne."
PASCAL. *Pensées*, part i., art. vi., s. 8.

VOL. IV.

LONDON:

WILLIAM BENNING & SON, 5, GREAT QUEEN STREET,
LINCOLN'S INN FIELDS.

1861.

PREFACE.

I. I HAVE endeavoured in the publication of this last volume of my Commentaries upon International Law, fully to redeem the pledge given in the first chapter of the first volume. (a)

Professional avocations have interrupted and delayed till now the complete execution of my original design.

The former volumes, in accordance with the plan of that design, treated of the relations, and the laws which govern the relations, between independent States, or, in other words, they were occupied with the consideration of *Jus inter Gentes,* or *Public International Law.*

This volume is devoted to the consideration of *Jus Gentium—Private International Law,* or *Comity:* that is, strictly speaking, the law which ought to govern the legal relations of individuals not being the subjects of the State which administers the law. Practically speaking, however, it embraces also the legal relations of persons domiciled, or, in some cases, only resident abroad ; and rights acquired abroad, or existing in objects situate abroad.

This subject has been treated of, till lately, under the title of the *Conflict of Laws*,—a title which I think has been justly censured as expressive of a limited and unsound view of this important portion of jurisprudence; but under which title so able a treatise has been written by Story, substantially, upon Private International Law, as, perhaps, to render some apology necessary on the part of any subsequent writer who publishes a treatise on the subject, even on the assumption that he adopts a sounder theory and a more correct title.

My apology, if one be needed, is, that the treatment of this subject was necessary to the completion of the plan upon which my Commentaries upon International Law were written.

II. The end of all justice, wheresoever administered, is correctly stated by the Roman lawyers, *suum cuique tribuere*—to give to each person, his own, his due, his right, his *jus*,—be he subject or foreigner.

The enquiry, What is the *jus* of an individual, shows that it must be attached to one of these predicaments : 1. to a Person; 2. to tangible or corporeal Property (*rei*); 3. to incorporeal Rights.

The *nature* of the predicament must be examined into as a *fact* before a *sentence* of what is just can be passed respecting it.

As the fact of relation is ascertained with greater accuracy, as the nature of it is considered with deeper wisdom, the juster will be the sentence pronounced upon it. The more cultivated the mind of the individual, the more accurate will be his judgements as to what is just; the more cultivated the mind of a people, the deeper will be their insight into the true nature of legal(*a*) relations, and the better will be their general definitions of what is just, or, in other words, their laws.

The variety of definitions of what is just, or the variety of laws which prevail in different States, arises in great measure from the different degrees of this culture in different States.

The general opinion of what is just, strengthened by custom and positive enactments, becomes the *jus civile* of a State.

But when many States agree, as all civilized States do, in their opinions of what is just with reference to many legal relations, the *jus civile* becomes to a great extent identical with a *jus gentium.* (*b*)

Thus, the Roman Law recognized two classes of *obligations;* those *juris civilis,* and those *juris gentium,*—and under the latter head ranked almost all *contracts.* (*c*)

These permanent and invariable relations, laid in the necessities and nature of man, may be modified, but cannot be annihilated, by positive law, when the intercourse of the subjects of different States brings these relations at different periods of time within the

---

(*a*) Perhaps *jural* would have been a better word. I have been deterred from using it by a dislike to introduce a new word without the sanction of any accredited English authority.

(*b*) *Vide post,* p. 421.

(*c*) " Ex hoc jure gentium omnes pæne contractus introducti sunt, ut emtio, venditio, locatio, conductio . . . . . et alii innumerabiles." *Inst.* l. i. t. ii. s. 2. *Vide post,* p. 422.

" Sed hæc quidem verborum obligatio dari spondes ? spondes pro_ pria civium Romanorum sunt, *ceteræ vero juris gentium sunt, itæque in-*

scope of different jurisdictions. A harmony, rather than a conflict of laws, is, therefore, to be presumed among civilized States, with respect to the administration of justice upon the most important interests of mankind.

But where the municipal laws of States differ, the ends of justice require that they should agree in the adoption of the law which ought, from the nature and reason of the thing, to govern the *jus* of a foreigner, whether they agree that it shall be the law of his own or of another State.

This practical harmony in the administration of justice, ought to be the object of the community of civilized States.

It is a triumph of barbarity when a municipal law is applied to a foreign legal relation or right, instead of the law which, from the nature and reason of the thing, ought to govern it. It is a false and unjust theory, that when States are independent, there must be, or ought to be, a conflict of laws; though this may be in certain instances inevitable.

A *jus* once acquired under the dominion of the law of one State, ought not to be invalidated by the accident, that the acquirer afterwards brings that *jus*, so to speak, physically, under the dominion of the law of another State. Reason and the interests of society require that its validity should, as a general rule, be equally recognized everywhere;—" Ex quo liquet," Huber says, " tunc rem non ex simplici jure

---

ter omnes homines sive cives Romanos sive peregrinos valent." Gaius, iii. 93.

civili sed *ex commodis et tacito populorum consensu,*
esse petendam : quia sicut leges alterius populi apud
alium directe valere non possunt : ita commerciis et
usui gentium promiscuo nihil foret magis incommodum,
quam si res jure certi loci validæ, mox alibi diversitate
juris infirmarentur." (*a*)

A difficulty does, indeed, sometimes arise from considerations of public policy, which prevent the application of the true abstract rule of law to the *jus* of
the private individual. There are cases of exception
which it is both morally and legally competent to
each State to specify for itself, and which therefore
mark the discrimination between Right and Comity ;
between Public and Private Interational Law.(*b*)

II. Let me add a word or two as to my Predecessors (*c*) in the cultivation of this branch of Jurisprudence.

The first labourers were naturally those Jurists,
who lived in the States composed of different pro-

(*a*) *Prælect.* II.

(*b*) Cicero, in a very remarkable passage, points out the distinction
(which is not to be found in the Repositories of the Roman Law); he is
explaining the *rationale* of *jus* :—

" Juris est omnis ratio nobis explicanda, quod dividitur in duas partes
primas naturam atque legem . . . atque hæc communia sunt naturæ
atque legis : sed propria legis et ea quæ scripta sunt, et ea quæ sive lit-
teris, aut *gentium jure,* aut majorum more, retinentur. Scriptorum autem
privatum aliud est, publicum aliud : *publicum,* lex, senatusconsultum,
fœdus : *privatum,* tabulæ, pactum, conventum, stipulatio. Quæ autem
scripta non sunt, ea aut consuetudine aut conventis hominum et quasi
consensu obtinentur, *atque etiam hoc in primis ut nostros mores legesque
tuedmur, quodammodo naturali jure præscriptum est."—Orat. Partit.*
s. 37.

(*c*) *Vide post,* Note to Chap. I.

vinces, partly governed by the Roman Law, partly by indigenous customary laws. *D'Argentré*, in treating of the customs of Brittany, and *Burgundus*, in treating of the customs of Flanders, discussed with care and perspicuity portions of the subject, and propounded various general rules, by which the selection of the proper law ought to be determined, where the rights of the individual appeared to be under the dominion of two different laws.

Paul and *John Voet* dealt also with the subject, rather inclining to a severe and rigid view of the inadmissibility of exterritorial laws.

Hertius, Chancellor of the University of Giessen, wrote a treatise of considerable repute, " *De collisione legum.*"

Rodenburgh, a distinguished jurist of Utrecht, proceeded much further than his predecessors in the scientific development of Private International Law, investigating, with great care and accuracy of thought, the principles which ought to govern the application of Statutes to the questions of property, to the form and the substance of the acts of men, and to their personal capacity. His disquisition was, however, necessarily limited, being subordinate to the question of rights incident to the *status* of Marriage; the consideration of which question was the object of his work.

Huber, in his Prælectiones on the Civil Law, pointed out the magnitude of the subject, and gave a valuable but meagre outline of its principles.

Rocco, in 1837, published a Treatise on this subject of great merit, under the title of an " Essay, on the use and authority of the laws of the Two Sicilies, considered in their relation to the persons and territories of Foreign States."

The variety and extent of the Colonies of Great Britain brought before her tribunals at home and abroad, especially during the present century, cases which rendered it necessary to consider upon what principles they ought to decide, whether the rights of parties ought to be governed by the law of the Colony or the law of England: but no considerable work on the subject appeared before the elaborate and voluminous commentaries of *Mr. Burge*, a work to which succeeding authors upon Private International Law have been much indebted.

The lawyers of the United States of North America were necessarily led from the same cause as the lawyers of the old Netherlands and of France before the Revolution,—namely, the existence of various States with various laws in one Commonwealth—to the study of this jurisprudence.

The learned essay of *Livermore* led to the elaborate and popular work of *Story,* which has exercised great influence, and obtained a very high authority in this kingdom, as well as in the country of its author.

I must, however, be allowed to remark that even *Story* wrote, the nature of his work being considered, too much in the spirit of an English Common Lawyer, and too little in the spirit of an International Jurist.

With the work of *Fælix*, *Story* does not appear to have any intimate knowledge : he makes no reference to *Rocco*, and with the essays of *Wächter*, and the last of the eight volumes of *Savigny*, he was necessarily unacquainted.

While preparing this volume for the press, I was glad to find that this Treatise of *Savigny* had attracted the attention of *Mr. Westlake*, whose recent work on Private International Law has taken its place in the legal literature of England.

Since the Commentaries of *Donellus*, to whom *Savigny* was deeply indebted, no more philosophical or profound work has appeared than the great work of *Savigny* on the system of Roman Jurisprudence, in its application to the particular law of his own country, Prussia, and to the general law of the European Continent. His eighth volume contains a separate Treatise on Private International Law, conceived in the same spirit, and executed with the same ability, as the great work of which it is a part. It has been constantly referred to in this work.

I cannot help expressing a hope that the Treatises of such jurists as those of *Puchta* and *Savigny*, which have the merits without the defects of German erudition, may one day become familiar to English lawyers.

III. Something let me say, in conclusion, as to the frequent and full reference made throughout this work to the jurisprudence of ancient Rome; till lately so little known, and so often misunderstood, in England.

The advantage to the jurisprudence of Comity which results from this study is twofold : First, a knowledge of the laws, not only of a most civilized people, but of a people which continually imported and incorporated into their administration of justice to foreigners, the rules and principles of foreign law, which the reason of the thing, and the nature of the relation, rendered applicable, when they manifestly rendered inapplicable, the strict civil law of the Roman citizen.

In the Institutes, the Digest, and the Code, we are therefore enabled to study a system of Jurisprudence which avowedly passed over the limits of the positive law of the State in which it sprung up ; a Jurisprudence intended to be applicable to the world.

Secondly, We study in it a *system* of Jurisprudence. Nothing can more advance the culture of Private International Law, than the study, not of the letter, but of the spirit, of Roman Jurisprudence, which, because it recognized the duty of applying to *jura* acquired without its limits, or by others than its own citizens, a law founded upon general principles, has become the basis of the law of Christendom.

The law of England and the United States of North America, is not properly called by *Story* the Common Law, in a Treatise on Private International Law.

If there be any Common Law of States upon this subject, it is, for the reasons already given, furnished by the Roman Law.

Huber justly remarks, that though you may look in vain for rules *eo nomine*, on the Conflict of Laws in the repositories of Roman Jurisprudence, yet you will find rules applicable to the subject. " *Regulæ tamen fundamentales,* secundum quas hujus rei (i. e. conflictus legum) judicium regi debet, ex ipso jure Romano videntur esse petendæ." (*a*)

(*a*) *Prælect.* II.

The sculptor and the painter, who are worthy of the name, study the works of the ancient masters, not as the object of literal and servile copy, but of reverential and careful enquiry into the principles of truth by which these works have been immortalized.

In like manner, the Jurist ought to study the Roman Law, searching into those principles of truth, which, under the guidance of an intimate and practical acquaintance with the nature of legal relations, have rendered it an everlasting monument of the people whose genius brought it forth.

THESE Four Volumes of Commentaries are now brought to an end. Of the various notices and criticisms upon the three already published, there are only two on which I wish, at parting with my reader, to make a remark.

I. The notice of Professor *Mohl,* (a) in his elaborate work on the History and Literature of Sciences connected with the Policy of States. I am gratified not merely by his favourable opinion generally of my work, but still more by his recognition of the soundness of the principles upon which the work is planned, and of the labour and pains expended upon it. He has travelled over the same road, and he knows the difficulties and toils of the journey. His criticism was written when the First Volume only had been published. I hope he will find that the defect which he points out is remedied, as far as the nature of the subject will permit, in the Second and Third Volumes.

(a) Die Geschichte und Literatur der Staatswissenschaften,—*Robert von Mohl,* I. 391. Erlangen, 1855. This work is in three volumes.

II. An essay on International Law in the last number of the *Edinburgh Review*. Of the Reviewer's criticism on my work I say nothing: but he has made, he thinks, a great discovery as to the opinions and system of *Grotius;* indeed, on this discovery he rests the merit of his review. This discovery is not only what is popularly called a *mare's nest*, but also unjust to the character of a very great man, and moreover likely to inflict an injury to the jurisprudence in which I take a deep interest.

These are the reviewer's words:—"The result has been to discover that the revolution wrought by him (*Grotius*) consisted in transferring the chief grounds of the law of nations from the ancient theoretic and territorial basis—somewhat mitigated by the family humanity of Catholicity—to the Protestant and personal ground of the human will. Hence the term *jus gentium voluntarium*, which *Grotius* had been the first to introduce, and which marks throughout his chaos of quotation and adoption the new voice of inspiration that gave him value and vitality."

The reviewer then remarks on the fact that all the writers since *Grotius* have been, without a single original exception, Germans, or generally of the Teutonic race. "Is it that the Germans were a people of no foreign intercourse, and no domestic stimulus from politics of public life?" "What, then, should lead these writers to agitate the law of nations?" "Is it, then, that that law, as now resolved into its *true principles, a law of personality, resistance, will, and warfare,* has anything congenial to this people?"

To call International Law "a law of personalty, resistance, will, and warfare," is a confusion of ideas which results in something very like nonsense; and the theory about German International Jurists is very indifferent history.

First. The existence of the German Confederation of States, Protestant and Catholic, supplies at once no very recondite reason why Germany should have produced the greater number of International Jurists.

Secondly. There *have been*, since the time of *Grotius*, French (I do not include *Vattel*), Italian, and Spanish writers of considerable authority upon International Law, to say nothing of those jurists who occupy a kind of border line between Public and Private International Law, of whom, as of the Roman Law, the reviewer would, I dare say, candidly admit, as is evident, that he knew next to nothing.

Thirdly. There is the very awkward fact that the most eminent and original of the successors of *Grotius* is to be found among the Dutch (the reviewer seems to have forgotten that *Grotius* was a Dutchman). Yes ; but the Dutch, the reviewer would say, are included in my category. Be it so ; does he seriously mean to say that the Dutch were "a people of no foreign intercourse, and no domestic stimulus from politics of public life ?" A little reflection would have reminded him of the notorious truth, that the exact reverse is historical fact.

Next, for the great discovery about *Grotius* himself. It is an error, and a mischievous error, because it tends to lower the authority of that great man, by weakening the basis upon which he placed the mutual obligations of States, as the basis of the Civil Law of a State would be weakened by one who denied that conscience enforced obedience to it.

In the first place, *Grotius* himself says, that in the use of the phrase *jus gentium voluntarium*, he means—to do what ? To introduce a Protestant discovery forsooth ? No ; to *tread in the steps of Aristotle !*

" Juris ita accepti optima partitio est, *qua apud Aristotelem exstat*, ut sit aliud jus naturale, aliud *voluntarium*, quod ille legitimum vocat, legis vocabulo strictius posito, interdum et τὸ ἐν τάξει constitutum." (Lib i. c. i. ix.)

In the second place, the reviewer altogether misapprehends the meaning of *jus voluntarium ;* it does not mean "the Protestant and personal ground of the human will." It means *instituted* as distinguished from *natural* law.

Jus voluntarium is, *Grotius* says, vel humanum vel divinum (*ib.* xiii.). Jus humanum he divides into (1.) jus civile ; (2.) jus gentium ; distinguishing the latter from *jus naturale*, in language which at the same time distinctly admits that the moral law of nature is the primary source of the Jus Gentium: "Latius autem patens est jus gentium, id est quod gentium omnium aut *multarum* voluntate vim obliquandi accepit; *multarum* addidi, quia vix ullum jus reperitur extra *jus naturale, quod ipsum quoque gentium dici potest,* omnibus gentibus commune." (*Ib.* xiv.).

This jus gentium is to be proved, he says, like the jus civile of a particular State, namely—(1.) by usage; (2.) by the writings of jurists (*usu et testimonio peritorum*).

In plain language *Grotius* says, International Law, apart from the consideration of the Law of God, (including that which is written on the conscience by the finger of God, and that which is especially revealed,) which is the fountain of all laws, is derived from the consent of independent States, which make up the community of States,—as the civil law is derived from the consent of the people, which makes up the community of that State ; and this consent of States in the matter of International Law is to be proved by *usage* and the *testimony of writers*, where there is no express law, as in the case of treaties,—as the Civil Law of a State is to be proved in the absence of express Statute or Code.

The human law of all societies is, of course, derived from human *will;* that is, from consent founded on human will. It really required no ghost or reviewer to tell us that—*Grotius* knew that every thinker and writer on jurisprudence for two thousand years had known this—he knew also that when he wrote, no discovery, Protestant or Catholic, was to be made in morality or religion—he knew that "all human laws are, properly speaking, only declaratory, that they may alter the mode and application, but have no power over the substance, of original justice." (*a*) And he, therefore, said in a passage the reviewer ought to have known, "in jure gentium jus naturæ includitur."

(*a*) *Burke,* xi. 351.

Wherefore, to represent *Grotius* as having excluded the jus naturale and the jus divinum from the sources of International Law, is a grave misrepresentation. As a matter of fact he has done no such thing, and nothing could have been more alien to his habits of thought than to have done so.

A Dutch writer, in a recent and very interesting commentary on the writers since the time of *Grotius*, says truly, " Post-quam juris gentium fundamenta (*Grotius*) posuerat in ipsâ naturâ, legibusque divinis in moribus, atque in pactis : ejus sectatores in duas (*a*) ferè abiere partes."

To represent *jus voluntarium*, explained as I have shown by *Grotius* himself, as a Protestant discovery, is an extraordinary error. It is an error also, though of less magnitude, to assert that *Suarez*, the Roman Catholic predecessor of *Grotius*, would never have admitted, as a source of International Law, this jus voluntarium ; because, though not in terms, in substance he has distinctly done so.

In a passage (cited in the Appendix, p. 494, to my first volume), speaking of the necessity of an International Law, *Suarez* says, " Et quamvis magnâ ex parte hoc fiat per rationem naturalem non tamen sufficienter et immediatè quoad omnia : ideoque specialia jura potuerunt *usu corundem gentium* introduci."

I have one more citation to make from *Grotius* himself, which perhaps puts this grave and fundamental error of the reviewer in the strongest, and I fear the least venial, light. The reviewer says, *Grotius* "made the *prime* source (of International Law) independent of God and providence." *Grotius* says, "*jure primo Gentium* quod et *naturale* interdum dicitur." (*b*)

Lastly, I will dismiss this mischievous and baseless notion of a Protestant discovery, which is to render the immutable

---

(*a*) *Van Hogendorf, Commentatio de Juris Gentium studio in Patriâ nostrâ post H. Grotium*, Amstelod, 1856.

(*b*) Cited vol. i. 15.

laws of eternal justice not binding between States, in the language of the Protestant *Wolff*, the Protestant successor of the Protestant *Grotius* : " Absit vero, ut existimes, jus gentium voluntarium, ab eorum voluntate ita proficisci ut libera sit eorum in eodem condendo voluntas, et stet pro ratione solâ voluntas, nùllâ habitâ ratione juris naturalis." (*a*)

The review teems with minor and, in a Reviewer, venial errors—e. g., as to Roman Law—the *Recuperatores*—the effect of Roman upon International Law—the English exposition of International Law in 1753 confounded with a German theory. These are errors comparatively insignificant.

But it is not insignificant to place, even in a review, International Law upon a false basis—to substitute what I must call the rubbish of " a law of personalty, resistance, will, and warfare," for the immutable foundation of everlasting justice—and to misrepresent *Grotius* as your fellow-labourer in the mischief.

(*a*) Cited vol. i. 26-7 of Commentaries.

CONTENTS.

b 2

CHAP. IV. A.

DEFINITION OF DOMICIL. Pp. 41—45.

CHAP. V.

CAN A MAN HAVE TWO DOMICILS? Pp. 46—52.

Whether a Man can have Two Domicils. Distinction between Domicil and Allegiance.

CHAP. VI.

CAN A MAN BE WITHOUT A DOMICIL? Pp. 53—56.

Whether a Man can be without a Domicil. A Vagabond. Original Domicil easily reverts. Children of unknown Parents; Where Domiciled.

CHAP. VII.

DIFFERENT KINDS OF DOMICIL. Pp. 57—59.

Domicil of Birth. Domicil by operation of Law.

CHAP. VIII.

NECESSARY DOMICIL—WIFE. Pp. 60—72.

Domicil by operation of Law or Necessary Domicil. The Wife.

CHAP. IX.

NECESSARY DOMICIL—MINOR. Pp. 73—90.

Necessary Domicil of the Minor: (1.) Legitimate; (2.) Illegitimate.

CHAP. X.

THE STUDENT—THE LUNATIC—THE SERVANT. Pp. 90—97.

Necessary Domicil of the Student—of the Lunatic—of the Servant.

CHAP. XI.

THE PUBLIC OFFICER. Pp. 98—139.

Necessary Domicil of Public Officer: Military and Naval; the Ambassador; the Consul; the Ecclesiastic; the Prisoner; the Exile; the Emigrant; a Corporation.

CHAP. XII.

CHAP. XIII.

CHAP. XIV.

CHAP. XV.

CHAP. XVI.

CHAP. XVII.

CHAP. XXIX.

CHAP. XXX.

CHAP. XXXI.

CHAP. XXXII.

CHAP. XXXIII.

CHAP. XXXIV.

CHAP. XXXV.

CHAP. XXXVI.

CHAP. XXXVII.

CHAP. XLIII.

RIGHTS RELATING TO SUCCESSION. Pp. 625—636.

What Forum has Jurisdiction over the whole question of Succession. By
what Law ought the Forum to decide—as to (1.) the legal capacity of
the Testator; (2.) the form of the testamentary Instrument; (3.) the dispositions contained in it; (4.) the construction or interpretation of it.
What Law ought to govern the rights of parties in a Succession *ab
intestato.*

CHAP. XLIV.

ADMINISTRATION OF JUSTICE IN THE CASE OF FOREIGNERS.
Pp. 637—652.

Civil and Criminal Law. Civil Law: 1. Voluntary Jurisdiction; Notaries;
Commissions; Litteræ Requisitoriæ. 2. Contentious Jurisdiction: Fo-
reigner Plaintiff; Defendant; Two Foreigners; Foreign Law; English
Law ; Chancery Law. Immoveable Property.

CHAP. XLV.

LAW OF PROCEDURE. LEX FORI. EVIDENCE, DIFFERENT KINDS OF.
PROOF OF FOREIGN ACTS— OF FOREIGN LAW. Pp. 653—670.

CHAP. XLVI.

FOREIGN JUDGMENTS. Pp. 671—694.

Practice of Comity as to the reception of; Foreign and English Law thereupon.

NOTE TO CHAPTER. Pp. 695—697.

Catalogue of the principal English decisions since 1830, upon the effect of
Foreign Judgments in England.

CHAP. XLVII.

LEX FORI. PROVISIONAL MEASURES. INTERDICTA. Pp. 698—702.

Injunctions of English Courts of Equity in favour of Foreigners.

CHAP. XLVIII.

GENERAL APPENDIX.

I.   Pp. 717—733.

II.   Pp. 734—751.

LIST OF PRINCIPAL AUTHORITIES

REFERRED TO IN THIS VOLUME.

A.

Abbott, Treatise of the Law relative to Merchant Ships and Seamen.
Addison's Law of Contracts, &c.
Ahrens, Phil. du Droit.
Allgemeines Landrecht für die Preussichen Staaten.
Argentræi Comment. ad patrias Britonum leges
Arnould, on Insurance.
Austrian Code, The.

B.

Barante, Ducs de Burgogne.
Barbosa, De Officio ex Potestate Episcopi.
Barbosæ et Tahoris loci communes Jurisprudentiæ.
Bartolus, in Codicem.
Bassevi, Annotazioni al Codice Civile Austriaco.
Bell's Commentaries on the Laws of Scotland (Shaw's Ed.).
Bishop on Marriage and Divorce.
Blackstone's Commentaries.
Blume, System des Deutsches P. Rechts.
Bouhier, Les coutumes du Duche de Bourgogne, &c.
Boulay Patey, Cours de Droit Comm.
Boullenois, Introduction génerale aux Coutumes des Duches, &c., d'Orleans.
       ,,   (L.) Traité de la personalité et de la realité des Loix, &c.
Brazilian Code.
Bright's Husband and Wife.
Brooks on Notaries.
Burge's Colonial Law.
Burgundus.

Burn's Ecclesiastical Law (Edit. Phillimore).
Byles on Bills of Exchange.
Bynkershoek, De Foro Legatorum.
                        Questiones Juris privati.

C.

Canon Law (*See* list of references to).
Carpzovius, Processus Juris.
Cassiodorus, cited by Miltitz.
Casaregis, Discursus legales de Commercio.
Chitty (Junr.), on Contracts (by Russell).
Cicero, De Off.
    „   De Legibus.
    „   Pro Balbo.
Cochin, Œuvres.
Code, The Roman (*See* list of references to).
Code de Commerce.
Code Civil of France.
Code Civil of Louisiana.
Code Napoleon, The (Rogron).
Code de Procedure Civil.
Coin de Lisle, Comment. Analyt. du Code Civil.
Coke on Littleton.
Cole on domicil of Englishmen in France.
Collectanea Juridica.
Cooper's Bankruptcy Laws.
Cujacius.

D.

D'Aguesseau, Cinquante-Septieme Plaidoyer.
Dalloz, Jurisprudence générale.
Daniel's Chancery Practice.
Demangeat, Histoire de la Condition Civile des Etrangers en France.
        „   Du Statut Personel, Revue Pratique de Droit Français.
Demolombe, Cours de Code Civil, &c.
Denizart, Collection de Decisions.
Desquiron (A. T.), Traité du Domicile et de l'Absence.
Devoti. jus canonicum.
Digest, The Roman (*See* list of references to).
Dictionnaire de Droit Canonique.
Dirksen's Manuale.
Domat—Loix Civiles dans leur Ordres Naturelles.
Donellus, De Jure Civ. Comment.
Duranton, Cours du Droit Français.

E.

Edwards' Admiralty Jurisdiction.

Emerigon, Traité des Assurances et des Contrats à la Grasse.

F.

Farinacius Consiliorum.

Ferguson's Reports of Consistorial decisions in Scotland.

Ferguson on Marriage and Divorce.

Fœlix, Traité de Droit International.

  ,,   Revue Etrangère.

Fonblanque, Treatise of Equity.

Frisquet, Traité Elementaire de Droit Romain.

G.

Gaill. Practic. Observ.

Gaillard (Nicias).

Gazette des tribunaux de France.

Gellius (Aulus).

Gothofred.

Grotius, De Jure belli et Pacis.

Günther, Europäisches Volkerrecht.

H.

Hargrave's Law Tracts.

Heffter.

Henry, Judgment in Odwin v. Forbes.

Hertius (I. N.), De Collisione Legum, &c.

Huberus, De Conflictu Legum.

I.

Institutes, The (*See* Roman Law, references to).

J.

Jenkins (Sir L.), Life of.

Justinian, Instit., Pand., Cod.

K.

Kent's Commentaries on American Law.

Klüber, Europäisches Volkerrecht.

Koch, Hist. des Traités de Paix.

L.

Lauterbach (Wolfgang Adamo).

Le Bret, Questions Notables.

Legat, Code des Etrangers, ou Traité de la Legislation Française concernant les
        Etrangers.
Lewis (Sir G. C.), Essay on Foreign Jurisdiction and the Extradition of
        Criminals (1859).
Loccenius.
Loerè, Legislation Civile de la France.
Lyndwood, Const.

M.

Mackeldey, Lehrbuch.
Marcardé, Commentary upon the French Code
Martens, Droit des Gens.
Mascardus, De Probationibus.
Massé, Le Droit Commercial dans ses Rapports avec le Droit des Gens et le
        Droit Civil.
Meier (D.), De Conflictu Legum.
Menochius, De Præsumptionibus.
Merlin, Repertoire de Jurisprudence.
        „   Questiones de Droit.
Meyer, Institutions Judiciares.
Miltitz, Manuel des Consuls.
Morrison's Dictionary of Decisions.
Muhlenbruch, Doctrina Pandectarum.

N.

Novellæ, The (See Roman Law, list of references to)

P.

Pardessus, Cours de Droit Commercial.
Park, on Insurance.
Pascal.
Pataille et Huguet, Code Internationale de la Proprieté Industrielle, Artistique,
        et Litteraire.
Peckius.
Pinheiro Ferreira, Notes sur Vattel.
Portula, Dizionario di diritto e di Economia, &c.
Pothier, Introduction Generale aux Coutumes D'Orleans.
        „   Traité du Contrat de Marriage.
        „   Traité des Obligations.
Prussian Code, The.
Puchta, Instit.
Puffendorfius, De Jure N. et G.
        „   Observationes Juris Universi.
Putnam's United States Digest.
Putter, Das Praktische Europäische Fremden Recht (Leipsig, 1845)
Puttlingen, Die gesetsliche Behandlung der Ausländer in Œsterreich

R.

Renouard, Des Brevets d'Intervention.

Revue Étrangere et Française de Legislation, &c.

Reports (*See* list of).

Robertson, on Personal Succession.

Rocco.

Roccus, De Navib.

Rodenburg, De Jure Conjugum.

Rogron, Code Napoleon.

Ross's Leading Cases of Commercial Law.

Rutherford's Inst. of Natural Law.

S.

Sanchez, De Matrimonie.

Sardinian Code, The.

Savigny, Geschichte des Romischen Rechts in Mittelalter.

    ,,   System des heutigen Romischen Rechts.

Schäffner (W.), Entwickelung des Internationalem Privatrechts.

Smith's Action at Law.

    ,,   Leading Cases.

Smith, on Contracts.

    ,,   on Mercantile Law.

Stair's Institutes.

Starkie, on Evidence.

State Trials, The.

Stephens' Commentaries.

Story, on Bills of Exchange.

    ,,   Conflict of Laws.

Struve (G. V.) Uber das positiv Rechtsgesetz in seiner Beziehung auf räumliche Verhältnisse.

Stypmannus.

Sugden's Vendors and Purchasers.

T.

Taylor, on Evidence.

Thöl, Das Handelsrecht, &c.

Toullier, Le Droit Civil Français suivant l'Ordre du Code.

Troplong, Le Code Explique.

    ,,   De l'influence du Christianisme sur le Droit civil des Romanis.

V.

Vattel, Droit des Gens.

Villefort, Des Crimes et des Delits Commis à l'Etranger.

Vinnius, ad Instit.

Voet (John), De Statutis Eorumque Concursu.

    ,, (P.), ad Pandect.

W.

Wächter, Die Collision der Privatgesetze, &c.; Archiv für die Civil Praxis.
Warnkonig, Inst. Jur. Civ.
Westlake's Private International Law.
Wheaton's Elements of International Law.
     ,,   History.
Williams (V.) on Executors.
     ,,   on the Law of Real Property.
Wolff, Jus Gentium.
Woodeson's Lectures.
Wynne's Life of Sir L. Jenkins.

Z.

Zouch, De Jure Feciali sive de Judicio inter Gentes.
Zacharia, Cours de Droit Civil Français.

LIST OF REPORTS.

ENGLISH.

SCOTCH.

B.

Bell, Murray, and Young's.

F.

Ferguson's (Consistorial).

S.

Shaw and Dunlap's.

IRISH.

B.
Ball and Beatty's.

D.
Drury's (Chancery).

J.
Jones and Latouch's.

M.
Millwood's Cases in Prerogative and Consistorial Court of Dublin.

AMERICAN.

A.
Alabama (The).
Arkansas (The).

B.
Barbour's.
Binney's.

C.
Cranch's.
Curtis's.

D.
Deane's (Vermont).

F.
Foster's (New Hampshire).

G.
Gallison's.
Gates'.
Gill and Johnson's.
Greenleaf's Cases in the Supreme Judicial Court of the State of Maine.

H.
Harris and Johnson's.
Howard's.

J.
Johnson's.

L.
Louisiana (The).

M.
Martin's.
Massachusetts.
Mason's (Circuit Courts of United States).
Miller's (Louisiana).
Missouri (The).

P.
Paige's (New York Chancery Cases).
Peter's.
Pickering's.
Putnam's United States Digest.
Story's.
Sumner's.

LIST OF CASES

CITED IN THIS VOLUME.

ENGLISH, SCOTCH, AND IRISH.

AMERICAN.

FOREIGN.

ERRATA.

Page 13, note (t), 1st line, *for* "constitutiones," *read* "constitutionesque;" *for*
"donos," *read* "bonos."
   31, note (a), 4th line, *for* "subjicatur," *read* "subjiciatur."
   64, note (i), *for* "Dalloy," *read* "Dalloz;" *for* "Rogion," *read* "Rogron."
   85, note (f), *for* "Dig. l. 3, 4," *read* "Dig. 50, t. 1, ss. 3, 4."
  128, note (x), 2nd line, *for* "Dig. L. xxii. s. 3," *read* "Dig. 50, t. i. s. 3."
  129, note (y), 2nd line, *for* "l. lix. s. 19," *read* "l. xlviii. t. 19, s. 17."
  160, note (i), 2nd line, *after* "contestatione" *read* "solâ."
  173, note (s), 2nd line, *for* "Code, t. xl. l. vii." *read* "Code, lib. x. t. xl. l. vii."
  234, note (a), 5th line, *for* "initio," *read* "insinuata."
  275, 12th line, *after* "was," *read* "to be made."
  333, 3rd line, *for* "fifth and sixth," *read* "fourth and fifth."
  375, 21st line, *for* "jure," *read* "juri."
  377, note (i), 6th line, *for* "Syloa," *read* "Sylva."
  408, 16th line, *for* "quorum," *read* "quarum."
  428, note (h), 7th line, *for* "Dig. l. t. xiv., &c." *read* "Dig. lib. ii. t. xiv., &c."
  436, note (t), 1st line, *for* "l. ii. t. xiv. 7, cf. eod. 15," *read* "l. ii. t. xiv. s. 45."
  460, 32nd line, *after* "alienigenæ" *read* "liberos."
  472, 28th line, *for* "alibi," *read* "alio."
  487, 5th line, *for* "those," *read* "these."
  494, note (e), *for* "Dig. l. l. t. xix., &c.," *read* "Dig. l. l. t. xvii., &c."
  495, note (h), the like correction.
  496, note (m), 1st line, *for* "26," *read* "27."
    „   „   „   3rd line, *for* "*Ib.* xxxv." *read* "*Ib.* xlv."
  499, 4th line, *after* "place" *read* "in which."
  533, 20th line, *for* "Pfundrecht," *read* "Pfandrecht."
  554, 1st line, *for* "debtor of the domicil," *read* "domicil of the debtor."
  559, note (c), *dele* xlviii. t. xi. s. 7.
  593, note (p), *for* "Dig. lxiv. t. 2," *read* "Dig. xiv. t. 2, s. 1."
  625, note (d), *for* "et l. xxvii., &c." *read* "et l. xxviii., &c."

ERRATA IN VOL. III.

Page 327, *for* "the ornament," *read* "an ornament."
  395, *for* "breach of Blockade," *read* "act of Blockade."
  587, *dele* note (b).

ADDENDA.

ALIEN. (Page 306).

THAT he has the rights of an English Patentee, see *Ollendorff* v. *Black*, 4 *De Gex & Smale's Rep.* 209; and *In re Schlumberger*, 9 *Moore's Privy Council Rep.* p. 14.

That when domiciled and naturalised in this country, he is subject to the same disabilities as is a natural born subject, and therefore is incapable of contracting a marriage which would have been void if contracted by a natural born subject, although valid by the law of his domicil of origin, and by the *Lex loci contractus*, see *Mette* v. *Mette, Swabey & Tristram's Probate & Divorce Rep.* vol. i. p. 417 (1859-60), and 28 *Law Journ. Rep. (Probate)*, 117.

OBLIGATIONS.—LOCUS REGIT ACTUM.
(Chap. xxxiii., p. 453.)

The Scotch Law appears at present to be in accordance with the European Law, as to the form of Testaments, and at variance with the English Law.

RECLAIMING NOTE.

The Trustees of William Purvis, Esq., v. *Lord Benholme's Interlocutor.*

"*30th June*, 1857.—The Lord Ordinary, having heard parties' procurators, and made avizandum, Finds, that the late William Purvis, Esq., a native of this country, died domiciled in Scotland in the year 1854: Finds, that the said William Purvis left a Trust Deed of Settlement in favour of the Pursuers embracing, *inter alia*, All lands and heritages that might belong to him at the time of his death: Finds, that this Settlement remained effectual and unrevoked, *quoad* All the heritable property belonging to the

d 2

Testator at the time of his death, situated in Scotland. Finds, that the disposal of the Testator's real property in the Netherlands, India, depends upon the validity of the testamentary writings which he executed in that country, to carry real property there: Finds that, by the law of Scotland, in which country the Testator died domiciled, the succession to his moveable property will depend upon the formality, *according to the law of the country in which they were executed*, of the testamentary writings executed by the Testator in the Netherlands, India, as constituting a last will and testament of moveable property;—and, with these findings, Appoints the case to be enrolled, that the proper steps may be taken for ascertaining the effect and validity of these writings by the foreign law.   (Signed)   H. J. ROBERTSON.

"*Note.*—The question of domicile, in reference to which further probation has been renounced, does not appear to be involved in much doubt.   The Testator was a native of, and lived the earlier years of his life in, Scotland.   He then went abroad, and after living for many years and after marrying abroad, he returned to this country with his wife and family in 1833, more than twenty years before his death.   He himself repeatedly went abroad after that period, leaving his family in this country, and returning to them from time to time.   The last five years of his life were spent exclusively in Scotland, where he died, and where he had property, both real and personal.   His letters, during this last period, indicate an intention of ultimately returning to the Netherlands, India, for the special purpose of greater intercourse with relations in that country.   But that plan was at best contingent; and it would rather appear that had he found an estate in this country to suit him, at a moderate price, he would have bought it, and given up the plan of settling abroad.   His later intention appears to have been to reside some years longer in this country, at all events for the education of his younger children, and as the climate of this country suited him better than that of the foreign country, it appears that he would have preferred that the intercourse of their families should have been attained by his relations returning to this country, rather than by his going out to them.

"2. The second and third findings do not require much notice. The Lord Ordinary cannot consider any of the latter testamentary writings, even if they revived to every effect the testament of 1823, as sufficient to revoke the conveyance of his Scotch heritable property, contained in the Trust Deed of 1834.   And upon the authority of the case of Thomson's Trustees, 18th December, 1851, and other cases, the Lord Ordinary thinks himself entitled to act upon this opinion, without requiring the opinion of foreign counsel.

3. The last finding involves a question of international law, in regard to which there may be a conflict between the law of Scotland and of other countries, especially of England.)

"The Lord Ordinary humbly adopts what he considers the Scotch view of the international question : and holds that a Testament is good and effectual to settle personal property, if drawn up conformably to the laws of the country in which it was executed, even although the Testator should die domiciled in a country in which other formalities would be required. He thinks that this view of the international question is supported by the authorities referred to, and by the opinions of the Judges in the case of *Leith* v. *Leith*, 6th June, 1848. With reference to this last case, it is to be observed that the Testator, Sir George Leith, died domiciled in Scotland. The English will, upon the effect of which the question turned, was executed by him during a temporary residence in England. None of the Judges seem to have doubted that such will was effectual, as a settlement of moveables. The real difficulty was as to its effect in revoking a settlement of Scotch real property—and had the intention to revoke been clear, a majority of the Judges would have given effect to it, even as a revocation of the Scotch Trust Settlement." (a)

PERSONAL PROPERTY.

If personal property is disposed of in a manner binding by the laws of the country in which it is, that disposition is binding everywhere, and it makes no difference that the goods were wrecked on the coast of the country where they have been disposed of, and were not intended to be sent thither by the shipper. (*See Cammell and others* v. *Sewell and others, Exch. Chamber*, 1859-60 ; *The Jurist*, vol. vi., N. S., 918, *Sept.* 15th, 1860).

LEX MERCATORIA. (Chap. xli. pp. 578—600).

By the law of England, and the general maritime law, the master of a ship has no power to sell either cargo or ship, except in cases of absolute and utter necessity.

The plaintiff was underwriter on a cargo of deals shipped in Russia for delivery to a party in England. The vessel having been stranded in Norway, the master wrote to the consignee stating the fact, and asking for instructions in the event of the ship being

---

(a) This case is now before the "Second Division," that is, it is appealed from.

entirely lost. On the receipt of this letter the consignee abandoned the cargo to the plaintiff, who accepted the abandonment, and paid as for a total loss. Before the receipt of any answer from the consignee, the master procured a survey to be made of the ship and cargo, on which occasion the surveyors recommended a sale of both, by public auction, as best for all parties. A sale was accordingly held by the sheriff, at the requisition of the master, previous to which, however, a person protested against the sale, producing to all parties a letter from the underwriters on the ship and freight, directing him to get the ship off, and repair her for sea; or, should that be impossible, to save as much of the cargo as he could, and dispatch it to its destination; the party who purchased the cargo also stating that he had received a letter from an insurance company, requesting him to demand the delivery of the cargo, on payment of the expenses. After the sale a communication was received by the master from the consignee, desiring him to make a protest of the loss of the ship and cargo, and inclosing a letter from the underwriters on the cargo, stating that they had written to a party to prevent a sale of it, and requesting him to carry out those instructions. The plaintiff did nothing to confirm or adopt the sale. The party who had protested against the sale then instituted a suit against the master and the purchaser in the Superior Diocesan Court at D., in Norway, to disavow the public auction, and compel the purchaser to deliver up the deals, or make compensation for the loss and damage; but the court, by its judgment, confirmed the public auction. It was stated, that by the law of Norway a sale, by the master of a ship, transfers the property to the purchaser, and the owner must look to the master for his remedy. Previous to this judgment the deals arrived in England, consigned to the defendant, who had made advances upon them to the purchaser; whereupon the plaintiff gave a written notice of the circumstances, and demanded the deals to be delivered up, which the defendant refused to do, and afterwards sold them. The plaintiff then brought the present action to recover the sum realised by the sale, declaring in trover, with indebitatus counts; and the defendant having pleaded, to the count in trover, not guilty and not possessed, and, to the indebitatus counts, never indebted—It was holden,

That assuming the law of Norway to operate to pass the property, in the circumstances, to an innocent purchaser, the subsequent bringing the deals into this country did not divest it.

That there was no reason why such should not be recognised, by the courts of this country, as the law of Norway. (*See Cammell and others v. Sewell and others, Exch. Chamber,* 1859-60; *The Jurist,* vol. vi. N. S. 918.)

COMMENTARIES

UPON

INTERNATIONAL LAW.

CHAPTER I.

JUS GENTIUM—PRIVATE INTERNATIONAL LAW.

I. *JUS INTER GENTES,* or, as it is sometimes called, Public International Law, has been the subject of the three preceding volumes. It remains to consider in this, the last volume of the whole treatise (*a*), *Jus Gentium,* or, as it is sometimes called, Private International Law, or Comity (*b*) (*Comitas*) (*c*).

II. We have seen, in the first of the foregoing volumes, that

---

(*a*) In redemption of the pledge given, vol. i. s. xvi.

(*b*) " Denique nonnunquam dum populus vicinus vicini mores *comiter* " vult observare et ne multa bene gesta turbarentur, de moribus sta- " tuta territorium statuentis inspecto effectu solent egreidi." *P. Voet, de Statutis eorumque concursu,* s. iv. 17.

John Voet, speaking of the rule that moveables are governed " lege " loci in quo eorum dominus domicilium fovet ubicunque illa verè ex- " titerent," observes, that in this case "de juris rigore, quasi gentium " omnium communi consensu relaxatum est sic ut *ex comitate* profecta " regula praxi universali invaluerit." *Tit.* iii., *ad Pandect.* p. 2.

So *Huberus, De Conflictu Legum,* s. 2, " id *comiter* agunt," &c.

The word occurs once in the *Digest ;* " liber autem populus est is," &c. " sive fœdere comprehensum est ut is populus alterius populi majesta- " tem *comiter* conservaret." Lib. 49. t. 15, 7, 1.

" *Une espèce* de droit des gens et de bienséance." *Bouhier,* cited by *Fœlix,* s. 11, p. 24, ed. *Demangeat*

" La conpiacenza vicendevole." *Rocco,* 119.

" Mutua compiacenza." *Rocco,* 120, 253.

(*c*) See a notice at the end of this chapter, of the Sources of Private International Law.

Sovereignty united with Domain (*dominium eminens*) esta-blishes, as a fundamental rule of International Law, the exclu-sive jurisdiction of a State over all persons, acts, and things, within its territories (*d*) ; and, of course, over suits and actions in Courts of Justice, civil or criminal, arising within these limits.

This is a proposition which does not only concern the natives of a territory, who are naturally subject to such a jurisdiction. There is no country, not only in Europe, but in the world, since the opening of China and Japan, in which there may not be foreigners, both transient and resident (*e*). Being allowed to enter a State, of which they are not natives, they have a strict right to be secured from injury while therein ; the ill usage of them, whether by positive mal-treatment (*f*)

(*d*) The exception of the ambassador, which is a matter *stricti juris inter gentes,* and not *comitatis juris gentium,* is mentioned, vol. ii. part vi. *Puchta, Instit.* i. 360.

(*e*) Civil laws, when they causelessly and unreasonably exclude foreign-ers either from coming into the territories at all, or from trading there, are inhospitable ; but these inhospitable civil laws are no otherwise con-trary to the laws of nations, than as this law, like the general law of nature, enjoins the duties of humanity and benevolence. Every nation has by the law of nations, as every individual has by the law of nature, a right to judge for itself how far its intercourse, either of the com-mercial or of the friendly sort, is likely to be detrimental to itself; so that to cut off either or both sorts of intercourse, will be no act of in-justice, though it will be wrong if it is done causelessly. A nation has a moral power to withhold its benevolence ; and they from whom it is withheld unreasonably, though they are not treated friendly, are not injured."—*Rutherford's Inst. of Natural Law* (2nd edit. 1832), p. 489.

(*f*) The *Jus Albinatus,* or *Albinagii* (*alibi natus*), or *droit d'Aubaine,* now happily abolished in all civilized states, whereby the Crown seized on the property of the deceased foreigners, was, perhaps, strictly speaking, a violation only of Comity; but it was on the confines of a legal as well as a moral injustice. Some relict of this barbarism appears still to linger in parts of Germany, in which it would seem that the foreign heir pays 10 per cent. of his inheritance to the State.—*Blume, S., des Deutsches P. Rechts,* s. 452. This is called *Gabella Hereditaria.*—*Mar-tens,* l. iii. c. iii. s. 90 ; *Vattel,* l. ii. c. viii. s. 112—114 ; *Merlin,* Rep. *Voce,* Aubain ; *Rocco,* p. 63, speaks of it in a manner worthy of the great

or by a denial of justice (*g*), may, and ought to be, resented by the State of which they are members. A refusal of redress in such cases would be a justifiable cause of war. If by long usage and custom they have been allowed to enjoy certain rights; and these, though originally the fruit of free concession, are violently, suddenly, and, without equitable notice, withdrawn from them; an injury is done to them, for which it is the duty of their own State to obtain reparation (*h*), the denial of which justifies a recourse to *reprisals* (*i*), or *war* (*j*), according to the exigencies of the case. But here the narrow province of International Right ends, and the wide domain of International Comity begins. For though the laws of every State are built partly upon general principles common to all States, *jus gentium*, they are also partly built upon positive enactments *jus civile;* and, though there is, moreover, a *speciale jus inter gentes* (*k*) common to all Christian States,

---

school of Neapolitan jurists, "l'albinato questa usanza derivata dalla barbarie delle nazioni," &c., were, he says, in force at Naples.

Pütter, Das Praktische Europäische Fremden Recht (Leipsig, 1845), *Erster Abschnitt,* 13. This is, generally speaking, a good little work; though the present English Law is incorrectly stated with respect to the operation of Domicil upon the wills of English subject, p. 23.

Rocco speaks of domiciled foreigners as having the same *private* rights as natives of the Two Sicilies. "Oggidì avvenga che quasi tutte le leggi della colta Europa ammettano i forestieri ad esercitare i diritti civili, gli respingono poi allora che si tratta di partecipare alle cariche dello Stato," (p. 39); but of *non-domiciled* strangers as enjoying only those rights which their country accords to the natives of the Two Sicilies, "Sol quando s'intrametta la *reciprocazione* fra i due Stati" (p. 40). Here he is speaking of "Esteri non-domiciliati," or as he afterwards calls them, "semplicemente residenti" (p. 59).

(*g*) France, however, has thought it consistent with Comity to refuse, as a general rule, to entertain suits between two foreigners in her courts of justice.— *Vide post.*

(*h*) In the case of rights secured by treaty and withdrawn in time of peace, the *casus belli* is, of course, beyond the reach of doubt, vol. iii. p. 47.

(*i*) *Vide ante,* vol. iii. pp. 11, 12.

(*j*) *Vide ante,* vol. iii. p. 47.

(*k*) *Vide ante,* vol. i. c. 1.

the practical application of those general principles and of this *jus speciale* may vary in different States. There is no universal positive law for all mankind. Each State has its own municipal code; though each code contains many principles common to all : and each individual is a member of the great family of mankind.

III. States becoming, under the blessed influence of Christianity and its attendant civilization, more and more impressed with a deeper sense of national duty, and with the principles of universal justice, having regard also to their reciprocal advantages and mutual interests (*mutuæ vicissitudinis obtentu—ob reciprocam utilitatem*) arising from the impartial administration of justice to the foreigner and the native (*l*), have tacitly agreed (*m*) to recognise and adopt certain common rules and maxims of jurisprudence, both civil and criminal, with respect to the individual foreigners sojourning within their territory, and with respect to the operation therein of the laws of a foreign State. "Usu exigente" (to borrow the language of the *Institutes*) " et humanis necessitatibus gentes " humanæ jura quædam sibi constituerunt" (*n*).

IV. This consent has manifested itself in various ways; in the decisions of Courts of Law, in writings of accredited jurists in acts of the executive authority (*o*), such as the

---

(*l*) " Le genti colte prestano mutuamente osservanza agli atti celebrati, e alle obligazioni e a' diritti nati nelle stranie contrade. E le qualità personali legittamente infisse nel luogo del domicilio si mantegono mai sempre intere col mutar che si fa dalla residenza e passaggiera dimora. Quantunque il diritto delle genti che *necessario* dai guispubblicisti si appella non ordini questa *vicendevole applicazione*, e autorità, delle leggi di uno stato sul territorio dell 'altro. Nissuna primitiva obligazione stringe le nazioni a riconoscere provvedimenti stranieri—nullameno *il diritto delle genti volontario*, il quale intende alla perfezione progressiva dei popoli altamente il richiede."—*Rocco*, iii. 2.

(*m*) See in *Wheaton's Hist.* 726-8, Mr. Webster's Letter, in which the difference between Comity and strict Right is much dwelt upon.—See 18 *Curtis's (Americ.) Rep.* 203.

(*n*) L. i. t. ii. 2.

(*o*) *Story*, s. 38, n. 1.

declaration with respect to the security of foreign merchants, on the breaking out of war, contained in the Magna Charta of England (*p*). More recently also, France, as will presently be seen, and some other nations, have incorporated into their national code express provisions relating to this subject.

But France had suffered before her first revolution—and the same may be predicated of England, and the United States of North America — a system of *Private International Law* (*Jus Gentium*) to grow up, partly out of the analogies furnished by the Roman (*q*) Civil Law (*r*), partly out of an enlightened application of the principles of their own municipal

---

(*p*) *Vide* vol. iii. p. 118.

(*q*) *Story* unfortunately, in my opinion, in a treatise on *International Law*, uses the words, "common law," meaning the English and North American Law; but the Roman Law is the "common law" of States.

(*r*) See preface, p. viii. to vol. I. of this work.

Early in the history of ancient Italy the intercourse between *Romans* and those who were *not Romans* created, of necessity, what was in substance an *International Private Law* or *Comity*, to which the name *jus gentium* ("quod apud omnes gentes peræque custoditur, juris gentium est") properly belonged, as distinguished from the *jus inter gentes*. The history of its growth from its introduction through the *annual* and *perpetual edicts* of the Prætor to its full development in the compilations of *Justinian*, in which it appears as the law of the Empire, is a most interesting subject, but far beyond the limits of any note. These compilations were naturally the principal storehouse from which the rules of modern Comity were taken; though, unfortunately, an ignorance of the history of the Roman Law, and a superficial acquaintance with its whole system, led especially, but by no means solely, in England, to many mistakes in the application of the rules of this jurisprudence; *vide post*, remarks on the misapplication of the maxims of law as to *nudum pactum* in our municipal law, and in Private International Law of *mobilia sequuntur personam—locus regit actum*, &c. See some good remarks on the Roman *Jus Gentium-Mommsen-Römische Geschichte*, i. 146; iii. 540; on the misapplication, *Wächter die collision der privotgesetze versehied. Staaten*, ii. ; (*in Archiv. für die Civilistische Praxis*, B. 24—242). That there are, however, rules on the subject of collision of laws to be found in the Roman Law, though defective and incomplete, see *Savigny*, viii. s. 344. *Justinian* introduced a real *jus gentium* by removing the distinction between *cives* and *peregrini* who belonged to the empire.—*Cod.* l. vii. t. 5-6.

jurisprudence, and of that of other countries, partly out of the general usages of commerce (s), aided by the reasoning of writers of all nations upon Public Law.

V. Upon the application of principles derived from these sources to the decisions of particular questions, the fabric of International Comity has been slowly, but steadily, reared; it is daily acquiring consistency and strength, and has already become a *Jus Gentium Privatum*, having for its object the decision of questions affecting the interest of individuals, as the *Jus Gentium Publicum*, or, more properly, *Jus inter Gentes* (t) has for its object the decision of questions growing out of the mutual relations of communities.

VI. In illustration of the position in the last paragraph, it may be observed that some modern codes of European States contain express provisions upon the subject of the general Civil *Status* of the foreigner within their territory. The French, the Austrian, and the Prussian codes all contain some enactments on this subject. The French code recognises distinctly an equality between the native subject and the foreigner, as to the enjoyment and capacity of acquiring civil rights (u). But on the subject of collision between native and foreign laws, it contains few special provisions, though some will be referred to hereafter in the discussion of foreign *Contracts* and *Testaments*.

The Prussian code contains an express acknowledgment of the principle that the foreigner has a right to the same

---

(s) The *Law Merchant* is both a part of Private International Law and of the Common Law of England. This advantage is mainly due to the Roman Law and its commentators. It will be the subject of a separate and distinct consideration in a later part of this volume.

Comity was wholly alien to the Feudal Law. See *Barante Ducs de Burgogne, Introd.*

(t) *Donellus* explains *jus publicum* as follows :—" Dicuntur res ad statum Reipublicæ pertinere, sine quibus aut civitas constitui, aut constituta stare incolumis non potest id enim *statum* cujusque rei vocamus, quo res stat et sine quo non consisteret. Itaque si cognoverimus, quænam eæ res sunt et quid de his juris sit simul *jus publicum* tenetimus."—*Donelli, de Jure Civ. Comment.* lib. iii. ch. v.

(u) *Code Civil*, Art. 3, 11, 13.

administration of justice as the native (*x*). Where an exception is made, it is with the intent of relieving the foreigner from the effect of the collision of local laws and usages to which the native is exposed. Savigny remarks that the doctrine dominant at the time of the compilation of this code, of *Personal and Real Statutes* had a marked influence on the terms of these texts of the law, and has led to important difficulties in their application, especially in the matter of *Succession (y)*.

The Austrian code resembles the Prussian in this matter, and contains similar provisions with respect to foreigners (*z*). There are codes of other nations (*a*), European and American, containing positive enactments relating to the validity and interpretation of *Contracts* and *Testaments* and Successions of Foreigners (*b*).

VII. Private International Law has been generally discussed in treatises bearing the title of "Commentaries upon the Collision or Conflict of Laws," a mode of treating the subject which is certainly not philosophical. According to Savigny, The natural order of thinking upon the subject is—to ask as to the rule of law to be applied the question what is the legal relation (*c*) which it is to govern? As to the legal relation, to what rule of law is it subject, or does it belong? The enquiry concerning the limits of territorial sovereignty or dependence, and concerning the difficulties and disputes arising from the demarcations of these limits, or from collisions, is in its nature a secondary and subordinate enquiry. Wächter (*d*), he adds, makes the just remark, that many

---

(*x*) *Allgem. L. Recht. Einleitung*, s. 23—35.

(*y*) *System des R. R.* viii. s. 361 (133).

(*z*) *Oester. Gesetzbuch*, s. iv. s. 33—37.

(*a*) *Vide post.*

(*b*) *Fœlix, Tr. dec. Dr. Int.* P. L. ii. t. i. c. ii. s. vii.—See too the Brazilian Code (1857), Consolidacao des Leis Civis, s. 5 (proof of birth, &c.) 34, 1260 ; 1266 (successions) s. 408 (*status* and age); s. 696 (contracts).

(*c*) So I have rendered the German word used by *Savigny* in this passage and familiar to the readers of *Puchta* and *Blume* viz., *Rechtsverhaltniss*,—it has been rendered "jural relation," but I think the word implies Right and Obligation, and *jural* is unknown to our language.

(*d*) *Wächter*, ii. 34.

writers who entirely separate the question as to the application of the law from the question as to the Collision, have
been thereby led into the error of giving upon two identical
questions contradictory answers (e).

VIII. The very interesting but very difficult question, What
are the limits assigned by the *Jus Gentium Privatum* to the
operation of the laws of one State within the territory of another?
necessarily involves a twofold consideration of the conflict of laws:
1. With respect to the different positive laws of different States;
2. With respect to the diversity of the practice of States, as to
recognising the authority of each other's laws, and giving effect
to them beyond their proper sphere. The expression itself—
Jus Gentium, or, *J. G. Privatum*—however convenient, and,
though open, perhaps, to less objection than any other expression, is yet not strictly accurate; and the use of it must not lead
us to forget that clear and important distinction between the
concessions of Comity and the obligations of Right, which
flow from the cardinal principles of International Law, viz. the
Equality and Independence of States, " Debitor," says the
Roman Law, "intelligitur is a quo invito exegi pecunia
potest" (f). One State may be lawfully compelled by force

(e) *Savigny*, viii. s. 344.

(f) *Dig.* l. l. t. 16—108.

The two propositions, viz.:—That the laws of foreign countries
are not admitted *ex proprio vigore*, but only *ex comitate*; and that the
judicial power will exercise a discretion with respect to the laws they
may be called upon to sanction, and, if they be manifestly unjust, or
calculated to injure the citizens of the State in which that power is
exercised, refused to sanction them, appear to have been very strongly
asserted by the Courts of the United States of North America in the
following cases :—

Blanbord v. *Russell*, 13 *Massachusetts Rep.* 1—6.

Prentiss v. *Savage*, ib. 20—24.

Tappan v. *Poor*, 15 ib. 419—422.

Ingraham v. *Geyer*, 13 ib. 146—7.

Cambridge v. *Lexington*, 1 *Pickering's Rep.* 506.

These cases are cited in *Curtis's United States Digest*, v. ii. p. 762, n. 46.

See also a leading case, *Saul* v. *His Creditors*, 17 *Marten's Americ.*
Rep. 569, 590 to 596.

to pay its debt to another member of the community of
States. But the favour or grace of Comity may not lawfully be exacted by force. And from the same authority
is derived the maxim so often cited on the subject, " Extra
territorium jus dicenti impunè non paretur " (g).

IX. The writer upon International Law is bound to draw
the distinction which has been mentioned between Comity
and Law. But having done so, and shown on what terms
Comity is admitted to govern the legal relations of the subjects of different States, he may and ought to insist that the
jus gentium, like the *jus inter gentes*, is built upon the hypothesis of a common law for a Commonwealth of States (h)—
"Sub diversitate judicum, una justitia" (i). And as the
National Jurist endeavours to apply rules of justice to cases
which come in contact with different laws of different independent portions or provinces of one integral State, so
ought the International Jurist to consider cases which come
in contact with the laws of different States of one Commonwealth, and to apply the like rules of justice. To both
the remark of Pascal is equally applicable, " Plaisante justice
qu'une rivière ou une montagne borne" (j) ; or, as it is admirably put by Cicero, " Qui autem civium rationem dicunt esse
habendum, externorum negent, bi dirimunt humani generis
societatum" (k). It is true that the National Jurist may, with
respect to different portions of one State, invoke the sanction
and enforcement of a common superior: while the international

---

(g) *Dig.* l. ii. t. ii. s. 20. A maxim relating to the limits of different
domestic jurisdictions borrowed from the *municipal* law of the Romans,
and applied, like others, on account of its instrinsic worth, by States
to each other. See remarks, vol. i. p. 31.

(h) *Savigny, R. R.* viii. ss. 348, 349. He remarks, justly, that this
theory of a community of States, and the constant tendency to adopt
a uniform practice upon the subject of Foreign Law, was unknown to
the Romans, and is due to the rapid intercourse among the subjects of
different states in modern times.

(i) *Cassiodorus*, as cited by *Miltitz, Manuel des Consuls*, i. 162.

(j) *Pensées*, art. vi. s. 8.

(k) *De Off.* lib. iii. c. 11.

Jurist cannot do this, for States have no common superior; but he finds a practical substitute in the pressure of the necessities, and mutuality of the exigencies, of States. Every invention of man and the age teems with such devices, which renders more easy and more quick the intercourse of the subjects of different States, increases this pressure, and strengthens this mutuality. To treat the foreigner and the native as entitled to a like measure of justice has become the manifest interest, as it has ever been the clear duty, of States. The vision of the great statesman and orator does not appear incapable of practical fulfilment to the Christian Jurist, who sees how marvellously time and space are, relatively to the past, annihilated, and how the remotest corners of the earth are becoming knit together by agencies unknown, undreamt of, by antiquity. The day may not be far off when civilized man, wherever he goes, "sese non unius circumdatum mœnibus loci, sed civem totius mundi, quasi unius urbis agnoverit" (*l*).

X. In England, the subjects (*m*) of the other States of Christendom have been, speaking generally, governed, in such cases as are mentioned in the last section, on the same principles of law as her own subjects of Scotland and of her Colonies. The *jus gentium* (said an eminent English civilian and judge in the last century,) is the law of every country"(*n*).

(*l*) *Cicero, de Legibus,* p. i. c. xx. 166.

(*m*) " And as the judges furthermore may informe the Lords, howe former lawes of this realme presentlie stand touchinge any matter there debated. For many they bee also informed by the Masters of the Chancery (of which the greatest number have alwaies been chosen men skillfull in the Civil and Canon Lawes) in lawes that they shall make touching forraine matters, whom the same shall accord with *Equitie, Jus Gentium,* and the Lawes of other nations."—*A Treatise of the Masters of the Chancerie,* date between 1596 and 1603. (*Hargrave's Law Tracts,* p. 309).

(*n*) *Scrimshire* v. *Scrimshire,* 2 *Consistory Reports,* 417.

Ruding v. *Smith, ib.* 384-6.

So *Lord Stowell* (in a prize case, it is true, but referring to the *Jus Gentium,* and not the *Jus inter Gentes*) : " This is the law not of the

The same may be predicated of other States, especially of Prussia, but not, as will be seen, without great deductions, of France (o).

XI. And it may be observed that this branch of jurisprudence has been, and is being, more scientifically developed than others, by judges and by jurists. It is a matter for rejoicing that it has escaped the Procrustean treatment of positive legislation, and has been allowed to grow to its fair proportions under the influence of that science which works out of conscience, reason, and experience, the great problem of Law, or Civil Justice. The judge who has to decide by what Law a particular Legal Relation, which comes into contact with the laws of divers States, shall be governed, ought to apply to this contested Legal Relation that local positive law to which it is, in its true nature, properly subject or appertaining, without distinguishing whether that law be the law of his own or of a Foreign State.

The State ought to permit its judge to treat the Foreign Law as one of the sources from which, in the particular case before him, he is to derive justice. It ought, as Lord Stowell observes, to make it a principle of its own law to adopt the law of the foreigner (p).

XII. Nevertheless, there are exceptional restrictions which limit, in a Commonwealth of States, the application of this principle of a Common Law; they grow out of the reason and nature of the thing. In every State there are various kinds of laws, the special nature of which is not in harmony with this principle.

To define the limits of these exceptional restrictions is among the most difficult tasks which can be imposed upon the jurist.

Court only, but of all Courts, and one of the first principles of *universal jurisprudence.*"—*The Betsy*, 1 *Robinson's Rep.* 94. So he speaks of " *The general rule of civilised nations*" as to derelict. *The Aquila, ib.* 20. " Salvage is a question of the *jus gentium,*" ib. 279 and vol. vii. 185.

(o) See *Fælix, Preface*, p. vii. (3me. ed.)

(p) *Dalyrmple* v. *Dalrymple*, 2 *Consistory Reports*, p. 39. *et vide post.*

XIII. These exceptional restrictions partake of (*q*) a political and (*r*) of a moral and religious character : for International Comity, like International Law, can only exist in its lowest degree among Independent States ; in its next degree among Independent Civilized States, and in its highest degree among Independent Christian States (*r*). There is a third class of these exceptional restrictions, namely, laws of a stringent, positive character, which are the peculiar growth of the peculiar institutions of a Foreign State,—an exotic incapable from its nature of being transplanted into a strange soil. Under these three categories it would seem that all these exceptional restrictions may be classed.

XIV. First, with respect to those of a political character.

The law of the Foreign State cannot be admitted into another State if it be contrary to any fundamental or constitutional law or usage of that State.

Under this head are included the following propositions :—

1. That the Foreign Law be not incompatible with the safety of the State.

2. That it be not prejudicial to the public interest of the State.

Under this head also may be mentioned the universal rule that, one State will not administer within its territory the Criminal Law of another : How far the generality of this proposition may have been qualified by Treaties on the subject of Extradition, and the practice of States thereupon, has been considered in a former volume of this work (*s*).

XV. Secondly—With respect to Exceptional Restrictions arising from Moral and Religious considerations, no Foreign Law which enjoins or sanctions an institution, custom or practice, at variance with the immutable Laws of Right written by

---

(*q*) *Savigny* R. R. viii. s. 349—365 (32—160).
Story, s. 28.
Fœlix, s. 15.
(*r*) *Vide ante,* vol. i. ch. 1.
(*s*) Vol. i. c. xxi.

the finger of God on the heart of man (*t*), or with those which have been the subject of His express Revelation can be admitted into a Christian State (*u*).

XVI. With respect to the Exceptional Restriction arising from considerations of the stringent positive character of the Foreign Law, a Law of this character, the peculiar growth of accidental circumstances, alien to the feelings, habits, and Laws of the State which would have to enforce it, has no claim to be admitted, on the ground of Comity, concerning which, in such a case as this, the rule of Huberus is sound. — "Quatenus sine præjudicio indulgentium fieri potest"(*x*).

XVII. A case may also be imagined not only where there is a conflict between the laws of the Foreign State and the State of the *forum*, but also, where it is a matter of doubt, which should prevail. In such a case, the tribunal of North American United States (*y*) have declared themselves strongly in favour of the law of the actual *forum.* Probably snch a case would be of very rare occurrence, but the principle of such a decision appears to the writer of these pages very questionable(*z*).

XVIII. The foregoing categories appear to comprise the prin-

(*t*) "Pacta quæ contra leges constitutiones vel contra donos mores fiunt nullam vim habere indubitati juris est."—*Cod.* l. ii. t. iii. l. vi.

"Pacta quæ turpem cansam continent non sunt observanda."— *Dig.* l. ii. t. xiv. 27, 4.

(*u*) *Vide ante,* vol. i. ch. iii.

(*x*) *De Conflict. Leg.* lib. i. tit. ii. s. 2.

Story, speaking of Assignments by Bankruptcy Laws, says, " Besides, National Comity requires us to give effect to such assignments only as far as may be done without impairing the remedies or lessening the securities which our Laws have provided for our own citizens," s. 414. He relies on the doctrine of *Huberus.— Vide post,* as to Bankruptcy and its effects in Foreign States.

(*y*) *Story,* s. 28 ; *Judgment of Mr. Justice Porter ; Martens' (Americ.), Rep.* 569—595, 596.

(*z*) The mischievous extent to which this doctrine may be easily pushed appears in the decision of the Louisiana tribunal in *Olivier* v. *Townes,* 2 *Martens' (Americ.),* N. S. *Report,* 93.

ciples which regulate the application, and restrain the enforcement of Foreign Laws, according to the Comity of States; whether that Comity be administered in Courts of Justice, or by acts of the Executive or of the Administrative authorities. Many illustrations of the possible application in practice of the restrictions may be imagined.

For instance,—no Christian nation (a) could be expected to tolerate Polygamy, or Incest, within its territory, because the persons practising it were subjects of a country which permitted such connections. Nor could a Christian nation, whose law regarded certain marriages as incestuous which other Christian nations sanctioned, be required to recognise the validity of such marriages in the cases of its own subjects, though celebrated in a country which permitted them.

No country which held the *status* of slavery to be abominable, and unwarranted by the laws of God and man (as most Christian nations do at this moment), would allow any title to property of this description to be set up, or any legal consequences to be drawn from it within her dominions.

XIX. In the case of the *Creole* (b), which formed the subject of a dispute between Great Britain and the United States of America in 1842, this doctrine was steadily maintained by the former power. That vessel, having been driven by stress of weather into the Bahamas, a British port, certain slaves on board her, who were being conveyed from one port of America to another, where the curse of slavery still exists, rose upon their master, overpowered him, and effected their escape.

(a) But a Christian State may possess a Heathen dependency, which it allows to continue under its own laws, and then, if the last Court of Appeal be in the Christian mother State, it must recognise the Heathen Law, even in the case of marriage. See, as partly illustrating this point, a recent decision of the Privy Council.—*Ardassar Cursetjee* v. *Perozeboye*, 10 *Moore's P. C. Rep.* 374. So it may allow an unchristian race, like the Jews, to live according to their own laws in the Christian territory. But these are questions rather of Public than International Law.

(b) See the case of the *Creole* considered by R. Phillimore, in a letter to Lord Ashburton, published in 1842.

The British authorities refused to allow any force to be used towards these persons, to compel them to return to slavery ;— the Comity of Nations, through which alone such force could have been exercised, did not require her to sacrifice a fundamental principle of her laws—namely, the inviolable right of personal liberty of all persons within her realms—in order to enforce therein the ordinances of another country.

Long before this period, and while Great Britain was still largely participating in the accursed traffic—from the guilt of which she had endeavoured, before the time of the last-mentioned occurrence, by every means in her power, to purge herself—in the year 1771, the decision of Lord Mansfield, in the famous case of Somerset, the Negro, had shown that she applied this vital maxim of her Constitutional Law, under circumstances of far greater embarrassment, rigorously against the interests of her own subjects. France appears to have held steadily the same doctrine (c).

XX. Again, no State can be expected to enforce the execution of any law which offends the religious feeling of the community—such, for instance, as the law that the descendants of a Jew, who had been converted to Christianity, should be excluded from the right of succession *ab intestato*, or such as the old Irish Popery Laws, branded with deserved infamy in the immortal writings of Burke (d).

XXI. No State would allow a foreigner to do any act with respect to another foreigner of the same nation, which act

---

(c) *Demangeat Du Statut Personel*, Revue Pratique De Droit Français, t. i. p. 57.

(d) *Vide ante* vol. ii. App. ii. Cases and authorities collected on the subject, of enforcing *Foreign Revenue Laws*. "Unfortunately (*Story* observes, s. 245) from a very questionable subserviency to mere commercial gains, it has become an established formulary of the Common (he means the English and American) Law, that no nation will regard or enforce the Revenue Laws of any other country ; and that the contracts of its own subjects made to evade or defraud the laws or just rights of foreign nations may be enforced in its own tribunals. Sound morals would seem to point to a very different conclusion."

would violate the law of the State, though permitted by the law of their own land. No foreigner, for instance, would be allowed to inflict any chastisement or cruelty upon his wife, or any member of his family or suite, because such chastisement or cruelty would be authorised by the law of the foreigner's native country.

XXII. The foregoing cases relate principally to the question of allowing the operation of Foreign Laws at variance with the religion or morality of the State. There are others in which the application of these laws is denied, because injurious to the public policy of the nation.

XXIII. Thus Great Britain and the United States of North America consider the allegiance of native subjects as indelible ; and though they allow them to be domiciled in another country, and will consider them as subjects of that country in many respects, e. g., with regard to their succession to personal property, to their contracts and other matters, they will not allow them so to incorporate themselves with another nation, as, in the event of war breaking out between the country of their domicil and of their birth, to allow them to bear arms against the latter. Prisoners of this description are considered as rebels, and not as lawful enemies.

XXIV. If a State, upon grounds which are supposed to concern the welfare and safety of the Constitution, impress a personal incapacity upon its Sovereign or its subject (e), to enter into a contract of a particular description, that State will not hold valid such a contract because it was executed in a foreign land, according to the Municipal Law of which it was legal and binding. England, by the Royal Marriage Act impressed a personal incapacity upon certain members of the Royal Family to contract a marriage except under certain conditions ; and the tribunals of this country refused to recognise a marriage duly and legally contracted, according to the *lex loci contractûs*, by a member of that family, in a foreign

---

(e) *Vide post*, Chapter on MARRIAGES.

land, but with respect to which these conditions had not been fulfilled : England has also, by the express provisions of a statute (*f*), rendered it unlawful for any of her subjects, "wheresoever residing," to be the possessor or purchaser of a slave even in any State. Upon this subject also an indelible personal incapacity is by this law impressed upon the Englishman, and though the penalty of infringing it cannot be inflicted upon him while he is resident in a State which permits slavery, it will reach him whenever he comes within the jurisdiction of England.

XXV. But where these Exceptional Restrictions do not apply, a State can then (to borrow the phrase of Vattel) perform an office for another nation without neglecting its duty towards itself : or rather Comity then assumes the character of a *Jus Gentium Privatum ;* the general principle of which cannot be more happily conveyed than in the language already referred to (*g*) of Lord Stowell's celebrated judgment in *Dalrymple* v. *Dalrymple,* where, deciding upon the validity of a Scotch marriage in an English Court, he said, "Being "entertained in an English Court it must be adjudicated "according to the principle of English law applicable to such a " case. But the only principle applicable to such a case by the "law of England, is, that the validity of the marriage rights "must be tried by reference to the law of the country where, "if they exist at all, they had their origin.

(*f*) 6 & 7 Vic. c. xcviii. s. 1.

(*g*) *Townsend* v. *Jamison,* 9 *Howard's Amer. Rep.* p. 407 ; 18 *Curtis's Amer. Rep.* p. 202. The following passages, from this judgment of the Supreme Court of the United States of North America, are worthy of all consideration :—

"It has become, as we have always said, a fixed rule of the *jus gentium privatum,* unalterable, in our opinion, either in England or in the States of the United States, except by legislative enactment,— when there is no positive rule affirming, denying, or restraining the operation of Foreign Laws, courts establish a Comity for such as are not repugnant to the policy or in conflict with the laws of the State from which they derive their organization."

"Having furnished this principle, the law of England "withdraws altogether, and leaves the legal question to the "exclusive judgment of the law of Scotland."

The principal sources of Private International Law are the following:—

I. Writers on General or Public International Law—they have rarely or very incidently touched upon Comity or Private International Law:
Grotius, pp. 416—593, 595, 675—697.

Puffendorfius, De Jure N. et G. l. ii. c. iii. p. 150, fol. ed.

Bynkershoek, De Foro Legatorum, c. 2.

Günther, Europäisches Völkerrecht, 30-31.

Zouch, De Jure Feciali sive de judicio inter gentes, iii.

Vattel, l. ii. c. viii.

Martens, Dr. des Gens, l. iii. c. iii. ss. 93, 98, 99, 100.

Heffter, s. 35.

II. Civilians or commentators on the Roman Law—they have occasionally dealt with this question:

Bartolus, in Codicem, l. i. c. *de Summâ Trinitate*, n. 13—51. This is the fountain of Private International Jurisprudence. Without a careful study of this Commentary, nobody can be thoroughly versed in the history of the progress of the principles of Private International Law. Who would have expected such a treatise in a *Gloss* on the words "cunctos populos" in a chapter *de Summâ Trinitate ?*

J. Voet, in his *Commentary on the Pandects*, l. i. t. 4, *De Constitut. Princ.*, at part ii. *de Statutis*, ss. 1—22.

Huberus, Prælect. ad Pandectas, treats *De Conflictu Legum* in an *Appendix* to lib. i. t. iii., *De Legibus*, ss. 1—15.

Mühlenbruch, Doctrina Pandectarum, l. i. c. iv., de ratione quæ inter plures leges vel concurrentes vel secum dissidentes intercedit, p. 148—159 (A.D. 1830.)

Puchta, Instit. I. 360, explains *Jus Gentium.*

Savigny, System des R. Rechts, I. s. 22 (112—119) explains *Jus Gentium*, showing how it affected the *jus civile*. Here *Jus Gentium* is in fact Comity. As to vol. iii. *vide post.*

III. Writers on Municipal Law treating incidently of Private International Law:

B. Argentræi, Comment. ad potius Britonum leges. The 218th Article of the Customs of Bretagne ordains that no one shall leave away from his natural heirs more than *one-third* of his immoveable property. Thereupon arose the question whether immoveables situated out of Bretagne ought to be included in this *third.* D'Argentré, in the sixth Gloss upon the 218th Article enters fully into the question of the collision of laws, pp. 601—620. The work was published after his death A.D. 1608.

C. Rodenburg, De Jure Conjugum. The question of the Collision of Laws is treated of at length in his *Præliminaria,* pp. 13—178 (A.D. 1653).

D'Aguesseau, xiii. 639, Memoire sur l'execution des Contrats passés et jugemens rendus en pay étranger, *ib.* 638; Memoire sur l'execution des jugemens entre les Souverains.

Massè, Le Droit Commercial dans ses Rapports avec le Droit des Gens et le Droit Civil, t. ii. c. 1. Des Relations Internationales Individuelles ou Du Droit International Privé (A.D. 1844).

Merlin, Repertoire de Jurisprudence *v.* "Etranger" and "Souveraineté."

Demolombe, Cours de Code Civil, tome i. tit. i. c. iii. *Quelle est la condition juridique des étrangers en France,* and tit. 3 *Du Domicile,* 1845, A.D.

Demangeat, Histoire de la condition civile des Etrangers en France, 1844, A.D.

Legat, Code des étrangers ou Traité de la legislation Française concernant les Etrangers, 1832, A.D.

Thöl, Das Handelsrecht, I., Einleitung, 1847, A.D.

Puttlingen, Die gesetsliche Behandlung der Ausländer in Œsterreich.

Kent's Comment. on American Law, I. 187.

Bell's Commentaries on the Laws of Scotland in relation to Mercantile and Maritime Law, vol. i. Introduction : vol. ii. p. 1294. International Law relating to Bankruptcy Ed. Shaw, 1858, A.D.

Cole on Domicil of Englishmen in France, 1857, A.D.

IV. Writers on Private International Law, *per se.*—

P. Voet, De Statutis eorumque concursu, ss. 4, 9, 10, 11, upon the Collision of Statutes (1661, A.D.)

J. N. Hertius, De Collisione Legum (1688, A.D.). *Comment. et opuscul,* vol. i. pp. 118—154.

L. Boullenois, Traité de la personalité et de la realité des Loix &c. (1766, A D.). It is a French translation with considerable additions of Rodenburg's work.—*D. Meier, De Conflictu Legum* (1810, A.D.).

G. V. Struve, über das positive Rechtsgesetz in seiner Beziehung auf räumliche Verhältnisse (1834, A.D.)

W. Shäffner, Entwickelung des Internationalen Privatrechts (1841, A.D.).

Pütter, Das praktische Europäische Fremdensecht, 1845, A.D.

Wächter wrote some excellent numbers "über die collision der

Privatrechtsgesetze," in a German publication entitled "Archiv für die Civilistische Praxis," 24th and 25th volumes (1841-2, A.D.).

Rocco, Dell 'uso e autorità delle leggi del Regno delle due Sicilie considerate nelle Relazioni con le persone e col territorio degli Stranieri (1837, A.D.).

Fœlix, Du Droit International Privé du Conflit des Lois de différentes Nations en Matiére de Droit Privé, last edition by M. Demargeat in 1856.

Henry, Judgment in *Odwin* v. *Forbes*, 1823, A.D.

Story, Commentary on the Conflict of Laws, last edit. 1857.

Burge, Commentaries on Colonial and Foreign Laws generally, and in their conflict with each other and the Law of England, 1838, A.D.

R. Phillimore, the Law of Domicil, 1847, A.D.

Westlake, Private International Law, 1858, A.D.

Savigny, System des heutigen Römischen Rechts Achtes Band, A.D. 1849.

This eighth volume of the author's great work is entirely occupied with Private International Law.

V. The decisions of Courts of Justice of Independent States upon questions involving a conflict of Laws.

VI. Lex Mercatoria of Independent States.

VII. Civil Codes of States into which express provisions on the subject of P. Int. Law have been incorporated.

CHAPTER II.

PLAN OF THE WORK.

XXVI. IN the former Chapter it has been stated that the Judge who has to decide as to a particular Legal Relation which comes into contact with the laws of divers States, ought, as a general rule, to arrive at his decision by applying to that particular Legal Relation that positive law to which it is, according to its true nature, properly subject. All positive law is derived from a State (a), that is, from a particular defined territory occupied by a particular people, governed by their own Ruler.

The enquiry, therefore, as to what positive law a particular Legal Relation is, according to its own nature, subject, necessarily involves the further enquiry as to the territory from which the positive law is derived. This necessarily leads to a further enquiry as to what are the ties which bind an individual (*persona*), and all that appertains to his personal rights (*Status, l'etat du droit, Rechtszustand*), to a particular territory so as to subject him to its laws.

XXVII. We may consider the individual (*persona*) *in himself*, with his personal rights, abstractedly; that is, without reference to other considerations than the actual place in which he corporeally exists or resides; and then these ties appear to be of a twofold character, arising out of—

1. Origin;
2. Domicil.

It is by reference to the positive law of his Origin or his Domicil, that the *personal state* or legal condition of the individual—his *status*—his *capacity* of *actually acquiring* or

---

(a) Vol. i. c. i.

being *passively the subject* of Legal Relations—is to be ascertained.

XXVIII. But we must also consider the individual with reference to his *acts*, and the Legal Relations which accrue therefrom : and then, in order to discover to what positive law these Legal Relations should be subject, we are led beyond the consideration of the particular territory to which, by Origin or Domicil, the individual may be attached.

The positive law of the territory in which the *acts* of the individual have been done, from which these Legal Relations have accrued, must be considered, and also the positive law of the territory of other individuals with whose Legal Relations his acts have brought him into contact.

These Legal Relations may be classified under the two great categories of—

1. Legal Relations of Family ;
2. Legal Relations of Things or Property.

XXIX. The positive law which should govern these Legal Relations, when they are in contact with divers positive laws, should be the positive law to which they are naturally subject ; or, as it is sometimes said, the law of the territory in which the Legal Relation has its seat.

XXX. Or it may be thus expressed : the individual is connected with positive law in a threefold manner, namely,

1. By his person ;
2. By his acts ;
3. By his property.

XXXI. In the present treatise it is proposed to consider both—

1. What law ought to govern the particular Right or Legal Relation which comes in contact with divers laws; and

2. What law by the consent of States does practically govern such Legal Relation.

The arrangement of the subject will be as follows :—To consider—

First, Origin and Domicil; and, as necessarily connected therewith, the Personal *Status* of the Individual.

Secondly, the Legal Relations arising from *Family*—under which head will be included—

    1. Marriage and Divorce.

    2. Legitimacy.

    3. Parental authority over

      a Persons ⎱ of Children.
      b Property ⎰

    4. Guardianship.

Thirdly, Property—under which head will be included

    1. Rights to specific things

      a Immoveables.

      b Moveables.

    2. Rights to compel certain persons to do certain things or Obligations—of which Contracts are a branch.

    3. Rights relating to Succession, whether *Testamento* or *ab Intestato.*

Fourthly, The rules which govern the *Form and Manner of Procedure* in actions or suits in which the subject of a Foreign State is Plaintiff or Defendant(*b*).

Fifthly, *Criminal International Law,* which concerns the *unlawful acts* of a subject of a Foreign State.

(*b*) This is treated of by *Fœlix* under Private International, but by *Savigny* as a matter of Public International Law, because the State is prosecutor. *Vide ante,* vol. i. c. xviii., Right of Jurisdiction over Persons. There has been quite recently an essay on this subject, written by the present Home Secretary, Sir George Lewis.

CHAPTER III.

ORIGO.

XXXI. The expressions "*Origo*"(a) and "*Domicilium*"(b), have been engrafted into all modern jurisprudence from the Roman Law.   Savigny (c), however, justly warns us against the danger of a false application of supposed technical expressions of that law, as connected with these words.

The warning, however, is not needed, or scarcely needed, as to the word *domicilium*, the Rules of Law respecting which have not been essentially modified by modern usage, and which in practice are correctly applied.

But with respect to the word *Origo*, the case is different. A greater danger of mistake exists as to it; not on account of any obscurity in the Roman decisions upon the subject, but because the modern *status* of the individual differs essentially from that which he possessed under the Roman Empire. This is a danger of which the practice of modern law scarcely admonishes us.

The word *Origo* is so easily translated into the words *place of birth* (*lieu de la naissance—Geburtsort*), that modern jurists (including among their number those who were acquainted with the true meaning of *Origo* in the Roman Law) have frequently so rendered it :—" The mere place of birth," Savigny says, " is an accidental circumstance without any

---

(a) *Origin. L'origine, Herkunft.*

(b) *Domicil. Domicile, Wohnsitz.*

(c) VIII. s. 350. The following slight sketch is chiefly taken from his large picture.

" legal influence whatever." The English lawyer, at least (*d*) is aware that this statement is too broad, inasmuch as the mere accident of birth in English territory is attended with most important legal consequences to the person born therein (*e*). The French lawyer knows that the individual who is domiciled in France may yet be, in many civil respects, considered as a foreigner. And in Switzerland (*f*), as Savigny himself afterwards remarks, there is a *jus originis* springing from *birth* in a particular *commune*, and a *jus domicilii*, from domicil in a *commune*, the former overruling the latter in the more important Legal Relations.

XXXII. Towards the close of the Republic and during the first centuries of her Empire, Italy, with the exception of Rome, consisted of a variety of urban communities which were called, for the most part, *municipii*, and *coloniæ*. Each of them possessed a kind of constitution of their own,—their own magistrates, their own jurisdiction, and sometimes their own legislation. Every inhabitant of Italy appertained either to Rome or to one of these urban communities.

The provinces, on the contrary, had originally very various constitutions; but had, in the time of the great jurists of the two first Christian centuries, become assimilated with the Italian communities. The general appellation of these urban commuities was *civitates* or *reipublicæ :* their domain was designated *territorium,* an expression which occurs often in the Justinian compilations, and sometimes *regio.* The *vici* were rural subdivisions of the *civitas.* The individual was bound to the urban community in two ways, 1st, by the

---

(*d*) *Vide post,* and see *Story,* s. 51—68, for the opinions of Foreign Jurists, which, in s. 81, he says lay down, "that the law of the domicil of origin, *or,* the law of the actual domicil, is of universal obligation as to the capacity, state, and condition of persons." Very unsatisfactory, it must be admitted.

(*e*) *Vide post.*

(*f*) *Ib.* s. 358. It is remarkable that this peculiarity appears to have no connexion with the Roman jurisprudence, *vide post.*

Right of Citizenship generally founded on birth (*Origo*) ; 2, by the Right of Domicil (*domicilium*) within the *territorium*.

XXXIII. There are certain passages in the Roman Law which classify the free inhabitants of the Empire as follows— (*g*) *Cives*, (*h*) *Latini*, (*i*) *Peregrini*, which classification at first sight appears to apply to each class a determinate positive law : but this is not so. The classification did indeed materially affect the capacity of individuals, *e. g.*, the *Cives* had *connubium* and *commercium*—the *Latini* had *commercium* only—the *Peregrinus* had neither: but the classification has no bearing on the consideration as to which entire system of positive law the individual was subject (*k*).

The tie which bound the individual to an urban community, or, speaking generally, municipality, whether it sprung from *origo* or *domicilium*, produced three effects or consequences.

1. It subjected him to a share of the *burdens and charges* (*Munera*) of the community.

2. It subjected him to the *jurisdiction* of the community (*forum originis vel domicilii*). The plaintiff (*actor*) was bound to institute his suit in the *forum* of the defendant (*rei*) but he might choose *the forum originis* or the *forum domicilii*.

3. It fastened upon him *the particular law* of the community as a *personal attribute* (*lex originis—domicilii*).

This last of the three effects or consequences, Savigny (*l*) points out, as of extreme importance. There is, he says, an intimate connection between all the three effects, but especially

---

(*g*) *Municipem* aut *nativitas* facit, aut manumissio, aut adoptio.—*Dig.* l. l. t. 1—1.

(*h*) *Cives* quidem *origo* manumissio allectio vel adoptio. *Incolas* vero . . . *domicilium* facit.—*Cod.* l. x. t. 39—7.

(*i*) *Muneris particeps*—but the exact primitive meaning of this word is doubtful ; it came to be the designation of all who, out of Rome, had rights of citizenship, their connexion with their particular community being generally expressed by the word *origo* or *patria*.

(*k*) *Savigny, ib.* s. 356.

(*l*) *Ib.* s. 356.

between the two last (*m*), which are to be regarded but as different sides of one whole— different appearances of the same local or territorial law to which the individual is subject.

The intimate connection between the *jurisdiction* of, and the *particular law* derived from, the Community is a principle which extends beyond the mere antiquarian consideration of the Roman Constitution; it lies, in fact, at the root of the existing Private International Law; it furnishes the true solution of the problem, what law shall govern that Legal Relation which comes in contact with the law of divers territories (*n*)?

XXXIV. The observations in the last section are applicable, it will be remarked, to the tie by which *Domicilium*, as well as that by which *Origo*, binds an individual to a State. In truth, the effect of mere Origin or Birth in binding the individual to a particular territory, and subjecting him to the law thereof, appears chiefly in the consideration of Public International Law, and has been treated of in an earlier volume of this work in a chapter upon "The Right of Jurisdiction over Persons" inherent in the government of every independent State (*o*). Also the collateral question as to the acquisition

---

(*m*) See, too, *Bynkershoek, De Foro Leg.* c. 2; *Forum competens,* founded by *origo et natura. Subjectio duplex,* 1 *rei,* 2, *personæ.*

(*n*) This appears to me to give fairly, as far as the English language will allow, *Savigny's* meaning.

(*o*) Vol. i. c. xviii. p. 345. "Right of Jurisdiction over Persons." In *Shedden* v. *Patrick,* 1 *Macqueen's House of Lords Cases,* 611, Lord Chancellor Cranworth observes, that in England, *independently of Statute Law,* and with certain exceptions, every one *born* abroad is an alien. See also, *Mr. Westlake's Private International Law,* c. ii.

The English Statutes are 25 Edw. III. stat. 2; 7 Anne, c. v.; 4 Geo. II. c. xxi.; 13 Geo. III. c. xxi.; 7 and 8 Vic. c. lxvi. s. 3.

English Leading Cases.—Bacon's case, Croke's Ch. Reports, 602.

Doe v. *Jones,* 4 *Durnford and East Rep.* 308.

Countess de Conway's Case, 2 *Knapp's P. C. Rep.* 364.

Count de Wall's Representatives Case, 6 *Moore's P. C. Reports,* 216.

These two last Cases, and *Bacon's* Case, were before the 7 and 8 Vic. c. lxvi., s. 16, of which makes the foreign wife of an Englishman

of a new and the loss of an old national character. The theory of *Domicil* has in fact, with few, but important exceptions, swallowed up the theory of *Origin* in all matters of Comity.

The effect of Origin is, however, still seen when the positive law of the State in which a man is born affixes an indelible incapacity upon its subject to do certain acts, and enter into certain obligations. Thus, in Switzerland the *jus originis* of the *commune* decides in preference to the *jus domicilii*, both the local positive law and the forum in suits concerning Divorce and Succession. The law of England renders an Englishman incapable of possessing a slave in any State, and certain members of its Royal Family from contracting marriages (*p*) in any State without certain previous consents. The law of England also applies the law of treason—though this is a matter of Public International Law—with great severity, affixing on all who *have been born* from parents who are not enemies (*q*) within its territory an indelible allegiance, and therefore, an indelible incapacity to bear arms against herself (*r*). So, with regard to incestuous marriages; under which head it is to be observed that the Law of England at present places marriages with the wife's sister, making, as it does, no difference between relations by consanguinity and by affinity (*s*).

---

an Englishwoman; and it has been holden in a criminal case that she cannot refuse this character, but must accept it with its advantages and disadvantages, *Maria Mnaning's Case*, 2 *Carrington and Kirwan's Rep.* 387.

(*p*) 12 *George* III. c. xi.

Sussex Peerage Case, 11 *Clarke and Finnelly*, 85.

(*q*) See this exception, *Calvin's Case*, 7 *Coke*, 18 a.

(*r*) See the celebrated case of *Æneas Macdonald*, 18 *State Trials*, 857. He had not been in Great Britain since his infancy, but he was born there. In 1745 he was taken in arms under a French Commission, and holden guilty of treason.

See too, *Drummond's case*, 2 *Knapp's P. C. Report*, 295, 311, 314.

Fitch v. *Weber*, 6 *Hare's Rep.* 65.

(*s*) *Story*, s. 86; from s. 113 (a) to 119 discusses the question condemning the English Law; though his reasoning at s. 116 (a) is strange.—*Sed vide post.*

This subject is further discussed in a later part of this volume, in which the law relating to Foreign Marriages is discussed.

XXXV. M. Demangeat, in his endeavour to answer the question, What the circumstance is which determines for each individual his personal law, justly observes, that if the domicil of the individual were always and necessarily identical with the territory of the State to which he belonged, it would be enough to say, by way of answer to the question, that the personal law of the individual is the law of the place wherein the individual is domiciled (*t*).

But it may happen in France that a person may be domiciled in France, and yet not cease to be *étranger :* for *incontestablement cela est possible*, M. Demangeat says: nay, he may be even domiciled with the permission of the French government, and yet remain *étranger*. In this latter case what would be his personal law?

M. Demangeat observes that when the personal law serves to disclose to us the intention of the individual, there is no difficulty in saying that it is the positive law of his domicil (*du domicile*), not the law of his Origin or State (*de la patrie*), which is his personal law; thus the French courts have decided that a domiciled foreigner, marrying without a marriage settlement, subjects himself to the *communauté légale* of the Code Napoleon. So, in the *succession mobilière*, the personal law of the Domicil is applied. The real difficulty is to ascertain the personal law when a question of *status* (*d'etat ou capacité*) arises. And M. Demangeat is, on the whole, of opinion, though, as it would seem with less confidence, that even in this case the personal law is the law of the Domicil,— (both of that *de facto* and of that under permission of the government (*u*),—that it was the intention of the compilers of the 13th Article of the Code Napoleon, that the foreigner, so domiciled, should be likened *en ce qui concerne le droit privé* to the

---

(*t*) *Revue Pratique De Droit Français.*—T. 1,n. 2, p. 65.
(*u*) " *Acquis dans toute la force du terme.*"

Frenchman, and if the concluding part of the 13th Article seems
to say that the French law is the personal law of the Frenchman,
the answer is that the Article contemplated the Frenchman
who was *resident*, but not the Frenchman who was *domiciled*
abroad. These observations, however, anticipate the consideration of the law as to personal *status* to which, perhaps, they
more properly belong.

XXXVI. Questions relating to the effect of the *lex originis*
upon the individual and his personal *status*, which may arise
between a State and her colonies (*x*) generally belong to the
department of Public rather than International Law ; while,
upon this question, with the above-mentioned exception, Private International Law refers to the *lex domicilii*, which is
the subject of the following chapter.

(*x*) Birth in an English colony is at present equivalent to birth
in England for all questions of origin as distinct from domicil.—
(*Donegani v. Donegani*, 3 *Knapp, P. C. Rep.* 63 ; *Re Adam*, 1 *Moore,
P. C.* 460.) But as to naturalization in colonies, see 10 & 11 Vic.
c. 83. It is possible that the power of self-legislation in the colonies
may give rise to serious questions, *e.g.* the validity of a divorce
decreed in England upon parties domiciled in a colony where a divorce
is illegal. The English Divorce Court would not, it is true, adjudicate
wittingly on such a case, but it might do so unwittingly. Various other
instances might be suggested.

CHAPTER IV.

DOMICIL.

XXXVII (a). We have now to consider the question of Domicil, the second of the ties which bind, or of the causes which subject, the individual to the jurisdiction of a particular territory (b).

" Questions of Domicil" (said Lord Chancellor Cottenham) " are frequently attended with great difficulty, and the circum- " stances which give rise to such questions are necessarily very " various ; it is of the utmost importance not to depart from " any principles which have been established relative to such " questions, particularly if such principles be adopted not only " by England, but generally by the laws of other countries"(c) ; and Cochin truly observes, " Les questions de domicile dé- " pendent d'un grand nombre de circonstances qu'il faut " réunir (d)."

Domicil is, therefore, principally a question of fact ; and though also, in some degree, a question of law, the former

---

(a) *Donelli Comment. de Jure Civili*, lxvii. c. ix. " Quis sit in jurisdictione competens judex : seu de foro competenti : seu *quod idem valet,* ubi quis agere vel conveniri debeat, ac primum de territorio, et causis cujusque jurisdictione attributis, c. xii." " Ubi subjicatur quisque ex personâ suâ jurisdictioni, tum quibus de causis : et in his primum *de domicilio."*

(b) " *Jus terrendi*—unde *territorium* dictum volunt."—*Ib.* cxii. 10.

(c) *Munro* v. *Munro,* 7 *Clarke & Finnelly's Reports of Cases in the House of Lords,* p. 876.

(d) *Œuvres,* t. 9, p. 124.

ingredient predominates—the contrary of which may be predicated of Origin (*e*).

XXXVIII. The Roman Law is the great repository of the principles of this, as of most other branches of civil jurisprudence. The Roman jurist bestowed great attention upon the different bearings of this question, and all the disquisitions and pains of modern lawyers have been engrafted upon the luminous investigation of the subject contained in the Digest and the Code.

XXXIX (*f*). The universal extent, indeed, of the Roman Empire, excluded the possibility of any question of domicil arising between the subjects of Rome and those of another kingdom; but the necessity of considering domicil, as between the inhabitants of different parts of the same kingdom, was forced upon their jurists by various circumstances, principally by the oppressive nature of the duties and responsibilities incident to the Decurionatus, or municipal office (*g*).   Under

---

(*e*) *Westlake*, 31, note a.

(*f*) In some of the earlier English cases, this has been alleged by counsel as a reason why little or nothing was to be found in the Roman law on the subject of domicil; one of the many proofs how very slight the acquaintance of English lawyers with that law has been. *Munroe* v. *Douglas*, 5 *Maddock's Rep.* p. 291. *Attorney General* v. *Countess of Dalhousie*, 7 *Clarke & Finnelly's Reports*, p. 840.

(*g*) In the time of the free Republic, the citizens, both of Rome and in the provinces, appear to have been divided into the classes of *cives optimo jure*, and *cives non optimo jure*, or *plebeian*. The former enjoyed the privilege of voting for the candidates to high offices, and of being eligible to them. The municipalities of the provinces were governed, as to their internal administration, by a Senate, called, first, *ordo decurionum*, subsequently *ordo* simply, and latterly *curia*, whose members were *curiales*, or *decuriones*. When Augustus permitted the *municipes* to send their suffrages in writing for the elections at Rome, he confined this privilege to the *decuriones*. From this time the name *municipes*, originally given to all the inhabitants, is used almost synonymous with *decuriones*. See Savigny, *Geschichte des Römischen Rechts im Mittelalter*, *Band. I.* c. 2.

System des R. R. viii. s. 353.

the Emperors, the *decuriones*, who collected the imperial taxes, became responsible for the payment of the fixed amount, and were compelled to supply the deficiencies from their own property. Each *decurio* was, moreover, considered as a guarantee for the solvency and good faith of his colleague, and for the successor whom he had presented to fill the office which he vacated. This grievous oppression made every citizen as anxious to escape as he had been formerly desirous to obtain the honour (*h*) ; but the law imposed upon every one who had his *domicilium* in a particular place, the necessity of filling the public offices, and discharging the duties incident to them in that place. So also with respect to the assessment and payment of taxes, Domicil was of much importance ; hence the *criteria* of it are more fully examined in the passages of the Digest and the Code which relate to these subjects—but not alone in these passages—for in discussing the question as to the difference between the " civis" and the " incola " (*i*) of a province—as to the Tribunal before which a person should be convened—when and under what modifications the doctrine of Prescription should take place—what causes excused the Tutor from accepting the office imposed upon him—in discussing these and various other subjects, the question of domicil was frequently brought under the consideration of the jurists of ancient Rome (*j*).

(*h*) " Sed si aliis rationibus domicilium in splendidissimâ civitate Laodicæorum habere probatus fueris, mendacium quo minus muneribus fungaris non proderit."—*Code* x. t. 40, s. 2.

(*i*) *Incolas* vero, *domicilium facit*, c. x., *de Incolis. Vide post.* To *Origo* belonged the expressions *municipes, jus originis, patria;* to *Domicilium*, the expressions *incolæ, jus incolatus, domus.—Savigny*, R. R. viii· s. 353.

(*j*) The following passages should be studied in the Digest and Code for an accurate acquaintance with the language of Roman jurisprudence on the subject of Domicil :—

Dig. i. t. 9, l. 11—De Senatoribus.

Dig. ii. t. 15, l. 8—De Transactionibus.

Dig. iv. t. 6, l. 28—Ex quibus causis majores viginti quinque annis in integrum restituuntur.

XL. It is the remark of a great jurist of the present day that the Canon Law, where it modifies the Civil Law, has obtained an European reception as general as that law itself (*k*).

Dissertations on the Law of Domicil under that system of jurisprudence were provoked by various causes—such as the prohibition imposed on the Presbyter to administer sacred rites to a person belonging to the congregation (*parochianus*) of another church—the law that a person in holy orders might become subject (*subditus et diocœsanus*) to the jurisdiction of a bishop *ratione domicilii* (*t*)—the law which, in order to check the encroachment of religious houses upon parochial churches, ordered a certain portion (*canonica portio*) of the ecclesiastical dues of sepulture to be paid to the parish church

---

* *Dig.* v. t. 1—De Judiciis et ubi quisque agere vel conveniri debeat.

* *Dig.* xxvi. t. 5—De Tutoribus et Curatoribus datis, &c.

Dig. xxvii. t. 2, l. 30—46, s. 2—De Excusationibus.

Dig. xlvii. t. 10, l. v.—De injuriis et famosis libellis.

* *Dig.* l. t. 1—Ad Municipalem et de Incolis.

Dig. l. t. 16, l. 190, 239—De verborum significatione ; *Dig.* xxiii. t. 2, l. 5—De ritu nuptiarum ; *Dig.* xl. t. 5, l. 28—De fideicommissariis libertatibus.

* *Cod.* vii. t. 33—De præscriptione longi temporis, decem vel viginti annorum.

* *Cod.* x. t. 39—De Incolis et ubi quis domicilium habere videtur, et de his qui studiorum causâ in aliâ civitate degunt.

Cod. vi. t. 23, l. 9, has this passage ; " si non *speciali privilegio patriæ tuæ* juris observatio relaxata est, &c. &c. nullo jure testamentum valet."

" De Interdictis et Relegatis et Deportatis." The Præses who *interdicted* a person *domiciled* in his province, had also the power to interdict him from the place of his *origin*.

The * denotes the most important passages.

(*k*) *Savigny, System des Römischen Rechts, Band.* 1, *Kap.* 111, s. 17, p. 75—" Denn auch dies hat eine-gleich Allgemeine Europäische Anerkennung gefunden, wie das Römische."

(*l*) *Lyndwood, Const. Oth. de Scrutinio Ordinandorum.* Gloss. i. *per Episcopum.*—(Oxford ed. 1679).

of the domicil of a deceased person, who had desired to be buried with the members of a religious fraternity. With reference to these and other subjects, rules were laid down, and opinions were given by Canonists how a domicil might be created, acquired and abandoned (*m*).

XLI. Savigny, in his learned work on the History of the Roman law in the Middle Ages, ascribes the growth of personal rights, and personal, as opposed to territorial laws, to the state of society which ensued on the conquest of the Roman Empire by the barbarians, after which both races lived together preserving their separate manners and laws. " The moderns," he observes, " always assume that the law to which the individual owes obedience is that of the country where he lives : and that the property and contracts of every resident are regulated by the law of his domicil. In this theory the distinction between native and foreigner is overlooked, and national descent is entirely disregarded : not so, however, in the middle ages, when, in the same country, and often indeed in the same city, the Lombard lived under the Lombardic, and the Roman under the Roman law" (*n*).

XLII. When the darkness of the Middle Ages began to disappear, and the pacific intercourse of European nations to increase, the subject of Domicil came to be discussed by writers on Public and International Law (*o*). As the subjects of one

---

(*m*) A very elaborate disquisition on the subject is to be found in the *Treatise Augustini Barbosæ* de officio et potestati Episcopi. Pars secunda Allegatio IV. p. 172 ; see also 6 *Decretal.* l. 3, t. 12, c. 2 ; *Decretal.* lib. 1, tit. 3, c. 29 ; see also *Dictionnaire de Droit Canonique,* tit. *Domicile,* and *Denisart. Domicile,* s. 40. See also the cases collected by *Mascardus,* in his great work " De Probationibus.' Conclusio dxxxv. v. 1.

(*n*) Vol. 1, c. 3. See also *Story's Conflict of Laws,* ch. 1, s. 2, note where this passage is cited.

(*o*) In the Great American case of the *Venus,* it was said by Mr. Justice Marshall, that " Grotius nowhere uses the word 'Domicil'" (8 *Cranch's Reports,* p. 278). This is a mistake, for the word is used by him, l. 2, c. 5. s. 24 ; the quotation is given at length in another part

kingdom began to migrate into and reside in other countries, the various questions, arising from a conflict between the municipal regulations of the original and adopted country, gave importance to the Law of Domicil, and rendered the maintaining a uniformity of rules respecting it in Christendom a matter of great consequence.

The circumstance which has most contributed towards producing this effect has been the universal and increasing value of *personal* property. The Roman law made but slight distinction between the rules applicable to personal and real property. This distinction issued from the maxims of the feudal code: from these, and from the comparatively insignificant value (*p*) of *moveables* or chattels, arose the maxim, generally received in Europe, that moveables followed the person (*mobilia sequuntur personam*); while land was governed by the law of the country in which it was situated (*lex loci rei sitæ*) (*q*). The progress of trade and commerce has since imparted to the law of chattels an interest and importance at least equal to that which regulates real estates.

XLIII. Of modern nations France, Italy, Holland, America,

---

of this work. But it is among the writers who followed in the track which this illustrious man had opened, that the word is of frequent occurrence, and the thing constantly discussed.

(*p*) *Blackstone's Commentaries*, chap. 24, book 2, " Hence it was that a tax of the *fifteenth tenth*, or sometimes a much larger proportion of all the *moveables* of the subject, was frequently laid without scruple, and is mentioned with much unconcern by our ancient historians, though now it would justly alarm our opuleut merchants and stockholders." Mr. Reeves remarks that chattels are scarcely mentioned as objects of importance in treatises or reports before the time of Henry VI.; *Hist. of English Law*, vol. 3, p. 15, s. 69. It is in the reign of Richard III. that the Duke of Buckingham urges his master to grant him "The Earldom of Hereford and the *moveables*."—*Richard III.*, act 4, sc. 2.

(*q*) All jurists of all countries agree in this position : so that, in the language of *Bynkershoek*, " Adeo recepta hodie sententia est ut nemo ausit contra hiscere." *Questiones Juris Privati*, lib. I, c. 16.

and Germany, (r) and lately England, have produced elaborate commentaries on the Law of Domicil, and, for a like reason, namely, the division of their territory into divers provinces, governed by divers customs and ordinances. In these countries no question could be more material to the individual than to ascertain to which law his person, his money, his dealings, and his testament were subjected by the place of his domicil; before the Revolution no less than two hundred varying and conflicting customs were furnished by the provinces of France. In the twenty-six United States of America, the subject, from

---

(r) These, among other writers, may be mentioned :—

Cujacius, On the 7 Code, t. 33, ⸢de Præscriptione, &c., on 27 Dig. de Excusationibus.

J. *Voet*, l. v. t. 1, s. 92, &c. Comment. on Dig 5, de Judicius, especially useful to those who wish to prosecute their studies further into the Civilians, from his frequent references to *Zangerus, Donellus, Christinæus,* and *Struvius.*

Bynkershoek—Questionis Juris Privati. l. 1, c. xxi.

Barbosa—De off, Episcopi, part 2, all. iv.

Mascardus—De Probationibus Concl. 535.

Carpzovius—Processus Juris, t. 3, a 1. Forum competens quodnam dicatur ratione domicilii.

Tractatio de Domicilio Eberhardina Præside, Wolfgang Adamo Lauterbach, 1663. This is, perhaps, not to be reckoned among the books generally accessible, but it contains the best *separate* treatise on Domicil which the Germans have produced.

Savigny—R. R. viii. s. 351—359.

Denizart—Collection de Decisions, tit Domicile.

Pothier—Introduction Generale aux Coutumes D'Orléans.

Merlin—Répertoire de Jurisprudence, tit. Domicile.

Domat—Loix Civiles dans leur Ordres Naturelles, t. 16, s. 3.

Toullier—Le Droit Civil Français suivant l'Ordre du Code, l. 1, t. 3, n. 362—378.

Locrè—Législation de la France, tome 3, liv. 1, tit. 3.

Story—Commentaries on the Conflict of Laws, ch. 3.

Kent—Commentaries on American Laws, part v., lecture 35 ; part vi. Lecture 37.

R. Phillimore—On the Law of Domicil.

Cole—On the Domicil of Englishmen in France.

Westlake—On Private International Law, ch. iii. on Domicil.

a similar cause, has undergone frequent and careful investigation. In England the consideration of it is of comparatively recent date (s). I find Sir Leoline Jenkins, speaking of Domicil in the reign of Charles the Second, as "a term not "vulgarly known" (t): and the answer of this learned civilian to the statement of the French lawyers, claiming for the Duchess of Anjou the succession to the Dowager Queen Henrietta Maria's goods, as having died domiciled in France, is the earliest exposition in England of the Law of Domicil which I have been able to discover. In this case, Sir Leoline Jenkins admitted, that the Law of a fixed domicil ought to regulate this disposition of the personal property of every deceased person (u). This doctrine was subsequently upholden by Lord

---

(s) See remarks of Lord Campbell, in *Advocate General* v. *Thomson*, 12 *Clarke and Finnelly's Reports* (House of Lords), p. 28, cited at length below.

(t) See his letter to King Charles the Second from Niméguen, 1676, as to the sentence pronounced by the Scotch Court of Admiralty, upon a Swedish vessel.—*Life of Sir L. Jenkins*, 2 vol p. 785.

(u) "Ne Merite pas le nom d'un domicile fixé et tel qui doit regler la succession soit qu'on en juge selon le droit de France ou selon celui de l'Angleterre ou bien selon le droit Romain qui est commun à tant de nations."—*Life of Sir L. Jenkins*, 2 vol. p. 668. But the earliest cases judicially decided in England, upon the question as to the disposition of the personalty of a person, whose domicil was in one place and personalty in another, were the cases of *Cholmley* v. *Cholmley*, 2 *Vernon's Reports*, 47, in 1688, and of *Webb* v. *Webb*, 1689, *Robertson on Personal Succession*, p. 105; in both which the Court of Chancery pronounced that the custom of London followed the person and prevailed over the custom of York, which was the law of the domicil. In these cases the deceased parties were freemen of London; and, as late as 1826, there has been a decision confirming this anomaly to the general law of domicil in favour of the custom of the City of London; *Onslow* v. *Onslow*, 1 *Simons's Reports*, 18.

Lord Hardwicke appears to have been the first judge who clearly laid down the law in England, "that the personal estate follows the person and becomes distributable according to the law or custom of the place where the intestate lived." This was in a case decided in 1744; *Pipon* v. *Pipon, Ambler*, p. 25; in *Thorne* v. *Watkins*, 2 *Vesey*, 35.

Chancellor Hardwicke, about the middle of the last century, and was finally confirmed by Lord Chancellor Thurlow, in the great case of *Bruce* v. *Bruce* (*v*), appealed from the Scotch Courts to the House of Lords in 1790. The opinions of these high authorities seem not to have reached Scotland in a fully authentic shape, and it required another decision of the House of Lords firmly to engraft this principle of jurisprudence upon Scotch law (*x*).

Of late years, the extent and variety of our colonial (*y*) dependencies, and the importance of the interests at stake, especially with regard to the marriage contract, governed by different laws in the north and south of the same kingdom, have produced a more accurate acquaintance with this branch of jurisprudence, in its application to British subjects ; while during the long maritime war which grew out of the French Revolution, it came also to be considered in its application to the subjects of other nations, in our courts of International Law (*z*).

The same judge in 1750, pronounced that the case of a Scotch personal succession was regulated by an English Domicil.

In *Sill* v. *Worswick*, 1 *H. Blackstone*, 665, Lord Chancellor Loughborough said, " It is a clear proposition, not only of the law of England but of every country in the world where law has the semblance of a science, that personal property has no locality.

(*v*) See note to *Marsh* v. *Hutchinson* 2 *Bosanquet and Puller's Reports*, p. 299.

(*x*) *Hogg* v. *Lashley* ; see *Robertson on Personal Succession*, pp. 126—150. The earlier decisions as to the law in Scotland seem to have been correct, but there had been, Mr. Bell says, " a very distressing versatility of opinion." *Commentaries on the Law of Scotland*, 1 vol. p. 683. It should appear, too, that the Ecclesiastical Courts had held the doctrine of the *lex loci rei sitæ* ; but see *Somerville* v. *Somerville*, 8 *Vesey*, 750 ; and the opinion cited above of Sir L. Jenkins.

(*y*) Mr. *Burge's Comment. on Foreign and Colonial Law*, vol. 1, c. 2, Chapter on Domicil; Mr. *Henry's Report of the Case of Odwin* v. *Forbes*, Appendix.

(*z*) See first of the standing Interrogatories administered in the time of war, 1 *Robinson's Admir. Reports*, p. 381. The decisions, however, of the Prize Courts on *Commercial* Domicil *in time of war*, are only *sub modo* applicable to domicil *in time of peace*. *Vide ante*, vol. iii. 128

XLIV. In the following pages, it will be attempted to collect together and set forth, under each division of the subject, those maxims of jurisprudence relating to the Law of Domicil which are contained in the sources mentioned above, namely, in the Roman and Canon law, in the opinions of European and American jurists, the decisions of European and American tribunals, with a more especial reference to the decisions of the various Courts of Justice in Great Britain.

It will be seen that this question has undergone much discussion in Westminster Hall, in the Ecclesiastical and Admiralty Courts, the Privy Council, the Courts of Equity, and the House of Lords.

CHAPTER IV. A.

DEFINITION OF DOMICIL.

XLV. THE definition of domicil, according to the Roman Law, is as follows :—

" Si quis negotia sua non in Coloniâ sed in municipio sem-
" per agit, in illo vendit, emit, contrahit, in eos foro, balinco,
" spectaculis utitur, ibi festos dies celebrat, omnibus denique
" municipii commodis, nullis coloniarum fruitur : ibi magis
" habere domicilium quam ubi colendi ruris causâ versatur,
" videtur" (a)..."In eo loco singulos habere domicilium non
" ambigitur, ubi quis larem, rerumque ac fortunarum suarum
" summam constituit, unde rursus non sit discessurus, si nihil
" avocet, unde, cum profectus est peregrinari videtur, quod si
" rediit peregrinari jam destitit" (e).

" Eam domum unicuique nostrum debere existimari, ubi
" quisque sedes et tabulas haberet, suarumque rerum constitu-
" tionem fecisset" (b). Domicilium re et facto transfertur non
" nudâ contestatione" (c).

" Donellus justly observes as to the first of these definitions,
" Sed majore venustate quam certitudine definitionis" (d).

(a) *Dig.* l. t. 1, 27.

(e) *Code* x. t. 40—7.

(b) *Dig.* l. t. 16, 203.

(c) *Dig.* l. t. 1, 20.

(d) " Nam illa" (he says) " sedem rerum suarum alicubi constituere ;
unde non esse discessurum si nihil avocet ; inde si quis profectus sit
eum peregrinari videri, quæ sunt in superiore descriptione ; si non
æqué incerta sunt atque illud alicubi domicilium, habere ut certé non
sunt ; incerta sunt tamen et adhuc illam questionem desiderant, unde
sedem alicubi ita constitutam intelligamus ex quo illo sequuntur quæ

XLVI. So that, according to a French civilian of high authority, "Those who have no intention of fixing their "domicil in a place, but are absent somewhere for convenience, "necessity, or business, by no lapse of time can create a domicil; "since neither the intention without the fact, nor the fact "without the intention, is sufficient for this" (e).

The definition of a modern French jurist is as follows:— "Domicil consists in the moral relation subsisting between a "man and the place of his residence, where he has fixed the seat "in which his fortune is administered, and the establishment of "his affairs. We say, the moral relation, because domicil does "not consist in physical existence, nor in an actual residence in a "place, but in the attachment contracted by a person for the "place which he has chosen for the centre of his negotia-"tions" (f). Whether this definition does, in reality, throw any clearer light upon the subject, may be well doubted.

XLVII. According to Vattel, "Domicil is an habitation "fixed in some place with an intention of remaining there "always"(g). Upon this an American judge remarks, "Pro-"bably the meaning of Vattel is that the habitation fixed in "any place, without any present intention of removing there-"from, is the domicil"(h); at least, he pronounces it "better

---

diximus. Pressiùs, igitur ac certiùs sic domicilium cujusquam rectè definietur; ut sit locus in quo quis habitat eo animo, ut ibi perpetuo consistat, nisi quid avocet."—L. xvii. c. xii.

(e) *D'Argentré ad Leg. Britonum. Art.* 9, n. 4. 'Quamobrem qui figendi ejus animum non habent, sed usûs, necessitatis aut negotiationis causâ alicubi sint protinus a negotio discessuri domicilium nullotemporis spatio constituent: cum neque animus sine facto, neque factum, sine animo ad id sufficiat." Cited by *Denisart*, tit. *Domicile, Story*, c. iii. s. 44.

(f) *Proudhom, Cours de Droit Français*, tome 1, p. 119, cited with approbation in "*Traité du Domicile, et de l'Absence, par A. T. Desquiron*, à Paris, 1812, p. 42."

(g) *Vattel, Droit des Gens*, l. i. c. xix. s. 218, du Domicile.

(h) *Putnam* v. *Johnson*, 10 *Massachusetts Reports*, p. 492, c. 486; see also *Story's Conflict of Laws*, c. iii. s. 43.

" suited to America." Vattel's definition is clearly inadequate to the notion of a principal (*i*) domicil received in British Courts of Justice.

XLVIII. Boullenois, in his Treatise on the Personalty and Realty of Laws, &c., says,

" Though it be true that man is born to be in motion, and " to traverse this earth which God has given him, he is not " made to dwell in all the places which necessity compels him " to traverse; he must have a place of repose, a place of " choice and predilection, a place of society, a place where " he can enjoy, with his family, the advantages of his " labours and cares : this place it is which we call Domicil, and " where a man, by a kind of fiction, belongs. He cannot be " said to belong to a place unless he be there in the spirit " and meaning of abiding there, and having his ordinary habi- " tation there" (*k*).

XLIX. Lord Alvanley commends the wisdom of Bynker- shoek (*l*) for hazarding no definition ; and it must be admitted, that among the various definitions (*m*) to be found in pub- licists, none are completely satisfactory. Donellus, after cri- ticising the definitions of the Roman Law, says, " Pressius " igitur et certius sic domicilium cujusque definietur—ut sit " locus in quo quis habitat eo animo ut ibi perpetuò consistat " nisi quid avocet" (*n*). Perhaps, however, the American Judges have been the most successful in their attempts, and from a combination of their *dicta* upon different occasions, we may arrive at a tolerably accurate definition in designating it " a " residence at a particular place, accompanied with positive or " presumptive proof of an intention to remain there for an

---

(*i*) See below Chapter V., " Can a man have two domicils ? "

(*k*) *Traité de la Personalité et de la Realité des Lois, Coutumes Statuts, par forme d'Observations*, Obs. 32, p. 40.

(*l*) *Somerville* v. *Somerville*, 5 *Vesey's Reports*, p. 750.

(*m*) See *Maltass* v. *Maltass*, *Robertson's Eccles. Reports*, p. 73.

(*n*) *Ibid.* l. xvii. c. 17.

"unlimited time"(o). Domicil answers very much to the
common meaning of our word "home;" and, where a person
possessed two residences, the phrase, "he made the latter his
"home," would point out that to be his Domicil(p).

L. All jurists agree that there must be both intention and
fact to constitute a Domicil. The French jurists seem to have
rather leant to the extreme doctrine of the Civil and Canon
Law, that, without intention, no length of time can constitute
a Domicil, to which, I shall have occasion to show in another
part of this Treatise, the law in England has been less inclined (q). It seems, however, to be universally admitted by
all jurists, that the fact is admitted only as a proof of the
intention (r); but, then, there are certain facts which the law

---

(o) *Guier* v. *Daniel*, 1 *Binney's Reports*, 349, note; "a residence at
a particular place accompanied with positive or presumptive proof of
continuing there for an unlimited time."

Ebbers v. *Kraft*, 16 *Johnson's Reports*, p. 128, " an indefinite intention of remaining."

The Frances, 8 *Cranch*, "a permanent settlement for an indefinite
time."

Johnson v. *Sundry articles of Merchandize, Peter's Condensed Reports
of Cases in the Supreme Court of the United States*, vol. iii. p. 171—" the
time is not so essential as the intent."

(*p*) *Wolff, Jus Gentium*, c i. s. 137, says, "domicilium dicitur habitatio aliquo in loco constituta perpetuo ibidem movendi animus—idio-
mate patrio dicitur *die Behausung*." This idiom, however, appears to
have been superseded in the German of the present day by the word
"*Wohnort*," and "*Wohnsitz*." The former word, is used by *Savigny* in his
last work, *System des Römischen Rechts, Band. V.* s. 243 (319, the latter
is said to be the correct expression, viii. s. 353, (58).

I find no trace of any Greek law on domicil. Cicero renders
" διϰῆσις " by domicilium." See the passage in Plato, περι νομων,, xii.
p. 206, translated by Cicero. *De Legibus*, l. ii. c. xviii.

(*q*) "Domicilium, domus, sedes domestica, *habitatio certa et diuturna*,"
is the not inelegant definition of *Forcellini, Lexicon curâ Facciolati*.
Some Etymologists derive *Domicilium* from " *domus* " and " *colo*."

(*r*) See *Locré Legislation Civile de la France*, tome iii l. i. t. iii.
Partie 2, p. 415.

considers as undoubted evidence of that intention—facts which may be regarded as speaking a language on this point, at least, equally entitled to belief with any declarations, oral or written, even of the person himself. This part of the subject will be discussed in considering the change of domicil, the criteria of which are nearly the same as those of its original existence (*s*).

(*s*) " Probatur mutatio eisdem ferè modis ac prima constitutio."— *Voet*, l. v. t. i. s. 9.

CHAPTER V.

CAN A MAN HAVE TWO DOMICILS?

LI. CAN a man have two Domicils? is a question which should be resolved at an early stage of any disquisition upon this branch of law.

The Roman Law answered in the affirmative (*a*), that is, when a man had so set up his household gods in both places as to appear equally established in both : and this answer, properly understood and qualified, is not incorrect, with reference to the International Law of the present day (*b*).

LII. It is the remark of Domat (*c*), and of other jurists, that though it may be difficult, or impossible, for a man to have two domicils, which shall be equally the centre of his affairs, according to the definition already given ; and though a man can have but one *principal* domicil, yet a man may have two or more domicils (*d*) for different purposes.   In the case of

---

(*a*) Though it was the boast of the Roman that he could not be the *civis* of another State : " Sed nos (Romani) non possumus et hujus esse civitatis et cujusvis præterea : cæteris omnibus concessum est."— *Cic. pro Balbo*, 12.

(*b*) " Viris prudentibus placuit duobus locis posse aliquem habere domicilium si utrubique ita se instruxit, ut non ideo minus apud alteros se collocásse videatur." *Dig.* 50, t. i. s. 5, *Ad Municip.*

(*c*) *Domat*, l. i. t. xvi. s. 6.
Duranton, Cours du Droit Français, l. i. t. iii. s. 357.

(*d*) " Mais on peut avoir deux domiciles dit la demoiselle de Kerbahu et n'est-ce pas ce qui a été jugé dans la succession du Prince de Guimené, par l'arrêt du 6 Septembre, 1670 ? Ainsi le Comte d'Hautefort pouvoit être domicilié à Paris et à Hauterive.   Deux responses fait cesser une pareille objection.   La premiere est *que si l'on pouvoit avair deux domi-*

Lord Somerville, the Master of the Rolls observed on the novelty of the question, as being "between two acknowledged "Domicils"(e), and upon the question " which of two Domicils " shall preponderate, or, rather, which is the Domicil, according " to which the personal estate shall be regulated ?" It cannot, therefore, be too carefully recollected, that Domicil is distinguished by the various situations to which it is applied (*f*); that is to say, the circumstances which will be of force to impress the character of a Domicil in one instance, will fail to do so in another.

LIII. The European and American Law require the characteristics of the *principal* (*g*) Domicil for cases of a testament, or distribution under intestacy.

---

ciles ce seroit par rapport à des objets tout differens ; ainsi l'une pourroit être un domicile de fait qui influeroit sur tout ce qui regarde directement la personne domicilée ; l'autre un domicile de droit et de volonté, qui décideroit du sort de la succession. Le cas est sans doute fort extraordinaire, et peut-être même que dans les regles il ne devroit point être admis," &c. *Cochin's* argument in the case of the Marquis d'Hautefort, *Œuvres,* t. iii, p. 327.

(*e*) 4 *Vesey's Report,* 750.

(*f*) *Mr. Chancellor Kent's Commentaries on American Law, Lecture* 37, s. 4, note—"There is a *political,* a *civil,* and a *forensic* domicil."

(*g*) " Le domicile de tout Français quant à l'exercise de ses droits civils est au lieu où il a son principal établissement."—*Code Civil,* t. iii. du Domicil. " A man can have but one domicil for the purpose of succession."—*Kent's Comment.* L. 37, s. 4, note.

So *Grotius* (in his opinion cited by *Henry*) says, " To the solution of this question, if we follow the written or Roman law and the commentators thereon, "originis domicilium est immutabile et ideo qui alibi habitat, consetur habere duo domicilia." — *L. Origine, C. de Municip. et orig. lib.* 10 *l. Assumptio. ff. ad Municip. et ibi Bart.* But this difficulty ceases if we consider the general custom of the Netherlands, nay even of the whole world at this time, "Secundum quam consuetudinum domicilium originis solâ voluntate mutatur ita ut originarius nullo modo maneat subjectus jurisdictioni originis : au consuetudini testimonium etiam prohibet *Gail,* l. ii. obs. 36, dicens eam et in Germaniâ et ubique obtinere." This, says *Henry,* does not extend to cases of allegiance : *Odwin* v. *Forbes,* Appendix, p. 197 ; and in an

LIV. The facts and circumstances which might be held sufficient to establish a commercial Domicil in time of war, and a matrimonial, or forensic, or political Domicil, in time of peace, might be such as, according to English Law, would fail to establish a testamentary or principal Domicil. "There "is a wide difference," it was observed in a judgment delivered in a recent case before the Judicial Committee of the Privy Council "in applying the Law of Domicil to contracts and to "wills" (h).

LV. It might, perhaps, have been more correct to have limited the use of the term Domicil to that which was the *principal domicil*, and to have designated simply as *residences* the other kinds of domicil; but a contrary practice has pre-vailed, and the neglect (i) to distinguish between the different

---

opinion from a Dutch jurist, cited by the same author, occurs this pas-sage : "Sed ista omnia ita non procedunt (cum locus originis det domicilii presumptionem secundum ante dicta pluribus tamen, puta tribus locis, quis domicilium habere possit) quin considerandum veniat an non et plurium domiciliorum jure frui quis possit *distinguenda vero hic sunt onera, munera, à successionis jure de hoc mono quæritur hic.*"—App. 193.

So, too, *Voet* : "Considerandum tamen eos qui quantum ad successio-nem aliosque effectus domicilium per negotiationem, tabernam, nudam habitationem, non constituisse intelliguntur, nihilominus quantum ad forum competens attinet illis in locis dum illic degunt rectè conveniri," &c. l. v. t. i, s. 98, De Judiciis, &c. See too *Ferguson's Report of Con-sistorial Decisions in Scotland*, p. 283 : "We indeed all know that, besides this permanent domicil, a man may have many domicils of action at the same time," &c. So the decisions known to the French law of the "Domicil du Secours," or pauper's domicil, "Domicile élu," a domicil chosen for the purposes of the execution of a particular act, and of the "domicile politique." See, too, the case of the Churchwarden— *Stephenson* v. *Langston*, 1 *Consistory Reports*, (*Haggard*), 379.

(h) *Croker* v. *Marquis of Hertford*, &c., Judicial Committee of Privy Council, 4 *Moore*, P. *Rep.* 339.

(i) See the *Discours* pronounced by *M. Malherbe* on the introduction of the Law of Domicil into the Code Civil : "Chaque individu ne peut avoir qu'un *domicile*, quoiqu'il, puisse avoir plusieurs *résidences.*" *Locré Législation de la France*, p. 452, t. iii.

subjects to which the Law of Domicil is applicable, has been the chief source of the errors which have occasionally prevailed on this subject.

LVI. Thus, in a case (j) brought before the Prerogative Court of Canterbury in 1823, Sir John Nicholl expressed a doubt whether a British subject was entitled so far *exuere patriam*, as to select a foreign in complete derogation of his British Domicil, which it was necessary he should do in order to render his property liable to distribution according to any foreign law; he considered this proposition as resting on no authority (k), and doubtful even upon principle (l). In a subsequent case, the same Judge held that there was no precedent for pronouncing that the property of a British subject, dying *intestate* in a foreign country in which he was domiciled, was distributable according to the law of that foreign country, or for holding that if such British subject be domiciled in a foreign country, he had not a right to make his will according to the law of the country of his *allegiance*, and not of his *domicil* (m).

"The gradation from *residence* to *domicil* consists both of circumstances and intention ;" see *Maltass* v. *Maltass*, 1 *Robertson's Eccles. Reports*, p. 75.

In the case of *Hogg* v. *Lashley*. The Lord Ordinary at first decided, "that there were two domicils at the dissolution of the marriage, one in London, the other in Scotland, but the last was the principal." The Court, however, altered the Interlocutor, and found that there was but one domicil in Scotland. *Morrison's Decisions*, 4619 ; *Robertson on Personal Succession*, p. 142.

(j) *Addam's Reports*, p. 19, and note to p. 15 ; *Curling* v. *Thornton*.

(k) M. *Fœlix* remarks, " En général les anciens auteurs ne parlent que du changement de *domicile*, en gardant la silence se le changement de *nationalité* : ce'st qu'alors les differentes provinces du même Etat étaient régies par des lois ou coutemes non uniformes, de manière que le simple changement de domicile plaçait l'individu sous l'empire d'une autre loi." *Traité du Droit International Privé*, l. i. t. i, xxix. note 1.

(l) *Stanley* v. *Bernes*, 3 *Haggard's Reports*, 373.

(m) By the 36th statute of George the Third, chap. lii. sec. 2, a duty is payable "for every legacy, specific or pecuniary, given by any will of any person out of his personal or moveable estate, or out of or charged

LVII. These opinions of Sir John Nicholl, however, were overruled by the High Court of Delegates (*n*), and the distinction between the domicil of allegiance and the domicil for testamentary purposes was repeated and firmly established (*o*) in the case of *Lord Hertford's* will.

LVIII. To these remarks may be added an extract from a judgment by Lord Stowell in the Admiralty Court, in which the true distinction is perspicuously taken.

---

upon his real or heritable estate. Upon this Act some most important decisions have been given: it is only necessary to mention two. 1, *In re Ewin*, 1 *Crompton and Jervis's Exchequer Reports*, p. 151 (A.D. 1830), decided that *American, Austrian, French,* and *Russian* stock, the property of a testator *domiciled* in England, *was* liable to legacy duty.

2. *Thompson* v. *The Advocate General*, 12 *Clark and Finnelly's (House of Lords) Reports*, p. 1, A.D. (1845), decided, overruling the Scotch Court of Exchequer, that legacy duty was *not* payable by the legatees named in the will of a British born subject who had died *domiciled* in a British colony, though the personal property was locally situate in Scotland, to which the statute extended. In this case Lord Campbell said, p. 28, " My Lords, I believe that if the Chancellor of the Exchequer, who introduced this bill into Parliament, had been asked his opinion he would have been a good deal surprised to hear that he was not to have his legacy duty on such a fund as this, where the testator was a British born subject, and had been domiciled in Great Britain, and had merely acquired a foreign domicil, and had left property that actually was in England or in Scotland at the time of his decease. The truth is, my Lords, that the doctrine of Domicil has sprung up in this country very recently, and that neither the Legislature nor the judges thought much of it; but it is a very convenient doctrine: it is now well understood; and I think that it solves the difficulty with which this case was surrounded."

(*n*) A further distinction, taken in the case of Lord Hertford's will, as to the law of Domicil not applying to personal property which was deposited in *different* countries, was overruled both by the Prerogative Court and the Judicial Committee of the Privy Council. See remarks of Lord Chancellor on this point in *Bempde* v. *Johnstone*, 3 *Vesey's Reports*, 198.

(*o*) It was never the custom of the Judges Delegate to give reasons in open court for their decision ; but in *Lord Hertford's* Case, Mr. Baron Parke declared that they had intended to lay down the rule broadly in *Stanley* v. *Bernes*.

It was a question as to the national character of the claimant of a vessel seized in the river Thames by the Marshal of the Admiralty. Lord Stowell said—" The question, therefore " comes to this, whether the claimant is, *quoad* this property, to " be considered as a *British* subject? For some purposes he is " undoubtedly so to be considered ; he is born in this country, " and is subject to all the obligations imposed upon him by his " nativity. He cannot shake off his allegiance to his native " country, or divest himself altogether of his *British* character, " by a voluntary transfer of himself to another country. For " the mere purposes of trade, he may, indeed, transfer himself to " another State, and may acquire a new national character" (*p*). This chapter should not be closed without mention of what has been considered, by high authority, the only possible case of two principal Domicils, which would arise in modern times.

LIX. At the end of his judgment in *Lord Somerville's* case, the Master of the Rolls observed, " I shall conclude with a few " observations upon a question that might arise ; and which I " often suggested to the Bar. What would be the case upon two " contemporary and equal domicils ; if ever there can be such a " case ? I think such a case can hardly happen, but it is pos- " sible to suppose it. A man, born no one knows where, or " having had a domicil that he has completely abandoned, " might acquire, in the same or different countries, two domicils " at the same instant, and occupy both under exactly the same " circumstances ; both country houses, for instance, bought at " the same time. It can hardly be said, that of which he took " possession first is to prevail. Then, suppose he should die at " one, shall the death have any effect? I think not, even in " that case ; and then *ex necessitate rei*, the *lex loci rei sitæ* " must prevail ; for the country in which the property is would " not let it go out of that, until they knew under what rule " it is to be distributed. If it was in this country, they would

---

(*p*) The *Ann*, *Dodson's Admiralty Reports*, p. 223 ; see also *Wheaton's Elements of International Law*, p. 159.

" not give it up until it was found that he had a domicil some-
" where."

LX. It appears that the case suggested by the Master of
the Rolls had occurred in France. In 1680, a question arose
as to the succession to the Prince de Guémené. The Prince
appears to have left an equal amount of moveables, at his
residence in Paris and at his residence on his estate, at Verger,
in Anjou. It must be presumed (for the statement in Merlin
is meagre), that, in other respects, an equal attachment to
both places was manifested. It was decided that the custom
of each place should regulate the succession to the goods
found therein ; in other words, that the *lex loci rei sitæ* should
prevail (*q*).

(*q*) *Merlin, Rep. de Jurisp.* t. 8 Domicile, s. 7.

CHAPTER VI.

CAN A MAN BE WITHOUT A DOMICIL ?

LXI. The Roman law (*a*) answered this question by saying, that it is difficult for any one to be without a domicil; but even this might happen; if a person having abandoned his domicil, should make a journey by sea or land, seeking a place wherein to establish himself, he might be without a domicil. And Domat adopts this view of the case.

LXII. But a different view has been taken by other (*b*) jurists, and, especially, by those of Great Britain and America. They hold that the former Domicil is not abandoned until a new one has been intentionally and actually (*animo et facto*) acquired.

" A third rule I shall extract," (said the Master of the Rolls, in the case of *Somerville*,) "is, that the Domicil of Origin is " to prevail, until the party has not only acquired another, but " has manifested and carried into execution an intention of " abandoning his former domicil, and taking another as his sole " domicil " (*c*).

A British-born subject had been employed as American consul at the Cape of Good Hope, and was engaged in a house of trade there. A ship belonging to him was taken by a British cruiser, on her voyage from the Cape to Europe. It was con-

---

(*a*) " Et verum est habere, licet difficile est quemadmodum difficile est, sine domicilio esse quemquam. Puto autem et hoc procedere posse si quis domicilio relicto naviget vel iter faciat quærens quo se conferat atque ubi consistat; nam hunc puto sine domicilio esse."—*Dig.* 50, t. i. s. 27, s. 2.

(*b*) *Duranton*, l. i. t. cxi. s. 360 ; *Story's Conflict of Laws*, ch. 3 ; *National Domicil*, p. 52.

(*c*) 5 *Vesey*, 787.

tended that he was not a Dutch merchant, as he had intended
to remove to America ; but Lord Stowell said—"A mere in-
" tention to remove has never been held sufficient without some
" overt act ; being merely an intention, residing secretly and
'undistinguishably in the breast of the party, and liable to be
"revoked every hour. The expressions of the letter in which
" this intention is said to be found, are, I observe, very weak and
" general, of an intention merely *in futuro*. Were they even
" much stronger than they are, they would not be sufficient ;
" something more than mere verbal declaration, some solid fact,
" shewing that the party is in the act of withdrawing, has always
" been held necessary in such cases" (*d*).

LXIII. (*e*) The original Domicil, and the native character
easily revert ; and, therefore, it has been laid down by the
American (*f*) Judges, that a person resumes his native character as soon as he puts himself *in itinere* to return to his
native country ; or, as Lord Stowell said of a belligerent, lurk-
ing under the disguise of a neutral, "the vice of his old cha-
" racter is revived."

And so in *Munroe* v. *Douglas*(*g*), it was laid down(*h*), by the
English Vice Chancellor, that an acquired Domicil "remains
" until a subsequent domicil be acquired, unless the party die
" *in itinere* (*i*) towards an intended Domicil." And in *Colville*

(*d*) The *President*, 5 *Robinson's Admiralty Reports*, 279. See, also,
the *Falcon*, 6 *Robinson*, p. 198.

(*e*) *La Virginie*, 5 *Robinson*, 99.

(*f*) This national character, which a man acquires by residence, may
be thrown off at pleasure by a return to his native country, or even by
turning his back on the country in which he has wended on his way to
another. It is an adventitious character gained by residence, and which
ceases by non-residence ; it no longer adheres to the party from the
moment he puts himself in motion *bonâ fide* to quit the country, sine
animo removendi.—The *Français*, 1 *Gallison's* (*Amer.*) *Rep.* 467—469.

(*g*) The *Phœnix*, 3 *Robinson*, 191.

(*h*) 5 *Maddock's Chancery Reports*, pp. 379—406.

(*i*) *Pothier* seems to think that the change is not effectual till the
actual arrival at the new place : " La volonté'de transferer notre domicile dans un autre lieu doit être justifiée. Elle n'est pas équivoque

v. *Lauder,* it was *observed,* on the Scotch Bench, that when the deceased (a native of Scotland) was at St. Vincent's his succession must have been regulated by the law of England; but after leaving that island, he must in the whole circumstances, be considered as *in transitu* to Scotland (*k*).

LXIV. (*l.*) A vagabond is said to be a person who, without travelling in quest of a Domicil, has really and truly no certain Domicil at all.

LXV. A familiar example occurs in the instance of Gipsies. In one of the cases recorded in Cochin, it appears that it was attempted to include a "comédien," a travelling player, under this class. Cochin, however, combatted this doctrine, declaring that every man was born with a Domicil, and that till he had acquired another *animo permanendi,* it would remain till his death (*m*).

---

lorsque c'est un bénéfice, une change ou un autre emploi non amovible qui nous y appele. En ce cas, *dés que nous y sommes arrivés nous y acquérons domicile et nous perdons l'ancien.*"—*Introd. Gen. aux Cout.* 13.

(*k*) *Morrison's Succession,* App. i. ; see this case below. *Craigie* v. *Craigie,* 3 *Curteis's Ecclesiastical Reports,* p. 445.

(*l*) *Domat.* l. i. t. xvi. s. 9. So it was argued in the *Duke of Guise's* case, that, being exiled from France, he had no domicil where he served as a general ; he would be a *vagabond*—which *D'Aguesseau* pronounced *absurdum.* See *Vattel,* l. i. c. xix. s. 219, *Des Vagabonds.* "Les *Vagabonds* sont des gens sans domicile. Par conséquent ceux qui naissent de parents vagabonds n'ont point de patrie : puisque la patrie d'un homme est le lieu où, au temps de sa naissance ses parents avaient leur domicile, ou l'Etat dont son père était membre alors, ce qui revient à la même chose: car s'établir pour toujours chez une nation, c'est en devenir membre au moins comme habitant perpétuel si ce n'est point avec tous les droits des citoyens. Cependant on peut regarder la patrie d'un vagabond comme celle de son enfant, en tant que ce vagabond sera censé n'avoir pas absolument renoncé à son domicile naturel ou d'origine." This is little more than a repetition of *Wolff's* language, *Jus Gentium,* c. i. s. 245.

(*m*) *Cochin Œuvres,* t. i. p. 184, pour Dame Louise Françoise de Samsons.

Carpzovius says, "Vagabundum nuncupamus eum qui nullibi domicilium contraxit habitationis, ita utnec forum sortiatur certum, originis

LXVI. In the leading American case of *Guier* v. *O'Daniel* it was contended, among other things, that Thomas Guier, being a seafaring man, a sort of vagabond on the ocean (*n*), was without a Domicil; but the Court held that his Domicil of origin remained.

The rule is laid down by one of the latest writers upon Private International Law, that children of unknown parents must be considered as domiciled in the territory where they actually are: this is said to be a rule generally acknowledged and received (*o*).

---

verò domicilium si quis usque velit, parùm efficiet si vagabundus ibidem non reperiatur, licet nec inficias eamus conveniri ipsum posse in domicilio naturali modo copia ejus haberi queat vel ex hoc ipso generali asserto: Vagabundum ubique conveniri, nec utitur exceptione incompetentiæ, qui est vagabundus," tit. iii. art. i. s. 65; *Processus Juris*, &c.

(*n*) *Guier* v. *O'Daniel*, 1 *Binney's* (*Americ.*) *Reports*, p. 349, note, *vide ante*.

(*o*) *Traité du Droit International Privé*, &c. par *M. Fœlix*, l. i. t. i. s. 29, note 2.

CHAPTER VII.

DIFFERENT KINDS OF DOMICIL.

LXVII. The kinds of Domicil are sometimes classed as follows. 1. The Domicil of Birth. (*Domicilium naturale*). 2. The Domicil by Operation of Law (*necessarium*). 3. The Domicil of Choice, where one is abandoned and another acquired. (*Voluntarium, adscititium—Domicile de Choix*) (*a*).

LXVIII. The Civilians generally use the expression Domicil of Origin (*domicilium originis*) as synonymous with Domicil of Birth (*domicilium nativitatis*). Though if the parents were on a journey, or temporarily absent from their own domicil, that, and not the accidental place of birth, was the domicil of the child. "The Domicil of Origin is that arising "from a man's birth and connections," according to the case of *Somerville* v. *Somerville* (*b*.)

LXIX. But this expression "Domicil of Origin" is incorrect, and tends to confound the distinct ideas of "Origin" and "Domicil." There is a time, indeed, when they happen to be,

---

(*a*) *Wolff*, c. i. s. 138, *Jus Gentium; Vattel*, t. i. c. xix. s. 218; *Pothier, Introd. Gen. aux Cout.* s. 12.

(*b*) "Exemplo senatorii ordinis Patris originem unusquisque sequitur."—*Code* 10, 31, 36.

" Est autem originis locus in quis natus est, *aut nasci debuit*. Licet forte re ipsâ alibi natus esset, matre in peregrinatione parturiente."— *J. Voet*, l. v. t. i. s. 91.

According to the law of England, even the children of aliens not at enmity with the Crown, if *born within the realm*, are natural-born subjects; and all children, whose fathers or grandfathers by the father's side, were natural-born subjects, are, with certain exceptions, deemed natural-born subjects themselves.—*Stephen's Commentaries*, vol. ii. p. 427.

identical; for instance, a child born in the State in which his father is domiciled, has, generally speaking, his Origin and his Domicil in that State : because, in the case of a person who has never *acquired* a Domicil, you must go back to the epoch when a Domicil was chosen for him ;—this epoch is the time of his birth.

This is the true meaning of "Origo" to which jurists have referred when they have spoken of the *forum originis.* Though they have sometimes confounded *Origin* with the accidental *place* of *birth*, and sometimes have not had a clear idea of the relation which modern *Origin* bears to the Roman *Origo* (c).

Savigny explains the matter in this way:—

The Romans called by the name *Origo*, the right of citizenship which a man acquired by his birth. The moderns call by the name of *Origo* the fiction that a man has a *Domicil* in the place at which his parents at the time of his birth had a domicil. This notion of *Origo* in modern law is equally applicable to the jurisdiction (d) as *forum originis,* and to the local law which attaches to the person, or *lex originis* (e).

The expression, therefore, *domicilium originis,* is, with reference to the language of the Roman Law, unintelligible, and confounds two distinct and independent ideas ; while, with reference to modern law, it signifies a *domicil* not founded upon choice, but upon descent from a parent, and therefore in some sort upon a fiction.

LXX. The effect of origin, as an ingredient in the consideration of the circumstances which constitute a change of domicil, will be discussed in a later chapter in which the " Domicil of Choice" finds its place.

See also *Kent's Commentaries, Lecture,* 25, vol. ii.; 5 *Vesey's Reports,* 750; *Traité du Droit International Privé, &c. par M. Fœlix* (Paris, 1843), l. i. t. i. xxii.

(c) *Savigny,* viii. ss. 350— 359.

(d) *Ib.* viii. s. 369 (103).

(e) *Ib.* viii. s. 459 (103).

LXXI. *Domicil by operation of Law* comprises two classes of persons : 1. Those who are under the control of another, and to whom the State gives the Domicil of another. 2. Those on whom the State affixes a Domicil—(i). By virtue of the employment or office they hold; (ii). By virtue of some punishment inflicted upon them.

LXXII. Under the first class may be reckoned the Domicil of—1. The Wife. 2. The Minor (i.) legitimate, and (ii.) illegitimate. 3. The Student. 4. The Servant.

Under the latter class may be reckoned—1. The Officer employed by the State, whether Civil or Military. 2. The Ecclesiastic. 3. The Prisoner. 4. The Exile. 5. The Emigrant.

CHAPTER VIII.

I. NECESSARY DOMICIL—WIFE.

LXXIII. We have now to consider the case of those persons who are comprised under the first class, the domicil of whom is determined by operation of Law.

LXXIV. 1st of the Wife.

The maxim of the Roman (a) and of Continental civilians, and of this country and of America, is, that, as the wife takes the rank, so does she the domicil, of her husband ; and the Widow retains it, by the same analogy (b), after the death of her husband. If, however, the widow marry again, her domicil will be that of her second husband ; and, according to the Canon law, she had a right to be buried in the place of sepulture belonging (c) to the domicil of her last husband (d).

(a) " Item rescripsèrunt mulierem quamdiù nupta est incolam ejusdem civitatis videri, cujus maritus ejus est, et ibi unde originem trahit non cogi muneribus fungi."—*Dig.* l. 50, t. 1, s. 38.   " Mulieres honore maritorum erigimus, genere nobilitamus, et forum ex eorum personâ statuimus et domicilia mutamus."—*Code* xii. l. 13 ; x. 40—9.

(b) " Vidua mulier amissi mariti domicilium retinet, exemplo clarissinæ personæ per maritum factæ." " Sed utrumque aliis intervenientibus nuptiis permutatur."—*Dig.* l. 50, t. 1, s. 22. " Si autem minoris ordinis virum postea sortitæ fuerint, priore dignitate privatæ, posterioris mariti sequentur conditionem et domicilium."—*Code* x. 40—9.

(c) " Mulier autem quæ plures viros habuit successivè, si sepulturam non eligat est cum viro ultimo, cujus domicilium retinet et honorem tumulanda."—*Decretal,* l. iii. t. 12, c. 3.

(d) " Ea quæ desponsa est ante contractas nuptias suum non mutat domicilium."—*Dig.* 50, t. 1, s. 32.   And *J. Voet* observes, " Quamvis multis in partibus juris nostri sponsa uxoris loco sit, veluti iu injuriis, dotis

LXXVI. This doctrine of the widow's title to the domicil of her husband, was successfully sustained by one of our most eminent civilians against the lawyers of France, in the question of the disputed succession to the personal property of Henrietta Maria, widow of Charles the First.

LXXVII. The French lawyers claimed the property for the Duchess of Anjou (e), her daughter, alleging that Charles the Second, the Duke of York, and the Princess of Orange (the other children), were excluded and disabled by the " *droit* " *d'aubaine*," which took effect because Henrietta Maria had died domiciled in France.

They reasoned in this manner ; that the Dowager Queen of England was a Frenchwoman, the daughter of Henry the Fourth, from whom she had received a " *dot*" of one hundred thousand crowns ; that having fled from England in 1645, she purchased a house in France, and lived there for twenty-five years, till the time of her death, visiting England only twice during that period, and dying in her French residence ; that she was, therefore, a domiciled native of France ; and that the acknowledged rule of " mobilia sequuntur personam" must be applied to the question of succession to her personal property.

LXXVIII. It was argued, on the other side, by Sir Leoline Jenkins, that it was a clear proposition of public law that the wife followed the domicil of her husband ; that she always continued to do so ; and that no length of absence from her husband could affect this right ; that the Queen Dowager of England originally went to France in obedience to the order of her husband, at the time when England was embroiled in civil war ; that she afterwards resided there for the sake of her health, having returned to France for the purpose of attending the marriage of her daughter to the Duke of Anjou ; that she

---

privilegio, dotali fundo aliisque, domicilii tamen intuitu contra est; cum desponsata ante contractas nuptias suum domicilium non mutat."—*L.* v. t. i. s. 92.

(e) Better known in our history as Duchess of Orleans.

had always herself considered England as her domicil; that there she had a palace (Somerset House), moveables, and officers, who received their wages there ; that during her absence she had laid out considerable sums in the reparation of Somerset House ; that her letters to her son, Charles the Second demonstrated that ill health alone prevented her from closing her life in London ; and, lastly, that it did not become France, which held that all the great nobles of the kingdom and officers of the Crown, were domiciled at Paris, the metropolis of the realm, to deny the application of the same principle to the Queen Mother of England, and to refuse to consider her as an integral part of the Royal Family of that Kingdom.

LXXIX. The reasoning of Sir L. Jenkins prevailed. It is obvious that the main argument is founded upon the widow's retention of the marital domicil : the point of her residence in France, having been for the most part that of an exile and compulsory, does not seem to have been much pressed, though it is glanced at ; but her latter residence is said to have been under the constraint of ill health (doit être estimée fortuite, passagère, et mesme contrainte par son indisposition) (f).

LXXX. The betrothed, though in many respects enjoying the privileges of the wife, according to the Roman and Continental law, remained, in respect to her domicil as before her betrothment.

LXXXI. I am not aware of any decided case upon the question of the domicil of a wife, divorced a mensâ et thoro ; but there can be little doubt, that in England, as in France, it would not be that of her husband ; but the one chosen for herself after the divorce (g).

(f) *Wynne's Life of Sir Leoline Jenkins, Judge of the High Court of Admiralty*, &c. &c. vol. i. (life), p. 19, vol. ii. (letters), pp. 665—70. Both the statement of the French lawyers and Sir Leoline's reply are in the French language.

(g) " Le domicile d'une personne est aussi celui de sa femme. Comme la femme dès l'instant de la celebration du marriage, passe sous la puissance de son mari, elle cesse, en quelque façon d'avoir *propriam personam,*

LXXXII. There is another exception to the general rule mentioned by French jurists : namely, that where the husband is under an interdict (*interdit*), or an idiot, or a madman (*h*), and the wife is appointed his guardian (*tutrice*), she may choose her own domicil ; and so, according to the same law, where the husband is transported, or condemned to an infamous punishment ; as would also, probably, be the case in England.

LXXXIII. The French Courts have most justly decided that the wife *legally separated* from her husband may choose her own domicil, " Considerant que, par la separation de corps la " femme a été deliée de l'obligation d'habiter avec son mari, " qu'il est évident qu'elle recouvre le droit de choisir un autre

---

et elle ne fait plus qu'une même personne avec son mari. Elle prend, dès cet instant, son domicile, celui de son mari devient le sien, et elle devient, dès ce jour, sugette aux statuts personels du lui de ce domicile, quoiqu'elle n'y soit pas encore arrivée. Ceci n'est pas contraire à ce qui sera dit ci-apres, que la translation de domicile d'un lieu à un autre ne peut s'effectuer que lorsqu'on y est arrivé, car ce principe a lieu à l'égard du domicile propre qu'une personne se propose d'établir, et non à l'égard de ce domicile que la femme ne s'établit pas elle-même; mais qu'elle tient de son mari. Lorsqu'une femme est separée d'habitation par un jugement, qui n'est suspendu par aucun appel ni opposition, elle peut s'établir un domicile qui lui devient propre. (This is the language of *Pothier's Introd. aux Coutumes*, p. 4). According to the existing *French Code*, tit. cxi. art. 108—La femme mariée n'a point d'autre domicile que celui de son mari.

M. Marcadé observes, in his recent *Commentary upon the French Codes* (last edition, vol. i. p. 287), " Il y a cependant une exception à la disposition de notre article, pour la femme separée de corps. Celle-c en effet, étant formellement autorisée par le jugement de séparation à habiter séparément de son mari, la doctrine et la jurisprudence, dans le silence de la loi, ont etabli qu'elle recouvrait, par là, le droit de se choisir un domicile propre ; c'était aussi-là, sous l'ancienne legislation le sentiment de Pothier."

(*h*) " Il est même un cas particulier" (says the same author) " où la femme mariée peut avoir son domicile propre, sans être separé de corps c'est quand le mari est interdit, et que sa femme est nommée sa tutrice. L'interdit, en effet, aux termes de notre article, ne peut avoir de domi-

"domicil où elle puisse transporter son établissment et la
"siége de ces affaires"(i).

LXXXIV. In the English Courts there have been decisions bearing upon the question of the domicil of the wife
when *living apart,* but not *legally separated,* from her
husband.

A married woman had power to appoint a fund by writing
under her hand or by will.   For thirty years previous to, and
up to the time of her death, she resided in Paris separate
from her husband; but there was no legal divorce or separation.   Her husband was domiciled in England.   She disposed
of the fund by testamentary paper, valid according to the
Law of France, but not witnessed so as to be valid in this
country.   The English Courts held that it was not a good
execution of the power, either as a will or as a writing under
her hand (k).

LXXXV. In the case of *Donnegal* (l) v. *Donnegal,* it
was said that a party may have two domicils, the one actual,
and the other legal ; and *primâ facie,* at least, the husband's
actual and the wife's legal domicil are one, wheresoever the
wife may be personally resident; and the residence of the
husband in London was held to found the jurisdiction of the

---

cile propre, il est domicilié chez son tuteur.   Le mari donc, dans notre
hypothèse, sera domicilié chez sa femme."

Cochin, in his argument on the *Duchess of Holstein's* case, observes,
"C'est qu'elle n'en pouvoit avoir d'autre que celui de son mari mais
depuis que, par la separation elle est devenue maîtresse du choix de son
domicile elle l'a fixé a Trelon," &c.—*Œuvres,* t. ii. p. 223.

The Sardinian Code allows, by implication, the wife, divorced *à mensâ
et thoro,* to choose her own domicil.   "La donna maritata non ha altro
domicilio che quello del marito, salvo che ne sia legittimamente separata
di corpo e d'abitazione."—*Codice Civile,* tit. iii. s. 71.

(i) *Arrêt du 23 Novembre,* 1848; *Dalloy Ann.* 1849, II. 9.

Rogton Code N, explique, I. 194-5.

(k) *In re Daly's Settlement* (May 7, 1858), Rolls Court.— *The Jurist*
vol. xxii. (June 19, 1858), note p. 525.

(l) 1 *Addam's Ecclesiastical Reports,* pp. 5, 19.

Consistory of London over the wife, who was resident in Ireland.

LXXXV. So in *Shackell* v. *Shackell* (*n*), a case in the Arches Court of Canterbury, the husband, who resided at Egham, cited the wife, who resided at Paris, in the Court of Arches, on the legal presumption that she was resident within the same jurisdiction as her husband.

LXXXVI. But the leading case is that of *Warrender* v. *Warrender*, in which the decision of the Scotch Court was affirmed on appeal to the House of Lords. The facts of this case, so far as they are important in their bearing upon this point, may be given in the words of the judgment delivered by Lord Brougham.

" Sir George Warrender, a Scotch Baronet, possessed of " large hereditary estates in Scotland, born and educated in " that country, and having there his capital mansion, where he " resided the greater part of the year, except when he held " office, or was attending his Parliamentary duties in England, " intermarried, in London, in 1810, with the daughter of the " Viscount Falmouth, Ann Boscawen, who was born and edu- " cated in England, and never had been in Scotland previous to " the marriage. After that event she was twice there with her " husband ; but, subsequently, he resided for the most part in " London, to discharge the duties of Lord of the Admiralty " and Commissioner of East India Affairs, offices which he " held from 1812 to 1819 inclusive. In the latter year, at the " end of much domestic dissension, a separation was deter- " mined upon, and an agreement executed by the parties, in " which, after setting forth, by way of recital only, their hav- " ing agreed to live separate, Sir George bound himself to " allow Dame Anne Warrender a certain annuity ; and it was " further agreed, that the agreement shall only be rescinded " by common consent, and in a certain specified manner. A

(*n*) Cited by the Judge in *Whitcombe* v. *Whitcombe*, 2 *Curteis' Eccles. Reports*, p. 352.

" letter was written by Sir George, bearing equal date with the
" agreement, and addressed to the trustees under the marriage
" settlement. In this he stated, that he had refused to insert
" any provision for her being allowed to live apart, in order that
" he might not be precluded from suing, if he chose, for resti-
" tution of conjugal rights ; but also stating, that it was not his
" intention ever to do so, or to interfere with or molest her in
" the choice of a residence. The marriage settlement had se-
" cured her a jointure upon the Scotch Real Estates ; upon which
" fact it is now admitted that nothing can turn, except that it
" may serve the better to shew the connection of the parties
" and the contract with Scotland. These are the facts, and the
" undisputed facts of this case; I say undisputed—for the
" attempts occasionally made in the course of the Appellant's
" arguments to create some doubts as to Sir George Warrender's
" Scotch residence and domicil, cannot be considered as per-
" sisted in with such a degree of firmness or uniformity, as to
" require a discussion and a decision of the point, in order to
" clear the way for the very important legal question which
" arises upon these plain and undeniable statements. In 1834,
" after the parties had lived separate for fifteen years, Sir
" George's residence being, during the latter part of the time,
" almost constantly on his Scotch estates, and Lady Warrender's
" varying from one country to another—a few months in
" England, generally in France, and occasionally in Italy, Sir
" George brought his suit in the Court of Session (exercising
" under the recent statute the consistorial jurisdiction formerly
" vested in the Commissioners) for divorce, by reason of adul-
" tery, alleged to have been committed by his wife. Lady
" Warrender took preliminary objections to the competency
" of the suit under three heads :—First, that the summons
" of divorce was not served on her at her husband's residence,
" so as to give her a regular citation. Secondly, that the Court
" had no jurisdiction, inasmuch as the wife's domicil was no
" longer her husband's after the separation. Thirdly, that
" even if the service had been regular, and the two domicils

" one and the same, and that domicil Scotland, the marriage
" having been contracted in England, and one of the parties
" being English, no sentence of a Scotch Court could dissolve
" the contract. To these several points I propose to address
" myself in their order.

"The first need not detain us long. It is clear that if the
" wife's Domicil is not in Scotland, her being cited or not cited
" at the mansion is wholly immaterial : and the minor objec-
" tion of irregularity merges in the exception to the jurisdic-
" tion ; and if the wife's Domicil was in Scotland, it must be
" her husband's, which, indeed, the objection supposes : and
" then the argument amounts to this, that Sir George should
" have served himself with a notice, by way of regularly serv-
" ing his wife."

After further discussing this objection, he proceeded :—
" We may, therefore, come at once to the serious and more
" substantial exceptions taken against the jurisdiction ; the first
" of which arises from the domicil, as affected by the articles of
" separation. Secondly, it is admitted on all hands, that in the
" ordinary case, the husband's domicil is that of the wife's also ;
" that, consequently, had Lady Warrender been either residing
" really and in fact with her husband, or been accidentally absent
" for any length of time, or even been by some family arrange-
" ment, without more, in the habit of never going to Scotland,
" which was not her native country, while he lived generally
" there, no question could have been raised upon the compe-
" tency of the action, as excluded by her non-residence. For
" actual residence—residence, in point of fact—signifies nothing
" in the case of a married woman, and shall not, in ordinary cir-
" cumstances, be set up against the presumption of law that she
" resides with her husband. Had she been absent for her health,
" or in attendance upon a sick relation, or for economical reasons,
" how long soever this separation *de facto* might have lasted,
" her domicil would never have been changed. Nay, had the
" parties lived in different places, from a mutual understanding
" which prevailed between them, the case would still be the

" same. The law could take no notice of the fact, but must
" proceed upon its own conclusive presumption, and hold her
" domiciled where she ought to be, and where, in all ordinary
" circumstances, she would be—with her husband. Does the
execution of a formal instrument, recognizing such an under-
" standing, make any difference in this case ? This is all we
" have here ; for there is no agreement to live separate. The
" 'letter' has, indeed, been imported into the agreement, and
" argued upon as a part of it. Now, not to mention that the
" instrument in which parties finally state their intentions, and
" mutually stipulate and bind themselves, is always to be re-
" garded as their only contract ; and that no separate or subse-
" quent agreement is to be taken into the account, unless it
" contains some collateral agreements ;   1. Admitting that
" we have a right to look at the letter at all, either as part
" of one transaction with the agreement, or as providing
" for something left unsettled in the principal instrument,
" and so collateral in some sort to the instrument itself, it does
" not appear that the tenor of the letter aids the Appellant's
" contention."

After dwelling further upon this point, the Learned Judge
proceeded—

" But let us suppose it to be an ordinary deed of separation ;
" that it contained a covenenant on the husband's part to permit
" the wife to live apart from him, and to choose her own resi-
" dence ; and let us consider what difference this would make,
" and whether or not this would be sufficient to determine the
" legal presumption of domicil.

" First of all, it must be admitted, that, even if the execution
" of such a deed gave the wife a power of choosing a residence.
" no new domicil could be acquired by her. The domicil which
" she had before marriage was for ever destroyed by that change
" in her condition. The dissolution of the marriage by divorce,
" or by the husband's decease, never could reunite her to her
" original or maiden domicil ; much less would this be effected
" by any such deed as we are supposing ; for that, by the utmost

" possible stretch of the supposition, could only give her the
" option of taking a new domicil other than her husband's ; and
" until she did exercise this option, her married or marital
" domicil would not be changed. Now, there is no evidence
" here of Lady Warrender having ever acquired any domicil
" after 1819, other than the one she had before the separation,
" that is to say, her husband's ; and this proof clearly lay upon
" her, for she sets up the separation, only conveying to her a
" power of choosing a domicil, and the production of the articles
" only proving that power to have been conferred upon her :
" unless she goes further, and also proves the exercise of the
" powers by acquiring a new domicil, she proves nothing. She
" only shews—and all the ample admissions we are, for the
" sake of argument, making, confess—that she had obtained the
" power or possibility of gaining a domicil other than her hus-
" band's, but not at all that she had actually gained such a
" separate domicil. The evidence in the cause is nothing to
" this purpose. It is, indeed, rather against than for the Appel-
" lant's argument ; it rather shews that she had done nothing
" like gaining a new domicil ; for she was living chiefly abroad,
" and in different places : but there is, at any rate, no evidence
" in the cause of her acquiring a separate domicil ; and, the
" proof lying upon her, it follows that, for all the purposes
" of the present question, her husband's Scotch Domicil is her
" own : but suppose we pass over this fundamental difficulty
" in her case, and which appears to me decisive of the exception
" with which I am now dealing, I am of opinion there is nothing
" in the separation, supposing it had ever been so formal and
" ever so full in its provisions, which can by law displace the
" presumption of domicil raised by the marriage, and subsisting
" in full force as long as the marriage endures " (n).

LXXXVII. And in accordance with the rule laid down in
this decision, in the case of *Whitcombe* v. *Whitcombe,* the
Judge of the Consistory of London pronounced the wife in
contempt, for the purpose of carrying on the proceedings of

(n) 2 *Clark & Finnelly's Rep.* p. 523.

the suit, in which the husband, living in the Diocese of London, had served a citation upon the wife, who was resident in the Diocese of Hereford (o).

LXXXVIII. But this rule, that the domicil of the husband is the domicil of the wife, is not to be pressed so as to make a fiction of law work a practical injustice.

The rule does not apply to a suit brought by the wife against the husband who has illegally separated himself from her.

The language of the Court of Massachusetts in *Harteau* v. *Harteau*, is as follows (p) :—

"This suggests another source of inquiry, that is, how far the

---

(o) 2 *Curteis*, 351. The citation was by Letters of Request to the Consistory of Hereford; but the principle is the same. The effect of the Matrimonial Domicil (not the place of the marriage) upon instruments of dower, rights of wife and children, is among the gravest and the most difficult questions belonging to the Conflict of Laws. According to the Roman Law—"Exigere dotem mulier debet illic, ubi maritus domicilium habuit, non ubi instrumentum dotale conscriptum est: nec enim id genus contractûs est, ut et eum, locum spectari oporteat, in quo instrumentum dotis factum est, quam cum, in cujus domicilium, et ipsa mulier per conditionem matrimonii erat reditura."—*Dig.* v. t. i. s. 65, *de Judiciis*. See this doctrine upholden in the case mentioned by *Puffendorf, Universi Juris Observationes*, cxxi.

See also the case of *Gambier* v. *Gambier, 7 Simon's Chancery Reports*, 263, and the two most important cases of *Hogg* v. *Lashley*, in the House of Lords, 6 *Brown's Parliamentary Cases*, 550, and *Saul* v. *his Creditors*, in the American Courts, 17 *Martin's Reports*. The former established, that parties married in England, where they had their domicil, by removing to Scotland, and fixing their domicil in that country, changed their own rights and the rights of their children, and subjected these to the rules of succession of the law of Scotland. The latter decided, that where married persons had removed from Virginia their matrimonial domicil, where no community exists, into Louisiana, where a community does exist, the acquests and gains, *acquired after their removal*, were to be governed by the laws of community in Louisiana.— *Story's Commentaries*, p. 153 ; *Robertson on Personal Succession*, pp. 142, 147, and note.

(p) *Harteau* v. *Harteau*, Judgment of Shaw, C. J., in the Supreme Judicial Court of Massachusetts (A. D. 1833).—*Pickering's (Amer.) Rep.* vol. xiv. p. 181.

" maxim is applicable, to this case, ' that the domicil of the
" ' wife follows that of the husband.' Can this maxim be true
" in its application to this subject, where the wife claims to
" act, and by law, to a certain extent, and in certain cases,
" is allowed to act, adversely to her husband ? It would oust
" the Court of its jurisdiction in all cases where the husband
" should change his domicil to another State before the Suit is
" instituted.

" It is in the power of the husband to change and fix his do-
" micil at his will. If the maxim could apply, a man might go
" from this country to Providence, take a house, live in open
" adultery, abandoning his wife altogether, and yet she could
" not libel for a divorce in this State, where, till such change of
" domicil, they had always lived. He clearly lives in Rhode
" Island : her domicil, according to the maxim, follows his; she
" therefore, in contemplation of law, is domiciled there to ; so
" that neither of *the parties* can be said to *live* in this Com-
" monwealth."

" It is probably a juster view to consider that the maxim is
" founded upon the theoretic identity of person and of interest
" between husband and wife, as established by law, and the pre-
" sumption that, from the nature of that relation, the home of
" the one is that of the other, and intended to promote,
" strengthen, and secure their interests in this relation, as it
" ordinarily exists where union and harmony prevail. But the
" law will recognize a wife as *having* a separate existence, and
" separate interests, and separate rights, in those cases where
" the express object of all proceedings is to shew that the rela-
" tion itself ought to be dissolved, or so modified as to establish
" separate interests, and especially a separate domicil and home,
" bed and board being *put* apart for the whole, as expressive of
" the idea of *home*. Otherwise, the parties in this respect
" would stand upon very unequal grounds, it being in the power
" of the husband to change his domicil at will, but not in that of
" the wife.

" The husband might deprive the wife of the means of *enforc-*
" *ing* her rights, and in effect, of the rights themselves, and of

" the protection of the Commonwealth at the same time
" that his own misconduct gives her a right to be rescued
" from his power on account of *his own* misconduct towards
" her (q).

(q) *Dean* v. *Richmond*, 5 *Pick.* 461; *Barber* v. *Root*, 10 *Mass. Rep.*
260.

CHAPTER IX.

NECESSARY DOMICIL—MINOR.

LXXXIX. The Minor may be either.—1. Legitimate, or 2. Illegitimate. The Legitimate may be either 1, emancipated, or 2, unemancipated.

XC. (a) The Domicil of the legitimate unemancipated minor, who is not *sui juris*, and whose *will*, therefore, cannot concur with the *fact* of his residence, is the domicil of the father, or of the mother during widowhood, or—though it will be seen this is a disputed point—of the legally appointed guardian.

XCI. It is an undisputed position of all jurists, that of his own accord, *proprio marte* (to borrow the expression of Bynkershoek), the minor cannot change his domicil. In our own country, this maxim was enunciated by Lord Alvanley, Master of the Rolls, in the case of *Somerville* v. *Somerville* (b), and in America, in the case of *Guier* v. *O'Daniel* (c). It should seem, from all analogy, to follow that such change may be effected by the parents or guardians of the minor.

XCII. But this question has undergone very full and elaborate discussion by the most distinguished jurists; and, though agreeing upon the general principle, they differ as to the exception from and limitations of it.

XCIII. Some, and no less than Denisart, have held, that neither mother nor guardian can change the domicil of a minor

---

(a) *Guier* v. *O'Daniel*, 1 *Binney's Americ. Report*, 349, note.

(b) 5 *Vesey*, 787.

(c) *Vide supra*.

whose father is deceased, but that, during his minority, he retains the paternal domicil ; and such, in the time of Denisart, appears to have been the law of the French Courts (*d*).

XCIV. 2. Others, like Bynkershoek, have held the doctrine broadly and without qualification, that it is competent to the mother or guardian to change the minor's domicil.

XCV. 3. Others, like Voet and Pothier, and Mr. Justice Story, conceive that the surviving parent may transfer the domicil of the minor from one place to another, except where such transfer is fraudulently made, not for the benefit of the minor, but in contemplation of his death, and for the sake of securing a larger share of the succession to him.

XCVI. 4. Others, and among them, Mr. Chancellor Kent, are of opinion, that they have the power of changing the minor's domicil, when acting reasonably and in good faith (*e*).

XCVII. 5. It seems agreed, that this power does not belong to the widow, if she marries again, and thereby loses her position as the head of the family of her former husband (*f*).

(*d*) *Denisart—Domicile*, s. 2, (case of the *Comte de Choiseul*) ; a comparison of the dicta of *Denisart, Pothier, and Merlin*, will show that the French lawyers were by no means agreed upon this point.

(*e*) See last edition of *Kent's Commentaries*, vol. ii. p. 227, Lect. 30, *note*, where it is said that, in the case of *The School Directors* v. *James*, 2 *Watts and Serg.* 568, it was held that, though the domicil of the *parent* was the domicil of the child, it was not necessary. So in the case of a *guardian*. The parent's influence in this case springs from the institution of marriage and families ; and the learned Chief *J. Gibson* followed the doubts of *Mr. Justice Story*, and he confined the power of changing the infant's domicil to the parent *qua* parent. It would rather seem to me, that, if there be no competent parent living, and the guardian be duly appointed, that he may and ought, when acting in good faith and reasonably in his character of guardian, to be able to shift the infant's domicil with his own, and that the foreign authorities to that point have the best reason on their side. The objection against the guardian's power in such a case appear to me to be too refined and speculative.

(*f*) " Minor children having the settlement of their mother do not, by the common law, acquire a new settlement gained by her marriage,

XCVIII. But these differences of opinion are applicable only to the question of *succession* to an intestacy; for all writers are of opinion, that the *forum* of the minor is that of the surviving parent or guardian.

XCIX. Bynkershoek (*g*), who has devoted a whole chapter to the consideration of this subject of the minor's domicil, mentioned several cases upon the question of the *forum*.

C. (1.) A native of Y., a minor, went to V., for the purpose of contracting marriage with a native of Amsterdam, obtained the citizenship of V., and caused the banns to be published there and there only, the law requiring that they should be published at the place of the domicil. The guardians of the minor dwelt at Y., and had sent their ward to H. for his education. They procured the marriage to be pronounced null and void, the banns not having been published either at Y., or Amsterdam, and the minor having been incapable of acquiring a domicil at V.

CI. (2.) A youth, born at H., lost both his parents. His guardian, who dwelt at the Hague, sent his ward to different places, and finally to Amsterdam, for the purpose of acquiring a knowledge of mercantile matters. While at this place, the youth determined to contract a marriage; and cited his guardian to appear and shew cause, if he had any, against his ward's marriage, before the tribunal of the Delegates of Matrimonial Causes, which was established at Amsterdam. The

---

although they remove with her to the place of such new settlement."— *Inhabitants of Freetown* v. *Inhabitants of Taunton, Massachusett's Reports*, vol. xvi. p. 51, c. 63.

" Les eufans suivent le domicile que leur mère s'établit sans fraude, lorsque ce domicile lui est propre et que demeurant en viduité elle conserve la qualité du chef de famille : mais lorsqu'elle se remarie quoiqu'elle acquière le domicile du second mari, en la famille duquel elle passe, ce domicile de son second mari ne sera pas celui de ses enfans, qui ne passent pas comme elle en la famille de son beau-père: c'est pourquoi ils sont censés continuer d'avoir leur domicile au lieu où l'avoit leur mère, avant que de se remarier, comme ils seroient censés le conserver, si elle étoit morte."—*Pothier's Introd. aux Coutumes*, p. 7, s. 19.

(*g*) *Quæst Jur. Privati*, l. i. c. xvi.

guardian made two replies to this citation, both null and invalid. First, he denied that a minor could proceed against his guardian in a matrimonial cause, incorrectly, Bynkershoek says; but this question does not concern our present inquiry. Secondly, that the marriage must be published, and the guardian cited at H., where the parents died, and the decree of Hadrian, already referred to, and which enacted, that those who were resident in a place, "studiorum causâ," did not acquire a domicil there; and that the principle of this law clearly embraced the cases of those who were resident "mercaturæ discendæ causâ." This answer, Bynkershoek is of opinion, was also bad; because though it be, generally speaking, true that a minor does not change his domicil by a residence, "studiorum vel mercaturæ causâ," it is so on the assumption that the minor has a domicil elsewhere; but he who has no domicil elsewhere, has his domicil wheresoever he is tarrying. The domicil of the parents of this youth did not affect the question; they were dead, and, according to Bynkershoek, their domicil died with them; and, on the other hand, the place where the marriage is about to be celebrated is the proper place to cite all contradictors.

CII. It will be observed, that in this case the guardian dwelt at the Hague; and the question is not raised as to whether the minor had the domicil of his guardian at the Hague, but of his deceased parents at H.

CIII. The opinion of Bynkershoek, as to the competency of the guardian to change the domicil of his ward, is in accordance with that of Christineus and Boulenois (h), but is at variance with that of Mornac and Pothier.

CIV. To this latter authority much deference is due; but the reasoning which supports his position does not seem to be forcible. "Minors (he says) do not form a part of the family "of their guardians, as children form a part of the family of

---

(h) Introduction Générale aux Coutumes des Duchés, &c. d'Orléans, ch. i. s. 17.

" their parents. Their position in the house of their guardian is " the same as if they were in the house of a stranger ; they are " there *ad tempus*, for the time during which their wardship " lasts. It follows, therefore, that the domicil of the guardian " is not their true domicil ; and that they cannot be considered " as having any other domicil than the paternal one until " such time as they shall be of an age to establish one for " themselves by their proper choice, and until they have actually " established it" (*i*).

CV. Cochin, on the other hand seems to assume it as an undoubted fact that the minor's domicil is that of his guardian, and continues so even when the minor is in the king's household, and an officer in the army (*j*).

CVI. Bynkershoek, Boulenois, and others, contend that the paternal domicil of the minor is extinct with the death of the father, though it may be, and is, *retained by a continual residence of the minor, under the sanction of the guardian, in the paternal habitation* (*k*) ; but these jurists are at a loss to conceive why the guardian should not have the power of

---

(*i*) The reasoning of *Duranton* is different; speaking of the modern law, he says, " Et si pour une cause quelconque le père survivant n'exercait point la tutelle, le domicile du tuteur séroit aussi celui du mineur. La loi (art. 108) ne le décide pas textuellement, mais il nous semble que tel est son esprit : l'établissement du domicile est dans l'intérêt de la personne puisque c'est là qu'elle exerce ses droits civils ; et comme dans l'espèce c'est le tuteur et non le père qui exerce ceux du mineur, il est conséquent de dire que le principal établissement de celui-ci est au domicile du tuteur."—*Cours de Droit François*, tome i. tit. iii. p. 103. *Du Domicile.*

(*j*) *Œuvres*, t. 6, 227, *case of Marquis de Saint Peter.*

(*k*) So *J. Voet*, (though he differs from *Bynkershoek* on this point), l. v. t. ii. s. 102, *De Judiciis*, &c. " Esse enim domicilium iis accensendum, quæ personalia sunt, ac morte personæ evanescunt, frequentius probatum est : eo quod ab animo et voluntate hominis in universum tum constitutio ejus tum continuatio dependet, dum ergo morte cessat voluntas ac per id etiam tolluntur ea quæ ab illâ pependerant voluntate."— *Quæst. J. P.* l. i. c. xvi. p. 177.

changing the minor's domicil: and Bynkershoek, especially, is of opinion, that to deny this power is to ascribe to the *domicilium originis* an efficacy with which neither modern practice nor the Roman Law invested it.

CVII. By the Code Napoleon (*l*), the domicil of the minor was that of his guardian : it would seem to follow, therefore, that under this system of law, the guardian might have changed the domicil of the ward. The same provision is to be found in the existing Code Civil ; and no doubt is entertained by modern writers as to this power of the guardian (*m*).

CVIII. Though Pothier's objection is couched in language which appears universally applicable to change of domicil by the guardian (*n*), the objection would seem to have been practically confined to cases where the transfer of the domcil varied, in the event of the minor's death, the rights of the representative (*o*).

CIX. As to the power of the surviving mother to change the domicil of her minor children, it had no existence in the Roman Law ; but Pothier unhesitatingly asserts its existence under the French Law, with this limitation, that the transfer must be made without any *fraudulent* intent ; and he adds, " It will be fraudulent, if there appears no reason for the

---

(*l*) *Code*, liv. 1. i. t. iii, c. 108, " Il *aura* son domicile chez ses père et mère ou tuteur." The *Civil Code of Louisiana* is to the same effect, art. 48, *Kent's Commentaries*, vol. ii. p. 227, note.

(*m*) *Merlin Répertoire de Jurisprudence*, tom. viii, *Domicile*, s. 3.

(*n*) *Merlin* says, that the only doubt under the old law was as to the case of a guardian who was also an *ascendant* relative of the minor, for that as to the case of a guardian who was a stranger in blood, or a *collateral* relation, it was unanimously admitted that he had no power to change the domicil of the minor. *Rép. de Juris.* t. viii. *Domicile*, s. 3.

(*o*) " Posse tutorem pupilli sui domicilium mutare, perinde ut potest parens superstes, nescio quisquam serio dubitaverit si successionis legitimæ causa non versetur, nam si hæc versetur multa disputatio est ut mox audies."—*Bynkershoek, Quæst. J. P.* 1. i. c. xvi.

" transfer of the domicil, except that of obtaining advantages
" with respect to the succession to the moveable property of the
" children."

CX. Those who agree with Pothier (p), liken this power of
the surviving parent to that which the guardian of an infant
possesses, of binding him by contracts bonâ fide entered into in
his behalf. Bynkershoek is of a contrary opinion ; he puts
the case of a minor, the succession to whose property would
be regulated according to a law which made his next of kin
heirs in the event of his death happening in the place of his
parental domicil, being removed by his guardian to another
place where a law prevailed which constituted the guardian
heir; and he affirms that this latter domicil cannot be impeached, though he admits that the minor could not of his
own will (proprio marte) have made the transfer.

CXI. He then supposes an objection to be taken that this
was a fraudulent defeating of the deceased parents' intention,
who left their child in a domicil, according to the law of
which they knew that, in the event of his death, his and their
relations would succeed to his property ; and he answers this
objection by remarking that it would have been competent
to the parents to have guarded against this contingency,
either by an anténuptial act or by a testament, and that as
they had not done so, the presumption was they would not
have objected to the effect of the transferred domicil; an
argument which has additional weight in a case where such
transfer had been effected by the surviving parent instead of
the guardian, for the presumption then would be very strong
" that the defunct parent loved the surviving partner of wed-
"lock better than any relations, and was, besides, perfectly
" aware that, the child having attained to puberty, could, under
" any change of domicil, dispose of his property by testament,
" according to his pleasure."

CXII. Some jurists have been of opinion, that the domicil
of the minor may be changed by the surviving parent or

(p) Burge's Commentaries on Colonial and Foreign Laws, vol. i. p. 39.

guardian, when by such transfer no third person is injured—when it is not made *in fraudem tertii* (q),—that in such cases it must be duly considered, *quo animo*, the transfer was made. And it has been said, that one of the indications of fraud would be, the state of health (r) of the minor at the time of his removal; that if he was sick and ill at such time, the presumption of fraud would be strong ; if he was well and stout, it would be otherwise. Bynkershoek treats (s) the objection and the example with scarcely suppressed ridicule, and meets them with strenuous contradiction, founded on the practical impossibility of ascertaining the real motives of the parties, the insuperable difficulty of defining the amount and nature of the illness during which a removal shall be held fraudulent, the uncertainty of the proofs, and other objections, which would throw the whole matter into such confusion that it would be a wiser rule of law to hold every transfer of a minor's domicil which caused an alteration in the succession to his property, fraudulent and illegal.

CXIII. Mascardus mentions the following case :—A boy was born in the parish of St. Peter's ; he was left an orphan under the guardianship of his great grandmother, who resided in the parish of St. Paul's, and there she took the minor to live with her, which he did for fourteen years, there attending the services, and there receiving the Sacraments of the Church. Nevertheless, he had always wished to remain in the parish of St. Peter's. He paid, it is said, tithes there and other eccle-

---

(q) So *Wolff*, maintaining the position that every one is at liberty to change his domicil, observes, " Quoniam tamen unicuique permittendum, ut voluntatem suam mutet, quamdiu nil agit contra jus alterius."—*Jus Gentium*, c. i. s. 189.

(r) Of this opinion is *J. Voet, Comm. ad Pandectas*, l. v. t. i. s. 100.

(s) " Sed quem vocas languentem et ægrotantem, non, putem si caput, si dentes doleant. Sed quid si febricula comes adsit ? Nescio, et lubrica res esset gradum morbi definire. Si simile quid placeret mallem omnem translationem domicilii, quæ successionem intestati mutat, habere pro fraudulentâ, nisi probetur, aliam fuisse mutandi domicilium causam."—*Bynk, ibid.*

siastical dues, and kept his name on the list of parishioners, and had a furnished house in the parish. When he became an adult he married, and told his guardian that it was his intention to take his wife to his own house (*proprios lares*), where everything was prepared for her reception. Before, however, this was accomplished, and at the age of eighteen, he died, having made his will, and expressed his desire to be buried in the burying-place belonging to a certain religious order. By the Canon Law, this order was bound to pay a certain part of the dues of sepulture to the parish church. The question arose, which church that was?—that of St. Peter's, the parish of his parents, and, as far as he could make it, his own, or of St. Paul, that of his guardian, and within whose authority he had died. Upon this question the Canonists were much divided, there being about the same weight of authority for either opinion (*t*).

CXIV. In a case argued in the Consistory of London, in 1752, it was mentioned as one of the acknowledged general principles of Domicil, that neither a mother nor a guardian could change the minor's domicil; but the point was not decided by Sir Edward Simpson, who then presided over that Court (*u*).

CXV. In 1817, the question of the powers of the surviving mother underwent very elaborate and able discussion in the High Court of Chancery, before Sir William Grant. Thomas Pottinger, a native of England, domiciled and died in Guernsey, the place of his domicil, intestate, leaving seven children living at his decease, four by his former wife, and three by his widow, who also gave birth to a posthumous child. The widow, after the death of her husband, was appointed guardian of the children by the Royal Court of Guernsey, and, in con-

---

(*t*) *De Probationibus Conclas.* XLVI. ss. 30, 35. "Utraque pars validissimis est fulcita rationibus—cui tamen adhæreas sententiæ tuum lector, esto judicium," *Mascardus* not very satisfactorily observes.

(*u*) *Scrimshire* v. *Scrimshire, Haggard's Consistorial Reports*, vol. ii. p. 405.

junction with another person, who was appointed guardian of
the children by the former marriage, sold the property of the
intestate, and invested the produce in the English funds;
after which she came to England with her children, and was
domiciled there. On the death of some of her children under
age, a question arose whether the shares of the property had
become distributable according to the laws of England, or of
Guernsey. The very eminent judge who adjudicated upon
this matter, observing upon the meagre information to be
derived from English Law upon the subject of Domicil, and the
necessity of resorting to the writings of foreign jurists for the
decision of most of the questions arising upon it, said, "Here
" the question is, whether after the death of the father, the
" children remaining under the care of the mother, follow the
" domicil which she may acquire, or retain that which their
" father had at his death, until they are capable of gaining one
" by acts of their own. The weight of authority is certainly
" in favour of the former proposition. It has the sanction
" both of Voet and Bynkershoek; the former, however, quali-
" fying it by a condition that the domicil shall not have been
" changed, for the fraudulent purpose of obtaining an advan-
" tage by altering the rule of succession. Pothier, whose
" authority is equal to that of either, maintains the proposition
" as thus qualified. There is an introductory chapter to his
" Treatise on the Custom of Orleans, in which he considers
" several points that are common to all the customs of France;
" and, among others, the Law of Domicil. He holds, in oppo-
" sition to the opinion of some jurists, that a tutor cannot
" change the domicil of his pupil; but he considers it as clear,
" that the domicil of the surviving mother is also the domicil
" of the children, provided it be not with a fraudulent view to
" their succession, that she shifts the place of her abode. And
" (he says) that such fraud would be presumed, if no reason-
" able motive could be assigned for the change.

" There never was a case in which there could be less sus-
" picion of fraud than the present. The father and mother
" were both natives of England. They had no long residence

" in Guernsey ; and after the father's death, there was an end
" of the only tie which connected the family with that island.
" That the mother should return to this country, and bring
" her children with her, was so much a matter of course that
" the fact of her doing so can excite no suspicion of an im-
" proper motive ; I think, therefore, the Master has rightly
" found the deceased children to have been domiciled in
" England (x). It is, consequently, by the law of this coun-
" try, that the succession to their personal property must be
" regulated " (y).

CXVI. It would appear that the very eminent judge who
decided this case, inclined to the opinion of Pothier in opposition to that of Bynkershoek, that the question of fraud
might be entered into in considering a change of domicil ;
but the decision can hardly be pronounced to be express upon
this point. It is said, " There never was a case in which
" there could be less suspicion of fraud :" but it is not said,
that if there were a suspicion of fraud, the Court would examine into it. In this case, it happened that the surviving
mother was also guardian, but the decision has reference to
her only as acting in the former capacity.

CXVII. With respect to the effect of the judgment in
Pottinger v. *Wightman*, it should be mentioned that in a
recent and very important case, adjudicated upon by the
House of Lords, Lord Campbell said, " I think that the case
" of *Pottinger* v. *Wightman* must be taken conclusively to
" have settled the general doctrine, that, if, after the death of

---

(x) *Pottinger* v. *Wightman*, 3 *Merivale's Reports*, p. 67. The principle
of this case has been adopted in America; *Holyoke* v. *Hoskins*, 5 *Pickering's Reports*, p. 20; *Kent's Commentaries*, vol. ii. p. 227, note.

(y) *Inhabitants of Woodend* v. *Inhabitants of Paulsbury*, *Lord Raymond's Reports*, vol. ii. 523; *Cumner* v. *Milton*, 2 *Salkeld's Reports*, 523;
Rex v. *Inhabitants of Boston Torfe*, *Burrow's Settlement Cases*, 49; *Rex*
v. *Inhabitants of Oulton*, *ibid.* 64; *Woodeson's Lectures*, pp. 278—9;
1 *Nolan's Poor Laws*, 236—76; *Pottinger* v. *Wightman*, 3 *Merivale's
Reports*, 79; *Kent's Commentaries on American Law*, vol. ii. p. 431,
note.

" the father, an infant lives with its mother, and the mother
" acquires a new domicil, it is communicated to the infant "(z) ;
and Lord Chancellor Lyndhurst made this observation, " the
" case of *Pottinger* v. *Wightman* appears to have been well
" argued and well considered, and must be held conclusive as
" to the mother's power to change the domicil,—which is a
" novel point in the law of England—unless there is some
" opposite decision."

CXVIII. According to the principles of the Scotch Law,
it should seem that the power of choosing a domicil would
vest in the minor on attaining puberty, at the same age as
would formerly have been sufficient to render the marriage or
the testament of a minor valid. Erskine says, " The persons
" of pupils are under the power either of their tutors or of
" their nearest cognates ; but the minor after pupillarity has
" the disposal of his own person, and may reside where he
" pleases "(a). Where the law of the country permits a minor
to dispose of personal property by testament, it would, of
course, allow him, by changing his domicil, to vary the succession to him in the case of an intestacy.

CXIX. The principle of the judgment in *Pottinger* v.
Wightman has been adopted by the American tribunals (b),
but I am not aware that any express decision has been delivered, either in the Courts of that country, or of England,
upon the question of the power of the guardian or tutor to
change the domicil of the minor. The present law of France
declares the domicil of the unemancipated minor to be that
of his father, mother, or guardian (c).

Mr. Henry, in his commentary upon the case of *Pottinger*
v. *Wightman* observes, that although the transfer of domicil
was held to be valid in that particular case, nevertheless,

(z) *Johnstone* v. *Beattie*, 10 *Clark & Finnelly*, p. 138.

(a) *Bk.* i. t. vii. s. 8.

(b) *Holyoke* v. *Hoskins*, 5 *Pickering's Reports*, 90, note.

(c) " Le mineur non émancipé aura son domicile chez ses père et mère
ou tuteur."—The last edition of the *Code Civil*, l. i. t. iii. s. 108.

inasmuch as wheresoever the law of Holland is in force, the children have a vested interest, he conceives no change of property or of domicil, by an executor or guardian would affect that (*d*).

CXX. What might be considered emancipation of a minor under the English Law may be doubtful ; but it seems clear at least that the marriage (*e*) of the minor would emancipate him, and give him the power of acquiring a new domicil (*f*).

CXXI. According to the old law of France (*g*), the minor preserved his paternal domicil, although his guardian was domiciled elsewhere ; and, if the minor died during his minority, his effects were disposed of according to the law of his fathers's domicil. Yet the minor might acquire a capacity of choosing his own domicil by being emancipated by the law, or by the sentence of a judge. It should seem from the following case, that such a capacity was acquired by entering into the military service.

CXXII. The Sieur Délattre, who served as an officer in the French army, passed the winter of every year at Dunkirk. He died at the age of eighteen. A question arose whether his domicil could be fixed at Dunkirk, or whether he was not bound to the domicil of his guardian at St. Omer, where his mother had been domiciled at the time of her death, and

---

(*d*) *Odwin* v. *Forbes, Henry's Reports*, p. 208, note, App.

(*e*) One of the cases allowed by the French Law ; see thereon, *Code Civil*, 1. i. t. x. c. 3.

(*f*) Whether a guardian validly appointed in any given country has an authority for the protection of the ward, and the administration of his personal estate everywhere *ex comitate*, is a matter of some dispute with jurists. The House of Lords held, in *Johnstone* v. *Beattie*, that the English Court of Chancery had jurisdiction to appoint guardians to an infant, although her domicil and all her property was in Scotland. Lords Brougham and Campbell *dissentientibus*. See this very important case, 10 *Clarke and Finnelly's Reports*, 43.— *Vide post.*

(*g*) *Denisart, Domicile*, s. 2. So the Roman Law, " Placet etiam filiumfamilias domicilium habere posse." "Non utique ibi ubi pater habuit, sed ubicunque ipse domicilium constituerit."—*Dig.* 1. 3, 4.

where his guardian was then domiciled. The disposition of his personality varied accordingly. The Court at Montreuil pronounced for the domicil of St. Omer; but the sentence was reversed by an "arrèt" (1769), which decreed in favour of the domicil of Dunkirk (h).

CXXIII. But Cochin was of opinion that the Marquis de St. Pater did not cease to have the domicil of his guardian by becoming the King's page, or by obtaining a company of infantry under the Dauphin (i).

CXXIV. So by accepting a benefice, or other office from which he is not removeable, or by entering into a house of commerce, with the consent of those under whose control he is, the minor becomes emancipated, and capable of acquiring a domicil of his own.

CXXV. By marriage, also, the minor may acquire, either the domicil of his wife, or, after marriage, (j), any domicil he may choose.

CXXVI. According to Pothier, the marriage must have been contracted with the consent of one of his parents or guardian; but it can scarcely be doubted that in Great Britain, a minor once married, whether with or without the proper consent, would be held capable of choosing his domicil (k).

(k) In the edition of *Denisart*, of 1787, it is said that it is difficult to see the "*motif*" of this "arrèt," and that it is only reprinted because it is in the former edition. Surely, however, the ground of the decree must have been that the Sieur's employment as an officer capacitated him to choose a domicil; and such, I find, is the opinion expressed in the last edition of *Merlin*, where this "arrèt" is characterised as one "qui a nettement jugé que le mineur emancipé pouvoit se choisir un domicile."

(i) *Œuvres*, t. vi. p. 227.

(j) "Il paraît en effet que le domicile occasioné par le marriage doit l'emporter sur celui de la naissance."—*Merlin Domicile* V. tome 8, p. 347.

(k) "Un mineur ne peut pas transférer à son gré son domicile: il le peut néanmoins en certains cas: 1, il peut en contractant marriage du consentement de ceux sous la puissance desquels il est, transferer son

CXXVII. It would appear from the following case that the Scotch Law would refuse equally to mother and guardian the power of changing the minor's domicil; for though the case of *Pottinger* v. *Wightman* is the only express decision in an English Court relative to a change of domicil during infancy, yet some very strong judicial dicta have been applied to this question in Scotland, though the case which gave rise to them was not decided upon this, but upon another point.

CXXVIII. It was brought in 1829, before the Court of Sessions in Scotland. Robert Alexander Paterson Wallace was born in Scotland; his father, Captain Wallace was also by birth a Scotchman, and an officer in the army, who had married Miss Oliver, an English lady, in England. The father named guardians to his child, one of whom, the maternal grandfather, Mr. Oliver, resided in England; another, Mr. Hathorn, resided in Scotland. The father died when the infant was of tender years, and the child was conveyed by his mother into England. She also died during the infancy of the child, who continued in England, under the charge of his maternal grandfather, one of his guardians, and was sent to English schools and to an English university. The bulk of the property consisted in stock of the Bank of Scotland. He occasionally visited that country, as well before as after he came of age. He purchased a small landed estate in Scotland after he had attained majority. He died at Hastings, in England, in 1824, aged twenty-two years and seven months, a bachelor and intestate.

His personal property was claimed, in the Courts both of England and Scotland, by his maternal grandfather as next of

domicile au lieu où il prend sa femme, et il peut même, depuis qu'il est marié, le transferer où bon lui semblera. 2, Un mineur peut transférer son domicile soit au lieu où il est pourvu d'un bénéfice où d'une charge, ou autre emploi non amovible qui démande résidence perpétuelle ; soit au lieu où, du consentement de ceux sous la puissance desquels il est, il formeroit un établissement de commerce."—*Pothier, Introduction aux Coutumes,* p. 6.

kin, according to the law of England ; and by his paternal
uncle and aunt, as his next of kin according to the law of
Scotland.

CXXIX. The Lord Ordinary (Cringletie) gave the following
note on the cause when he pronounced his Interlocutor.

"3rd December, 1829.   The Lord Ordinary regrets that
"the parties have thought it necessary to detail the circum-
"stances of Captain Wallace's marriage with Miss Oliver in
"England, and the terms of his contract of marriage with that
"lady : as to the Lord Ordinary they appear not to have the
"least bearing on the cause.   A man by marrying in England
"an Englishwoman does not thereby become domiciled there :
"nor is it necessary that he should reside a day there for that
"purpose : far less does he make his children domiciled there
"by the mere act of marrying in England.   The lady resides
"in a certain parish for a specified time to enable her te be
"married in the church of it, and an oath must be made that
"such has been her residence and domicil otherwise she requires
"a special licence to be married." (The Lord Ordinary here
further illustrated this position by an anecdote respecting his
own marriage).   "Captain Wallace having been a Scotchman
"in the army, did not acquire any domicil by marrying there,
"but returned to Edinburgh where he sold out of the army,
"lived there for some time, and died here.   There can, there-
"fore, be no doubt that he died here domiciled as a Scotchman.
"As to his son, R. A. Wallace, it is admitted that he was born
"in Edinburgh, and went to England with his mother.   Even
"had there been no contract made before he was permitted to
"accompany her, the Lord Ordinary could have no doubt that,
"had he died in pupillarity, his legal domicil of Scotland would
"not have been changed by his residence in England : a pupil
"has no *persona standi*, has no will in law, and he cannot act
"for himself—could not fix his domicil—cannot make a will.
"*But the matter is quite changed when he passes the years of*
"*pupillarity*.   As a domiciled Scotchman he is entitled to act
"for himself with the consent of his curators : *he is entitled to*
"*live where he pleases :* for curators have no control over his

" person." (In support of this position the passage in Erskine already referred to was cited.) "The defenders seem totally " to have lost sight of this principle. They state their case as if " Mr. Hathorn could have prevented R. A. Wallace from living " in England; as if he placed him there, and was at the ex- " pense of his education there : when it is quite plain that it was " Mr. Hathorn's indispensable duty to advance the minor's own " funds to him, for a suitable and reasonable maintenance and " education. Still, residence merely for education may be ques- " tionable how far it constitutes a domicil to govern succession. " *But when education is over, when a man attains majority,* " *and still resides in England, making only short visits to* " *Scotland, having no house of his own in which he lives in* " *Scotland, and dies in a house in England of his own—* " the Lord Ordinary confesses that he thinks there is little room " for doubting what must be held to be his domicil. From the " admitted facts in the case the question appears to have been " fairly tried in a competent Court in England; and a question " may arise how far it is proper or competent to try it again " here; and whether an appeal from the English judgment " would not be the mode to obtain redress "(*l*).

The matter was subsequently settled by compromise, and the proceedings in the Court of Scotland withdrawn.

CXXX. The proceedings in England, to which the Lord Ordinary referred, took place in 1825, before the Prerogative Court of Canterbury, where the same parties, viz., the paternal uncle and aunt on the one side, and the maternal grandfather on the other, respectively claimed administration. Sir John Nicholl decided in favour of the latter, finding the domicil of the deceased to be English, and founding this opinion entirely on the evidence that the deceased had chosen a domicil for himself after the attainment of his majority. The point as to whether or no a domicil could be changed during infancy was not alluded to by the judge. (*m*)

(*l*) *Robertson on Personal Succession*, p. 201, note.

(*m*) There is no report of this important case, but a summary of it is given in *Robertson's Personal Succession*, p. 275, note.

CXXXI. According to the Roman Law(*n*), it devolved on the Prætor to settle the place of abode and education of the minor.

CXXXII. The illegitimate minor, according to the doctrine of the Roman Law (*o*), obtained the domicil of his mother; and this doctrine seems to have been generally recognized in Europe.

CHAPTER X.

II. THE STUDENT.

CXXXIII. The maxim of the Roman Law upon this head has been generally adopted by European jurists; namely, that those who sojourn in a particular place for the purpose of prosecuting their studies, do not acquire a domicil in that place. Ten years are the period specified in the Roman Law, during which no domicil was created; and the inference seems to be, that if they continued to stay there after the lapse of that time, a domicil would be acquired. It was further provided by that law, that no father who frequented the scene of his son's studies should obtain a domicil there. This doctrine, therefore, was especially applied to minors: the principle of it would, however, appear to include majors (*p*).

(*n*) "Solet Prætor frequantissimè adiri, ut constituat, ubi filii, vel alantur *vel morentur*, non tantum in postumis, verum omnino in pueris." *Dig.* lib. xxvii. t. 2. *Pr. ubi pupillus educari vel morari debet.* "Si disceptetur ubi morari vel educari pupillum oportent, causâ cognitâ id Præsidem statuere oportebit."—*Ibid.*

(*o*) "Ejus qui justum patrem non habet prima origo a matre."—*Dig.* 50, t. i. s. ix.; *Story's Conflict of Laws*, ch. iii. s. 46.

(*p*) "Nec ipsi qui studiorum causâ aliquo loco morantur domicilium ibi habere creduntur, nisi decem annis transactis eo loco sedes sibi constituerint, secundum epistolam Divi Adriani nec pater qui propter filium studentem frequentiùs ad eum commeat."—*C.* x. t. xl. s. 2.

There has been a decision upon the point in America; *The Inhabitants of Granby* v. *Inhabitants of Amherst.* According to this case, a student of a college does not change his domicil by his occasional residence at college; (a settlement case), *Massachusetts Reports*, vol. vii. p. 1. *Putnam* v. *Johnson and others* decided that a student in the Theological

III.—THE LUNATIC.

CXXXIV. The power of the guardian with respect to the domicil of the lunatic and the idiot, seems to fall under the principle already discussed of his power with respect to the domicil of the minor (q).

CXXXV. By the old law of France the lunatic either preserved the domicil of his origin, or that which he had last chosen before he had been placed under the care of a *Curator*. By the Code Civil the domicil of the *Tutor* (*tuteur*) determines that of the lunatic (r).

CXXXVI. That a similar rule obtains in (s) England seems a reasonable inference from the following case (t).

George Morrison was born and resided in England. In July, 1742, he lent £2,100 to his nephew the Earl of Sutherland, then in London, who granted bond for it in the English form. On a commission of lunacy in England Mr. Morrison was afterwards found to be a lunatic, and two grants were

---

Institution at Andover, being of age and emancipated from his father's family, is entitled to a vote in that town for the election of senator, 10 *Massachusetts Reports*, p. 492, c. 488.

(q) *M. de Desquiron* observes, "Il tombe sous les sens que le majeur qui est frappé d'interdiction perd l'administration de ses biens, parcequ'il est reconnu dans un état de foiblesse qui l'assimile aux mineurs non émancipés : des lors il cesse à avoir un domicile parcequ'il a perdu la qualité necessaire pour manifester sa volonté. *Traité du Domicile*, p. 94, s. 94.

(r) "Le majeur interdit aura son domicile chez son *tuteur*." Code Civil, art. 108. In the first edition of the Code the word was "*curateur*." See *Duranton's Cours du Droit François*, l. i t. iii. s. 371 ; *Merlin's Rép. de Jurisp* t. viii. tit. du Domicile, s. iv.

(s) Mr. Westlake remarks that this is the modern French rule, because the uniformity of the present law in France has deprived the domicil of its effect on the distribution of property after death ; and this may be the reason. *Westlake*, p. 47-8.

(t) Mr. Westlake is of a different opinion. *Ibid.*

issued under the Great Seal ; one by which the custody of the person of the lunatic was granted to Sir Nicholas Bayley : the other by which the custody of the estate and effects of the lunatic was granted to Walter Baynes and Penelope, his wife, the brother in-law and sister of the lunatic.   These last, as such committees, brought an action upon the bond against the Earl of Sutherland in the Court of Session.   In defence, he contended that the lunacy had not been established in Scotland : that the law upon the subject was different in the two countries : and that the rules of distribution of the personal estate of lunatics were also different.

CXXXVII. The question was argued several times before the Lord Ordinary.   The defendant contended that the Lord Chancellor had no power to direct the management of any estate *extra territorium*.   The pursuers answered that *statuta personalia loci domicilii* must bind everywhere, and that *mobilia sequuntur personam*, and are regulated by the law of the place of domicil.   The pursuers applied to the Lord Chancellor, stating their process and defences : that the debt was in danger, and praying that the Committee might have access to the lunatic to obtain a power of attorney from him to authorise them to sue for this debt.   This application the Lord Chancellor granted.   The power of attorney was accordingly obtained, and the Committee then insisted upon both titles.   The Court of Session (21st June, 1749) found that there was no sufficient title produced to carry on the action, and therefore sustained the defence.   But this judgment was reversed upon appeal to the House of Lords, and, it was "de-"clared that there was a sufficient title in the appellant, George "Morrison, to carry on the action commenced by the appellant, "and that the same be sustained at the instance of the said "Morrison" (*u*).

(*u*) This account of *Morrison's* case is taken from *Robertson's Personal Succession*, pp. 113, 114.   The exact grounds of the decision may be doubtful, but the inference from *Lord Hardwicke's* reference to it in *Thorne* v. *Watkins*, 2 *Vesey*, sen 35, certainly is, that it was decided

CXXXVIII. In *Leith* v. *Hay*, (1811), the Court of Sessions sustained an action in Scotland upon the bond granted to the King by the committee of an *English* lunatic and his sureties, such *commitee and sureties being domiciled in Scotland.* In this action decree was granted for payment of the bond, and the money was directed to be paid into the Bank of Scotland upon a receipt, till, upon application to the Lord Chancellor, his Lordship should "direct in what manner the money so to be paid shall be remitted to the proper officer of the Court of Chancery for the benefit of the estate of the said lunatic." Mr. Robertson remarks, that there is nothing in the report with regard to the domicil of this lunatic.

CXXXIX. In *Lord Annandale's* case, where the English Domicil prevailed rather by the weakness of the Scotch Domicil than by its own strength, the question was glanced at but not decided (*x*). The Lord Chancellor said, "Wherever he" (Lord Annandale) "had a place of residence that could not be referred "to an occasional and temporary purpose that is found in Eng- "land and no where else. I am not clear that the period of his "lunacy is totally to be discarded, but I will take him to have "died there" (*y*).

IV.—THE SERVANT.

CXL. We have now to consider the case of the Servant. A combination of *fact* and *intention,* has been said to be necessary for the constitution of a Domicil, and this principle

---

upon the great principles of law. The American Courts however, appear to hold that the power of guardians over their ward's property does not extend to property in Foreign States. *Story's Conflict of Laws,* p. 416.

(*x*) There were, however, two commissioners of lunacy, one in England and one in Scotland, and two curators appointed, one in each country.

(*y*) *Bempde* v. *Johnson,* 3 *Vesey,* 198.

would seem to preserve to the domestic servant the Domicil which he possessed before entering into service.

CXLI. According to Voet, however, the presumption founded on experience is, that the domestic servant has abandoned his native domicil without any intention of returning to it; and, therefore, has acquired another domicil, which must be the domicil of the master with whom he is living. He likens the case of servants to that of tutors, who, he thinks, acquire the domicil of the pupils with whom they reside, and to that of the freed men (*liberti*) among the Romans, who acquired the domicil of their patrons; between these freed men and the modern domestic servant Voet conceives a very close analogy to subsist (*z*).

CXLII. But it is a question much depending upon the particular circumstances of each case. If a servant, having quitted his domicil of origin, remains for a long period of time at one particular place in the employment of several masters, and has collected together in that place his earnings, the legal presumption would be the abandonment of the original, and acquisition of a new domicil. But a contrary presumption would flow from the circumstances of his having been known to return several times to the place of his birth in the interval

---

(*z*) "Famulos ancillasque nostrates quod attinet, etsi liberi sint et certâ mercede conducti nobis operas prætent, nec familiæ nostræ perpetuò addicti sint, *tamen vix est ut existimemus eos proprium retinere domicilium*, quippe à quo plerumque eos secedere animo non revertendi experientia testatur. Quin potius eos ex domicilio domini cui ministrant censeri, et competens sortiri forum suadent juris rationes: si enim nuncii scholarium ac ministri cum scholaribus studiorum causâ degentes, ex personâ eorum, quibus ministrant forum sortiantur privilegiatum, et ex quali quali domicilio ac jure scholarium in loco studiorum æstimentur (*auth. habita C. ne filius pro patre*), cur non cessante illo foro privilegiato, in loco domicilii dominici propriè sic dicti convenirentur, ratio non est. Cui accedit quod et liberti Romani, utcunque liberi, patronorum suorum non originem modo sed et domicilium sequebantur, quos tamen in obsequiis et operis præstandis non longè a famulis hodiernis constat," &c. *Voet*, i. t. v. s. 96.

of his servitudes to different masters, and of his having deposited his savings and property there; the intention of preserving his original domicil would be fairly deducible from this conduct.

CXLIII. Claude Doumayron, born near Rhodès, quitted his country soon after the death of his father, and came to Paris. He remained there for twenty years in the capacity of servant to the Sieur Bergeret, and in that service he died. The question was, whether the succession to his personalty (*la succession mobiliaire*), should be ruled by the custom of Paris, or by the Roman Law (*droit écrit*). He was held to have been domiciled at Paris. The number of years and the uninterrupted residence seem to have been the foundation of this decision of the French tribunal (*a*).

CXLIV. Nicholas Sautereau had his domicil of origin in Burgundy; he came to Paris while a minor: during his stay there he served as a kind of steward (*régisseur*) to different masters, but especially the family of Bonvelles. He was sent by one of his masters, in that capacity, to Ferraques, near Lisieux, and there he died. Five advocates decided that he had never lost his domicil of origin, and that his succession must be regulated by the custom of Burgundy, because the nature of his employments at Paris and Ferraques were not such as to acquire for him a domicil. " He lived " (they said) "by his " masters' wages, was subject to their wills, and was under the " necessity of following them whithersoever they went." He had, in fact, never enjoyed a state of liberty requisite to enable him to found a domicil (*b*).

CXLV. An ancient custom exempted all persons domiciled at Nevers (*c*) from the payment of certain duties in the trade of corn and wine. Berger, a domestic servant of a lady, and Berthaut, who acted in the same capacity to a religious order

---

(*a*) Denisart, *Collection de Décisions, &c. Domicile*, s. 11, ed. 1787.

(*b*) Denisart, *ibid.*

(*c*) Merlin, *Rép. de Jur. Domicile*, IV. 2.

of the community, claimed this exemption. The Advocate General, however, unhesitatingly pronounced against their claim upon the ground that, as domestic servants, they could not have acquired any domicil. His opinion was confirmed by an "arrêt" of Parliament with respect to Berger. With respect to Berthaut, they allowed him one month to prove — 1st, that when the demand for duty was made upon him, he was actually domiciled at Nevers; Secondly, that he paid the "taille"; Thirdly, that he was married and had a wife and children; 4thly, that he had always traded in corn and wine; and in the event of his failing in such proof, they confirmed the sentence of the Advocate General (d).

CXLVI. The Code Civil expressly declares that every person of full age who is in the habit of acting as a servant or a workman to another, if he reside in the same house as his master, shall be held to be domiciled therein (e).

CXLVII. According to the Prussian Law and to Savigny, hired servants (*Dienstboten*—*serviteurs à gages*), day labourers on an estate (auf einem bestimmter Landgute bleibend arbeiten-den Tageslohnern—journaliers constamment occupés dans un domaine rural), apprentices to a particular master (*bei einem bestimmter Handwerksmeister arbeitenden Gesellen*—*ouvriers qui exercent leur métier chez un maître*) have the domicil of their employers (f).

CXLVIII. The slave, of course, would have no domicil but

(d) It was said by the *Attorney General*, in the case of the *Countess of Dalhousie* v. *MacDowall*, that a servant who followed his master for a particular service, did not thereby lose his domicil of origin. 7 *Clark and Finnelly's Reports*, p. 331.

(e) *Art.* 109. "Les majeurs qui servent ou travaillent habituellement chez autrui ont le même domicile que la personne qu'ils servent, ou chez laquelle ils travaillent lorsqu'ils demeurent avec elle dans la même maison."

(f) *Savigny* viii. s. 353.

Preussiche Allge. Gerichtsordnung, I. ii. s. 13.

that of his master, but the manumitted person was held by the Roman Law to have acquired the domicil of the manumittor. (*g*)

(*g*) *Dig.* 50, t. i. s. 27, which says, "Ejus qui manumisit municeps est manumissus non domicilium ejus sed, patriam secutus." S. 22 says, "filii libertorum libertarumque ut liberti paterni patroni et manumissoris domicilium, aut originem sequuntur."—"Cives quidem origo manumissio, allectio, vel adoptio facit." *Code* x. 40—7.

CHAPTER XI.

V.—THE PUBLIC OFFICER.

CXLIX. So much was the liberty of the freeman to choose his own domicil respected by the Roman Law, that it was not allowed to be restrained by any act of another private individual (*a*). If a legacy was left to a freeman on condition that he fixed his domicil in a particular *civitas*, the condition was set aside (*b*).

CL. But it was fully competent to the Law of the State, or the Public Law, to place restrictions upon this liberty ; and the Roman Law—followed in this, as well as in other regulations relating to Domicil, by modern Law—has affixed a particular domicil upon certain public servants (*c*) of the State, and upon certain criminals (*d*).

CLI. This leads us to consider the domicil of the Public Officer of the State. The existing French Code has laid down the following rules respecting the domicil of the Officer, Civil or Military, employed in the Public Service of the State (*e*).

(*a*) Nihil est impedimento quo minus quis ubi velit habeat domicilium ei quod interdictum non sit."—*Dig.* lib. l. t. i. 31.

(*b*) Titio centum relicta sunt ita, *ut a monumento meo non recedat,* vel *uti in illâ civitate domicilium habeat.* Potest dici non esse locum cautioni, per quam jus libertatis infringitur. Sed in defuncti libertis alio jure utimur. *Dig.* l. xxxv. t. i. 71, s. 2.

(*c*) "Miles ibi *domicilium* habere videtur ubi meret, si nihil in *patriâ** possideat."—*Dig.* lib. i. t. i. s. 23, 1.

  * *Vide ante* as to meaning of this word, p. 26, n. (*i*) ; 33, n. (*i*)

(*d*) "Relegatus in eo loco, in quem relegatus est, interim necessarium domicilium habet."—*Dig.* lib. l. t. i. 22, 1.

(*e*) Duranton, *Cours du Droit Français,* l. i. t. iii. du Domicile. *Merlin, Rep. de Juris Domicile,* iii. *Du Domicile des Fonctionaires Publics*

1. If the office be conferred for the life of the holder, and irrevocable, the law fixes his Domicil in the places where its functions are discharged, and admits of no proof to the contrary. "For the law," says Denisart, "will not presume an "intention contrary to an indispensable duty"(*f*).

2. If the office be of a temporary and revocable nature, the law does not presume that the holder has changed his original domicil, but allows the fact that he has done so to be established by the usual proof.

CLII. The authority of Denisart, under the old Law of France, would seem to warrant a third division, namely, that of those public officers whose service does not compel them to such close residence, but, perhaps, to only half a year's residence or to a residence of alternate months; they, according to the high authority of Denisart, are *presumed* in law to be domiciled at the place of their vocation (*dans le lieu ou il se sont consacrés à des fonctions publiques*): but it is a presumption, capable of being repelled by proof, that the seat of

---

(*f*) Il y en a dont le devoir indispensable exige qu'ils aient leur domicil dans tel lieu, parcequ'il faut qu'ils s'y trouvent tous les jours et presque à toute heure; tel est le lieutenant civil du châtelet de Paris. Il en est d'autres qui ne sont pas astreints au même devoir, quoiqu'ils aient aussi des fonctions particulière: tel est un trésorier de France. En conséquence, il est impossible quelle lieutenant-civil du châtelet n'ait pas son domicile à Paris; au lieu qu'il n'est pas impossible qu'un trésorier de France soit domicilié ailleurs, que dans la ville où se fait l'exercise de son office. On ne sauroit avoir égard en matière de domicile à une intention contraire à un dévoir indispensable. C'est pourquoi quand même un lieutenant-civil se diroit dans tous les actes qu'il passeroit domicilié dans un château, où auroit sa femme et ses enfans, il n'en seroit pas moins domicilié à Paris, &c." *Denisart, Domicile*, c. ii. s. 5. This rule applies to those who are comprised under the 109th article of the *Code Civil*, according to which, "L'acceptation de fonctions conferées à vie emportera translation immédiate du domicile du fonctionnaire dans le lieu où il doit exercer ses foctions." *Merlin* remarks upon the equivocal character of the expression "conferées à vie," which, he says, is designed only to mean "fonctions *irrevocables*." —*Rép. de Jur. Domicile* iii.

his family affairs, the residence of his wife and family, is elsewhere, and that he has described himself, in all legal instruments, as belonging to his ancient domicil, and not to that which he has acquired by virtue of his employment.

CLIII. The presumption was repelled in the case of *Lord Somerville* (g). His residence in London, after he had been elected one of the sixteen peers of Scotland, was held to be no proof of his Domicil there being occasioned by his Parliamentary duties. So the office of "grand-mâitre de eaux et "forêts" was not held to prevent the law of the original domicil from operating in the case of *M. de Courteval*, chiefly on the ground that the office did not compel more than a visit of two or three months during the course of the year to the department, and not a fixed residence (h).

CLIV. The case of *Mr. Bruce* (i) should be mentioned as belonging to the first division. He left Scotland when young, and after being several years in the navy, in the year 1767 went to the East Indies (j) in the military service of the Company, and continued there till his death, in 1783, having risen to the rank of major. In many letters to his friends in Scotland he expressed an anxious desire to return and spend the remainder of his life in his native country : particularly he wrote to that purpose a few months before his death, and he was in the course of remitting home his money, meaning soon to follow, when he died. Lord Chancellor Thurlow confirmed the judgment of the Scotch Court, which had pro-

---

(g) *Somerville* v. *Somerville*. *Vide supra.*

(h) *Cochin. Œuvres,* t. ix. p. 124.

(i) *Brown's Cases in Parliament,* vol. vi. p. 566. 2 *Bosanquet and Puller's Reports,* 230.

(j) *Voet,* remarking that a domicil is not created when a person " negotiationis peragendæ causâ alicubi commoretur," adds, " quâ rá- ratione responsum quoque aliquando fuit, eum qui in Indiam Orien- talem profectus fuit domicilium non amississe, quod tamen nostris moribus ex novissimo jure de iis qui Indiam Orientalem petunt quo- dammodo mutatum est," &c. l. v. t. i. s. 87.

nounced Mr. Bruce to be domiciled in India, and therefore, by fiction of law, in the province of Canterbury. It was said by counsel, in *Somerville* v. *Somerville,* that "*Mr. Bruce entered* "*into the India service, not the King's service. A great* "*deal turned upon that : for he was bound to reside in* "*India, and could not reside elsewhere except by the leave of* "*the Company, and, consequently, for a temporary pur-* "*pose.* Therefore by entering into that service, he was con-"ceived to have abandoned his original domicil, and to have "gained a new one. It did not depend upon the place in "which he lived in India. That was not inquired into. It "turned upon his residence in India under an obligation that "was to last during his whole life, unless put an end to." And it is difficult, upon any other suggestion than that contained in the foregoing remarks to account for the little weight which seems to have been ascribed to the circumstances of birth, declarations of intention, and the absence of any fixed home elsewhere.

CLV. The case of *Dr. Munroe* (*k*) seems also to fall within this principle. He was born in Scotland, and educated there to the profession of a surgeon. At the age of nineteen he went out to Calcutta to practice, and in 1771 *was appointed assistant surgeon to a regiment in the East India Company's service.* On the 6th of May, 1789, he was appointed full surgeon in the Company's service ; *in 1811, he was ranked as surgeon in His Majesty's service ; but it was only local rank.* He was married in India in 1797. In March, 1813, he made his will, and added a codicil thereto on the 22nd September, 1814. He left India in January, 1815, with a determination, as the plaintiff contended from his letters when in India, to spend the rest of his days in Scotland, and arrived in England in the following June, where he took a house, and, owing to ill-health, became undetermined whe .

(*k*) *Munroe* v. *Douglas,* 5 *Maddocks' Reports of Cases in Chancery,* 379—406, before Sir J. Leach, Vice Chancellor.

ther he should continue to reside in England, or spend his
days in Scotland.   In July, 1816, he went on a visit to Scotland, and died at his friend's seat there in August, 1816.   By
his will he had given property to his wife to the amount of
£1000 a year and upwards, and made dispositions in favour
of his nephew and nieces; but he had not disposed of the
remainder of his property, amounting nearly to £60,000; and
the question was whether Dr. Munroe at his death was to be
considered as domiciled in Scotland, or whether he was, as the
defendants contended, to be considered as domiciled in England, the distribution of the property being by law much more
in favour of the plaintiff in the former case than in the latter.
Many *letters* were given in evidence, written by the Doctor
during his residence in India, to show that his determination
was to spend his latter days in Scotland, and some *passages in
his will* were relied on as indicative of that intention.   Letters also and *conversations* were in evidence to prove that,
after the Doctor's return from England, his health was such
that he was doubtful whether he should spend his days in
England or Scotland; and clear evidence was adduced that
when he went to Scotland after his return from India, it was
only on a visit, and without an intention of then permanently
residing there.   It was very elaborately argued before the
Vice Chancellor: that learned Judge said, "It was settled
" by the case of *Major Bruce* that *a residence in India for
" the purpose of following a profession there in the service
" of the East India Company* creates a new domicil.   It is
" said that, having afterwards quitted India in the intention
" never to return thither, he abandoned his acquired domicil,
" and the *forum originis* revived.   As to this point I can
" find no difference in principle between the original domicil
" and an acquired domicil, and such is clearly the under-
" standing of Pothier, in one of his passages which has been
" referred to.   A domicil cannot be lost by mere abondonment.
" It is not to be defeated *animo* merely, but *animo et facto,*
" and necessarily remains until a subsequent domicil be ac-
" quired, unless the party die *in itinere* toward an intended

" domicil. It has been stated that, in point of fact, the tes-
" tator went to Scotland in the intention to fix his permanent
" residence there; but his statement is not supported by evi-
" dence. It has also been stated that the testator, knowing he
" was in a dying state, went to Scotland in order to lay his
" bones with his ancestors; but this, too, is clearly disproved.
" It may be represented as the certain fact here, that, when
" this gentleman left England on his visit to Scotland, he
" had formed no settled purpose of permanent residence
" there or elsewhere; that he meant to remain a few
" months only in Scotland, and to winter in the south of
" France, and with this fluctuation of mind on the subject
" of his future domicil, he was surprised by death at the house
" of a relation in Scotland. I am of opinion, therefore, that
" Dr. Munroe acquired no new domicil after he quitted India,
" and that his Indian Domicil subsisted at his death. A
" domicil in India is, in legal effect, a domicil in the province
" of Canterbury, and the Law of England, and not the Law
" of Scotland, is, therefore, to be applied to his personal
" property."

CLVI. The point of the obligation to reside in India being
incidental to the holding a commission in the Company's service, as well as the general character of the Anglo-Indian
officer, underwent much discussion in a very recent case
(1843), in the Prerogative Court of Canterbury, in which Sir
Herbert Jenner Fust delivered the following judgment:—

CLVII (*l*). "The question relates to the domicil which is to
" determine on the validity of a paper purporting to be the
" will of Colonel J. Craigie, who died on the 23rd of Novem-
" ber, 1840, at Hatchett's Hotel, Piccadilly. The will is dated
" in the month of October preceding; it is in the shape and
" form of a Scotch deed, a holograph, subscribed by the de-
" ceased, but not attested by any witnesses; and, conse-
" quently, as it was made since 1840, if the deceased is to be

---

(*l*) *Craigie* v. *Lewin*, 3 *Curteis's Ecclesiastical Reports*, p. 435.

" considered as a domiciled British subject, the will is invalid
" for want of a due attestation ; if on the other hand, he is to
" be considered as a domiciled Scotchman, then the Law of
" Scotland must determine on the validity or invalidity of this
" paper as a will.

" The question in the present case is not, whether the
" Domicil of this person was Indian or English, for the Law of
" England and India are now the same, as regards the validity
" of wills ; whether it was so at the time when the act of the
" 1 Vict. c. 26, passed, does not matter in this case, *because*
" *an act was shortly after, January, 1838, passed by the*
" *Legislature in India, assimilating the Law of India in*
" *respect to wills to that of England;* there is no necessity,
" therefore, to consider, whether the Domicil was English or
" Indian, provided it was not Scotch. This leads the Court
" to inquire into the history of this gentleman. He was born
" in the year 1786, in Scotland ; his parents were Scotch, and
" they also were of Scotch descent ; he remained in Scotland,
" indeed was never out of that country, until 1804, when he
" went to India in the East India Company's military service,
" in which he had obtained a commission as a lieutenant of a
" regiment of native infantry. By birth, descent, and gene-
" alogy, therefore, his Domicil was clearly and decidedly Scotch,
" and he did not abandon that domicil until he became of age,
" when he acquired an Indian, or, as one counsel has called it,
" an Anglo-Indian Domicil. Having entered into the service
" of the East India Company, and having attained his age of
" twenty-one whilst in that service, his Domicil became Indian,
" or Anglo-Indian ; for it is the same thing. In India he
" remained until 1837, with two exceptions ; he was in Eng-
" land in 1819 until 1820, and he was also at the Cape of
" Good Hope from February, 1824, until October in the same
" year. On the first of these occasions, when absent from
" India, he did not visit Scotland ; it is said, in explanation,
" that he came to England on a special mission from the
" Marquis of Hastings, the duties of which fully occupied his

time. On the second occasion, when at the Cape of Good Hope, his Domicil was clearly Indian. During the visit of the deceased to England in 1822, he married an English lady. I do not think this fact of any importance; it merely amounts to this—that, being a domiciled Indian, he married whilst being on a visit to England: he carried his wife back with him to India; he had children by her, and he lived in India from that time until the year 1837, when he came over to England on the customary leave of absence, but still retaining his commission in the East India Company's service: he came on a three years' leave of absence, though, it is stated, that such leave is renewable for two years more; so that he had every prospect of remaining in this country for five years: he applied for renewal of leave of absence on two occasions, and obtained it; this would have carried his leave of absence down to March, 1841; he died in November, 1840. Now it is said this leave of absence being granted as a matter of course, the deceased had every expectation that before its expiration he should have succeeded to a commission of full colonel in the service, which would have precluded the necessity of his returning to India, to which it is admitted he had a decided aversion. If he did not return to India on the expiration of his leave of absence, or previously attain his full rank, he must have quitted the service of the East India Company (33 Geo. III. c. 55). Now it appears, that the deceased had no intention of abandoning his commission, unless he became a full colonel; he must, therefore, at this time, 1837, have contemplated the possibility, if not the probability, of being obliged to return to India, if only for a short period. It appears, that on his arrival in this country, in 1837, after remaining in England a short time, the deceased proceeded direct to Scotland, and arrived there in the October of that year, and he continued in Scotland until August, 1839, living, whilst there, in furnished houses: it further appears that, during the time of his residence, he contemplated the purchase of a house in Edinburgh; he wished to take a lease of a house for seven

' years, and offered to take such a lease of a particular house ;
' but it had been purchased by another party, to whom he
' offered £100 to give up the bargain, and not being able to
' succeed in effecting his wishes, in August, 1839, he quitted
' Scotland, and by the advice of his medical attendant, came
' to London ; from thence he went to Plymouth, and lived
' there, or in that neighbourhood, in furnished houses, until
' the death of his father in 1840, when he left Plymouth, and
' again went to Scotland to attend his father's funeral; he
' remained in Scotland until October in that year, when he
' returned to London, and died at Hatchett's Hotel in No-
' vember, 1840, being at the time about to join his wife and
' children at Plymouth. This is the statement on behalf of
' those who desire to support the Scotch Domicil ; on the
other side, there is very little difference in the statement of
the facts, the affidavits scarcely vary the case at all; they
all coincide in the fact that the deceased did express an
intention of taking up his abode in Scotland, in his wish to
take a particular house in Edinburgh, that he offered £100
to the purchaser of the lease to give up the bargain; that
as late as 1840, he again expressed a wish for the same
house, or of purchasing some other house in the neighbourhood of Edinburgh ; and that he was desirous of sending his
son to study with some civil engineer in that neighbourhood.
These circumstances are undoubted ; from them I think the
Court can come to the conclusion that if everything had
turned out according to the deceased's own wishes, he would
have taken up his residence in Scotland : no one can look
to his letters without seeing that he had a decided preference for the country of his birth : unfortunately his wife had
a different opinion ; she preferred residing in England, and
she at last persuaded the deceased that such residence
would be better for themselves and children. It appears
to me, that having left Scotland in 1839, he did not go
back until 1840, and then only to attend his father's
funeral, and when that ceremony was over, he returned to
England.

" These are the facts of the case, so far as is important to the present question ; but the Court will have to refer more particularly to the exhibits, before coming to a conclusion on the case. Now, I do think that, if all circumstances had combined to favour the deceased's wishes, he would have taken up his residence in Scotland : but still the question remains, whether there was an abandonment of the Indian Domicil, and if there was the *animus* and *factum* of a domicil in Scotland. It was properly asked by the counsel for Mr. Craigie, when was it that the Indian Domicil was abandoned, and the Scotch acquired ? The answer, or the tenor of the answer to the question was, at the time when the deceased went to Scotland in 1837, that he then went there for the purpose of remaining ; in short, that he did it *animo manendi*, with the intention to preclude all question as to his domicil : that he took up his residence there *animo et facto*. The question then remains for the Court to determine—it being an admitted fact that the deceased went to Scotland in 1837, and remained there until 1839—whether he went there *animo manendi ;* the solution of that question depends very much on his peculiar situation at the time ; whether he was in a condition to abandon his acquired domicil in India : for if he was not in a condition to abandon his Indian Domicil, the intention, even if to a certain extent complete by the fact of his having come to this country, *animo manendi*, if he could possibly remain, would not be sufficient to change the domicil ; if the deceased was not in a condition to carry his intention into effect, that is, if his remaining in this country was dependent on circumstances, which might be such as to render it incumbent on him to return to India, that is, if certain events did not give him an opportunity of finally quitting the service. In 1837, when the deceased arrived in this country, he retained his commission in the East India Company's service; he not only came on leave of absence for a distinct period ;—it signifies not whether there was a greater or less probability, or whether, as a mere matter of course, his time

' of absence would be extended for two years more—he was
' still absent on leave; he retained his commission in the
' Indian army, his regiment was in India, and his military
' establishment there : he had quitted India only for a tem-
' porary purpose ; not with a fixed determination to abandon
' it altogether, but with the intention to return, unless on the
' happening of a particular event, namely, his attaining the
' rank of full colonel, before his leave of absence expired.

" The question is, whether a person having a fixed domicil,
' and having quitted it with the proposed intention of return-
' ing, although such intention may be annulled by the happen-
' ing of a particular event, can by law be said to have aban-
' doned that domicil; this is the important part of the case ;
' did the deceased, when in 1837, or in 1839, he went to
' Scotland, go there *animo manendi,* or did he merely go
' there to remain, so long as the rules of the service in India
' would permit, and no longer? Now all the correspondence
' and the affidavits tend to shew that he contemplaced return-
' ing to India; he might have continued to live in Scotland
' during the whole of the time of his leave of absence, but
would that have been a residence *animo et facto ?*—the
animus would only be whilst his absence from India permitted, for if he did return to India, his Indian domicil
would revert—perhaps I should not say *revert,* because it
would never have been divested. When the deceased came
to this country, he quitted India on a temporary absence,
which might be converted into a permanent quitting, by a
certain event happening in the interval between the time of
the commencement of his absence and the time for his return ; I cannot think that the fact that he was absent from
India, when he was looking to a probable return, can be said
to be quitting that country *animo manendi* in another : he
was indeed in another place, but for a temporary purpose
only. Now, up to 1839, when he last quitted Scotland, his
domicil was India. I cannot conceive that, by having left
India under the circumstances mentioned, he had divested
himself of the domicil acquired by his commission in the

East India Company's service; in 1839, he went to Plymouth with his wife and family, he resided there, although only in furnished lodgings. If the question was between a Scotch or an English domicil I should decide for the Scotch domicil, notwithstanding his returning to England, and living there in furnished lodgings, and although, as has been argued, he had at one time expressed a wish to purchase a house near Plymouth; and although his actual residence was so far in this country, except for a short time when he went to Scotland on his father's death; and although he died in the act of returning thence to join his wife and family in this country. The important question is, what is necessary to constitute a change of domicil. There must be both *animus et factum;* that is the result of all the cases. This case must depend on its own circumstances; the principles on which it is to be determined are the same in all cases, and that principle extracted from all the cases is this, ' That ' 'a domicil once acquired remains until another is acquired, or ' 'that first abandoned ;' I admit all that has been said in this case, that length of time is not important; one day will be sufficient, provided the *animus* exists : if a person goes from one country to another, with the intention of remaining, that is sufficient; whatever time he may have lived there is not enough, unless there be an intention of remaining.

" It is now my duty to consider the effects of the exhibits, and of the particular circumstances stated in the affidavits, ' for the purpose of shewing the grounds on which the Court ' thinks that the deceased had not abandoned his Indian Domicil : he retained his establishment in India, his connection with his regiment, of which he remained lieutenant-colonel, still continued ; he was bound by the rules of the service ' to rejoin his regiment at the expiration of his leave of absence.

" Now, admitting the fact of actual residence in Scotland, ' from 1837 until 1839, and the wish for a fixed and permanent residence in Scotland ; admitting that the deceased had 'a decided preference for Scotland, and that, if peculiar circumstances did not interfere to prevent him carrying that inclination into effect, he would have settled in a house in that country; still he had not at the time of his death placed himself in such a situation as to enable the Court to say that he had abandoned his Indian Domicil, and acquired a permanent domicil in Scotland: the deceased had not abandoned his Indian Domicil, he could not do so without resigning his commission, he did not intend to do so unless he obtained the rank of full colonel. Although the bias of his inclination was to live in Scotland, and, even if he had remained there during all the time he was absent from India on leave, I should still have held that by retaining his commission, which might, and probably would, have compelled him to return to India, the deceased had not abandoned his Indian Domicil. If so, then can it be said that he had abandoned that domicil? His connection with that country, which originally gave him his Indian Domicil, still remained in full force; it was indeed liable to be dissolved by his attaining his full rank.

"Looking to all the circumstances of the case, I think it is distinguished from all those cases which counsel have most judiciously abstained from going into; they have all been considered here often and often. I think the Indian Domicil was not abandoned, but that the deceased was still domiciled in India. If he had died in Scotland that would not in the slightest degree have changed my opinion; he was domiciled in India: if the question had been, whether he was domiciled in England or in Scotland, if that point had been in *equilibrio*, the place of birth and origin might have turned the scale.

" I think there is quite sufficient in this case to enable the Court to determine that the Indian Domicil, which the deceased had acquired, did remain at the time of his death: when I look for the *animus* and the *factum*, I do not find sufficient to enable me to say that the deceased had dissolved his connection with India; and I think, under all

" circumstances, that the Scotch Law cannot determine on the
" validity or invalidity of this will."

CLVIII. The liability to recall preserved the Anglo-Indian
Domicil in this case. It is of course possible, however, that
the liability may be so remote in any service that it may be
not a practical liability, and this might affect the consideration
of Domicil (*m*).

CLIX. The decision in the case of *Sir C. Douglas* appears
to have been founded upon the principle that by entering
into the military service of a foreign country you acquire a
domicil in that country. The circumstances (*n*) were these.
He left Scotland in 1741, at the age of twelve, with a view to
enter into the navy. From that time to his. death he was in
Scotland only four times : 1st, as captain of a frigate ; 2ndly,
to introduce his wife to his friends, on which occasion he staid
about a year; 3rdly, upon a visit; 4thly, when, being appointed to a command upon the Halifax station, he went in
the mail coach to Scotland, and died there in 1789. He was
not for a day resident there in any house of his own. Under
those circumstances, it was difficult to contend that he retained
the domicil during all that time in a country with which he
had so little connection. He had no estate there, no mansion-
house ; he was not a peer of that country (*o*). There was
nothing but the circumstances of his birth and his death ; and
upon those circumstances, and because he had an occasional
domicil there, the Court of Sessions determined that he was
domiciled in Scotland. He married in Holland, and had a
sort of establishment there ; he commanded the Russian navy

(*m*) *Forbes* v. *Forbes*, 1 *Kay's Rep.* 64, 16 *Jurist*, 642. *Sed vide post,*
Hodgson v. *De Beauchesne.*

(*n*) *Ommaney* v. *Bingham, before the House of Lords*, 18th March,
1796. See argument of counsel, 5 *Vesey's Reports*, p. 757, case of
Somerville.

(*o*) See *Lord Redesdale's Speech on the Strathmore Peerage Case*, for
the distinction between the Peer of the Realm and the Lord of Parliament. *Wilson and Shaw's Appeal Cases*, vol. iv. *Appendix* V. p. 91.

for about a year, and was afterwards in the Dutch service; he had no fixed residence in England till 1776, when he took a house at Gosport, in which, when on shore, he lived as his home. That was the only residence he had in the British dominions. Whenever he went on service he left his wife and family there, and he always returned to that place. His third wife was a native of Gosport. Before his visit to Scotland, in November, 1786, Sir C. Douglas had written to his sister— " Be pleased to observe, that I do not engage to build my " tabernacle in Scotland; and if it should, some time hence, " prove convenient to me to establish myself elsewhere, be- " cause of service or otherwise, I shall probably remove the " whole of my family," &c. He stayed in Scotland till September, 1789, returned to London and Gosport, where Lady Douglas resided; in 1788 he went for a few months to Scotland; in 1789, he went to Edinburgh alone, and died there two days after his arrival, in furnished lodgings, of an apoplexy. In his will he spoke of his dwelling-house at Gosport. Under these circumstances the cause came before the House of Lords. The Lords considered the circumstance of his death in Scotland, going there only for a few days, as nothing. The Lord Chancellor expressed himself to the following effect :—

"The reasons assigned in support of the decision of the " Court of Session are by no means satisfactory. His dying " in Scotland is nothing; for it is quite clear the purpose of " going there was temporary and limited; nothing like an in- " tention of having a settled habitation there. The interlocu- " tor says he had an occasional domicil there: but the ques- " tion never depends upon occasional domicil: the question is, " what was the general habit of his life? It is difficult to " suppose a case of exact balance. *Birth affords some argu-* " *ment, and might turn the scale, if all the other circum-* " *stances were in equilibrio;* but it is clear in this case, his " circumstances, his hopes, and sometimes his necessities, fixed " him in England. His taste might fix him at Gosport in the " neighbourhood of a yard, a place also convenient to him in

" the pursuit of his profession. Upon his visit to Scotland by
" a letter he guarded his sister against the hope of his settling
" there."

The Counsel in the case had argued that " the words of the
" Civil Law, ' Larem rerumque ac fortunarum summam,' can-
" not be translated better than by the expression of that letter,
" that he had no thought of setting up his tabernacle there :
" it means the main establishment."

The Counsel further argued that " it became important to
" determine the domicil in that case; because, by a codicil,
" he had imposed a condition in restraint of marriage upon a
" legacy to his daughter with a gift over to other children ;
" and it was contended that the condition was void by the
" Law of Scotland, but good by the Law of England, on account
" of the gift over. If Sir Charles Douglas had died in the
" Russian or Dutch service, his property must have been dis-
" tributed according to the Law of Russia or Holland ; for
" he had made himself a subject of those countries, and by his
" establishment there, had lost his establishment in Scotland."
And then Counsel said that " *His original Domicil having*
" *been abandoned, when he afterwards entered into the ser-*
" *vice of this country he became domiciled here, as a Russian*
" *or Dutchman would on entering into our service.*" This
last proposition, though made *arguendo*, appears to me a
correct exposition of the law. (*p*)

CLX. It was said, indeed, that this case was decided rather
with reference to the weakness of the Scotch, than to the
strength of the English Domicil. The Lord Chancellor closed
his decision on *Lord Annandale's* case with the following
comments on that of *Sir C. Douglas.*

CLXI. (*q*) " The case last determined in the House of
" Lords is the case of *Sir Charles Douglas.* I particularly
" had the benefit of hearing all the arguments so well pressed
" in this cause, and also at the bar of the House in that. It fell

(*p*) The doubt expressed in the note, 5 Vesey (Jr.), p. 782, does not
materially affect it. The case of *Curling* v. *Thornton*, referred to, has been,
as to this point, long over-ruled. *Et vide post*, s. clxviii., and cases in note.

(*q*) *Bempde* v. *Johnstone*, 3 *Vesey*, p. 200.

" to my share to pronounce the judgment, but it was much
" more formed by Lord Thurlow, and settled in concert with
" him : the general course of the reasoning he approved. It
" was one of the strongest cases ; for there was first a deter-
" mination of the Court of Session upon the point. Great
" respect was due to that. They had determined the point.
" The judgment was reversed. It came before the House with
" all the respect due to the Court of Session upon the very
" point, and under circumstances that affected the feelings of
" every one ; for the consequences of the judgment the House
" of Lords found themselves obliged to give, were harsh and
" cruel. If the particular circumstances raising very just senti-
" ments in every mind, could prevail against the uniformity of
" rule, it is so much the duty of Courts of Justice to establish,
" there could be no case in which the feelings would have led
" one farther. *Lord Annandale's* case is not near so strong.
" The habits of Sir Charles Douglas were military ; he had
" no settled property ; his life had been passed in very differ-
" ent parts of the world ; if the consideration of his Original
" Domicil could have had the weight that is attempted in this
" case, it would have had much more there ; for there was less
" of positive fixed residence there than in this case. At one
" time he was in Russia, at another in Holland, and in a fixed
" situation as commander of a ship in the Russian and Dutch.
" service. His activity rendered him not much settled any-
" where. It was necessary to take him where he was found.
" The cause had this additional circumstance, that he hap-
" pened to die in Scotland, the place of his birth ; but, un-
" doubtedly, he went there for a very temporary purpose, a
" mere visit to his family when going to take a command
" upon the American service. That is so strong a case that
" it makes it rather improper in me to have said so much."

CLXII. These cases are clearly founded upon the peculiar
nature of the East India Company's service. As long as a
person was engaged in it, he held an irrevocable office, binding
him to residence in a certain country.

The principle upon which these cases were decided, though
the East India Company has ceased to exist, is still applicable

to similar cases. In fact, upon the same principle it was held by the House of Lords, in the case of *Sir C. Douglas*, that persons who enter in the military service of a *foreign* State acquire the domicil of that State (*q*).

CLXIII. It remains to be considered, whether the domicil of a person employed in the military service of his *own* country, is changed when, in the discharge of his functions, he is compelled to reside in a foreign land.

CLXIV. The language of the Roman Law is, "the soldier "would seem to have his Domicil in the place where he serves, "if he possess nothing in his own municipality"(*r*). But it seems clear that if he had had any property in his own municipality he would have been allowed a double Domicil, that of his own municipality and place of serving (*s*).

CLXV. In the curious case mentioned by Puffendorff (*t*), respecting the instrument by which the dowry of the wife was confirmed being governed by the law of the husband's Domicil, it was said that this Domicil, which was in Bremen, was in no way affected by the husband's having served as a soldier in Hamburgh, and having resided there.

CLXVI. The leading foreign case is that of the *Duke of Guise.* This illustrious person, who was, by virtue of his inherited title, the Premier Lay Peer, and by virtue of the Archbishopric of Rheims, the Premier Ecclesiastical Peer of

---

(*q*) " If Sir C. Douglas had died in the Russian or Dutch service, his property must have been distributed according to the law of Russia and Holland ; and when he afterwards entered into the service of this country, he became domiciled here, as a Russian or Dutchman would on entering into our service."— *Vide ante*, pp. 74—5.

(*r*) " Miles ibi domicilium habere videtur ubi meret, si nihil in *patriâ* possideat."—*Dig.* 50, t. i. 1. xxiii. *Vide ante.*

(*s*) *Domat, Book* 1, t. xvi. s. ii.

(*t*) "Sed postea maritus militaria stipendia civitatis Hamburgensis meruit ibique habitavit, quamquam hoc facto nondum apparabit domicilium eum mutâsse," &c.—*Puffendorf, Observationes Juris Universi.* Obs. CXXII. Dotem creditoribus hypothecam, &c.

France, after becoming a member of the famous League (*u*), and signing the Treaty of Sedan, was expatriated, and entered as general into the service of the King of Spain and the Emperor of Austria. During the time of his residence at Brussels, he contracted a marriage, the validity of which depended upon his Domicil.

The marriage had been solemnized by the Vicar General of the Army; but it was especially provided by the Ecclesiastical Law then in force in the Pay Bas, that the Vicar General's power (*x*) should cease when the soldier or officer resided in a place where they might be said to have a fixed domicil (*domicilium fixum*), and that in such case, the soldiers should receive the Sacrament of the Church from the ordinary minister; and that the nobles who returned to their ordinary residence should be emancipated from the control of the Delegate, and placed under that of their Bishop. This last position, D'Aguesseau argued, was decisive against the validity of the Duke of Guise's marriage. "Will it be contended" (said that great jurist) "that Monsieur de Guise had no "Domicil, or that he had it not at Brussels? To say M. de "Guise had no Domicil is *absurdum*; it would be to make "the General of the Armies of the Emperor, and of the King "of Spain, a *vagabond*. To say that his Domicil was not at "Brussels is *absurdius*: all who serve the King of Spain "in Flanders cannot be considered as domiciled elsewhere "than in the capital of the Pays Bas; as, for example, Paris "is the reputed Domicil of all the great lords who have no "other in point of fact " (*y*).

(*u*) *Ligue confédérée pour la Paix Universelle de la Chrétienté.*

(*x*) "Similiter omnes nobiles et alii inferiores, qui cessante exercitu, habent sous ordinarios in iis partibus, quando subsistunt iis in locis ubi est fixum eorum domicilium, censentur subditi eorumdem locorum ordinariis, etiamsi alioqui habeant officia et stipendia ratione dicti exercitus." This was the article of the Papal *bref*, upon the construction of which the case principally turned.

(*y*) *D'Aguesseau, Cinquante-Septième Plaidoyer* (A.D. 1700), t. v. p. 448.

CLXVII. William Macdonald, a native of Scotland, acquired a considerable plantation in Jamaica, where he had resided about fifteen years. In 1779, he was appointed lieutenant in the seventy-ninth regiment of foot, at that time quartered in the island : he also obtained the command of a fort in it. In 1783, he obtained leave of absence for a year, that he might return to Scotland for the recovery of his health. He died a few months after his arrival. The seventy-ninth regiment was by this time reduced. He had no effects in Scotland, and his only property in England consisted of two bills, which he had transmitted from Jamaica before he left it, in order, as was said, to purchase various articles for his plantation. His father intromitted with the funds in England. The rights of the parties turned upon the question, whether William Macdonald had his domicil in Jamaica or in Scotland. It was offered to be proved that the deceased meant to have returned to Jamaica, if his health had permitted, and that he had no intention of residing in Scotland. The Lord Ordinary found the succession was to be regulated by the Law of Scotland, in respect that William Macdonald died in Scotland, his native country, where he had resided several months before his death. A reclaiming petition having been presented, the Court was of opinion that the Domicil of William Macdonald was in Scotland, and that the proof offered was incompetent, and, therefore, unanimously refused the petition without answers. Some of the Judges came to be of opinion that the Domicil of the deceased was in Jamaica, but a considerable majority retained their former opinion. The ground of this decision, Mr. Burge observed, must have been that his commission in the army necessarily rendered the continuance of his residence in Jamaica uncertain (z).

CLXVIII. The proposition that the officer has the Domicil of the State which he serves applies, of course, equally

(z) *Morrison's Dictionary of Decisions*, vol. vi. p. 4627, tit. *Foreign*. *Burge's Commentaries on Foreign and Colonial Law*, vol. i. pp. 47, 48.

to the Naval and Military Service. The ship of war is part of the territory of the State (a). If the Foreign State possess territories with distinct jurisdiction and laws (b) the officer will have his domicil in that subdivision of the State which he serves (c).

CLXIX. If this case be compared with that of *Sir Charles Douglas*, it will place the difference between the effect of the general service of the Crown and the particular service of a Company, or of a Foreign State, upon the question of Domicil, in a clear light.

CLXX. There had been several cases of military testaments decided in the Prerogative Court of Canterbury under the new Wills' Act, in which it seems always to have been asumed that the domicil of the officer was unchanged by his serving the Crown in foreign parts (d).

But during the present year the Judicial Committee of the Privy Council in England (e) have given a decision upon the question of the domicil of the soldier, which goes a great, if not the entire way to the proposition that the domicil of a military person so long as he continues, whether on half-pay or not, in the service of the Crown, can never be changed, but must, necessarily, be in England. This decision was mainly founded on the liability, however remote, to be called into active service.

The judgment was also remarkable for a judicial notice of

(a) *Vide ante* vol. i. s. 366.

(b) Vol. i. ch. ii.

(c) *Ommaney* v. *Bingham*, 5 *Vesey R.* 757, *Dalhouise* v. *M'Donal*, 7 *Clarke and Finnelly's R.* 817, *Brown* v. *Smith*, 15 *Beavan Rep.* 444.

(d) In the goods of *C. E. Phipps*, officer on service at Berbice, 2 *Curties' Ecclesiastical Reports*, 368. *Whyte* v. *Repton*, officer at New Brunswick, 3 *Curteis*, 818. The term soldier, however, in the clause of exemption in the new Wills' Act, has been held to apply to those engaged in the East India service. In the goods of *Donaldson*, 2 *Curteis*, 386.

(e) *Hodgson* v. *De Beauchesne*, A.D. 1859. Reversing decision of the Courts below.

the inapplicability of the *dicta* of Prize Courts, as to the domicil of neutrals and belligerents, to cases of domicil during peace.

Time, which is the great ingredient in the former class of cases has generally much less and sometimes no weight in the latter class, a distinction too often not adverted to in the decisions of English Courts.

VII.—THE AMBASSADOR.

CLXXI. The (*f*) most important class of public officers whom the law exempts from the presumption of Domicil attaching to continuous residence in a particular place, are :—

Ambassadors (*g*).—No position of International Law is, as has been shewn, better established than that which preserves to the Ambassador in a Foreign State the Domicil of the country which he represents. The important legal consequences flowing from this doctrine, with respect to the celebration of marriage and the birth of children, are well known.

CLXXII. But if a State choose to employ as Ambassador the services of a foreigner domiciled in the State to which he

---

(*f*) " Les ambassadeurs, les commissaires départis, les gouverneurs et commandans de provinces, les officiers militaires, et les susdits, n'acquièrent point nou plus de domicile dans le lieu où se fait l'exercice de leurs fonctions par la seule résidence qu'ils y font encore qu'elle soit continuelie, *lorsqu'il est prouvé par d'autres circonstances plus fortes qu'ils ont un domicile dans un autre lieu.*"—*Denisart*, Domicile 4. It would appear from this last sentence, that, according to *Denisart*, the *primâ facie* presumption, even in these cases, was in favour of the *actual* domicil. See *Wheaton's Hist.* 245.

" Legatus non est civis noster, non incola, non venit ad nos ut domicilium, hoc est rerum et fortunarum suarum sedem transferat ; peregrinus est qui apud nos moratur ut agat rem principis sui."—*Bynk. de foro legat,* c. viii.

(*g*) " Ita legatus etsi per multos, immo plurimos annos cum familiá suâ degat in aliquâ aulâ, et in urbe domum propriam possideat, non tamen propterea domicilium ibi habet."—*Wolff, Jus Gentium,* c. i. s. 187.

"L'envoyé d'un prince étranger n'a point son domicile à la cour où il éside.'—*Vattel,* l. i. c. xix. s. 218. See also s. 217.

is Ambassador, it is probably a sound proposition of law that *his* Domicil is not changed (*h*).

CLXXIII. The privilege of the Ambassador extends to those domiciled in his family, and (*i*) resident with him, but there is no authority for saying that he can impart it to strangers.

CLXXIV. *Petreis* v. *Tondear* was a cause of nullity of marriage instituted in the Consistory of London, on the ground that it was not celebrated in the parish church, or in a place where marriages had been usually solemnised according to the provisions of the English Marriage Act. The validity of the marriage was contended for on the plea that it had been celebrated in the chapel of the Bavarian Ambassador, which was to be considered as a part of the country to which that Ambassador belonged : the marriage, it will be seen, was not contracted between two English subjects. On the other side, the case of *Heinville* v. *Fierville* was cited, in which a marriage of a minor, solemnized without consent, in the Venetian Ambassador's chapel in 1783, had been set aside by the Consistory of London.

CLXXV. In the course of his judgment Lord Stowell observed, " The principal objection, however, is that this act of " Parliament will not operate under the circumstances of the " case ; for that the house and chapel is to be considered as " the country of the person residing there to which our law " will not extend. But the authority of the case which has " been cited, sufficiently decides this question, so as to oblige " me to admit this libel. The party who proceeds was in the " suite of the Spanish Ambassador, and not of the Bavarian : " and the other party though she has the name of a foreigner, " is not described as being of any Ambassador's family, and " has been resident in this country four months, which is much " more than is necessary to constitute a matrimonial domicil " in England, inasmuch as one month is sufficient for that

---

(*h*) *Heath* v. *Samson*, 14 *Beavan's Rep.* 441.

(*i*) *Vattel, Droit des Gens*, l. iv. c. ix. ss. 118, 120, 124.

under the act of Parliament. Supposing the case, therefore, to be assimilated to that of a marriage abroad between persons of a different country, it is difficult to bring this marriage within the exception, as this woman is not described as domiciled in the family of an Ambassador. Taking the privilege to exist (which has, perhaps, not been formally decided), I may still deem it a fit subject of consideration, whether such a privilege can protect a marriage where neither party, as far as appears at present, is of the country of the Ambassador, and where one of them has acquired a matrimonial domicil in this country, and where it is not shewn that she had been living in a house entitled to privilege during her residence in England. On these grounds I shall admit the libel. The matter may receive further illustration of facts which may entitle it to further consideration." The cause, however, appears to have been discontinued (k).

CLXXVI. Mr. Henry quotes the following case and opinion from the *Nieuw Nederland's Advys Boek*, 1 vol. 165, as important in its bearing upon the Domicil of Ambassadors :—

" A. (l) born at Amsterdam, and the Dutch Consul at
" Smyrna, being about to intermarry with B. at Smyrna, they
" both appeared before the Chancellor of the Dutch nation at
" that place, and entered into an anténuptial contract or set-
" tlement of their respective property : some years after the
" wife dies, leaving two children, and without having disposed
" of her half of the joint property, which by the settlement
" she was entitled to do. One of the children died soon after
" the mother at Smyrna : the question was, under the law
" of which place, whether of Smyrna or Amsterdam, the wife's
" share should be regulated or disposed of."

CLXXVII. On this the following opinion was given :—
" The undersigned, having considered the case proposed and

(k) *Consistory Reports*, vol. i. p. 139. See vol. ii. p. 386, *Ruding* v. *Smith*.

(l) *Odwin* v. *Forbes*, *Henry's, Rep.* p. 204, *Appendix*.

" the question arising therefrom, is of opinion (under correc-
" tion) that, since A. was born at Amsterdam, and only re-
" siding at Smyrna in the service of the Government, he must
" be considered as still residing at Amsterdam : since it is
' clear in law that, by residence in a foreign country under a
' commission, especially when this is only for some years and
' not perpetual, no Domicil is contracted ; the reason of which
' is evident, namely, that to the constituting of a fixed Domicil,
' it is not sufficient that a person resides in this or that place,
' but that he must have the intention at the time, of making
' it his fixed and permanent abode during his life, according
' to Voet, *ad tit. Dig. et Judiciis et ubi quisque, no.* 97 *et* 98 ;
' and even were a man to remain ten or more years in a place,
' still he cannot be said to have had there his fixed Domicil,
' so long as it was considered by him as a temporary residence
' (*mansio temporaria*), as by example in a commission ;
' whence it follows, that the marriage celebrated by A. at
' Smyrna, the place of his residence, so far as concerns the
' community of profit and loss during this marriage, must be
' considered as having taken place at Amsterdam, according
' to the doctrine of *Goris.in Advers. Jur. Tract.* 1, *de Socie-*
' *tate Conjug. cap.* 6 n. 4, 5, 6, *et* 9, where he shews also that
' this has been so decided in Portugal. With him also agrees
' Van Wezel, *de Connub. Bonorum, Societ. Tract.* 1, n. 100,
' where he says, that a native of Utrecht being in Friesland,
' whether under commission from his State or not, and there
' marrying, must be considered to have married in the com-
' munity of goods, notwithstanding that community by mar-
' riage in Friesland does not extend beyond the use of the
' goods, and by no means over the goods themselves ; which
' is also confirmed by Van Someren, *de Repres.* c. 3, s. 13,
' *et de Jure Novere, c* 3, § 4 ; see also Bergandas, *ad Consue-*
' *tud. Fland. Tr.* 2, n. 11, 12 ; and no wonder, since it is
' an indisputable rule that a wife follows the dignity of the
' Domicil, and the forum of her husband, according to the *lex*
' 65, *dig. de Judiciis et ubi quisque.*

" So, as we have before shewn, the aforesaid Consul A. must

be considered as yet dwelling at Amsterdam, his birth-place; hence it follows that this marriage must be held as contracted according to the custom which has prevailed of old in Holland, by which, so soon as the marriage is celebrated, a community of goods is induced and takes place, not only with respect to the property possessed by the parties respectively at the time, but also all future acquired property; which effect of marriage, by the custom of Holland, can only be avoided by an express anténuptial contract, *disertis verbis.* Therefore, as the succession of foreign Ministers, and consequently of their wives, must be regulated according to the law of their Domicil, as Professor Voet shews under the title of the *Digest. Senat. Consult. Tertull. n.* 34; so he cites in support of this doctrine a case taken from the 3d *Hollandsche Consultatien, consult.* 4, whereby it appears that a certain married woman having died at Utrecht while residing there with her husband, a Hollander by birth, who was the Dutch Commissary at Munster, she must be considered as having died in Holland, and therefore, the succession in her goods must be regulated according to the custom of Holland, and also by the 113 *Consult.* of the *Nederland's Advys Boek, b.* 3, *p.* 268. It appears that a deputy ' from the province of Guelderland to the States-General ' having died intestate at the Hague, after several years' ' residence there, in that office, he was not understood ' to have lost his original Domicil by this residence, and ' his property was divided between his widow and ' children, according to the custom of Guelderland; and ' furthermore, as it appears that one of the children of this ' marriage is dead, leaving the said A. his father, him sur- ' viving, the said parent is by the law of Holland entitled to ' the half of this child's share in his mother's property; nor ' can it be objected that this child was born and died at ' Smyrna, since this child according to law must be held to be ' born and have had his fixed Domicil at the birth-place of ' his father, *viz.* at Amsterdam, according to Grotius, in his ' Introduction to the Law of Holland, *lib.* 2, *part* 26, *n.* 4,

" who says that in such cases, in Holland, is followed the law
" of succession of the place where the deceased child's parents
" had their fixed Domicil, which in this case, as we have seen,
" was, and is yet, the city of Amsterdam ; for this father of
" the child did not withdraw himself from this city of his own
" will, in order to choose another Domicil, but only on account
" of his office and commission; and in this case no one,
" however residing at another place, is said to change his
" Domicil.

" Thus advised at Leyden, 6th July, 1731."

CLXXVIII. Mr. Henry likens the case of the party in this
opinion to that of *Lord Somerville*, which has been already
referred to, considering the former a strong confirmation of
the latter, and expresses his surprise that no mention should
have been made in the discussion of that case to the law in
the Digest, which gave to senators a Domicil (*m*) in the city
where they exercised their functions, while it retained their
Domicil of Origin, upon the principle that the dignity conferred
on them was rather an addition to than a diminution of their
existing Domicil.

(*m*) " Senatores licet in urbe domicilium habere videantur tamen et
ibi unde oriundi sunt habere domicilium intelligentur, quia *dignitas*
domicilii adjectionem potius dedisse quam permutasse videtur."—
Dig. lib. i. t. ix. c. 11 de Senatoribus.

Voet, in commenting on this text, remarks, " Nom et senatores Ro_
manos domicilii jus in municipio unde oriundi retinuisse ante dictum
est adeo ut in urbe domicilium *magis habere* viderentur quam *reveré
haberent.*"—*De Judiciis et ubi quisque*, l. v. t. i. s. 98.

This passage does not appear by the report to have been specifically
cited, but it was argued, that "his residence for the purpose of Parliamentary duty, on being elected one of the sixteen Peers of Scotland,
in 1790, according to *all the law on the subject*, would have no effect."

According to the Canonists, the Senator was domiciled at the place
where he exercised his functions.

" Senator etiam aut aliter quivis officialis perpetuus alicujus principiis
quamvis ejus loci in quo senatorium exercet dignitatem minimè sit civis
(*ex text. in* l. civis, C. de incolis, lib. 10), domicilium tamen illic ac-
quirere tenet *Anna* filius rescribens," &c. &c.—*Barbosa de Officio ex
Potestate Episcopi, Alleg.* iv. s. 34.

CLXXIX. So, under both the ancient and modern Law of France, it has been held that the peerage does not give the Domicil of the capital and residence of the court to the person ennobled by it (*n*).

CLXXX. The Consul, in the case cited from Mr. Henry's work, does not appear to have been engaged in the trade of the country where he exercised his functions, or to have been a native of that country; otherwise the law would have taken a very different view of his domicil.

CLXXXI. In the case of *the Indian Chief* (*o*), the law is most clearly laid down by Lord Stowell. "I am" (he said) " first reminded that he was American Consul, although it is " not distinctly avowed that his consular character is expected " to protect him : nor could it be with any propriety or effect, " it being a point fully established in these Courts that the " character of consul does not protect that of merchant united " in the same person. It was so decided in solemn argument, " in the course of the last war, by the Lords, in the case of " *Mr. Gildermester*, the Portuguese Consul in Holland, and of " *Mr. Eykellenburg*, the Prussian Consul at Flushing. These " were again brought forward to notice in the case of *Mr.* " *Fenwick*, the American Consul at Bordeaux, in the be- " ginning of this war, on whose behalf a distinction was set " up in favour of American Consuls, as being persons not " usually appointed as the Consuls of other nations are, from " among the resident merchants of the foreign country, but " specially delegated from America, and sent to Europe on " the particular mission, and continuing in Europe principally

---

(*n*) " La seule qualité de duc et pair ne donne point de domicile à Paris, lieu reconnu pour être celui de la demeure du roi, parcequ'elle ñ'exige point une residence habituelle auprès de sa Majesté," so decided, *Merlin* says, is the case of the Prince de Guémené, 1670, and to the edition of 1826, he adds this note, "Il n'y a plus de duchés-pairies, mais le même décision paraît devoir être appliquée aux pairs de France actuels." *Merlin, Rép, de Juris, Domicile* III. 4.

(*o*) 3 *Robinson's Admiralty Reports*, p. 29.

" in a mere consular character.　But in that case, as well as
" the case of *Sylvanus Bourne*, American Consul at Amster-
" dam, where the same distinction was attempted, it was
" held that, if an American Consul did engage in commerce,
" there was no more reason for giving his mercantile character
" the benefit of his official character than existed in the case
" of any other Consul.　The moment he engaged in trade the
" pretended ground of any such distinction ceased; the whole
" of that question therefore is as much shut up and concluded
" as any question of law can be" (*p*).

CLXXXII. It may here be observed that the Domicil of
Origin is not changed, either by residence in the house of the
Ambassador, or within the lines of an army quartered in a
foreign country, or by remaining on board any vessels (*q*) of
the native country.

CLXXXIII. The Ambassador is allowed to retain the
domicil of his own country, because he is the representative of
his Sovereign, and it should seem that the same privilege
would be, *a fortiori*, extended to the Sovereign himself, if
such an occasion should occur for its application.　What, for
instance, would have been considered the Domicil of James
the Second of England, or of Charles the Tenth of France,
during the later years of their respective lives?　It has been
stated that the English Domicil of Henrietta Maria was
strongly contended for on the ground of her being an integral
part of the Royal Family of England.

VIII.—THE ECCLESIASTIC.

CLXXXIV. The Domicil of the beneficed Ecclesiastic (*r*)
has been always held to be the spot in which his benefice is

(*p*) See too *Maltass* v. *Maltass*, *Robertson's Rep.* 79 ; *Gout* v. *Zimmer-
mann*, 5 *Notes of Cases*, 440.

(*q*) *Wheaton's Elements of International Law*, p. 150—1. *Vattel*, liv. i.
c. xix. s. 216—17.

(*r*) *Denisart, Domicile* 4, c. ii. s. 6.

situated. Neither the bishop nor the *curé* were considered to have changed the Domicil of their benefice by the exercise of their functions at the residence of the King or of independent Sovereign companies. The longest possible absence " from the diocese or the parish, from whatever cause or with " whatever intention, was held insufficient to effect a change " of Domicil."

CLXXXV. On this principle the testaments of bishops, under the old French law, was ruled by the custom prevailing in their diocese. Canons, however, and members of an ecclesiastical corporation, were not bound by so strict a rule, because their functions could be supplied by others, and they were under no obligation to a continual residence (*s*) ; and, therefore, if a canon held an office in some independent Sovereign company, which did require continual residence (*t*), his Domicil was considered to be in that place and not where his canonry was (*u*).

IX.—THE PRISONER.

CLXXXVI. By the law of all European countries, the prisoner preserves the domicil of his country.

CLXXXVII. In a case tried before the Judge of the Prerogative Court in Ireland (Dr. Radcliffe), the deceased party,

---

(*s*) Le vrai domicile d'un évêque est dans le chef-lieu de son diocése quand même il passerait une grande partie de l'année à Paris ou ailleurs."- *Merlin Rép. de Juris, Domicile* III. 6.

(*t*) " Tertio modo habito respectu ad ordines suscipiendos quis subjectus est episcopo diæcesis, in quâ beneficium ipse habet, et potest ab illo ordinari, seu ab alio de ejus licentiâ, quamvis alias ei alio modo subditus non sit. Clericus enim habet domicilium, et est civis illius Diæcesis, in quâ situm est ejus beneficium, dum illud possidet."— *Barbosa*, Alleg. 14, s. 42.

(*u*) The functions, however, which the celebrated Abbé Dubois performed at Paris were not considered to be of this class, and his domicil was pronounced to be at Beauvais.

about whose domicil a discussion arose, had been an Irishman by birth, where he had also resided, and had property, as he had, however, in England, where he died in prison. The learned Judge observed, " Now, how does he describe himself " in both wills, as well that relied on by the impugnant as that " by the intervenient ; not as late of Wrexham or Hammer- " smith, or, generally, as of any part of England, but as late " of the city of Dublin, in Ireland, but then a prisoner in " the King's Bench Prison. It could not be supposed that " he acquired a domicil in England, by residence within the " rules or the walls of the King's Bench Prison ; all such resi- " dence goes for nothing " (v).

X.—THE EXILE.

CLXXXVIII. With respect to the Exile, there would appear to be two conflicting texts of the Roman Law, one promulgating " that the relegated person had in the place of his " relegation a necessary domicil *ad interim;*" the other, " that, he could have a Domicil in the place from which he " was relegated " (x).

(v) *Milwood's Reports of Cases in Prerogative and Consistorial Court of Dublin,* vol. i. p. 191—2. " The Learned Judge sustained this position by reference to the rule of Roman Law, and to the case of the *Marquis of Annandale, Bempde* v. *Johnson,* 3 *Ves.* 198. But with submission to the learned Judge, the latter case cannot be said to "decide that a residence in any place by constraint operates nothing in a question of domicil," however true that position may be. Lord Annandale had been confined in England as a lunatic during the latter part of his life, and the Lord Chancellor's remark is, " I am not clear that the period of his lunacy is totally to be discarded."

" L'exilé ni le prisonnier ne sont jamais présumé avoir perdu l'esprit des retour, quelque temps qui se soit écoulé depuis le moment où ils ont été privés de leur liberté. Ils conservent par conséquent le domicile qu'ils avoient alors.—*Denisart, Domicile* 3.

(x) " Relegatus in eo loco in quem relegatus est, interim domicilium necessarium habet."—*Dig.* L. xxii. s. 3, *ad Municipalem.* " Domicilium

CLXXXIX. It is justly, however, observed by Merlin, that the conflict between the two laws is to be reconciled by recollecting that there were two kinds of relegation known to the Roman Law : 1, temporary ; 2, perpetual ; and that it is quite clear that the latter text cited applies only to the former of these punishments (*y*). Even the temporary exile would, under that law, have been held to have a fixed domicil in the place of his relegation, though still to have preserved his Original Domicil.

---

autem habere potest et relegatus in eo loco unde arcetur ut Marcellus scribit."—L. xxvii. s. 3, *ibid.* See also l. lix. s. 19, *de Pœnis.* "Item quidam ἀπολιδες sunt, hoc est sine civitate ut sunt in opus publicum perpetuo dati, et in insulam deportati, ut ea quidem quæ juris civilis sunt, non habeant, quæ vero juris gentium sunt, habeant." By "jus gentium " is meant " Private" not " Public International Law."

(*y*) Compare, too, the reasoning of *Barbosa*—" Relegatus retinet domicilium in eo loco ubi habitat relegationis causâ ex text. quem ad hoc clarum suspicor *in l. filii liberorum,* sec. *relegatus ff. ad municip.* cujus verba sunt. Relegatus in eo loco in quem relegatus est, interim domicilium habet ; ad quod dicendum impellet dict: illa, *interim,* verboque illo *necessarium,* nam quamvis post quæsitum domicilium mutari possit, attamen dum quæsitur et retinetur, abesse debet animus ab eo discedendi, et ideo destinatus animus illique permanendi adesse dicitur, prout requiritur ad quærendum domicilium, ut supra dicitur. Non tamen obliviscar Ulpiani auctoritatem *in l. ejus qui manumissus sec. final. ff. ad municip.* quâ probatur relegatum domicilium retinere eo loci unde arcetur habere, ubi *gloss. ultim.* exponendo illa verba *unde arcetur,* dicit, id est, in quo : sed hujusmodi Ulpiani responsio nullam affert contrarietatem cum Paulo Jurisconsulto in *d. sec. relegatus ;* rejectâ enim glossæ distinctione dicentis in perpetuo relegato planum esse quod in dicto sec. *relegatum* asserit Paulus Jurisconsultus, alios non ita, quasi insinuat tunc procedere Ulpiani dictum ; tenendum igitur est relegatum domicilium habere eo loci unde arcetur. scilicet ab eo unde trahit originem, et in eo loco in quem relegatus est, exclusâ denique intelligentiâ de exulatu in perpetuum, propter dictionem, *interim,* de quâ in *d. sec. relegatus,* de quo tamen *vide Petr. Greg. in Tract. de Beneficiis,* cap. 36, num. 20. *Campanil,* d. cap. 8, num. 25."—*Barbosa de Officio et Potestate Episcopi,* Alleg. IV. s. 35.

CXC. The French jurists, however, have no doubt that, for the purposes of testamentary succession, his Original Domicil would be alone considered. Acting on this interpretation of the Roman Law, they classed persons condemned for a term of years to the galleys in the same category with respect to their Domicil as people absent on a long voyage, and therefore considered them as retaining the Domicil of Origin.

CXCI. It is equally clear, in spite of two sentences passed during the time of the French Revolution to the contrary, that the person banished (z) for life, (*deporté*), whether for a civil or political offence, loses his Original Domicil. It cannot be doubted that the same sentence would be passed in England with respect to persons transported for life.

XI.—THE EMIGRANT.

CXCII. The Fugitive from his country on account of civil war is held not to have lost his intention of returning to it, and therefore still retains his Domicil in his native land (a).

(z) *Merlin, Rép. de Jur. Domicile* IV.   " Relegatus integrum suum statum retinet, et dominium rerum suarum, et patriam potestatem, sive ad tempus, sive in perpetuum relegatus sit.   Deportatio autem ad tempus non est."—*Dig.* 48, t. xxii. l. xviii.   The præses had, latterly power given him to *interdict* a person *domiciled* in his Province, not merely from the Province, but also from his place of origin.

(a) *Mascardus*, after stating the ordinary presumption of law, remarks, " Preterra illud sic velim limites, ut non procedat, quando quis aliquo metu impulsus, res, familiamque suam alibi transtulerit: non enim ibi durante metu domicilium contraxisse præsumitur: ita decisum fuit a *Pet. de Ubald, in d. tract. de Cano. Episcop. et Paroch,* c. vii. vers. octavo, quæsitur post num. 9, ubi quæstionem illam diremit, Parochianus est quidam nescio cujus Ecclesiæ in rure sitæ, quæ in cujuspiam civitatis dominatu erat: hic bello hostiumque immanitate quæ ibi flagrabat, coactus, unâ cum domesticis et supellectili, ne sibi aliqua vis inferretur domicilium mutavit, illique commigravit Parochiæ, quæ in illâ erat urbe constructa.   Hic, dum mors immineret, cuidam

CXCIII. This proposition was fully established in France towards the beginning and about the middle of the last century, with respect to the English who followed the fortunes of James the Second after his abdication. "The English," (says Boullenois), "who following King James the Second, " sheltered themselves in France, have been maintained in " their laws; they may make wills, as to the form (b), as it is " practised in England, and their wills, clothed with this for- " mality, are esteemed valid in France."

CXCIV. It is of course possible that the Prisoner, the Exile, the Emigrant, or the Fugitive, may, by continuing to reside in a country after the coercion has been withdrawn, and after his power of choice has been restored to him—like the minor who resides in a place after his minority has ceased—acquire a Domicil therein.

CXCV. Both these points were considered in a case which, in the year 1838, was brought before the Prerogative Court of Canterbury.

---

tertiæ Ecclesiæ nescio quid legavit ibique se humari legit. Quæro igitur cum in parochiâ parochialis Ecclesiæ in illâ urbe positæ deces- serit, cui parochiali Ecclesiæ canonica debeatur? Debebiturne paro- chiali Ecclesiæ constitutæ in civitate ubi ille mortuus est, an vero parochiali Ecclesiæ sitæ ruri, cujus moriens erat Parochianus? Debe- bitur profecto canonica parochiali Ecclesiæ rurali, *etenim cum e rure discesserit ob hostium metum, non desiit esse parochianus Ecclesiæ rus- ticanæ: nec domicilium mutâsse præsumitur et si omnino cum suis in urbem sese contulerit, cum eo consilio e villâ non abierit, ut perpétuo urbem incoleret quod nimirùm requiritur ut censeatur domicilium mu- tâsse,"* &c. &c., citing *Ulpian, Paul, and Celsus. De Probationibus Concl.* DXXXV. s. 26—29, vol. i. p. 249.

"Hanc tamen decisionem intelliges" (says *Mascardus,* referring to the passage last cited) "ut procedat quando durante metu rus non se con- tulit, verum secus esset, si postquam metus cessaverit in urbe remanserit : tunc enim mutâsse rurale et urbanum domicilium legîsse præsumitur," &c.—*Ibid.*

(b) *Le Traité de la Realité et Personalté des Statuts,* t. i. tit. ii. c. 3. See also *Denisart,* t. i. tit. "Anglais." Both cited, *Collectanea Juridica,* vol. i. p. 329 ; in *Monsieur Target's Opinion on the Duchess of Kingston's will.*

CXCVI. The facts of this case (c) were thus stated by the Judge, (Sir Herbert Jenner), "that the deceased, Guy Henri " du Vol, Marquis de Bonneval, died at the age of seventy-one, " on the 22nd of September, 1826, in Norton Street, Fitzroy " Square (London) : that the will in question was made in " the English form, and was executed for the purpose of dis- " posing of the property in England alone, being confined " simply to that ; that he also made a will in 1826, at Paris, " by which he disposed of his property in France, and that " he thereby constituted the Vicomte de Bonneval, his " nephew, (son of the party before the Court, the Comte de " Bonneval), sole and universal heir : that the deceased was " born in France, in 1765, of French parents, and continued " to reside there till 1792, when he left that country in conse- " quence of the Revolution : that his parents were of high " rank, and that he succeeded to estates in France, and was " President à Mortier in the Parliament of Normandy ; that " on his leaving France, in 1792, he proceeded first to Ger- " many, and afterwards to England, and continued to reside " here till 1814 or 1815, during which time he received an " allowance from the government of this country as a French " emigrant : that, on the return of the Bourbons, he repaired " to France, and it is stated, on behalf of his brother, (who " asserts the French Domicil), that the deceased went to " France in 1814, and that, on the escape of Buonaparte from " Elba, he came again to this country, but returned to France " in 1815 : that, from 1815, (according to the statement of " the brother), he continued to reside in France, occasionally " visiting this country, till 1821, when he became entitled to " certain property, under the will of his aunt, including the " château and estate of Soquence in the district of Rouen, " and, in 1823, he succeeded to part of the estate of his " mother ; that from 1814 to 1827, he was actively engaged in " the settlement of his property and family affairs in France ;

(c) De Bonneval v. De Bonneval, 1 Curteis' Ecclesiastical Reports, 856.

" that he agreed to purchase of his brother part of his
" paternal property, which had been confiscated under a
" decree of the French Government, and to part of which
" property he was entitled. It is further stated that, in the
" deed of purchase of these estates in 1827, made at Paris,
" the deceased is described as ' residing usually at the château
" ' of Soquence,' and that, in a decree of the Court of Appeal
" at Caen, he is described as ' living on his rents, and domiciled
" ' in the commune of Sahurs, district of Rouen.' The act or
" petition goes on to state that, in 1825, the deceased received
" compensation as a French emigrant for the property con-
" fiscated at the Revolution, and that, from 1815 to 1821, he
" resided on his property in France, and took up his Domicil
" in the château of Soquence, and maintained it till his death ;
" that, from 1815 to 1821, he made occasional visits to Eng-
" land, and, in 1821, he took a house in Norton Street, in
" which he resided when he came to England, but that such
" visits (which is not denied by the other side) were in-
" terrupted for several years together ; that, in 1834, he came
" to England, but with the intention of returning again to
" France ; that he was rated as proprietor of the property at
" Soquence to the electoral contributions of the district ; that
" he exercised his political rights as a French subject, and con-
" stantly described himself, and was described in legal pro-
" ceedings, as domiciled in France, and there are entries in
" the Register of Mortgages at Rouen, from 1827 to 1836, in
" which he is so described ; that the deceased was a Marquis
" of France, and by the will of 1826, disposing of his property
" in France, he directs his nephew, out of certain estates in
" France, to form a *majorat*, to serve as an endowment to the
" title of hereditary Marquis, granted to their ancestors about
" 1680, and to settle the same upon the heirs male of their
" name, by order of primogeniture and proximity to the elder
" branch. These are the grounds upon which the brother
" contends that the deceased was domiciled in France, and,
" consequently, that the validity of the will must be deter-
" mined by the law of that country.

" On the other side, it is alleged that the deceased came to
" this country in 1793, and that, with certain exceptions, he
" ever after resided here, down to the time of his death ; that
" in June, 1814, the deceased took the lease of a house in
" Mortimer Street, Cavendish Square, for the term of eight
" years; and, in 1820, he took the lease of another house
" in Norton Street for forty-four years, for which he paid
" £360 premium, and a rent of £40 per annum, putting
" himself to considerable expense in fitting up and furnishing
" the house, which he continued to occupy till his death,
" keeping up an establishment of servants there, and spoke
" of the house as his 'home.' The act denies that on his re-
" turn to France, he was generally, or principally, resident
" there from 1814 to 1841, and alleges, that in 1821 he had
" no house in France, but went there merely to visit his
" friends and relations, and to obtain compensation for his
" losses; that after he became entitled to the château and
" estate of Soquence in 1821, he was involved in lawsuits in
" France, which he was compelled frequently to visit, passing
" considerable portions of time there ; and, in order to give
" validity to acts done there, he was obliged to describe him-
" self as of a certain residence in that kingdom ; but, from
" 1834 to the time of his death, he continued permanently to
" reside in this country without paying a single visit to France,
" though not prevented from doing so by ill health, or by any
" other circumstance than his uniformly avowed preference
" for a residence in this country ; and that in 1834, the name
" of the deceased was included in the list of persons entitled
" to vote at the election of members of Parliament for the
" borough, and that he at all times kept his property in Eng-
" land wholly distinct from his property in France. In the
" reply, it is alleged that the deceased kept up an establish-
" ment at Soquence, and that at his death, a correspondence,
" consisting of about 1200 letters, dated from 1818 to 1835,
" and from different persons and places, was found at his
" château at Soquence carefully preserved and classed, and that
" the family papers and plate were deposited there ; that the

" house in London was kept for his convenience when here,
" and, in case of new disturbances in France, of which he ex-
" pressed fears; and that he exercised in France the political
" rights of a French subject."

CXCVII. The learned Judge then referred to the principles
of law laid down in *Somerville* v. *Somerville,* and continued
—"Applying these principles to the case now to be decided,
" there is no doubt that the Domicil of Origin of the deceased
" was France; for there he was born, and continued to reside
" from 1765 to 1792; and he left that country only in conse-
" quence of the disturbances which broke out there.   He
" came here in 1793; but he came in the character of a
" Frenchman, and retained that character till he left his
" country in 1814; for he received an allowance from our go-
" vernment as a French emigrant.   Coming with no intention
" of permanently residing here, did anything occur while he
" was resident here to indicate a contrary intention?   It is
" clear to me that, as in the case of exile, the absence of a
" person from his own country will not operate as a change of
" domicil : so, where a party removes to another country, to
" avoid the inconveniences attending a residence in his own,
" he does not intend to abandon his Original Domicil, or to
" acquire a new one in the country to which he comes to avoid
" such inconveniences.   At all events, it must be considered
" as a compulsory residence in this country: he was forced to
" leave his own, and was prevented from returning till 1814.
" Had his residence here been in the first instance voluntary;
" had he come here to take up a permanent abode in this
" country, and to abandon his Domicil of Origin—that is, to
" disunite himself from his native country—the result might
" have been different.   It is true, that he made a long and
" continued residence in this country; but I am of opinion
" that a continued residence in this country is not sufficient to
" produce a change of domicil; for he came here avowedly as
" an emigrant, with an intention of returning to his own
" country as soon as the causes ceased to operate which had
" driven him from his native home.   He remained a French-

" man ; and if he had died during the interval between 1798
" and 1815, his property would have been administered ac-
" cording to the law of France.

" Up to 1814, then, he had not acquired a domicil in this
" country ; the connection with his native country was not
" abandoned : from whence, then, is the Court to collect that
" he had at any time acquired a domicil in this country, by
" any act manifesting an intention to do so ? I can find no
" fact beyond the mere residence in this country till 1814, and
" his taking the lease of a house for eight years, which would
" be a strong fact to shew intention, if followed up by a con-
" tinued residence here. But what is the fact ? In 1814 the
" Bourbons were restored ; and, as he returned to his own
" country after taking this house, the inference is that he did
" not intend to reside here, but took the house with a view of
" securing a residence of his own if he should be forced to
" return hither : and it turned out that his apprehensions
" were not ill-founded. He remains in France during the
" greater part of the interval between that time and 1821.
" It is alleged that he was employed during these visits in
" settling his family affairs, and it has been argued that his
" return to France was not in order to resume his French
" Domicil, an argument which might have some force if he
" had lost his French Domicil. But the question is, had he
" abandoned his French Domicil? I am of opinion that he
" had not abandoned his French Domicil, nor acquired one in
" England, up to 1814 or 1815."

CXCVIII. The learned Judge proceeded to observe that
there was no evidence as to the period from 1815 to 1821,
during which he resided in England; and that the evidence
with respect to the periods of time during which the deceased
resided in England and France respectively, was very loose :
but it was proved that he left England in 1828, and resided
entirely in France for three years and a half, and that he was
again absent from England for eight months, and that in a
contract for the sale of some property, he was described as
" residing usually at the château de Soquence, near Rouen ; "

and that between 1830 and 1834, he had been frequently seen to proceed up the river by the steam-boat to Rouen. The learned Judge concluded with these observations, " Now, " under the circumstances, it appears to me that there is no " evidence to shew that the deceased ever acquired a domicil in " this country. I see nothing but the fact of the taking of the " lease of a house in Norton Street in 1820, for a long term " undoubtedly, but which does not appear to denote anything " more than an intention of providing a place of occasional " residence in this country. But up to 1820, he had acquired " no domicil here, and during the subsequent time he was " absent in France for several years : there is nothing there- " fore, to shew that he had abandoned his Original Domicil, " and taken up his *sole* Domicil (for that is the expression used " in *Somerville* v. *Somerville*,) in this country, although he " kept two female servants in this country : yet—when I find " that he kept an establishment at Soquence ; that he had " plate and furniture worth £1,200 ; that his family papers " and his correspondence were deposited there, the letters " classed and arranged ;—his having a house here can have been " only for an occasional residence in England, even if he " divided his residence between the two countries, or even if " he spent the greater part of his time here : but all the evi- " dence as to his continual residence in this country is that he " resided here from 1834 to 1836 ; though it does not appear " that he did not intend to return to France. I do not con- " sider that in this case, any more than in *Somerville* v. " *Somerville*, the declarations made by the deceased at differ- " ent times, that he preferred a residence in this country, can " be a ground upon which the Court is to rest its judgment ; " the domicil cannot Depend upon loose grounds of this sort, " where there are documents which shew that the party looked " to France as his home. Unless the evidence was nicely " balanced, the Court would pay no regard to such declara- " tions, shewing a preference for a residence in this country, " and not a decided intention to abandon his native land, and " take up his residence here."

CXCIX. The Court having then alluded to the circumstance of the deceased's description in legal documents—of his having exercised political rights in France—of his being a registered voter in England—of his refusing contribution to certain French rates, (concerning which no judicial decision had taken place,)—proceeded, "I am, therefore, of opinion, "that the deceased continued a domiciled French subject to "the time of his death, and, consequently, that the validity or "invalidity of his will must be determined by the French "tribunals, and not by this Court" (d).

CC. This point of residence under constraint *as an exile*, seems to have been quite applicable to the succession to the goods of Henrietta Maria, which is mentioned in another part of this work.

CORPORATION.

CCI. (e) The definition of Domicil which has been given above, and every other definition, is founded upon the habits and relations of the natural man ; and is therefore, of course, inapplicable to the artificial and legal person whom we call a Corporation.

It is, nevertheless, necessary for the purposes of justice, that an artificial Domicil should be assigned to this artificial person, and one formed on the analogy of natural persons.

In most cases there is a clear and palpable connection be-

(d) The practice of the Court in these cases is thus stated:—"The precise form in which the Court must pronounce its sentence is this: That the deceased, at the time of his death, was a domiciled subject of France, and that the Courts of that country are the competent authority to determine the validity of his will, and the succession to his personal estate ; and, as in the case of *Hare* v. *Nasmyth* (2 *Addams*, p. 25), the Court suspends proceedings here as to the validity of the will, till it is pronounced valid or invalid by the tribunal of France."

(e) *Savigny* viii. s. 354.

tween the territory and the legal person, *e. g.* municipalities, churches, hospitals, colleges, and the like.

More difficulty arises in the case of companies and societies, formed for the purpose of carrying on commerce and traffic, to which it is difficult to assign a definite seat, as in the case of traffic carried on by means of steamboats, railways, and electric telegraphs, which may be connected with and pass through different territories, as every Rhine steamer, and almost every German railway does : and in these cases, one of two things must happen, viz., either a domicil must be specified in the charter of their constitution (*f*), or the court which exercises jurisdiction with respect to it, must determine, by artificial rules, which is the central point of the enterprise (*g*) and make that the Domicil.

CCII. The leading English case upon this point, is the *Carron Iron Company* v. *James Maclaren and others.* It was a question of domicil for the purposes of jurisdiction[i] The case travelled through the Rolls Court to the House o Lords : and the result of it seems to be that a company, according to English Law, may have two domicils for the purposes of jurisdiction ; but that such a domicil cannot be created by the agency of a person who has no concern whatever in the management of the affairs of the company, although he be employed in selling its goods. The doctrine of Principal and Agent had more influence on this decision than the ordinary rules of Domicil.

(*f*) This has been done in the case of various Prussian and Saxon Railways.—*Savigny, ib.*

(*g*) "Den mittelpunkt der Geschäfte; le centre de l'entreprise."— *Ibid.*

CHAPTER XII.

DOMICIL OF CHOICE.

CCIII. It remains to consider the Domicil of Choice, which may be conveniently considered under the question of Change of Domicil, the subject of this chapter.

CCIV. It may be taken as a general maxim of European and American Law (a) that every person *sui juris* is at liberty to choose his Domicil and to change it according to his inclination.

CCV. An exception should, perhaps, be made now, as in the time of Grotius, with respect to the subjects of Russia(b).

CCVI. According to the Roman Law, if the change of abode were made to avoid discharging the offices, or paying the taxes of the place of domicil, two things were required,

---

(a) Nihil est impedimento quo minus quis ubi velit, habeat domicilium quod ei interdictum non sit. *Dig.* 50, t. 1, s. 31, *ad Municip.* Domicilium re et facto transfertur non nudâ contestatione, sicut in his exigitur, qui negant, se posse ad munera ut incolas vocari. S. 20, *ibid.* Incola jam muneribus publicis destinatus, nisi perfecto munere, incolatui renuntiare, non potest. S. 34, *eod.* Non tibi obest, si cum incola esses, aliquod munus suscepisti, modo si antequam ad alios honores vocareris domicilium transtulisti.—*Code* x. t. 40, l. i. *de Incolis. Vide ante.*

(b) *Grotius* says (l. ii. c. v. s. 34, *De Jure Belli et Pacis*), " Solet hic illud quæri an civibus de civitate abscedre liceat, veniâ non impetratâ. Scimus populos esse ubi id non liceat, ut apud Moschos : nec negamus talibus pactis iniri posse societatem civilem, et mores vim pacti accipere. Romanis legibus, sultem posterioribus, domicilium quidem transferre licebat : sed non eo minus qui transtulerat municipii sui muneribus obligabatur : verum in quos id constitutum erat, ii manebant intra fines imperii Romani : atque ea ipsa constitutio specialem spectabat utilitatem tributariæ præstationis."

that the change of domicil should be real and *bond fide ;* another, that it should have been made before the nomination to the office or the assessment of the tax had taken place.

CCVII. Questions as to change of domicil may be classed under two divisions,—1. Change of Domicil from one town or one province to another within the same country; 2. Change of Domicil from one country to another. But as the same principles apply to both, it will be convenient to consider them together.

CCVIII. Whenever the facts and circumstances are such as to beget a doubt, whether a domicil has been required or not, recourse must be had to probable conjectures (c) (*conjecturæ probabiles*), and, though all cases must in a great measure be dependent on their particular circumstances, yet it is most important to bear in mind that the opinion of jurists and the decisions of Courts of Justice have impressed a character upon certain circumstances as affording the best criteria of Domicil, as legal presumptions of the intention of the party deduced from his acts. " In allegations" (says Lord Chancellor Cotten- " ham) " depending upon intention, difficulties may arise in " coming to a conclusion upon the facts of any particular case ; " but those difficulties will be much diminished by keeping " steadily in view the principle which ought to guide the de- " cision as to the application of the facts" (*d*).

(c) "Quoties autem non certo constat ubi quis domicilium habeat, et an animus sit inde non discedendi, ad conjecturas probabiles recurrendum, ex variis circumstantiis petitas, etsi non omnes æquè firmæ, aut singulæ solæ consideratæ non æquè urgentes sint, sed multum in iis valeat judicis prudentis et circumspecti arbitrium."—*J. Voet,* l. v. t. i. s. 97. *De Judiciis,* &c. "Dans les faits que les lois Romaines signalent comme des signes caracteristiques de domicile."—*Duranton,* p. 100, t. i. See, too, the speech of the Avocat-Général in the case of Mademoiselle de Choiseul.—"Mais comment connaître le fait de l'habitation réelle ; comment avoir des preuves de la volonté ? &c. &c. Les juges ne peuvent donc en décider que par des *conjectures.*"—*Denisart, Domicile,* 11.

(*d*) *Munro* v. *Munro,* 7 *Clarke and Finnelly's Reports of Cases in the House of Lords,* p. 877.

CCIX. The circumstances which appear principally to be relied upon as affording evidence of the intention (*animus manendi*) are the following.

CCX.   1. Place of Birth and Origin.

2. Oral and Written Declarations.

3. The Place of Death.

4. The Place of Wife and Family.

5. The House of Trade.

6. The depositary of Family Papers and Memorials.

7. The Mansion House.

8. Description in Legal Documents.

9. Possession and exercise of Political Rights and Privileges.

10. Possession of Real Estate.

11. Length of residence and lapse of Time.

CHAPTER XIII.

CRITERIA OF DOMICIL.—I. PLACE OF ORIGIN.

CCXI. The Domicil resulting from Origin is to be distinguished, as has been always observed, from the accidental place of birth, which affords a much fainter kind of presumption (*a*). The place of Origin continues to be the Domicil until it be changed either by those who have the power to change it, as in the case of pupillage, or by a party *sui juris*.

CCXII. The doctrine of the Civil Law is explicit. " Let " each person follow the origin of his father ; " that is, each person legitimately born ; for the doctrine is equally explicit that " whoever has no lawful father, his first origin is deemed " to be from his mother " (*b*).

CCXIII. In *Bruce* v. *Bruce* (*c*), the first case of Domicil brought before the House of Lords, Lord Chancellor Thurlow said, " a person's Origin, in a question of where is his Domicil ? " is to be reckoned as but one circumstance in evidence which " may aid other circumstances; but it is an enormous proposi- " tion that a person is to be held domiciled where he drew his " first breath, without adding something more unequivocal."

(*a*) *Guier* v. *O'Daniel*, 1 *Binney's Reports*, p. 349 (American). The Lord Chancellor said, in *Sir C. Douglas's case*, " Birth affords some argument, and might turn the scale if all other circumstances were *in æquilibrio*." *Ommaney* v. *Bingham*. See note to *Lord Somerville's case*, 4 *Vesey's Reports*. *Marsh* v. *Hutchinson*, 2 *Bosanquet and Puller's Reports*, p. 219.

(*b*) " Exemplo senatorii ordinis. Patris originem unusquisque sequatur. *Cod.* X. t. xxxii. l. xxxvi. " Ejus qui justum patrem non habet, prima origo a matre."—*Dig.* 50, t. i. l. ix.

(*c*) *Note to Marsh* v. *Hutchinson*, 2 *Bosanquet and Puller*, p. 231.

And in *Bempde* v. *Johnson* (*d*), Lord Chancellor Lough-borough said that he laid "the least stress" upon the place of birth taken alone; though, in conjunction with the place of education and connection, it had great weight : and in the case of *Ommaney* v. *Bingham*, alluded to in the House of Lords, in 1793, in *Somerville* v. *Somerville,* "birth affords some " argument; and might turn the scale, if all the other cir- " cumstances were *in equilibrio*" (*e*).

CCXIV. In *Lord Somerville's* case the Master of the Rolls observed, " The third rule I shall extract is, that the Original " Domicil, or, as it is called, the *Forum Originis* or the " Domicil of Origin is to prevail until the party has not only " acquired another, but has manifested and carried into execu- " tion an intention of abandoning his former Domicil, and " taking another as his sole Domicil. I speak of the Domicil " of Origin rather than that of Birth : for the mere accident " of birth at any particular place cannot in any degree affect " the Domicil. I have found no authority or dictum that gives, " for the purpose of succession, any effect to the place of birth. " If the son of an Englishman is born upon a journey in " foreign parts, his Domicil would follow that of his father ; " the Domicil of Origin is that arising from a man's birth and connections " (*f*).

(*d*) 3 *Vesey's Reports,* 198.

(*e*) " Inficias haud eundum, quin in dubio unusquisque domicilium in ipso potiùs originis loco, quam alibi præsumatur habere : cum enim ab initio jus domicilii a patre in filium translatum sit, atque ita filius secutus sit domicilium habitationis paternæ, consequens est, ut is, qui id mutatum contendit, hoc ipsum probet ; cum in eodem statu res una-quæque mansisse credatur donec contrarium demonstratum fuit."— *J. Voet, ub. supra.* s. 92.

(*f*) 5 *Vesey's Reports,* p. 750. See too *De Bonneval* v. *De Bonneval,* 1 *Curteis' Ecclesiastical Reports,* 863.

" Quando ignoratur origo alicujus, an scilicet sit hujus vel illius civitatis et loci, præsumitur esse illius in quâ fuit alitus et educatus," was the opinion of *Bartolus,* in opposition to that of *Andreas Alciatus,* and is adopted by *Menochius. De Præsumptionibus,* XXX. s. 25, p. 1038.

CCXV. The leading case in English Law upon the question of the preponderating influence of Origin, where the scale is nearly equally balanced between two domicils, is the case of *Lord Somerville,* which has just been mentioned.

CCXVI. Lord Somerville's father was born in Scotland, and died domiciled in that country. Lord Somerville, the son, was born in Scotland, and at the age of nine or ten years, was sent into England, remained a year at Westminster School, and was sent from thence into France, to complete his education. In 1745, he entered the army as a volunteer, and was present at the battles of Preston Pans and Culloden. In 1763, he left the army and resided at Somerville House, in Scotland : he then went abroad ; returned in 1765, on account of his father's illness, and after his father's death in that year, stayed about six months longer in Scotland, and then came to London, and manifested an intention to reside a considerable part of the year in London, also to keep up his establishment in the family mansion in Scotland, and divide, as nearly as possible, the year between each residence. It was held by the Master of the Rolls, after a most elaborate and protracted argument, that the Domicil of Birth had never been abandoned, that Lord Somerville died, as he was born, a Scotchman. In this case, the Domicil of Origin was also the seat of his principal establishment.

CCXVII. In the valuable opinions, or rather decisions, of Grotius, and other Dutch lawyers, upon questions of Domicil, selected by Mr. Henry, in his Appendix to the case of *Odwin* v. *Forbes* (g) is the following:—Titius, whose Domicil of Origin was Hanover, lived for some time (probably less than ten years) at Hamburgh, making that place the centre of his mercantile transactions : from Hamburgh he betook himself to Paris, and after living there a short time, he died, a bachelor

---

Alciatus gave his opinion, " civem illius civitatis aliquem præsumi in quâ habitare reperitur," *eod.,* and this is considered the *first* presumption, however slender, by modern Courts of Justice.

(g) P. 192.

and intestate. It appeared, among other things, that he had made no declaration of intending to change his Domicil of Origin, and that he had exercised no rights of citizenship at Hamburgh, where his moveable property was found at his death. It was decided, that his Domicil of Origin had never been lost, and that his property must be distributed according to the law of Hanover.

CCXVIII. In the American case of *Catlin* v. *Gledding* (*h*), a person had abandoned his Original Domicil and citizenship, but afterwards returned to the home of his mother's family; and the circumstance of birth was held material, by that eminent jurist, Judge Story, as fixing the required domicil.

CCXIX. Lord Stowell says (*i*), "It is always to be remem-" bered, that the native character easily reverts, and that it " requires fewer circumstances to constitute domicil in the case " of a native subject than to impress the national character " on one who is originally of another character;" but the acquired Domicil must be *finally* abandoned before the Domicil of Origin can revert (*k*).

CCXX. In the case of *Chiene* v. *Sykes*, determined by Sir W. Grant in 1811, the facts of the case were these:—Robert Chiene was born at the Scotch town of Crail and was a natural child. He was educated at Crail, residing with his mother. About eighteen years of age he went to sea; he returned to Crail in the year 1784, spent a twelvemonth on shore, and then resumed his occupation as a seaman. He returned to Crail in the year 1802, and resided there till his death, which happened in November of that year. It

---

(*h*) *Vide infra*.

(*i*) *La Virginie*, 5 *Robinson's Admiralty Reports*, 99. "The sin of the old character is revived," he observes in *The Phœnix*, 3 *Robinson*, p. 191. [The necessary caution as to applying the authorities of case in the Prize Courts has been already pointed out.] *Note to Munroe* v. *Douglas*, 5 *Maddock's Reports*, p. 394.

(*k*) *Craigie and Craigie* v. *Lewin and others*, 3 *Curteis' Ecclesiastical Reports*, 405.

appeared that, some years before his death, he had caused to be purchased for him and his brother a dwelling-house, gardens, and some other property at Crail, which had previously belonged to their father. At first he rented a house at Crail, in which he resided for some months, and afterwards removed to the one he had purchased, after it had undergone some repairs, and resided therein till his death. It further appeared that he had married a person who lived in Philadelphia; but had written letters, from which his own intention of residing at Crail was to be inferred. The Master to whom the question was referred, found that Chiene was domiciled in Scotland. The Domicil of Origin was, perhaps, the prominent feature in this case; but the seafaring life of the individual must not be lost sight of as a fact of considerable significance.

CCXXI. So in the leading American case of *Guier* v. *O'Daniel* (*l*), the Judge, after observing that Guier was a seafaring man, says, " Employments of the most opposite cha-
" racter and description may have the same effect to produce
" a domicil. A man may be alike domiciled, whether he
" supports himself by ploughing the fields of his farm, or the
" waters of the ocean. It is not exclusively by any particular
" act that a domicil is acquired; but by a train of conduct
" manifesting that the country in which he died was the place
" of his choice, and, to all appearance, of his intended resi-
" dence. The sailor who spends whole years in combating
" the winds and waves, and the contented husbandman, whose
" drowsy steps seldom pass the limits of his farm, may, in
" their different walks of life, exhibit equal evidence of being
" domiciled in a country. Every circumstance in the conduct
" of old Guier and his son Thomas, taking into view the
" unsettled life of the latter, afford the fullest proof that they
" were both domiciled in Delaware. If the proof be stronger
" in either case, it is in the case of Thomas, who though
" employed in traversing the globe from clime to clime,

(*l*) 1 *Binney's Reports*, p. 349, note.

" stantly returned to Wilmington, the source and centre of
" his family, the seat and abode of his friends and connections.
" His 'heart untravelled,' appears to have been universally
" fixed on the spot to which he was attached by the strongest
" ties of interest and the strongest obligations of social duty ;
" and never for a moment to have pointed a wish to any other
" country" (m).

CCXXII. The inference from both these cases is strongly
in favour of the Domicil of Origin, where the person is one
who " occupies his business on the great waters ;" and, in
Abington v. *Barton* (another American case,) it was said,
" a seafaring man, having lands occupied by himself or his
" servants, or hired people, although frequently absent on
" long voyages, has always been considered as having his
" residence on his lands, and as not losing his Domicil by
" following his profession" (n).

CCXXIII. The old French Law inclined greatly in favour
of the Domicil of Origin, and required the concurrence of a
number of circumstances to establish the fact of a transference
of domicil.

CCXXIV. Mademoiselle Clermont de St. Agnan (o) had her
Domicil of Origin in Maine.   After the death of her mother,
she came to Paris in 1742 ; there she had an hotel, a Swiss,
her other servants, her furniture, her papers ; she paid the
capitation tax, and enjoyed the privilege of a citizen with
respect to the rights of receiving goods free of municipal
duties ; kept Easter there (*elle y fit ses Pâques*).   But she
was in the habit of passing the summer (*la belle saison*) on
her property at St. Agnan ; and, as in various municipal acts
she was described as domiciled in Maine, although she had
resided nineteen years in Paris, where she died in 1761, she
was judicially declared to have preserved her Original Domicil.

(m) See also *The Phœnix*, 3 *Robinson*, 189.

(n) *Massachusetts' Reports*, vol. iv. p. 312.

(o) *Traité du Domicile et de l'Absence, par A. T. Desquiron*, p. 70, c. i.
s. 36. *Denisart, tit, Domicil*, 1—5.

CCXXV. In the following opinion it was held by the Dutch jurists that a person residing out of the Domicil of Origin, but only with the intention of carrying on trade there, is understood still to retain his Domicil in his birth-place. The case was as follows : Cornelius Van Leeuwen, born a citizen of Utrecht, of which place his father and mother were also citizens, was, at the age of fourteen, sent to Spain to be instructed in commerce and the office of a factor, where he remained ten years, without however taking a house, or forming any domestic establishment, but merely boarding and lodging. However, on his return from Spain, he had, in order to preserve his right of citizenship at Utrecht, taken a room there and kept up fire and light as required by the custom. He afterwards died intestate at Amsterdam, but his body was removed to Utrecht and interred there. On the question, as to which place was to be considered as his Domicil, De Witt gave the following opinion :—" The undersigned " having considered the above case, and the question thereout " arising, it seems (under correction) that the aforesaid " Cornelius Van Leeuwen must be considered to have had his " Domicil at Utrecht, and to have only peregrinated to Am- " sterdam for the sake of trade ; and, since he was buried at " Utrecht (p), although he died at Amsterdam, he must be " presumed to have wished to preserve his Domicil in *loco* " *originis*, so long as it does not appear that he had altered it " *cum animo manendi ;* and that also by dwelling in another " place, *extra locum originis*, a man is not understood to " have changed his Domicil, except such dwelling is done " with the intention or will to remain there without a wish to " return again *ad locum originis*. Since a domicil is only " acquired by acts, and cannot be had otherwise than by the " disposition shewn to continue the dwelling there, or make it " a permanent residence, and a man is understood only to

---

(p) Most probably by his direction, but it does not appear in the case.

" live at a particular place, and not to found his Domicil in
" that spot who only resides there, though for several
" years, for the mere purpose of trade or business, or to
" effect any particular object, and by such dwelling or
" residence no *domicilium civitatis* or " *incolatus* is ac-
" quired.   Elbert Leoninus (*q*), (*Consil.* 54. *circa* n. 2),
" when he speaks of foreign merchants residing at Ant-
" werp for the purposes of commerce, 'tradens pro regulâ
" ' domicilium non contrahi ex solâ habitatione negotiendi
" ' causâ facta.'   Since, therefore, the intestate has not
" shewn any disposition to charge his Domicil of Origin at
" Utrecht, which appears, by presumption in law, until the
" contrary is shewn : that, on his return from Spain, he rented
" a room there, and kept up fire and light; and that he took
" no house at Amsterdam, he must, although he died there,
" be considered as having his Domicil at Utrecht " (*r*).

CCXXVI. To the same effect was a decision of the Cour de
Cassation in France, in the case of *General Destaing*. The
question was, whether that officer at the time of his death in
Paris was domiciled at that place or at Aurillac, where he had
been born and undeniably domiciled for the greater part of
his life. The question was tried first before the tribunal,
" de première instance de la Seine," and that Court decided
in favour of the domicil at Paris, on the ground that the
General had not resided at Aurillac for fifteen years ; that
he had resided at Paris for some months previous to his
decease ; that he had many times manifested an intention of fixing his principal establishment there, and of purchasing a house for that purpose ; so that there was *animo et
facto* a change of domicil. But the Cour de Cassation
reversed this judgment, principally on the ground that the
facts alleged were not sufficiently distinct and positive to

(*q*) Many authorities are cited for each proposition in this opinion,
which I have been compelled to omit.

(*r*) *Henry, Appendix,* 201—3. See too *Voet, ad Pandectas,* lib. 38,
n. 34, where this case is also cited.

counterbalance the presumption in favour of the Domicil of Origin at Aurillac (s).

CCXXVII. The legal presumption in favour of the Original Domicil was also very strongly illustrated in a recent case brought by appeal from the Scotch Courts to the House of Lords (t). It was an action of declaration of legitimacy, brought by the appellent, Mary Munro, for the purpose of establishing that she was the lawful daughter of Sir Hugh Munro, of Fowlis, and as such the heiress in entail entitled to succeed to the estates of Fowlis. Sir Hugh succeeded to the baronetage and estate on the death of his father in 1781; he attained his full age in 1784; he took an active share in the management of his own estates, and was frequently an attendant at the sittings of the Town Council at Fortrose, to which he was admitted a member soon after becoming of age. In 1785, 1787, 1788, he visited the continent, but always returned to Scotland, where he resided not at the family mansion, Fowlis Castle, but at Ardullie, a house belonging to his mother. He resided with her till 1794, when, in consequence of some disagreement with her, he left Scotland professedly on a short visit to London. In November of that year he became acquainted with a Miss Mary Low, in London; he took apartments for her in Bolsover Street, Oxfort Street, and there on the 4th of May, 1796, the appellant was born. He afterwards took a house, on lease, in Gloucester Place, Portman Square, where he and Miss Low resided together till 1801. In September of that year he married her at the parish church of St. Mary-le-bonne, according to the form of the ritual of the Church of England. He continued to reside in England for some months after his marriage, but then broke up his establishment in Gloucester Place, and went to Scotland, and there introduced his wife and daughter to his friends and connections. In August, 1803, Lady Munro and two

---

(s) *Traité du Domicile*, p. 52.

(t) *Munro* v. *Munro*, 7 *Clarke and Finnelly's Reports of Cases in the House of Lords*, p. 842.

female attendants were drowned while bathing on the shore near Fowlis Castle. Rumours having been afloat that Miss Munro was under a legal incapacity to succeed as heiress to the entailed estates, the suit for declaration was brought to determine that question. The majority of the Scotch Judges pronounced her illegitimate. The Lord President thought the Domicil of the father did not fix the *status* of the child ; and was also of opinion that if it did, then the Domicil was altogether English; and therefore the child was indelibly impressed by the law of England with illegitimacy. Six of the other Judges thought the child legitimated by the subsequent marriage on the ground that the Domicil was *Scotch.* Six others thought the Domicil was *English*, and, therefore, that the appellant was illegitimate ; from the decree of illegitimacy Miss Mary Munro appealed to the House of Lords.

CCXXVIII. Lord Chancellor Cottenham having laid down the rule of law in Scotland to be " that the Domicil of Origin " must prevail, unless it be proved that the party has acquired " another by residence, coupled with an intention of making that " his sole residence, and abandoning his Domicil of Origin," proceeded to consider the evidence with reference to this rule. After observing that the case of *Lady Dalhousie* v. *Mac Dowall* (which had been argued, and as involving the same points of law as *Munro* v. *Munro*, stood over for judgment with that case) presented no difficulty, as in that case the Scotch Domicil had clearly not been abandoned, he proceeded —" In the case of *Munro* v. *Munro* the difficulty is ap-" parently greater, because there was a residence in England " of many years ; but the only period to be considered is from " the father quitting Scotland, in 1794, to the time of the " marriage in 1801. There was a sufficient reason, indepen-" dently of any intention of changing his Domicil, for his " leaving Scotland in 1794. His family house was not in a fit " state for residence, and he had failed in effecting a proposed " arrangement with his mother, by which he wished to obtain " for his own use the house where she lived. There is no " ground for supposing that he at that time intended to abandon

" Scotland; the reverse is proved by the first letter he wrote
" after his arrival in London, (3rd of September, 1794), in
" which he gives directions about keeping some land in grass,
" the only farming he takes pleasure in, and about clothes-
" presses for his dressing-room at Fowlis.   In November,
" 1794, he occupied the office of Deputy Lieutenant of Ross-
" shire.   In 1795, on the 9th of February, he gave directions
" for the preparation of a will in the Scotch form ; and in a
" letter of the 14th of June, he states his intention of being
" in Ross-shire at the end of the month, which, by subsequent
" letters, it appears, was prevented by an attack of illness.
" He, in a letter of the 1st of September, 1795, expresses his
" regret at having been prevented going to Scotland ; and in
" a letter of the 14th of September he says, he shall be there
" next summer ; and in a letter of the 18th he says, that he
" shall, after Whitsuntide next, take the management of his
" estate into his own hands.   Similar expressions occur in
" many letters of 1795 and 1796.   In a letter of the 7th of
" October, 1796, he says, ' I shall be in Ross-shire next year,
" ' and, should unforseen events oblige me to defer my jour-
" ' ney,' &c.; and in a letter of the 27th of October, he directs
" the payment in kind of hens and eggs to be continued, say-
" ing, ' when at home I shall have occasion for them.'   Many
" letters in 1797 speak of his intended journey to Scotland,
" and in one of the 25th of November, 1797, he says, ' My
" ' journey to Ross-shire, so long and often retarded by
" ' circumstances which I could not foresee, is now, by the
" ' advice of my friends here, given up till next summer.'
    " It appears that before this time, that is, in 1794 or 1795,
" the connection between the Appellant's father and mother
" had been formed, and she was born in September, 1796,
" which may well account for the continued postponements of
" his intended journey to Scotland : but he does not appear
" ever to have abandoned the intention ; for in a letter of the
" 28th of March, 1798, to a person in Scotland, he says that
" he expects very soon to be able to write him the time at
" which he proposed to himself the pleasure of seeing him.   In

" 1799, 1800, and 1801, he gives directions for the fitting-up
" of his family residence in Scotland, and for that purpose
" sends large quantities of furniture from London, and in
" September, 1801, he marries the Appellant's mother ; and by
" letter of the same year, speaks of his intention of coming to
" Scotland.   In a letter of the 15th of April, 1802, he says,
" ' I have resolved to be at Fowlis as soon as the house, which
" ' is painting and papering, can be inhabited ; but as these
" ' things do not depend upon my wishes, I cannot fix posi-
" ' tively any time.   I hope to be in Edinburgh in July or
" ' August.'   He accordingly went to Scotland that year with
" his family, and resided in his family house at Fowlis, and
" there continued till 1808, the Appellant's mother having
" died there in 1803.   Lord Corehouse, who entered much
" into this part of the case, in commenting on this corres-
" pondence, asked this question, ' Do these expressions, when
" ' read in connection with the context, import that he was to
" ' return to Scotland with a view to settle permanently there,
" ' and to live at the castle at Fowlis during the rest of his
" ' life ?   The very reverse is manifest.'   And then he observes
" upon expressions used indicating that the promised visit to
" Scotland would be short.   These observations would be
" highly important if the question was whether, by his subse-
" quent residence in Scotland, he had acquired a new domicil
" there, but they do not appear to me to touch the question,
" whether he had abandoned the Domicil of Origin in that
" country, which can only be effected by evidence of an inten-
" tion to do so accompanying the act of a residence elsewhere.
" If he ever formed such an intention, to what period is the
" adoption of that resolution to be referred ?   In order to
" be of any effect upon the present question, it would be
" at some time prior to September, 1801, the date of the
" marriage.
" That he took a lease of the house in Gloucester Place, and
" formed an establishment there, has been much relied upon ;
" and, in the absence of better evidence of intention as to his
" future Domicil, might be important as affording evidence of

" such intention, but cannot be of any avail, when from the
" correspondence, the best means are afforded of ascertaining
" what his real intentions were. The having a house and an
" establishment in London is perfectly consistent with a domi-
" cil in Scotland. This fact existed in *Somerville* v. *Somer-*
" *ville,* and in *Warrender* v. *Warrender.* Taking, therefore,
" the rule of law as to the Domicil of Origin to be what I have
" before stated, and applying the evidence to that rule, I do
" not find it proved that the Appellant's father acquired a new
" domicil in England with the intention of making that his
" sole residence, and abandoning his Domicil of Origin in Scot-
" land."

2. AS TO ORAL AND WRITTEN DECLARATIONS.

CCXXIX. To these evidences of the intention—the indispensable element of true Domicil—the civilians (*u*) have always attached great importance. The French Code enacts that the proof of intention shall follow upon an express declaration, made either to the municipality from which a person removes, or to that to which he transfers his Domicil ; and that

---

(*u*) "Declaratur autem animus ille vel expressè vel tacitè. Expressè si quis verbis vel literis profiteatur se in civitatem aliquem vel regionem eà intentione habitatem venîsse ut ibi perpetuo esset. Atque de tali declaratione si constat, frustrà de voluntate domicilium constituendi dubitatur, sed quamprimùm actualis habitatio accedit, statim eo ipso momento domicillum censetur constitutum. *Carp.* lib. ii. *Respons.* 21, n. 15, etsi summam rerum nondum eò transtulerit *Mœv. ad.* i. L. lib. i. tit. ii. n. 28, è contrariò, si quis animum suum declaraverit se nolle ibidem domicilium constituere, et perpetuò manere : non contrahit domicilium licet per multos annos ibidem subsisteret et etiam majorem partem eò attulisset. (See below this doctrine denied by *Lord Stowell* in a prize case.) Nam in his quæ ab alicujus animo dependent, simplici illius dicto credendum et potius ad expressam declarationem, quam factum respiciendum est communiter tradunt Doctores *Amoya d.* 101, *Mascard. de Prob.* vol. i. *cond.* 434, n. 3, *non obstât* l. ii. *C. ubi Senator vel. Clariss.* ea enim loquitur de casu dubio nos verò de certo."
—*Tractatio de Domicilio Eberhardina,* s. 29, Præside *Lauterback.*

in the absence of such proof from express declaration, recourse shall he had to the consideration of the circumstances of the case (*x*).

CCXXX. From the case of *Munro* v. *Munro*, which has just been cited, it has been seen what great weight in the balance of evidence has been given by the highest legal authority in Great Britain to statements of intention made in *letters* written by the party whose Domicil is in dispute. It would be useless therefore to multiply inferior authorities upon this point.

CCXXXI. The English Courts appear generally to ascribe but little value to *oral* declarations.

CCXXXII. In the case of *Lord Somerville* the declarations seem to have rather inclined the balance towards the English Domicil. To some of his friends (according to the report in the case) he declared repeatedly, that he considered his residence in London only as a lodging-house and temporary residence during the sitting of Parliament; but he spoke of Scotland as his residence and home, where he was born, and with the warmth of a native. About a month before his death Colonel Reading urged him to make a will, for the sake of his natural children ; upon which he said he meant to take care of them, and also of his brother's younger children. Soon after this conversation, he told Colonel Reading that he had seen his nephew, Sir James Bland Burgess, who had alarmed him by telling him that, if he had died without a will, his personal estate would be divided among the several branches of his family, which he would much deplore ; and afterwards, he said that he should soon go to Scotland, and

---

(*x*) "103. Le changement du domicile s'opérera par le fait d'une habitation réelle dans un autre lieu, joint à l'intention d'y fixer son principal établissement. 104. La preuve de l'intention resultera d'une declaration expresse, faite tant à la municipalite du lieu qu'on quittera, qu'à celle du lieu où on aura transféré son domicile. 105. A défaut de déclaration expresse, la preuve de l'intention dependra des circonstances."—Code Civil, t. iii. *Du Domicile.*

would then make his will. He died in about a month after this conversation. Elizabeth Dewar, who had been house-keeper at Somerville House, in her depositions stated that she had heard the intestate say he was an Englishman; that though in Scotland, he was educated in England; his connections were English; ho had no friends in Scotland, and everything he did was after the English fashion. The deponent had heard him say that his reason for going to Scotland was that he might be at his estate; that he did not like it, but he had promised his father, when dying, that he would live one half of the year in Scotland, and the other half in England; that he considered himself an Englishman; that his estate in England was preferable to that in Scotland; that he preferred England, and would never visit Scotland, except on account of the promise to his father; and that he did not care though Somerville House was burnt: and this he frequently said in conversation with the witness. In spite of these declarations, the Scotch Domicil was sustained by the judgment.

CCXXXIII. It is clear law that the expressions of an intention not to renounce a domicil, cannot prevail against the intention and facts collected from the acts of the person, if those are otherwise sufficient to constitute a domicil abroad (y).

III.—THE PLACE OF DEATH.

CCXXXIV. In England and America the place of death seems to have been considered a circumstance of very slight moment; it is admitted however to afford a *primâ facie* presumption (z), though of a faint kind: for it has been well said, "the question of Domicil, *primâ facie*, is much " more a question of fact than of law. The actual place " where he is, is *primâ facie* to a great many purposes his " Domicil. You encounter that if you shew it is either con-

---

(y) *Re Steer*, 28 *Law Journal, Exch.* 22.

(z) "Taking the place of the deceased's death to be *primâ facie* the place of his domicil."—*Burton v. Fisher*, (*Prerogative Court of Dublin*,) 1 *Milward*, p. 187.

" strained, or from the necessity of his affairs or transitory,
" that he is a sojourner, and you take from it all character
" of permanency" (a).

CCXXXV. In the leading American case, *Guier* v. *O'Daniel*,
Président Rush said, "A man is *primâ facie* domiciled at the
" place where he is resident at the time of his *death* : and it
" is incumbent on those who deny it to repel the presumption
" of law, which may be done in several ways. It may be
" shewn that the intestate was there as a traveller, or on
" some particular business, or on a visit, or for the sake of
" health ; any of which circumstances will remove the impres-
" sion that he was domiciled at the place of his death." And
in *Ommaney* v. *Bingham* (b) the House of Lords considered
the circumstance of Sir C. Douglass' death having taken place
in Scotland (whither he had gone only for a temporary and
limited purpose) as nothing. In *Dr. Munroe's* case (c), it was
urged that the testator, knowing he was in a dying state, went
to Scotland in order to lay his bones with his ancestors : the
Vice Chancellor took notice of the argument, but said the fact
was disproved.

CCXXXVI. In *Somerville* v. *Somerville*, the Master of
the Rolls observed, "It was contented, in favour of the
" English Domicil, that in such a case as that of two domicils.
" and to neither any preference, (for it cannot be contended
" that the Domicil in Scotland was not at least equal to that
" in England, except the *lex loci rei sitæ* is to have effect),
" the death should decide. There is not a single dictum from
" which it can be supposed that the place of the *death* in such
" a case as that shall make any difference. Many cases are
" cited in *Denisart* to shew that the *death* can have no effect,
" and not one that that circumstance decides between two
" domicils. The question in these cases was, which of the

(a) *Bempde* v. *Johnson*, 3 *Vesey's Reports*, p. 201.
(b) *Binney's Reports*, p. 349, note.
(c) See below.

" two domicils was to regulate the succession, and without any
" regard to the place where he died " (d)?

CCXXXVII. In *Johnson* v. *Beattie*, (the case already alluded
to, in which the House of Lords held that the English Court
of Chancery had jurisdiction to appoint guardians to an infant
who happened to be in this country, but whose property and
Domicil were Scotch), Lord Campbell said (e), " It must be
" remembered that all her (the mother's) own property, as
" well as the child's, was situate in Scotland ; that she went
" to reside there on her husband's death ; that she came to
" England only on account of her health and her child's ;
" that all the tutors appointed by her husband resided in
" Scotland ; and that there can be no doubt her daughter
" would return to occupy the mansion of her ancestors. I see
" no reason to think that, in case she should recover her
" health and her daughter should be brought back to Scot-
" land, she had permanently adopted England as her place of
" residence, although her father resided at Chester. She
" undoubtedly expected *to die* in England, and she gave
" directions that her body should be buried in England ; but
" this was in her last sickness, of the fatal termination of
" which she had a foreboding. The question is, whether she
" had taken up her permanent residence in England, in case
" she should recover her health and strength ? If, instead of
" Albion Street, Hyde Park, she had gone for her health to
" the Island of Madeira, where her husband died, and had
" written letters stating that she should *die* there, and had
" given directions that she should be buried there, although
" she had *died and been buried* there, unquestionably her
" Scotch Domicil would never have been superseded." And
so, in a recent case, Sir H. J. Fust remarked, " If he had
" died in Scotland, that would not in the slightest degree have
" changed my opinion that he was domiciled in India" (f).

(d) 5 *Vesey's Reports*, p. 783.

(e) *Clarke and Finnelly's Reports*, vol. x. p. 138.

(f) *Craigie and Craigie* v. *Lewin and others*, 3 *Curteis' Ecclesiastical Reports*, p. 449. See further mention of this case below.

In the case of *Cornelius Van Leeuwen* (*g*), referred to above, the place of death was held to be of no avail in the consideration of his Domicil, though his directions to be buried at a particular place, being the place of his Origin, seem to have had some weight ascribed to them.

CCXXXVIII. In the case of the *Marquis de Gassion*, referred to under the next section, the place of death, and that of making the will were held slight presumptions.

CCXXXIX. The presumption would, however, be stronger, where the place of death was also the place of Origin. It was the circumstance most strenuously insisted upon by Cochin, in the case of the *Marquis de Saint Pater*, who had spent much of his time at Paris, as well as in the province of Maine, where he was born, and where he possessed a large, if not the largest, amount of his property (*h*).

IV.—PLACE OF WIFE AND FAMILY.

CCXL. The Roman lawyers were very careful to distinguish a mere habitation (*habitatio*) (*i*) from a Domicil (*domicilium*).

(*g*) Sec. 1.

(*h*) "Secondement, le Marquis de Saint Pater est mort dans cette même province du Maine, après y avoir passé les derniers tems de sa vie. Si dans l'intervalle il y avoit des preuves d'un domicil fixé à Paris, la circonstance de l'habitations dans les derniers tems, et de la mort dans le domicile d'origine, suffiroit pour prouver un esprit de retour à ce domicile, et pour effacer les preuves contraires qui s'élèveroient dans les tems intermédiares. La nature éclateroit dans ses dernières démarches ; et ses opérations sont si vives que la loi ne balanceroit pas un momeut à en reconnoître toute l'autorité."—*Cochin, Œuvres*, VI. 231.

(*i*) " Illud certum est neque solo animo atque destinatione patris familias, aut contestatione sine re et facto, domicilium constitui, neque solâ domus comparatione in aliquâ regione, neque solâ habitatione sine proposito illic perpetuò morandi : cum Ulpianus à domicilio habitationem distinguet, dum asserit, legem Corneliam inj..riarum de domo vi introitâ *ad omnem habitationem in quâ paterfamilias habitat, licet ibi domicilium non habeat*, pertinere, &c. See *Voet*, l. v. t. i. s. 98, citing l. lex *Cornelia*, 5 s. si tamen 5 ff. de injuriis, &c., and other passages of the Civil Laws.

They held that the mere purchase of a house did not indicate any intention of acquiring a new domicil, much less the purchase of a shop, or of a place for the deposit of goods.

CCXLI. And their opinions have been adopted by all European jurists.   But if a person places his wife and family and "household gods," (under (*k*) which class heirlooms, pictures, and muniments, might reasonably be included), in a particular place, the presumption of the abandonment of a former domicil, and of the acquisition of a new one, is very strong (*l*).

CCXLII. In *Sir C. Douglas's* case (*m*), the circumstance that wherever he went on service (which he did in divers countries and under divers governments), he left his wife and family in England, and always returned to them there, was held to be one of the criteria which marked his Domicil; though the principal circumstance was his dying in the English service.

CCXLIII. In *Bempde* v. *Johnson*, (the case of the *Marquis Annandale*), the Lord Chancellor ascribed considerable importance to the fact of marriage. "In the latter part of his "life" (he says) "his Domicil, *de facto*, was unquestionably in "England; during the latter part of it, and from an epoch "remarkable enough when contracting a second marriage and "forming a new family at that period, all the circumstances "of his family point much more to England than to Scot- "land" (*n*).

CCXLIV. The Marquis de Gassion was born in Bearne, where he had his Domicil of Origin. He afterwards resided a long time in Paris, and he had also a residence at Pau, where he made his will. He died at Pau, and the question was, whether the *Original* Domicil at Bearne had been super-

---

(*k*) See argument in *Somerville* v. *Somerville*.

(*l*) "Accedit (says *Grotius*, in an opinion cited by *Henry*) altera conjectura ex invectione familiæ et bonorum," &c.   *Odwin* v. *Forbes*, p. 198, *Appendix*.

(*m*) *The Ann Smith, Dodson's Admiralty Reports*, p. 224.

(*n*) *Bempde* v. *Johnson*, 3 *Vesey's Reports*, 201.

seded by a *real Domicil* at Paris, or at Pau. It appeared that he had married there, that the marriages of his children took place there, and that he had described himself in a power of attorney as "de présent à Pau, mais démeurant à "Paris." The facts of his having died at Pau, and made a will there, were not held sufficient to shew a change of domicil, whilst the other circumstances were held to have proved a Domicil *animo et facto* at Paris (*o*).

CCXLV. "He is not a married man" (*p*) (said Lord "Stowell, in the case of the *Phœnix*), "holding any con- "nection with that place by the residence of his wife and "family." It was held, however, by the same high authority, that, in the case of a North Briton by birth, personally resid- ing in America, having been admitted a citizen of the United States and engaged in American trade, the mere circumstance of leaving a wife and family in Scotland would not avail to retain his national character. Dr. Story is of the same opinion : —"If a married man has his family fixed in one place, and "he does his business in another, the former is considered the "place of domicil" (*q*).

CCXLVI. In the following American cases, the wife and family were much considered as criteria of Domicil.

Mellen, C. J., said (*r*), "If, according to legal principles, "Isaac Stanton, the pauper, is to be considered as having "*resided, dwelt,* and *had his home* in Parsonfield, on the "21st of March, 1821, then he gained a settlement by virtue "of the act (*s*) passed on that day relating to the settlement "and support of the poor. It appears that from 1800 or

---

(*o*) *Burge's Commentaries on Colonial and Foreign Laws*, vol. i. p. 40. Some cases in *Denisart, Domicile.* s. 19.

(*p*) 3 *Robinson*, 139.

(*q*) *Conflict of Laws*, p. 50.

(*r*) *Cases in the Supreme Judicial Court of the State of Maine. The Inhabitants of Parsonfield* v. *Perkins*, Pauper Case, April, 1824. *Green-leaf*, vol. ii. p. 414.

(*s*) *Stat.* 1821, c. cxxii. s. 22.

" 1801 to 1817, he lived with his wife and children in Par-
" sonfield, with the exception of a short time, during which he
" resided in another town, about the year 1812; that, in 1817,
" he separated from his wife and family, and has never had
" any connection with them since; though he has continued
" generally to reside in Parsonfield, sometimes employed in
" his trade of a mason there, and in adjoining towns, and
" sometimes idle (as mentioned in the exceptions) (t).   It
" appears also that, with the exception of nearly a year, the
" wife and children have lived and kept house in that town.
" From these facts, what is the legal conclusion as to the domicil
" of the pauper?   It is clear that, during all the time that he
" resided in Parsonfield, and *lived with his family*, he dwelt,
" in the strictest sense of the words, and *had his home* in that
" town.   In this situation he was in 1817, and since that time
" he has generally resided there.   There is no fact in the case
" tending to shew that he has ever contemplated a residence in
" any *other* town, or has in any manner lost his right as a
" townsman on an election of state, county, or town officers,
" so far as residence could give or effect such right.   Nor is
" there any fact by which it appears that he may not return
" to and live with his family whenever he may be inclined to
" do so : or, in a word, that he may not resume his rights as
" the head of his family and former home at his option.   As
" he has not become domiciled in any *other* town, and for the
" other reasons suggested, we are of opinion that his Domicil in
" Parsonfield must be considered as continuing and existing
" when the act was passed : of course he then gained a legal
" settlement in that town, and the defendant was not guilty of
" the violation of any law in bringing the pauper into the town
" of Parsonfield, and leaving him there, as alleged in the
" writ. We sustain the exception, and the verdict is set
" aside."

(t) Brought by bill of exceptions from the Court below, whose judgment was reversed.

CCXLVII. In another American case (*u*), the circumstance of the person whose Domicil was disputed, being unmarried had great weight with the Court. It was a case of assumpsit on a promissory note, and there was a plea to the jurisdiction that the defendant is not a citizen of Rhode, as set forth in the writ, and issue thereon.

At the trial it appeared in evidence that the defendant was a native citizen of Rhode Island ; and that his mother, his father being dead, still resided in Providence, in that State, on the family estate. The defendant was a young unmarried man, and was in partnership in New York for some time. This commercial house in New York had failed ; and, upon that failure, he returned and resided with his mother at Providence. At the time of the service of the writ he was engaged as a clerk in the store of his brother in the State of Connecticut. But he made frequent visits to his mother in Providence, and no act appeared to shew any intention of a permanent domicil in Connecticut. Upon these facts the case was submitted to the Court by Searle for the plaintiff, and R. W. Greene for the defendant.

Story, J.—" The opinion of the Court is, that the defendant " is a citizen of Rhode Island, and that the plea is not main- " tained. His birth was in that State; the family estate is " there, and his mother remains on it. The defendant is un- " married. While he was resident at New York on business, " he may be deemed to have acquired a citizenship there, as he " probably intended a permanent domicil. But when the " house failed, he gave up his residence in New York and " returned to his mother's family. Under such circum- " stances he must be presumed to have regained the family " Domicil, and to have returned to his native allegiance. " The native character and Domicil easily revert, and fewer " circumstances are necessary to establish it than a foreign " Domicil. Upon his return from New York he re-acquired

---

(*u*) *Catlin* v. *Gladding*, 4 *Mason's Report of Cases argued in the Circuit Court of the United States, Rhode Island.*

" his native citizenship. What evidence is there that he has
" since changed it? It does not appear that he had any
" intention of becoming a citizen of Connecticut. For aught
" in the case his engagement may be merely temporary until
" he can get other business, and without any intention of
" changing his Domicil. *The case might have been different
" if he had had a family, and removed with them* into Con-
" necticut. Such an act would afford *primâ facie* evidence
" of a change of permanent domicil. The judgment must,
" therefore, be for the plaintiff."

CCXLVIII. In the case of *Cornelius Van Leeuwen*, referred
to above, the absence of any domestic establishment, and the
mere boarding and lodging of the person in the place where
his trade was carried on, were the chief circumstances relied
upon to shew that no domicil had been acquired in that
place (x).

CCXLIX. In America, owing probably to the habit of the
country, little, if any, stress seems to have been laid upon
the fact of a person being only a boarder or a lodger at a
place. "On a question of domicil" (it was said by President
" Rush), "the mode of living is not material, whether on rent
" at lodgings, or in the house of a friend. The apparent or
" avowed intention of *constant* residence, not the manner of
" it, constitutes the Domicil" (y).

V.—HOUSE OF TRADE.

CCL. In the foregoing cases, the circumstances of marriage
and family were not encountered by presumptions arising from
a second establishment, in which the person's business was
carried on. But even in these cases, it is said by great autho-

---

(x) See p. 149.

(y) *Guier* v. *O'Daniel*, 1 *Binney's Reports*, p. 349, note. See too the case
of the *United States* v. *The Penelope*. *Peters' Admiralty Decisions*, 450.
In *Craigie* v. *Craigie*, furnished lodgings were treated as no criterion of
domicil. 3 *Curteis' Ecclesiastical Reports*, p. 447.

rity that the locality of the wife and family would be the better criterion of the Domicil.

CCLI. Dr. Story says (z), " If a married man has his family " fixed in one place, and he does his business in another, the " former is considered the place of his Domicil."

CCLII. He relies for this position upon the text of the Roman Law, as adopted an denforced by French Jurists ; but not upon any decided cases in the Courts of England or America.

CCLIII. It is, however, an opinion in some degree confirmed by Grotius, who, deciding the Domicil of an intestate in the Netherlands, observed that the Law of Embden will not prevail; " for although his partnership firm was there, yet " he had no habitation there ;" and in the case of *Van Leeuwen*, as has been shewn, the house of trade was not held to counterbalance the Domicil of Origin.

CCLIV. The following case is selected by Henry from the "*Appendix ad Hollandsche Consultatien*," as one in which the testator had clearly abandoned his Original Domicil : the principal evidence of his having done so was his carrying on his business elsewhere.   " L. G., a North Hollander by birth, " having, for more than thirty years, fixed his residence at " Dantzick, without change, and carried on his business there, " made his will, conformably to the solemnities required by " the law of that place ; whereby, after leaving some legacies, " he left the rest of his property to his heirs *ab intestato*, " without declaring who they were. His property consisted " in merchandise, outstanding debts, rights of action, and im- " movable property, both at Dantzick and North Holland ; " and the question was, whether the law of the *domicilium* " *habitationis* or of the *domicilium originis* should prevail " as to the succession."

CCLV. The opinion of counsel was as follows :—As it appears that L. G. for upwards of thirty years has dwelt at Dantzick until his death, without any indication of a wish to return to his birth-place, it is, therefore, manifest that he

---

(z) *Commentaries on the Conflict of Laws*, c. iii. p. 51.

must be understood to have renounced this, and to have fixed his Domicil at Dantzick (*per textus express. in l. ejus* 27, § 1, *ff. ad Municip. l.* 7, *cod. de Incolis*) " nam ibi quis domici-
" lium habere intelligitur ubi larem et fortunarum summam
" constituit unde (rursus) non sit discessurus si nihil avocet."
Whence it follows that the said L. G. having thought proper to appoint as his heirs, his heirs *ab intestato*, must be understood to have meant those who, according to the law of his *domicilium habitationis*, would succeed (*a*).

CCLVI. " No position" (says Lord Stowell) " is more estab-
" lished than this, that if a person goes into another country
" and engages in trade and resides there, he is, by the law of
" nations, to be considered as a merchant of that country,"
that is to say, as domiciled there (*b*).

CCLVII. Many passages in the luminous commentary on International Law contained in the reports from which this case is cited, shew the anxious care with which that great Judge invariably guarded this position: thus, recent establishment was held to constitute a domicil where intention of making a permanent residence was proved upon the party (*c*).

CCLVIII. No fugitive visits to the native country were allowed to counteract the presumption of domicil arising from a regular course of employment in a foreign country and trade (*d*).

CCLIX. The Consul who traded in the country where he resided was not permitted to cover his mercantile with his official character (*e*). A neutral subject found residing in a foreign country was presumed to be there *animo manendi*, and if a state of war brought his national character into question, it lay upon him to explain the circumstance of his residence (*f*).

(*a*) *Henry*, case of *Odwin* v. *Forbes*, Appendix, 209.

(*b*) *The Indian Chief, Robinson's Admiralty Reports*, vol. iii. p. 18.
The Matchless, 1 *Haggard*, 103.   *The Rendsburg*, 4 *Robinson*, 139.   *The President*, 5 *Rob.* 279.

(*c*) *The Diana*, 5 *Robinson*, 60.

(*d*) *The Vriendschap*, 4 *Robinson*, 168.

(*e*) *The Indian Chief*, 3 *Robinson*, 27.

(*f*) *The Bernon*, 103.

CCLX. The owner of a landed estate, who confined himself to the shipment of its produce, was said not to stand exactly on the same footing as a general merchant retaining a Mercantile Domicil by his house of trade (g).

CCLXI. The cases referred to which contain the enunciation of this doctrine were indeed cases occurring in time of war, and at a time when it was often a matter of great difficulty to discover the trader in the enemy's commerce, who sought to disguise himself under the garb of a neutral, or to retain his native character. They were cases of Commercial Domicil; and, in the first place, it must be recollected that, with respect to cases of this description, it has been held that there may be transactions so radically national as to impress the national character, independently of the *local residence* of the parties (h). The doctrine contained in these and other cases decided by Lord Stowell, was formally and judicially recognised by the Supreme Court of the United States, in the great case of the *Venus*, Rae, master (i). But, as has been already observed, further evidence of the *animus manendi* will generally be required to fix a Testamentary Domicil in time of peace (k).

VI.—DEPOSITARY OF PAPERS AND MUNIMENTS.

CCLXII. It may be that a man may have two places of residence, in different countries, and spend his time, with his family, equally, or nearly so, at both.

CCLXIII. In this case, one criterion of domicil will be the having deposited at one of the two places his most valuable papers and muniments, and also, according to the civilians (l), the most valuable part of his goods; though money in the funds would be an exception to this rule,

---

(g) *The Dree Gebræders*, 4 *Robinson*, 235.

(h) *The Vigilantia*, 1 *Robinson*, 12—15. *Boedes Lust*, 5 *Robinson*, 233. *The Phœnix*, *ib.* 20.

(i) 8 *Cranch's Reports*, p. 279.

(k) *Wheaton's International Law*, vol. i. p. 159.

(l) " Sed si de animo expresso non constet, et aliquis in diversis locis

little, if any, inference of Domicil being deducible from their locality.

CCLXIV. From the accidental place of debts, bills of exchange, &c., no presumption arises. In *Bruce* v. *Bruce*, Lord Chancellor Thurlow, overruling on this point the Court of Scotland, observed, "that he professed not to see how the " property could be considered in England. It consisted of " debts owing to the deceased, or money in bills of exchange " drawn on the India Company. Debts have no *situs ;* they " follow the person of the creditor."

And in the case of *Lord Somerville,* already referred to, the Lord Chancellor said, "it is hardly possible to contend " that money in the funds, however large, shall preponderate " against his residence in the country and his family seat."

VII.—THE MANSION HOUSE.

CCLXV. Another principal criterion in cases of double residence, has been the existence of a mansion-house. It has been shewn that a mere habitation, or dwelling house, constitutes a presumption of domicil of the slightest kind. In *Lord Somerville's* case (in which there was a conflict between two acknowledged domicils), the Master of the

---

bona habeat, ibi præsumitur habere domicilium, ubi maxima patrimonii quantitas sita, nam in dubio ibi videtur habere animum potissimum commorandi."—*Barbosæ et Taboris loci communes Jurisprudentiæ,* l. iv. c. li. *De Domicilio.*

"Quando vero versamur in dubio, ut si incola nunquam declaravit velit necne in loco domicilium contrahere, ibi tamen *bonam partem bonorum suorum* transtulerit dicendum erit ex eo solo præsumi domicilium contractum." Opinion of *Bartolus,* adopted by *Mascardus,* who adds, however, "illud vero, quod modo diximus, præsumi domicilium contractum, quod quis alibi *majorem partem bonorum suorum* transtulerit, ita intelliget, ut ex illâ translatione solâ non probetur domicilium quod erit alibi esse extinctum, cum quis possit habere domicilium pluribus in locis."—*Mascardus de Probationibus, Concl.* DXXXV. *s.* 22—4 vol. i. p. 248.

To the same effect, *Farinacius Consiliorum,* lib. i. consil. 75, n. 168.

See note to *Marsh* v. *Hutchinson,* 2 *Bosanquet and Puller's Rep.* p. 219.

Rolls observed, " that from a particular period Lord Somer-
" ville had determined not to abandon his *mansion-house :*
" so far from it, he made overtures with a view to get
" apartments in Holyrood House : from which I conjec-
" ture, that, if that application had been granted, he might
" have been induced to spend more time than he did in
" Scotland. He came to London. I will not inquire how
" soon he took a permanent residence there ; *but I admit*
" *from that time he manifested an intention to reside a con-*
" *siderable part of the year in London, but also to keep his*
" *establishment in Scotland, and to spend, as nearly as pos-*
" *sible, half of the year in each.* He took a lease of the house
" evidently with the intention to have a house in London
" as long as he lived, with a manifest intention to divide his
" time between them." Then, after repudiating the notion,
that the circumstance of the death should decide the question,
and alluding to the cases collected by Denisart, he proceeds,
" the fair inference from these is, that a person, not under an
" obligation of duty to live in the capital in a permanent
" manner, as a nobleman or gentleman having a mansion-
" house, his residence in the country, and visiting the metro-
" polis for any particular purpose, shall be considered domi-
" ciled in the country. On the other hand, a merchant,
" whose business lies in the metropolis, shall be considered
" as having his Domicil there, and not at his (*m*) country
" residence. *It is not necessary to enter into this distinc-*
" *tion, though I should be inclined to concur in it.* I there-
" fore forbear entering into the cases of *Mademoiselle Cler-*
" *mont de St. Aignan* (*m*) and the *Comte de Choiseul* and
" the distinction as to the acts of the former describing her-

---

(*m*) Compare the language of *Farinacius*, " Quod eo magis procedit
quia hæc mobilia non erant in loco Subiaci perpetuo permausura, sed
ad tempus tantum : cum Paulus illac accesserit recreationis causâ ad
effugiendos calores æstivos, &c. et quia non censentur esse ejus loci in
quo sunt illa quæ ad tempus tantum sunt in eo loco, sed dicuntur esse
illius loci ad quem revocanda sunt."—*Consiliorum,* l. i. consil. 71, n. 2.

(*n*) *Vide infra.*

" self as of the place of the country," and, he adds, " it is of " no consequence whether more or less money was spent at " the one place or the other, living alternately in both."

CCLXVI. As a proof that the Domicil of the Marquis de Saint Pater was in Maine, and not at Paris, Cochin urges that at the latter place were " his household, his domestic servants, his " furniture, all that he had need of for daily use—all, in one " word, which the Law calls *instrumentum domesticum ;* " " whereas, at Paris he had lived either in a friend's house, " or in an 'hôtel garni'" (*o*).

CCLXVII. In the case of *Balfour* v. *Scott,* which is cited in the report of the foregoing case, it was proved that Mr. Scott, whose Domicil was disputed, had intended completely to abandon his Domicil in Scotland. Twelve years before his death, he had dismantled his mansion-house and broken up his establishment, leaving only a gardener there. He paid two or three visits to Scotland, but on such occasions resided with his friends ; and during the latter period of his life, even these visits were discontinued. He had invested all his money in the funds. It was held by the House of Lords that the Domicil of Origin in Scotland had been abandoned.

CCLXVIII. In the case of the *Dowager Queen Henrietta Maria,* her palace of Somerset House was urged as a far stronger criterion of Domicil than the house she possessed at Paris (*p*).

CCLXIX. In the case of *Sir Charles Douglas,* before referred to, there was no mansion-house, or even estate, to corroborate the Domicil of Origin, circumstances which were much

---

(*o*) *Cochin,* tome 6, p. 231, " en un mot, ce que la loi appelle " *instrumentum domesticum,*" and p. 233, " On a trouvé des meubles dans l'appartement de Paris : mais on en a trouvé une plus grande quantité à Loresse, et *des meubles qui indiquent le véritable domicile ;* savoir, toute la batterie de cuisine, le linge ordinaire, tant de table que des chambres, et généralement tout ce qui compose, si on peut parler ainsi, tout l'attirail d'une maison."

(*p*) *Life of Sir L. Jenkins,* vol. ii. p. 669.

insisted upon by counsel in distinguishing it from the case of *Lord Somerville.*

CCLXX. In *Lord Annandale's* case, there was also no mansion-house ; there was evidence only that he had stamped with his foot upon the ground of his Scotch estate, and said, " Here I built my house !" The absence of the mansion-house was a material fact in the case; for Lord Annandale, like Lord Somerville, was one of the sixteen Scotch peers.

CCLXXI. So, too, it has been said that in the more recent case of *De Bonneval* v. *De Bonneval,* the establishment and ancestral château of the deceased in France were very important ingredients in the decision that the Domicil was French, and a long lease of a house in London which was kept by two female servants, was not held to be any counterpoise to the inference of Domicil deducible from the family mansion. Though the learned Judge said, "his taking the lease of a house for " eight years would be a strong fact to shew intention if it " had been followed up by a continued residence there."

CCLXXII. On the other hand, much stress was laid upon the fact that his correspondence, extending over a long period of time, and the family plate and papers were kept at his château in France. In the case of *Sir George Warrender,* his having "his capital mansion" in Scotland was considered among the principal circumstances which fixed his Domicil in Scotland (*q*). Letters addressed to a person at a particular place are very slight, if any, evidence of domicil, though the answers to them may be (*r*).

CCLXXIII. In the case of the *Marquis de Saint Pater,* a sort of Journal written in his own hand, and entitled " Mémoire de mes voyages et séjours à Paris," was strongly urged as a proof that Paris was *not,* and that Loresse was his

---

(*q*) 2 *Clark and Finnelly,* p. 520.

(*r*) " On ne peut prouver le séjour d'une personne dans un lieu uniquement parcequ'on lui a adressé des lettres dans le même endroit; ce ne seroit que par ses réponses qu'on pourroit le justifier."—*Cochin, Œuvres,* t. vii. p. 301.

Domicil. It was said to bring the latter place directly under the definition of the Roman Law, and so was the fact that all his title deeds and valuable papers were kept at Loresse (s).

CCLXXIV. In the very important case of *Munro* v. *Munro* (t), before referred to, Lord Chancellor Cottenham, commenting upon the various evidences of intention evinced by the conduct of Sir Hugh Munro, observed " That he took a lease of the house in Gloucester Place, and formed an estab- " lishment there, has been much relied upon, and, in the " absence of better evidence of intention as to his future " Domicil, might be important as affording evidence of such " intention, but cannot be of any avail, when from the corres- " pondence, the best means are afforded of ascertaining what " his real intentions were. The having a house and an estab- " lishment in London is perfectly consistent with a domicil in " Scotland. This fact existed in *Somerville* v. *Somerville*, and " in *Warrender* v. *Warrender*."

CCLXXV. In this case of *Munro* v. *Munro* it was proved that the family mansion was undergoing repair, and that furniture had been purchased for it. It was urged in the argument in *Lord Somerville's* case, that family pictures might, in some degree, denote the family mansion, and be considered as answering to the *lares* of the Romans.

VIII.—DESCRIPTION IN LEGAL DOCUMENTS.

CCLXXVI. Lord Somerville was described in the books of the Bank of England as of Henrietta Street, Cavendish Square, but it was successfully contended in argument that this was merely the designation of the broker, and could furnish no inference.

CCLXXVII. In *Curling* v. *Thornton*, the circumstance of Colonel Thornton's having applied for and obtained a royal

---

(s) "Unde cum profectus est, peregrinari videtur, et quo si rediit, peregrinari jam destitit."— *Code*, t. XL. l. vii.

(t) 7 *Clark and Finnelly*, 881.

ordinance assuring to him certain privileges so long as he resided in France, and a territorial title, was not held by Sir John Nicholl to weigh in the scale against the circumstances of his Domicil of Origin, and of his houses containing family papers and valuable moveables, which were in England.

CCLXXVIII. But it is to be remembered that the opinion of this learned Judge, that a British subject could not select a foreign, in complete derogation of his British Domicil, pervades this case, and that such opinion has been subsequently pronounced erroneous.

CCLXXIX. In *De Bonneval* v. *De Bonneval* the Court observed, " I am not inclined to pay much attention to the " descriptions of the deceased, in the legal proceedings in " France, for it may have been necessary, as the proceedings " related to real property, that he should describe himself as of " some place in that kingdom."

CCLXXX. In the *Marquis de Gassion's* case, already referred to, this description in a power of attorney as " de " présent à Pau, mais demeurant à Paris," seems to have influenced the decision that his Domicil was at the latter place.

CCLXXXI. The weight due to this species of evidence must very much depend upon the particular circumstances of each case ; but it would rarely be safe to discard altogether the consideration of it.

CCLXXXII. It should be observed that French lawyers appear to have always laid considerable stress upon it.   Thus, in the case of the *Marquis de Saint Pater*—as a preface to which Cochin has prefixed the title, " Where ought the Domicil " of a deceased to be fixed who has varied in his declarations?" —and where the question was, whether the Marquis was domiciled at Paris, or in Maine, the notarial acts in which he is described as "demeurant à Paris," or "demeurant à Loresse," &c., are carefully summed up ; and it was urged that the greater number of these acts described him as "demeurant à Loresse " (*u*).

(*u*) " Il faut convenir que le nombre des actes qui le déclarent de-

IX.—THE POSSESSION AND EXERCISE OF POLITICAL RIGHTS
AND PAYMENT OF TAXES.

CCLXXXIII. These circumstances have been considered as strong tests of Domicil by the Roman law (*x*) and by the civilians, but have had perhaps less weight given to them in England than in continental Europe (*y*).

---

meurent à Loresse est bien supérieur à ceux qui indiquent une demeure à Paris."—*Cochin, Œuvres,* t. vi. p. 231.

(*x*) " Dictæ expressæ declarationi domicilii constituendi equipollet illa, si quis in civitate aliquâ jus civitatis *das Burgerecht* impetraverit et ibi habitaverit, vulgo *da einer verburgert oder Erbschuldigung geleistet häusslich und beständig gesessen ist.* Requiritur autem copulativè, ut quis ibidem, non solum jus illud impetraverit sed etiam actualiter habitet."—*Tractatio de Domicilio* (1663) p. 27, t. xxx, and authorities there cited.

(*y*) " Si quis, &c. omnibus denique municipii commodis, nullis coloniarum fruitur : ibi magis habere domcilium quam ubi colendi causâ diversatur." See passage from the *Digest* cited above, and *Menochius,* " Illud tamen observandum est, quod etsi quis nomine, dicitur civis origiuarius ob id, quod in civitate natus sit, vel privilegio creatus civis, attamen ut commodis et privilegiis civitatis fruatur, habitare in ipsâ civitate atque ita domicilium in eâ habere et cum aliis civibus onera sustinere debet." And then quoting the authority of other civilians, " et idem ego ipse respondi, *in cons.* 390, &c., dixi civem hunc non sustinentem onera esse impropriè civem et secundum quid ; " and he adds the authority of other civilians, and the decisions in the " Rota Romana," " qui scripserunt civem originarium aliquem non esse, nisi parentes ibi domicilium contraxerint et civitatis munera subierint ; ita et olim apud Romanos civis Romanus dicebatur is, qui etsi natus esset Romæ attamen domicilium Romæ in ipsâ urbe contraxîsset, ac qui tribum et bonorum potestatem adoptus esset."—*Lib.* 6 *Præsumpt.* XXX. s. xxiv. p. 1037.

Mascardus, says unhesitatingly, " Preterea mutare et constituere domicilium in eâ urbe is præsumitur qui privilegium impetravit quo jus civitatis petebat."—*De Probationibus, Concl.* 85, s. iv. p. 249.

See also the opinion of the Dutch lawyers, cited by *Henry* in his Appendix, p. 193, from the *Hollandsche Consultatien,* vol. iii. consult. 138, " ubi exemplum affert ejus, qui cum escet civis Mediolanensis per

CCLXXXIV. In the case of *De Bonneval*, mentioned above, the Court observed, " I am inclined also to pay very " little attention to the statement as to his exercise of political " right in France, or to his being registered as a voter here : " being a housekeeper, he was registered here as a matter of " course. It is stated that he resisted, with success, the con- " tribution to some French rates, which a person resident in " France was liable to ; but the grounds are not stated, and it " is too loose a reasoning, that because all French subjects are " liable to such rates, and he successfully resisted them, there- " fore he was not domiciled in France. It must be shewn that " the question came regularly before the French tribunals, and " that he was held not to be a domiciled subject of France" (*z*).

CCLXXXV. It may be doubted, however, whether, if the circumstance has been so proved, it would have very mate- rially influenced the decision of the question. In the Ameri- can case of *Guier* v. *O'Daniel*, the President Rush said, " It " is, I think, extremely doubtful whether voting and paying " taxes are in any way necessary to constitute a Domicil, " which, being a question of General Law, cannot depend on " the municipal regulations of any state or nation. Voting " (in America) is confined to a few counties, and taxes may " not always be demanded."

CCLXXXVI. And in the English case of *De Bonneval* v. *De Bonneval*, the circumstance of successfully resisting the payment of French rates was held no proof of the English Domicil, no judicial decision having been pronounced upon the legality of the refusal.

CCLXXXVII. The Law of Domicil is not to be confounded with the Law of *Settlement* which may obtain in any country. In an American case, entitled "*The Inhabitants of Cam- bridge* v. *the Inhabitants of Charlestown*," a citizen of Ver-

---

multos annos autem Genuæ vixisset, *et non subisisset aliqua onera*, tan- quam civis Genuensis statuit eum ibi non fixîsse domicilium."

(*z*) See case of *Curling* v. *Thornton*, cited above.

mont having resided in a town in that state for ten years, and having paid taxes more than five years, was held to have acquired a settlement in such town, although he left his wife and children upon a farm at Vermont, and occasionally visited them there, and once tarried with them five or six months during the term (a).

CCLXXXVIII. In the following case (decided, it must be remembered, in the Prize Court), (b) the citizenship conferred by the United States upon a British subject, appears to have been a principal ingredient in deciding that his Domicil was American, and, in conjunction with his personal residence, and the character of his ship, to have overpowered the presumption arising from the residence of his wife and family in Scotland, that his National Domicil had been retained. The peculiarity of the case, and the high authority of the Judge, seem to warrant its insertion at full length in this place.

Ann, Smith. This ship, under American colours, was seized in the river Thames, by the Marshal of the Admiralty, on the 1st of August, 1812. A claim was given by the master, who was also sole owner of the ship, describing himself to be a British subject, and, as such, entitled to the benefit of the Order in Council of November, 1812, directing the restitution of British ships under the American flag. It appeared that he was a native of Scotland, and that his wife and family resided in that country, but that he had himself been admitted a citizen of America about sixteen years ago, upon taking an oath that he had been sailing out of an American port for two years; that from the year 1799 till 1805, he had been connected with a house of trade at Glasgow, which had an establishment at New York, and another at Charlestown, and that he had occasionally resided at each of the last-mentioned places; that he had purchased this vessel at public auction in America, and had made three voyages in her, the

---

(a) *Massachusetts Reports*, vol. xiii. p. 501.

(b) *Vide ante.*

two first from Charlestown to Kingston in Jamaica, returning each time in ballast; and the last from Charlestown to the river Thames. The question was, whether, from the residence and employment of this man, he was, *quoad* this vessel, to be considered a British subject.

CCLXXXIX. Sir W. Scott gave judgment. "This ship, " when seized by the Marshal in the river Thames, was under " the American flag; but, according to the account given by " the master, was not furnished with the American, or, indeed " with any pass whatever. It is very difficult to conceive that " this was the true state of the case, since the ship was not " only American built, but likewise American owned, as far at " least as the ostensible character of the claimant is concerned; " for, though he could not altogether throw off his allegiance " to his native country, he had been admitted a citizen of the " United States. I cannot conceive, therefore, why the pass " was not granted, or what obstacle prevented this man from " obtaining so important a document. I must presume that " the vessel was furnished with an American pass; but, sup- " posing the case to be otherwise, still, if the ship was furnished " with the documents usually granted to American ships, the " same rule of law must be applied as if she had been furnished " with a regular flag and pass. The ship must be conclusively " held to be American property, and, consequently, subject to " condemnation.

" It is said, however, that this ship is protected by the Order " in Council issued on the 28th of November, 1812, by which " it is directed, that ' all vessels under the flag of the United " ' States of America, which are *bonâ fide* and wholly the " ' property of his Majesty's subjects, and not purchased by " ' them subsequent to the date of hostilities on the part of " ' the United States of America, and which shall have been " ' detained in port under the embargo, or shall have sailed to " ' or from the ports of this kingdom previous to the know- " ' ledge of hostilities, and shall have been captured on such " ' voyage, shall be restored to the British owners, upon satis- " ' factory proof being made to the High Court of Admiralty,

" ' or the Courts of Vice Admiralty, to which they shall be
" ' taken for adjudication, that the said vessels are *bonâ fide*
" ' and wholly the property of his Majesty's subjects as afore-
" ' said, and had been engaged in trade as above described.'
" A claim has been given for this ship by Mr. Smith, describ-
" ing himself to be a British subject ; and, if he is a British
" subject, he will, under this Order in Council, be entitled to
" restitution.

" The question, therefore, comes to this, whether the claim-
" ant is, *quoad* this property, to be considered as a British
" subject.   For some purposes he is, undoubtedly, so to be
" considered.   He is born in this country, and is subject to all
" the obligations imposed upon him by his nativity.   He cannot
" shake off his allegiance to his native country, or divest him-
" self altogether of his British character, by a voluntary trans-
" fer of himself to another country.   For the mere purposes of
" trade, he may, indeed, transfer himself to another State, and
" may acquire a new national character.   An English subject
" resident in a neutral State, is at liberty to trade with the
" enemy of this country in all articles with the exception of
" those which are of a contraband nature ; but a trade in such
" articles would be contrary to his allegiance.   Now, the ac-
" count which he gives of himself is, ' that he was born at
" ' Falkirk, in Scotland ; that during the last seven years he
" ' has been chiefly at sea, but, when at home, he has lived,
" ' and still lives, at Bathgate, in the shire of Linlithgow, in
" ' North Britain ; that he is a subject of our Sovereign Lord
" ' the King, but, about sixteen years ago, he was admitted a
" ' citizen of the United States of America for the purpose of
" ' commerce only.'   Why, this transaction is for the purpose
" of commerce.   According to his own account, then, he ceased
" to be a British subject for commercial purposes.   He goes
" on to say, ' that he was admitted for the purpose of covering
" ' a ship of his own, to enable her to sail without risk of
" ' capture, and he was so admitted by the magistrates of Phila-
" ' delphia, on oath being made that he had sailed out of an
" ' American port for two years ; that he hath never been ad-

" ' mitted a burgher or freeman of any city or town, but from
" ' the year 1799 to the year 1805, the deponent having been
" ' connected in a house of trade at Glasgow, which had a
" ' house at New York, and another at Charlestown, in South
" ' Carolina,' so that from the year 1799 to the year 1805, he
" might, as far as he was connected with the house at Glasgow,
" and for that particular branch of his trade, be considered a
" British subject.   But, since that time, I understand him to
" say that he has withdrawn altogether from that connection.
" He says afterwards, in answer to the ninth interrogatory,
" ' that he is a North Briton by birth ; and, when he is at
" ' home, his place of residence is Bathgate, in the shire of
" ' Linlithgow, in North Britain, where his wife and family
" ' reside, and where he, the deponent, hath always resided
" ' from the time he was ten or eleven years of age, when he
" ' was not at sea or in foreign parts.'   The affirmative part of
" his history, as far as it goes, shews that he lived very much
" abroad, and principally at New York or Charlestown, in
America.   True it is that he had no house in either of these
places, but he was there a single man.   It is not the mere
" circumstance of leaving a wife and family in Scotland that
" will avail him for the purpose of retaining the benefit of his
" national character.   He cannot be permitted to take the
" advantage of both characters at the same time, and in the
" same adventure.   The utmost that can be allowed to him is
" that he should be entitled to the one character or the other,
" according to the circumstances of the transaction.   When
" the vessel herself is American-built, when the personal resi-
" dence of the owner, as far as he has any, is in America, (for it
" does not appear that this man at all resided in Scotland,) it
" would be difficult to say that it could be any other than an
" American transaction.   Since the purchase of this ship by
" Mr. Smith, he has made three voyages, two of them to
" Kingston, in Jamaica, and one to the port of London ; but
" to the ports of Scotland he has never sailed, nor does it
" appear that he has even visited his wife and family in that
" country.   He has been sailing constantly out of American

" ports, and his prevailing destination has been to the West
" Indian Islands. It is quite impossible that he can be pro-
" tected under the Order in Council, which applies only to
" those who are clearly and habitually British subjects, having
" no intermixture of foreign commercial character. It never
" could be the intention of his Majesty's Government that the
" benefit of this Order should be extended to a person who has
" thrown off his allegiance, and estranged himself from his
" British character as far as his own volition and act could
" do. I am of opinion that Mr. Smith is not entitled to the
" benefit of the Order in Council, and therefore I reject the
" claim."

CCXC. The case of *Stanley* v. *Bernes*, has been already referred to as being the first case in which it was decided that a
British subject, domiciled in a foreign country, cannot make a
valid will unless it be executed according to the forms prescribed by the law of that foreign country. In this place it is
only necessary to state the facts of the case, upon which Sir
John Nicholl said there was little if any controversy, and he
states them thus :—" The testator (Mr. Stanley), a native of
" Ireland, went, in 1770, to Lisbon, and there engaged in busi-
" ness as a merchant : soon afterwards, he married a lady, a
" Portuguese by birth, though of Irish parents and a Roman
" Catholic. In order to contract that marriage he professed
" the Roman Catholic religion. In 1798 he obtained letters
" of naturalization as a Portuguese subject, and, in 1808, when
" the French were in possession of Portugal, it is alleged that
" he was treated as a Portuguese subject; that is denied, and
" it is, on the other side, alleged that he was treated as a British
" subject. The manner, however, in which the French treated
" him is not very material to the decision of this case. Before
" their arrival he had placed a large part of his property in
" his son's name, who was born in Portugal ; but the will
" recites ' that it was a fictitious measure as a security against
" ' the French.' The testator had four children by his wife,
" but only the present party survived him. His wife, having
" become insane, was removed from Portugal to Ireland, where

" the connections of both resided. She was there supported
" by an allowance paid out of the property of the deceased,
" placed, as already mentioned, in the possession of his son.
" The deceased, in 1808, removed from Lisbon to Madeira, and
" continued to reside in that island till his death in 1826."
Such being the state of the facts, it was argued, on the one
side, that fifty years' residence, confirmed by change of religion,
marriage, and naturalization, had rendered him a Portuguese
subject, and that Portuguese Law must govern his will. On
the other side it was contended that residence without intention would not destroy the Domicil of Origin ; that during his
life and death he had been considered as a British subject; or
that, if he were domiciled in Portugal, he still had the right of
a British subject to dispose of his property by a will made in
the English form.

CCXCI. Sir John Nicholl seems to have doubted whether
Mr. Stanley was a domiciled Portuguese, but decided that
he had a right to make his will according to British Law.
This decision was reversed by the Delegates, who held Mr.
Stanley to have been domiciled in Portugal (c), and, therefore, obliged to make his will according to the law of that
country (d).

CCXCII. *Thomas Moore* died at Alicant, in Spain. His
father was a natural-born British subject ; his mother was born
in Spain, but was the daughter of a British subject, and died
in London. The father, George Moore, was principal of an
eminent mercantile house at Alicant ; his son, Thomas, was
born there in 1775 ; after passing his childhood in Spain, was
educated at Thoulouse and Liege, ultimately became the head
of the house at Alicant, and continued to his death to be there
domiciled : in 1817, he ceased to have any connection with

(c) *Stanley* v. *Bernes,* 3 *Haggard's Ecclesiastical Reports,* 431.

(d) The last case on this subject was that of *Freeman* v. *Bremer,*
lately decided by the Privy Council. This case, and the law on this
subject, will be considered presently.

mercantile business. He had been in England from 1807 to the middle of 1812 ; from the beginning of 1813 to the latter end of 1818 ; again in 1815, and in 1821, when it was said that he intended to return, and had frequently so declared. He died at Alicant in 1830. The question was, whether his testamentary papers were subject to the Law of Spain or of England. In favour of the latter position, it was alleged that he was entitled, under existing treaties with Spain, to the privilege of a British subject ; there were letters from the deceased, shewing that he considered himself, and claimed to be considered, as a British subject.

CCXCIII. It was argued that the case fell under the principle of *Stanley* v. *Bernes*, and that the deceased must be considered as domiciled in Spain. The Court seemed at first to doubt whether there might not be a distinction between this case and that of *Mr. Stanley*, inasmuch as Mr. Stanley was naturalized in Portugal, and took all the advantages of a Portuguese subject ; whereas, though the deceased had made a long residence in Spain, yet it was alleged that he resided under the faith of a special treaty, and always claimed to be considered as a British subject ; and that cases of Domicil did not depend upon residence alone, but on a consideration of all the circumstances of each particular case.

CCXCIV. But, when the cause came to a final hearing, it seems that the counsel, the King's Advocate (e) of the day, declined to argue the question raised by the treaty, and Sir John Nicholl said, " The deceased may have been a subject of both " Great Britain and Spain ; but the question is where was he " domiciled at his death ? for though he might occasionally " visit England, and make a considerable stay there ; though " under a special Act of Parliament (7 Anne, c. 5, explained by " 4 Geo. 2, c. 21), his father being a British subject, he was " entitled to certain privileges, and to be considered for certain " purposes as a British subject (when it was convenient to him,

_____

(e) 4 *Haggard's Ecclesiastical Reports*, 346 ; and see *Dr. Lushington's* remarks in *Maltass* v. *Maltass*, 1 *Robertson Ecc. Rep.* 79.

" he certainly seems to have claimed that character), yet
" by birth he was a Spaniard, and by education, by trade
" and commerce, by residence at his death, he was domiciled
" in Spain, &c., the *lex domicilii* must govern the case." (*f*)

CCXCV. *The Duchess of Kingston,* whose case has been
already referred to, resided in France, and though not a naturalized subject, had obtained permission from the King of
France, under letters patent, registered in the Parliament, to
acquire, possess, and dispose of property. She made her will
in a form valid in England, but invalid in France; and it was
sustained upon the ground that she had retained her English
Domicil (*g*).

X.—POSSESSION OF REAL ESTATE (*h*).

CCXCVI. Cochin, in his argument in the case of *The
Marquis of Hautefort,* denies that a landed estate derived
from inheritance, is any proof of Domicil (*i*).

CCXCVII. So in the case of *The Dree Gebrœders,* Lord
Stowell said, that landed estate alone had never been held
sufficient to constitute Domicil, or fix the national character of
the possessor who is not personally resident upon it (*j*).

CCXCVIII. In the case of *Warrender* v. *Warrender,*
Lady Warrender had been infeft in real estate in Scotland,

(*f*) *Moore* v. *Darral and Budd,* 4 *Haggard's Ecclesiastical Reports,*
p. 353.

(*g*) *Collectanea Juridica,* vol. i. 329, contains the opinion of *Monsieur
Target* referred to by *Sir John Nicholl, Curling* v. *Thornton,* 2 *Addam's
Report,* p. 22.

(*h*) Aus dem so eben bestimmter Begriff des Wohnsitzes ergiebt sich
die wessentliche Verschiedenheit desselben von blossen Aufenthalt so
wie von Grundbesitz."—*Savigny,* viii. s. 353.

(*i*) " Un homme est-il domicilié dans une terre parcequ'il l'a eue par
le succession de son pere ?" *Œuvres,* t. iii. p. 328—9.

See also on this point various cases collected, in which the succession
to real or heritable, and also as to personal estate, was involved in the
same decision, c. viii. s. ii. *Robertson on Personal Succession.*

(*j*) 4 *Robinson, Ad. Rep.* 235.

in pursuance of her marriage contract; but it was admitted, the Scotch Domicil could not be supported on that ground (*k*).

XI.—LENGTH OF TIME.

CCXCIX. Among the most important criteria of Domicli must be reckoned the *length of time* during which the residence has continued in a particular place.

CCC. This question may be best considered under two divisions.

1. Where the presumption of the new Domicil, arising from long residence, is not counteracted by any contrary presumption arising from the special object or purpose of the residence, or by any declaration or other indication of an intention to return to the Domicil of Origin.

2. Where it is so counteracted.

CCCI. Many of the civilians (among them Accursius, Baldus Bartolus) held that residence for ten years (*decennalis habitatio*) created a legal presumption of change of Domicil, while some thought that it was in every case a matter for the discretion of the Judge (*judicis relinquendum arbitrio*), to be exercised with due regard to the place and condition of the person (*juxta loci et personarum conditionem* (*l*). Some States of modern Europe have fixed, by positive statute, the time within which a Domicil shall be acquired.

CCCII. In the following case, (extracted from the *Hollandsche Consultatien*, Vol. 2, p. 42), lapse of time was held to have effected a tacit abandonment of a former domicil. L. G., a North Hollander by birth, having for more than thirty years fixed his residence at Dantzick, without change, and carried on his business there, made his will conformably to the solemnities required by the law of that place: whereby, after leaving some legacies, he left the rest of his property to his heirs *ab intestato*, without declaring who they were. His pro-

---

(*k*) 2 *Clark and Finnelly's Reports*, S. P. 502-3—521.

(*l*) *Mascardus de Probat., Concl.* DXXXV. s. xii. p. 248.

perty consisted in merchandize, outstanding debts, rights of action, and immoveable property, both at Dantzick and North Holland : and the question was, whether the law of the *domicilium habitationis*, or *originis*, should prevail as to the succession. The opinion of the Dutch jurist was, " As it appears " that L. G. for upwards of thirty years has dwelt at Dantzick " until his death, without any indication of a wish to return to " his birth-place, it is therefore manifest that he must be un- " derstood to have renounced this, and fixed his Domicil at " Dantzick, relying upon the text in the Digest, which has been " already cited (*nam ibi quis domicilium habere intelligitur* " *ubi larem et fortunarum summam)*" (*m*).

CCCIII. In an American case, entitled *Elbers and Kraffts* v. *The United Insurance Company* (*n*), this question of time was much considered. Spencer, J., delivered the opinion of the Court. " The plaintiff claims for a total loss on the ground " that the vessel having sailed on the voyage was never heard " of afterwards ; and, a year and a day having elapsed, she is " presumed to be lost. The claim is resisted : 1st, because " there is no proof that the vessel ever sailed ; 2nd, that " there was a breach of the warranty as to the Swedish owner- " ship of the goods insured. Kraffts having lost his Swedish " and acquired an American character by being domiciled here.

" The last point will be first considered.

" The plaintiffs had a mercantile establishment as partners " in St. Bartholemew's several years prior to February, 1814, " and it is proved also that Kraffts came to this country " for the recovery of his health in 1811, and has ever since " continued toreside here,being occasionally at New York, " Philadelphia, andBaltimore, having agents at those places " who generally corresponded with, and transacted the business " of, the house of Elbers and Kraffts, at St. Bartholemew's—

(*m*) " Civis etiam quis efficitur longâ atque diuturnâ habitatione quâ domicilium constituitur," says *Menochius de Præsumptionibus de Præsumpt.* XXX. s. xxiii, p. 1037.

(*n*) *Johnson's Reports of Cases in the Supreme Court of Judicature in the State of New York*, (Jan. 1819.)

" Kraffts having himself, in one instance, in 1813, made a
" purchase of a produce for the house, which he shipped to it,
" when Kraffts was present at New York; that his agent
" there advised and consulted with him on the business of
" the house, and constantly kept the house in St. Bartholo-
" mew's advised of the business transactions in this country,
" and that Kraffts applied to T. Roger, one of his agents in
" New York, saying he wanted an agent in Philadelphia,
" and received letters to Bohlen and Co. upon that subject.
" It does not appear that he had any counting-house.

" It is an established principle, not only in the Prize
" Courts, but also in the Common Law Courts, that ship-
" ments made by merchants actually *domiciled* in the
" enemy's country at the breaking out of the war, partake
" of the nature of the enemy's trade, and, as such, are sub-
" ject to belligerent capture. The only question is, whether
" Kraffts was temporarily here, or whether he was here
" *animo manendi*. He having remained in the United
" States for such a length of time, the presumption of
" law is that it was his intention to reside here perma-
" nently; and he is bound to explain the circumstance of
" his residence to repel that presumption. This is the doc-
" trine of the British Admiralty Court (o), and it is founded in
" good sense and the plainest principles of polity. The fact of
" a person residing in a country for a considerable period, leads
" to the conclusion that he has adopted it as his residence. If
" the real fact be otherwise, he alone can shew it. Kraffts
" came to this country for his health; but he has not shewn
" that the state of his health required his continuance here.
" We find him on one occasion actually purchasing a cargo to
" be sent to St. Bartholomew's, constituting a commercial agent,
" and superintending the concerns of the house by advising
" with and consulting with the agent of the house in relation
" to their business with the firm. Indeed, there is no proof
" that Kraffts ever talked of returning to St. Baholomew's, or

---

(o) 1 *Rob.* 102.

" that he ever explained himself to any one, that he was here
" for mere temporary purposes."

The learned Judge then cited, with approbation, *The
Yonge Klassima*, 5 Rob. 299, and Judge Story's remarks in
*Livingston and Gilchrist v. Maryland Insurance Com-
pany*, 7 Cranch, 542, and proceeded—

" It seems to me not to admit of a doubt that, by the well
" understood law of nations, the facts disclosed in this case, and
" the absence of all proofs that Kraffts was here temporarily,
" or that he intended to return at any future time to St. Bar-
" tholomew's, are decisive that *he had an indefinite intention
" to remain here*, and especially as he was actually engaged
" in superintending the business of his house in their concerns
" in this country.   The warrantry is therefore broken and
" plussed.   The property insured would have been liable to
" belligerent capture and condemnation."

CCCIV. The following observations of Lord Stowell are
" worthy of the most careful attention. He says—" Of the
" few principles that can be laid down generally, I may ven-
" ture to hold that time is the grand ingredient in constituting
" Domicil. I think that hardly enough is attributed to its
" effects ; in most cases it is unavoidably conclusive : it is not
" unfrequently said that if a person comes only for a special
" purpose, *that* shall not fix a domicil. This is not to be
" taken in an unqualified latitude and without some respect
" had to the time which such a purpose may or shall occupy :
" for, if the purpose be of a nature that *may probably,* or
" *does actually,* detain the person for a great length of time,
" I cannot but think that a general residence might grow on
" the special purpose. A special purpose may lead a man to
" a country where it shall detain him the whole of his life.
" A man comes here to follow a lawsuit : it may happen, and
" indeed is often used as a ground of vulgar and unfounded
" reproach (unfounded as matter of just reproach, though the
" fact may be true,) on the laws of his country, that it may last
" as long as himself. Some suits are famous in our judicial
" history for having even outlived generations of suitors. I

" cannot but think, that against such a long residence, the
" plea of an original special purpose could not be averred :
" it must be inferred in such a case that other purposes forced
" themselves upon him, and mixed themselves into his original
" design, and impressed upon him the character of the country
" where he resided. Suppose a man comes into a belligerent
" country at or before the beginning of a war : it is certainly
" reasonable not to bind him too soon to an acquired character,
" and to allow him a fair time to disengage himself; but if he
" continues to reside during a good part of the war, con-
" tributing by payment of taxes and other means to the
" strength of that country, I am of opinion that he could not
" plead his special purpose with any effect against the rights
" of hostility. If he could, there would be no sufficient guard
" against the fraud and abuses of masked, pretended, original
" and sole purposes of a long-continued residence. There is a
" time which will estop such a plea ; no rule can fix the time
" *a priori*, but such a time there must be. In proof of the
" efficacy of mere time, it is not impertinent to remark that
" the same quantity of business which would not fix a domicil
" in a certain space of time, would nevertheless have that
" effect if distributed over a larger space of time. Suppose an
" American comes to Europe with six contemporary cargoes,
" of which he had the present care and management, meaning
" to return to England immediately : that would form a
" different case from that of the same American coming to any
" particular country of Europe with one cargo, and fixing him-
" self there to receive five remaining cargoes, one in each year
" successively. I repeat that time is the great agent in the
" matter : it is to be taken in a compound ratio of the time
" and the occupation, with a great preponderance of the
" article of time : be the occupation what it may, it cannot
" happen but with few exceptions, but that mere length of
" time shall not constitute a domicil " (*p*).

(*p*) 2 *Robinson's Adm. Reports*, pp. 224—5.

CCCV. It is true that these observations are directly applied to the case of a *commercial* Domicil in the time of war, which may be more easily acquired than a *testamentary* Domicil; and the proposition, that "a general residence may grow on "a special purpose," if intended—from the context, the analogy of the lawsuit, and the absence of any qualification—to be held as universally true of all kinds of domicil (*q*), cannot be so considered in England after the case of *Hodgson* v. *De Beauchesne* (*r*).

CCCVI. The following dicta of the American judges upon this point, are worthy of observation :—" In questions on " this subject, the chief point to be considered is the *animus* " *manendi*, and Courts are to devise such reasonable rules

---

(*q*) " Quodnam autem temporis spatium, aut quantus, annorum numerus ad hunc diurnitatem requiratur, doctores, valdè inter se digladiantur Plerique judicis arbitrio id relinqunt, ut ex loci etpersonarum conditione ac qualitate vel breviori vel longiori termino dijudicet, (*Zangerus* and *Menochius* are here cited and compared with *Mascardus* and *Mævius*).   Quidam existimant etiam solo decennio domicilium contrahi, et ad hoc probandum adducunt (2 C. de incolis), cui hanc rationem jungunt, quod per diuturnum tempus, decem scilicet annorum, domicilium præscriptum esse censeatur, *Ernest. Cothm.* vol. i. resp. 21, b. 4, *et Warmser*, exerc. 4, q. 10, p. m. 152.

Qui etiam argumentis Zangeri ita respondet, " *Non imus inficias, minori etiam tempore domicilium constitui posse ita tamen, ut aliæ conjecturæ et circumstantiæ tacitè contracti domicilii concurrant.   Tunc autem non tam ex temporis ratione, quam potius ex ipsis conjecturis et circumstantiis tacitè contractum æstimabitur.   Verum impræsentiarum quando quæritur, an decennium ad contrahendum domicilium necessarium sit; Aliis conjecturis minimè opus est, sed sufficit solius temporis decursus.*   Sed priorem sententiam tutiorem esse arbitratur etiam *Du. Carpsov.* l. ii. t. ii. resp. 22, n. 5."—*Tractatio de Domicilio Eberhardinæ* 1663.   *Tubingæ.*

" Lorsqu'on ne connoît pas la cause pour laquelle quelqu'un est allé demeurer ailleurs qu'au lieu de son domicile, sa volonté d'y transferer son domicile peut se prouver tant par la longueur du temps qu'il a commencé d'y demeurer, que par d'autres circonstances, qui sont laissées à l'arbitrage du Juge."—*Pothier, Introd. Gen. aux Coûtumes*, p. 6.

(*r*) *Vide post.*

" of evidence as may establish the fact of intention. If it
" sufficiently appear that the intention of removing was to
" make a permanent settlement, or for an indefinite time, the
" right of Domicil is acquired by a residence even of a few
" days " (s). Again, " Every man is viewed by the law of
" nations as a member of the society in which he is found.
" Residence is *primâ facie* evidence of national character:
" susceptible, however, at all times, of explanation. If it be
" for a special purpose, and transient in its nature, it shall not
" destroy the original or prior national character; but if it be
" taken up *animo manendi*, then it becomes a domicil, super-
" adding to the original or prior character the rights and
" privileges, as well as the disabilities and penalties, of a
" citizen—a subject of the country in which the residence is
" established."

CCCVII. And in the same case it was laid down, " An
" inhabitant, or resident, is a person coming into a place with
" intention to establish his Domicil or permanent residence,
" and in consequence actually resides. The time is not so
" essential as the intent, executed by making or beginning the
" actual establishment, though it is abandoned in a longer or
" shorter period " (t).

CCCVIII. So, in the case of *Stanley* v. *Bernes*, the declarations of Mr. Stanley of his intention to return to England,
were outweighed by his residence of fifty years in Portugal (u).

CCCIX. The object of the residence in these cases was not
special, the purpose was not temporary, so as to bring it
within the rule of the civilians, exempting all such cases from
the application of the legal presumption of Domicil. The mer-

---

(s) *Peter's Condensed Reports of Cases in the Supreme Court of the
United States*, vol. iii. p. 171. Note to *The Frances, Boyer, Master*.
reported also (8 *Cranch*, 363). See also *The Diana*, 5 *Robinson, Adm.
Rep.* 60.

(t) See *Johnson* v. *Sundry Articles of Merchandize*, 6 *Hall's American
Law Journ.* p. 68.

(u) 3 *Haggard's Eccl. R.* 373.

chant engaged on a special and limited venture; the student who resides for the sake of prosecuting his studies; the individual detained by the prosecution of a lawsuit; the officer employed by the State in a particular service, all fell under this exception of the civilians (x), because they were held to retain their intention to return to their Domicil of Origin.

CCCX. When Grotius (y) is commenting on the opinion of the civilians, that ten years constitute a legal presumption of Domicil, he observes, that this applies to cases of doubt; but if the intention to adopt a new domicil was made evident, a single moment sufficed for the creation of a new domicil. And it should also be observed that, if the person who came to a country for a special purpose, continued to reside there after the object of the special purpose is satisfied: e. g. the student after the prescribed time of attendance at the university was over; the merchant after his venture was made; then a counter presumption arose that the person so remaining intended to adopt a new domicil (z).

CCCXI. Still the question has been agitated whether length of time may not establish a new domicil, even in cases where the intention has been already declared of not abandoning the Domicil of Origin.

CCCXII. Upon this point there would be, perhaps, some variety of opinion, and some difference between the decisions of European and English jurists.

CCCXIII. It has been said by some civilians, that where

(x) "Et primum dicendum est *habitationem* et *domicilium* inter se differre. Nam *domicilium* habere quis dicitur in loco qui animo ibi commorandi perpetuò habitat. Is verò qui pro emptore aliquâ ex causâ, puta studiorum, vel litis vel simili commoratur, *habitare* dicitur."—*Menochius de Præsumpt. Præs.* XLII. p. 1053.

(y) See *Henry's Appendix*, p. 198. Neither again is it any objection, " quod decennio quæratur domicilium," since it does not thence follow, "quod minore tempore non quæratur : sed quod in dubio decennium per se sufficit ad probandum domicilium, alioqui, si de voluntate appareat, vel uno momento, domicilium constitutum intelligitur."

(z) See *Mascardus, Ibid.*

a person retained the intention of returning to his former Domicil, a thousand years would not suffice to establish a new one.   "So," (says Mascardus(*a*), himself no mean authority,) "I was taught by the chief of all interpreters of the law, by "Bartolus."

CCCXIV. Locré, it has been already remarked, speaks of a case decided by the Parliament of Paris, that a person who had been absent for fourteen years retained his Domicil, by a correspondence intimating his intention to do so (*b*).

CCCXV. The Judge of the Prerogative Court observed, in a recent case, "Length of time will not alone do it ; intention "alone will not do ; but the two taken together do constitute a "change of domicil.   No particular time is required ; but when "the two circumstances of actual residence and intentional "residence concur, then it is that a change of domicil is "effected " (*c*).

CCCXVI. The French and Sardinian Codes (*d*) enact,

(*a*) "Amplius secundo loco limitabis ut non procedat si ille haberet animum recedendi, etiam tunc et per mille annos non contrahitur domicilium, ut in scholari, sic me docuit juris interpretum *Coryphæus*, Bart. quæsit. in prin. ff. de Lega 3," &c.

Mascardi de Probat., Concl. DXXXV. s. xiii. p. 249.

"Nulla tempora constituunt domicilium aliud cogitanti."—*DArgentré* Commentarii in patrios Britonum leges seu consuetudines generales Ducatûs Britaniæ, Art. 449.

(*b*) *Legislation Civile de le France*, tome iii. l. i. t. iii. Partie II p. 414.

(*c*) *Collier* v. *Rivaz*, 2 *Curteis' Ecclesiastical Reports*, p. 859.

(*d*) "Le changement de domicile s'opérera par le fait d'une habitation réelle dans un autre lieu, joint à l'intention d'y fixer son principal établissement." See Articles 103, 4, 5, of the Code Civile, l. i. t. iii. and Locré's Legislation de la France, tome iii. Code Civil, pp. 414—47, where the discussion is set forth at length.   Napoleon took an active part in it.   "Le Premier Consul dit, qu'au premier mouvement de de volonté n'est qu'un caprice, et qu'on ne peut regarder l'intention comme formée, que lorsqu'elle a été réfléchie, et qu'elle s'est maintenue pendant un temps suffisant pour qu'on puisse la croire solide ; qu'ainsi on peut l'éprouver par un délai."

" that a man's change of domicil shall be effected by the fact
" of an actual (real) habitation in another place, combined
" with the intention of fixing there his principal establish-
" ment."

CCCXVII. When this article was submitted to the French
Council of State for adoption, a discussion took place upon the
propriety of fixing a certain definite period, before the lapse of
which a new domicil could not be acquired ; but it was said to
be provided for, as far as was practicable, by the words "*habitation réelle;*" and subsequent articles enacted that the law
would consider as proof of intention, a declaration made to
the municipality of the Domicil abandoned, and to that of the
Domicil acquired ; that, where no such declaration exists, the
proof should depend upon circumstances.

Cambacérès thought the question one of great difficulty, but inclined
against fixing a definite period.

So the Sardinian Code enacts, " L'abitazione reale trasferita in un
altro luogo, con intenzione di fissare in questo il principale stabilimento,
produrrà cangiamento di domicilio."—*Codice Civile*, l. i. t. iii, Del Domicilio, s. 67.

CHAPTER XIV.

MISCELLANEOUS POINTS.

CCCXVIII. There are a few miscellaneous points which seem worthy of consideration before the subject of Domicil is brought to a conclusion.

CCCXIX. These miscellaneous points embrace the consideration of

1. Domicil in Factories.
2. Domicil under a Treaty.
3. Domicil in Mahometan Countries.
4. Domicil in a Country where it is regulated by Enactments of the Government.

I.—DOMICIL IN FACTORIES.

CCCXX. It seems to be a well established position of International Law, that the Original Domicil is not lost by residence in a factory belonging to the countrymen of that Domicil, but allowed to be established in a foreign country (a).

CCCXXI. Such factories are considered to be in the same category as the Ambassador's house, or the vessel of war in a foreign harbour, and to be protected by the same fiction of law, viz., that they are parts of the country which they represent.

CCCXXII. In the case of *The Danous*, however, a British-born subject, resident in the English factory at Lisbon, was

---

(a) 3 *Robinson's Admiralty Reports, The Indian Chief*, p. 28. See below.

allowed the benefit of a Portuguese character, so far as to render his trade with Holland, then at war with England, but not with Portugal, unimpeachable as a legal trade (b).

CCCXXIII. In Smyrna, and other places of the Turkish dominions, the control over and disposal of their property, its exemption from the municipal laws of the place, and many other privileges, by which the laws of their own countries are preserved to them, have been secured by treaty to European merchants (c).

II.—DOMICIL UNDER TREATIES.

CCCXXIV. So the Original Domicil may be preserved by the effect of a treaty.

CCCXXV. Mr. Maltass was a British subject, born at Smyrna in 1764. When about six years of age, he was sent to England for his education, but returned to Smyrna at the age of fourteen. He made another visit to England in the year 1826, and remained there about two years. After his return to Smyrna he served a clerkship in a mercantile house there, and finally established a house of trade there, under the name of J. and W. Maltass, and in which house he was one of the partners at the time of his death in 1842. He left two wills, one dated October 22nd, 1842, the other, 10th June 1834.

CCCXXVI. The former will was not executed according to the provisions of the recent statute in England (d); the latter, having been made previous to that law, would have been held a valid instrument in England.

(b) 4 *Robinson's Ad. Reports*, p. 255, n. 6.

(c) Upon the History of European Factories and Consulates, see an excellent and most laborious work, "*Manuel des Consuls*," in two volumes, by *Alex. de Miltitz*, published in London and Berlin, 1837.

(d) 1 *Victoria*, c. xxvi.

CCCXXVII. The will of 1842 was first propounded in the Prerogative Court of Canterbury, and it was contended that British merchants in the Ottoman dominions were governed by a peculiar code (*e*) of civil and criminal law, which was neither that of England nor of Turkey, but framed upon the custom of the Levant with respect to European subjects in the Ottoman dominions (*f*). That, on the one hand, they were exempted by treaty from the Turkish Law, which allowed no will to be made by a Turkish subject, but divided his property between his relations in certain fixed proportions ; and, on the other, they were not affected by the recent statute in England. That the will in question being a holograph in the testator's own handwriting, was a valid instrument, according to the *jus gentium*, and according to the Law in England before the passing of the late statute.

CCCXXVIII. The Judge, however, held, " that if the de-" ceased was domiciled in Turkey, he would make no will at " all ; if he was a British subject, he must make a will accord-" ing to the Testamentary Law in England," and the allegation propounding the paper was rejected (*g*).

CCCXXIX. At a subsequent period the former will of 1834 was propounded ; and it was pleaded, that by certain articles of peace between England and the Ottoman empire, made and concluded at the Dardanelles in the year 1809, the property of any Englishman, or other subject to that nation, or navigating under its flag, who should happen to die within the Turkish dominions, shall be given up to the persons to whom the deceased may have left them by will, or to the British Consul.

CCCXXX. The Judge held the admitted facts in the case to be these. That the deceased was born at Smyrna, of British parents ; that he passed his boyhood in England for the pur-

---

(*e*) See *Wheaton's International Law*, p. 156, s. xii.

Ruding v. *Smith*, 2 *Haggard's Consistory Reports*, p. 386.

(*f*) This was not pleaded, but contended in argument.

(*g*) 3 *Curteis' Ecclesiastical Reports*, 233—5.

pose of his education; that he went back to Smyrna, where his father was engaged in trade ; that he had been for many years occupied in commercial pursuits ; and was a member of a firm established at Smyrna, but which was dissolved a considerable period before his death ; that there was no positive evidence that the deceased had been engaged in trade during the latter years of his life ; that he had married at Smyrna, was constantly resident there, and died there, leaving a widow and children.   The Judge considered the deceased to be domiciled in England, but observed that his judgment did " not " affect the question of Domicil, if the deceased was in the " legal sense domiciled in Turkey ; and if the Law of Domicil " does prevail, the Law of Turkey, in conformity with the " treaty, says that in such case, the succession to personal " estate shall be governed by the British Law; if he was not " domiciled in Turkey, but in England, then the Law of Eng- " land prevails *proprio vigore :*" he, therefore, pronounced in favour of the will of 1834.

CCCXXXI. The case of *Moore* v. *Darell and Budd* (h) was cited, in argument, by the counsel contending for the Turkish Domicil of Mr. Maltass.   In that case, a treaty was *pleaded* between Spain and England, by one article of which it was agreed that the goods of the subjects of one King who shall die in the dominions of the other, should be preserved for the lawful heir, and certain other privileges granted ; yet, nevertheless, Mr. Moore had been held to be a · domiciled Spaniard.

CCCXXXII.   But in *Mr. Maltass's* case, the Judge observed, " As to the case of *Moore* v. *Budd*, I conceive that " my opinion does not militate against that case, or the con- " struction of the treaty with Spain.   This Court was of " opinion that the will there propounded was invalid by the " Law of Spain, and, though more doubtfully, by the Law of " England.   It held that the deceased was domiciled in Spain,

---

(h) 4 *Haggard's Ecclesiastical Reports*, p. 350.

" never mentioning the treaty. Indeed, not even in the argu-
" ment was the treaty alluded to ; no allegation on that point
" was given in ; no answers were taken. The King's Advo-
" cate of the day declined to argue the point, and not a
" single word appears in that case upon the construction of
" the treaty" (i).

III.—DOMICIL IN MAHOMEDAN COUNTRIES.

CCCXXXIII. It was contended in the case of *Mr. Maltass*,
that the European International Law of Domicil would not
be applicable to the residence of Christian subjects in Mahometan countries.

CCCXXXIV. The following passage was cited from Lord
Stowell's judgment in *The Indian Chief.* "It is to be remem-
" bered that, wherever a mere factory is founded in the Eastern
" parts of the world, European persons trading under the
" shelter and protection of their establishments, are conceived
" to take their national character from that association under
" which they live and carry on their commerce. It is a rule
" of the Law of Nations, applying particularly to those coun-
" tries, and is different from what prevails ordinarily in Europe,
" and the Western parts of the world, in which men take their
" present national character from the general character of
" the country in which they are resident ; and this distinc-
" tion arises from the nature and habits of the countries. In
" the Western parts of the world, alien merchants mix in
" the society of the natives ; access and intermixture are
" permitted ; and they become incorporated to the full
" extent. But in the East, from the oldest times, an immis-
" cible character has been kept up ; foreigners are not

(i) The learned Judge (*Dr. Lushington*) had been counsel in the
cause.

" admitted into the general body and mass of the society
" of the nation ; they continue strangers and sojourners
" as all their fathers were, '*Doris amara suam non inter-*
" *misceat undam,*' not acquiring any national character
" under the general sovereignty of the country, and not
" trading under any recognised authority of their own original
" country, they have been held to derive their present cha-
" racter from that of the association or factory, under whose
" protection they live (*j*)."

CCCXXXV. With respect to establishments in Turkey, it
was declared, in the case of *Mr. Fremeaux*, during the war of
1782, that a merchant carrying on trade at Smyrna, under the
protection of the Dutch Consul at Smyrna, was to be considered
as a Dutchman (*k*).

CCCXXXVI. The case of *The Angelique* was brought by
appeal from the Prize Court before the Lords of Appeal, in
the year 1801.   " It was the case of a ship and cargo taken
" on voyage from Madras to the Spanish settlement of Manilla,
" and claimed on behalf of Armenian merchants, resident in
" Madras.   It was asserted on the part of the claimant, that a
" trade of this nature had been carried on by this peculiar
" class of merchants, under the knowledge and permission of
" the government of Madras ; and that it had in former wars
" also been a trade specially privileged by the East India
" Company's governing officers in India, and by the Spanish
" government at Manilla.   It appeared, also, that there had
" been a subsequent permission of the Governor of Madras,
" Lord Clive, and of the Governor General, Lord Mornington,
" for the carrying on a similar trade, granted to the claimant
" in this case—and the application stated that it had been
" usual to trade in this manner, without consulting govern-
" ment ; but that the application was now made in conse-

(*j*) 3 *Robinson's Admiralty Reports*, pp. 28—9.
(*k*) *ib.*

" quence of the capture of *The Angelique*. It was said
" farther, that there was a legal opinion of the Attorney
" General of Madras, under a certificate from Lord Morn-
" ington and Lord Clive, and the persons constituting the
" council at Madras, stating their opinion of the legality of
" the trade, and representing the extreme hardship of the
" case to the Vice Admiralty Court of the Cape of Good
" Hope."

CCCXXXVII. After a very full hearing, the Court of Appeal
were of opinion that, by the general law, all foreigners resident within the British dominions incurred all the obligations
of British subjects—that there was nothing to distinguish this
particular class of merchants, in point of law, from the general
rule ; that, whatever doubt might be entertained, whether the
East India Company might not, in wars in India originating
with them, under the power of their charter, relax the operation of war so far as to license the trade of individuals with
such an enemy, they could unquestionably have no such
power in respect to a trade carried on with a general and
public enemy of the Crown of Great Britain ; that it would
on that account be useless to admit the claimants to prove, as
it was offered, the fact of a tacit, or acknowledged, permission
from the Governor in Council in India. The Court seemed
to admit that the trade in question might be a very lucrative
trade, in a public point of view, as it was the means of carrying the silver received by the Armenian merchants in Manilla
for the exports of the Company's manufactures, on to China,
where it was vested as a fund for the purchases made by the
East India Company, the private merchants taking in payment bills on the Company in India. They thought that, on
these grounds, there might, perhaps, be reasons for making
particular regulations in future for such a trade ; but, being of
opinion that, as it was in the power of the Crown alone to
declare war, so it rested with that authority only to dis-
pense with its operations, they affirmed the sentence of
the Vice-Admiralty Court, and condemned the ship and

cargo as the property of British subjects taken in trade with
the enemy.

" Being possessed with a conviction of the *bonâ fide* conduct
" of the parties, and considering that they had been led into a
" mistake, under a public misapprehension prevailing in India,
" even on the part of the governing persons there, the Court
" directed the expenses of the suit to be paid out of the pro-
" ceeds" (*l*).

CCCXXXVIII. The opinion of the Attorney-General at Madras, referred to in the above case, so far as it bears upon the
present question, appears to have been as follows :—" In the
" year 1688, a treaty or agreement was entered into between
" the Old Company and the Armenian nation ; by which the
" latter, in consideration of their changing the ancient course
" of their trade to Europe, (till then carried on to a great
" extent by the way of Turkey), and sending their goods on
" the Company's ships to London, by which the customs were
" expected to be greatly increased, were granted, within the
" Company's limits, all the privileges enjoyed by British sub-
" jects; and were licensed to trade to and from Europe in the
" Company's vessels on equal terms. For many years before
" this, they had had a free and uninterrupted trade to Manilla
" (from which the Company were excluded by the treaty of
" Madrid, in June, 1670), and this commerce was by the
" agreement allowed to be carried on directly from the Com-
" pany's settlements, in any ships which had their permission
" to trade. Having been before received as neutral subjects of
" Persia, or as temporary subjects of the Mogul empire, the
" residence of some Armenian families in the Company's fac-
" tories was not, from the nature of the factories, considered
" by the Spaniards as a circumstance of sufficient weight to
" exclude them from the port of Manilla, or a reason for
" depriving them of their ancient advantages of trade, by
" treating them as English subjects. It is now one hundred

(*l*) *The Angelique*, 3, *Robinson's Ad. Rep. App* 8.

" years since the treaty or agreement was entered into,
" and during that period the Armenians have continued
" to be received at Manilla, as they had at all times before,
" as subjects of Persia or the King of Delhi : and in
" the various wars we have had with Spain since 1688,
" though coming directly from our ports, they have uni-
" formly been considered and treated by the Spaniards as a
" neutral nation " (*m*)

CCCXXXIX. In the case of *Maltass*, the factory was not
pleaded ; but Lord Stowell's expressions were relied upon to
prove that no Christian would acquire a domicil by residence
in a Mahometan country ; that "the immiscible character" (*n*)
(to borrow his happy expression) would prevent the acquisition of a domicil.

CCCXL. The learned judge who decided the case of *Mr.*
" *Maltass* observed, " I give no opinion, therefore, whether
" a British subject can or cannot acquire a Turkish Domicil ;
" but this I must say, I think every presumption is against
" the intention of British Christian subjects voluntarily be-
" coming domiciled in the dominions of the Porte. As to
" British subjects, originally Mussulmen, as in the East
" Indies, or becoming Mussulmen, the same reasoning does
" not apply to them, as Lord Stowell has said, does apply in
" cases of a total and entire difference of religion, customs,
" and habits " (*o*).

(*m*) 3 *Robinson's Admiralty Reports*, App. B. pp.7—9, and note to p. 7.

(*n*) In another case *Lord Stowell* said, " It has been argued that it
would be extremely hard on persons residing in the kingdom of Mo-
rocco, if they should be held bound by all the rules of the Law of Nations, as it is practised amongst European States. On many accounts,
undoubtedly they are not to be strictly considered on the same footing
as European merchants ; they may on some points of the Law of
Nations be entitled to a very relaxed application of the principles
established by long usage between the States of Europe holding an
intimate and constant intercourse with each other," &c.—*The Hurtige
Hane*, 3 *Robinson's Admiralty Reports*, p. 325.

(*o*) *Maltass* v. *Maltass*, 1 *Robertson*, 81. *Eccles. Rep.* See some inter-

IV.—DOMICIL, WHERE IT IS REGULATED BY THE STATE.

CCCXLI. Where the Government of a country prescribes a certain form, whereby a stranger shall be admitted to establish his Domicil therein, and to enjoy all the civil rights of a native subject, can a stranger, without the permission of Government, acquire a domicil in such country?

CCCXLII. In France, where such a law exists, the question —so far as it relates to rendering the person so domiciled *justiciable* by a French tribunal—has been judicially decided in the affirmative. On the 25th of March, 1819, B., banker of Amsterdam, but residing at Paris, was condemned to pay E., banker of Paris, 251,782 francs, by the Tribunal of Commerce at Paris. B. refused obedience to the order, and was imprisoned. He then demanded to be set free, chiefly because, being a stranger, he could not have a domicil in France without the royal authority, and the proceedings having treated him as domiciled, were therefore null. The case was decided against him in the Civil Tribunal of the Seine, in the "Cour Royal" of Paris, and in the "Cour de Cassation," (the last Court of Appeal), on the ground that a stranger could have a *de facto* domicil and residence, although according to the 13th article of the Code Civil, he could not have a domicil *de jure* without the authority of Government (*p*), and could not enjoy the privileges of a domiciled subject.

---

locutory remarks of the present Judge of the Prerogative Court, as to domicil in the settlement at Hudson's Bay. *Notes of Cases,* vol. iv. pp. 561—3. *In the goods of Sutherland, deceased.*

(*p*) *Merlin, Répertoire de Jurisprudence,* t. viii. p 359, *Domicile* IV. The case cited is in *M. Merlin's Questions de Droit,* t. v. p. 431, *Domicile* V. *Vide post* as to *Merlin's* supposed change of opinion as shown in edit. of 1827, *Rep.* t. v. p. 16 *Domicile,* s. 13. cf. with t. vi. p. 303 Etranger X.—with last edit. 1828 of *Rep.* t. xviii. p. 540 *v. Testament.*

CCCXLIII. This case only established that a person so domiciled was *justiciable* by the French tribunal; but the reasoning of it seems equally valid to prove that a *principal* domicil may be *de facto* acquired by a person who was not himself entitled to the privileges of a domiciled subject. Nevertheless, as will presently be seen, this proposition is very far from being incorporated into the administration of French Law : it would perhaps rather seem that the contrary proposition has obtained the sanction of the highest French authorities.

CCCXLIV. The case of *Collier* v. *Rivaz* appears to support this conclusion. In that case, the testator (Mr. Ryan), an English-born subject, died *de facto* domiciled in Belgium, leaving a will executed before 1830, that is, at a time when the Code Napoléon was in force in Belgium and Holland, then one kingdom; the will was valid according to the English, but not according to the Belgian Law ; but the testator had not obtained the proper authority requisite for the establishment of such a domicil as would entitle him to civil rights in the kingdom of the Netherlands. Two advocates, one practising in Holland, and one in Belgium, deposed to the effect that, "the successions " of persons—who, however long they might have been " resident, not having obtained the royal authority to reside " there, being considered as mere foreigners—would be go- " verned by the laws of their own country, and would be " upheld by the Courts of Belgium, if those Courts were " called on to decide." The Court of Probate in England, finding, upon the evidence of these two advocates, that the foreign country in which the testator was domiciled would uphold his testamentary disposition, decreed probate of the same (*q*).

CCCXLV. The following remarks, however, of the Judge

(*q*) *Collier* v. *Rivaz*, 2 *Curteis' Ecclesiastical Reports*, p. 885.

who decided the foregoing case, are worthy of attention.
" Now (*r*) three witnesses have been examined with respect to
" the Law of Belgium, as applying as well to the acquiring of
" a Domicil in Belgium as to the law with respect to the execu-
" tion of testamentary instruments.

" With respect to Domicil acquired, it is quite clear, accord-
" ing to the evidence of these persons, that no Domicil, ac-
" cording to the Law of Belgium, can be acquired, unless the
" authority of the ruling powers is obtained to authorize the
" persons who apply for that authority to continue in that
" country ; that, unless that authority is obtained, he is liable
" to be removed at any time ; that, having obtained that
" authority, he then becomes to all intents and purposes a
" subject of Belgium, and has a right to remain there and
" enjoy the privileges of a natural born subject. But it may
" be a different question, whether a person who has not ob-
" tained that authority—a mere resident there—is to be con-
" sidered as a foreigner, simply having a residence and not a
" Domicil. I think it is very doubtful whether the Dutch and
" Belgian lawyers understand the same thing, from the evi-
" dence given with respect to Domicil—whether they do not
" consider that a person to become domiciled, must have deni-
" zation, that which is equivalent to our naturalization, and
" they do not mean simply Domicil for the purpose of su cces-
" sion or anything of that description, but they consider that a
" person in order to become domiciled, must place himself by
" the authority of the government in the same situation as a
" Belgian subject, and have the rights and privileges of that
" country.   But I think it is not necessary to inquire
" into this, because I think we have the conclusive evidence
" of two witnesses as to that which is necessary to give
" validity to the testamentary dispositions of persons who
" reside there, but have not acquired all the rights of Belgian
" subjects."

(*r*) *Ibid.* pp. 859—60.

CCCXLVI. The authority of this decision in *Maltass* v. *Maltass*, has been shaken by the judgment of the Privy Council in *Bremer* v. *Freeman*: and yet, this last decision will be found, on examination, to have done little or nothing towards the adjustment of this vexed and difficult question.

In *Bremer* v. *Freeman*, the testatrix, an English lady domiciled, *de facto*, at Paris, made her testament in the English form, disposing of property which was, with an inconsiderable exception, entirely English or Anglo-Indian.

The testament was ultimately pronounced to be invalid as far as it related to personalty, while it was admitted to be valid in its relation to freehold property in India. The Prerogative Court of Canterbury had decided that the testament was a valid disposition of personalty. This sentence was reversed by the Judicial Committee of the Privy Council.

The principal arguments in favour of the testament were, that the testatrix was not domiciled in France according to the French Code, and, therefore, was not domiciled, *de jure*, there at all: that the *testamenti factio* was a matter *juris positivi* or *civilis*, and not *juris gentium* — that Pothier (s) had expressly declared so: that the French Code did not admit the foreigner domiciled without *autorisation* to *civil* French rights. That the Law of England adopted in these cases the Law of France, and that, according to the French Law, the English Law governed the testament.

The principal argument against the validity of the testa-

(s) "Il est vrai que ces personnes ne sont pas capables du droit civil, qui n'a été établi que pour les citoyens, tel que le droit des testaments, des successions, du retrait lignagers ; mais elles sont capables de ce qui appartient au droit des gens, telles que sonts toutes les conventions."— *Traité de la Communanté.*

ment was, that by Domicil in these cases was meant Domicil *de facto*, and according to the general *jus gentium* or *lato sensu*, and not *de jure* or according to the positive provisions of a particular code upon the subject. It was conceded that the Law of England did adopt the Law of France (*t*); but it was contended that this law pronounced the testament invalid because it was executed by a person domiciled, *de facto*, in France, and not according to the forms prescribed by the French Law.

French advocates and jurists of great eminence were ex·amined by both parties to the suit, for the purpose of proving the French Law to be as respectively alleged by them.

A great number of decisions (*u*) also were cited by both parties for the same purpose (*x*). It is a maxim of English Law that foreign Law must be proved as a *fact* in each case, though the practice has varied as to how far it is competent to the judge to form his own opinion from the perusal of writings of authority, whether Codes of Law, or treatises on jurisprudence (*y*).

(*t*) It does not seem certain whether in the simple case of a *de facto* domicil of an Englishman in a foreign State, the English Court would ascribe any weight to the opinion of foreign *experts* as to what con-stituted a *de facto* domicil according to the law of the foreign State. The practice on this case has not been uniform.

(*u*) It was contended by the party setting up the validity of the tes-tament that an investigation of these decisions would show that they were, in fact, all opposed to the French Domicil : there were exceptions ; but these ranged themselves generally under two heads ;—1. Where *French interests* were concerned—a strange, but I fear, undoubted exception ; 2. Where both parties had *consented* to the fact of the Domicil, and the dispute had arisen upon some collateral or emergent matter.

(*x*) The authorities of both kinds will be found collected together in the report of the case in the Prerogative Court, *Deane's Reports*, 198, 202, and of the case before the Privy Council, 10 *Moore's P. C. Rep.* 312—357.

(*y*) *Vide post*, where the *Form and Manner of Procedure* are dis-cussed.

The result of the foreign evidence taken in this case was certainly embarrassing. The opinions of the French advocates were directly at variance with each other. The judicial precedents were equally conflicting.

And—what worse confounded the confusion to the English judges—some of the French lawyers who deposed *against* the validity of the testament, founded their opinion entirely on the maxim *locus regit actum*, and not upon the Domicil being French.

The Judicial Committee of the Privy Council considered that they were sitting as a French Court, to decide upon a question of French Law. Their Lordships said :—

" This Domicil being established in evidence, the burden is " thrown on the respondent to prove that the will, in the " English form, is sanctioned by the Municipal Law of France. " He must show, upon the balance of the conflicting evidence " in the cause, that the wills of persons, so domiciled, in that " form, are allowed by that Law. This is the important ques- " tion, and the only one of any difficulty in the case. Much " evidence was produced of the Law of France on both sides ; " the *vivâ voce* testimony of experts in the science and prac- " tice of the law, vouching and referring to the Code Napoleon " decrees, and to known treatises. Some of these last have " been since brought forward and referred to without objec- " tion on either side ; and their lordship's have to decide on " the whole of this (for the most part) very unsatisfactory, " confused, and conflicting evidence, whether they are con- " vinced that this will, executed in France, in the English " form, is valid.

" On the part of the Respondent, five persons, practising in " the French Courts, stating themselves to be experienced in " the Law of France, were examined : on the part of the " Appellant, three. It is to be lamented that, from the very " nature of the case, we cannot satisfy ourselves by the per- " sonal examinations of these witnesses as to the weight due " to each of them ; and a proper sense of professional delicacy " precludes them from giving evidence as to the merits of each

" other. We are compelled, therefore, to decide the disputed
" question with inadequate means of judging of their profes-
" sional eminence, their skill, and knowledge. It is to be
" remarked, speaking with all respect to those gentlemen,
" that the rule of International Law which all English lawyers
" consider as now firmly established, namely, that the form
" and solemnities of the testament must be governed by the
" law of the Domicil of the deceased, does not appear to be
" recognised, or at least borne in mind, by any of them. Nay,
" in *Quartin's* case, both the Cour Royale and the Cour de
" Cassation, expressly decided that the will must be in the
" form and with the solemnities of the place where it is made
" on the principle that *locus regit actum* (z) : an error
" which is ably exposed, in the opinion of M. Target, in the
" *Duchess of Kingston's* case (Coll. Jur. p. 323). The
" three witnesses called for the Appellant, Messrs. Frignet,
" Senaed, and Paillet, all maintain the same doctrine. If this
" position were really true, the case of the Appellant would
" prevail ; but the other witnesses do not maintain the same
" doctrine. Of the five experts examined for the Respondent,
" three, Messrs. Blanchet, Hebert, and de Vatismesnil, all think
" that the will, either in the form required by the Law of the
" Domicil of Origin, or the place where the party dwells, is
" valid ; a position which, by English lawyers, is certainly
" now considered to be exploded since the case of *Stanley* v.
" *Bernes* " (y).

(z) The extent to which this principle prevails on the Continent,
could scarcely have been present to their Lordship's minds." "Actui
lex formam dat" (says *Hertius*) "quando negotium aliquod ad usum
civitatis certis circumscribit solemnitatibus puta cum de loco de tempore
de modo actûs statuit, *e.g* ut *testamenta his aut illis solemnitatibus
fiant*," &c."—*De Coll. Leg.* s. 4, p. 7. " Or che dire " (says *Rocco*) "se lo
straniero intenda fare nel regno alcun contratto con altri pur forestiero
ovvero con qualuno de' nazionali nostri, *e voglia delle sostanze sue
disporre* per via di *testamento* ? . . . . Il principio generale cui fa
uopo trarre dietro è, doversi seguitare le formalità del luogo ove l' atto
si celebra, *locus regit actum*."

(a) *Bremer* v. *Freeman*, 10 *Moore, P. C. Rep.* p. 361.

CCCXLVII. It is manifest that a judgment pronounced upon "very unsatisfactory, confused, and conflicting evidence," can constitute no precedent for any other case, and that the whole question still remains open for discussion.

An unsuccessful attempt was made to oppose the practical execution of the sentence by tendering proof that it was not what it purported to be—a correct exposition of the *French Law*. For the purpose of obtaining this proof, the President of the Civil Tribunal of the Seine was requested by the defeated party to name the French advocates most competent to form an opinion as to whether the sentence of the English Privy Council did or did not correctly expound the French Law. He named ten gentlemen. The admitted facts of the case were laid before them, and they unanimously declared that the will was valid, and not invalid, according to the French Law.

This evidence, however, which was taken *ex parte*, and after the sentence had been pronounced, was not permitted to be produced before the Privy Council ; but, nevertheless, it is not improperly mentioned in this place : (*b*) though, of course, it is open to the observation that the other side might possibly have produced an equal amount of testimony in support of the sentence.

CCCXLVIII. The foreign jurist will, no doubt, be surprised to learn that the maxim *locus regit actum*, which he has always considered as incontrovertible, is erroneous when applied to the form of testaments, though correct when applied to the form of contracts. The truth is, that the English lawyers and judges early committed themselves to the opposite maxim ; and, true to the English rule of adhering to what has been once determined, have never been able to escape from the fetters which they had, with less knowledge than they now possess of Foreign and Roman Law, imposed upon themselves. On the other hand, the English lawyers and judges

---

(*b*) See note at the end of this chapter.

must have learnt, with at least equal amazement, the little value which French tribunals, even of the last resort, attached to judicial precedent.   A French lawyer deposed, as a witness, to the comparatively insignificant effect of mere judicial precedents upon subsequent cases, and on being asked by the perplexed English lawyer " what are our judicial decisions then good for ? " received the concise and remarkable answer, " they " are good for those who get them." Never were the opposite characteristics of the legal mind of the two countries more clearly shewn, and perhaps, it might be added, the defects of both (c) :—the obstacle to the melioration of law presented by the inflexible adherence to a judicial precedent on the one hand ; and on the other, the great uncertainty of law arising from the disregard of judicial ⁓precedent, and the habit of applying an independent consideration of law, as well as fact, to every case which is brought into a court of justice.

CCCXLIX. It was, perhaps, rather taken for granted in *Bremer* v. *Freeman*, that an individual who *has* complied with the forms prescribed by the Law of a foreign State for the attainment of Domicil, becomes, unquestionably, domiciled in that State. But Rocco, (d) no mean authority, says that this is not necessarily true : that an individual may have complied with this prescribed form, and have enjoyed all civil privileges appertaining thereto, and yet have retained his ancient Domicil : the *animus revertendi* to which may never have deserted him.

(c) *Vide post*, " Form and Manner of Procedure."

(d) "E può in fine accadere che il forestiero come che ammesso a stabilir vel regno il domicilio non abbia per tanto inteso di abbandonare l'antico ; abbia mai sempre serbato la intenzione di far ritorno nella sua patria," 148.

"A dir briève egli userà nel regno di tutti que diritti i quali non tengono allo stato della persona e fra quelli et che il riguardano, il godimento o la privazione ne verra regolata secondo le norme del *suo vero* domicilio," 155.

The foreign jurist has always ascribed more weight than the English jurist to *intention*, as the principal ingredient of Domicil ; and the instance just cited, affords, perhaps, as strong an illustration as could be furnished, of the preponderating influence of this element in continental jurisprudence.

CCCL. We cannot close these observations on the operation of the French Code upon the general Law of Domicil, without adverting to a remarkable passage in the *last* edition, (1828), of *Merlin's Répertoire de Jurisprudence.*

After observing that the question no longer presented itself under the Civil Code, at least upon the wills of Frenchmen, he says :—

" But the question remains open, (*entière*), in respect to " holograph wills made in France, by foreigners domiciled in " countries where the laws do not admit that mode of " making a will, *and by which they dispose of property* " *situate in those countries :* ought the tribunals of those " countries to declare them valid according to French Law, or " to annul them according to the Domiciliary Laws of the " testator ?"

Here, the question on Merlin's mind was, not whether the foreign court would recognize as valid the will of a foreigner made according to the forms of his Personal Statute, which follows him wherever he goes, but whether the foreign Court would recognize as valid the will of a foreigner made in the holograph form, where his own Laws do not admit it.

CCCLI. Another question of difficulty might arise from the regulation of the Law of Domicil by the State. Suppose that the Government of a country, Russia for instance, forbade its subjects, to establish a Domicil out of their native land, and a subject nevertheless *de facto* established a Domicil in a foreign country, and died there, what law would the country in which he died apply to the distribution of his personal property—that of the country of his Domicil *de jure*, or of his Domicil *de facto ?* It should seem the Law of the Domicil *de facto* (*e*), but the case would be open to some argument on the other side (*f*).

(*e*) *Vide ante*, p. 38, and *note*, as to the peculiarity of the custom of London prevailing over the Law of the Domicil.

(*f*) According to the Sardinian Code, no domicil in a foreign country, however long and permanently established, will, *of itself*, avail to prove that the person establishing it had abandoned the intention of returning to his native country, and so incurred the forfeiture of his civil rights.—*Codice Civile*, c. ii. Della privazione dei diritti civili, s. 34.

NOTES ON THE FOREGOING CHAPTER.

I.

The cases on Domicil have of late years been very numerous, both in the English, Irish, and Scotch Reports, and in those of the N. A. United States; but in many of them no new principle or new application of old principle is contained.

The reader will find a great collection of American cases in *Curtis' United States Digest*, vol. ii. p. 102, and *Putman's U. S. Digest*, vol. v. p. 153 ; and may also refer to the following English cases not expressly referred to in the preceding pages :—

Attorney-General v. *Napier*, 6 *Exchequer Reports*, 217.

Laneuville v. *Anderson*, 17 *Jurist*, 511, 2 *Spinks' Rep.* 53, 9 *Moore's P. C. Rep.* 325.

In re Wright's Trust, 25 *Law Journal* (*Chancery*).

Cockerell v. *C.*, 2 *Jurist*, N.S. 621, 727.

Hoskins v. *Matthews*, *ib.* 216.

Attorney-General v. *Fitzgerald*, 3 *Drew's Reports*, 610.

Forbes v. *Forbes*, 1 *Kay*, 341.

M'Cormick v. *Garnett*, 4 *De Gex. M. and G.'s Rep.* 278.

Re Daly's Settlement, 22 *Jurist*, 525 (*d.* 856).

Brown v. *Smith*, 15 *Beavan's Rep.* 448.

Robins v. *Paxton and Dolphin*, 30 *Law Times*, 310.

Erskine v. *Wylie*, 31 *Law Times*, 171.

Wicker v. *Hume*, 4 *Jurist*, N.S. 933.

Re Dons's Estate, before V. C. Kindersley (1858).

Re Muir, deceased (1859).

Lord v. *Colin* (1859).

Re Bernard Mette, deceased (1859).

Campbell v. *Beaufoy* (1859).

II.

In *Bremer* v. *Freeman*, the following authorities on Foreign and French Law were cited :—

WRITERS.

Niciäs Gaillard in Dalloz, Jurisprudence Generale (1851), Pt. I. p. 38.

Coin de Lisle, Comment. Analyt. du Code Civil, p. 35.

Troplong, le Code Expliqué, t. xviii. p. 378.

Pardessus, Cours de Droit Commercial, p. 773.

Duranton, Cours de Droit François, t. i. pp. 95—291.

Demolombe, Cours de Code Civil, l. i. t. i. c. iii. pp. 332—335.

Demangeat, Condition Civile des Etrangers, p. 369.

Zachariæ, Cours de Droit Civil François, t. i. pp. 278—280.

Merlin, Rep. de Jurisprudence Etranger, s. 10, 2 *Domicil*.

JUDICIAL DECISIONS.

Lynch's case, Sirey's Reports (1851).

Thornton v. *Curling, Dalloz Reports* (1827).

Baron deMecklembourg's case { *Gazette des Tribunaux* (1856)..
{ *Le Droit* (1856).

D'Abaunza's case, Sirey (1842).

Princess Poniatowsky v. *Le Normand* (1811), *Dalloz Recueil Alpha-bétique*, t. iii. p. 348.

Andre v. *Andre* (1844), *Recueil Périodique de Dalloz* 2. 1851.

Verity v. *Mackenzie, Dalloz Rep.* (1847).

Breul's case, Gazette des Trib. (1852).

———— *Appeal, ib.* (1853).

Lloyd v. *Lloyd, Sirey* (1849).

Onslow v. *Onslow, Dalloz* (1836).

De Veine v. *Routledge, Sirey* (1852).

Browning v. *De Narye or Veyne, Dalloz* (1853).

Olivarez', case, Le Droit (1854).

Laneuville and Anderson's ease, Gaz. des Trib. (1855).

Church v. *Cargill, Dalloz Rec. Alphabet.* vi. p. 474 (1811).

Houseal v. *Colon, Dalloz Rec. Period.* (1838), 2—137.

Appleyard v. *Bachelor, ib.* (1847), 2—170.

The Husband C. or Czarnecki's case, ib. (1848), 2—149.

Appeal Court of Cassation, ib. (1849), 1—256.

Collett's case, Gaz. des Trib. (1855).

Fraix's case, Le Droit (1856).

Scottowe's case, Gaz. des Trib. (1856).

Upon these cases the following notes were prepared on behalf of the party supporting the will :—

LYNCH *v.* LYNCH.—This was the only case decided by the French Courts, in which, when the advocates in the case of *Bremer* v. *Freeman and Bremer* were examined, the question of the law regulating the succession of a foreigner who had died in France had been brought forward distinctly. The decree in that case was made by the Imperial Court of Paris on the 13th of March, 1850, relating to the succession of Francis Lynch, and the Court refused to entertain the settlement of the succession of the deceased, on the ground that he had not been naturalized a Frenchman; that he had not even obtained from the king the right to establish his Domicil in France; and the Court declared that consequently he died an Englishman, and that his fortune being wholly personalty must be governed by the Law of England; he leaving no French heirs.

THORNTON *v.* CURLING.—The converse of the decision in *Francis Lynch's* case had been decided by the Court of Cassation (the highest Court of Appeal) in the case of *Thornton* v. *Curling* in 1826. The Court held that the succession of Thornton, an Englishman, and the validity of his will were subject to the Law of France, on the ground that he had obtained the authorization of the Government to establish his Domicil there.

BARON F. DE MECKLENBOURG'S CASE.—After the hearing of the cause of *Bremer* v. *Freeman and Bremer*, but before the decree was pronounced, the case of the *Baron Frederick de Mecklenbourg*, a German, which is mentioned in the Judgment, was decided by the French Courts. In that case the Tribunal of the Seine found that it resulted, from all the facts and documents produced, that he had his principal and indeed sole establishment in Paris; and held that he had died domiciled at Paris, and that his succession opened there, though he had not been authorised to establish his Domicil in France.

The decision was appealed from to the Cour Impériale de Paris, on the ground that the deceased had not been naturalized a Frenchman, nor had obtained the authorization of the Government to establish his Domicil in France under the 13th Article of the *Code*, and the *Court reversed the decision.*

CARLIER D'ABAUNZA'S CASE.—Under a Law of the 17th of April, 1832, Art. 14. (see *M. Coin de Lisle's Exhibit 6, Joint Appendix*, p. 155,) a foreigner not domiciled in France is liable to arrest for debt. M. Carlier D'Abaunza was arrested by his creditor under that law, and the Civil Tribunal of the Seine refused to set aside his arrest, and held that the prolonged residence of a foreigner, and even his marriage in France, could not enable him to obtain the rights resulting from the establishment of the Domicil, which can only take place in the terms provided by the Article 13 of the *Civil Code*, *i.e.* with royal authorization. On appeal, the Imperial Court of Paris confirmed the decision, holding that the Appellant had not proved that he was domiciled in France.

THE PRINCESS PONIATOWSKI'S CASE.—In this case, which was one of arrest, the arrest was upheld by the Imperial Court of Paris, by decree of the 16th of August, 1811, on the ground that the Princess was a foreigner, and did not prove a domicil in France, established conformably to the Article 13 of the *Civil Code*.

ANDRE *v.* ANDRE.—In this case, in which the Court of Douai, by decree of the 12th of July, 1844, held that the French tribunals were not competent to take cognisance of purely civil obligations contracted between foreigners when the defendant declines their jurisdiction, the Court observed as follows, "Whereas a residence more or less prolonged in France cannot constitute a Legal Domicil, since, according to the terms of the Article 13 of the *Civil Code*, a foreigner cannot acquire such a domicile in France, unless in virtue of an Ordinance of the King."

VERITY *v.* MACKENZIE.—This was a decree of the Court of Cassation, by which, notwithstanding the deceased (whose succession was in question) had resided for forty years in France, the Court would not allow itself to be competent to adjudicate, by reason of the interests on all sides being of foreigners only. (See the *Evidence of M. Blanchet, Joint Appendix of Case before P. Council*, p. 139.)

BREUL'S CASE.—Breul was a Hanoverian. He resided for more than thirty years in Paris, and *married there a Frenchwoman*, in 1847. He died at Paris, in 1851, having made his will, in which he asked himself whether, by the fact of his having married without a settlement, there was a community of goods between him and his wife conformably to the French Law. He disposed of his property in either alternative. On the question being brought before the Civil Tribunal of the Seine, the heirs of the deceased objected to the competency of the Tribunal. The Tribunal held that the 13th Article of the *Civil Code* had not for its object to determine the conditions which a foreigner must fulfil in order to acquire a domicil in France; and on the ground of the *de facto* Domicil, and of the * interests of two Frenchwomen being involved, the Court overruled the objection of incompetency, and retained the cause for decision.

In the Appeal to the Imperial Court of Paris, the question was, whether there was community of goods between the husband and wife under the Articles 1393 and 1400 of the *Code?*

The Court held that Breul being a foreigner did not prevent the application of those Articles. That foreigners, capable of stipulating in all contracts, *tenant du droit des gens*, as that in question, may, in marrying in France, accept tacitly the rule of community. That undoubtedly the *de facto* Domicil ought to have an importance distinguishing it from a simple residence, but that it was not necessary that it should have been authorized by the Government in the terms of the Article 13 of the *Code*, since the object of that authorization is to confer on the foreigner all the civil rights belonging to natives; and those rights are not necessary for the regulation of matrimonial conventions, which are purely of the *droit des gens*.

---

* By Article 14 of the *Civil Code*, Frenchmen are enabled to cite before the French Courts foreigners, even those not in France; and it is held on this Article, that the French heir or creditor of a foreign succession can bring before the French Courts the questions that interest him.

The Court of Appeal thus adopted the distinction between civil rights (which would include the right of making a will declared by Article 25 of the *Code Napoléon* to be a civil right) and matrimonial contracts, purely of the *jus gentium*.

LLOYD's CASE.—This is also one of tacit convention for community of goods between husband and wife.

The Imperial Court of Paris held that a domicil, as established under Article 13 of the *Code*, is not required for the purpose of matrimonial agreements, which belong purely to the *jus gentium*. And as to the legitimation by Lloyd of his natural children, the Court, in admitting an unauthorised domicil as a ground for presuming the intention of the parties to have been to submit to the French Law of community of goods ; does not mean that such a domicil can give him the French personal status. Accordingly it validates the legitimation of the natural children, notwithstanding the English Law, which the Court considers was still the status of Lloyd, but on the ground that he had entered into an engagement with the mother to do so, and that this woman, being a Frenchwoman, was authorized by her status to legitimize her children, and that the latter cannot be legitimate as regards the mother, and illegitimate as regards the father.

The Court orders the distribution of the succession among the children. Its reasons for so doing are omitted in the Report; but as the Court declares that there was a tacit agreement that the French Law and all its effects should be carried out with respect to the legitimation of the children and its effects under the French Law, it considers it to have been agreed that they should have the rights which the French Law reserves to children in the succession of their parent, and not be thrown back on the English Law and treated as bastards, and thus lose the object of the legitimation.

ONSLOW's CASE.—Onslow was an Englishman by birth, who had become naturalized in France within the terms of a Law of the 30th of April, 1790. The question was, whether he had acquired a legal Domicil in France, notwithstanding subsequent laws requiring other conditions ? The Court of Riom held that he was naturalised ; that moreover he had acquired a domicil in France before the *Code*, of which he could not be deprived by any conditions under the *Code*. It then expresses an opinion, not called for by the case, that even under the *Code* a domicil can be acquired without any authorization ; and " on these grounds" the Court gave judgment.

The Court of Cassation on Appeal, held that Onslow had been naturalized a Frenchman under the Law of 1790, and that the Court of Riom had made a just application of that law—the violation of which was the sole ground of appeal.

In this case Onslow had married a Frenchwoman in 1783, and had resided continuously in France up to his death in 1829. All his property was in France, and all his children, *i. e.* all the parties in the cause, were French.

ROUTLEDGE *v.* DE VEINE or CONNOLLY'S CASE.—A holograph will, made by Connolly, an Englishman settled in France, of his real and personal property in that country, in favour of his adulterine children, was set aside by the Court of Paris at the suit of Madame de Veine, *an illegitimate daughter*, who had become French by her marriage with a Frenchman, on the ground that it did not in all respects comply with the provisions of the French Code.

The Court finds that the succession being both real and personal, Madame de Veine had on that ground an interest in disputing the will —that the succession had been opened in France—Connolly having resided there upwards of twenty years, and having placed there his fortune and his establishment ; but these facts are given as a ground of the succession, which was real as well as personal, opening in France, *i. e.* for giving competence to the French Courts, not for its being governed by the French Law. The reasons given by the Court for subjecting the personal property to the French Law is, that the personal property being in France, and Madame de Veine being French, it would be a violation of the principle of national sovereignty, and of the protection due by the Law to natives, if in such a state of things the property, personal as well as real, was not governed by the French Law.

The Court declares, moreover, that this lady is entitled, as a Frenchwoman, to the benefit of Art. 2 of the Law of 1819.

Under the *Civil Code*, and until that Law, a foreigner could only inherit in France in case the French were admitted by treaty to the same right in his country.

The Law of 1819 did away with that restriction. By Art. 1, foreigners are to inherit in the same manner as the French ; and by Art. 2, in case of the heirs of a succession being both Frenchmen and foreigners, the former may take out of the property in France the value of the share from which they are excluded in the property in foreign countries on any ground whatever by virtue of the Local Law.

This Law is construed to give a French person the right of requiring the application of the French Law to the succession, even personal, of any foreigner, whether domiciled or not in France. Hence the illegitimate daughter of Connolly having become French by her marriage, was entitled to have her father's succession treated as a French succession. The will was set aside as not being in the form required by the Law of France, where it was made, and the succession was held to be governed by the French Law.

On an Appeal to the Court of Cassation, the Court declared (see p. 57 of reported cases) that if all that relates to the status of the Testator, to the extent and limit of his rights and his capacity, is regulated by the personal statute which follows the person, it is otherwise in respect of the solemnity of the document, and of the exterior form, which are regulated by the Law of the country where the Testator disposes ; and that thus the holograph will made by a foreigner in France, and of which execution is demanded before the French Tribunals, can only be declared valid, provided it unites all the conditions of form required by French Legislation.

The Court dismissed the appeal, on the ground of no law having been violated by the Court of Paris in pronouncing for the nullity of the will, as not made in the holograph form determined by the French Law.

OLIVAREZ' CASE.—His personal estate in France was held subject to the French law, and the Court of Bordeaux expresses an opinion that a foreigner can acquire a Domicil of Succession without authorization.

Olivarez, a Dane, came to France whilst yet a minor, with his mother, who was his guardian, his father being dead : his mother married a Frenchman and became French. This gave the minor a complete French Domicil, the minor having the same Domicil as his guardian. He died in France soon after his majority.

Two of his heirs were French, his mother and sister both French by their marriages.

Madame Gomez, the sister of the deceased, as French, was entitled to the application of the French Law under the Law of 1819, and the presence of French interests rendered it impossible to follow the usual rules of Domicil, as will appear from the case of succession of the sister of Oliverez, Madame de Vivanco, decided by the same Court the same day.

This lady had married a Spaniard, established at Bilbao, and died a minor, having by will left her property to her mother ; the Spanish Law, which the Court says was her personal statute, and the treaties between Spain and France, permitting her to make such a will. Madame de Vivanco only left in France some personal property, her share in her brother's estate. The Court found that she was domiciled at Bilbao, and referred the settlement of her succession to the Courts of that place.

LANEUVILLE v. ANDERSON.—Madame Laneuville, a Frenchwoman, a legatee under the holograph will of Mr. Wm. Anderson, an Englishman, cited the Testator's nephew before the Tribunal of Paris, in order to obtain an order for putting her in possession of the goods and valuables of the Testator situate in England and Ireland. She also made M. Guichard, a legatee under a subsequent will, and who had taken up his residence at Dublin, a party to the proceeding.

The nephew, M. Guichard, objected to the competency of the Court; but the Court overruled the objection, and the Court of Paris, on Appeal, upheld the decision. The Court, in giving its reasons, observed that the Art. 14 of the *Code Napoléon* is a direct consequence of the principle of Sovereignty; that the Art. 59 of the *Code of Civil Procedure*, applicable exclusively to successions opened in France, and regulated by French Law, does not derogate from the rule laid down for protecting the Frenchman in his claims against the foreigner.

CHURCH *v.* CARGILL.—The defendant, an Englishman, resident in France, being cited before the French Court, objected to its competency as not being the Court of his Domicil. The Court of Cassation held the citation valid, distinguishing between a domicil conferring political or civil rights, which can only be obtained by conforming to Article 13, and the *de facto* Domicil of every foreigner who is residing in France, which is sufficient for a citation.

Here the Court of Cassation allows that a Domicil *de fait*, which it assimilates to a mere residence, is enough for giving jurisdiction to the Courts. The reason being the Article 5 *C. Procéd. Civil*, cited by Coin de Lisle :—" In personal matters the defendant shall be summoned to appear before the Tribunal of his Domicil, and if he has no Domicil then before that of *his residence.*

HOUSEAL *v.* COLON. This was a case of arrest. The Imperial Court of Paris, in giving judgment, says, " Considering that by Article 14 of the Law of 1832, foreigners not domiciled in France are subjected to arrest for debt, and that a foreigner can only be considered as having a Legal Domicil on proving that he has the authorization of the Government for establishing that Domicil."

APPLEYARD *v.* BACHELOR.—In this case the Court of Rennes treated the Domicil of a foreigner in France as a civil right to which he can only be admitted in conformity with Article 13.

CZARNECKI'S CASE.—Czarnecki was a Polish refugee, banished for life from his own country, in which his condition was that of a person civilly dead. He had established himself as a Printer at Saintes, in France, and married a person of that place. His wife applied to the Tribunal of Saintes for the separation. The Tribunal pronounced the separation. On Appeal by the husband, the Imperial Court of Poitiers reversed the judgment—considering (says the Court) that the wife of Czarnecki does not show that her husband has been authorized to establish his Domicil in France—that the Frenchwoman who marries a foreigner follows the condition of her husband and becomes a foreigner.

In support of the appeal to the Supreme Court from this decision, it was said that Czarnecki, being civilly dead in Poland, the Courts of that country would not recognise, as having any effect in Poland, the engagement he entered into elsewhere, that he had thus no country, and that his only judges were those of Saintes.

The Court of Cassation dismissed the Appeal. It held that the Article 59 *C. Procéd* relative to citations, does not alter the incompetency of the French Courts with respect to proceedings affecting the status of persons.

COLLETT's CASE.—The Court of Cassation decided that the French Tribunals are competent to make a decree on application for a separation of a husband and wife, foreigners, legally authorized to establish their Domicil in France.

FRAIX's CASE.—The language of the Imperial Court of Paris can leave no doubt of its opinion that no establishment in France, however long, can constitute a domicil. Fraix was a Savoyard, who had been settled for forty years in Paris earning his living as a Commissionnaire, when he married his second French wife, without making a settlement The question was, if he must be held to have married under the French community of goods. The Court found that when he married he had established himself in France, and had altogether abandoned his native country. It held that he was married under the Law of French community. It was true the Court declares that Fraix had not been authorized to establish his Domicil in France, but a domicil was not necessary to make the communauté applicable, which is presumed to have been the intention of the parties when they fixed themselves in France.

SCOTTOWE's CASE.—An Englishman, described as a rich proprietor in the Department of the Loiret, where he had long been settled, and whose first and second wives were both French, legitimated, on his second marriage, the natural children he had by his second wife, and then sought, by virtue of Article 960 of the *Code*, which revokes donations in favour of strangers in case of children subsequently, to set aside an annuity he had settled on another person. The validity of the legitimation was disputed on the ground of the English Law not admitting it. On the other hand, proof was given that in England the status of a person is determined, not by the law of his country, but by that of his *de facto* Domicil. The *de facto* French Domicil was not denied; but Article 13, and the fact of Scottowe being an Englishman, were relied on against the validity of the legitimation. The Court of Orleans, confirming the decision of an inferior Court, held that the legitimation was void as contrary to the English Law.

OLIVAREZ' CASE.—This is a very recent decree of the Court of Cassation on Appeal from the Imperial Court of Bordeaux. The Court of Bordeaux had decided that at the time of her decease Madame De Vivanco was not domiciled at Bordeaux, but at Bilbao ;—that by the terms of the Article 110 of the *Code Napoléon*, the place where the succession opens is determined by the Domicil ; that thus the succession of Madame De Vivanco was opened in Spain ; that her succession was personal only, and remained subject to the Law of the Domicile ; and that the Article 2 of the Law of the 14th of July, 1819, was not applicable.

The Court of Cassation reversed the decision, and the Court states in its decree, that neither the rule laid down by the Art. 110 of the *Code Napoléon*, in virtue of which the opening of a succession is determined by the domicil, nor the rule which provides, conformably to the Art. 3 of the same *Code*, that the status and the capacity of persons shall be regulated by the national law forming their personal statute, ought, in any case, to be an obstacle to the execution of the Law of the 14th of July, 1819 ; and that the French Tribunals, and not the foreign Tribunals, are competent to maintain in virtue of that Law, in respect to goods situate in France, the right reserved by the French Laws to French coheirs.

This case shows how the established rules of the French Courts are set aside by them in favour of French persons under the Law of 1819.

The following cases were cited by the party opposing the will in addition to those cited on the other side :—

QUARTIN.—*Court of Cassation.*—This decision upheld the holograph will of a foreigner made in France, and here again the Court of Cassation held that the Court appealed from had not, in applying the rule of *locus regit actum*, violated any law. The Court says (see p. 25 of Appellant's case) that *the form of a will is governed by the law of the country where the Testator disposes ; for otherwise the foreigner would, when out of his own country, be prevented from making his will, in consequence of the impossibility of having recourse to the forms required by the Law of his Domicil ; the laws determining the forms in which a will is to be made do not affect the capacity of the Testator, but only the external solemnities which are to accompany the expression of his wishes.*

The property in that case in France was personalty (see p. 22 of Appellant's case), and nothing is said as to any property elsewhere.   The

Civil Tribunal of the Seine (whose decree was upheld by the Royal Court of Paris) says in its decree (see p. 23), *Whereas the property composing the succession of Quartin existing in France is purely personal, and personalty in principle follows the condition and capacity of the person;* and the Court recognised and applied to the will the personal statute of the Testator. It is thus clear that if he had died intestate, the Court would have applied his personal law to his succession : and it is by no means to be inferred from the Court of Cassation rejecting the Appeal, on the ground that the Court of Paris had not violated any law by upholding the holograph will, that the Court would have set aside an Englishman's will made in the forms prescribed by his personal law disposing of personalty following his capacity, and not situate in France.

D'HERVAS.—*Court of Cassation.*—A Frenchwoman, in 1812, married a Spaniard at Madrid, and thereby became a foreigner. Soon afterwards the parties came to and established themselves in France, and acquired real estate there.

In 1820 the wife acknowledged herself indebted jointly with her husband to M. Bonnar, and as security she mortgaged the estate belonging to her.

The wife pleaded nullity of the obligation, on the ground that it was not valid by the Spanish Law.

The Court of Paris held that, there being clear evidence of a Domicil *de facto* in France, the contract was to be judged according to the French Laws.

The Court of Cassation said in its decree that the question in that case did not relate to the status of Madame D'Hervas (the wife), but to the validity of a contract entered into in France by a foreigner who had a domicil there, and was the owner of realty there.

In the next *attendu* the Court says that if the 3rd Article (of the *Code*) declares that the laws concerning the status and the capacity of persons govern Frenchmen, even when resident in a foreign country, it does not contain any similar or analogous disposition in favour of foreigners resident in France, whence it results that the decree attacked cannot have violated that Article.

Unless a very qualified meaning is to be attached to that *attendu* of the Court, it is overruled by the later decisions of the same Court in the cases of Connolly and Quartin, in which the doctrine is clearly recognized that whatever relates to the status of the foreigner, and to the extent and limitation of his rights and of his capacity, is governed by the personal statute, which follows the person wherever he goes.

In the next *attendu* the Court says that realty possessed by foreigners in France is, according to the terms of the same Article, governed by the French Laws.

There was, therefore, in that case, a *de facto* Domicil, sufficient for the regulation of contracts of the *jus gentium*, and, moreover, the contract related to realty in France, as to which the 3rd Article of the *Code* says, "Realty, even that possessed by foreigners, is governed by the French Law."

DUBOIS DE CHEMANT.—*Court of Paris.*—This case was decided in 1836. The Testator, a Frenchman by origin, died at London a naturalized Englishman.

A decree of 26th of August, 1811, deprived the Frenchman naturalized in a foreign country without the authorization of the French Government, of the enjoyment of his civil rights and of the ownership of his property—and the Court decided in this case, that that decree had been abrogated by the Law of the 14th July, 1819, which abolished the *droit d'aubaine*, and grants to the foreigner the power of disposing and of receiving in France.

The Court of Cassation decided that thus the Testator, who had become a foreigner by his naturalization in England, had had since the Law of 1819 the capacity of disposing of his property situate in France. And the Court further decided that his succession was to be governed by the Law of England, which had become the Law of his Domicil.

DE BONNEVAL.—*Court of Cassation.*—This case was decided in 1843. The Court of Cassation rejected an Appeal from the Royal Court of Rouen, which had decided that the will of a Frenchman made in England, in compliance with the forms prescribed by the English Law, was a valid will within the terms of the 999th Article of the *Civil Code*, which enables a Frenchman in a foreign country, either to make his will in the holograph form, or by authentic act, with the forms used in the place where that document is drawn up.

Here follows the letters of the President and opinion of the French Advocates referred to at p. 211.

No. 70.   Paris le 16 Juin 1857.
Tribunal de 1re Instance du Departement de la Seine.
Cabinet de M. le Président.

Monsieur,

Par votre lettre datée du 15 Juin, 1857, vous me demandez de vous indiquer plusieurs des avocats les plus anciens et les plus éminents du barreau de Paris, à l'effet de vous donner une consultation sur des difficultés élevées à l'occasion de l'ouverture en France d'une succession Anglaise ; je ne vois aucun inconvénient à répondre officieusement à votre demande, en conséquence voici les noms des avocats dont la connaissance et la capacité peuvent vous inspirer une entière confiance.

M. M. de Vatimesnil, Demangeat, Chaix d'Est Ange, Berryer, Dupin Paillard de Villeneuve, Bethmont, Odillon Barrot, Marie et Lionville.

Veuillez recevoir, Monsieur, l'assurance de mes sentiments les plus distingués.

Le Président du Tribunal civil de la Seine.

Monsieur Digweed, Avocat Anglais,   BENOITCHAMPY.
Rue du Colisée, 3, Paris.

Devant le " Judicial Committee " du très Honorable Conseil Privé de sa Majesté.

BREMER v. FREEMAN et BREMER.

Dans les biens meubles de Fanny Calcraft, celibataire, decedée.

ONT comparu personnellement Antoine Francois Henri de Vatimesnil, Avocat à la Cour Imperiale de Paris, Ancien Avocat-Général à la Cour de Cassation, Ancien Ministre de l'Instruction Publique, demeurant à Paris, Rue St. Dominique, St. Germain ; Charles Demangeat, Docteur en Droit, Avocat, Professeur à l'école de Droit de Paris, demeurant Rue d'Enfer, No. 11, à Paris ; Eugene Bethmont, Ancien Ministre de Justice, Ancien Président du Conseil d'Etat, Ancien Batonnier de l'Ordre des Avocats, demeurant à Paris, Rue des Capucines, No. 3 ; Pierre Antoine Berryer, Ancien Batonnier de l'Ordre des Avocats, demeurant à Paris, Rue Neuve des Petit Champs, No. 64 ; Felix Silvestre Jean Baptiste Lionville, Batonnier de l'Ordre des Avocats, demeurant à Paris, Rue des Moulins, No. 19 ; Camille Hyacinthe Odilon Barrot, Avocat à la Cour Imperial de Paris, Ancien Garde des Sceaux, Ancien Président du Conseil des Ministres, demeurant à Paris, Rue de la Ferme des Mathurins, No. 24 ; Alexandre Thomas Marie, Avocat à la Cour Imperiale de Paris, Ancien Batonnier, Ancien Ministre demeurant à Paris, Rue Neuve des Petits Champs No. 64 ; André Marie Jean Jacques Dupin, Avocat à la Cour Imperiale de Paris, Ancien Procureur Général à la Cour de Cassation, Ancien Président de la Chambre des Deputés, demeurant à Paris, Rue du Bac, No. 118 ; Adolphe Victor Paillard de Villeneuve, Avocat à la Cour Imperiale de Paris, Membre du Conseil de l'Ordre des Avocats, demeu-

rant à Paris, Rue Louvois, No. 4 ; et Gustave Adolphe Chaix d'Est
Ange, Avocat à la Cour Imperiale de Paris, Avocat de la Maison de l'Em-
pereur, Ancien Deputé demeurant à Paris, Rue St. George, No. 15 ; et
ont separément fait Serment, Qu'étant informés que Fanny Calcraft,
la défunte, était née à Calcutta aux Indes orientales, en l'année 1795, et
qu'elle était l'enfant legitime de parens Anglais, Qu'elle a commencée
à resider animo manendi à Paris en l'année 1838, et qu'elle a fait son
testament dans cette ville en 1842, conformément à la loi Anglaise,
Qu'elle est morte à Paris en 1853, Qu'elle n'était pas naturalisée en
France, Qu'elle n'avait pas obtenu du gouvernement Francais l'autorisation d'établir son domicile en France aux termes de l'article 13 du Code
Civil de ce Pays, Ils sont positivement d'avis que d'après le loi Française la défunte n'a jamais acquis en France un domicile de nature à
faire régir par la loi de ce pays son testament ou la forme de son testament, Que conséquemment si ce testament est fait en conformité avec la
loi Anglaise, la défunte ne seroit pas jugée être morte intestat.

BERRYER,
     Ancien Batonnier.
CH. DEMANGEAT.
MARIE,
     Ancien Batonnier.

L. DE VATIMESNIL.
DUPIN,
     Ancien Batonnier.
BETHMONT,
     Ancien Batonnier de l'Ordre des
          Avocats de Paris, &c.
FELIX LIONVILLE,
     Battonier.
ODILON BARROT.
PAILLARD DE VILLENEUVE.
G. CHAIX D'EST ANGE.

CHAPTER XV.

JUS PERSONARUM—STATUS.

CCCLII. We have now considered the nature of Origin and Domicil, two personal ties which bind the individual to a particular territorial jurisdiction.

This consideration, however, has not carried us far on the way to the goal which is the end of our enquiry, viz., what positive law ought to govern the legal relations of a foreigner? Even if this law were, which it is not, necessarily identical with the jurisdiction of the *forum*, there are other causes or sources of that jurisdiction besides Origin and Domicil.

When Donellus is speaking, in his admirable Commentaries on "ubi subjiciatur quisque ex personâ suâ jurisdictioni," he says, "jure communi omnino *quatuor res* sunt quæ eos qui "*ex personâ suâ* conveniuntur jurisdictioni ejus, apud quem "agitur subjiciunt: quæ eædem faciunt ut judicis jurisdictio sit "de eâ re de quâ agitur ; sive ut sit competens judex quem "quærimus : apud quem propterea quique agere et conveniri "debeat. *Sunt autem hæ res totidem subeundæ juris-* "*dictionis causæ* :—

"1. *Domicilium* litigatoris in territorio judicis consti- "tutum.

"2. *Obligatio* quâ de agitur ibi contracta.

"3. *Res* ita sita de cujus *proprietate* aut *possessione* agitur.

"4. *Judicium* ibi apud eum judicem cæptum (a).

CCCLIII. With reference however to this citation from Donellus, and to this mode of ascertaining what is the Law,

---

(a) Lib. xvii. c. xii.

Under this last head is established the position, that a person who has instituted a suit cannot afterwards decline the forum.

by enquiring what is the forum, it must be observed that though in the Roman Law and in the Law of Christendom there exists, generally speaking, an intimate connection between the jurisdiction, or *forum*, to which a legal relation is subject, and the Law which ought to govern that relation ; nevertheless, it cannot be said that the two are necessarily identified : there are cases clearly arising, for instance, out of *obligations*, in which the choice of a particular local law may be an integral part of the engagement, and in which the forum may be wholly different (*b*).

CCCLIV. But, though by an investigation into these other sources of jurisdiction, namely, the *obligatio* and the *res sita*, we might be led to a full, though circuitous consideration of the law which ought to govern all the legal relations of the foreigner, we shall more naturally and readily arrive at the same end by a somewhat different road. In the foregoing chapters we have considered the individual as merely existing in a certain place, and so, to speak in the abstract ; we must now proceed to consider him as a legal person, both passively the subject of legal relations, and actively capable of acquiring them.

We advance, therefore, to the next step in our enquiry, by considering what is the *jus*, or what are the legal relations of which the person is the centre, and round whom they are grouped ?

The same great civilian, speaking "de jure privato," says, " dicitur omne jus quo utimur, vel ad *personas* pertinere, " vel ad *res*, vel ad *actiones*. Quod enim *nostrum* est consistit " in *personâ* cujusque et rebus *extra personam positis* : obti-" nendi autem ejus ratio est in *actionibus* (*c*) id est in judiciis " quibus *nostrum* consequimur id quod *nostrum* cujusque " duplex est, est enim id quod verè et propriè nostrum est et " est quod nobis debetur—ita jus nostrum cujusque seu

---

(*b*) *Savigny* viii. s. 356. 359—360.

(*c*) *Actus*, distinct from *actiones*. *Vide infra.*

" quod nostrum est duabus his rebus continetur (*d*) eo *quod* " *propriè nostrum est* (*e*) et *obligatione.*"

He proceeds to enquire what the ingredients are which make up what we call *our own* (quod propriè et verè *nostrum* est) and he discovers that they are Rights (1) attaching to our Persons and (2) to the Things external to them. As to the former he says, " In personâ cujusque id nostrum est quod tribuitur " personæ id est, *quod cuique ita tribuitur ut is id habeat* " *in sese etiamsi desint res cœteræ externæ.* Hæc a naturâ " quatuor sunt, vita, incolumitas corporis, libertas, existi- " matio."

But these Personal Rights may suffer diminution, and the mode of their existence constitutes the *status* of each individual. :—" *Status*" (he defines) (*f*) " est *conditio personæ* " cujusque—jus, facultas vivendi et faciendi quæ velis quæ ei " conditioni tribuitur." You enquire into the *status* in order to ascertain the *jus personæ*: the one is cause, the other " effect :—et status conditio causa est : jus personæ illius " statûs et conditionis effectus" (*g*).

CCCLV. Under the term *Status* (*etat Stellung*) are properly included in this treatise, all questions relating to the personal condition of the individual, (*h*) *e. g.*, whether he be a slave or a free man ; all questions relating to legitimacy, minority, capacity of entering into any contract, whether of marriage, the contract of contracts, (*seminarium Reipublicæ*)

(*d*) *De Jure Civili,* 1. 2. c. vii. 35.

(*e*) " *Actionum* verbo hoc genus persecutionum intelligi non autem hominum *actus* ut Connanus interpretari tentat, &c.," *ib.*

(*f*) *Ib.* cap. ix.

(*g*) The title in the Pandects " *de Statu*'' is identical with the title in the Institutes " *De jure Personarum.*"

(*h*) *Savigny, R. R.* i. (397—400 pages) condemns a modern improper use of this expression denoting as a particular personal capacity or condition, which is not the sense of the word in the Roman Law. It especially applies to the individual in all the relations of family, and is, he thinks, identical *with jus personarum.*

Rocco, c. xix. p. 409 &c., is not very satisfactory or precise on this head.

or into others of an inferior order, – all these questions carrying with them others emergent from and incident to them.

But before we consider the operation and efficacy allowed by the Comity of States to laws affecting the *status* of foreigners, it will be expedient to make some mention of the *Statutes* or the *Statuta* which occupy so prominent a position in the writings of continental jurists, both of ancient and modern times.

CHAPTER XVI.

STATUTES.

CCCLVI. The endeavours of jurists to find a satisfactory solution of the great problem of Private International Jurisprudence, viz. :—ought any, and, if any, what laws, to be allowed an efficiency and operation beyond the territory of the lawgiver?—led eventually to the famous category of (1) *Personal*, (2) *Real*, (3) *Mixed Statutes*. Any work on the *Jus Gentium* which omitted all notice of this ancient and celebrated division, would be censurable on the double ground of historical imperfection, and of omitting to explain to its readers the meaning of technical terms, without a knowledge of which the writings of jurists would be, for the most part, unintelligible.   is true, nevertheless, that the examination will not lead to the satisfactory result of ascertaining firm and clear landmarks in this branch of the science of law; for it must be admitted, First, that the division itself has always encountered much opposition. Secondly, that it is built upon an ambiguous and unsteady principle. Thirdly, that in the application even of this principle, jurists have proceeded in an arbitrary and uncertain manner ; and, lastly, that they have been far from unanimous upon some of the most important questions arising out of the division. Still, some notice of this division is a necessary part of the task undertaken by the writer of these pages ; though it need not enumerate or classify every variety of opinion which the subject has called forth.

CCCLVII. From the time of the writers (*postglossatores*) who succeeded to the earliest commentators on the Civil and Canon Law (*glossatores*), up to the doctrine conveyed in the axioms " statutum territorium non egreditur,"—" statutum " non porrigitur vel se non extendit extra territorium statu- " entis,"—" efficacia statuti ad territorium statuentis restricta

" est," has universally prevailed in the civilized world. The doctrine originated in Italy—the cradle of law—which also after it became divided into separate principalities, furnished the name " *Statutum*," and the first commentators upon it. The German commentators of the 16th century built upon the Italian foundation, which was, in fact, the principle of exclusive territorial sovereignty, expressed in the axioms which have just been cited. The *Statutum* was the positive law—the *Jus Civile* of that exclusive territorial sovereignty.

CCCLVIII. The great Italian jurist, Bartolus, may be said to have planted, about the middle of the 14th century, that threefold division of the *Statutum*, which, towards the end of the 16th century, had ripened into the scientific form which it has ever since worn.

Bartolus wrote, among others, a commentary on the words " cunctos populos," which are the two first words of the First Title of the First Book of the Roman Code (*a*).

CCCLIX. He propounds for consideration two questions (*b*), not stated with great accuracy, or very carefully distinguished from each other.

1. *An Statutum, porrigatur extra territorium ?*

2. *An effectus Statuti porrigatur extra territorium statuentium ?*

He founds his reply to these questions upon citations from the Roman Law, which do not, when carefully examined, always support his positions.

CCCLX. First, as to a *Statutum* affecting *Contracts* (*a*)

(*a*) *Cod.* l. i. t. 1. " De Summâ Trinitate et fide Catholicâ et ut nemo de eâ publicè contendere audeat." " *Cunctos populos* quos Clementiæ nostræ regit imperium in tali volumus religione versari quam divum Petrum Apostolum tradidisse Romanis religio usque adhuc ab ipso initio declarat."

(*b*) I have given the heading of this remarkable commentary, with all its subdivisions, in the note to this chapter. I have added the *ipsissima verba* of that part of the text which is most pertinent to the subject of this work ; but, for the analysis which follows here, I am chiefly indebted to *Wächter*, 272, note 79.

—as to their *Form*—the *Statutum* of the place of the contract is to be applied : even when the contract is made abroad, and the action upon it brought at home. (β) A like rule is applied to the *effects* which belong to the nature of the contract. An exception, however, is made in the case of contracts relating to Marriage and Dowry : in these the law of the husband's domicil is applied. (γ) But as to matters *quæ oriuntur ex post facto propter negligentiam vel moram,* (in which *prescription*) is included, if a definite place of payment (*locus solutionis*) be specified, the law of that place prevails ; otherwise, the law of the place where the action is brought.

Secondly, as to the *Statutum* affecting *Testaments.* Bartolus enquires whether a stranger can legally make his Will according to the *forms* of the State in which he is? and the answer is in the affirmative, unless the law of that State have reserved these forms as the special privilege of its own citizens. A testament so validly executed is valid everywhere, and operates upon property in other States.

Thirdly, as to the *Statutum* affecting the *capacity* to make a Will. The laws of the State are not to govern foreigners who happen to make their Wills their *quia* statuta non possunt legitimare *personam* non subditam nec circa ipsam personam aliquid disponere. But it is not so with respect to the *solennitas actus*—that belongs to the jurisdiction in whose *territorium* it has been adopted.

Fourthly, if the right to a particular thing be in question, then *statutum loci ubi res est* must be applied. Nevertheless, Bartolus arbitrarily modifies this position when he considers the second question *an statuta porrigant effectum secum extra territorium* ; for on this he lays down the following positions :—

(A). A *Statutum which prohibits an individual from doing certain things* follows him into a foreign State when it is *favorabile, i.e.,* made for the advantage of the individual ; but not when it is *odiosum ;* for instance, a *Statutum* that a daughter shall not inherit, does not extend to property in a foreign State.

(B) A *Statutum* which *confers a capacity, i.e.,* which enables an unemancipated child to make his testament, or a spurious child to inherit, has no extra-territorial effect. The individual so capacitated can make no use of his privilege out of the State, nor affect, by means of it, property in another State, especially if thereby *alteri civitati prœjudicatur.*

(C) As to *succession ab intestato*—the *Statutum* of the place in which the property is, governs this matter ; but then the character of the *Statutum* is to be considered : if it be *in rem conceptum, e. g., bona veniant in primogenitum,* then it applies to the property of the foreigner, situate in the State : but not if the *Statutum* be *in personam conceptum, e. g.,* that *primogenitus succedat,* because *dispositio circa personas non porrigitur ad forenses.*

CCCLXI. Such is the outline of the famous commentary out of which was afterwards elaborated the generally accepted division of Statutes which has been already mentioned, and concerning which it now remains to make some observations.

CCCLXII. The division of *Statuta* adopted since the close of the 16th century and the writings of *Argentrœus* or *D'Argentrè* (c), has been into

      1. Statuta personalia.
      2.   „   realia.
      3.   „   mixta.

Statuta personalia purported to be those positive laws which had for their principal object the *person* and his *status,* although they might collaterally and indirectly affect his property.

Statuta realia, purported to be those positive laws, which had for their principal object *immoveable property :* although

---

(c) *Bertrand D'Argentrè,* presided over the principal Tribunal of Rennes—flourished in the middle of the 16th century—wrote *Commentarios in patrios Britonum léges, seu consuetudines generales Ducatûs Britanniæ.*

1 *Voet,* s. 2—4.

Savigny, viii., s. 361.

they also might indirectly and collaterally affect the persons.

Statuta mixta, (*d*) which had not for their principal object *persons* or *things,* but the *acts* and *obligations* of individuals: according to some jurists, only *the form* of these *acts* and *obligations:* according to others, not only their *form,* but their *matter and substance (vinculum obligationis)* of the latter. *Statuta mixta* included, also, all that related to the legal establishment and enforcement of claims: according to many jurists, *actions,* or the form and mode of procedure in legal acts, whether judicial or extra-judicial: according to other jurists, they referred to both Persons and Things: *conjunctim de utrisque* (*e*).

CCCLXIII. Though the limits of these respective *Statuta* have been narrowed by some, and extended by other jurists, and a great difference of opinion and divergence of practice has always prevailed in their application to particular cases; still, on the whole, and practically speaking, they may be summed up as follows (*f*) :—

Personal Statutes attach to all persons domiciled in the territory of the statute-making authority, and ought to be recognized and applied by the judgment of a foreign tribunal.

Real Statutes attach to all immoveable property, and ought to receive a similar recognition.

Mixed Statutes apply to all acts (*handlungen-actes*) done in the territory of the statute-making authority, and the law of that territory ought to be applied to them.

CCCLXIV. This chapter may not improperly be closed by a reference to the opinions of three modern jurists, of great celebrity upon the subject of it.

(*d*) *P. Voet De Statutis* t iv. civ., No. 4, says:—"Mixta dicentur meo sensu quæ licet forte vel in rem vel in personam loquerentur, non tamen principaliter de re vel de personâ disponant, verum de modo et solennitate in omnibus negotiis et causis sive judicialibus sive extra-judicialibus adhibenda." See *Fœlix,* s. 21.

(*e*) So *Burgundus, Rodenburg, Boullenois.* See *Fœlix,* s. 21.

(*f*) *Savigny,* viii. s. 361.

The Italian *Rocco* adheres to the twofold division into Personal and Real Statutes, but rejects the category of Mixed Statutes : the subject of them, he says, should be transferred either to Personal or Real, according as the Person or the Property be the predominant element or principal object (*g*).

The French *Fœlix* adopts the threefold division, understanding by Mixed Statutes, *acts* or *obligations*, and thereby assimilating the division to that transplanted from the commentaries of Gaius into the Institutes " omne jus vel ad personas per-" tenet vel ad res vel ad actiones" for "actiones" or suits (demandes) the effect, Fælix substitutes " acta" or "obligationes" which he designates the cause (*h*).

The German *Savigny,* the prince of modern jurists, pronounces the division to be capable of the most various meanings and applications, and, therefore, of course, to contain some true doctrine.   But he rejects the division for himself as altogether unsatisfactory, and, on account of its ambiguity, unsafe as a basis of Private International Law ? (*i*)

It must not be supposed, however, that though these eminent men differ so widely as to the philosophical truth of the division in question, that they differ as widely upon the expediency and equity of the doctrine which it was the intention of the framers of this division to enforce.   This is not the case : they are substantially unanimous upon the most material points of Private International Law.   For instance, all are agreed as to what law ought to govern the *Status* of the Individual in a foreign State : and it should be observed here, that the terms *Personal Statute* and *Status* are nearly identical in their signification (*k*).

" Les Statuts personnels" (D'Aguesseau says), " sont ceux qui " affectant la personne qui forment ce qu'on appelle son *état,*

(*g*) " In somma le legge miste non esistono.   Sono elle o reali o personali a secondo che le cose o le persone ne sieno l'obietto principale e diretto."—p. 23.

(*h*) Sec. 21.

(*i*) VIII. s 361.

" qui le rendent incapables non pas de disposer de tels ou tels
" biens, mais de contracter de faire tels ou tels actes : en sorte
" que l'acte est nul en soi et indépendamment de son exécu-
" tion" (*l*).

This observation leads us to the consideration of the Law
which governs the *Person* and his *Status*, the subject of the
next chapter.

(*x*) *Œuvres* t. iv. (*ed. Pardessus*) p. 281, &c.; 34 *Plaidoyer*. Cited
also, *Fælix*, s. 22.

NOTES ON THE FOREGOING CHAPTER.

The edition of Bartolus which I have used, is the one published Venetiis MDCII., a fine copy belonging to the College of Advocates at Doctor's Commons. It will be seen that the part interesting to the student of Private International Law, begins at the 14th section of the following heading to the chapter ; but I have given the heading entire, partly on account of its novelty to the English reader.

De Summa Trinitate—Bubrica Lex Prima.

1. Relativum quis ponitur declarative, augmentative, et restrictive.
2. Lex non debet esse ludibrio.
3. Verbum volo, quandoque inducat dispositionem.
4. Relativum, quis, vel qui, est relativum substantiæ.
5. Religio, quo modo sumatur, et quid nobis afferat.
6. Usuræ quando possunt de mente et voluntate juris civilis exigi et ut interesse peti, N. S.
7. Minus malum permittitur, ut evitetur majus.
9. Dementia alia vera, alia ficta.
10. Argumentum de perjurio ad hæreticum, quando procedat.
11. Heretici hodie sunt infames, et repelluntur a testimonio.
12. Infames de facto, quando possunt testificari.
13. Hæretici qua pæna puniantur.
*14. Statutum loci contractus quo ad solemnitatem ejus attenditur.
15. Quo ad ordinem litis inspicitur locus judicii.
16. Locus contractus circa dubia quæ oriuntur tempore contractus, secundum naturam ipsius inspicitur, fallit in dote-num. 17.'
18 Statuta quædam circa dubia quæ oriuntur post contractum, propter negligentiam, vel moram quæ attendantur.
19. Statutum loci viri, quo ad lucrum dotis inspicitur.
20. Restitutio ex læsione contingente in ipso contractu, quando petitur, quod statutum attendatur.   Forensis delinqens in loco, secundum quæ statuta puniatur.
21. Statutum quod testamentum coram duobus testibus possit fieri, valet et nu. 22.
23. Solennitas publicandi testamentum potest per statutum minui, et mutari.
25. Statutum circa ea, quæ sunt voluntariæ jurisdictionis comprehendit forenses.

26. Statutum quod filius familias, possit testari, non comprehendit filium familias ibi testantem.

27. Statutum ubi res est sita, servare debit.

28. Statuta et consuetudo laicorum quando ligerit clericos, et servare debeant in curia episcopi.

29. Statuta contra privilegia clericorum dicuntur esse contra liberta tem ecclesiæ.

30. Consuetudo laicorum in his quæ pertinent ad processum, servatur in foro ecclesiastico.

31. Statutum quod testamenta insinuentur, ligit clericos.

32. Statutum quandoque porrigit suum effectum extra territorium.

33. Statutum quod filia femina non succedat, cum sit prohibitorium et odiosum, non trahitur ad bona alibi sita.

34. Statutum permissum quando habeat locum extra territorium.

35. Instrumenta confecta a notario extra territorium, faciunt ubique fidem.

36. Testamentum conditum coram quatuor testibus, secundum dispositionem statuti loci, valet, etiam quo ad bona sita extra territorium.

37. Lex potest facere, quod quis decedat pro parte testatus, et pro parte intestatus.

38. Statutum habilitans personam, quando trahatur extra territorium et nu. 41.

39. Actus voluntariæ jurisdictionis, non possunt exerceri extra jurisdictionem concedentis, qui sit inferior a principi, nu. 40.

41. Aditio hæreditatis porrigit effectum suum extra civitatem et nu. 43.

42. Consuetudo Angliæ, quod primogenitus succedat in omnibus bonis, quando trahatur ad bona alibi sita.

44. Statutum punitivum, quando porrigat effectum suum extra territorium.

45. Delinquens in loco, efficitur de jurisdictione loci.

46. Forenses duo existentes in exercitu Perusino, si in territorio Aretino delinquant.

47. Statutum punitivum simpliciter loquens, quando comprehendat civem delinquentem extra territorium, ad hoc ut possit contra eum procedi et puniri secundum statuta suæ civitatis et num. 48.

49. Cauntela in formanda inquisitione contra civem delinquentem extra territorium.

50. Pæna imposita quando extendat effectum suum extra territorium judicantis.

51. Publicatio bonorum au extendatur ad bona alibi sita, et ad uem dominum pertineat.

The 14th Section begins as follows :—

" Nunc veniamus ad Gloss. quæ dicit *Quod si Bon.* &c. cujus occasione videnda sunt duo : et primò utrum statutum porrigatur extra territorium ad non subditos.—Secundò utrum effectus statuti porrigatur extra territorium statuentium.

" Et primò quæro quid de contractibus. Pone contractum celebratum per aliquem forensem in hâc civitate litigium ortum est et agitata lis in loco originis contrahentis cujus loci statuta dicent servari vel spectari? Quam illa quæstiones sunt multum revolutæ omissis aliis distinctionibus plenius quos Doctores dicant hic distingue.

Aut loquimur de statuto aut de consuetudine, quæ respiciunt ipsiùs contractûs solennitatem aut litis ordinationem aut de his quæ pertinent ad jurisdictionem ex ipso contractu evenientis executionis.

Primo casu inspicitur locus contractûs (ad. l. si fundus de evic. cl. l. 2 quem ad test ap.)

Secundo casu aut quæris de his quæ pertinent ad litis ordinationem et inspicitur locus judicii ab † aut de his quæ pertinent ad ipsiùs litis decisionem et tunc aut de his quæ oriuntur secundum ipsiùs contractûs naturam tempore contractûs aut de his quæ oriuntur ex post facto propter negligentiam vel moram. Primo casu inspicitur locus contractûs‡ et intelligo locum contractûs ubi est celebratus contractûs non de loco in quem collata est solutio. Nam licet fundus debeat solvi ubi est tunc inspicitur locus contractûs. Fallit in dotem § ut, &c. propter rationem ibi positam in textu.

Secundo casu aut solutio est collata in locum certum aut in pluribus locis alternativè ita quod electio sit actoris, aut in nullum locum quia promissio fuit facta simplicitur.

---

* Every position in the text of Bartolus professes to be built upon *dicta* of the Roman Law. *Wächter* and *Savigny* have, however, clearly shown that these *dicta* frequently do not support the positions in the text.

Dig. xxi. t. 2. 6. si fundus venierit, ex consuetudine ejus regionis in quâ negotium gestum est pro evictione caveri oportet."

Cod. vi. t. 32. 2. " Testamenti tabulas ad hoc tibi à patre datas ut in patriam perferantur affirmans, potes illuc perferre ut secundum leges moresque locorum insinuentur."

† *Dig.* xxii. t. v. 3, *in fine.* " Quod ad testes evocandos pertinet diligeniæ judicantis est explorare quæ consuetudo in eâ provinciâ in quâ judicat fuerit, &c."

‡ Refers again to *Dig.* xxi. t. 2. 6. and to *Dig.* xl. iv. t. 7. 21. " contraxisse unsquisque in co loco intelligitur in quo, ut solveret se obligavit."

§ *Dig.* v. t. 1. 65. " exigere dotem mulier debet illic ubi maritus domicilium habuit non ubi instrumentum dotale conscriptum est."

Primo casu inspicitur consuetudo quæ est in illo loco in quem est collata solutio.*

Secundo et tertio casu inspicitur locus ubi petitur, †.

Ratio prædictorum est quia ibi est contracta negligentia seu mora."

Then Bartolus proceeds to say:—

" Ex prædictis possunt solvi multæ quæstiones," and he gives an example :—" Statutum est Assissii unde est mulier ubi est celebratus contractus dotis et matrimonii, quod vir lucretur etiam partem dotis uxore moriente sine liberis ; in hâc verò civitate Perugii unde est vir statutum est quod vir lucretur dimidium, quid spectabitur ? certè statutum terræ viri."

And shortly afterwards another example occurs :—" Aut quis vult petere restitutionem ex læsione contingente in ipso contractu tempore actûs et inspiciamus locum actûs aut ex læsione contingente post actum ex aliis negligentiis ut morâ, et inspiciamus locum, ubi est illa mora contracta ut ex prædictis apparet : et sic si esset in loco Judicii inspiciamus locum Judicii." He then considers the other subjects mentioned in the sections of the heading to his chapter ; but a sample, longer, perhaps, than is justified by the size of this volume, has already been given to the reader.

---

* Refers to *Dig. sed* (pace tanti viri) *quære Cod.* iv. 2 si certum petatur, l. x. *Dig.* xxiii. 6, &c.

† Refers to authorities already cited.

CHAPTER XVII.

THE PERSONAL STATUTE—STATUS—JUS IN PERSONA POSITUM.

CCCLXV. The subject of this Chapter is the consideration of what Law shall govern the Personal *Status* (a) of the individual in a foreign State—the *jus positum in personâ ipsâ cujusque* (b) ; or, in the language of continental jurists, what State is to furnish the *Personal Statute* of an individual commorant in a foreign State.

It is clear that the consideration of the Law which governs the capacity of the individual to acquire legal relations precedes, in the natural order of things, the consideration of the Law which is to govern the legal relations when acquired.

CCCLXVI. Is, then, this Law to be the Law of the Foreigner's Origin (*Originis*)? the Law of his Domicil (*Domicilii*)? the Law of the place in which the act has been done, or the contract entered into, which occasions the enquiry (*lex loci actûs vel contractûs*) or, the Law of the place in which he happens to be at the time when the question is raised (*lex fori*) ?

CCCLXVII. The due investigation of this subject requires the following arrangement :—To consider—

1. The doctrine which prevails out of England and the United States of North America.

2. The doctrine which prevails in England and the United States of North America.

(a) Or, in the language of *Story*, "the capacity, state, and condition of persons."—Ch. iv. s. 50.

(b) *Donellus*, I. i.

3. The limitations which confine the application of both doctrines.

CCCLXVIII. First, as to the doctrine which prevails out of England and the United States of North America ; an over-whelming majority of authorities upon the subject pronounce that the Law which governs the *Status* is the Law of the Domicil (c) :—a great majority pronounce that if the *Domicil of Origin* has been abandoned, and a new one *acquired*, the law of the latter—that is, the law of the *actual Domicil*—ought to govern.

CCCLXIX. It is not, however, contended that the law of the new Domicil has any *retroactive effect on obligations contracted, or acts done* under the Law of the old Domicil. It is, of course, assumed that such acts and obligations are of a private and not a public character (d) ;—that they concern the individual, and not the State.

CCCLXX. It is obvious that this proposition as to the paramount authority of the law of the actual Domicil may, unless, indeed, it be universally incorporated into the Municipal Law of each State, tend to a collision of laws in various ways: —

1. Between the Law of the Origin, or the Domicil of Birth, and the Law of the actual Domicil ; when the sentence of the latter requires execution in the country of the former.

(c) *Savigny*, viii. s. 362.   *Rocco*, p. iii. "*le qualità personali* legittamente infisse vel luogo del domicilio si mantengono mai sempre intere col mutar che si fa della residenza e passagiera dimora."—P. 147. "Il principio cui vuolsi tener fermo si è come abbiam detto di sopra che le legge personali del domicilio accompagnano gl'individii in tutti i luoghi nella terra"—what can be stronger? *Fœlix*, s. 27 :—"La loi personelle de chaque individu, la loi dont il est sujet quant à sa personne et celle de *la nation dont il est membre* .... la loi de cette nation est sa loi personelle depuis le premier moment de son existence physique." This, it will be observed, however, is Law of Origin, not necessarily of Domicil.

(d) The Scotch Courts pronounced a divorce upon a marriage contracted between English persons in England, when marriage was indissoluble, on the ground that marriage is a contract of a *public* character, and that the incidents of it must be subject to the laws of the country in which the contracting parties reside.

2. Between the Law of Origin and of the Domicil, and the Law of the place where the contract is entered into, or the act done.

3. Between the Law of the Domicil and the Law of the place in which the thing adjudicated upon happens to be situate.

It is the more necessary to mention these modes of collision, because in Story's elaborate and learned work, the *Conflict of Laws*, they are not always very clearly discriminated (*e*).

CCCLXXI. The position, however, already stated, viz.: that the Law of the Domicil determines the *Status*, and, therefore, travels with the person, binding on him all its capacities and incapacities, wherever he goes, rests, as an abstract proposition, upon a very largely preponderating authority of jurists,—upon the recognition of it by courts of justice,—and has, moreover, been expressly incorporated into the positive legislation of the principal States on the European Continent.

CCCLXXII. By the Code Civil of France it is enacted, " Les lois concernant l'état et la capacité des personnes régis- " sent les Français même residant en pays étranger."

It is true that this law in its terms affects French *citizens* only, and does not expressly declare that the *Status* and *capacity* of the *foreigner* commorant in France will be governed by the law of the foreigner's country. But it clearly appears from the discussions which preceded the incorporation of this article into the Code, that such was the intention of the framers of the law : such, too, has been holden to be its effect by the highest authorities in France, and by the decisions of the first tribunals in that State (*f*).

CCCLXXIII. Belgium adopts the Law of France in this matter, and so do the cantons of Geneva, Vaud, and Berne.

(*e*) Cf. ss. 55, 70, 73, 77, 81, 83, 94.

(*f*) *Fœlix*, p. 44, l. 1, t. 1, s. 32, cites *Pardessus, Toullier, Caboin, Merlin.* This last author observes :—" Du principe que les lois Fran-

CCCLXXIV. The Austrian Code (g) provides that the personal capacity of the Austrian subject shall be governed by the Law of his Domicil as to transactions in another country ; and with respect to foreigners, that their personal capacity shall be determined according to the laws of their country, and, that their country shall be taken to be the place of their Domicil, and, if they have no proper Domicil, the place of their birth (h) ; unless the Austrian Law shall have, as in the case of slavery and serfdom, specially provided otherwise.

CCCLXXV. The Prussian Code of Laws (*Das Allgemeine*

çaises concernant l'état et la capacité des personnes régissent les Français même residant en pays étranger, il suit tout naturellement que, par reciprocité, les lois regissent l'état et la capacité des étrangers les suivant en France, et que c'est d'apres ces lois que les tribunaux Français doivent juger s'ils ont ou n'ont pas tel état s'ils sont capables ou incapables."—*Répertoire* v. *Loi*, s. 6, n. 6,

The discussion arose on the first part of the third article "Les Lois obligent ceux qui habitent le territoire."

The doctrine in the text is maintained by an arrêt of the Cour Royale of Paris, 1836 ; by another of the 25th November, 1831 ; by one of the Cour Royale of Bordeaux, of 15th July, 1841 ; by a judgment of the Tribunal de Première Instauce at Paris, in 1842. There is a decision of the Cour Royale at Paris, 15th March, 1831, which is of a contrary tenor ; but, the circumstances of the case were peculiar.

Savigny, viii. p. 146, agrees with *Fœlix*.

(g) *Œsterr. bürgerliche Gesetzbuch*, 1811.

(h) Die gesetzliche Behandlung der Ausländer in Œsterreich, von *D. Püttlingen*, s. 47.

Savigny, viii, s. 363.

Fœlix, ubi supra.

Savigny, viii. s. 363. Zustand der Person an sich. (*Fortsetzung*).

Savigny, viii. s. 362, is most decided and uncompromising in maintaining the law of the Domicil as the true law for deciding the *Status*.

"Meine meinung geht also vielmehr dahin, das Jeder in seinen personlichen Zustanden stets nach dem Recht seines Wohnsitzes zu beurtheilen ist; ohne unterschied, ob daruber im Inland oder im Ausland geurtheilt werde; eben so ober auch ohne unterschied, ob die persönliche Eigenschaft au sich, oder die rechtliche Wirkung derselben, beurtheilt werden soll."

Landrecht) enacts as its fundamental proposition, " That the " personal qualities and capacities of a man are to be deter- " mined according to the laws of the Judicial Tribunal to " which his true and proper Domicil" (*eigentlicher Wohnsitz* " —*domicile réel*) is subject."

This proposition relates to Prussian subjects, and does not distinguish between the exercise of their capacity at the place of their Domicil, or elsewhere. With respect to foreigners the same law provides as follows : —" The subjects of Foreign " States who live in this country are to be judged according " to the aforementioned enactment."

CCCLXXVI. It will be seen hereafter that these principles, both of the Austrian and Prussian Law receive some modification in their application to questions concerning the validity of contracts—modifications which have for their excellent object the maintaining the substantial and real intention of the engagement.

CCCLXXVII. The Bavarian Code provides that *in causis merè personalibus*, recourse shall be had to the Law of the Domicil.

The Code of the Grand Duchy of Baden adopts the rule of the French Code, with a most material exception, as to all questions relating to contract—an exception which has a tendency to assimilate the Law of Baden to that which prevails in Great Britain and North America.

CCCLXXVIII. The law of Holland appears to contain a yet greater infraction of the general principle ; for it provides that the Dutch Laws relating to the Status, shall bind the Dutchman in every other country ; but, that the foreigner, resident in Holland, shall be subject to the Dutch Law only, and not to the law of his Domicil.

CCCLXXIX. As to the Italian States.

Sardinia adopts in her Codice Civile the three propositions of the third Article of the French Code ; and, it is presumed, would apply them also to foreigners.

The *Papal States* enacted, in 1836, that the Personal Law of the Domicil followed the subject of it everywhere.

The *Two Sicilies*, according to the opinion of M. Fælix, resemble the Dutch ; because—though they incorporate into their Code the three propositions above referred to ; of the French Code—they, by their fifth Article, declare that the laws are binding on all who dwell in the land, whether they be citizens, domiciled strangers, or sojourners ; and do not accompany the statement with the reservation as to " les " lois *de police et de sûreté*" of the French Code. Yet, no author lays down the rule that personal qualities depend on the Law of the Domicil more strenuously than Rocco (*i*) the principal Neapolitan writer on the Conflict of Laws, and on whose authority M. Fælix is in the habit of relying.

CCCLXXX. *Russia* appears to have no law analogous to or resembling the third Article of the French Code, but to contain provisions in the same spirit and to the same effect as those already referred to in the Dutch Law. The Russian enactment as to the foreigner is (103) " Pendant tout le " temps de son sejour il est soumis, quant a la personne et ses " biens, aux dispositions des lois Russe, et a droit de leur pro- " tection." Though in the preliminary title of the new Civil Code of Poland the third Article of the French Code is introduced (*k*).

(*i*) " Le qualità personali legitimamente infisse nel luogo del domicilio si mantengono mai sempre intere col mutar che si fa della residenza e passagiera dimora. Quantunque il diritto delle genti, che necessario dai Gius-pubblicisti si appella, non ordini questa vicendevolc applicazione e autorità delle leggi di uno stato sul territorio dell altronessuna primitiva obligazione stringe le nazioni a riconoscere provedimenti stranieri nullameno il diritto delle genti volontario il quale intende alla perfessione progressiva dei popoli, altamente il richiede."—*Rocco.* 113—14.

(*k*) *Fælix ubi supra.*

The *Révue Etrangère et Française De Legislation* &c. t. 3, contains a translation of that part of the Russian Code which relates to " *Legislation Internationale de l'empire Russe.*" P. 550 contains the provisions respecting " *Etranger en Russie.*"

CCCLXXXI. Secondly, we have to consider the doctrine on the subject of the Personal *Status* which prevails in England and the North American United States. The jurisprudence of the United States of North America, and, in some respects, that of England also, differs materially from the doctrine of the codes and jurists of the European continent (*l*).

It is, indeed, true that the *Status* of persons with respect to acts done and rights acquired *in the place of their Domicil*, and contracts made *concerning property situated therein*, will be governed by the law of that Domicil ; and that England and the United States will hold as valid or invalid *such* acts, rights, and contracts, accordingly as they are holden valid or invalid, by the Law of the Domicil. But this proposition is very far from being equivalent to the proposition of the French Code, viz. :—that the Laws which concern the status and capacity of persons govern Frenchmen, even when resident in a foreign country (*m*).

CCCLXXXII. The state of jurisprudence presented by the practice of the English and American tribunals upon the question of the *Personal Status* of foreigners will be found very unsatisfactory, whether it be considered with reference to Comity, as being at variance with the law of the rest of the Christian world, or with reference to its own domestic jurisprudence, being marked by painful and clumsy inconsistencies.

No impartial person can rise from the perusal of Story's fourth chapter on the " Capacity of Persons," occupying nearly one hundred and thirty closely printed pages, without a sense of the confusion into which the legal relations of mankind are plunged in a great measure, though certainly not altogether, by the peculiarity of what is called the "*Common Law*."

CCCLXXXIII. It will be necessary in the following chapters to consider whether there are or are not grave

---

(*l*) *Story*, s. 101—106.
Burge 1, p. 132.
(*m*) *Vide post*.

discrepancies between the English and Continental Law on the subject of *Status, e. g.,* in the chapters relating to disabilities incident to minority. It will be sufficient, in this place, to notice the principal features (*n*). Story—pressed by the weight of his own *erudition*—knowing how much the law of the United States of North America differed from that of the rest of Christendom on this point, and anxious to defend "the Common Law," is driven to the necessity of making such statements as these :—" The truth, however, " seems to be that there are, properly speaking, no universal " rules by which nations are, or ought to be, morally or politi- " cally bound to each other on this subject : whatever rules it " may adopt, or whatever it may repudiate, will be alike the " dictate of its own policy and sense of justice : and whatever " it may allow or withhold, will always be measured by its " own opinion of the public (*i. e.* the domestic) convenience " and benefit, or of the public prejudice and injury arising " therefrom."

These observations are made, generally, it must be remarked, not with respect to the particular exceptions demanded by the public policy of the State ; but with respect to personal qualities of a general nature : and it is obvious that if his doctrine be sound, there is an end, altogether, so far as *Status* is concerned, of a *Jus Gentium* and of Private International Law, founded upon the theory of a community of States. It is a matter of indifference (Story says) whether a country suffers the *Status* of foreigners to be governed by the Law of their Domicil or not—whether it adopt the Law of their "actual Domicil" according to "the more general doctrine;" or, according to "the "stricter doctrine," it adopt the Law of "the Domicil of Birth :" probably the former, he says, is the safer and most convenient rule. But surely this is a false standard and a Lesbian measure. The question, in matters of this *universal* character —in which no consideration of imperial policy or constitutional law is concerned,—is, what does universal justice demand ? not

what does the supposed convenience of a particular State require. See the consequence. The Court of Louisiana (o), in a celebrated and leading case, came to the monstrous conclusion, viz. :—that they would recognise the personal disability of a foreigner in a case of minority, where it was contrary to their own law on the subject, if such recognition helped to sustain a contract with an American citizen ; but if it had the opposite effect, they would refuse to recognise it —in the one case the *lex domicilii*, in the other, the *lex loci contractûs* ought to govern. Now, Story is at a loss to understand this decision, he says :—" Such a course of decision cer-
" tainly may be adopted by a *government* if it shall so
" chose. But, then, it would seem to stand upon mere arbitrary
" legislation and positive law, and not upon principle. The
" difficulty is in seeing how a *court*, without any such positive
" legislation, could arrive at both conclusions." But if, in the case of a foreigner, a court may mete out justice according to its opinion of what is best for " the public conveniences " of its own State, the difficulty does not seem great. " Public con-
" venience," considered altogether apart from private justice, may point out, as it appears to have done, the adoption of both principles, though absolutely repugnant to each other.

It is very remarkable that the same Court appears previously to have laid down in substance, the general European Doctrine, " that the Laws of the Domicil of Origin govern the
" state and condition of the minor into whatever country he
" removes." (*p*) and " that personal incapacities communi-
" cated by the laws of any particular place, accompany the
" person wherever he goes" (*q*).

The Court appears to have departed from this doctrine in later cases ; but they are remarkable as being, I believe, the only instances in which the European Doctrine of *Status* has

---

(o) *Saul* v. *his Creditors*, 17 *Martin* (*Americ.*) *Rep.* 596.

(p) *Story*, s. 77.   *Barrera* v. *Alpuente*, 18 *Martin* (*Americ.*) *Rep.* 69.

(q) *Ib.*, s. 78.   *Le Breton* v. *Fouchet*, 3 *Martin* (*Americ.*) *Rep.* 60.

been maintained by a Court in the United States of North America.

An English President of the Court of Demerara and Essequibo, Mr. Henry, (r) in giving judgment on a plea of English certificate of bankruptcy in bar, in a foreign jurisdiction, to the suit of a foreign creditor, observes as follows:—
" Again, the effect which one country gives to the laws of
" another, is further shewn in the case of prodigals, minors,
" idiots, lunatics : these qualities accompany the person every-
" where, when attached to him by a competent jurisdiction in
" his own country, so far, that the foreign judge will confirm
" them as to property in his own jurisdiction." And the learned judge in the preface to the report of his judgment remarks, " although the universal admission of Foreign Law in
" any State would be highly dangerous, yet, the knowledge
" and admission of it in those cases which are of an *univer-*
" *sal nature,* as those of bankruptcy, idiotcy, lunacy, majority,
" minority, (s) marriage, and wills, and which necessarily affect
" the intercourse of different States with each other, would,
" for many reasons to be seen in the course of the work, be
" highly desirable and advantageous to commercial inter-
" course" (t). And again, " personal universal qualities of
" whatsoever kind, by virtue of the third general proposition,
" and the Comity of nations, accompany the person every-
" where" (u).

CCCLXXXIV. But the English Courts have been supposed to hold that certain incapacities attached by the Law of their

---

(r) *Henry on Foreign Law; Odwin* v. *Forbes* (1823, A.D.). This important judgment was confirmed on appeal, and was dedicated, *by permission,* to Sir W. Grant. It is, or was, entitled therefore, to every respect. Yet, some of the principles contained in it have been, as will be seen, entirely departed from.

(s) This is not to be reconciled with *Ruding* v. *Smith,* 2 *Consistory Reports,* 391—2.

(t) *Henry on Foreign Law,* pp. 8 and 9, *Odwin* v. *Forbes.*

(u) *Ib.* p. 5.

Domicil to minors, do not necessarily travel with them into other countries : and to have pronounced Contracts of Marriage (*x*) as well as contracts for loans of money(*y*) by English persons, valid, according to the *lex loci contractús*, but invalid according to the Law of the English Domicil, to be valid contracts in England. While, on the other hand, they have holden that certain incapacities, attached by the *lex domicilii*, do travel with the individual, and have refused to recognise the validity of a second marriage contracted by English persons, during the life of the first wife, after a divorce by a foreign State of an English marriage : (*z*) they have also refused to recognise the validity of an English marriage abroad, within the prohibited degrees of affinity (*a*).

So they have refused to recognize marriages contracted abroad in evasion of the English Statute, respecting the Royal Family (*b*).

And the English Courts have also made the following irreconcileable decisions. They have holden that the legitimacy of a person depends on the Law of his Origin or Birth(*c*): and yet, that a person legitimate by that law (*d*) may be incapable of inheriting *real* estate in England, because he was not legitimate for that purpose (*e*).

The English Law would probably respect the *patria potestas* of a foreign father, (*f*) that is within all reasonable limits :

(*x*) *Dalrymple* v. *Dalrymple*, 2 *Consistory*, 54, supposed to be the leading case, *sed vide post*, as to how far the supposed doctrine is explained and affected by *Brook* v. *Brook*.

(*y*) *Male* v. *Roberts*, 2 *Espinasse*, N. R. p. 163.

(*z*) *Conway* v. *Beasley*, 3 *Haggard's Reports*, 639.

Lolly's Case, 1 *Russell and Ryan's Cases*, 239.

(*a*) *Brook* v. *Brook*, 3 *Smale and Grainger's Reports*, 48.

(*b*) *Duke of Sussex's Case*, vide post.

(*c*) In re *Wright's Trust*, 2 *Kay and Johnson's Rep.* 575. *vide post*.

(*d*) *e. g.* legitimate *per subsequens matrimonium*—*vide post*.

(*e*) *Vide post*.

(*f*) *Johnstone* v. *Beattie*, 10 *Clarke and Finnelley's Rep.* 114; *vide post*.

while it appears to have refused to recognise the authority of a foreign guardian of an infant, (*g*), or of a foreign curator (committee) of a lunatic (*h*).

CCCLXXXV. The result of this examination of the Law of England, and of those States of the United States of North America which have adopted that law, is, that these countries do at present, on principle, refuse to recognize universally the *personal statute* or law of the *Status*, imposed by a foreign Domicil, and are at variance in this particular, with the usages of the other States of Christendom (*i*).

CCCLXXXVI. Thirdly; it remains to consider the limitations to the doctrine which prevail both as to the Foreign and and English Law, as to the recognition of a foreign personal *Status*.

CCCLXXXVII. And first, as to the limitations, which are admitted even by the State, which applies the Personal Law of the Domicil to the individual wheresoever he may be.

Savigny divides these limitations into two classes :—

A. Where the Law affecting the *Status* belongs to that anomalous class of positive and absolute laws which are without the limits of the community of Law among independent States ; and under this head he enumerates the following cases.

a. Where the Personal Law of the Domicil permits polygamy.

β. Where it incapacitates on the ground of heresy.

γ. As to Ecclesiastical Corporations of foreigners—they would be subject to the restrictive Laws of the foreign State in which they acquire property : and *vice versâ*, would not carry with them the restrictive laws of their Domicil into a State which had no such laws.

(*g*) *Johnstone* v. *Beattie,* 10 *Clarke and Finnelly's Reports,* 114, *vide post.*

(*h*) *Sylva* v. *Da Costa,* 8 *Vesey,* 316, *Re Houstoun,* 1 *Russell's Rep.* 312, *vide post.*

(*i*) *Sed vide post, Brook* v. *Brook,* as to English Law.—*Story,* s. 103.

δ. If the Law of a State declares Jews incapable of acquiring immoveable property, it will affect foreign Jews who are not so incapacitated by the Law of their Domicil.

In some portion of the eastern department of France, Jews are not allowed to become creditors by loan of money except under some very severe restrictions.

This law would affect foreign as well as native Jews (k).

The foregoing limitations of the General Law of Domicil are founded upon the fact that the Personal Law which is to be applied has a character of positive and rigorous obligation (l).

The following limitations are founded upon the peculiarity of a particular institution of a State which is not recognised by the general community of States.

a. Of this class is the incapacity of acquiring legal rights attached to *civil death* by the Law of France and Russia. The State which has no such law would not recognize this Law of the Domicil, Savigny says. And yet it would be difficult to distinguish this case from that of the incapacity of a monk to inherit, which Savigny seems to think would be enforced by a State which did not recognize monastic institutions.

β. Of this class, too, are the disabilities which belong to a state of slavery in a State which does not recognise this accursed condition.

CCCLXXXVIII.—B. The second class of limitations which Savigny applies to the general adoption of the Personal Law of the Domicil, are derived from cases, which, inasmuch as they do not relate either to the capacity of being the passive subject of

---

(k) *Wächter* II. 173.

Fœlix, p. 147.

Seuffert Archiv für Entscheidungen der obersten Gerichte in den deutschen Staaten, B. 1, N. 35.

Savigny viii. s. 365.

(l) " Eine streng positive und zwingende natur" *Savigny, Ib.*

rights or to the capacity of actively acquiring them, do not, properly speaking, affect the application of the rule ; or in other words, are only apparent, and not real limitations of it. Such are—

1. Peculiar rights of a privileged class of nobility with respect to the acquisition of, or succession to, immoveable property.

The question whether or no a foreign nobleman shall be admitted to the privilege, has clearly no reference to general principles of Law at all; it is a question as to the Law on which that particular class of privileges is founded.

2. The same may be predicated of certain privileges (m) belonging to ecclesiastical establishments, and the public treasury (which is, of course, the national treasury only), when creditors in a case of bankruptcy.   This is a matter belonging exclusively to the Laws of Bankruptcy (n).

3. With respect to the *restitution* of minors : this has lost its primitive character of a restraint on the capacity of acting ; and, with reference to the application of the Law of Domicil, is to be rather classed among the grounds of impugning a juridical act (o).

4. So with respect to the privilege which protects minors against all prescriptions under thirty years.   This has no connection with a restraint on the capacity of acting ; it does not fall under the principle of applying the Law of the Domicil, but under the rules which relate to prescription.

CCCLXXXIX. Such are the only limitations which Savigny admits to the universal recognition of the Personal Law of the Domicil.

The English and North Americans *e converso* admit the Personal Law of the Domicil only as an exception to the universal recognition of the *lex loci actûs vel contractûs* (p).

(m) *Privilegien im concurs.*

(n) *Wächter* II. ss. 179, 181.

(o) *Ib.*, ss. 174, 179.

(p) *Story*, ss. 102, 103.

The nature of these exceptions (*q*) has been already mentioned. Both kinds of limitations or exceptions will be considered in the following Chapters, which treat of the validity of obligations, contracts, acts done, and rights acquired by a foreigner. With the consideration of all these subjects the question of *Status* is more or less intimately connected.

(*q*) *Vide ante*, pp. 12, 13, 14.

CHAPTER XVIII.

MARRIAGE.

CCCXC. We have now arrived at the Second Branch of the General Subject of this Work ; namely, the Legal Relations arising from Family (a).

The Legal Relations arising from Property affect the person through the medium of external circumstances, which are within the scope of individual option.

The Rights and Duties incident to Family, accrue to persons in great measure arbitrarily, and without their choice.

CCCXCI. Under this title are to be considered :—

1. Marriage and Divorce.
2. Legitimacy.
3. Parental Authority.

In this chapter it is proposed to consider the Principles and Rules of Comity respecting Marriage.

CCCXCII. The Legal Relations arising from Marriage, have, in all countries, been affected, not only by the principles of morality, which are universal, but by Religious and Political opinions, which are not universal ; and, therefore, it would be natural to expect, on this subject, the intervention of many obstacles to the universal prevalence of those general rules which it is the great object of Comity, the handmaid of Civilization, to effect. On the other hand, the great importance of mutually maintaining and acknowledging these Legal Relations has approached so nearly to a necessity as to counteract, to some extent, the tendency to a discordant practice, which religion or politics might create.

CCCXCIII. These remarks apply with particular force to

(a) *Vide ante*, p. 23.

all questions connected with the validity of the Marriage
Contract itself.

The question as to the validity of this, as of inferior contracts, involves two considerations :

1. The external formalities, or the outward form of the
Contract.

2. The capacity of the contractors.

CCCXCIV. (1.) With respect to the outward form (b) : just
considerations of the immense importance attaching to the
validity of that Contract which is the foundation of the State
and the nursery of the Commonwealth (c), have induced all
civilized nations to recognize universally the principle *locus
regit actum.*

That the law of the place of celebration is binding as to the
outward form is a *recepta sententia* of Private International
Law.

CCCXCV. (2.) With respect to the capacity of the persons
contracting the *de facto* marriage.

Upon this important question there is a great and lamentable difference in the laws and judicial decisions of different
States.

(b) First among the Canonists on this subject is *Sanchez, de Matri-
monio, Lib.* iii. *Disp.* 18, s. 10, n. 26—28.

Among the numerous civilians of the seventeenth century (the cases
usually referred to), the two Voets.

P. Voet, de Statutis et eorum concursu, s. 9, cl. ii.

J. Voet, ad Pandectas, l. xxiii. t. ii. s. 4.

For modern writers see—

Schauffer, S. Kap. ss, 99, 100, 101, 102, 103.

Pütter, ss. 36—43.

Wächter, s. 23.   Archiv. für die Civ. Prax. 6, 25, 184—7.

Savigny, R.R. viii. 337—357.

Fælix, Revue Etrangère, 1841, t. viii. p. 433, des mariages contractés
en pays Etranger.

Story, Conflict, ss. 80, 81, and ch. v.

(c) It is the parent, not the child, of civil society. "Principium
urbis et quasi seminarium reipublicæ" (Cii. de Off. 1, 17).   Lord Stowell
in *Dalrympie* v. *Dalrymple,* 2 *Consistory Reports,* p. 63.

CCCXCVI. The Courts in England (d) have decided that a marriage valid between parties according to the *lex loci contractûs* is valid everywhere.

Did they mean, thereby, merely to affirm what has been already said, namely, that the form and the rites of the contract were to be governed by the *lex loci;* or did they mean to affirm that—though one or both of the parties to the contract might be incapable, by the Laws of his or her Domicil, by reason of minority, the absence of paternal consent, or for any other reason not of the character already mentioned, as taking the case, on special grounds (e), out of the consideration of Comity—did they mean to affirm the validity of the marriage, even though the marriage has been contracted avowedly in *fraudem legis domesticœ,* by parties who have left their own country for the express purpose of evading its laws and returned directly afterwards to it? Is, nevertheless, the marriage, once duly contracted according to the forms of the country in which it is celebrated, for ever after binding in England?

CCCXCVII. Certainly, ever since the decision of Lord Stowell in *Dalrymple* v. *Dalrymple* (f) ; indeed, since the earlier decision of the Judges Delegate, in *Harford* v. *Morris* (g), it has been the general opinion among lawyers in England and the United States of North America (h) that marriages

---

(d) There are four classes of English statutes on the subject of Marriage :—

1. The General Marriage Statutes (26 Geo. II. c. 33, 4 Geo. IV. c. 76).

2. The Statutes regulating the Marriages of Dissenters, or those which enable persons to marry without the aid of any religious rite (6 & 7 Will. IV. c. 85).

3. The Statute declaring the invalidity of Marriages contracted within the prohibited degrees of affinity and consanguinity (5 & 6 Will. IV. c. 54).

4. The Statute affecting the Marriages of the Royal Family, or of the descendants of King George the Second (12 Geo. III. c. xi).

(e) *Vide ante,* pp. 15, 16, 17.

(f) 2 *Consistory Rep.* 59 (A.D. 1811).

(g) 2 *Ib.* 423 (A.D. 1776).

(h) *Story,* s. 123a—6.

contracted abroad by English domiciled subjects, like the
Gretna Green or Scotch Marriages, for the purpose of evading
the English Law, were valid in England, if valid *lege loci contractûs.*

But in the year 1857, this general opinion received a great
shock. In that year Mr. Vice-Chancellor Stuart and Mr. Justice Cresswell decided that a marriage celebrated during a
temporary residence in Denmark between an English widower
and the sister of his deceased wife, being null by the statute
5 & 6 William, was not valid, although valid by the Law of
Denmark, the *lex loci contractûs.*

This decision did not necessarily affect the general question
of the validity of marriages duly contracted abroad ; because
the case of an incestuous marriage fell under the category
of exceptional cases (*i*), in which Comity did not require the
adoption of the Foreign Law. But incidentally, and in the
course of the judgment, it was denied that even where the case
was not of this exceptional character, the Courts of England
had ever laid down the doctrine that marriages celebrated
abroad in *fraudem legis domesticæ* were valid, because valid
legi loci contractûs. The validity of the Gretna Green or
Scotch Marriages, was said to afford no proof to the contrary, because the English statute, which it was certainly the
object of the fugitives to evade, contained an express provision
whereby Scotland was excluded from its operation ; and
Mr. Justice Cresswell said :—" I have, therefore, come to the
" conclusion that a marriage, contracted by the subjects of a
" country in which they are domiciled, in another country, is
" not to be held valid, if, by contracting it, the laws of their
" own country are violated."(*k*).

The decision of the other learned judge, Mr. Vice-Chancellor
Stuart, was founded more entirely, if not altogether, upon the
marriage in question being positively prohibited by the law
of England as *contra bonos mores :* but he agreed with Mr.

(*i*) *Vide ante* p. 12.

(*k*) *Brook* v. *Brook,* 3 *Smale and Giffard's Reports,* 481 (A.D. 1857).

Justice Cresswell in his remarks upon the Gretna Green or Scotch Marriages.

CCCXCVIII. The case in which this judgment was delivered has been carried by appeal to the ultimate tribunal of the House of Lords, and will probably be affirmed or reversed before this volume be published; in which event the decision of the House of Lords will be noticed in the Preface or the Appendix to this work.

CCCXCIX. In the meanwhile, the conclusion at which Mr. Justice Cresswell arrived as to the foreign marriage of English subjects generally is of the utmost importance. The direct consequence of it may be to place the English Law in accordance with that of the Continent, and at variance with that of the United States of North America. It appears to adopt the sound principle of Private International Law as to Personal Statutes, or qualities impressed upon persons by the Law of this Domicil, namely : " Quando " lex in personam dirigitur respicienda est ad leges illius civitatis, " quæ personam habet subjectam." It seems to bring the law on the Contract of Marriage in harmony with the law which governs every contract. " It was admitted" (Story (l) says, speaking of the contrary doctrine maintained by the Court of Massachusetts and by himself), " on that occasion by the " Court, that the doctrine is repugnant to the general principles " of law relating to contracts : for a fraudulent evasion of, or " fraud upon the laws of the country where the parties have " their Domicil would not, except in the Contract of Marriage, " be protected under the general principle." It matures into a sound judgment the hint of the great jurist and judge, Lord Mansfield. "It has been laid down" (Lord Mansfield said) " at the bar, that a marriage in a foreign country must be " governed by the law of the country where the marriage " was had ; which in general is true. But the Marriages in " Scotland of persons going from hence for that purpose were " instanced by way of example. They may come under a " very different consideration, according to the opinion of

" Huberus and other writers (*m*)." It brings the law upon marriage into harmony with some of the ablest decisions of English Judges, as to the legitimation of children born after marriage of Domiciled Scotchmen and Englishmen which will be presently considered more at length (*n*).

* The following observations upon the judgment of Mr. Justice Cresswell had been printed before the case of *Simonin* v. *Mallac* (*o*) had been argued before the Court of Divorce. In the course of his argument upon that case, the author of this work cited the judgment of Mr. Justice Cresswell in *Brook* v. *Brook* as an authority for the position that the English Courts ought to hold invalid a Marriage contracted in England, according to the English Law, but contrary to the French Law, by two French subjects domiciled in France.

The Judge Ordinary, Sir Cresswell Cresswell, however, expressly and distinctly repudiated this construction of the language, which, when Mr. Justice Cresswell, he had used in the case of *Brook* v. *Brook ;* that language, he said, was to be construed *secundum subjectam materiam*, and did not go beyond the proposition that the Court of the Domicil had a right to recognize incapacities affixed by the Law of the Domicil as invalidating a contract entered into in another country between parties belonging to that Domicil ; and that nothing he had said affected in any way the proposition contended for, namely, that the Court of the place of the Contract of Marriage ought to recognize the incapacities affixed by the Law of the Domicil on the parties to the Contract.*

CCCC. A singular case growing out of the Marriage Contract illustrates the difficulties which may arise on this subject between a Christian State and a heathen dependency.

It has been holden that the Supreme Court of Bombay *on its Ecclesiastical side* has no jurisdiction to entertain such a suit,

---

(*m*) *Robinson* v. *Bland*, 2 *Burrow's Reports*, 1079,1080.

(*n*) *Munro* v. *Munro*, 7 *Clarke and Finnelly's Rep.* 782, *Lord Cottenham.*

In re Wright's Trust. 3 *Kay and Johnson's Rep.* p. 419.

(*o*) Judgment will be noticed in Preface or Appendix.

as there existed such a difference between the duties and obligations of a matrimonial union among Parsees from that of Christians, that the Court, if it made a decree, had no means of enforcing it, except according to the principles governing the Matrimonial Law in England, which were in such a case incompatible with the laws and customs of the Parsees (o).

CCCCI. The Law in France, upon the foreign marriage of Frenchmen, may be briefly stated as follows :—

First, by the 170th (p) article of the Code Civil, it is enacted that, (1) " a marriage contracted abroad between a " French subject or between a French and a foreign subject, " shall be valid, if celebrated according to the forms in use in " the country of its celebration—*provided* (2) that it has " been preceded by the notices prescribed by the 63rd article " in the title *des actes l'état civil* ; and, *provided,* (3) that the " Frenchman have not contravened the regulations contained " in the preceding chapter" (q).

With regard to the *forms*, as has been already said, France applies, like other nations, the rule *locus regit actum.*

It should, however, be mentioned here, that though a French Diplomatic Agent or Consul may lawfully marry two French subjects abroad, it has been holden in France that he cannot marry a French subject and a foreigner, because he has no authority or jurisdiction over the latter (r).   But, with

---

(o) *Ardaseer Cursetjee* v. *Perozeboye*, 10 *Moore's Privy C. Rep.* p. 374.

(p) *Code Civil,* Art. 170. " Le mariage contracté en pays étranger entre Français, et entre *Français* et étrangers, sera valable, s'il a été célébré dans les formes usitées dans les pays, pourvu qu'il ait été précédé des publications prescrites par l'art. 63, au titre des Actes de l'état civil, et que le Français n'ait point contrevenu aux dispositions contenues au chapitre précédent (C. 47, 48)."

(q) *Titre Cinquième,* Du Mariage, Art. 144, 164.

(r) *Revue Etrangère,* t. viii. p. 435. Des Mariages contractés en pays étranger-par *Fœlix,* ch. i. 2, 2, citing *Duranton,* Cours de droit Français, t. ii. Nos. 234, 235, arrêt de la Cour de Cassation du 10 Août 1819 (*Sirey* 1819, I. 492). Jugement du tribunal de la Seine du 30 Décembre, 1837 (*Gazette des Tribunaux du* 31.)

respect to the capacity of the contracting parties, it is clear, from the citation already made from the Code, that France does not agree with England upon this point; and this becomes more certain as we unravel the provisions of their 170th article.

CCCCII. Secondly,—By the 63rd article (s) it is enacted, that the marriage must be preceded by two public notices (*publications*), made, with an interval of eight days, before the door of the Domicil of the future husband; that Domicil being the place of his residence for the last six months, in France. If he be, relatively to his marriage, subject to the control of others, the notice must be made before the door of the domicil of such persons. The French subject who has preserved his French Domicil, must cause these notices in France to precede his marriage in a Foreign State.

CCCCIII. Thirdly,—Moreover, he must comply with the requisitions contained in the chapter on marriage, in the Code Civil (art. 144, 164). The husband must be of the age of eighteen, or the wife of fifteen; he must have consented; be unmarried at the time; his future wife must not be within the prohibited degrees; he must have obtained the consent of his *ascendants* or of the *family council*, (*conseil de famille*).

CCCCIV. The question, how far the absence of these public notices, (*publications*), and the previous reference to ascendants, (*actes respectueux*), affect the validity of a marriage celebrated abroad does not appear to have received

---

(s) *Revue Etrangère, ib.*

Code Civil, Art. 63. " Avant la célébration du mariage, l'officier de l'etat civil fera deux publications, à huit jours d'intervalle un jour de Dimanche, devant la porte de la maison commune. Ces publications, et l'acte qui en sera dressé, énonceront les prénoms, noms, professions et domiciles des futurs époux, leur qualité de majeurs ou de mineurs, et les prénoms, noms, professions et domiciles de leurs péres et mères. Cet acte énoncera, en outre, les jours, lieux et heures où les publications auront été faites : il sera inscrit sur un seul registre, qui sera coté et paraphé comme il est dit en l'art. 41 et déposé, à la fin de chaque année, au greffe du tribunal de l'arrondissement. (C. 94, 95, 166s. 192, 193.)"

an uniform judicial interpretation in France (*t*). But it does appear that the *Cour de Cassation*, on the 6th of March, 1837, and the *Cour Royale of Angers*, on the 12th of January, 1838, have decided (*u*), (the second being only a re-production of the first), that a marriage wanting these preliminaries, is absolutely void.

The language of the arrêt of 1837, is here given in its own words :

" Attendu que l'on ne peut pas interpréter l'article 170 du " Code Civil, sur les mariages contractés à l'étranger, par " les dispositions du même Code relatives aux mariages " célébrés en France : que, si ces derniers peuvent être " déclarés valables, lorsqu' il n'y a eu ni publications, ni " actes respectueux, c'est parce que la loi trouve sa sanction " dans les peines qu'elle prononce contre les officiers de l'état " civil qui auraient précédé à la célébration ; tandis que, " pour les mariages contractés a l'étranger, comme les mêmes " dispositions pénales ne pourraient atteindre les officiers pub-" lics, la loi n'avait d'autre moyen de donner une sanction à " ses prescriptions, qu'en frappant le mariage lui-même " d'invalidité ; que s'il en était autrement, il suffirait à des " Français de passer à l'étranger pour affranchir leur mariage " de toutes les conditions imposées par les lois Françaises, et " pour, en s'abstenant des publications et des actes respec-" tueux exigés, se soustraire, soit aux oppositions des tiers-" soit à l'autorité de la puissance paternelle."

CCCCV. The high authority of M. Fælix is opposed to the soundness of this judgment ; and his argument concerning the whole question, viz., the effect of the non-observance of the formalities prescribed by the French Law in nullifying a marriage contracted without these formalities in a foreign State, with a foreigner, appears irresistible ; a question, it must be admitted, of no mean importance to the subjects of all other States, and especially to the near neighbours of France, among whom these marriages are most frequently contracted.

(*t*) *Revue Etrangère*, p. 436.
(*u*) *Ib.* 439.

The reasoning of M. Fælix is to this effect :—

The *Arrêt* above cited, declares that the non-observance of the prescribed preliminary formalities, renders the marriage null and void, for two reasons.   1. That the French Law cannot punish the officers of another country, and therefore it can only mark its sense of the violation of Law by striking at the validity of the marriage—an argument which is not very satisfactory or convincing to foreigners.   2. That, otherwise, French subjects might evade the French Law, as to marriage.

To the first reason he replies that the fact of its being impossible to inflict a fine or punishment upon the officer of a foreign State can never justify an entire alteration in the Law, and introduce a power, which would not otherwise exist, of nullifying a marriage ; that such doctrine would lead to monstrous consequences : and that it is clear that the authors of the Code never intended that the marriage should be set aside whenever the officer of the State before whom it was contracted was the subject of and resident in another country.

The true exposition of the Law is, that if the non-observance of these particular preliminaries would not nullify the marriage of a Frenchman if contracted *at home*, they will not nullify it if contracted *abroad*.

The question, therefore, is, would the non-observance of the preliminaries—these *publications*, and *actes respectueux*— vitiate the marriage in France ?   The answer is in the negative, whether the *object*, the *letter*, or the *spirit* of the Law be considered.

The *object* of the 170th Article was to apply to French Marriages, wheresoever celebrated, two fundamental principles of French Law :—

a. That the form of Acts or Contracts is governed by the Law of the place where they are entered into.

β. That the Laws which concern the state or capacity of persons,—*i. e.* Personal Statutes,—govern French subjects, even while resident in a foreign State (*x*).

(*x*) Art. 3.—" Les lois de police et de sûreté obligent tous ceux qui habitent le territoire. (I. 5s).

The *letter* or text of this Law employs very general terms. The reference to the 63rd Article, and to the first chapter of the Title on Marriage, only applies to French subjects abroad the Laws existing at home respecting Marriage.

If it had been intended to establish, in the 170th Article, an objection to the 3rd Article, it would have been expressed, and not left to conjecture.

The particular words "provided that" (*pourvu que*), implies an indispensable condition (*condition irritante*); so the absence of these preliminaries necessarily nullifies the marriage.

But Merlin agrees with Fælix in interpreting this language to mean only that *there are cases* in which this non-observance *may* influence the annulling of the Marriage, on the ground of *clandestinity*; and the Court of Appeal at Brussels decided to this effect, 28th July, 1848 (*y*).

As to the *spirit* of the Law : all legislators have recognized a distinction in the nature of the conditions required for the due solemnization of a marriage, some being deemed of an *essential*, some of a *precautionary* character. The Code establishes a complete system upon this subject. There is no

---

"Les immeubles, même ceux possédés par des étrangers, sont régis par la loi Française.

"Les lois concernant l'état et la capacité des personnes régissent les Français, même résidant en pas étranger. (C. 47, 48, 170, 2063.)"

(*y*) *Merlin's Rep.*, v. *Bans de Mariage*, 2.

Questions de Droit, v. *Publication des Mariages.*

"Les conditions que cet article impose au moyen des mots pourvu que, sont aussi relatives et s'appliquent aussi à la contravention aux dispositions que renforme le chapitre I., sous lequel se trouvent, non-seulement des dispositions dont l'inobservation entraîne la nullité absolue et irréparable du mariage, mais aussi des dispositions dont l'inobservation peut non-seulement se réparer mais vient même à disparaître par le seul laps de temps ; que, par conséquent, on ne peut induire du contenu littéral de l'article 170, que toute contravention indistinctement à l'une des dispositions du chapitre I., emporte nécessairement et per se, une nullité absolue. . . . ."—*Revue Etrang. ib,* 440—41.

reason for supposing that it meant to depart from that system in the case of marriages contracted *abroad*.

CCCCVI. Adopting, then, the sound and well-reasoned opinion of M. Fælix, that the non-observance of these preliminaries only which nullify a marriage contracted in France, nullify it when contracted abroad, the very important question remains, what are these?

The question may be answered generally and specifically. Generally, it may be said, in the language of the Cour Imperiale of Paris, which tried, in 1856, the case of M. Léfebvre, that no defect of these publications will invalidate a foreign Marriage, unless this defect be surrounded and further contaminated by a real clandestinity (*entouré, entaché d'une veritable clandestinité*) (*z*).

(*z*) The case is reported, *Gazette des Tribunaux*, 2 *Mars*, 1856. The judgment was as follows :—

" Attendu, en fait, que les père et mère de Lefebvre ont connu son mariage et qu'ils y ont consenti ;

" Qu'ils l'ont ratifié depuis son accomplissement ; que cette ratification résulte :

" Premièrement.   D'actes, déclarations, expressions de volonté maintes fois reiterées et impliquant le consentement le plus formel ;

" Deuxièmement.   De ce qu'ayant connu le mariage, ils sont demeurés plus d'un an sans l'attaquer et ne l'attaquent même pas aujourd'hui ;

" Que Lefebvre lui-même est demeuré plus d'un an sans attaquer son mariage depuis l'époque où il a été contracté, époque a laquelle il avait déjà l'âge competent pour consentir lui-même son mariage ;

" Attendu qu'aux termes de l'article 183 du Code Napoléon, les faits ci-dessus énoncés créent contre Lefebvre, comme ils créeraient contre ses père et mère eux-mêmes, une fin de non-recevoir ;

" Attendu qu'il résulte du texte et de l'esprit de la loi que le défaut de publications avant le mariage contracté à l'étranger n'est pas, à lui seul, une cause de nullité de mariage ;

" Que le defaut de publications ne peut contribuer à faire prononcer la nullite d'un mariage que lorsque ce mariage a été entaché d'une veritable clandestinité :

" Attendu que le mariage des époux Lefebvre, loin d'avoir été contracté clandestinement, a été entouré de toute la publicité necessaire ;

CCCCVII.   To answer the question specifically it should be observed—

First, a Marriage contracted by a French subject abroad, may be impeached in the terms of the 191st Article (a) on the ground that it has not been *publicly* contracted (*contracté publiquement*).

The text of this article not expressly pronouncing that the marriage is null, because the 63rd, 166th, and 167th articles have been contravened, leaves a large latitude to the discretion of the Judge, to consider whether there has been the requisite *publicity* or not; and the absence of the *publications* and *actes respectueux*, may or may not be adminicular to the proof of non-publicity or *clandestinity*.

They are not, however, necessarily so ; and the French Tribunals have held that these formalities have been enacted by

---

" Que ce serait à Lefebvre, demandeur, de prouver la clandestinité ; qu'il ne rapporte aucunne preuve ni justification à cet égard ;

" Que la publicité résulte des formes mêmes dans lesquelles le mariage a été célébré ;

" Qu'elle résulte, en outre, des toutes les circonstances qui ont precédé et accompagné ce mariage ;

" Declare Lefebvre mal fondé en sa demande, l'en déboute, et le condamne aux dépens.'

M. Lefebvre est appellant de ce jugement.

I have not learnt whether the appeal was prosecuted, or what was the result.

In the case of the succession of *M. J. P. Pescatore*,* the Civil Tribunal of the Seine declared itself divided, and therefore expressed no opinion on the validity of a marriage of French persons in Spain, which the next of kin of the husband applied to set aside as clandestine and void under the French Law, and void, also, by the Law of Spain, the priest who officiated being neither the Parochus of the parties, nor duly authorized under the Decree of the Council of Trent.

(a) Art. 191.—" Tout mariage qui n'a point été contracté publiquement et qui n'a point été célébrê devant l'officier public compétent, peut être attaqué par les epoux eux-mêmes, par les père et mère, par les ascendans, et par tous ceux qui y ont un intérêt né et actuel, ainsi que par le ministère public." (C. 75, 165, 170.—T. C. 121.)

---

the 191st article, in order to prevent an infringement of the fundamental provisions of the above-mentioned first chapter; and that where the Court is of opinion that these have not been infringed, the marriage, in spite of the absence of the *publication*, will be pronounced *valid* (*b*).

On the other hand, where it is proved that the marriage was contracted abroad *in order* to escape from the prohibitions of the French Law—where, in fact, it was intentionally clandestine—it will be pronounced *invalid* (*e*).

Secondly. The marriage of a Frenchman under 25, and of a Frenchwoman under 21 years of age, may be annulled, under the terms of the article 182 (*d*). But it has been held, that the absence of the *actes respectueux*, prescribed in articles 151, 152, 153, (*e*) do not generate a nullity (*f*).

(*b*) *Rev. Etrang. ib.* 441—45. Arrêt de la Cour d' Appel de Bruxelles, 18 Juin, 1828, *Table générale* v. *Mariage*, No. 6.

(*c*) Arrêt de la Cour de Cassation, 12 Février, 1833, et 6 Mars, 1837.

(*d*) Art. 182.—" Le mariage contracté sans le consentement des père et mère, des ascendans, ou du conseil de famille, dans les cas où ce consentement était nécessaire, ne peut être attaqué que par ceux dont le consentement était requis, ou par celui des deux époux qui avait besoin de ce consentement." (C. 148 s. 201, 202.)

(*e*) Art. 151.—" Les enfans de famille ayant atteint la majorité fixée par l'art. 148, sont tenus, avant de contracter mariage, de demander, par un acte respectueux et formel, le conseil de leur père et de leur mère, ou celui de leurs aïeuls et aïeules, lorsque leur père et leur mère sont décédés, ou dans l'impossibilité de manifester leur volonté." (C. 157.— T. 168.)

Art. 152.—" Depuis la majorité fixée. par l'art. 158 jusqu'à l'âge de trente ans accomplis pour les fils, et jusqu'à l'âge de vingt-cinq ans accomplis pour les filles, l'acte respectueux prescrit par l'article précédent ; et sur lequel il n'y aurait pas de consentement au mariage, sera renouvelé deux autres fois, de mois en mais ; et un mois après le troisième acte, il pourra être passé outre à la célébration du mariage." (C, 157, 158.—T. 168.)

Art. 153.—" Après l'âge de trente ans, il pourra être, a défaut de consentement sur un acte respectueux, passé outre, un mois après à la célébration du mariage."

(*f*) *Rev. Etraug. ib.* 444.

Thirdly (g). Marriages contracted abroad, within the French prohibited degrees, are invalid in France.

CCCCVIII. If the validity of a marriage contracted abroad, be impeached in France, the defendant is entitled to plead the same defence as if it had been contracted in France, and invoke for this purpose the (h) 183rd and (i) 185th articles of the Code.

Although, by article (k) 171, a French marriage abroad ought to be transcribed on the public Registry of Marriages, in the place of the Domicil of the French husband, three months after his return home, yet, no penalty is attached to the omission; and before the registration, both parties may claim the civil rights of marriage (l).

CCCCIX. France possesses no written law in the Code Civil, or elsewhere, as to marriages contracted in France between foreigners, or between French subjects and foreigners (m); the question is therefore subjected to the general principles of French jurisprudence.

(g) *Rev. Etrang.* 442.

(h) Art. 183.—"L'action en nullité ne peut plus être intentée ni par les époux, ni par les parens dont le consentement était requis, toutes les fois que le mariage a été approuvé expressément ou tacitement par ceux dont le consentement était nécessaire, ou lorsqu'il s'est écoulé une année sans réclamation de leur part, depuis qu'ils ont eu connaissance du mariage. Elle ne peut être intenté non plus par l'époux, lorsqu'il s'est écoulé une année sans réclamation de sa part, depuis qu'il a atteint l'âge compétent pour consentir par lui-même au mariage."

(i) Art. 185.—"Néanmoins le mariage contracté par des époux qui n'avaient point encore l'âge requis, ou dont l'un des deux n'avait point atteint cet âge, ne peut plus être attaqué, 1° lorsqu'il s'est écoulé six mois depuis qui cet époux ou les époux ont atteint l'âge competent; 2° lorsque la femme qui n'avait point cet âge, a concu avant l'échéance de six mois."

(k) Art. 171.—"Dans les trois mois après le retour du Francais sur le territoire du royaume, l'acte de célébration du mariage contracté en pays étranger sera transcrit sur le registre public des mariages du lieu de son domicile." (C. 40*s.*)

(l) 8 *Rev. Etrang.* 446—7.

(m) *Ib.* 448—457.

These marriages, therefore, as to *form*, depend upon the French Laws already cited : *locus regit actum* is the principle applied to them.

These marriages, as to all that concerns their *substance* and their intrinsic validity, depend upon the Law of the foreigner's Domicil. All that relates to the *status* and *capacity* of the foreigner to contract, is governed by this Law. *Statutum personœ sequitur personam* (*n*) is the principle applied to these cases.

CCCCX. Thus, the marriage of a subject of Wurtemburg, by the Law of which State a subject is incapable of marrying before his twenty-fifth year is completed, would be held invalid if contracted before that period, though contracted in France, which permits, as has been said, marriage at the age of eighteen or fifteen years.

CCCCXI. Again, by a Law of Bavaria, (12th July, 1818,) and of Wurtemburg, (4th September, 1818,) the subjects of these kingdoms are forbidden to marry abroad, without the permission of their respective governments.

A marriage by such subjects in France, without such permission, would be pronounced null and void in that country.

CCCCXII. The French subject, therefore, who marries a foreigner, in France, is exposed to the great risk of having his marriage annulled, on account of the provisions of a foreign law, of which he is wholly ignorant.

The French authorities appear to have vainly endeavoured to remedy this evil,—first, by requiring every foreigner, *non*

(*n*) The English lawyers are in the habit of supposing and enunciating that the English and Foreign Laws are agreed as to the doctrine "*mobilia sequuntur personam*" (*Bremer* v. *Freeman and Bremer*, A.D. 1857, J. C. of Privy Council) ; but they do not know, or forget that the foreign lawyers held also, and conjointly with it, the doctrine "*statutum personale sequitur personam*." The word " *persona*," therefore, conveys to the English and the foreign lawyer a very different meaning. *Vide post* as to the case of the testament made according to the Law of the Domicil.

naturalisé, to produce a certificate from the legal authorities of his Domicil, as to the absence of any legal impediments to his proposed marriage (*o*).

This scheme was thwarted, sometimes, by there being no officer at his Domicil qualified to give such a certificate ; for it seems, whimsically enough, never to have occurred to the French authorities that an analogous officer to the French *Maire* might not exist in other countries.

Sometimes, the officer of the Domicil refused to comply with the requisition.

This state of things was attempted to be remedied by a very strange regulation (*p*).   An *acte de notoriété* was, in the

---

(*o*) Dans plusieurs états limitrophes ou voisins de la France, la loi défend aux regnicoles de se marier en pays étranger sans l'autorisation du gouvernement, sous peine de la nullité de leur mariage.   Il résulte de là que les habitants de ces pays, attirés en France par l'activité de l'industrie ou par la richesse du sol, y ont épousé des Françaises sans avoir obtenu cette autorisation.   S'ils veulent ensuite retourner dans leur patrie, leurs femmes et leurs enfans s'en voient repoussés comme illégitimes.   Un tel état de choses impose au gouvernment Français le devoir de recourir à quelques précautions própres à assurer la validité de ces mariages contractés de bonne foi par des femmes qui, après l'accom·plissement de toutes les formalités requises par les lois Françaises, ont dû compter sur la protection de ces lois.   Le moyen le plus efficace me paraît être d'exiger de tout étranger, non naturalisé, qui voudra désormais se marier en France, la justification, par un certificat des autorités du lieu de sa naissance ou de son dernier domicile dans sa patrie, qu'il est apte, d'après les lois qui la régissent, à contracter mariage avec la personne qu'il se propose d'épouser.   En cas de con·testation, les tribunaux compétents seront appelés à statuer."—8 *Rev. Etrang.* pp. 449, 450.

(*p*) S'il y avait impossibilité d'obtenir le certificat d'aptitude prescrit par les instructions, parce que l'autorité du lieu de la naissance ou du dernier domicile du futur époux en pays étranger refuserait de délivrer une attestation de cette nature, on pourrait y suppléer par un acte de notoriété sous la forme indiquée dans l'article 70 du Code Civil.   Cet acte devrait être soumis à l'homologation préuve par l'article 72, s'il contenait en même temps l'attestation de l'impossibilité où la future se trouverait de se procurer son acte de naissance."—*Ib.* pp. 451, 452.

form prescribed by the (q) 70th article of the Code Civil, being afterwards ratified or subjected to *homologation* according to the 71st article (r).

This led to grievous abuses, and was intrinsically absurd; for this *acte* was satisfied by the appearance of seven individuals, taken from any class, swearing that the foreigner had applied in vain to the authorities of his Domicil for the proper certificate.

M. Fælix is of opinion that these attempts, though they have rendered *de facto* marriages of foreigners in France a matter of great facility, have by no means contributed to strengthen the validity of the marriage bond.

Marriages contracted on the faith of these *jugements d'homologation* are frequently only phantoms of a real marriage (*simulacre de mariage*). For instance, when the Laws of the foreigner's Domicil enact nullities unknown to the French Law; when the *acte de notoriété* is silent as to nullities recognized by the French Code, such as the prohibited degrees ; or when the *acte* announces the fact of there being no consent on the part of the parents.

At all events, M. Fælix thinks that foreign countries which hold that Personal Laws follow the person into a foreign land, will not consider that these nullities are cured by judgments of homologation (s).

(q) Art. 70.—" L'officier de l'état civil se fera remettre l'acte de naissance de chacun des futurs époux. Celui des époux que serait dans l'impossibilité de se le procurer, pourra le suppléer, en rapportant un acte de notoriété délivré par le juge de paix du lieu de sa naissance, ou par celui de son domicile."

(r) Art. 71.—" L'acte de notoriété contiendra la déclaration faite par sept témoins, de l'un ou de l'autre sexe, parens ou non parens, des prénoms, nom, profession et domicile du futur époux et de ceux de ses père et mère, s'ils sont connus : le lieu, et autant que possible, l'époque de sa naissance, et les causes qui empêchent d'en rapporter l'acte. Les témoins signeront l'acte de notoriété avec le juge de paix ; et s'il en est qui ne puissent ou ne sachent signer, il en sera fait mention." *Ib.* t. v, 16.

(s) " Le certificat exigé par la circulaire du 4 Mars 1831, est sans objet à l'égard des sujets du roi de Sardaigne, suivant la législation qui

CCCCXIII. The law respecting the marriage of foreigners in the U. S. of North America and France, and the wide difference between the jurisprudence of the two countries upon this point, have been mentioned.

The former, it has been seen, disregards the disabilities, with certain exceptions, imposed by the Personal Law of the Domicil, and looks only to the *lex loci contractûs*. The latter considers these disabilities as incapacitating the subject of them from marrying anywhere, and invalidates the *de facto* marriage which has been celebrated in defiance of them.

CCCCXIV. It may be well to remark here that the Law on Marriage generally admits, with respect to countries, of a division into two classes :—

1. Those countries in Europe and elsewhere, which have adopted, upon this point, the principles of the French Code, either literally or in the main.

2. Those which have derived their jurisprudence in this matter from a wholly different source.

CCCCXV. In the former class are Belgium, the Provinces on the Left Bank of the Rhine, the Duchy of Berg, the Kingdom of the Netherlands, the Grand Duchy of Baden, the Kingdom of the Two Sicilies.

The second class comprises the other countries of Europe.

CCCCXVI. With respect to the particular question which is now under discussion, namely, by what laws the marriage of foreigners, or of subjects elsewhere than in the place of their Domicil, is governed ? it is to be further remarked—

That, with respect to both these points, the countries which

---

les régit." M. le garde des sceaux ajoute que "les mariages des Sardes pour être valables, doivent être autorisés par le droit canonique, et de plus célébrés dans toutes les formalités du culte qu'ils professent ; mais que, comme la loi Française ne permet pas que le mariage religieux précède le mariage civil, il suffira désormais, à l'égard des sujets sardes qui désireraient se marier, de constater leur capacité légale d'après le droit canonique, et de prévenir en outre les futurs des conditions requises par le legislation étrangère."—8 *Rev. Etrang.* pp. 455, 456.

had been incorporated into and were detached from France (*pays détachés*), in 1814, 1815, have adopted the rules of the Code Civil which have been already mentioned.

CCCCXVII. *Rhenish Bavaria* (*t*) has a Royal Ordinance containing provisions analogous to the circular of the French *Garde des sceaux*, dated 4th March, 1831.

CCCCXVIII. *The Netherlands* reproduce in their 158th and 159th Articles the 170th and 171st Articles of the French Code, which have been already discussed.

CCCCXIX. *The Grand Duchy of Baden,* by the 23rd Article of its Code enacts that in the case of a marriage contracted by a *Badenite* abroad, he ought to be furnished with the permission of his Government, must not contravene Article 13 of the Baden Code, and must observe the formalities *legis loci contractûs.*

The *Baden* husband is bound, on his return home, to certify to the minister of the church at his Domicil the marriage celebrated abroad; and the foreigner married in the Duchy is liable to the same obligation.

A marriage contracted by a Badenite abroad, without the permission of his Government, appears not to be invalid, but to entail the loss of the rights of citizenship.

The regulation of Badenite marriages in Switzerland, and of Swiss subjects in Baden, has been the subject of a Treaty between Switzerland and Baden; the general effect of which is to prevent marriage between the subjects of the two States, without the previous production of a regular permission from the proper authority of the Domicil. If the marriage be not

---

(*t*) " Tout étranger qui se propose de contracter mariage devant l'officier de l'état civil, dans notre province Rhénane, avec une femme originaire de cette province, présentera au sous-préfet un certificat des autorités compétentes de son domicile, qu'il est apte à contracter mariage. Lorsque le sous-préfet trouvera ce certificat en règle, quant à la forme et quant à son contenu, il le revêtira de son visa. Le certificat ainsi visé sera remis, avec les autres pièces, à l'officier de l'état civil, qui en fera mention dans l'acte de mariage, et il demeurera annexé aux actes de l'état civil."— 8 *Rev. Etrang.* pp. 816, 817.

celebrated within two months from the date of the permission, the permission must be renewed.

CCCCXX. According to the law in Austria, the *personal capacity* (*Status*) of the parties contracting marriage is to be decided by the Law of their own country ; the *formalities* are to be decided partly by Austrian, partly by foreign Law, accordingly as the marriage was contracted between two foreigners, between a foreigner and an Austrian, in Austria or in a foreign land.

Betrothals, whosoever the parties to them may be, have no binding effect or legal consequences in Austria.

Every foreigner about to marry, either with an Austrian subject or another foreigner in Austria, must, before his marriage, furnish the proper authority with evidence of his personal capacity to enter into the contract.

That evidence may be supplied by a certificate, properly attested and sealed, as the case may require, from the proper foreign authority.

In Vienna itself there are certain directions connected with the police authorities to be complied with as necessary preliminaries to the marriage of foreigners. These directions have for their object to ascertain that the requisite consents have been obtained.

There is a particular provision in the Austrian Law respecting foreign *minors*. It is as follows :— When a minor, who is a stranger, seeks to contract a marriage in the Austrian States, and cannot produce the necessary consent (that is, of his father, guardian, or court of justice), the Austrian tribunal to which he is subject, according to the nature of his Domicil, will name a curator, whose duty it will be to declare, before the proper tribunal, his consent or his opposition to the proposed marriage. This tribunal will then decide the question of allowing or refusing license for the marriage, in the same manner, and on the same principles, as it would decide the question in the case of a subject (*u*). Special instructions are

---

(*u*) *Hofdekret*, 17 *Juli*, 1813.

given to clergymen to apprize themselves, according to the proper legal forms, that the due consents have been given, before they solemnize the marriage of a foreigner.

It seems that an Austrian woman who marries a foreigner, does not, *ipso facto*, acquire permission to emigrate with him ; but must obtain a separate and distinct license for this purpose.

The marriages of the subjects of Bavaria (*x*) and of the Canton des Grisons (*y*) with Austrians, are the subjects of reciprocal legislation which forbid these intermarriages without the express permission of the States of the respective parties to the contract.

Austrian subjects are not forbidden to marry abroad ; and such marriages are valid unless they contravene the provision of the 4th article of the Civil Code of Austria (Das Oesterreichische Burgerliche Recht).   The proper *publications* must, therefore, have been made in the Austrian Domicil, or a dispensation must have been obtained : none of the *prohibitions* contained in the Code must have been violated ; or a dispensation from them must have been obtained (*z*).

In one word, observes M. Fælix, the 170th article of the French Code is applicable to Austrians marrying abroad (*a*).

Hungarians may marry in the Austrian States without any special permission from the authorities of their own country. They may marry abroad, according to the forms of the *lex*

(*x*) *Hofkanzleidekret*, 30 *Octob*. 1827.

(*y*) 10 *Mai*. 1828.

(*z*) 8 *Rev. Etrang.* p. 703.

Das Oest. Gesetzbuch. As to minors, s. 49. Some rules applicable to children *legitimated* by a subsequent marriage, and to *adopted* children, ss. 160, 162, 183.

As to natural children, s. 50.

As to individuals whose *majority* is not a matter of *notoriety*, s. 78.

The remedy for consents unjustly withheld, ss. 52, 53.

As to consents requisite for soldiers, s. 54.

As to Jews, s. 124.

a) 8 *Rev. Etrang.* 878.

loci contractûs, if these forms be conformable to the Hungarian Laws (*b*).

CCCCXXI. With respect to Prussia—*Foreigners* not naturalized, are not allowed to contract marriage unless the requisite notice—the publication of banns in fact—has been made in the place of their Domicil; or, if this cannot be effected, strictly speaking, credible proof of a judicial or material certificate must be produced, that the Law of their Domicil offers no impediment to the marriage. Nevertheless, it seems that the oath of a person intending to reside in Prussia—but who has not resided a full year—that there is no impediment, will satisfy the Prussian authorities. If, however, he has been settled, and resident in Prussia for more than a year, it will suffice that banns be put up, as in the case of a native subject in the parish of his residence (*c*).

(*b*) 8 *Rev. Etrang.* 879.

(*c*) 7 *Rev. Etrang.* 159 ; *Ib.* 879.

Allgemeines Landrecht für die Preussichen Staaten, 2 *Theil.* i. tit. iii. *Abschnitt, Von der Vollrichtung einer gültigen Ehe,* ss. 136, 172.

§ 143.—Auch ein Fremder, der in Königlichen Landen getraut sein will, muss sich in der Parochie seiner Heimath aufbieten lassen.

§ 144.—Kann er dies nicht bewerkstelligen : so muss er durch gerichtliche oder beglaubigte Notariatszengnisse nachweisen, dass an dem Orte seiner Heimath kein Ehehinderniss wider ihn bekannt sei.

Anh § 68.—Bei den neu angekommenen Kolonisten, die sich noch kein Jahr in den Königlichen Staaten aufgehalten haben, genüget der Eid, dass sie noch unverehelicht sind, und dass ihnen auch kein sonst Ehehinderniss bekannt sei.

§ 145.—Hat aber ein Fremder sich in hiesigen Landen niedergelassen, und länger als ein Jahr darin aufgehalten : so ist das Aufgebot in seiner hiesigen Parochie, so wie bei Eingeborenen, hinreichend.

§ 169.—Dass die Frauung nicht von dem gehörigen Pfarrer vollzogen worden, macht die Ehe selbst nicht ungültig.

§ 170.—Wer aber, um die Gesetze des Landes unwirksam zumachen, in fremden Landen sich trauen lässt, hat, ausser den übrigen rechtlichen Folgen der Nichtigkeit oder Ungültigkeit einer solchen gesetz widrigen Ehe (Abschn. 10), auch noch eine fiskalische Strafe von Zehn bis Dreihuundert Thalern verwirkt.

Native subjects of Prussia are not forbidden to marry abroad; and the marriage, according to the *lex loci*, is valid, provided that it have not been contracted abroad in order to defeat the Prussian Law (*d*).

If it be, the marriage may be pronounced null; and a pecuniary fine inflicted on the contravener.

The omission to publish the banns does not nullify the marriage; but entails, except in particular cases, a pecuniary fine on the party omitting it.

CCCCXXII. *Foreigners* may marry in Bavaria—their capacity to enter into the contract being decided by the Law of their country.

Native subjects of Bavaria, however, are actually forbidden to marry abroad, and such marriages are held to be void, and the party punishable by imprisonment.

It seems, however, that the extraordinary severity of this law is mitigated in practice, by ratifications of these marriages, obtained from the Bavarian administrative authorities, under the powers of an enabling ordinance, subsequent to the prohibitory Law.

The Law itself does not extend to Rhenish Bavaria (*e*).

CCCCXXIII. The marriage of *Wurtemburg* subjects abroad, without the permission of the Crown, is void. In other respects, the Wurtemburg Code resembles the Baden Code on this subject (*f*).

CCCCXXIV. In *Saxony*, the Law nullifies the marriage of a subject abroad in those cases only in which the Law would nullify them in Saxony. It punishes with imprisonment of fifteen days, parties marrying abroad with intent to evade the Laws of their country. (*g*)

(*d*) It therefore behoves every foreigner about to marry a Prussian to study carefully the prohibition rendering a marriage null or invalid, (nichtig-ungültig) especially in the case of soldiers : they are set forth 10 *Abschnitt*, ss. 933, 1014.

(*e*) 8 *Rev. Etrang.* 280—3.

(*f*) *Ib.* 883.

(*g*) *Ib.* 884.

CCCCXXV. In *Hanover*, a foreigner must, previous to his marriage, certify by proof from the authority of his Domicil, to the proper authority in Saxony, that no impediment exists to his returning home with his wife to his Domicil (*h*).

CCCCXXVI. The rules of the *Electorate and Grand Duchy of Hesse*, appear to be of much the same character as those of Prussia (*i*).

CCCCXXVII. In Nassau, the marriages abroad of Jews only, without consent of the government, are held invalid (*k*).

CCCCXXVIII. By the Law of *Denmark, Norway, Schleswig*, and *Holstein*, marriages contracted abroad are valid, though they contravene the prohibitions of the Danish Law ; but the contraveners are subject to punishment. It appears, however, that on proof of the marriage having been contracted abroad designedly *in fraudem legis patriæ*, it will be pronounced null (*l*).

CCCCXXIX. By the Law of *Sweden*, subjects may marry abroad, but are bound to register within a given time their marriage settlements in Sweden, under pain of the *settlements* being null (*m*).

CCCCXXX. *Russia* appears not to prohibit marriages abroad of its subjects, or of strangers at home, though it has some stringent regulations with respect to the marriages of its subjects belonging to the diplomatic profession (*n*).

CCCCXXXI. As has been observed, the Code of the Kingdom of the *Two Sicilies* (*o*) has been modelled on that of France ; but the former does not now contain the 170th article of the French Code, though it does contain the 171st, and therefore M. Fælix argues the subjects of the Two Sicilies are not prohibited from marrying abroad.

(*h*) 8 *Rev. Etrang.* 884.
(*i*) *Ib.* 884—5—6.
(*k*) *Ib.* 886.
(*l*) *Ib.* 887—8.
(*m*) *Ib.* 888.
(*n*) *Ib.* 888—9.
(*o*) A.D. 1819.

CCCCXXXII. *Sardinia* allows her subjects to marry abroad ; but the marriage must be celebrated according to the rites of the Roman Church, so that a marriage in France or England before a civil officer would be invalid (*p*).

In fact the 64th and 108th articles of the Sardinian Code, form a *statutum personale*, which is held to follow the subject everywhere ; and in this matter there is a formal denial of the rule, "*locus regit actum.*" (*q*).

If, however, the Sardinian subject has acquired a *bonâ fide* Domicil in a foreign country, it seems that his marriage, according to the *lex loci*, would be held valid ; and the Sardinian Laws require that before *two foreigners* can be married in that State, they shall have acquired a *bonâ fide* Domicil.

MARRIAGE—GENERAL REMARKS ON VALIDITY OF.

CCCCXXXIII. The investigation which has been pursued into the Codes and Common Law of the principal Christian States, leads us to the conclusion that the following maxims of jurisprudence prevail upon the matter of the validity of the marriage of subjects abroad :—

1. The broad principle maintained by the United States of North America—but not, according to the decision of Mr. Justice Cresswell in *Brook* v. *Brook*, by England,— namely, that the *capacity* of the parties as well as the *formalities* of the contract, are to be decided *lege loci contractûs*, and not *lege domicilii*.

2. The principle maintained by France, generally by the States of the European Continent, namely, that the *capacity* of the parties is to be determined by the law of their own

---

(*p*) Quære, however, whether the contract would not be so far considered in Sardinia as to enable the Church to compel the solemnization of a marriage between the contracting parties *in facie ecclesiæ*.

(*q*) 8 *Rev. Etrang.* 877. "Bien antérieur au mariage."

State, and that a marriage valid *lege loci contractûs* may be held invalid *lege domicilii* on account of the want of capacity, though it be duly celebrated *according* to the *formalities legis loci contractûs.*

3. The principle adopted by States which recognize the *lex loci contractûs* as binding in all cases but those *in fraudem legis domesticæ.*

To these categories might be added that arising out of the Bavarian Law, which theoretically prohibits, though it practically allows, its subjects to marry abroad; and that arising out of the Sardinian Law, which allows its subjects to marry abroad, but only according to the Roman ritual.

CCCCXXXIV. Story (*r*) dwells emphatically upon the probable evil resulting from the French Law. "It will be "no matter of surprise," he says, "if hereafter we shall find "a Frenchman with two lawful wives—one, according to the "Law of the place of the Marriage, and the other according to "that of his Domicil of Origin" (*s*). He might have extended his remarks to Austrian, Prussian, and, perhaps, to English Law.

But, Fælix (*t*) maintains as stoutly that the French Law

(*r*) *Conflict of Laws,* s. 124.

(*s*) Continental nations of Europe allow a much greater extent and force to the *parental* power (their ideas of which were mainly derived from the Roman law), than Great Britain or the United States of America.—*Story,* s. 90.

(*t*) § 88.—*Pothier* says, "Tout ce que nous avons dit jusqu' à présent sur la nullité du mariage célébré hors de la présence et sans le consentement du Curé des parties, a lieu, quand même le mariage auroit été célébre en pays étranger par des François, lorsqu'il paroît que c'est en fraude de la loi qu'ils y sont allés. En vain diroient ils que la forme des contrats se regle par les loix du lieu où ils se passent ; que leur mariage ne s'étant pas fait en France, mais en pays étranger, ils n'ont pas été obligès d'observer les loix prescrites en France pour la forme de leur mariage. La réponse est, que la celebration du mariage en face d'Eglise par le propre Cure, n'est pas une pure forme d'acte ; c'est une obligation que nos loix imposent aux parties qui veulent contracter mariage, à laquelle les parties qui y sont sujettes,

on this point is in conformity with the principles of International Law, as Mr. Justice Story can support the opposite conclusion.

CCCCXXXV. Moreover, if England did, as Story supposes —and as, before the case of *Brook* v. *Brook*, was generally supposed—maintain the Law of the place of contract when it contravened the personal Law of the Domicil,—it must be admitted that she would not be consistent in her administration of the Law upon this all-important subject of Foreign Marriage.

The *Marriage* of the Englishman in Scotland, contracted avowedly *in fraudem legis*, she holds good : but the *Divorce* of English persons pronounced in the same country, she not only holds bad, but subjects the parties, if the divorce be of an English Marriage contracted by domiciled English persons, and the parties marry again on the faith of the legal divorce, to criminal punishment (*u*), and bastardizes their issue ; while in another part of the same kingdom the marriage is good, and the children are legitimate.

CCCCXXXVI. The great advantage of looking to the *lex loci contractûs* alone for the validity of the Marriage, is the simplicity of its principle, namely, to maintain, at the cost of all other considerations, the sacredness of the Marriage bond, and the consequent legitimacy of children.

It has been forcibly contended that it is for the general interest of mankind that this principle should be main-

---

ne peuvant se soustraire, en allant en fraude se marier dans un pays étranger.

" Il en seroit autrement d'un mariage qu'un Français qui se trouveroit avoir, sans fraude, sa residence dans un pays étranger, ou il n'y a pas d'exercise de la Religion Catholique, auroit contracté avec une femme Catholique, et qui auroit été célébré dans la Chapelle d'un Ambassadeur Catholique par l'Aumônier ; ce mariage seroit valable, n'y ayant pas en ce cas de fraude, et le mariage n'ayant pu être célébré autrement."— *Pothier, Traité du Contrat de Mariage,* tom. iii. p. 4, c. i. s. 2, n. 363.

(*u*) *Vide post.*

tained at the cost of all others. It must, however, be maintained at a very considerable cost, inasmuch as it practically facilitates and encourages the violation of other laws and of other rights, such as those of the parents (x). The professed policy of the English Statute (y) governing the marriage of English subjects in England is—however little practical effect it may have—to uphold the bond of Marriage, and to deprive the contracting party who violates his native Law of all pecuniary emoluments, as the course which best reconciles the two objects of maintaining the sacredness of an obligation—the interest of which so seriously affects third parties—and of vindicating the majesty of the violated domestic Law.

CCCCXXXVII. It should, moreover, be stated that by far the greater number of jurists, civilians, and canonists on the continent, ancient and modern, are in accordance upon the point of considering personal incapacity as invalidating the marriage ; while, on the other hand, the weight of this most valuable species of authority (z) is in favour of maintaining the principle

---

(x) *Story*, s. 51—68. *Paul* and *John Voet* appear to be almost the only jurists of eminence who confine the authority of the *personal statute* to the domicil of the party, and allow it no *extra* territorial operation.

(y) 4 Geo. IV. c. lxxvi. s. 23.

P. Voet, De Stat. s. 4, c. ii. p. 137 (ed. 1661).

J. Voet, ad Pand. l. i. t. iv. s. 7. p. 40.

Meier, however, maintains the doctrine of the English Law.   2 D. p. 34.—" Nuptiarum enim celebratio, tanquam actus a nullo causâ alio pendens, loci in quo perficitur, legibus consentanea esse debet; quare si de facultate contrahentium atque de solemnitatibus observandis causa, quæritur, jurium in isto loco obtinentium rationem esse habendam existimamus.

(z) *Story*, s. 122, cites *Sanchez* De Matr. t. iii. Disp. 18, s. 10, n. 26, 28.

John Voet, ad Pand. l. xxiii. t. ii. s. 4, &c. (which were relied on in the case of *Scrimshire* v. *Scrimshire*, cited above).

Paul Voet, de Stat. s. 9, c. ii. n. 9.

Bouhier, cout. de Bourg. c. xxvii. ss. 59—66.

Hertius, de collis. Oper. l. iv. art. 10.

Merlin, Rep. Marriage, s. 1.

See, too, *Pütter*, Fremdenrecht, s. 39.

that the formalities are governed *lege loci contractûs* (*a*).
It follows, as a necessary consequence, from the fact that the
preponderance of the authority of jurists is in favour of upholding the *Personal Statute*, at the expense of the validity of the
Marriage, that the same authority should be adverse to the
validity of marriages contracted, not only at variance with a
Personal Statute, but also *in fraudem legis domesticæ.*

CCCCXXXVIII. It is important to observe, that—though
the proposition *locus regit actum* be applicable to the formalities attending the celebration of a marriage,—the converse
of this proposition is not necessarily true, viz. :—that if a marriage abroad be *not* celebrated according to the formalities
legis loci, it is void.

The general practice of nations is to allow parties to choose
which formalities they will adopt, those of their Domicil, or
those *legis loci contractûs*, and to hold the marriage valid if
celebrated according to the formalities of either the one or the
other.

The Court of Appeal at Dresden held that, where the parties observed the forms of their Domicil, the marriage, though
celebrated abroad, was valid, the Domicil being the proper and
permanent seat of the marriage (*b*).

Upon this point the opinion of Lord Stowell is very valuable
as far as English marriages abroad are concerned. He says:—
" It is true, indeed, that English decisions have established the
" rule, that a foreign marriage, valid according to the law of
" the place where celebrated, is good everywhere else; but they
" have not *è converso* established that marriages of British sub-
" jects, not good according to the general law of the place where

---

(*a*) *Story*, s. 123.

Huberus, l. i. t. iii. ix.

Bouhier, cont. de Bourg. c xxviii. ss. 60, 61, 62.

P. Voet, de Stat. 9, c. ii.

J. Voet, ad Pand. l. xxiii. t. ii. s. 4.

Pothier, Traité du Mariage, n. 263, in the passage cited above.

(*b*) *Savigny*, viii. s. 381 in fine, and note *q*. The rule *locus regit
actum*, he says, is only *facultative* and *optional*, and not *indispensably
necessary*. " Dieses ist denn auch meist anerkannt worden."

" celebrated, are universally, and, under all possible circum-
" stances, to be regarded as invalid in England. It is, therefore,
" certainly to be advised that the safest course is always to be
" married according to the Law of the country; for then no
" question can be stirred : but if this cannot be done on
" account of legal or religious difficulties, the Law of this
" country does not say that its subjects shall not marry abroad.
" And even in these cases where no difficulties of that insuper-
" able magnitude exist, yet, if a contrary practice had been
" sanctioned by long acquiescence and acceptance of the one
" country that has silently permitted such marriages, and of the
" other that has silently accepted them, the courts of this
" country, I presume, would not incline to shake their validity
" upon these large and general theories, encountered as they
" are by numerous exceptions in the practice of nations." (c)

CCCCXXXIX. Lastly, upon this subject of the formalities
being governed *lege loci contractûs,* the opinion of Savigny (d)
should be mentioned.

He is of opinion that the rule *locus regit actum,* is applicable to the forms of marriages; but still he thinks it a grave
question, whether, when the Law of the Domicil requires an *Ecclesiastical* ceremony, and the *lex loci contractûs* demands a
proceeding before the *Civil* Magistrate only, a compliance with
the latter Law would satisfy the Law of the Domicil : and he
advises parties who have been so *civilly* united, to be *ecclesi-
astically* married afterwards at the place of their Domicil.

This proceeding, he says, must, according to the Common
Law of Germany, validate retrospectively the marriage.

His advice is, of course, inapplicable, as he says, to the case
of foreigners who, being previously married, become domiciled
in the land which requires the religious ceremony.

(c) *Lord Stowell, Ruding* v. *Smith,* 2 *Consist.* 390.
(d) *Savigny,* viii, s. 380, v. 35.

CHAPTER XIX.

MARRIAGE—EFFECTS ON PROPERTY.

CCCCXL. (a) The maxim of the Roman Law, that the home of the husband becomes, immediately on marriage, the Domicil of the wife, was expressed in very forcible language. The woman, said that law, if she be absent, cannot be married by letter or by proxy, "deductione enim opus esse " in mariti non in uxoris domum, *quasi in domicilium* " *matrimonii* " (b).

It is well said by Savigny, that in this language is expressed not any peculiar characteristic of the positive Law of Rome, but a recognition of the relation which necessarily, and universally, springs from the general nature of the institution of Marriage. All States, accordingly, Christian and Heathen, appear to have founded their Marriage Laws upon this principle, as their basis—that the home of the husband is the Domicil of the wife.

CCCCXLI. It may be useful to state the various questions of law which have been raised, and variously solved by various jurists, on the effect of Marriage upon the property of the wife.

CCCCXLII. These questions of *law* presuppose, however,

(a) *Rocco*, p. 294, b. 6, 7.
Savigny, viii. s. 379.
Fœlix, l. ii. t. i. c. ii. ss. 90, 91.
Story, c. vii. Marriages—Incidents to.
1 *Burge, Comm. on For. and Col. Law*, Pt. I. c. vii. Effect of marriage on the property of the husband and wife, and c. vi, s. 2.
Westlake, p. 352, &c.
(b) *Dig.* lib. xxiii. t. ii. 5.

a certain state of *facts* with respect to the *Marriage,* the *Property,* and the *Domicil* of the parties, which it is of importance to notice.

Firstly, as to the Marriage :—

I. The Marriage has taken place either —

1 Without any express contract :

2 Or, with an express contract.

Secondly, as to the Property :—

The property has been acquired,—

1 Before the marriage :

2 Or, after the marriage.

Thirdly, as to the Domicil :—

1. It is either the same as it was when the marriage was contracted :

2. Or, it has been changed, and a new one acquired subsequently to the marriage.

CCCCXLIII. Upon one or other of these states of facts, the following questions of law have been raised :—

1. Assuming that the marriage has taken place *without express contract,* is the law which governs the property of married persons a Real or a Personal Statute ? in other words, is it the *lex rei sitæ,* or the *lex domicilii* of the husband ?

2. Is the law founded on the doctrine of a *tacit contract,* between husband and wife ? or, does it spring, *proprio vigore,* from the relations of Marriage ?

3. Does this law affect property acquired after, as well as before, the marriage ?

4. If, after the marriage, a new Domicil shall have been acquired in a State which has a law respecting the property of married persons other than, and different from, the law of the State which was the *domicilium matrimonii*—is the Law of the old or the new Domicil to govern the question ?

5. If the Law of the new Domicil, does it govern both kinds of property—that acquired before and that acquired after the marriage ?

U 2

6. If the Law of the husband's Domicil allow, in the absence of any express contract, two modes of regulating the conjugal association as to property, as in France, where there is *le régime de la communauté* and *le régime dotal*—is it in the power of the husband or of the wife to choose which of the two modes shall prevail in the case of their marriage?

7. Assuming the marriage to have taken place under *express contract*, how does this fact affect the answer to the foregoing questions?

8. By what Law is the *express contract* to be interpreted? the Law of the place in which it was contracted? or, the Law of the place in which it is to be executed? *lex loci contractûs?* or, *lex domicilii matrimonii?*

CCCCXLIV. *a.* The answers which these questions have received from the jurists, the judges and the legislators of States, the basis of whose jurisprudence is the Roman Law, have not been uniform.

β. In England and Ireland, and in the United States of North America, which have adopted the English Law, these questions have been but little discussed till lately ; and then chiefly in England : and there have been, as will be seen, points of important difference between England and the United States in the exposition of the Law upon this subject.

CCCCXLV. *a.* With respect to the jurisprudence which is founded upon the Roman Law,—

First, Where the marriage has taken place *without any express contract*, the opinion soundest in principle and supported by the best authorities is thus expressed :—" Dic indis-" tinctè quod ad effectum et decisionem jurium matrimonii, " *ubi non fuit specificatum nec facta relatio ad alium* " *certum,* inspiciatur locus domicilii habitationis viri desti-" natæ tempore matrimonii (*c*)."

This rule prevails almost universally with respect to *moveable* property, and is adopted equally by those who build the Law

---

(*c*) *Lib.* 1, *C. de Summâ Trin. tit. Concl. de Stat.* cited 1 *Burge,* 248.

of the Matrimonial Domicil upon the theory of a tacit contract (*d*), and of those who adopt the doctrine that, *proprio vigore*, the Law of the husband's Domicil prevails, inasmuch as persons marrying without express contract are presumed to marry with reference to the Law of the husband's Domicil.

But with respect to immoveable property, the civilians differ greatly, first, as to the premiss whether the Law of the Community be *personal* or *real ;* secondly, as to the premiss whether there be or be not a tacit contract; and lastly, they differ in the conclusions drawn from the same premiss. The soundest conclusion, and the most consistent with the general system of Comity adopted by continental writers, appears to be, that the Law of the Community extends to real property, where the *lex rei sitæ* does not prohibit it from doing so (*e*).

CCCCXLVI. But, if the husband change his Domicil after marriage—

1. How does it affect property already acquired under it, or, as the civilians speak, *jus quæsitum ?*

The weight of authority preponderates greatly in favour of the proposition that the rights of the husband or wife which have been once constituted by the Law of the Matrimonial Domicil remain unaffected by any subsequent change of Domicil.

Some authorities, Meier and Wächter, for example, make an exception in the case where the Law of the new *patria* expressly forbids, by positive law, the rights acquired under the old *patria.* But the force of reasoning and principle is against this exception.

The general proposition is maintained equally by those who do and who do not maintain the theory of the tacit contract. The former say that a *tacit*, like any other, contract, cannot be affected by the change of Domicil or National *Status* of the parties to it. The latter maintain that the interest of

---

(*d*) *Savigny* throws his great weight into this soale, viii. s. 379 ; " Diese Meinung halte ich für richtig."

(*e*) See authorities collected by *Fœlix, Burge*, and *Story.*

the conjugal union demands certainty in the relations of property which flow from it, and that it is not to be tolerated that
the husband, who has the absolute power of changing the
National *Status* of himself and his wife when he pleases, should
also have the power of modifying, for the sake of his own private and personal advantage, the settlement of property made
by the Law at his marriage (*f*).

CCCCXLVII. Does the Law of the Matrimonial Domicil
affect property acquired subsequently to the marriage, after
the original Domicil has been lost and a new one obtained?
A question certainly of no mean difficulty.

"In the opinion of the greater number of jurists" (Mr.
Burge observes), "not only the property which had been
"acquired by the husband and wife before their removal
"from their Matrimonial Domicil, but even that acquired in
"their new Domicil, is subject to the Law of the Matrimonial
"Domicil (*g*)."

The highest French authorities and the decisions of the
French Courts support this position.

The Court of Paris in 1849, and the Court of Cassation in
1854, decided, conformably to the opinion of Fælix, that *le
régime matrimonial* once established, ought not to be affected either by a change of National *Status* or of Domicil
on the part of the husband (*h*). Therefore, the French Courts
have holden in the case of an Englishman, who, having
married without express contract, established himself and
became naturalized in France, and who had purchased in
France, *conjointly with his wife,* property considered by the
Law of France as *immoveable,* that he obtained this property
solely to himself, because such was the English Law, which
was the Law of the Matrimonial Domicil.

A stronger instance of the application of what appears to

(*f*) *Fælix*, s. 91, and authorities there cited.

(*g*) 1 *Burge Comm.* Pt. I. c. vii. s. 21.

(*h*) *Fælix*, s. 91.

the writer of these pages to be a sound maxim of the *jus gentium* cannot well be imagined (*i*).

CCCCXLVIII. Of the three opinions, namely:—

1. That in the absence of express contract, the Law of the Matrimonial Domicil governs always and everywhere, all property of the married parties, as the necessary legal result of the tacit contract between them :

2. That there is no such tacit contract, but that the Law of actual Domicil governs the property, and therefore in the event of a change of Domicil, there may be a new law affecting the property :

3. The intermediate opinion, that there is no tacit contract, but that a change of domicil does not affect property already already acquired, but only property acquired under the new domicile :

Savigny declares, that he adopts without hesitation the first opinion, and reasons to the following effect :—

The first opinion is in accordance with the natural feeling of right and justice. It was competent to the wife— before marriage a free agent—to have insisted upon any stipulations which she liked, as a condition of her consent to the contract. She has not chosen to do so, but has relied, instead, upon the Law of the Matrimonial Domicil, and she has naturally counted upon the continuance of that Law. Subsequently to the execution of the contract, the husband, in the exercise of his undoubted right, changes his Domicil : and thereby subjects their joint property to the operation of a new Law.

If the wife consent to this, *cadit quæstio*, as lawyers speak ; for she might by a new contract modify her rights. But, if she does not consent, is it competent to one party to the contract to alter, by his single will, the conditions of it, and so as to injure the other party ? It is to prevent the possibility of such an injustice, that the doctrine of the tacit contract is

---

(*i*) See *M. Demongeat's* note to his edition of *Fœlix* (1856), t. i. p. 197.

maintained.   The impugners of this doctrine have always recoiled from this argument.

But, in truth, the same goal may be reached by a different way.   In every contract, be it express or tacit, the conformity of two wills is supposed ; both parties, therefore, ought to know and understand the subject of their agreement.

CCCCXLIX. But, at the celebration of a marriage, can it be said that both parties, more especially that the wife, understood the Law of Property? Certainly not; and therefore, the presumption of a tacit contract is inadmissible.   But then it is to be remembered, that the voluntary submission of the parties is the foundation of the authority of the local law ; that voluntary submission may be expressed negatively, as by the absence of contradiction.   In the case, however, of the disagreement of husband and wife, there is no such voluntary submission to the local law of the new Domicil ; therefore, there is no foundation whatever to rest a change of the rights of the conjugal union even in the opinion of those who hold that the local law and not the contract governs the question.   A different doctrine, therefore, leads us to the same result as the tacit contract ; namely, the unchangeableness of the Law of the Matrimonial Domicil.   Another way of stating the matter is, that those who maintain this unchangeableness, not on the ground of a *tacit contract,* but on the ground of the right accruing from the Law of the Original Domicil, seem to adopt the doctrine of a *fictitious contract,* such as prevails in the case of the *pignus tacitè contractum,* which does not require that the parties should clearly understand the consequence of their act : It is a mere difference of expression.   The essential point is, that each party has a distinct definite right independent of the arbitrary will of the other (*k*).

CCCCL. Savigny points out the injustice and cruelty of the doctrine that the change of the husband's Domicil affects property already acquired, by this illustration :—A rich man

---

(*k*) *Savigny,* viii. s. 379.

marries a poor woman, and, by the Law of the Matrimonial Domicil, marriage creates a community of goods in the widest sense. He afterwards transfers his Domicil to a State in which the Law of the Dotal Régime (*Dotal-recht*) prevails ; and the wife, according to this doctrine, loses, without her consent, the portion of property which she has already acquired.

Savigny, nevertheless, agrees with Wächter, that, if in the new Domicil there prevailed a law of the most rigorous obligation and exclusive character—a law for instance, which forbade a marriage to be contracted, except under the Dotal Régime, and that no stipulations relating to a marriage otherwise contracted, should be executed in the territory ; such a law would constitute an odious but binding exception. Of the existence of such a law he is happily ignorant (*l*).

CCCCLI. The Law of the kingdom of Prussia is in its general character, and with some subordinate exceptions, in accordance with the opinion expressed by Savigny, and holds, that the Law of the Matrimonial Domicil is always and everywhere binding.

CCCCLII. What effect has the change of Domicil on immoveable property?

The great majority of foreign jurists hold that the Law of the Matrimonial Domicil affects immoveable property, and remains unaltered by the change of Domicil.

We have seen, in the case recently cited, how strongly the French Tribunals hold this opinion. And it certainly appears to be the legitimate conclusion from the premiss that the Law of the Matrimonial Domicil is, in the absence of express contract, the Law which governs the Marriage Contract, whether this premiss be founded on the hypothesis of a tacit contract, or on the hypothesis of a voluntary submission to the Law of the Matrimonial Domicil.

CCCCLIII. According to the French Law, persons may be

(*l*) *Savigny*, viii. s. 379.

married under (1) *communauté de biens,* or (2) the *régime dotal.* And the best authorities hold, that, in the absence of any express stipulation to the contrary, it is for the Law of the Matrimonial Domicil to decide under which of these two the marriage was contracted.

But, if that Law decide in favour of the *régime dotal,* the questions remain, (1) what property is dotal? (2) what is the condition of the dotal property (*biens dotaux*)? *e. g.,* is it alienable or not? and by reference to what law are these questions to be answered? Fælix and some authors are of opinion that here the *lex sitûs* governs; because these are matters under the control of the *Real* Statute (*m*).

M. Demangeat (*n*) shows very forcibly the inconsistency and weakness of this opinion, and observes that the third article of the Code "les immeubles même ceux possédés pas *les étrangers, sont régis par le loi Française"* does not apply to a case where the judge is simply called upon to interpret the intention of contracting parties ; and that the French Tribunals have more than once decided that this article of the Code was not applicable to the case of an Englishman who had married without contract, and had afterwards purchased immoveable property in France. He says, those who hold the contrary opinion, are influenced by the maxim of the Roman Law, "*interest Reipublicæ mulieres dotes salvas habere,"* and consider the question of the alienability or inalienability of Dotal Property, as a matter of public order. He denies that the Roman maxim framed to encourage second marriages, is applicable to Christian States ; and maintains strongly the authority of the Law of the Matrimonial Domicil over all immoveables everywhere, except, indeed, in States which have, by express positive law forbidden, as a matter of public

---

(*m*) *Fælix,* s. 60.

(*n*) Note to *Fælix,* s. 90.

See, also, *M. Demangeat's* essay already cited.

Du Statut. Personnel.

Rev. Prat. de Dr. Français, pp. 59, 60, 61.

policy, the application of this Law to immoveables, within the limits of their territory (o).

CCCCLIV. The answer to the two last questions (7, 8,) propounded, will be easily anticipated.

(7) Where there has been an express contract, the stipulations contained in it are everywhere of binding force.

(8) With respect to the interpretation of such a contract, it must be according to the Law of the Matrimonial Domicil: nor in this case is there even the *presumption* which arises in the case of other contracts, that the parties intended to refer to the *lex loci contractûs* (*p*).

CCCCLV. β. Upon the subject of the property of married persons, we have now considered the opinions of jurists, and the decisions of judges, in those States of the European Continent whose jurisprudence is founded on the Roman Law. We have now to consider the Law of England and of the United States of North America upon the same subject: and first, as to the latter country.

CCCCLVI. The United States of North America are governed partly by the English; partly, that is, in Louisiana, by

---

(o) *Rocco* is very clearly of the same opinion, "S'immagini che si stipuli in Napoli un contratto di matrimouio—con le forme e le solennità chieste dalle leggi nostre. S'immagini ancora che i conjugi e massime il marito possedano alcuna proprietà *immobiliare* vel territorio Francese. Poste le cose dette di sopra, senza alcun dubbio questo contratto al pari degli altri, come la pruova della convenzione avuta fra i consorti e delle mutue loro obligazioni e diritti, avrà effetto eziandio sopra i beni collocati nell' estere contrade."—Pp. 294-5.

(p) En général (*M. Demangeat* observes), pour interpréter un acte dont les clauses sont obscures, pour suppléer à ce qu'il y a d'insuffisant dans l'expression de la volonté des parties, on recourt à la loi du lieu ou l'acte a été passé : il est, en effet, assez naturel de presumer qui c'ést à cette loi que les parties ont voulu se référer. Mais en matière de conventions matrimoniales la même présomption ne s'applique plus, et l'on ne tient pas compte de ce que, par événement, ces conventions aurait été passées a le mariage lui même célébré ailleurs qu' au lieu du domicile du mari."—*Rev. Prat., ubi supr. p.* 59.

the Roman Law. In Louisiana the Law of the *communio bonorum*, between husband and wife, prevails. Some of the important questions which have been already discussed in this chapter have been the subject of decisions in the tribunal in that State before its present Revised Code was passed, which contains special provisions thereupon.

CCCCLVII. The Supreme Tribunal of Louisiana has holden—

1. That the Law of Community is a Real Statute relating to Things rather than Persons.

2. That where there is an Express Contract, that governs all previously acquired property.

3. That where there is no Express Contract, the Law of the Matrimonial Domicil governs the subject.

4. In both cases all property acquired after marriage by persons who have, since their marriage, come to dwell in Louisiana, is governed by the Law of Community which prevails in that State.

5. It is not competent to persons residing in Louisiana to enter into a marriage contract which provides that the effects of it on their property shall be governed by a foreign Law. In the case which elicited this decision, the marriage was celebrated in the State of Louisiana (*q*).

6. A man ran away with a young lady (*r*), a minor of thirteen years of age. Both of them, at the time, were domiciled in Louisiana. They were married, without the consent of her parents, at Natchez, in Mississippi, and they then returned to Louisiana. The wife afterwards died, while they were living in that State; after her death, her mother claimed her property, as it would descend by the Law of Louisiana. The court pronounced in favour of her claim, on the double ground—

a. That the parties had the State of Louisiana in contemplation of their contract.

(*q*) *Bourcier* v. *Lancese*, 3 *Martin's* (*Americ.*) *Rep.* 587, *Story*, s. 179.
(*r*) *Le Breton* v. *Nouchet*, 3 *Martin's* (*Americ.*) *Rep.* 60—73.

β. That the minor could not remove the incapacity which the Law of her Domicil (Louisiana) had affixed upon her, to the detriment of a citizen of Louisiana. By that law a minor who marries cannot give away any part of his property without the sanction of those whose consent is necessary for the validity of the marriage. By the Law of the Domicil, the mother was entitled to the inheritance of her child. It was not the Municipal Law of Mississippi which was to govern the case; but International Law, according to which personal incapacities, affixed by the Law of the Domicil, travel with the person whithersoever he goes (s).

7. A marriage settlement, executed in another State, where the parties at the time resided, and where the property was situated, if valid by the laws of the place where made, cannot be affected by the subsequent dwelling of the parties in another State (t).

CCCCLVIII. Story says that these doctrines of the Louisiana Courts will, "most probably, form the basis of " the American jurisprudence on this subject " (u). And he lays down the following propositions (x) as those which, though not universally established or recognized, are no where gainsaid by "domestic authority," and ought to be adopted.

(1.) "Where there is a marriage between parties in a " foreign country, and an express contract respecting their " rights and property, present and future, that, as a matter

---

(s) This doctrine is the reverse of what *Story* has holden on the validity of foreign marriages *in fraudem legis domesticæ*, and identical with that of Continental Jurists and *Brook* v. *Brook* (*vide ante*); therefore *Story*, though he adopts these Louisiana decisions as the general Law of the North American United States, says ' ' upon some of the doctrines of which, as stated by the Court, there, perhaps, may be reason. to pause ; but the grounds are, nevertheless, stated with great force."—*Story*, s. 180.

(t) *Young* v. *Templeton*, 4 *Louis Rep.* 254.
Story, s. 182. a (last ed.)

(u) *Ib.* s. 183.

(x) *Ib.* s. 184, 5, 6, 7, 8.

" of contract, will be held equally valid everywhere, unless,
" under the circumstances, it stands prohibited by the Laws
" of the country where it is sought to be enforced. It will
" act directly on moveable property everywhere. But, as to
" immoveable property in a foreign territory, it will, at most,
" confer only a right of action, to be enforced according to
" the jurisprudence *rei sitæ* (*y*).

(2.) "Where such an express contract applies in terms, or
" intent only, to present property, and there is a change of
" Domicil, the Law of the actual Domicil will govern the
" rights of the parties as to all future acquisitions (*z*).

(3.) "Where there is no express contract, the Law of the
" Matrimonial Domicil will govern, as to all the rights of
" the parties to their present property in that place, and as
" to all personal property everywhere, upon the principle
" that moveables have no *situs*, or rather, that they accompany
" the person everywhere. As to immoveable property, the
" Law *rei sitæ* will prevail (*a*).

(4.) "Where there is no change of Domicil, the same rule
" will apply to future acquisitions, as to present property.

(5). "But, where there is a change of Domicil, the law of
" the actual Domicil, and not of the Matrimonial Domicil,
" will govern as to all future acquisitions of moveable property;
" and, as to all immoveable property, the law *rei sitæ* (*b*).

(6.) "And here also, as in cases of express contract, the
" exception is to be understood, that the Law of the place
" where the rights are sought to be enforced, do not prohibit
" such arrangements; for, if they do, as every nation has a
" right to prescribe rules for the government of all persons
" and property within its own territorial limits, its own Law,
" in a case of conflict, ought to prevail (*c*)."

(*y*) *Story*, s. 184.
(*z*) *Ib.* s. 185.
(*a*) *Ib.* s. 186.
(*b*) *Ib.* s. 187.
(*c*) *Ib.* s. 188.

CCCCLIX. It remains to consider the Law of England upon the subject of this Chapter, which is not, in every respect, identical with the propositions laid down by Story.

The effect ascribed by that Law to a foreign marriage, must be considered, both as to Personal and Real Property. And, first it may be well to state, briefly, the Domestic Law of England—independently of any express contract—upon an English marriage with respect to both kinds of Property.

CCCCLX. Speaking generally, by the Common Law of England, all the Personal Property of the wife—how large that category is will be considered hereafter—whether it accrues to her before or after her coverture, is conferred by marriage, in the absence of express contract, upon the husband.

Practically, however, this rule of the Common Law seldom operates to the injury of the wife; for Courts of Equity allow the wife to have a separate and independent estate in whatever property or interest is secured to her through the medium of a trustee; provided, that the intention of the grantor be distinctly declared, that she should have it to her *sole and separate use.* And, if the wife become, during her coverture, entitled to any equitable property, *not* settled to her sole and separate use, though the Courts of Equity allow the husband to claim it as his own, they will not assist his claim, except on the condition of his making an adequate provision for her out of the fund, unless she already enjoys a competent settlement, or freely consents to its being paid over to him without condition.

CCCCLXI. As to that peculiar portion of Personal Property called chattels real, the law is, that, as to terms of years and other chattels real, of which the woman is possessed at the time of the marriage, or which accrue to her during coverture, the husband becomes, by the marriage, possessed of them in her right; and he is entitled, not only to the profits and the management during their joint lives, but he also may dispose of them, as he pleases, by any act during the coverture; and they are liable to be taken in execution for his debts; and, if he survives her, they are absolutely his;

but he cannot devise them by will : and, if he makes no disposition of them in his lifetime, and she survives him, they remain to her at his death, by virtue of her original title, and shall not go to his executors (d).

CCCCLXII. As to Real Property, the law is, that all freeholds of which the wife is seised at the time of the marriage, or afterwards, are by law vested in the husband and wife, during the coverture, in right of the wife. During their joint lives, the husband is entitled to the profits, and has the sole control and management; but cannot convey or charge the lands for any longer period than while his own interest continues. If her real estate be an estate of inheritance, whether fee simple or fee tail, and he had actual seisin thereof, and there has been a child of the marriage born alive and capable of inheriting the property, the husband, upon the wife's decease, becomes solely seised of such estate for his life, and is said, in that case, to be tenant by the courtesy of England. But, subject to these limited rights of the husband, the freeholds of the wife are not affected by the marriage, and continue to belong to her and her heirs (e).

CCCCLXIII. In England there are two modes of providing for the wife out of the husband's *real* estate :—

I. By Dower.

II. By Jointure or Settlement; that is, what has been called *express contract*.

1. Dower is the provision made by the Common Law, for the support of the wife, and the nurture and education of younger children.

It is thus described by Littleton (f) :—"Tenant in Dower "is, where a man is seised of certain lands or tenements "in fee simple, fee tail general, or as heir in special tail, "and taketh a wife and dieth, the wife, after the decease

---

(d) *Stephen's (Blackstone's) Comm.* vol. ii. p. 300.
(e) *Ib.* p. 299.
(f) S. 36.

" of her husband, shall be endowed of the third part of
" such lands and tenements as were her husband's at any
" time during the coverture, to have and to hold to the
" same wife in severalty by metes and bounds, for the term
" of her life, whether she hath issue by her husband or no,
" and of what age soever the wife be, so as she be past
" the age of nine years at the time of the death of her
" husband " (h).

CCCCLXIV. 2. The other mode of providing, in England,
for the wife's maintenance, is by *jointure*, or settlement.
" The rule of the Common Law, that the widow's acceptance
" of a collateral satisfaction of or out of lands in which she
" was not dowable, was no bar to her title to dower in those
" to which that title attached (i), united with the inconve-
" nience which would have ensued after the passing of the
" Statute of Uses (k), induced the Legislature, by that act,
" to enable the husband to bar effectually the wife's right
" to Dower, by making a provision for her before marriage
" in lieu of it, and which is known by the name of her Join-
" ture " (l).

The statute enacted that where purchases or conveyances
had been, or should be, made of any lands, tenements, or
hereditaments, by or to the use of the husband and wife in
tail, or to, or to the use of, one of them in tail, or for their
lives, or the life of the wife, for her jointure, every woman
married, having such jointure made, should not claim, nor
have any title to Dower to the residue of the lands, &c.,
which at any time were her husband's by whom she had
jointure " (m).

In the construction of this Statute, Courts of Law, having
reference to the widow's title to Dower, in lieu of which

(h) *Bright's Husband and Wife*, vol. i. p. 321.

(i) *Co. Littleton*, 36 b.

(k) 27 Hen. VIII. c. 10, s. 6.

(l) *Bright's Husband and Wife*, vol. i. p. 433.

(m) *Ib.*

jointures were substituted, have required the jointure, as in time of commencement, certainty, interest, &c., to be as beneficial to the widow as her dower (*n*).

CCCCLXV. As to the application of this Law to *aliens*, it is to be observed that, formerly, in England, the wife of an alien, unless she was Queen Consort, was excluded from Dower. And, if she were made a denizen, her Dower did not attach upon estates previously disposed of by her husband, denization having no retrospective effect; but it was otherwise, if she were naturalized. Afterwards, all alien women, married by license of the king, were, by special statute, entitled to Dower in the same manner as English women. And now, by recent statute (*o*), the rights of natural born subjects are extended to all alien women married to any natural born subjects or persons naturalized (*p*).

CCCCLXVI. The decisions of the English Tribunals establish, as a maxim of English Jurisprudence, that where there is an express contract, it is governed, as to its construction, by the Law of the Matrimonial Domicil.

CCCCLXVII. In *Dues* v. *Smith* (*q*)—one of the early cases—the Master of the Rolls, in 1822, made an Order that money belonging to the wife be paid to the husband, the parties being subjects of Denmark, and the Law of that country not requiring a settlement.

CCCCLXVIII. In the case of *Anstruther* v. *Adair* (*r*), it was decided by Lord Chancellor Brougham, in 1834, that where a contract is made between persons domiciled in a foreign country, and in a form known to the Law of that country, the Court, in administering the rights of parties under it, will give it the same construction and effect as the foreign Law would have given to it. Where, therefore,

---

(*n*) *Bright's Husband and Wife*, vol. ii. p. 435.

(*o*) 7 & 8 Vic. c. 66.

(*p*) *Bright, on Husband and Wife*, 322.

(*q*) *Jacob's Rep.* p. 544.

(*r*) *Anstruther* v. *Adair*, 2 *Mylne & Keene*, p. 513 (A.D. 1834).

a domiciled *Scotchman* is entitled, in *Scotland*, by virtue of a Marriage Contract executed there, and in the *Scotch* form, to receive whatever property accrued during coverture to his wife, this Court will enforce his right, as against any such property coming within its jurisdiction, and will not raise an English equity for a settlement in favour of the wife, in opposition to the provisions of the Scotch contract.

CCCCLXIX. In *Byam* v. *Byam*, in 1854, the Master of the Rolls, in his judgment, observed :—"This is a cause, the " object of which is, to obtain from the Court its opinion " upon the construction to be put on certain articles of " Marriage, entered into between Major-General *Byam* and " his wife, then *Miss Temple*, at *Florence*, in the month of " September, 1829. Properly speaking, a marriage settlement " ought to be executed in pursuance with those articles, " carrying their executory provisions into effect. The parties, " however, are desirous to avoid that expense, and this " object may be accomplished by obtaining from this Court " a declaration as to the true meaning of the articles, upon " which declaration the parties will be able to act, with- " out causing a formal instrument to be prepared and " executed. . . . . .

"The articles were executed at *Florence*, and were drawn " up in the *Italian language ;* a translation, however, is " verified, for the purposes of this cause, and it is not dis- " puted ; and, indeed, it is so expressed in the body of the " deed itself, that this is an instrument entered into between " English subjects, and to be construed according to English " rules of construction " (s).

CCCCLXX. English subjects may agree that their contract shall be according to a Foreign Law. In the case of *Este* v. *Smyth* (t), before the Master of the Rolls, in 1854, it appears that doubts were raised whether a marriage between English

---

(s) 19 *Beavan's Rep* p. 62.
(t) 18 *Beavan's Rep.* p. 112.

subjects, at the British Embassy in Paris, would be recognized as valid by the French Tribunals, and whether an ante-nuptial settlement, in the French form, followed by such a marriage only, would be held operative in *France*. In this case a Marriage Contract was entered into in *Paris* between two English subjects, according to the formalities required by the French Law, in anticipation of a marriage to be solemnized "*suivant la loi.*" A valid English marriage took place at the Embassy, but no marriage ceremony took place according to the French forms and solemnities.

It was holden that the marriage "*suivant la loi,*" was fulfilled by the English marriage, and *that the settlement, being to regulate an English marriage, was valid here,* notwithstanding that, according to the French Law, the marriage and the settlement might be inoperative; it was therefore decided in this case, contrary, it will be remembered, to the decision of the American Court (*u*), that English subjects, on their marriage, may stipulate that their marriage rights shall be regulated by the Law of a foreign country, and this Court will enforce such a contract.

CCCCLXXI. In a very recent case the proposition—that the Marriage Contract is regulated by the Law of the Domicil of the parties at the time when the contract was entered into— was laid down as an unquestionable maxim of English jurisprudence (*x*).

CCCCLXXII. In *Duncan* v. *Cannon* (*y*), the Master of the Rolls, in giving judgment, reviewed all the former decisions. He said :—"The question, as it appears to me, may be properly " thus stated :—*Did the change of Domicil superinduce a* " *disability in the wife to give a receipt not existing by the*

(*u*) *Vide ante*, p. 300.

(*x*) *In the matter of Wright's Trusts* (1856)—*Kay & Johnson's Rep.* vol. ii. p. 595.

(*y*) 18 *Beavan's Rep.* p. 128.

" *Scottish law ? I am of opinion that it did not,* and that
" to hold that it did, would be, in reality, to hold that the
" construction of the contract is different in *England* from
" what it is in *Scotland.* When these parties entered into
" the Marriage Contract, they agreed that the joint receipt
" of the wife and husband should be a good discharge to
" any person who paid to them after-acquired property of
" the wife. This is, in my opinion, the effect of the contract,
" as established by the opinions of the Scottish lawyers. It
" is, as it appears to me, a part of the contract, according
" to the construction of the Law of the country which governs
" it, that the married woman may, in this respect, act as a
" *femme sole,* and give, or concur in giving, a receipt. If
" I am right in considering this to be a question of con-
" struction, this settles the matter. If the English words,
" 'that the after-acquired property should be for the sole
" ' and separate use of the wife absolutely,' had been inserted
" in this contract, she could, according to the English Law,
" have given a good receipt for the money, and she might
" have dealt with it as she pleased, and might have autho-
" rized it being paid to her husband. Such words were not
" inserted in the contract, because they are not words used
" in such instruments according to the Scottish form ; but
" the evidence shows that the words used in the contract
" have, in *Scotland,* so far as regards the extent of the
" interest of the wife in this property, the same effect as
" would have been given in an English settlement to the words
" I have above suggested, if they had been introduced. To
" create a disability in one of two parties to a foreign contract,
" not existing according to the law which governs the con-
" tract, solely by reason of the change of Domicil of the
" contracting parties to a country where such a disability
" exists, appears to me to be contrary to the principles
" governing such cases. It would be, I think, to hold that a
" contract is to bear a different meaning according to the
" place where it is acted upon. I do not find that any

" of the cases cited lead me to the conclusion that such
" a disability would be produced by such a change of
" Domicil.

" The cases principally relied upon, appear to me to confirm
" this view of the case. In *Faubert* v. *Turst*, (z) a gentleman
" and lady had married in Paris, and had entered into a Mar-
" riage Contract. It was admitted, that the custom of Paris
" would not follow them to London, whither they had gone to
" reside ; but the Court held, that the true construction of the
" contract was, that the custom of Paris should regulate the
" distribution of their estate. This made the question of
" domicil immaterial, (a) and then the Court acted upon that
" contract. In a late case of *Este* v. *Smyth*, (b) I acted on the
" same principle. The case of *Lashley* v. *Hogg*, (c) establishes
" the same principle. *The Custom and Law of the Country*
" *will follow the Domicil, but only where the contract of the*
" *parties is silent ; where the contract governs the distribution*
" *or the payment, this must be the same wherever it is acted*
" *upon.* The case of *Macdonald* v. *Macdonald* (d), which
" was cited, only shows that the duties and obligations of
" persons must vary with the change of Domicil, but this only
" so far as they are not bound by contract. *Don* v. *Lipp-*
" *mann* (e), merely establishes this proposition, that, though a
" foreign contract must be construed as it would be in the
" country which governs it, the mode of enforcing it must be
" according to the Law of the country in which that event takes
" place ; and that, on this principle, the Law of Prescription
" obtaining in the country where the contract was sought to be

---

(z) 1 *Bro. P. C. (2nd ed.)* 129.

(a) *Westlake*, 360.

(b) 18 *Beavan's Rep.* 112.

(c) Reported in the Appendix to Mr. Robertson's work on *Suc-cessions.*

(d) 8 *Bell, Murray, & Young's Rep.* 830.

(e) 5 *Clarke & Fin. Rep* 1.

" enforced, must prevail ; in fact, it was there held not to be a
" question of construction of contract, but of the mode in which
" it should be enforced.

" The case of the *Duchess of Buckingham* v. *Winter-*
" *bottom (f)*, which is peculiar, does not appear to me to affect
" the general proposition I am now stating; and the case of
" *Anstruther* v. *Adair (g)* supports the view that *the Court,*
" *administering the rights of parties under a foreign con-*
" *tract, will give it the same effect as the Law of that country*
" *would have given to it, whatever may be the Domicil of the*
" *parties to it ;* and I acted in this view in the case of *Este* v.
" *Smith (h).*"

CCCCLXXIII. It may be received, therefore, as a maxim of
English jurisprudence, that change of domicil does not affect
the construction of an express Contract of Marriage.

CCCCLXXIV. In a later case, *Watts* v. *Schrimpton (i)*,
before the Master of the Rolls, in 1855,—it appeared that an
Englishwoman married a domiciled Frenchman. Articles
were, previous to the marriage, executed in the English form,
by which the wife became entitled to 200*l.* a year. Her
husband afterwards separated from her, and subsequently the
French Court condemned her for adultery. It was holden
that the Contract of Marriage was English, and that the rights
of the parties were to be regulated by the English Law, and
further property of the wife having fallen into possession, and
the moral conduct of both parties being reprehensible, the
income of the fund was ordered to be equally divided between
them.

CCCCLXXV. According to this case, property, therefore,
not included in the express contract, is governed by the Law
of the *actual* Domicil.

(*f*) 13 *Bell, Murray, & Young's Rep.* 830.

(*g*) *Mylne & K. Rep.* 513.

(*h*) 18 *Beavan's Rep.* 112.

(*i*) 21 *Beavan's Rep.* p. 97 (A.D. 1855).

CCCCLXXVI. The foregoing cases belong to the category of marriages accompanied by an express contract as to property. There can be no reasonable doubt that the same principle is applicable to property accruing to married persons which has not been the subject of express contract—the principle, namely, that the Law of the Matrimonial Domicil will govern the rights of the husband and wife, as to their property.

CCCCLXXVII. That such is the English Law seems to have been assumed by the analogy adopted in the following case, which related immediately to the ex-territorial effect of a foreign sentence in a matter of commission of banruptcy (k). In this case, Lord Meadowbank observed, " I remember the judgment in " *Struther's* case being pronounced. I can tell your Lord- " ships that it was a most important case, though I thought it " went a step beyond the rules of International Law. For it " was formerly a principle that a judicial transfer only " operated *intra territorium*, and had no binding influence " beyond it. So much had this been the known understand- " ing of the Law of Scotland, that I remember struggling " with difficulty at the bar, in a case where the English " assignees had obtained a decree against their debtor, to " enable them to prevail over a subsequent arrestment. The " question was, whether the commission was a proper mode " of transferring the Dominion in *Scotland.* I succeeded in " the case. The Court held that there was a title to pursue, " but that it required the interposition of the Scotch magis- " trate to give it effect ; that, in short, I had a good title, if I " chose to render it effectual. I remember, I thought that it " was a difficult thing to deviate so far from principle as to " transfer property in Scotland without regard to our own " forms and rules, and without an intimation of the assign-

---

(k) *The Royal Bank of Scotland and others (Creditors)* v. *Cuthbert and others (Assignees, &c).—Rose's (Bankruptcy) Rep.* vol. i. p. 481. *Appendix* (A.D. 1813).

" ment or anything done to attach the property according to
" our own Law. But, what I yielded to, was the considera-
" tion that it had been recognized as Law by judgments of
" the Chancellor for so long a period that it might be con-
" sidered as a principle of the Law of Nations. *Equiparating*
" *this case, to the ordinary case of transference by contract*
" *of Marriage, when a lady of fortune, having a great*
" *deal of money in Scotland, or stock in the banks, or public*
" *companies there, marries in London, the whole property*
" *is, ipso jure, her husband's. It is assigned to him. The*
" *legal assignment of a marriage, operates without regard*
" *to Territory, all the world over.* Feeling this, and seeing
" the predominant, the irresistible necessity, in point of
" expediency, of adopting the rule that *Lord Hardwicke*
" adopted in one of the cases mentioned in the papers, I, for
" one, am bent to the necessity of giving effect to the principle,
" where a departure from it would be attended with such
" inextricable confusion."

CCCCLXXVIII. The same principle seems to have been the
foundation of the recent case of *M'Cormick* v. *Garnett*, (*l*) in
which it was decided that where a husband and wife are
domiciled in *Scotland*, in which country a wife has no equity
to a settlement, the English Court will order payment of the
wife's legacy to an assignee of the husband.

CCCCLXXIX. There does not appear to have been any
English decision upon the point, whether in the absence of an
express contract (*m*), and in the event of a change of Domicil,
the Law of the *actual Domicil*, or of the *matrimonial
Domicil*, should govern the property of married persons, nor
whether a distinction is to be made between property accruing
before and after the change of Domicil.

(*l*) 5 *De Gex, M. &. G.* p 278 (*before the Lords Justices*, 1854).

(*m*) In the case of *Watts* v. *Shrimpton*, mentioned above, there had
been an express contract, *vide supra*, p. 311.

It seems to the writer of these pages, that, as to property accruing before the marriage, it must obviously be considered that the wife's rights have vested, and cannot be affected by any subsequent conduct or acts of the husband: and that the same principles will, on examination, be found applicable to property acccruing after the marriage: in other words, that the reasoning of Savigny, and of the jurists who agree with him, is both superior to that of Story, and more in harmony with the English decisions which have been just mentioned.

CHAPTER XX.

MISCELLANEOUS INCIDENTS TO MARRIAGE.

CCCCLXXX. In the last chapter, the effect of Marriage upon the property of married persons was considered : in this it is proposed to notice some miscellaneous incidents to the contract.

CCCCLXXXI. (1.) Does a change of Domicil affect the *Status* of the married parties ?

" Whatever contrariety of opinion," Mr. Burge (*a*) observes, " may exist, respecting the effect of a change of Domicil " on rights of property acquired under the Law of the " Matrimonial Domicil, there is a general concurrence " amongst jurists (*b*) in holding that, although the Law which " confers those rights, powers, and capacities, is strictly a " Personal Law, yet its influence exists so long as the parties " remain subject to it by retaining their Matrimonial Domicil. " When they quit that Domicil, and establish another, their " *Status* is governed by the Law of the latter, and their " capacities and powers are those which that Law confers."

CCCCLXXXII. President Bouhier (*c*) maintains an opposite opinion, on the ground that the *Status* of the wife ought not to depend on the caprice of the husband. Such a doctrine, he contends, flies in the face of the rule of Law which does

---

(*a*) I. 253.

(*b*) *Rodenburgh, de jure,* tit. 2 ch. 1. p. 105.

J. Voet de judiciis, l. 5, t. i. n. 101.

Boullenois, t. 1 tit. i. c. 2. Obs. iv. p. 61.

Pothier, Intr. c. 10 tit. i. n. 13, p. 2.

(*c*) *Les coutumes du Duche de Bourgogne avec les observations du President Bouhier,* c. xxviii, 3.

Burge, I. 257.

not allow a right once duly acquired, to be taken away without the consent of the person possessed of it. It cannot be said that a wife *submits* herself even tacitly to the Law of the new Domicil; she only obeys.

Merlin, in his first edition, adopted this opinion; and in his second (not a solitary instance), rejected it, and admitted that the *Status* must be governed by the Law of the actual Domicil (*d*).

CCCCLXXXIII. An important case, upon the principle now under discussion, was decided in the Court of Session in Scotland, in 1846. In this case it was sought to compel an English mother to *aliment* a child born in Scotland. The following remarks were made by the Judges as to the effect of Domicil upon *Status*, and the recognition of that effect by the country in which a person, domiciled elsewhere, happened to be. The Lord President said:—" I have " great difficulty, moreover, in holding that her liability is " to be determined by the Law of Scotland; and I *am rather* " *inclined to the opinion that she has the Status of an* " *Englishwoman, and that it is the Law of the country of* " *her Domicil that must determine her obligations now.*"

Lord Mackenzie, in the same case, said:—"But the incli- " nation of my opinion is to hold that she is not subject " to the Law of this country. The child was certainly born " in Scotland; but the mother long since removed to England " and acquired an English *Status*. If an English couple " were to come here and acquire a Scotch Domicil, they " would not import the English Law of *Status* with them, " with the view of excepting them from the obligation to " aliment children, imposed upon parents by the Law of " Scotland. In the case of Maidment, where an English " mother was sought to be made liable to a child in aliment,

---

(*d*) *Merlin*, t. i. s. 10, pp. 532-3.

Burge, I. 257.

(*e*) *Macdonald* v. *Macdonald*; *Bell & Murray, Cases &c. in the Court of Session*, vol. viii. (2nd series), p. 331.

" according to the Law of Scotland, the point was not argued
" On the whole, I think we ought to know what is the
" Eng'ish Law as to the liability of children and parents in
" regard to aliment."

Lord Fullerton said:—"*It has been, indeed, contended
" that the claim originated at the child's birth, when the
" mother was subject to the Scotch Law, and that it
" remained in abeyance till the circumstances of the child
" sanctioned a claim for aliment. But the obligation to
" aliment is not a contingent debt of this sort. There was
" no debt contracted at birth.* The foundation of the claim
" is, that, after the birth, circumstances arose which warrant
" a demand for aliment; but the obligation only comes into
" existence at the time when the necessity or poverty of the
" child requires the relief. *Therefore, it is the law of
" England, the Law of her Domicil now, which must
" declare the extent and measure of her liability;* and if
" the case is to be further proceeded with, we must take
" the opinion of English lawyers as to the Law of England" (*f*).

Lord Jeffrey said:—"*The whole duties and liabilities of
" Personal Status are undeniably changed according to
" the Law of every new Domicil.* With regard to the
" subsisting and current obligations arising from *Status*, the
" Law of the country where the duties are to be fulfilled
" must be clearly the Law to measure their extent; and,
" therefore, if, by the Law of England, this claim cannot be
" sustained, we must refuse to give it force " (*g*).

It is important to observe that this judgment was mainly
founded on the position that the obligation—on the part of
the mother—to aliment, was not an obligation contracted at
the *time of the birth of the child*, but arose from *subsequent*
circumstances. This decision is, therefore, not inconsistent

(*f*) *Macdonald* v. *Macdonald; Bell and Murray, Cases &c. in the
Court of Session,* vol. viii. (2nd series), p. 836.

(*g*) *Ib.* p. 837.

with the doctrine presently to be considered, that the Law of the place of residence may enforce certain obligations arising out of the Marriage Contract.

CCCCLXXXIV. (2.) With respect to the *obligations* contracted by a wife. They may be contracted in a State in which her husband may not be domiciled, and by the Law of that State the wife's incapacity, or the husband's, may be greater or less than by the Law of his Domicil. Here again Mr. Burge observes (*h*) :— "According to the doctrine held " by all jurists (*i*), the wife retains the incapacity to which " she was subject by the Law of the husband's Domicil ; and, " therefore, the validity of an obligation, in respect of her " capacity, and of the nature of the authority to be given by " the husband to enable her to act, must be determined by " that Law, and not by the Law of the place in which the " obligation was contracted."

(3.) With respect to *gifts between husband and wife.*

This question is also to be decided by the Law of the husband's Domicil ; it is a matter connected with, and dependent upon, the *Status*, and governed, therefore, by the Personal Law.

On this ground was founded a recent and important *arrêt* of the Court of Paris (*k*). A foreigner, domiciled in France, made a gift to his wife conformably to the 1096th Article of the Code Napoléon. The Court held the gift valid, although the *lex rei sitæ* did not allow such a gift between married persons.

CCCCLXXXV. The old Roman Law (*l*) rigorously forbade all gifts between husband and wife as tending to substitute

---

(*h*) I. 258.

(*i*) *Rodenburgh, de jure,* tit. ii. c. 1, N. 1.

Boullenois, t. ii. tit. iv. c. ii, Obs. 46, p. 467.

Pothier, Traité des Obligations, par. 2, c. vi, s. 3, n. 389.

(*k*) 6 February, 1856, *Rev. Pratique, De Dr. Fr.* t. i. p. 59. n. 2. *Demangeat's Essay.*

(*l*) "Moribus apud nos receptum est, ne inter virum et uxorem

sordid considerations for those of love and duty, as the motive of performing the obligations of marriage.

Savigny (*m*) admits here, in exception to his general rule, that the Law of the Matrimonial Domicil should prevail, that States which adopt a Law on these moral grounds, are warranted in applying it to the exclusion of all other Law. If, therefore, at the period of a "*donatio inter conjuges*," their Domicil be in a State which forbids it, the gift is null ; but, if their Domicil be in a State where it is not so forbidden, it is valid ; for it cannot be said that persons, in whose Matrimonial Domicil, at the time of their marriage, such a prohibitory Law prevailed, had tacitly contracted that they would never, under any circumstances, make gifts to each other. The prohibition is a simple restriction, *ab extra*, on the liberty of both parties to the contract, and not a condition to which the parties voluntarily submit themselves by the *factum* of their marriage.

On the other hand, Savigny is of opinion, with Rodenburg (*n*), J. Voet (*o*), and Meier (*p*), that this prohibitory Law is not to be applied to all *immoveable* property situate within the territory, but possessed by married persons domiciled in a country where no such prohibition prevails. The intent and object of the prohibitory Law are not to protect the property of married persons against injury from mutual gifts, but to maintain the purity of morals in the married

---

donationes valerent. Hoc autem receptum est ne mututo amore invicem spoliarentur, donationibus non temperantes, et profusâ erga se facilitate."...*Dig.* lib. 24, t. 1, s. 1.

"Majores nostri inter virum et uxorem donationes prohibuerunt amorem honestum solis animis æstimantes, famæ etiam conjunctorum consulentes, ne concordia pretio conciliari videretur : neve melior in paupertatem incideret, deterior ditior fieret." *Ib.* s. 3.

(*m*) viii. s. 379 (4.)

(*n*) Tit. ii. c. 5, s. 1.

(*o*) *In Pand.* xxiv. i. s. 19.

(*p*) iii. p. 44.

state. The legislator, moreover, addresses his· law to married persons dwelling within his territory, and not to foreigners.

Savigny's opinion, therefore, agrees with the decision of the French Tribunal cited in the foregoing section.

CCCCLXXXVI. (4.) With respect to the *authority of the husband over the wife* (*l'autorité maritale*).

The rule laid down in general terms by jurists is that this authority is also a question of Personal Law. It is manifest, however, that the Law of the place of residence, whether it be identical or not with the Law of the Domicil, must, in many instances, prevail. " Marriage is a contract " (as has been said) " *sui generis* " (*q*) ; many of the obligations and rights incident to it must be governed by the public Law of the State. For instance, the question of whether any, and if any, what amount of force, control, or chastisement, may be exercised by a husband to a wife, must be under the cognizance of the Law of the place of *residence*. So, too, it should seem, must be complaints as to the violation of the conditions of the marriage bond.

For instance, if the husband deserts his wife, refuses her maintenance, or ill treats her by violence, she has a right, *jure gentium*, to redress in the tribunals of the place where they reside.

CCCCLXXXVII. So, too, it would seem, that the Courts of the place of residence ought to be open to suits brought by commorant foreigners for the purpose of compelling a performance of the obligations of marriage ; for instance, suits for the *restitution of Conjugal Rights*. Such seems to have been the opinion of the English Courts in the remarkable case of *Connelly* against *Connelly* (*r*). On this ground, also, Jews, whose Marriage Contract was subject to their own peculiar Laws, and who were, in this respect, treated

---

(*q*) *Fergusson on Marriage and Divorce*, 399 ; *Lord Robertson's Judgment*.

(*r*) *Vide post*, " Divorce," 7 *Moore*, P. C. Rep. 438.

altogether as foreigners, have been permitted to obtain redress for the violation of the obligations of the Marriage Contract in the ordinary Matrimonial Courts of the country (s)·

CCCCLXXXVIII. Whether the principle that the Law of the place of residence is applicable to the enforcement of the rights and obligations, and to the general protection of married parties, can be so far extended as to include the power either of absolutely or of partially annulling the contract, will be considered in the following Chapter upon the effect of Foreign Divorces.

CCCCLXXXIX. The Domicil of the wife, is, as has been seen, as a general rule, for all purposes identical with the Domicil of the husband. How far the misconduct of the husband may affect this general rule has been already considered (t).

CCCCXC. According to English Law, a wife cannot bind herself by any contract made during coverture, because she has no separate existence; she and her husband being, in contemplation of Law, but one person. The fact of her husband being a foreigner, residing abroad, will not render her liable for any contract (u); unless, indeed, he be a foreigner belonging to a State at war with England. In such a case, as he cannot lawfully sue or contract in England, it seems that his wife may do' so as if she were unmarried (x).

(s) *Lindo* v. *Belisario*, 1 *Consistory R.* 216.

D'Aguilar v. *D'Aguilar*, 1 *Haggard's R.* 273.

(t) *Vide ante*, chapter viii.

(u) *Faithorne* v. *Lee*, 6 *Mau. and Selwyn, R.* 73.

Lewis v. *Lee*, 3 *Barnewall & C.* 291.

(x) *Barden* v. *Keveobery*, 2 *Meeson & Welsby, R.* 61.

Smith, on Contracts (ed. *Malcolm*), 236—237.

CHAPTER XXI.

DIVORCE—FOREIGN SENTENCE.

CCCCXCI. That portion of Private International Law which relates to Divorce ought, perhaps, strictly speaking, to form a part of the consideration of the effect given by Comity to the sentences of Foreign Tribunals (a), a subject which is treated of in a later part of this volume. But it seems more practically convenient to examine this question in connection with the Law on Marriage.

CCCCXCII. The Contract of Marriage differs from all others in this, among other incidents, that it cannot be broken at the mere will and pleasure of the parties who entered into it (b).

In every Christian State, which permits either the entire or the partial dissolution of the Marriage Bond, the intervention of the public authority, in the shape of a judicial sentence, is necessary.

CCCCXCIII. Christian States have been unanimous in recognizing, subject to the limitations and exceptions which have been mentioned, the general principle, that Marriage celebrated according to the *lex loci contractûs*, is valid everywhere. But Christian States have been and are far from unanimous in recognizing the principle that a dissolution of the contract pronounced by the tribunal of one State is valid in another. Marriage has been said to be a contract *juris gentium*, but the dissolution of it has not been considered as *jure gentium* binding on all States.

(a) So *Merlin* mentions under *Q. de Droit—Divorce*, s. viii. "Les tribunaux Français peuvent ils annuler un Divorce prononcé par jugement en pays étranger;" but refers to "*l'article Jugement*," s. xix.

(b) See note at the end of this chapter as to the Roman Law on Divorce.

It is, indeed, a question of private right, but one indissolubly united with public order. The religious and moral elements which are the basis of the Marriage Contract (c) bring the Law relating to its dissolution under the category of those exceptional restrictions to the admission of Foreign Law which have been mentioned at the outset of this volume (d). The question is one more of *Status* than of *Contract.*

CCCCXIV. Upon this difficult and most important matter there has obtained, and still obtains, great and lamentable discord, both in the opinions of jurists and the decisions of Courts.

CCCCCXCV. This discord has principally appeared in the consideration of the following questions:—

1. What *forum* ought to take cognizance of the question of Divorce—the *forum* of the Matrimonial Domicil—of the actual Domicil—of the husband only—or of the wife only—or of either?

2. What Law ought the *forum*, if it entertain the suit, to apply? The *lex fori*, or that of the matrimonial or the actual Domicil? If the latter, that of the husband or the wife?

3. Ought a State, the Law of which does not permit Divorce, to recognize (d) a Divorce, decreed in another State between persons belonging to that State?

(c) It is said by a judge of the North American United States, that "regulations on the subject of Marriage and Divorce, are rather parts of the *criminal* than the *civil* code, and apply not so much to the contract between the individuals as to the personal relation resulting from it, and to the relative duties of the parties to their standing and conduct in the society of which they are members ; and these are regulated with a principal view to the public order and economy, the promotion of good morals, and the happiness of the community." *Mr. Justice Sewell* in *Barber* v. *Root*, 10 *Massach. Rep.* 265.

(d) *Vide ante*, xii, xiii, xiv, xv.

Mr. Burge says of Marriage, "as its dissolubility or indissolubility is no part, express or implied, of the Contract of Marriage, but is an incident to the *status* of husband and wife after it has been constituted by such a contract, it must be determined by the laws to which the *status* is subject." 1 *Burge, Col. & For. Laws*, 618.

Cf. ib. 102, 244.

4. Ought a State, the Law of which does permit Divorce, to recognize a Foreign Divorce between its own subjects, or between one of its own subjects and a foreigner ?

5. Ought a State, the Law of which permits Divorce upon certain grounds, to recognize a Foreign Divorce which had been obtained upon other grounds by its own subjects ?

CCCCXCVI. Savigny (e) lays it down as an incontrovertible proposition that the only competent *forum* is that of the *actual Domicil* of the husband ; and the only Law to be applied, that of his Domicil. His opinion is founded on considerations of the moral element of laws relating to Divorce, which clothes them with a rigorous and positive character; he considers them as belonging to that class of laws which appertain to the public policy of each State ; laws which each State therefore enacts without regard to other States.

It was upon this principle that when in 1814 and 1816, Prussia introduced her Code for the first time into her newly-acquired provinces beyond the Elbe, it was ordered that, with respect to existing Marriages, Divorces should be governed by this Code, and not by the Law in force when the marriage was celebrated : the order was indeed accompanied by an exception (praised by Savigny on account of its justice and moderation) that a Divorce should not be allowed in those cases in which the fact constituting the ground of the Divorce, and admitted to do so by the Code, should have taken place under the jurisdiction of the Foreign Law, which did not recognize this fact as constituting a ground of Divorce.

When the French Code was introduced into Belgium and Piedmont, during the period of their incorporation into the French Empire, it was decided by the tribunals of these States, that a Divorce ought to be granted under the provisions of that

---

(e) VIII. s. 379 (6) ; s. 396 ; s. 399 (II. 1).

The recent decision in *Yelverton* v. *Yelverton* (Dec., 1859), by the Judge Ordinary, in England, arrives at *Savigny's* Conclusion, through other premises, viz., "actor sequitur forum rei." *Vide post.*

Law on account of facts which had happened previously to the introduction of it (*f*).

CCCCXCVII. Savigny's position rests, no doubt, upon sound principle, and is supported by the best legal analogies; but it requires, nevertheless, explanations, and cannot in justice be always, and under all circumstances, rigorously applied.

In the first place, what is meant by the *actual* Domicil of the husband?—a *forensic* Domicil; that is, one more easily acquired than a testamentary Domicil—one which certainly does not require the intention to remain permanently in a particular place, and yet, perhaps, one which is not satisfied by a mere residence adopted for the purpose of founding a jurisdiction; to establish, indeed, this distinction in practice is, in the absence of any positive law on the subject, extremely difficult.

What are the *criteria*, which establish a *bonâ fide residence* as distinguished from *Domicil* (*g*)? Where are they laid down?

It is not easy to answer these questions. The French Law, as will presently be seen, attaches great importance to foreign *naturalisation*, admitting that in such cases the *Status* of the Frenchman is lost.

In Scotland a positive law specifies the duration of residence which renders a foreigner amenable to a suit for Divorce in a Scotch Court (*h*). Here the distinction between *domicil* and *residence* is remarkable. A plea that the residence was *in fraudem legis domesticæ* is inadmissible in Scotland, for by specifying the duration of residence it shuts out all consideration of *Foreign Domicil* (*i*).

(*f*) *Merlin, Rep. Effet Rétroactif*, s. 3, s. 2, art. vi.
Westlake, s. 359.

(*g*) See the recent case of *Yelverton* v. *Yelverton*. December, 1859, *Probate Court*.

(*h*) After forty days' residence a citation may be legally served on his *dwelling-place*; but he may be *personally* cited the moment he sets foot in Scotland. *Utterton* v. *Pewsh, Fergusson's Consist. Rep.* 23.

(*i*) See *Geils* v. *Geils*, 1 *Macqueen's H. of Lord's Rep.* 275.

In England a positive law requires a certain amount of evidence before a Marriage can be solemnized by Episcopal license or banns, but no positive law as to the time of residence requisite to found the jurisdiction of an English Court. The subject is at present in a state of much perplexity and uncertainty in England ; but, according to a recent judgment (*k*) of the Divorce Court, the residence of the wife alone is insufficient to found the jurisdiction of an English Court in a suit against a husband, who has not been and is not residing within the limits of the State to which the Court belongs. It should be added that in this case the Marriage also had been contracted out of England.

In the United States of North America a contrary doctrine has been maintained by their tribunals ; and surely such a doctrine may be maintained with no small show of reason.

The general doctrine, that the Domicil of the wife is legally that of her husband rests upon the basis that it is the legal duty of the wife to dwell with her husband wherever she goes ; but if he commits such an offence against the marriage state as renders her cohabitation morally, and perhaps also physically impossible, he has destroyed the basis upon which the general doctrine rests, and has entitled, or rather compelled, her to establish *for the purposes of obtaining justice against him at least,* if not a separate Domicil, in the full sense of the term, a separate *forensic Domicil;* otherwise the husband may easily take, what all sound jurisprudence abhors, advantage of his own wrong.   He deserts or ill-treats his wife, or pollutes with adultery his marriage-bed, and betakes himself to a country where no tribunal taking cognizance of such offences exists, and leaves his wife to starve in ignominy and wretchedness in a country which has tribunals which take cognizance of such offences against the marriage state, but which on a theory, the basis of which is wanting in the particular case, refuses to administer justice to her, even though its own subject (*l*).

(*k*) *Yelverton* v. *Yelverton, vide supra.*
(*l*) *Vide ante,* p. 70, s. lxxxviii (printed *before* the decision in *Yelver-*

CCCCXCVIII. According to the Law of France, M. Fælix tells us, the French wife married to a foreigner, may institute a suit for Nullity of Marriage before the French Tribunals. He rests this proposition on the due interpretation of the 14th Article of the Code (m). The foreigner who contracted Marriage with her bound himself at the same time by the obligation of incident to that contract ; among them was the obligation of liability to a suit for Nullity of the contract itself.

M. Demangeat thinks that the better argument is that the wife who institutes such a suit sustains by the fact of its institution, the proposition that she has never lost her character of a Frenchwoman, and, therefore, is entitled to invoke the 14th Article of the Code (n).

CCCCXCIX. (2.) As to the law which the *forum* ought to apply.

It seems clear upon all sound principles of jurisprudence that the *forum* can only administer the *lex fori* (o) upon Divorce.

In the first place, the parties to the Marriage Contract derive from it no right to a Divorce : it is not, as in the case of contract for transfer of property, a question of rights already existing before the contract is brought into a court of justice (*p*). In the second place, all remedies, as will be seen

---

ton v. *Yelverton*), and the leading American case, *Harteau* v. *Harteau*, there referred to. See too, *Bishop on Marriage and Divorce*, ss. 729—732. See too, *Lord Eldon's* remarks in *Tovey* v. *Lindsey*, 1 *Dow's. Rep.* 119, 138, and the reasoning of *Lord Lyndhurst* and *Lord Brougham* in *Warrender* v. *Warrender*, 2 *Cl. and Finnelly's Rep.* 488.

(m) *Code Civil*, 14, "L'étranger même non resident en France, pourra être cité devant les tribunaux, pour l'exécution des obligations par lui contractées en France avec un Français ; il pourra être traduit devant les tribunaux de France pour les obligations par lui contractées en pays étranger envers des Français."

(n) *Fælix*, s. 175, p. 337 of *M. Demangeat's* edition, see note (6).

(o) This proposition is strongly affirmed by *Justice Sewell*, in *Barber* v. *Root*, 10 *Massachusets* (*Americ.*) *Rep.* 265.

(p) See this well stated by *Mr. Westlake*, s. 351.

hereafter, depend on the *lex fori*, not on the *lex loci contractûs*.

The notion which appears to have been entertained by some of the Scotch judges (*q*) that the Scotch Tribunals might decree an English Divorce *a mensâ et toro*, a remedy unknown to Scotch Law, to English subjects resident in Scotland, was wisely over-ruled by the Superior Court.

This notion of the Scotch judges was that a *less* remedy than that allowed by the *lex fori* could be administered. The notion that a *greater* remedy than that allowed by the *lex fori*, *i. e.*, a Divorce *a vinculo* by the Tribunal of a State which allowed only a Divorce *a mensâ et toro*, on the ground that the Law of the Matrimonial Domicil allowed the former, remains to be promulgated. The true question is whether the *lex fori* is to be applied at all, not whether any other Law be applicable.

D. (3.) (*r*) To this question the answer seems on principle to be clearly in the affirmative ; the foreigners, in this hypothesis, come into a Foreign State with a particular *Status* affixed to them by the foreign Law of the State to which they belong. The only ground upon which this *Status* could be refused recognition would be, that it was contrary to the public policy or morality of the new State ; but it seems clear that the residence in that State of *two* foreigners, as single persons, is not a case of this description : what the former *Status* of these parties was is a matter of private history in no way affecting the State in which they happen to be now resident.

The question as to the past arises on the attempt of either foreigner to re-marry, which, it will be seen, the French Law does not allow (*s*).

(*q*) *Duntzee* v. *Levett, Fergusson's Consist. Rep.* 68.

(*r*) *Vide ante*, p. 323.

(*s*) *Wächter* says, " If a citizen of our State marries a divorced person belonging to another State, our State ought to decide according to the Laws of the foreign State, whether the divorce were invalid or not,

To the converse of this case, namely, the *Status* of polygamy among foreigners resident in a Christian State, very different considerations apply. A case, however, it must be admitted, of no mean difficulty to a Christian State which possesses oriental dependencies and recognizes in them oriental habits and laws (*t*).

Nor is the question of the operation of a Divorce granted by a *third* State upon foreigners resident in another State concluded by the observations which have been made (*u*).

DI. (4). This is the question (*x*) which has raised the fiercest and most important controversy ; States have refused to recognize Foreign Divorces, on the ground that the *lex loci contractûs* governs the Contract of Marriage ; and that indissolubility is of the essence of that contract ; and also on the ground that such recognition would be contrary to the fundamental policy of the realm.

States have recognized such Divorces on the ground that they relate to a question of *Status*, not of *contract*, and that the Law of the Actual Domicil governs questions of *Status*.

DII. In France, the Law of the 8th of May, 1816, ren-

---

but, acccording to the Laws of our own State, whether it was competent to our citizen to marry a divorced person." See s. 23, p. 2, of his article on " die Collision der Privatrechtsgesetze, &c., p. 187 of *Vol. 25 of Archiv für die Civil. Praxis.*

(*t*) The French Law, according to *Merlin*, would permit the Mussulman's polygamy with his own countrywomen, but not with Frenchwomen, on the ground that the *personal statute* rendered their marriage unlawful. *Questions de Droit—Divorce,* xiii. p. 370. *M. Demangeat* thinks that the Mussulman could not contract such a marriage, even with his own countrywomen, *in France,* and as to his marriage in his own country, "je n'oserais pas dire que nous devons les considerer, sauf la première, comme absolument non avenues : tout au moins faudrait-il voir là, en quelque sorte des mariages putatifs, et appliquer par analogie les art. 201 et 202: si par exemple la question de légitimité des enfans si présentait devant nos tribunaux.

(*u*) See in next chapter, *Lord Stowell's* remarks on this head.

(*x*) *Vide ante,* p. 324.

dered Marriages indissoluble for the future ; but it conceded
the power of re-marriage to persons already divorced during
the interval between the passing of this Law (*y*) and that of
the 20th September, 1792, which authorized Divorce (*z*).

The use which Merlin makes of this fact for the purpose of
solving the problem now before us, is remarkable. It proves,
he says, that the legislature of France did not consider the
Divorces decreed during the interval above mentioned, as
" *nuls dans le for interieur,*" that is, as contrary to the
immutable laws of morality.

The new Law of Prohibition was therefore to be construed
—as affecting French persons only--as enacting an *impedi-
mentum personale,* not *generale* (*a*).

Merlin, therefore, is very strongly of opinion that an
Englishwoman duly divorced in her own country, might lawfully marry in France, a Frenchman, during the lifetime of
her former husband, upon just the same principle as a
Frenchwoman divorced before the Law of 1816, might lawfully re-marry during the lifetime of her former husband.
Merlin, however, admits that the French tribunals have very
solemnly decided the reverse. Sir John Milley Doyle had
been divorced by an act of the English Legislature. His
divorced wife sought to be married in France, to a Frenchman. The *Maire* refused to marry these parties. They had

─────────────────────────────

(*y*) After a severe struggle in the Legislative body, the Crown and
the Chamber of Peers voting for giving the Law a retroactive effect
on this point.

(*z*) " Thereby reviving," *Merlin* says, " the *old* Law of France."—*Qu.
de Droit—Divorce,* xii.

(*a*) But *M. Demangeat* says, " Il suffit de repondre que le legislateur
de 1816, ne pouvait pas tenir pour non avenus les divorces prononcés
antérieurement entre François, tandis que la France est toujours libre
de ne pas admettre chez elle l'application d'une loi étrangère. De plus
dans un cas le scandale ne pouvait se produire que pendant un tems
limité à partir de 1816, tandis que dans l'autre il pourrait se produire
indéfinement, tant qu 'il restera dans le monde une législation qui con-
sacre le divorce."—*Revue Pratique de Dr. Fr.* t. i. p. 57, n. 1.

recourse to the *Tribunal de Première Instance du Departement de la Seine*, which affirmed the *Maire's* refusal. They appealed to the *Cour Royale*, of Paris, which affirmed the sentence of the inferior Court (*b*).

On the ground above mentioned, and solely on that ground, *Merlin* maintains that both judgements enunciated bad law.

M. Demangeat disagrees with Merlin, and agrees with these decisions: he considers that it is clear law, that a

---

(*b*) The judgment of the first French Court is as follows :—" Attendu que, si le mariage, sous le rapport de la capacité des contractans et des formalitiés qui doivent y être observées, est régi par la legislation du pays dans lequel il est contracté ; il est régi, quants aux effets qu' il produit sous le rapport de l'état des personnes, par les principes du droit naturel et du droit des gens ;

" Que c'est par cette raison que les étrangers mariés, en suivant les lois et les usages de leurs pays, jouissent en France de l'état d'époux, et leurs enfans, de l'état d'enfans legitimes ;"

Qu' à la difference du mariage, le Divorce n'est pas admis par toutes les nations, que même, parmi celles qui l'ont autorisé, ses effets varient suivant les différentes legislations : les unes déclarant indistinctement les deux époux capables de contracter un nouveau mariage ; les autres, au contraire, donnant cette faculté à l'époux innocent, et la refusant à l'epouse coupable ;

Attendu que la loi civile, en France, dispose qu'.on ne peut contracter un nouveau mariage avant la dissolution du premier, et que la loi Française ne reconnait plus le Divorce comme un moyen de dissolution de mariage ;

" Attendu qu' il suit de la qu' une personne engagée dans les lieus d'un premier mariage, même contracté en pays étranger, ne peut, à la faveur d'un Divorce que la loi Française ne reconnait pas, et dont les tribunaux Français ne sauraient apprécier les effets, contracter un second mariage en France ;

" Qu' ainsi le maire du troisième arrondissement de Paris, en refusant de passer outre à la celebration du mariage de Mary Bryan avec le Sieur Mausion, n'a fait qu' une juste application de l'Art. 147 du Code Civil ;

" Le tribunal déboute Mary Bryan et le Sieur Mausion de leur demande." . . . .—*Merlin, Qu. de Dr.* xiii.

Foreigner divorced in his own country, cannot re-marry in France, during the lifetime of his wife (c).

DIII. Merlin (d) propounds among others, the following questions, on the subject of Foreign Domicil.

1. If two French persons, subject as such to the Law rendering Marriage in France indissoluble, leave their country and become naturalized in a State which permits Divorce, can they dissolve their Marriage by means of a Divorce founded on mutual consent?

2. Can one of these persons institute a suit against the other for the purpose of obtaining a Divorce?

3. Can one of them found his application for a Divorce upon facts which happened before his naturalization, and that of the other party to the Marriage Contract?

4. If a husband alone become naturalized in a foreign State, may he obtain a Divorce from his wife by mutual consent?

5. May he, being alone naturalized, obtain a Divorce?

Merlin answers the two first questions unhesitatingly in the affirmative. It is not, he says, the Law at the time the Marriage was contracted, but the Law at the actual moment of the dissolution (loi du moment actuel), which governs the question.

As the Law of a particular period (loi du temps) has no effect on the past, so the Law of a particular place (loi du lieu) (e) has no operation beyond the limits of the State which enacts it. The Law of the new State in which they are naturalized has the same effect upon their Marriage as a new Law in their old country, passed subsequently to their Marriage, would have had upon it.

(c) La jurisprudence paraît been fixée en ce sens (Dev. Car. 49, 2, 11). Revue Pratique de Dr. Fr. t. i. p. 57.

(d) Qu. de Droit—Divorce, XI.

(e) It is not improbable that this passage in Merlin may have suggested to Savigny the arrangement of his eighth volume—the work so often referred to in these pages.

The third question he answers equally in the affirmative (*f*).

The fifth and sixth questions he has unhesitatingly answered in the negative. It is true, he says, that there is a general maxim that the wife follows the condition of the husband, but it would be a great error, he adds, to infer from this maxim the consequence that a woman who has either become French by marriage, or was born French, can lose her *status* and quality as a Frenchwoman, by the naturalization of her husband alone.

Equally erroneous would be a similar inference from the doctrine, that the wife has no other Domicil than that of her husband; Laws relating to *status* and *capacity* are not governed by the mere Law of Foreign Domicil; apart from foreign naturalization, it is presumed, Merlin means.

DIV. It has become the clear and settled doctrine, in spite of one or two judgments to the contrary, of the United States of North America, (*g*) that their tribunals are competent to decree Divorces without reference to the Law of the place in which the Marriage was contracted, or to the Law of the original Matrimonial Domicil.

In consistency with this doctrine, it appears that they recognize a Foreign Divorce of American subjects (*h*).

DV. The Scotch Courts hold the same doctrine. Divorce, they say, relates to a matter of *Status*, and it is the duty and right of each country to decide—without reference to the *lex loci contractús*, or the Domicil, or to the allegiance of the married parties—upon questions of *Status*, simply as questions

---

(*f*) As he had previously done in his *Répertoire de Jurisprudence* under the title *Effet retroactif*, s. 3, s. 2, Art. 6.

(*g*) *Bishop*, s. 759.

Story, s. 230*a*.

(*h*) Chief Justice Gibson's judgment in *Dorsey* v. *Dorsey*, 7 *Watts'* (*Americ.*) *Rep.* 347.

See, too, *Maguire* v. *Maguire*, 7 *Dora Rep.* 181.

affecting the public welfare and order (*i*). It seems difficult to
say how this proposition can be maintainable with respect to
two foreigners entering Scotland for a temporary object, and
that object the defeating the Laws of their own Domicil,
such foreigners meaning to return, and actually returning as
soon as they have effected this object, to their own country.

But, so the Scotch Superior Courts have ruled ; and there
has been no appeal from this ruling to the House of Lords,
though the English cases hereafter mentioned, show, that
out of Scotland, or at least in England, these decisions
would not be respected. Nevertheless, the House of Lords
sitting as an Appellate Scotch Court, *might* sustain the
validity of a Scotch Divorce of an English Marriage for Scotch
purposes, and yet refuse to sustain it for English purposes,
sitting as an Appellate English Court. It scarcely required
the great powers of Lord Lyndhurst (*k*) to display the dis-

(*i*) " We give the remedy of Divorce for adultery (said the Scotch
judge, Lord Glenlee) because the parties are husband and wife, and not
with relation to the constitution of Marriage."

(*k*) " It must be admitted that the legal principles and decisions of
England and Scotland stand in strange and anomalous conflict on this
important subject. As the laws of both now stand, it would appear
that Sir George Warrender may have two wives ; for, having been
divorced in Scotland, he may again marry in that country ; he may live
with one wife in Scotland most lawfully, and with the other equally
lawfully in England ; but only bring him across the border, his English wife may proceed against him in the English Courts, either for
restitution of conjugal rights, or for adultery committed against the
duties and obligations of the marriage solemnized in England : again,
send him to Scotland, and his Scottish wife may proceed, in the Courts
in Scotland, for breach of the marriage contract entered into with her
in that country.

" Other various and striking points of anomaly, alluded to by my
noble and learned friend, are also obvious in the existing state of the
laws of both countries; but, however individually grievous they may
be, or however apparently clashing in their principles, it is our duty,
as a Court of Appeal, to decide each case that comes before us according
to the law of the particular country whence it originated, and accord-

graceful consequences of this unseemly conflict between the two portions of the same empire.

Scotland, is of course, bound on her own principles of jurisprudence, to recognize the validity of a foreign Divorce between Scotch persons.

DVI. With respect to England, the decisions upon the subject of foreign Divorces are so remarkable, and the recent change of her domestic Law is so important, that it is proposed to consider this subject separately in the following chapter.

DVII. As to the fifth and last question, (*l*) the answer must depend upon the nature of the theory which the State applies to foreign Divorces.

A State which held that the incapacity to be divorced, except for reasons admitted by the original Matrimonial Domicil, was of the nature of a *personal statute*, ought certainly to hold a foreign Divorce on any other grounds than those admitted by the original Matrimonial Domicil, to be null and void. So a State which holds that a Divorce is a matter affecting public order and morality, is not found to recognize a foreign Divorce between its subjects founded upon reasons which it had not sanctioned by its own jurisprudence, whether these subjects had or had not been, at the time of obtaining the foreign Divorce, domiciled in the State which granted it.

On the other hand, a State which does *not* hold the doctrine of the *personal statute* above mentioned, and which does *not* hold that Divorce is such a question of public order and morality that no change of Domicil can give a foreign State jurisdiction over it, ought to recognize the sen-

---

ing to which it claims our consideration; leaving it to the wisdom of parliament to adjust the anomaly, or get rid of the discrepancy by improved legislation." *Warrender* v. *Warrender* (1835) (Judgment of *Lord Lyndhurst*), 2 *Clarke and Fin. Rep.* 561.

(*l*) *Vide ante*, p. 324.

tence of a foreign State over persons at the time domiciled within its territory, though her own subjects, and though she does not sanction the grounds of that Divorce by her domestic Law.

DVIII. There are some miscellaneous points, the notice of which may not unfitly close this chapter.

1. The English, Scotch, and North American United States Courts agree in the doctrine, that the place in which the offence was committed (*locus delicti*), whether in the State in which the case is brought, or in a foreign State, is immaterial (*m*).

2. Whether the Domicil of the parties at the time the offence was committed, be, or be not immaterial, is a more disputed question (*n*). But the more generally received doctrine in the three States which have been just mentioned, is in favour of the immateriality of *this* Domicil. The question has been more agitated in the North American United States than in England and Scotland ; but it has, as Mr. Bishop (*o*) observes, seldom been matter of direct judicial discussion.

3. It seems clear, that States which recognize the validity of a foreign Divorce, must recognize the incidents to it, such especially as its effects upon personal and real property.

The effect upon the former ought to be the same with that on the personal property in the State which decreed the Divorce.

The effect upon the latter must depend upon the *lex rei sitæ*, according to the prevalent doctrine as to real property.

If the *lex rei sitæ* visit Divorce with certain consequences, and recognizes a foreign Divorce, it ought to ascribe the same effects to it as to a Divorce by the Domestic Law (*p*).

(*m*) *Bishop on Marriage and Divorce*, s. 740.

(*n*) *Ib.* s. 741, 2, 3, 4.

(*o*) *Ib.*

(*q*) Cf. *Story*, s. 230 *b*.

THE ROMAN LAW ON DIVORCE.

The history of the Civil Law of Rome as to Divorce is very interesting, and very often misunderstood. The primary object of the old law was to preserve the perfect liberty of the subject with respect to contracting Marriage—not to encourage Divorce; traces of the old law appear in the *Dig.* l. xlv. t. i. 134, "inhonestum visum est vinculo poenæ matrimonia obstringi sive futura sive jam contracta," *Code* l. v. t. iii. 14, neque ab initio matrimonium contrahere, neque dissociatum reconciliare quisquam cogi potest, unde intelligis, liberam facultatem contrahendi atque distrahendi matrimonii transferri ad necessitatem non oportere. l. viii. t. xxxix. 2, " Libera matrimonia esse antiquitus placuit, ideoque pacta *ne liceret divertere* non valere, et stipulationes quibus poenæ irrogentur ei qui quæve divortium fecisset, ratas non haberi constat." It seems clear that the liberty of Divorce was rarely resorted to before the year 553, A. U. C. The scandalous frequency of Divorce after this period is well known to all readers of Plutarch, Tacitus, Cicero, Juvenal, Plautus, and Seneca. Augustus appears to have imposed some limitations upon it. Nor even after Christianity became the religion of the State, was Divorce abolished. Constantine did not absolutely prohibit Divorce, but limited the causes of it. The Council of Arles, A.D. 314, spoke doubtfully. St. Ambrose thought the language of the Gospel obscure, and that error on the point might be venial. Theodosius repealed the limitations of Constantine. Justinian restored, reluctantly, it is said, much of the license of Divorce which had disgraced pagan Rome, *Novell.* 117, c. 8. *de justis divortiorum causis marito permissis* ; *Novell.* 134, c. 10 ; *Novell.* 140.

The differences between the Roman and Greek Churches on the subject of Divorce are well known. The recent alteration of the Law of England upon Divorce was effected *Ecclesiâ inconsultâ* as much as the Law of France in 1792.

Cf. *Savigny,* VIII. s. 399, II. 1.

Troplong, De l'influence du Christianisme sur le droit civil des Romains, Chapitre VI. Du Divorce.

CHAPTER XXII.

FOREIGN DIVORCE—ENGLISH LAW.

DIX. The English Law upon Divorces obtained by the sentence of a Foreign Tribunal has been reserved, on account of its moment and peculiarity for consideration in this chapter.

The fundamental public policy of England, with respect to the question of Divorce, has recently undergone an entire change ; the bearing of which ought, it should seem, upon all sound principles of Comity, materially to affect the decisions of her tribunals upon the validity of Foreign Divorces.

The question, of course, still remains whether England will allow an English Marriage between English persons, or between an English person and a foreigner, upon *other grounds* than those which in her recent legislation she has declared to be proper causes of Divorce ; but the argument that *any* Divorce is contrary to the public policy—an argument hitherto of no mean weight—is in all reason, justice, and common sense entirely taken away.

DX. There are three divisions under which the English Law with respect to the validity of a Foreign Sentence of Divorce may be considered.

a Foreign Sentences of Divorce *a mensâ et toro*.

β Foreign Sentences of Divorce *a vinculo matrimonii*, before the recent Statute legalising Divorce.

γ Foreign sentences of Divorce since the passing of the Statute.

DXI. (*a*). Upon the question of the effect due in England to a Foreign Sentence of Divorce *a mensâ et toro*, it is safe to use the language of Lord Stowell :—

" Something " (he observed) " has been said, on the doc-
" trine of law, regarding the respect due to foreign judgments ;
" and, undoubtedly, a sentence of separation, in a proper Court,

" for adultery, would be entitled to credit and attention in
" this Court; but I think the conclusion is carried too far
" when it is said that a sentence of Nullity of Marriage is
" necessarily and universally binding on other countries.
" *Adultery and its proofs are nearly the same in all coun-*
" *tries. The validity of marriage, however, must depend,*
" *in a great degree, on the local regulations of the country*
" *where it is celebrated.* A sentence of nullity of marriage,
" therefore, in the country where it was solemnized, would
" carry with it great authority in this country; but I am not
" prepared to say that a judgment of a third country, on the
" validity of a Marriage, not within its territories, nor had
" between subjects of that country, would be universally bind-
" ing. For instance, the marriage, alleged by the husband,
" is a *French* marriage ; a French judgment on that Marriage
" would have been of considerable weight; but it does not
" follow that the judgment of a Court at Brussels, on a mar-
" riage in France, would have the same authority, much less
" on a Marriage celebrated here in England. Had there been
" a sentence against the wife for adultery in Brabant, it
" might have prevented her from proceeding with any effect
" against her husband here; but no such sentence anywhere
" appears " (a).

DXII. In an earlier case, the sentence of the Parliament of
Paris, declaring a Marriage null, had been pleaded, not as a
bar, but as evidence of the French Law on a Marriage Contracted in France. The suit in England was for a Restitution
of Conjugal Rights (b).

DXIII. The effect of a Foreign Sentence was also much
discussed before the Arches Court of Canterbury, and the

(a) *Sinclair* v. *Sinclair*, 1 *Consist.* 297.

Lord Hardwicke is reported to have said that the sentence of a
competent Court in France on the *validity* of a marriage was, by the
Law of Nations, conclusive.

Roast v. *Garwin*, 1 *Vesey*, R. 157.

(b) *Scrimshire* v. *Scrimshire*, 2 *Consist.* 411, A.D. 1752.

Judicial Committee of the Privy Council in the recent and very important case of *Conolly* v. *Conolly*.

In this case, the wife pleaded in bar to a suit for a restitution of conjugal rights by the husband, that she and her husband had both, subsequently to their Marriage, entered into religious orders, and agreed to live apart; and that the Court at Rome had decreed their separation.

It was contended on the other side—

1. That being Americans by origin, and not domiciled at Rome, the Court there had no jurisdiction.

2. That the pretended sentence was no sentence of a Court.

3. That the sentence of a third country was not binding here.

4. That the husband had a right to enforce the original obligations of the Nuptial Contract.

No objection, it should be observed, had been taken to the jurisdiction of the English Court. The Court of Arches rejected the plea in bar. The Appellate Court of the Privy Council allowed the wife to amend her plea, by stating that she and her husband were domiciled at Rome at the time when the alleged sentence was passed; and that by the Law of their American Domicil (the *lex loci contractûs*), that sentence would be held valid; but gave no opinion as to what the effect of such further pleading might be (*c*).

DXIV. (*β*). With respect to Foreign Sentence of Divorce *a vinculo* before the passing of the recent Statute.

The Courts in England have refused to acknowledge the validity of any sentence of Divorce *a vinculo matrimonii,* pronounced upon an English Marriage celebrated in England between English born subjects (*d*). They have, however, indirectly recognized the validity of a Scotch sentence of Divorce *a vinculo matrimonii* (*e*), in a case where the Marriage had been celebrated in England, and the parties to which

---

(*c*) *Conolly* v. *Conolly*, 7 *Moore's Privy C. Rep.* 332.

(*d*) *Lolley's Case,* 1 *Russ. and Ry. C. C. Rep.* 237.

(*e*) *Warrender* v. *Warrender,* 9 *Bligh Rep.* 89 ; 2 *Cl. and Fin.* 488 ; *vide post.*

were a Scotchman by birth, property, and connections, though frequently resident in England, and an Englishwoman. They had been separated for some time, and at the time of the Divorce, the husband was living almost wholly in Scotland, and the wife in France.

Perhaps, quite strictly speaking, there cannot be said to have been any direct English decision upon a case in which the parties were married in England, and having afterwards acquired *a bonâ fide Domicil animo et facto* in another country, were there, after the acquisition of such Domicil, divorced *a vinculo matrimonii* according to the *lex loci* by a competent tribunal (*f*).

In the celebrated case of *Lolley*, the husband went from England to Scotland, and, without having acquired a Domicil (*g*), procured a Divorce *a vinculo* there, and then married another wife. Lolley was found guilty of bigamy by the twelve judges, and a part of the criminal punishment was actually inflicted upon him.

DXV. In subsequent cases both Lord Chancellor Eldon (*h*) and Lord Chancellor Brougham (*i*) appear to have considered the judgment in *Lolley's* case as going the whole length of deciding that a Foreign Divorce could not operate to dissolve an English Marriage ; and the additional condition of the divorce being between *English parties* does not appear to have

---

(*f*) See Dr. Lushington's remarks in *Conway* v. *Beazley*, 3 *Haggard's* R. 646.

This case, as well as that subsequently [alluded to of *Macarthy* v. *Decaix*, were decided in the early part of 1831.

But Dr. Lushington and Lord Brougham appear in these cases to have taken rather different views of the *extent* of the decision in *Lolley's Case*.

(*g*) See *Lord Cranworth's* remarks in *Dolphin* v. *Robins*, 1859.

(*h*) *Tovey* v. *Lindsay*, 1 *Dow.* R. 124-5.

(*i*) *Macarthy* v. *Decaix*, 2 *Russ. and Myl.* R. 619-20.

See, however, Lord Brougham's explanation in *Warrender* v. *Warrender*, of his remarks in this case of *Macarthy* v. *Decaix*.

been engrafted upon that decision till the case of *Warrender*
v. *Warrender.*

DXVI. It has been observed that for more than a century
the Scotch Courts have holden that, without reference to the
country where the Marriage was celebrated, if the parties were
resident, this residence may fall far short of a legal Domicil (*k*). In Scotland it has, since the Reformation at least, been
competent to the Scotch Court to divorce *a vinculo matrimonii;* and since the decision (*l*) of the House of Lords
and of the Twelve English judges, the Fifteen judges of
Scotland have, nevertheless, expressly re-affirmed this to be
the Law of Scotland.

DXVII. The observations of Lords Brougham and Lyndhurst in *Warrender* v. *Warrender* (*m*), it can hardly be
denied, shook, to a certain extent, the doctrine of *Lolley's*
case, though the authority of that case was, as will be presently
seen, recognized in the recent case of *Dolphin* v. *Robins.*

DXVIII. But, at all events, the case of *Warrender* v.
Warrender, decided in 1835, contains the opinion of Lord
Brougham, that a sentence of Divorce *a vinculo matrimonii,* pronounced by the country where the parties were
domiciled, ought, even in the case of an English Marriage,
upon principles of Comity, to be recognized in this country.
The reasoning of the learned judge applies more forcibly to
the case of a *Scotch Divorce* of a *Scotch Marriage* between
English subjects. The English Courts having recognized the
authority of Scotland to complete the obligation of the marriage tie, ought, it is argued, to acknowledge its competency
to dissolve it on the principle of the maxim, " Unumquodque
" dissolvitur eodem modo quo colligatur :" and it is said with
great force as to the opportunity which a strict adherence to

---

(*k*) *Conway* v. *Beazley*, 3 *Haggard's* R. 646.

(*l*) The case of *Edmiston* referred to by Lord Lyndhurst in *Warrender* v. *Warrender,* 9 *Bligh*, 150-51.

(*m*) The Lords in *Warrender's Case* considered themselves as a *Scotch*
Court of Appeal from a *Scotch* Court.

the Law of Scotland with respect to the dissolution of the contract would give to the violators of the English Marriage Law, "This objection comes too late," after the decisions which have established that the Scotch Marriage of English parties avowedly *in fraudem legis*, is valid; that there is no sense in complaining of the evasion of English Law, which would arise from supporting Scotch Divorces, and sanctioning the evasion of English Law by upholding Scotch Marriages, which entirely, as in the case of minors, subverts it.

" If " (says Lord Brougham) " in a matter confessedly not clear, and very far from being unincumbered with doubt and difficulty, we find that manifest and serious inconvenience is sure to result from one view, and very little in comparison from adopting the opposite course, nothing can be a stronger reason for taking the latter. Now surely it strikes every one that the greatest hardship must occur to parties, the greatest embarrassments to their rights, and the utmost inconvenience to the courts of justice in both countries by the rule being maintained as laid down in *Lolley's* case. The greatest hardship to parties; for what can be a greater grievance than that parties living *bonâ fide* in England, though temporarily, should either not be allowed to marry at all during there residence here, or if they do, and afterwards return to their own country, however great its distance, that they must be deprived of all remedy in case of misconduct, however aggravated, unless they undertake a voyage back to England, ay, and unless they can comply with the parliamentary forms in serving notices? the greatest embarrassments to their rights; for what can be more embarrassing than that a person's *Status* should be involved in uncertainty, and should be subject to change its nature, as he goes from place to place; that he should be married in one country, and single, if not a felon, in another—bastard here, and legitimate there? the utmost inconvenience to the Courts; for what inconvenience can be greater than that they should have to regard a person as married for one purpose, and not for

another ; single and a felon, if he marries a few yards to the
southward—lawfully married if the ceremony be performed
a few yards to the north ; a bastard when he claims land,
legitimate when he sues for personal successions ; widow,
when she demands the chattels of her husband, his concubine when she counts as dowable of his land (n)?"

*   *   *   *   *   *   *   *

" I have now been commenting upon *Lolley's* case on its
own principle—that is, regarding it as merely laying down a
rule for England, and prescribing how a Scotch Divorce
shall be considered in this country, and dealt with by its
Courts. I have felt this the more necessary because I do
not see, for the reasons which have occasionally been adverted to in treating the other argument, how, consistently
with any principle, the judges who decided the case could
limit its application to England, and think that it did not
decide also on the validity of the divorce in Scotland. They
certainly could not hold the second English marriage invalid
and felonious in England without assuming that the Scotch
divorce was void even in Scotland. In my view of the present question, therefore, it was fit to show that the Scotch
Courts have a good title to consider the principle of *Lolley's*
case erroneous even as an English decision. This, it is true,
their Lordships have not done ; and the judgment now under
appeal is rested upon the ground of the Scotch Divorce
being sufficient to determine the marriage-contract in Scotland only.

" I must now observe, that, supposing (as may fairly be concluded) *Lolley's* case to have decided that the Divorce is
void in Scotland, there can be no ground whatever for holding that it is binding upon the Scotch Courts on a question
of Scotch Law. If the cases and the authorities of that Law
are against it, the learned persons who administer the system
of jurisprudence are not bound to regard—nay, they are
not entitled to regard—an English decision, framed by

(n) 9 *Bligh's Rep.* 130.

" English judges upon an English case, and devoid of all
" authority beyond the Tweed."

DXIX. The cases which intervened between that of *Lolley*
and that of *Warrender* were, first, *Macarthy* v. *Decaix* (*o*), in
the Court of Chancery, the case of a Danish Divorce. The
husband, a Dane by birth and domicil, married in England an
English wife. They afterwards both became domiciled in
Denmark. Lord Eldon hesitated, and said he could not take
it as settled by *Lolley's* case ; that the marriage was not,
for English purposes, dissolved by the Danish Divorce ; but
Lord Brougham becoming Lord Chancellor, decided against
the validity of the Divorce on the authority of *Lolley's* case.
Lord Brougham's subsequent remarks in *Warrender's* case
are not consistent with this judgment ; and the authority of
it appears now, at all events, since the passing of the recent
Statute, to be doubtful. Secondly, in the same year as
Macarthy v. *Decaix*, the case of *Conway* v. *Beazley* (*p*)
was decided by Dr. Lushington in the Consistory of London,
in which that learned judge held that a Scotch Divorce
did not annul an English Marriage ; but he observed :—
" My judgment, however, must not be construed to go one
" step beyond the present case ; nor in any manner to
" touch the case of a Divorce pronounced in Scotland, who,
" though married when domiciled in England, was, at the
" time of such Divorce, *bonâ fide* domiciled in Scotland ; still
" less between parties who were only on a casual visit to Eng-
" land at the time of their marriage, but were then and at the
" time of the Divorce *bonâ fide* domiciled in Scotland."

This question Dr. Lushington did not consider to have been
decided by the case of *Lolley* (*q*).

DXX. (γ). With respect to Foreign Sentence of Divorce
since the passing of the recent Statute.

(*o*) 2 *Russell & Mylne's Rep.* 614.

(*p*) 3 *Haggard's Eccles. Rep.* 642.

(*q*) In the case of *Tovey* v. *Lindsay*, 1 *Dow's Rep.* 117, in 1813,—an
appeal from Scotland to the House of Lords on a question of jurisdiction,—no decision was given.

In 1858, the Law of England underwent a change of the greatest moment. It is not too much to say that no law has been passed since the Reformation so vitally affecting the social and moral condition of this realm. By that Law Marriages were, for the first time, rendered dissoluble. Before this Law Marriages had been dissolved by special acts of Parliament, the passing of which bore testimony to the general Law of indissolubility : this *privilegium* was certainly open to the gravest objections, and was on principle indefensible ; but its practical effect upon the social and moral state of the people was inconsiderable. The practical effect of the present Law is certainly not inconsiderable, though yet but in the infancy of its domestic operation. With respect to its international operation it surely ought, upon sound principles of Comity, to lead to a recognition of Foreign Divorces of English subjects *domiciled abroad* for the same causes at least which the *lex patriæ* allows to be grounds of Divorce—namely, adultery, on the part of the wife ; cruelty and adultery, or desertion and adultery, on the part of the husband.

Since the passing of the Statute, the following case has been decided ; but the Scotch Divorce, it will be observed, had in this case been decreed before the passing of the Statute.

A domiciled English husband married in England a wife, in the year 1822 ; they separated by mutual consent in 1839. In 1854, the husband went to Scotland—his wife followed him. After a few weeks' residence, sufficient according to the Scotch Law, to found the jurisdiction of the Scotch court, the wife sued the husband for adultery, and obtained the decree of a Scotch Court, dissolving the marriage. The husband had not at the time a Domicil, but only a temporary residence in Scotland.

The wife afterwards resided at Paris, and married a Frenchman in that country. The House of Lords held, affirming the decision of the Court of Probate, that the Scotch Divorce had not dissolved the English marriage. (*r*)

(*r*) 1 *Swabey & Tristram*, 37 ; and 7 *House of Lords Reports*, 390.

The circumstances of the case were such as to show, that the Divorce was effected by gross collusion. Lord Kingsdown said, " It is clear, therefore, it was mere mockery and collu- " sion from beginning to end." Lord Cranworth, who spoke first and gave the judgment of the Lords in detail, (s) said, " My " Lords, the very learned judge of the Court of Probate, " rejected the allegation of the Appellant, on the ground that it " stated no case impeaching the validity of the will and codicil " propounded by the Respondents. The grounds on which the " Appellant relied were, that by the proceedings in Scotland " the Marriage with the Appellant was dissolved so as to enable " the deceased to contract a new Marriage in 1854, with " General de Pontes, a domiciled Frenchman, and became " herself domiciled in France, and so continued from the time " of her marriage till her death, and that while so domiciled " she made the will of 23rd of June, 1856, in the mode " required by the Laws of the country of her Domicil, which " therefore was a valid revocation of the will and codicil of " April, 1854. The Appellant further contended that, even if " the Divorce was not valid so as to enable the deceased to " contract a second marriage, still it operated as a Divorce " a mensa et toro, and enabled her to select a Domicil of her " own, and that in fact she did select France as her Domicil, " where she lived and died. The learned judge of the court " below was of opinion that the English Marriage was not " dissolved by the Scotch Divorce, and that so the deceased " remained up to the time of her death the wife of the Appel- " lent whose Domicil was and had always been in England ; " that his Domicil was her Domicil, and that the will or alleged " will of June, 1856, not having been executed in the mode

---

(s) In this judgment it was decided that the Scotch sentence of *divorce a vinculo* could not operate as a *divorce a mensâ et toro* in England. Also it should be observed that Lord Cranworth's opinion inclined to admit that a wife *domiciled a mensâ et toro*, may have a separate domicil from her husband. Lord Kingsdown expressed an opposite opinion : this question was not, however, decided.

required by our laws, had no effect on the will and codicil of
1854. He further held that the Scotch decree did not
operate as a divorce *a mensâ et toro*, and so made a decree
rejecting the allegation. The same arguments were renewed
and urged with great ability at your Lordships' bar. But
they failed to convince me, or, as I believe, any of your Lordships who heard the case. On the first question, the validity
of the Scotch Divorce to dissolve the English Marriage, the
decision in *Lolley's* case is conclusive. It was, indeed, contended in the argument here that *Lolley's* case did not necessarily govern that now under consideration, for that since
that decision the principles applicable to this question have
been materially changed by the Statute 9 Geo. 4, c. 31. But
this seems to me altogether a mistake. In *Lolley's* case it
appeared that he, having been married in England, afterwards went to Scotland, and while he was there, *not having
become a domiciled Scotchman* (for that must be assumed
to have been the state of the facts), his wife obtained a
Scotch decree for a Divorce on the ground of adultery committed by him in Scotland. After the decree was pronounced he returned to England and married a second wife
at Liverpool. This was held by the unanimous opinion of
the judges to be bigamy, on the ground ' that no sentence
' or act of any Foreign Country or State could dissolve an
' English marriage *à vinculo matrimonii*,' meaning, I presume, could dissolve the matrimonial *vinculum*, and that no
Divorce of an Ecclesiastical Court was within the exception in 1 Jac. 1, c. 11, s. 3, unless it was the Divorce of a
Court within the limits to which the 1 Jac. 1 extends.
The exception to the Statute 1 Jac. 1 was ' of any person
' divorced by sentence in the Ecclesiastical Court.' It was
contended here that the decision might have been different
if the case had arisen since the 9 Geo. 4, c. 31, which repeals
the Statute 1 J. 1, c. 11, and by sect. 22 again makes bigamy
a felony, but with a proviso that the enactment shall not
extend to any person who at the time of the second
Marriage shall have been divorced from the bond of the

" first Marriage. It was said that the Scotch Court was not
" the Ecclesiastical Court contemplated by the Statute 1
" Jac. 1, and that so Lolley was not within the exception
" contained in that Statute, but that, as he had been in fact
" divorced he would now have been within the proviso of the
" Statute 9 Geo. 4, c. 31. This, however, is evidently a mis-
" take. He was not, and could not, be divorced : for, accord-
" ing to the express opinion of the judges, no Court can
" dissolve the bonds of an English Marriage. *Lolley's* case
" has been frequently acted on. In the case of *Conway* v.
" *Beazley*, Dr. Lushington, after much consideration, acted on
" it, treating it as settled law where there is no *bonâ fide*
" Domicil in Scotland, meaning by *bonâ fide* Domicil a real
" Domicil, and not a Domicil assumed merely for the purpose
" giving jurisdiction. And I believe your Lordships are all
" of opinion that it must be taken now as clearly established
" that the Scotch Court has no power to dissolve an English
" Marriage where, as in this case, the parties are not really
" domiciled in Scotland, but have only gone there for such a
" time as, according to the doctrine of the Scotch Courts, gives
" them jurisdiction in the matter. Whether they could dis-
" solve the Marriage if there be a *bonâ fide* Domicil is a
" matter upon which I think your Lordships will not be
" inclined now to pronounce a decided opinion."

DXXI. No mention is made in this judgment of any alteration effected by the recent Statute in the Law of England with
respect to the general recognition of Foreign Sentences of
Divorce on English subjects.

It seems clear, however, that the question whether England
will recognize a Foreign Sentence of Divorce upon English
subjects domiciled in the State of the *forum* which pronounced it, is yet, unhappily, undecided.

It has been already stated that the argument of such Divorces being *contra bones mores* (*t*), or of then falling under

---

(*t*) That is, at least, of foreign divorces granted upon *the same
grounds* as those specified in the recent statute. The argument might

the class of the exceptional restrictions (*u*) which prevent the admission of Foreign Laws and Sentences cannot be now righteously advanced by England.

And where no such obstacle presents itself, the principles of Comity would lead to the recognition of the Foreign Sentence.

---

yet, though much weakened, be used against the recognition of foreign divorces decreed on *other* grounds.

(*u*) *Vide ante*, s. 12, &c.

CHAPTER XXIII.

PATERNAL RIGHTS.

DXXII. The next question arising from the relations of Family is that of the *Patria Potestas*, or *Paternal Rights* (a). The continental nations of Europe recognize an extent of Paternal Power, derived from the Roman Law, which is unknown to the Common Law of Great Britain and of the United States of North America; and this fact is used by Mr. Justice Story, as an argument for adhering to the rule that in the case of Marriages the *lex loci contractûs* shall prevail.

DXXIII. The Paternal Power is to be considered with respect to

1. The Person, } of the Child.
2. The Property, }

With respect to the Person, the Private International Law of Germany throughout its various States upon this subject, appears to declare, as a general rule, that the same rights are accorded to the parents and children of strangers, which they can, by legitimate proof, satisfy the proper German authorities they possessed in their native country, or in the country of their Domicil (b) at the time when the Paternal or Filial relation was called into existence.

(a) *Story*, ss. 25, 90, 455, 456, 462, 463.

Pütter II. ss. 48, 61. Von den Eltern und Kindesrechten der Fremden.

Savigny, VIII. ss. 380, 396.

Merlin's Rep., Puissance Paternelle.

(b) " Als Vaterland des Fremden wird aber jener Art erklärt, dessen Gesetzeu derselbe, vermöge seiner Geburt als Unterthan unterliegt."

Püttlingen, ss. 47, 48, citing *Allg.* 6 *G. B.* s. 34.

" Die Enstehung der väterlichen Gewalt durch Zeugung in der Ehe,

DXXIV. It is quite clear, however, that no country would tolerate such an exercise of a parental authority, however warranted by the Law of the Origin or Domicil, as actually *violated* the Law of the land. Upon this point Wächter (c), though his illustration from the supposed Law of England is ridiculous (d), speaks with firmness and accuracy.

DXXV. The limitations under which the *patria potestas* of a foreign father over the *person* of his child is admitted in England may be well gathered from the following remarks of Lord Chancellor Cottenham (d) :—

" It was urged that the Court must recognize the authority
" of a foreign tutor and curator, because it recognizes the
" authority of the parent of a foreign child. This illustration
" proves directly the reverse ; for although it is true that the
" parental authority over such a child is recognized the autho-
" rity so recognized is only that which exists by the Law of
" *England.* If, by the Law of the country to which the par-
" ties belonged, the authority of the father was much more
" extensive and arbitrary than in this country, is it supposed
" that a father would be permitted here to transgress the
" power which the Law of this country allows? If not, then
" the Law of this country regulates the authority of the
" parent of *a foreign child living in England* by the Laws
" of England and not of the Laws of the country to which the
" child belongs (e)."

DXXVI. With respect to the operation of Parental relations upon the Property of the child, according to the ancient Roman Law, no child under the Paternal power was capable

---

so wie deren denkbare Anfechtung ist zu beurtheilen nach dem Gesetz des Ortes, an welchem der Vater zur Zeit der Geburt des Kindes seinen Wohnsitz hatte."—*Savigny*, s. 380.

" E palese che lo statuto che definisce la patria potestà è personale, al pari dello statuto che fissa la minore età et la interdizione."—*Rocco*, 416—17.

(c) *Wächter, Die Collision* &c., s. 23, *in fine.*

(d) *E. g.* that a man cannot in Germany, as he may in England (!), sell his wife in the market-place.

(e) *Johnstone* v. *Beattie,* 10 *Clarke and Finnelly's Rep.* 114.

of acquiring property for himself—his acquisitions belonged to his father. This rule of law received many limitations in the course of time, as in the case of the *castrense peculium* and the *bona materna.* The general law, however, remained in force till the time of Justinian, who abrogated it entirely, and allowed the child to be the proprietor of his own acquisitions (*e*) ? Savigny expresses an unhesitating opinion that the parental relations are governed by the law of the Domicil of the Parents — not by the law of the place in which the child was born. A change of domicil, therefore, might be followed by a change of law in this matter (*f*). The reason for this opinion is, that the laws which regulate the acquisitions of children, being more or less a restriction upon the natural capacity of acquiring, belong to the individual *Status* (*g*), which is, according to Savigny's doctrine, always dependent on the Law of the Domicil ; and this affects all the children—those born before as well as those born after the domicil has been acquired (*h*). This rule of law is incorporated into the Prussian Code.

DXXVII. Much discussion has taken place among continental jurists as to whether the Paternal Power extends to *immoveable* as well as to *moveable* property ; or, as they phrase it, whether the law be *personal* or *real.*

(*e*) *Cod.* de bon. quæ, lib. vi. 6—61.

Inst. per quas pers. VIII. 1. 2. 9.

Savigny, 396.

(*f*) Dagegen sind die Vermögensverhältnisse zwischen dem Vater sind den Kindern zu beurtheilen nach dem Gesetz, welches an dem *jedesmaligen Wohnsitz* des Vaters besteht, so das also eine Veränderung des Wohnsitzes auch eine Veränderung dieser Verhältnisse nach sich ziehen kann."—*Savigny, ib.* s. 380.

" Im Europäischen Völkerrecht richtet sich die Verfügungs Befugniss des Vaters über das Einkommen vom Vermögen seiner Kinder nach dem Richt des Landes wo die dazu gehörigen Sachen sich befinden, sein Genuss desselben, Nutzniessung, &c. (i. e. *usufructus*) nach dem Rechte ihres Wohnorts."—*Pütter,* s. 54.

(*g*) *Savigny, ib.* s. 389.

(*h*) *Ib.* s. 396.

Story (*i*) collects and examines these opinions. Bretonnier, Hertius, Bouhier, Le Brun, D'Argentré, maintain that the Paternal Power is *altogether personal*, and extends to immoveable property in a foreign country. On the other hand, Froland, Boullenois, and the high authority of D'Aguesseau (*k*) are against the extension of the Parental Power to immoveable property. Merlin strives to steer a middle course between both opinions.

DXXVIII. Savigny (*l*), following Schäffner, altogether disapproves of the maxim of the English and American Law, that the *lex rei sitæ* and not the *lex domicilii* governs all questions, and, therefore, this one among the number, relating to immoveable property (*m*).

DXXIX. It would seem to be an inference from the only decision which has been given in an English court of justice, that the Parental Power, with respect to the *personal* or *moveable property* of minors was considered by English Law as depending upon and changing with the domicil. The case of *Gambier* v. *Gambier* (*n*) was as follows :—

" In 1818, the late Earl of Athlone in Ireland, and Count
" de Reade in Holland, married, at Paris, Miss Hope, who
" was possessed of large personal property. The earl was
" domiciled in Holland, Miss Hope was born at Amsterdam,
" of English parents, and, at the time of her marriage, declared
" her domicil to be at the Hague.

" At the time of the marriage, a marriage-contract was there
" executed in the Dutch form, making certain provisions, and,
" among other things, provision for the distribution of the
" wife's property in the event of her husband surviving her.

(*i*) *Conflict of Laws*, s. 455, &c.

(*k*) *Story* cites all these authorities; but see also authorities cited by *Rocco*, p. 26.

(*l*) S. 380, N. C.

(*m*) *Birthwhistle* v. *Vardill*, 7 *Clarke and Finnelly's Reports*, 911.

(*n*) 7 *Simon's Reports*, 263— 270.

" They afterwards removed to and became domiciled in Eng-
" land, and had children born there. The wife died ; and by
" her death the children became entitled, under a judicial
" compromise in Holland, to one-fourth of certain property of
" the wife in the public funds. By the French Code, which
" is the Law of Holland also, when children are under the age
" of eighteen years, their surviving parent has the enjoyment
" of their property until they attain that age; and the father
" insisted that as the children were under that age, and the
" marriage contract and judicial compromise, under which
" they took one-fourth, were both made in Holland, the
" children must take it, *subject to his Paternal Rights, by the
" Law of Holland*. The Vice-Chancellor held that the father
" was not so entitled. He said, ' The rights of the plaintiffs
" are not derived under the settlement made upon their mother's
" marriage with Mr. Gambier; but under the judicial compro-
" mise, which I must consider as a judicial decree which
" adjudicated that the children were entitled to one-fourth of
" their mother's personal estate. They take by virtue of
" that judicial decision; the contract is entirely out of the
" question.'

" By the Code Napoleon, which is the Law of Holland, as
" well as of France, when children are under the age of
" eighteen, their surviving parent has the enjoyment of their
" property until they attain that age. *But that is nothing
" more than a mere local right, given to the surviving
" parent, by the law of a particular country, so long as the
" children remain subject to that law; and, as soon as the
" children are in a country where that law is not in force,
" their rights must be determined by the law of the country
" where they happen to be. These children were never sub-
" ject to the Law of Holland; they were both born in this
" country, and have resided here ever since.* The conse-
" quence is, that this judicial decree has adjudged certain pro-
" perty to belong to two British-born subjects domiciled in
" this country; and so long as they are domiciled in this

" country, their personal property must be administered
"according to the law of this country. *The claim of their*
"*father does not arise by virtue of the contract, but solely*
" *by the local law of the country where he was residing at the*
" *time of his marriage ;* and, therefore, this property must be
"considered just as if it had been an English legacy given to
"the children ; and all that the father is entitled to is the
"usual reference to the Master to inquire what allowance
"ought to be made to him for the past and future maintenance
" of his children (*o*)."

DXXX. The Judicial Committee of the Privy Council
decided, in the case of *Sherwood* v. *Ray* (*p*), that the Ecclesiastical Courts in England adopted that part of the Canon
Law, " which abrogated the *patria potestas* of the Civil Law,
"and placed the parental authority in this respect in the
" hands of their spiritual guides ; and that part of the Canon
" Law which takes away the control of parents over the mar-
"riage of their children is undoubtedly in force in this coun-
" try, the marriage of males of fourteen years and of females
" of twelve being unquestionably valid by the Law of England,
"before the Marriage Acts, with or without the consent of the
" parents (*q*)."

DXXXI. (*r*) *Adoption* and *Emancipation* are Legal Relations founded on the Roman, and unknown to the English Law ;
but, whatever consequences, affecting the *Status*, flow from

---

(*o*) *Gambier* v. *Gambier*, 7 *Simon's Rep.* 269.

(*p*) 1 *Moore's P. C. Rep.* 398.

(*q*) See in next chapter the leading case of *Alicia Race*, as to guardianship by nurture of the widow.

(*r*) *Fœlix*, s. 33, observes of the *Statut Personel*, " Cette loi regit le
mode de constater l'état civil elle regit également les effets de la puissance
paternelle, en ce qui concerne la personne des enfants la manière de
constituer le tuteur ; elle indique les personnes qui peuvent être ap-
peleés à cette fonction civile, et elle définit les pouvoirs du tuteur : elle
determine les cas ou l'emancipation peut avoir lieu."

them, according to the personal Statute or Law of the Domicil, ought to be recognized in other countries; subject always to the exceptions to this general rule, which have been already mentioned.

CHAPTER XXIV.

ILLEGITIMATE CHILDREN—POLICY OF STATES.

DXXXII. (*a*) The question as to the *Status* of children born out of lawful wedlock, the parental power which can be exercised over them, the rights which they can claim at the hands of one or both of their parents, constitute some of the most difficult problems, both of Private Right and of Public Law.

The question in all its bearings, is one which certainly much concerns the well-being of the State ; for it greatly affects the general morality of the people, upon which the security of all States is built.

The public policy of States has looked at this question from two distinct points of view—always of course with the same object, that of checking the frequency of the crime. In truth, the whole question borders upon the considerations of *Criminal* International Law.   At the same time it would be absurd to apply the *lex loci* (*b*) *delicti commissi* to settle the question of the obligations of the parents toward the child. (*c*)

In some countries, it has been sought to obtain this moral end, by enlarging and strengthening the claims of the child upon the father, as a punishment of the male offender ; in

---

(*a*) *Story*, s. 93, 94.

Burge, Commentaries on Foreign and Colonial Law.   I. Pt. 1, ch. iii. s. 3, pp. 101—6.

Savigny, VIII. 399—3.

Rocco, pp. 416—20.

Pütter, ss. 58—63.

(*b*) *Savigny, ib.* s. 374.

(*c*) This is clearly stated by *Seuffert*, and adopted by *Schäffner*, *Entwickelung des Internationales Privatrecht*, s. 98.

others by narrowing, or, as in France, (*d*) altogether taking away the claims of the mother or the child upon the father, as a punishment of the female offender. In both cases, the Law has a *moral* end in view, and therefore it falls under the category of the exceptions to the operation of the general rule of Comity, that is to say, the *Status* of the illegitimate child will be determined by the Law of the land in which he is living, without reference to the Law of the Domicil of either of the parents at the time of the birth of the child.

DXXXIII. Thus, if an attempt was made by the mother, who had been a domiciled concubine in a country where concubinage was a legal *Status*, to enforce before a French Tribunal either a claim of affiliation or any other claim growing out of the *Status* of concubinage, such a claim would be rightly rejected by the French Tribunal, inasmuch as its recognition would militate against a *moral* principle of French Law (*e*). *Savigny* remarks, that this principle has been incorporated into the Prussian Code.

DXXXIV. In these remarks, the *factum* of the illegitimacy of the child has been assumed; but, if the *factum* itself be in dispute, a most difficult question of Private International Law arises, and, with respect to which, the decisions of that Law are far from satisfactory. The shape which this question has generally assumed, has been that of the "*legitimatio per* " *subsequens matrimonium.*"

The maxims of the Roman Law, "*Pater est quem nuptiæ*

(*d*) *Code Civil*, art. 340.—"La recherche de la paternité est interdite."

Savigny defends this law on the ground that the subject of it, properly speaking, is not the personal *status*, but a matter of public policy and positive law; and he remarks that the same principle is incorporated into the Prussian law.—*Savigny*, VIII. s. 399 and s. 374, n. *a*.

(*e*) This presumption of law, Savigny observes, is founded on the dignity and sanctity of marriage—unmarried *concubitus* does not fall under this principle: the father, if not necessarily uncertain, may be so, and the possibility furnishes a complete defence to a charge of paternity.

" *demonstrant,*" (*f*) and " *cum legitimæ nuptiæ factæ sint*
" *patrem liberi sequuntur,*" (*g*) are universally recognized ;
but the question, what are "*justæ,*" or "*legitimæ nuptiæ,*"
has been, and still is, a subject one of much dispute amongst
jurists.

DXXXV. (*h*) Foreign jurists, with few exceptions, hold the
doctrine, that the question of the *Status* of the child depends
upon the Law of the Domicil of his parents.

But the circumstances, as is well observed by Story, may be
very various, admitting and requiring very important distinctions in the application of this general doctrine ; and he
suggests the following cases as illustrative of this remark.

1. The case of a child born before marriage in the Domicil
of his parents, who afterwards intermarry in that Domicil,
according to the Law of which the child is legitimated by the
subsequent marriage.

2. The case of a child born under all these circumstances,
but whose parents marry in another State, where there is
no such law of subsequent legitimation.

3. The case of a child born before marriage in the Domicil
of his parents, the law of which does not admit retroactive
legitimation by a subsequent marriage, and *they, being there
married,* afterwards acquire a new domicil, by the Law of
which such subsequent marriage does legitimate the child.

4. The case of a child born before marriage in the Domicil
of his parents, the Law of which does not allow legitimation
by a subsequent marriage, and they acquire a new domicil, the

---

(*f*) *Dig.* l. ii. t. iv. 5. " Pater vero is est quem nuptiæ demonstrant."

(*g*) *Dig.* l. i. t. v. 10, *de statu hominum.*

(*h* Their opinions are collected and given at length by *Story,* s. 93,
&c.; but he is not quite clear or correct in s. 936, when he says that
because most jurists hold the validity of the marriage to depend on the
lex loci celebrationis, therefore they hold that the *status* of the child
ought to depend upon the same law. States differ very much, as has
been shown, with respect to the validity of the marriage being solely
dependent upon the *lex loci*; nor is the difficulty quite met by the quali-
fying woids, " at all events if the parents were then domiciled there."

law of which does allow such legitimation, and they are there married.

To these instances, another may be added :

5. The case of a child born illegitimate in a State which does not admit legitimation by subsequent marriage ; but the father is domiciled in a State which does admit such legitimation, and he afterwards, retaining his original domicil, marries the mother in the State, the law of which does not allow such legitimation (*i*).

DXXXVI. The conflicting jurisprudence of England and Scotland, the entire variance of two parts of the same empire as to the Law which governs the most important moral and social relations of the inhabitants, has caused this question of legitimacy by subsequent marriage, as well as the question of Divorce, to be elaborately and solemnly discussed in the courts of inferior and superior jurisdiction of Great Britain.

DXXXVII. In the leading case of *Birthwhistle* v. *Vardill*, (*k*) the House of Lords, after a re-hearing, having the unanimous advice of the twelve judges, decided, with respect to a son born of Scotch parents in Scotland before marriage, who afterwards intermarried in that State, and thereby legitimated the son in Scotland, that he was incapable of inheriting *immoveable* property in England.

The Judges expressed their opinion as follows :—

" It is said for the appellant, that according to the rule we " adopt, if he is born in lawful wedlock, he fulfils every con- " tract required of him. Now, they say he is born in lawful " wedlock, because, by a presumption of the Scottish Law, a " presumption *juris et de jure*, there was a marriage anterior " to his procreation. It is by force of this presumption that " he is legitimate : by this fiction he is born within the pale " of lawful matrimony. We know that this fiction is, by " respectable writers on the Scottish Law, represented as

---

(*i*) *Vide post, in re Wright's Trust.*
(*k*) 7 *Clarke and Finnelly's Rep.* 895.

" accompanying the legitimation *per subsequens matri-*
" *monium.* But we do not concede the *consequence deduced*
" *from it,* as applicable to the present question. The question
" is, what *the Law of England* requires; and, as we are
" advised, the Law of England requires that the claimant
" should actually, and in fact, be born within the pale of
" lawful matrimony ; we cannot agree that the prescription
" of a foreign jurisprudence, contrary to the acknowledged
" fact, should abrogate the Law of England, and that by such
" a fiction a principle should be introduced which, upon a
" great and memorable occasion, the legislature of the king-
' dom distinctly rejected : your Lordships will perceive that I
' allude to the statute of Merton. It would seem strange to
" introduce indirectly, and from *comity to a foreign nation,*
" a rule of inheritance which may affect every *honour* and all
" the *real property* of the realm, which rule, when proposed
" directly and positively to the legislature they directly and
" positively negatived and refused ; a refusal that, in England,
" has obtained the approval of every succeeding age (*l*)."

DXXXVIII. It is, perhaps, difficult to say that the English
Law, which allows a child born *the moment after* the marriage
ceremony has been performed to be legitimate, promotes a
higher standard of morality, than the ancient law of the
Church adopted by Scotland and most Continental States,
which allows legitimation *per subsequens matrimonium* ; or
that the Statute of Merton, considering the epoch at which it
was passed, or, rather, proclaimed, and the object of the Barons

---

(*l*) *Story* (88, 89, 93, 94) is wholly unable to reconcile the decision in
Birthwhistle v. *Vardill* with the cases of *Munro* v. *Saunders,* 6
Bligh's N. Rep. 483, of *Shedden* v. *Patricke,* 6 *Bligh's N. Rep.* 489, of
The Strathmore Peerage, 4 *Wils. and Shaw's Rep. App.* 89, 95, in which
cases it has been decided that a person *illegitimate* by the law of the
domicil of his birth is illegitimate in England ("*his* domicil of birth "
is an ambiguous expression, *vide post, in re Wright's Trust*) ; the reasoning of Lord Brougham *against* the decision in *Birthwhistle* v. *Vardill,*
deserves careful study, 9 *Bligh's N. Rep.* 73 ; *S.C.* 2 *Clk. and Finnelly's
Rep.* 584.

who proclaimed it, ought to be holden in very great esteem. Unquestionably, the state of the Scotch and English Law, both on this subject and on the question of divorce, is disgraceful to the jurisprudence of a civilized country. It is to be remembered that the judges founded their refusal to give full effect to the Foreign Law upon a question of *Personal Status*, upon the express ground that the recognition of it in this case would contravene a fundamental law of the country, and, therefore, be without the pale of Comity (*m*).

DXXXIX. In other recent cases (*n*) it has been holden by the House of Lords, that a child born before marriage of parents domiciled in a State, the law of which did not allow legitimation *per subsequens matrimonium*, would not become legitimate, for the purpose of inheriting *immoveable property*, by the marriage of his parents in another country, which did allow legitimation *per subsequens matrimonium ;* and it was intimated that the change of the domicil of the parents to the States where the marriage was celebrated would not have altered the decision.

DXL. The Law of France differs in this matter from the Law of England (*o*). It has been decided that a bastard cannot be made legitimate if at the time of its *conception* or *birth* the parents were incapable of *contracting* to legitimize

---

(*m*) So Littledale, J., observed on this case in the King's Bench.

" The very rule that a personal status accompanies a man everywhere is admitted to have this qualification, that it does not militate against the law of the country where the *consequences* of that *status* are sought to be enforced."—5 *Barnewell and Cresswell's Rep.* 455.

This ground does really constitute the defence of the judgment. In England, it is to be recollected, consequences of great political and constitutional moment flow from territorial possession.

(*n*) *Munro* v. *Saunders*, 6 *Bligh's Reports*, 468.

Rose v. *Rose*, 4 *Wilson and Shaw's Reports*, 289, and *App.* pp. 33, 89.

Story, s. 93.

(*o*) *Merlin, Quest. de Droit*, " *Legitimation*," s. 2, n. 1. The case of *De Conty.*

the child after its birth. But this does not seem to mean an incapacity of the law of the parents' domicil, but such a personal incapacity as a previous marriage. Story remarks that the result of these two cases seems to be, that the law of the place of the birth of the child, and not the law of the place of the marriage of the parents, decides whether a subsequent marriage will legitimate the child or not (p). But a recent and most important decision by Vice-Chancellor Wood in an English Court of Equity conclusively establishes that, in England, the law of the domicil of the father at the time of the birth of the child decides the question of legitimation.

DXLI. The substance of this decision was that a domiciled Englishman, being the putative father of an illegitimate child, born in France of a French woman, and afterwards becoming domiciled in France, cannot, on his subsequent marriage with the mother of the child, legitimatize the child under the provisions of the French Law so as to enable it to share in a bequest to his children contained in the will of a person in England.

The reasons for this decision were—

1. That marriage, being a personal contract, is like other personal contracts regulated by the law of the domicil of the party.

2. That the law of the domicil of the putative father attached to the child at its birth, and by that law its bastardy was indelible.

3. That by the Law of France a bastard cannot afterwards be made legitimate, if, at the time of its conception, the parents were incapable of contracting to legitimatize the child after its birth, and a domiciled Englishman could not bind himself to such a contract.

4. That by the Law of France a bastard can never be made legitimate, if it is uncertain who was the father ; and a domiciled Englishman by the law of this country cannot, for

---

(p) The opinions of the Scotch judges, whose decision the House of Lords reversed, in *Rose* v. *Rose*, contain much argument in favour of an opposite conclusion.

civil purposes, be more than the *putative* father of a bastard child (*q*).

DXLII. (*r*) *Legitimation by the authority of the State,* evidenced by some public act, as in England by an Act of Parliament, or in other countries by the decree of the Sovereign (*per rescriptum principis*), might give rise to an international question of some nicety, though reason and principle are in favour of the recognition by other countries of such legitimation, where it is valid *lege domicilii.* As to immoveable property, the rule respecting such legitimation would, perhaps, be liable to the same restrictions as the legitimation by sentence of a court of justice. The authority of Schäffner (*s*), however, is opposed even to this limitation ; he is of opinion that the *legitimatio per rescriptum principis* is good and valid everywhere, if good and valid by the law of the domicil, and that the *lex loci rei sitæ* has no bearing upon the question, which is one purely of *Status.*

(*q*) *In the matter of the* 10 & 11 Vict. c. 96, *and In the matter of the Trusts of the Will of Joseph Wright, deceased* (April, 1856, V. C. Wood), 2 *Kay and Johnson's Rep.* 595 ; *S.C. The Jurist,* vol. ii. n. 72, *New Series,* May 24, 1856.

Vide post, Appendix to this Chapter for the judgment in this case.

(*r*) *Pütter,* s. 60.

(*s*) *Entwickelung des Intern. Privatrechts,* s. 40. "Die Frage scheint unbedingt bejaht werden zu mussen." He cites *Anton. de Roselli's tract. de legit.* (*in Oceano juris*) i. 2. n. 24.

Voet, de Stat. s. 4, c. iii. s. 15, p. 138.

Le Bret, questions notables, liv. 3, *decis.* 7 ; *Boullenois,* i. 64.

APPENDIX TO CHAPTER XXIV.

The judgment of Sir W. P. Wood, so far as it refers to the cause *In re Wright's Trust*, on account of its great importance, is here given at length. It is taken, with a trifling correction, from the Jurist of May 24, 1856 :—

Here it is important in the first place to observe that William Wright's domicil by birth was English ; that his stay in Scotland, during which his first marriage took place, was but for a very short time ; that he then returned to and resided in England up to the decease of his first wife in 1821, at Collumpton, in Devonshire. She appears to have managed all his affairs, to which he throughout his life paid but little attention ; and on her decease he was astonished to find himself very much involved. Upon this he ultimately went to Dunkirk, whether under his own or an assumed name is in dispute, but, without doubt, for the purpose of avoiding his creditors, though with the honourable intention, which he fulfilled, of paying them off. That was in July, 1823. Mrs. Williams was born in December, 1824, the fruit of an intercourse which must have taken place in March, 1824. Now, the immediate question presents itself, what was William Wright's domicil in December, 1824 ? It was English beyond a doubt. The original cause of his leaving England was his being in debt, and his debts were not cleared off until 1836. In the interval, up to that time, there is no evidence of any declaration of an intention to return or not. The ceremony being performed in March, 1824, by an English clergyman is no very strong evidence on a question of domicil, but it shows a certain predilection. It is said that he took a house in St. Omer about this time, on lease. But if he did so, it is no strong evidence. His debts were still unpaid, and he continued living near the coast, taking a house for short limited periods, which he might consider would coincide with the time of payment. There is, therefore, in my opinion, nothing to shew that his domicil was other than English in 1824. Before 1832, however, but long after the birth of this child, he went to reside in Paris, and there is then some evidence of his intention to fix himself in France, and acquire a domicil in that country. If he had remained clearly and indisputably a domiciled Englishman, the case would be too clear for argument, for the state of the English Law, as applied to the case of Mrs. Williams, utterly precludes any subsequent legitimation. But I have had some doubts whether I should not desire further evidence as to the subsequent domicil ; and *in order to avoid putting the parties to that delay and expense, I have considered what would be the result assuming that*

William Wright had from 1832 *acquired a French Domicil;* for if I should come to the conclusion that that would make no difference, then, of course, the further evidence as to his subsequent domicil would be unnecessary. *I hold that at the time of the conception and of the birth of Mrs. Williams, William Wright was a domiciled Englishman;* but that his domicil is doubtful at the date of the marriage at the Ambassador's chapel in 1841, and of the marriage in the French form in 1846; and then *the question is, when an Englishman residing abroad, and having a putative child while a domiciled Englishman, afterwards becomes a domiciled Frenchman, and contracts these two marriages successively,* how this Court is to deal with persons who are clearly subjects of the country before whose tribunal the question comes to be determined? One point as to the Law of Domicil is, that every man carries about in his person the law of his own country as to personal contracts, and that it signifies nothing what may be the law of the foreign country in which he may happen to be residing. Marriage, indeed, must, in general be celebrated according to the law of the country in which it takes place; but in general the rule is, as to all personal contracts, that the Law of Domicil is to prevail. It was settled at a very early period, in *Conty's Case,* cited in *Munro* v. *Munro,* (*ubi sup.*) when the House of Lords was sitting in appeal on a Scotch case, and, therefore, as a Scotch Court; and they held that a domiciled Scotchman, having a child by an Englishwoman in England and afterwards marrying her, that child was by the Scotch Law legitimated. In the case of *Conty,* to which I have referred (*Guessière, Journ. des Princ. Aud. des Parl.,* tom. ii. b. 7, c. 7; *Burge's Co. Col. & For. Laws,* 106), a domiciled Frenchman, residing temporarily in England, married an Englishwoman, and the French Courts decided according to the same doctrine. On the other hand, I believe it is the law both in France and England, that if a person, admittedly of English Domicil, were in France to have connection with a Frenchwoman, the child, the result of that connection, would, if nothing more took place, be illegitimate. Then the question is, whether the additional circumstances which I have here to consider make any difference. I am not aware that these circumstances have ever before been the subject of judicial cognizance, viz., that the father should be a Domiciled Englishman at the time of the birth, and a Domiciled Frenchman at the time of the marriage. That distinguishes it from *Lloyd's Case* (*ante,* note), for there the Court treated the father's Domicil of Origin as doubtful. It was, therefore, not so difficult to hold that he was a domiciled Frenchman at the time of the birth in 1826, when he had already resided there for several years, and with other circumstances more favourable to a French domicil than are to be found here. I have examined what is the ground or theory as to subsequent ceremonies of marriage both according to the French Code, as also the Roman Law—of authority in France as it is in Scotland. But the course of decisions in France have cleared several points more than in Scotland. In the first place, the Roman Law clearly proceeds wholly upon the fiction that the subsequent marriage evidences a consent to have passed at the time of the connection of which the child was born ; and accordingly Merlin in his *Repertoire* shews how the old Roman Law found great difficulty when an intermediate regular marriage with somebody else, as in *Kerr* v. *Martin* (*ubi sup.*), had taken place between the birth of the child and the subsequent marriage of the parents ; and it considered such intermediate marriage to be an obstacle to the legitimation of the child ; because, if upon the subsequent ceremony and declaration before witnesses the parties should be held to have been married, in fact, from the time of their first connection, the intermediate marriage was an adultery, and that offspring spurious. The settled rule, however, now acknowledged in France is as laid down in *Pothier on the Marriage Contract* (part v. c. 2, s. 3, art. 421). He says, " The fiction of retroaction is not absolutely necessary for legitimation ; it is enough if it can be supposed at the time of the connection the parties had that connection in view of the marriage which they then proposed to contract, that one of the parties afterwards changed his intention of marrying another person ; but that after the dissolution of that marriage the original parties at length executed their first intention." That principle seems to be considered as now settled in France, and adopted by Merlin. But the whole retrospective or other action in legitimating the offspring must rest on some contract in some way or other. The Roman Law seems to have put it on this intelligible ground, viz., that the connection resulting in the birth of a child was an inchoate contract, which the parties intended to fulfil ; but that if interrupted, *e. g.*, by an intermediate marriage with another, so that either of the parties to the inchoate contract put it out of his or her power to carry it out, that put an end to the contract altogether. *And so far the Roman and present French Law are alike—that if the parties are at the time of the conception, or of the birth, under a disability to fulfil the contract, as, for instance, if either of them be married at the time of conception, although free to contract a marriage at the time of the birth, that child cannot afterwards be legitimated.* And so in the case of a person in priest's orders, &c. There is another point not unimportant. It has been decided, and Merlin gives the case in wich it has been so held, that although one party, for instance, the woman, were entirely ignorant of any impediment, *e. g.* of an existing matrimonial engagement on the part of the man, yet that that makes no difference, and the child can never be legitimated. Except for that decision it might have been doubtful whether the French code intended to rest on the want of contract at the time of conception, or on the deeper immorality of the act as preventing the subsequent legitimation of the offspring of adulterous intercourse ; which latter course has been assigned by many older authorities.   But this decision shews that the French doctrine as to these cases rests wholly on contract.   There is still one other point as to the French Law which it is material to notice, viz., that it has been determined, that although the party may, at the time of his subsequent marriage, recognize the child as his own offspring, still, if it can be shewn that the child was not his own offspring, or if the matter rest even in doubt, there can be no legitimation.   In the "Répertoire" (*Merlin*, tom. xvii. p. 37, art. "Légitimation," sect. ii. s. 2) there is a case where Antoine Salnove, marrying Maria Laurent, wished to legitimate the offspring ; but the only evidence of paternity was his own declaration, "Qu'il y avait en bonne part," and no legitimation took place.   As to the law of England in the case of children born out of matrimony, there can be no doubt.   In *Birthwhistle* v. *Vardill (ubi sup.*), Lord Brougham, who was most in favour of the legitimacy, admitted that since the Statute of Merton, when it was enacted that instead of sending to the ordinary open writs of inquiry, viz., " whether such an one were the 'legitimate child,' writs were substituted desiring him to inquire ' whether such an one were born in wedlock,'" (from an apprehension that the canon law predilections of the prelates might lead them to put their own meaning on the earlier form of writ,) it is a rule of our law, that a child born out of wedlock can be the child of no person with English Domicil except its mother.   It is impossible for any Englishman to acquire any relation or connection with it, except for certain purposes of the criminal law ; and nothing done at any subsequent period by the father can improve the condition of that child.   The case of an Englishman domiciled in a foreign country, and having intercourse with a woman. a native of that country, is to a certain degree new.   In *Sheddon* v. *Patricke (ubi sup.*) no such point arose.   There it is quite clear (in the first case of *Sheddon* v. *Patricke, ubi sup.*) that the domicil of the man was assumed to be American, from some passages in Lord Redesdale's judgment.   But in the second case of *Sheddon* v. *Patricke,* (*ubi sup.*), the Court, for the purpose of trying whether there had been any fraud in suppressing the fact that the father was a domiciled Scotchman at the time of the conception, though living in America, assumed that fact, *i.e.*, assumed that he was a domiciled Scotchman ; and then it was held, in the result, that the child could only make out a title to hold lands in England by claiming the benefit of the statute, which declares all persons to be natural-born subjects who are children of fathers born within the allegiance of this Crown.   The question which the House of Lords had there to determine, therefore, was,

what was the paternity of the child?   Could he say that he was
born of a British father?   And they held that he could not; Lord
Redesdale saying, in language quoted by Lord St. Leonards, "The law
of America touched him at his birth, and he was and remains a base-
born American subject." Lord Brougham says that you must indeed
follow the law of domicil, but that a subsequent marriage between the
parents of a bastard did not effect legitimation *ab initio*—that it did
not fix the father with the relation of paternity *ab initio*. He thought,
therefore, that the legitimation did not take place until the date of the
subsequent marriage, and that the law of America having once claimed
the child as born in that allegiance, nothing subsequently done by the
parents could affect that allegiance, which would be affected if their
marriage could affect the paternity of the child; and that he was from
the beginning an alien.   This question does not necessarily involve the
question of indelibility of bastardy.   It may well be held that the
comity which one nation generally extends to the decisions of another
does not extend to this question of lineage.   That is a question which
each nation may well decide for itself; and that question scarcely came
at all under consideration in *Sheddon* v. *Patricke*.   It was a good deal
discussed in *Munro* v. *Munro;* and there are some very important observations of Lord Cottenham addressed to that in 7 *Cl. and Fin.* 872.
Lord Cottenham clearly holds that, in dealing with the case of a domiciled Scotchman, he carries the law of his domicil always about with
him as to personal contracts, and that the accident of the place of the
child's birth is of no consequence.*   The present is the converse case,
viz., that of the child of a domiciled Englishman living in France.
Nothing can be founded upon the fact of the mother being French.   If
that could be so, then it would be an important circumstance in considering the case of a natural child born in this country of a French
mother; which clearly it would not.   Then we have Lord Cottenham's
declaration, that the domicil of the man, and the consequences of that
domicil, are not to be affected by the law of the country in which the
child may happen to be born.   A doubt seems often to have been entertained whether the place of the birth of the child ought not to be taken
to determine the domicil ad hoc of the parents.   That may be traced in
the question of the Lord President in *Munro* v. *Munro*, in his judgment
in the inferior court.   "I cannot see," he says, "what the domicil has
to do with it.   The child was born in England; whether the father
were Turk or Scotchman is immaterial."   That, however, proved to be

---

* The law of the country where the marriage is celebrated ascertained its validity;
the law of the country of domicil regulated its civil consequences.   But if the place
of the marriage be not material, still less can the place of the birth be so considered.

an erroneous view. The question was tried in France so long ago as 1672, in the case of *Conty (ubi sup.*). In *Munro* v. *Munro*, Lord Cottenham dealt with the case entirely on the ground of the domicil of the parents; and the same principle seems to have been in the mind of Lord Redesdale in *Sheddon* v. *Patricke*. (And see, also, Lord Redesdale's observations in *The Strathmore Peerage Case*, 4 Wils. and Sh. App. 94.) *Merlin*, in another able work, "Questions de Droit," (vol. ix. p. 171, art. "Légitimation," s. 1,) notices the conflict between the French and English law on this point. It has caused me some doubt to find this sort of distinction made, viz., that there is a difference when the child is born in a country where bastardy is indelible, and when he is born in a country where it is not so. But since I have come to the conclusion that it is the law of the domicil of the parent alone, and not the law of the country of the child's birth, which is to govern, I have felt that this doubt may be disregarded. The law of domicil in such a case as this, fastening upon the child at the time of birth, shews very strongly that this must be so. For the child is driven to this difficulty —as a domiciled French citizen it claims to be legitimate, and points for its father, to whom? To a domiciled Englishman. But in that case the child is obliged to concede, that, following the domicil of its father, it had from its birth an English domicil, and, being born before marriage, is an illegitimate English-born child, and as such incapable of ever establishing here any connection with its putative father. And even according to the French rule, that where there is any obstacle preventing the contract supposed by the French doctrine the child cannot afterwards be legitimated, there is something to be urged. For here an Englishman is in this predicament—he cannot enter into such a contract legally, according to the law of his domicil. His language, upon its being suggested to him to enter into such a contract, must be that he cannot do it; that no act of his (except a previous legal marriage) can make the child his; that it must be and for ever remain the child of nobody. And it would be immaterial that the woman was ignorant of the English law in this respect, on the same principle as that case which I have already cited from Merlin. So, also, that other case, cited by Merlin, to shew that the French Courts will not permit legitimation where the paternity is doubtful, is of the same tendency, and shews that the doctrine of legitimation of children born out of wedlock cannot be applied in our English courts, where the paternity is not only doubtful in some cases, but absolutely null in all. There are, however, other circumstances and arguments in this case which would lead me with equal clearness to the same conclusion, that the law which in France permits the legitimation of base-born children has no application in these courts, in this particular case at all events. It is clear to me that the code requires that the child should be recognized by both the parents, either at the time of marriage or before, if it was not done in the act of birth, in order to complete legitimation. The recognition by one parent alone will not do. Now, it is said that there was here the recognition ; but because the act of birth was clearly by the father alone, reliance is placed upon what took place at the marriage in 1846, where such a statement was "paraphé," *i. e.*, marked with the initials of both parents. Now, it is clear from *Merlin* (Répertoire, vol. xvii. p. 37), that the recognition in the act of birth ought to be by both parents. "It is unanimously agreed," he says, "that a new recognition is not required before the marriage, if the father and mother have both appeared at the act of birth." Then the next event is the marriage in 1841 at the English embassy. It is argued that that was a nullity, all the parties having a French domicil at that time. Even if that were so, the act of 6 Geo. IV. (*ante*) is quite express, and gives a sanction to all British subjects so marrying, whether domiciled or not. I must hold that to be a good marriage. There may be difficulties in cases where the English law lays a positive bar to a union not forbidden by the law of the country in which both the parties are domiciled— *e. g.*, where a man marries his deceased wife's sister in any foreign country. I apprehend that in this case, although the many interpositions required by the French law were not observed, I am obliged to hold this to be the real marriage, and consequently the ceremony of 1846, as far as the marriage was concerned at all events, to be a nullity, and at this, the real marriage in 1841, there was no recognition. M. Crémieux, in his opinion, which has been taken in this case, has assumed the domicil throughout to be English. M. Du Tilleul's argument to the same seems founded on the erroneous assumption that no French domicil can be acquired without letters of permission from the government. The inconvenience which would result from my coming to any other conclusion than that to which I have come would be extreme. In a case like the present, a grandfather disposing of his property in favour of his son for life, with remainder to his son's legitimate children who should survive him, might be quite aware that the son's family was in this condition, viz., that he had two legitimate children, was a widower, and cohabiting with a woman by whom he had several natural children. Could it be reasonably intended or contemplated by the grandfather that the son might, at any time after his decease, go and domicil himself in France, marry his mistress, and thus bring in all his natural children to share with the two born in wedlock ? It may be said that that is already the law in France and in Scotland. But the question is, whether it is fair to apply such a doctrine in construing the will of an Englishman. A testator might justly complain if our law, which does not permit such a thing to be done directly, were to allow it to be brought about by a sidewind, by the father going abroad. I ask the question which Lord Cottenham asked in *Munro* v. *Munro (ubi sup.)*, can the question of the legitimacy of the child of an Englishman be affected by the place where the child is born? Answering this question in the negative, I think it unnecessary to require any further evidence as to the subsequent domicil of William Wright, since, even if that were French, I should be against the legitimation of Mrs. Williams. I have looked into the case of *Ashford* v. *Tustin* (Sir J. Parker, V. C., July 28, 1852, only reported in Lovell's Monthly Digest, 1852, p. 389,) the papers in which were handed to me. That was merely the old case of *Munro* v. *Munro*. An Englishwoman domiciled in France formed an illicit connection with a Frenchman, who afterwards married her. In such a case the French law was held to apply, which declares that she was his wife from the first connection, and the legitimated child born before wedlock was held to be entitled along with the children born in wedlock. But that was not the case of an Englishwoman at all. . . . ."

CHAPTER XXV.

GUARDIANSHIP.

DXLIII. Guardianship is the next Relation of Family which requires consideration (b).

This subject admits of two principal divisions :—

First, as to the choice or constitution of the Guardian.

Secondly, as to his power when chosen or constituted.

The last head is again divisible into considerations respecing—1, the person ; 2, the property of the Ward.

The Ward may be either a minor (c), or a lunatic (d), or a person placed under the control of a Guardian on account of his excesses—a category not recognized by the Law of England.

DXLIV. And, first, with respect to the choice and constitution of the Guardian.

Upon the general question, Vattel says that " It belongs to

(b) *Savigny*, VIII. s. 380, s. 396, iii.

Rocco, pp. 52—59, 241—245, &c.

Fœlix, l. ii. t. i. c. ii. iv. *des Quasi-contrats.*

Pütter, s. 62, III. *Von den Fremden Vormundschaft.*

Wächter, s, 23.

Schœffner, s. 41.

Story, ch. xiii. s. 492—506.

As to questions of *Domicil* between Guardian and Ward, *vide ante*, ch. ix.

See, also, *De Martens, Droit des Gens*, l. iii. ch. ii. s. 98.

(c) *Fœlix*, ss. 88, 456.

" Ainsi en France " (he says) " la nomination des tuteurs d'un mineur est rangée dans la categorie des actes de jurisdictions volontaire."

(d) *Vide post*, distinction between contentious and voluntary jurisdiction.

"the domestic judge to nominate tutors and guardians for "minors and idiots. The law of nations, which regards the "common advantage and the harmony of States, requires "therefore that such nomination of a tutor or guardian be "valid and recognized in all States in which the ward may "have business to transact" (*où le pupille peut avoir des affaires*).

The reason and the law of most modern States are stated with great perspicuity by Vinnius :—"Tutela ex eorum nu- "mero est" (he says) "quæ *in genere* et quasi in *abstracto* "sunt *juris gentium*, et in *concreto juris civilis.* Nam ut "ineuntis ætatis inscitia atque imbecillitas alterius provec- "tioris prudentiâ atque arbitrio constituatur ac gubernetur, "juri naturali conveniens est, quod et apud omnes gentes "procul observatur. At forma regendi, qualitas personæ "tutoris, ejusque constituendi modus, potestatis, quam habet, "circumscriptio, hæc omnia sunt juris civilis, prout quæque "civitas ordinaverit (*e*)."

DXLV. The reason of the thing seems to point out that guardianship, in its origin, was an institution of natural law : "Impuberes autem in tutelâ esse naturali jure conveniens est : "ut is qui perfectæ ætatis non sit alterius tutelâ regatur (*f*) ;" the institution rises indeed on account of its intrinsic import- ance to the dignity of a public concern (*munus publicum*), but its root is in the natural relation of family.

The Guardian is put over the person and property of the Ward ; he ought to be a person chosen by the family, and out of the family, as having a natural interest in the protection of both. Such was the doctrine of the Statesmen of France, as appears in the discussions which preceded the introduction of the law upon this matter into the Code Napoleon. They bor- rowed in this, as in other respects, their wisdom from Domat, who considered guardianship as belonging to the class of obligations

---

(*e*) *Comment. Instit. Tit. de Atilian. tut* cited *Rocco*, p. 54.
(*f*) *Instit.* l. i, t. xx—xxvi.

contracted without positive convention, imposed, like that of parental duty, by the eternal laws of nature and the interests of all civilized society, which do not suffer the abandonment of orphans; and he laid down that it was according to natural feeling that the Guardian, both for person and property, should be chosen out of the connections of the Ward.

DXLVI. This subject has, in fact, been considered by all nations, unless we except the earliest periods of ancient Rome, as appertaining in a greater or less degree to considerations of Public Policy, as well as to those which concern Private Rights.

Throughout Germany it has obtained almost exclusively the former character. The State interferes to exercise, by the appointment of a Guardian, that care over the helpless and imbecile, which is one of the primary objects of its institution; nor is this public character of Guardianship affected by the circumstance that some of the consequences of this public trust fall under the category of Private Rights (g).

DXLVII. The jurisprudence of the Kingdom of the Two Sicilies upon the reception of the Law of Foreign Guardianship is, as on other matters of Comity, enlightened and just.

This jurisprudence ranks Guardianship among the *munera publica*, indeed, but those *quæ respiciunt rem privatam*, and, therefore, though it excludes foreigners from the discharge of offices affecting the Government of the State (*rem publicam*) it admits them to the discharge of the office of the Guardianship with some just limitations. Foreigners are, as a general rule, recognized as Guardians over the persons both of

---

(g) The subject is very fully treated in the *Institutes*.

Lib. i. t. 13, *de tutelis.*

,, t. 14, *qui testamento tutores dari possunt.*

,, t. 15, *de legitimâ agnatorum tutelâ.*

,, t. 17, *de legitimâ patronorum tutelâ.*

,, t. 19, *de fiduciariâ tutelâ.*

,, t. 20, *de Atiliano tutore.*

,, t. 21, t. 22, t. 23, *de curatoribus,* t. 24, 25, 26.

foreigners and of native subjects; but in cases where the interests of native subjects are concerned those foreigners only who have by some public act of the State been admitted to a domicil in the State, and not those who are merely residents (*semplicemente residenti*) (*h*).

DXLVIII. Whatever may be the differences in the Positive Laws of different States with respect to the mode of constituting a Guardian, the rule of International Comity imperatively demands that a Guardian duly constituted according to the Law of the Domicil of the Ward should be recognized as such by all other countries.

In the case of the minor that domicil is usually identical with that of the deceased father. The case of the lunatic will be presently considered.

Secondly, with respect to the power of the Guardian over the *person* of the Ward.

The jurisprudence of England upon almost every branch of subject of Foreign Guardianship has been sometimes unsatisfactory and at variance with the principles of International Comity (*i*). Still more so is the jurisprudence of the United States of North America. In them the rights and powers of Guardians are considered as bounded by the locality in which they are constituted, and as not extending in any degree to their Wards in other States; upon the same reasoning and principle, it is said, as those which circumscribe the Power and Right of the Foreign Executor or Administrator. This, to be sure, seems barbarous enough (*k*).

(*h*) *Rocco*, 59.

(*i*) *Johnstone* v. *Beattie*, 10 *Clk. and Finnelly*, leading case, in which an unsuccessful attempt was made to establish the authority of a foreign Guardian over a Ward; but in this case Lords Brougham and Campbell were opposed to Lords Lyndhurst, Cottenham, and Langdale.

Lord Hardwicke had been inclined to a more liberal view, *Ex parte Otto Lewis*, *Vesey Sen.* 298; but see *Syloa* v. *Da Costa*, 8 *Vesey*, 316.

(*k*) *Story*, *ib.* citing *Morrill* v. *Dickey*, 1 *Johns.* (*Americ.*) *Ch. Rep.* 153; *Kraft* v. *Vickery*, 4 *Gill and Johns.* (*Americ.*) *Rep.* 332.

DXLIX. The House of Lords in England have holden, though scarcely, however, it would seem, in harmony with other decisions on the subject, and overruling the decisions of the Scotch Courts, that the authority of an English Guardian sufficed for the institution of a suit respecting the personal property of his ward in Scotland (*l*).

DL. According to Lord Kames (*m*) the Scotch Law holds that the appoinment of a guardian or curator in England is recognized as effectual in Scotland : not, however, meaning to extend their doctrine to immoveable property of the Ward (*l*).

The doctrine of this case has not been sanctioned by the United States of North America.

DLI. According to the Law of England, there are certain general principles (*n*) applicable to—

(1). Guardianship by Nature ;

(2). Guardianship by Socage ; and,

(3). Guardianship by Nurture ; the first and last of which are often confounded, and used in a loose and indeterminate sense.

At the Common Law,

1. *Guardianship by Nature* is of the heir apparent only (and not of all the children), and belongs to the father and mother and other ancestor standing in that predicament to the infant. It lasts until twenty-one years of age, and extends no further than the custody of the infant's person.

2. *Guardianship by Socage* arises wholly out of tenure,

(*l*) *Story*, s. 499, collects the authorities of civilians, and of most English and Scotch cases.

Morrison's Case, 4 *Durnford and East, Rep.* 140 ; 1 *Henry's Blackstone*, 667—82.

Westlake, s. 402.

(*m*) *Equity*, b. iii. c. viii. s. 1, p. 325.

Ib. s. 4, p. 348, cited by *Story*, s. 503.

(*n*) See *Mr. Hargrave's* learned note, 66, ss. 12 and 13 to *Co. Litt.* 88, 6.

and exists only when the infant is seised of lands or other hereditaments lying in tenure and in socage. It extends to the person and all the estates (including the socage estates) of the infant, and lasts until the infant arrives at the age of fourteen. It belongs to such of the infant's next of blood as cannot have by descent the socage estate, (o) in respect to which the guardianship arises by descent, without any distinction between the whole blood and the half blood.

3. *Guardianship by Nurture* occurs only when the infant is without any other guardian, and none can have it except the father or mother. It lasts until the age of fourteen years, and extends only over the person. (*p*)

DLII. The Guardian by nurture is entitled to the custody of the child; and a writ of *habeas corpus* is the proper proceeding on the part of such guardian, to recover the custody of the child improperly detained from him.

The Common Law for this purpose recognizes no distinction as regards the discretion of the children between the ages of seven and it should seem *sixteen.*(*pp*) This Court, therefore, will not, where a child between those ages has been brought up under a writ of *habeas corpus*, obtained by the mother, a widow, who was the Guardian for nurture, examine the child in order to ascertain whether there is mental capacity sufficient to exercise a choice, and, if so, the wishes of the child; but will at once restore the child to the custody of the guardian, unless it appears that the guardian, either by past immoral conduct or a want of *bona fides* in making the application, or by having some illegal intention or purpose in view, has forfeited her right to the custody of the child.

(o) The jealousy of the feudal law disqualifying on the ground that the Civil Law qualifies for guardianship, viz., the guardian's contingent interest in the estate.

(*p*) 1 *Blackst. Com.* 461, 462; 2 *Fonbl. Eq.* b. 2, pt. 2, ch. ii. s. 2, n(*h*).

(*pp*) See *The Queen* v. *Howse*; *The Queen* v. *Hopkins*; decision of Lord C. J. Cockburn, after consultation with all the other judges, *Queen's Bench, Nov.* 20, 1860; *fourteen* appears to have been the age formerly fixed upon; see next page, *Case of A. Race.*

In the leading and recent cases of *Alicia Race* (q) and *The Queen* v. *Howse*, (qq) these doctrines were very solemnly laid down by the Queen's Bench ; it was holden in the former case that the intention of the mother, herself a Roman Catholic, to remove the child from a Protestant establishment, to a Roman Catholic seminary, is not enough to affect her right to the custody of the child as Guardian for nurture, though the father of the child lived and died in the Protestant faith, and had brought up his children in the same faith ; there being no directions of the father, by will, that the children should continue to be educated as Protestants.

The jurisdiction of the Court of Chancery, however, extends to the care of the person of the minor until he attains the age of twenty-one, so far as is necessary for his protection and education ; and to the care of his property, for its due management and preservation, and proper application for his maintenance.   It is upon the former ground principally, that is to say, for the due protection and education of the infant, that the Court interferes with the ordinary rights of parents, as guardians by nature, or by nurture, in regard to the custody and care of their children. (r)(s)

DLIII. Thirdly, with respect to the power of the Guardian over the property of the Ward.

And here it is first to be observed that not only English lawyers, but all jurists, make a great distinction between the Guardian's power over *moveable* and over *immoveable* property in a foreign land.

With respect to *moveable* property continental jurists are, for the most part, of opinion that inasmuch as by intendment of law it is holden to be in the domicil of the owner, therefore the law of the domicil of the Guardian, the legal representative of the owner, must govern *in every country* the rights and

---

(q) *Ex parte Alicia Race, Law Journal*, vol. xxvi. N. S. (Queen's Bench, 1857), p. 169.   (qq) See note to last page.

(r) *Story on Eq. Jurisprudence*, ch. xxxiv. s. 1341, p. 527.

(s) The Divorce Court has followed the decisions at Common Law.

powers of the Guardian over the moveable property of the Ward (s).

This is certainly the true language of international justice ; but it does not, at first sight, appear to be the language of the tribunals of England and the United States. They require that a fresh authority to act as Guardian be conferred by their own tribunal (*forum gestæ administrationis*) : " There " are few decisions" (observes Story) " upon the subject, pro- " bably because the principle has always been taken to be " unquestionable (!), founded upon the close analogy of Foreign " Executors and Administrators (t)."

It is to be observed, however, that though these countries differ from the rest of the civilized world (u) in holding a new authority to be requisite in the case of a foreigner in respect to moveable as well as immoveable property, there is no reason to suppose that such an authority would be denied to the person already clothed with the authority of Guardian in his own country—the analogy, as will be seen, of the Foreign Executor or Administrator leads to the opposite con- clusion. The practice is justified by the allegation, that Comity may, in both instances, require you to clothe the foreign officer with the power necessary for the execution of his office in the foreign country, but that in both instances the State has a right to take care that its own subjects are not debarred from an opportunity of vindicating their claims upon the *property* in the country wherein it, moveable or immoveable, is situate (x).

(s) As to the authority of Guardians to recover property of the infant out of the jurisdiction, see *Scott* v. *Bentley,* 1 *Kay and John-son's Rep.* 281.

(t) *Ib.* s. 504a.

(u) " Vorzüglich schwankend ist die Praxis in den Ländern des Eng- lischen Rechts, indem in diesen theilweise besondere Vormundschaften bestellt werden nicht bloss über das unbewegliche, sondern aud über das bewegliche auswärts liegende Vermögen."—*Savigny, ib.* s. 380.

(x) It is clear, from the following extract, that *D'Aguesseau* classed

In a recent English case (*y*), it appeared that A. B., the infant daughter of a British subject, who had emigrated to and had procured letters of naturalization in America, and *who had married an American lady,* whose real estate A. B. inherited, after an injunction had been granted by the Supreme Court of New York, to restrain the removal of the infant from that jurisdiction, and after the appointment by the Surrogate of New York of a maternal aunt as guardian, had been clandestinely removed from her residence and brought to England by paternal relatives, the English Court, on petition by

---

Guardianship among *Real Statutes,* and probably authorizes the doctrine of my text :—

" Ce que caractérise véritablement un statut réel, et ce que le distingue essentiellement du statut personnel, n'est pas qu'il soit rélatif à certaines qualités personnelles, ou à certaines circonstances personnelles, ou à certaines événemens personnels, outrement il faudroit dire que tous les statuts qui concernent *la puissance paternelle, le droit de garde, le droit de viduité, la prohibition aux conjoints* de s'avantager l'un et l'autre, sont autant de statuts personnels, et *cependant il n'est pas douteux dans notre jurisprudence, qu'on les considère tous, comme des statuts réels, dont l'exécution se règle non par la loi du lieu du domicile, mais par celle du lieu où les biens sont situés.* Le veritable principe dans cette matière, est qu'il faut distinguer si le statut a directement les biens pour objet, ou leur affectation à certaines personnes, et leur conservation dans les familles, ensorte que ce ne soit pas l'interêt de la personne dont on examine les droits ou les dispositions, mais l'intérêt d'un autre dont il s'agit d'assurer la propriété ou les droits réels, qui ait donné lieu de faire la loi ; ou si au contraire toute l'attention de le loi s'est portée vers la personne, pour décider en general de son habilité au de sa capacité générale et absolue, comme lorsqu'il s'agit des qualités de majeur, ou de mineur, de père, ou de fils légitime ou illégitime, d'habile ou inhabile à contracter pour des causes personnelles. Dans le premier cas le statut est réel ; dans le second, il est personnel ; c'est ce qui est assez bien expliqué dans ces mots de D'Argentré ' Cum statutum non simpliciter inhabilitat, sed ratione fundi aut juris realis alterum respicientis extra personas contrahentes, toties hanc inhabilitationem non egredi locum Statuti.' "—*D'Aguesseau,* tom. iv. cited by *Rocco,* 26.

(*y*) *Dawson* v. *Jay* (1854), *Jurist, N. S.* 39 ; *S. C.* 2 *Smale and Grainger's Rep.* 199.

the maternal aunt claiming the custody of the infant, and on cross petition by the paternal relatives praying the appointment of other guardians, appointed the maternal aunt and two paternal relatives guardians.

The order of the Surrogate of New York, it was said, appointing a guardian, will be recognized, and treated with the respect due, by the Comity of nations, to the order of the foreign Court; but it does not confer on the appointee the office of guardian in this country.

DLIV. Fourthly, as to the power of Guardians over immoveable property.

Upon this point the English Law is in accordance with the greatly preponderating opinion of foreign jurists (z), in holding that the *lex rei sitæ* is to govern, and that the guardian must obtain the sanction of the local authority to intermeddle with or in any way administer or deal with the *immoveable* property of the Ward.

Savigny (a) throws the weight of his great authority into the opposite scale. He denies that either with regard to principle or the general practice (meaning, it is presumed, of the German States), that the *lex rei sitæ* ought to govern the power of the Guardian. He maintains that the law is not a *Real* but a *Personal Statute;* that the whole Guardianship is one authority governed by one Law, that of the Domicil, and not parcelled out into as many laws as there are countries in which the property of the Ward may be situate.

DLV. The Prussian Law is in accordance with the opinion of this distinguished jurist. It is, indeed, admitted by Savigny that a great practical difficulty arises when the real property of the Ward is scattered over different territories; the solution which he proposes and which appears to have been adopted in Prussia, is that in these places ancillary or subordinate Curators or Guardians should be appointed under the

---

(z) Collected by *Story*.
(a) VIII. s. 380, numer. 2.

general superintendence of the one Guardian constituted according to the Law of the Paternal Domicil.

Such an arrangement is not altogether inconsistent with the principles of the Roman jurisprudence upon the same subject, which, when the property of the Ward was scattered and the Guardian was to be nominated, not by testament or by the written law, but by the living authority, appointed one for the *res Italicœ* and another for the *res Provinciales.*

DLVI. Prussia has entered into treaties with her immediate neighbours upon this subject to the effect that, generally speaking, the Law of the Domicil of the Ward shall govern the appointment of the Guardian ; but that it shall be competent to the foreign authority to elect between appointing a separate or an ancillary Guardian for the real property of the ward *subject* to their jurisdiction.

DLVII. This system of appointing ancillary or subsidiary Guardians is, after all, very germane to the English practice respecting Foreign Administrations of *personal* property ; and if the English Courts, as has been already suggested, follow the same rule respecting Foreign Guardians, the violation of Comity would be more in theory than in practice.

DLVIII. A case upon the conflict of the powers and rights of Guardians, decided by the Supreme Court of Berlin, is fit to be inserted in this place :

A Ward of good family lived in Bavaria, under guardianship. He possessed property in a part of Rhenish Prussia, to which no ancillary Guardian had been appointed. The Bavarian Guardian bought some property of his Ward in the ordinary way of purchase and not under the peculiar limitations and restrictions required by the French Code (*b*), which is the Law of Rhenish Prussia. The Ward having attained his majority, reclaimed the property, on the ground that the

---

(*b*) *Savigny, Dig.* l. 26, t. 7, 39.
   Ib. l. 26, t. 5, 27.
   Code Civil, art. 457—460.

sale was illegal. The claim seems to have been rejected on two grounds:

1. That these limitations and restrictions were parts of one indivisible system of laws respecting guardianship; and it was clear that other parts of this system were *ex necessitate rei* inapplicable to the Bavarian Ward.

2. That under any view of the law these restrictions and limitations were, as a matter of fact, only applicable to parts of that property which was without the Bavarian dominions. (c)

DLIX. With respect to the *obligation* to undertake the office of Guardian, and the ligitimate *excuses* for declining it, these must depend upon the Law of the Domicil of the Ward; they are unknown to the English Law. So must the amount of the guarantee or security required by the State for the due execution of the office, *e. g.*, whether that security shall be given upon property *dehors* the jurisdiction which imposes it. (d)

DLX. The question relating to the Guardian's power of changing the Domicil of his Ward has been already discussed. (e)

DLXI. There seems to be no reason why a different rule of practice should govern the case of the Guardian, or Committee, according to the phraseology of English Law, of the *Lunatic*.

The case of a conflict of laws upon this subject, even from its nature, but rarely occurs. Such a one did, however, take place not long ago in Paris. Mr. Dyce Sombre, who had been placed under the care of Guardians or keepers by the Lord Chancellor of England, to whom the constitution of that country confides the care of lunatics, escaped to Paris, and,

---

(c) *Savigny, ib. Bassenheim* v. *Raffauf,* 1847 (*urtheil des Cassation shofes zu Berlin*).

(d) *Rocco,* 241-2-3.
Savigny, ib. s. 380—3.

(e) *Vide ante,* chap. ix. p. 73.

declaring himself to be sane, invoked the aid of the authorities there. He was claimed by the agent of the Committee appointed by the English Lord Chancellor ; but the French authorities refused to give him up ; tried the case over again at Paris, causing him to be inspected by French physicians, and, on their verdict of his sanity, allowed him to live in France without restraint. The English Court, of course, retained possession of his property. It is certainly difficult to defend this proceeding at Paris upon the principles of International Comity.

DLXII. In some countries in accordance with the provisions of Roman Jurisprudence, a Guardian is assigned to the Prodigal; the appointment of such a Guardian ought to be respected in other countries, though such an appointment might not be holden to affect the capacity of the Prodigal Ward to deal with *immoveable* property situate in a country to whose jurisprudence such a guardianship was unknown.

The French Courts refused, in 1836, to give effect in France to the decrees (*f*) of the native tribunal which had placed the estates of the Duke of Brunswick under a curatorship, upon the double ground that, as far as the *law* was concerned, the sentence was not supported by the proofs of *private* prodigality required by French Law, and could not be applied to French property ; and as far as *public* and *political* considerations

---

(*f*) Cf. *Titre* xi. c. ii. 489—92, of the French Code. The title is " *De l'interdiction*," which Rogron explains thus : " L'Interdiction est l'état d'un individu déclaré incapable des actes de la vie civile, et privé par suite, de l'administration de sa personne et de ses biens."—*Rogron, Code Napoléon expliqué*, i. pp. 375, 489 : " Le majeur qui est dans *un état habituel d'imbecillité de demence* ou *de fureur*, doit être interdit même lorsque cet état presente des *intervalles lucides*." It appears that *le majeur* includes *le mineur—Rogron*, i. p. 376; *Sirey*, 30, ii. 218, 492 : "Toute demande en interdiction sera portée devant *le tribunal* de première instance." *Le tribunal* Rogron explains as that " du domicile de la personne dont on provoque l'interdiction," i. 378.

were concerned, they were inapplicable to property without the jurisdiction of the native Court (g).

DLXIII. The principle and practice of the English Law receive illustration from the judgment delivered in the matter of *John Houston.*

This was a case of a petition for a commission in the nature of a writ *de lunatico inquirendo,* by an illegitimate sister of the supposed lunatic and her husband.

The insanity of the individual was not denied; but it was stated as an answer to the application, that a commission of lunacy had issued, and was now in force against him in *Jamaica,* where his property was situated, and where till lately he had resided; that three persons had been appointed his Committees in that island; that he had been brought over to this country for the sake of his health; that Clarke, one of his Committees, had accompanied him, in order to take care of his welfare and comfort; that, under these circumstances, a commission in England was not necessary for the protection of the lunatic and his property, and, therefore, ought not to be granted.

The Lord Chancellor :—" The Commission now existing in " Jamaica is no reason why a Commission should not issue " here. On the contrary, it is evidence of the absolute neces- " sity that there should be somebody authorized to deal with " the person and estate of this lunatic. While the lunatic is

---

(g) *Pütter,* s. 63.

Fœlix, Memoire relatif aux débats élevés devant les tribunaux au sujet de l'interdiction de S. A. le Duc Charles de Brunswick, 1838.

Fœlix, Droit Int. Pr. ss. 33, 89.

In the last paragraph he says, " l'individu *interdit* dans son pays, et par la rendu incapable l'est aussi en pays étranger," citing

Boullenois, tit. i. c. ii. obs. 4, pp. 51, 59, 174.

Denisart, v. " prescription."

Rocco, p. 436, and other authorities.

" here, no Court will have any authority over him or his pro-
" perty, unless a Commission is taken out (*h*)."

DLXIV. Here we close the consideration of the effect of
Foreign Law upon the Rights and Duties incident to the
Relations of *Family.* (*i*)

(*h*) *In the Matter of Houston,* 1 *Russell's Reports,* 312.
(*i*) *Vide ante,* pp. 22, 23.

CHAPTER XXVI.

RIGHTS RELATING TO PROPERTY.

DLXV. It was stated in the early part of this volume (*a*) that the Third Division of it would be occupied with the Legal Relations arising from Property; and that under this head would be included—

1. Rights to specific things:

a. Immoveables.

β. Moveables.

2. Rights to compel certain persons to do certain things, or Obligations of which Contracts are a branch.

3. Rights relating to Succession, whether *Testamento* or *ab Intestato*.

DLXVI. It is the Rights to Specific Things, both Immoveable and Moveable, that we are now about to consider.

In other words, the jurisprudence of Private International Law relating to the *acquisition* and *alienation* of property by foreigners now presents itself for our consideration.

So much, however, of the doctrine of that branch of jurisprudence depends upon or is affected by the distinction between *Moveable* and *Immoveable Property* (*b*), that on that account alone a clear understanding of the meaning of these terms is indispensable to the jurist. But with respect to the English jurist, there is another very important reason, viz. :—

1. That the terms *mobilia* and *immobilia* appear to have been generally considered by English lawyers as identical with

---

(*a*) P. 23.

(*b*) *Vide post* as to Bankruptcy.

" *realty* " and " *personalty*," in the English Law ; for instance, the maxim most frequently cited in cases of testamentary Domicil, is " mobilia sequuntur personam ;" this maxim is borrowed from foreign jurisprudence, but conveys a very different idea to the continental jurist and the English lawyer. If the term *mobilia* be identical with *personalty*, and as such it appears to have been always used, the notion that a leasehold property of a thousand years would be a part of the moveables which followed the person never presented itself to the mind of a foreign jurist ; but such is the necessary inference from the decisions in the English Courts.

An English subject dying *de facto* domiciled in France and leaving only a will executed in the English form would, according to the recent decision of the Privy Council, die intestate, and it would, therefore, follow that his leasehold property in England—in fact, all his interests in English land not amounting to freehold would be governed by and distributable according to French Law.

At least no distinction has, as yet, been taken between, what in England are called *personal* and *real chattels*, of an Englishman domiciled abroad.

Perhaps this consequence of the Law of Domicil, as laid down by English courts of justice, was hardly foreseen. It is the result of borrowing a maxim of Foreign Law and applying it to subjects of English Law, to which the maxim did not apply in the system of jurisprudence from which it was taken. The terms *mobilia* and *persona* are applied as identical with *personalty* and *person.* But *mobilia* in Foreign Law is not identical with *personalty* in English Law, and *persona* in Foreign Law means a person clothed with certain indelible attributes, and is very different from the naked word person in English Law.

DLXVII. According to the English Law the subjects of property are divided into things real and things personal.

Personal things—with which we are alone now immediately concerned—are chattels. Chattels are subdivided into

1. Chattels Real.

2. Chattels Personal.

But both are personal property or estate.

DLXVIII. Chattels Real are those estates which are less than freehold—that is, less than an estate of inheritance or for life in lands or tenements of free tenure.   Chattels real, therefore, comprise (c)—estates for years, that is, for *any fixed* or determinate time—*e. g.*, for a thousand years.

This peculiarity of English Law arose out of two facts—namely,

1st, That, in feudal times, estates for years were very precarious, and subject to be defeated in various ways.

2ndly, That (at first) they were usually for very short periods. Chattels Reals included also

(2.) Estates at Will.

(3.) Estates by Sufferance.

DLXIX. Chattels Personal may be subdivided into (1) Corporeal, and (2) Incorporeal.

1. Corporeal are all moveable things, *e. g.*, animals, money, goods.

2. Incorporeal are *patent rights, e. g.*, exclusive rights of selling and publishing particular contrivances of art; *Copyright,* the exclusive right of publishing and selling particular works of literature—a chattel which has become of late years a great favorite of International Law.

Among incorporeal chattels are to be reckoned also chattels which are not in *possession,* but in *action ;* that is, where a man has not the enjoyment, actual or constructive, of a thing, but a right to recover it by a suit at law, which the English Law calls a *chose in action, e. g.*, debts, money due on a bond, a right to damages for non-performance of an agreement—things that are *in potentiâ.* not *in esse.*

DLXX. The Roman Law more than once refers to and

(c) *Stephen's Blackstone,* vol. i. c. v. *of Estates less than Freehold.*
Vol. ii. pt. ii. *of Things Personal.*
Vol. i. p. 262, *Vaughan Williams on Executors and Administrators*—as to what were *bona notobilia* under the former testamentary law of England.

recognizes a distinction between two classes of moveables—
namely,

1. Those destined to remain constantly fixed at a certain
place, and

2. Those in their nature of unfixed character, and only
temporarily or accidentally deposited at a particular place.

In treating "De hæredibus instituendis," Ulpian (d) remarks,
" *Rerum* autem *Italicarum vel Provincialium* significatione
" quæ res accipiendæ sint ? videndum est.   Et facit quidem
" totum voluntas defuncti : nam quid senserit spectandum
" est : veruntamen hoc intelligendum erit, *rerum Italicarum*
" significatione eas contineri, *quas perpetuo quis ibi habuerit,*
" *atque ita disposuit ut perpetuo haberet.*   Ceteroquin si in
" tempore aliquid transtulit in alium locum, non ut ibi haberet,
" sed ut denuo ad pristinum locum revocaret, neque augebit
" quo transtulit neque minuet unde transtulit.   Utputa de
" Italico patrimonio quosdam servos miserat in provinciam,
" forte Galliam, ad exigendum debitum vel ad merces com-
" parandas, recursuros si comparassent : dubium non est, quin
" debeat dici ad Italicum patrimonium eos pertinere debere
"   .   .   .   Quæ res in proposito quoque suggerit ut
" Italicarum rerum esse credantur hæ res, quas in Italiâ esse
" testator voluit.

" Proinde et si pecuniam miserit in provinciam ad merces
" comparandas, et necdum comparatæ sint ; dico, precuniam,
" quæ idcirco missa est, ut pro eâ merces in Italiam adve-
" herentur, Italico patrimonio adjungendam : nam et si dedisset
" in provinciâ de pecuniis quas in Italiâ exercebat ituras et
" rendituras, dicendum est, hanc quoque Italici patrimonii esse
" rationem.   Igitur effici dixi, ut merces quoque istæ, quæ
" comparatæ sunt, ut Romam veherentur, sive provectæ sunt eo
" vivo, sive nondum, et sive scit, sive ignoravit ad eum here-
" dem pertineant, cui Italicæ res sint adascriptæ."

So, again, in treating "de actionibus emti et venditi,"
Ulpian says—

" Fundi nihil est, nisi quod terra se tenet.   Aedium autem

(d) *Dig.* 1. xxviii. t. v. s. 35, s. 3—5.

" multa esse, quæ ædibus affixa non sunt, ignorari non oportet,
" utputa seras, claves, claustra ; multa etiam defossa esse,
" neque tamen fundi aut villæ haberi utputa vasa vinaria,
" torcularia, quoniam hæc instrumenti magis sunt, estiamsi
" ædificio cohærent. Sed et vinum, et fructus perceptos villæ
" non esse constat." (e)

Scævola, in the book "de pignoribus et hypothecis," observes—

" Debitor pactus est, ut quæcunque in prædia pignori data,
" inducta, invecta, importata, ibi nata paratave essent, pignori
" essent. Eorum prædiorum pars sine colonis fuit, eaque
" actori suo colenda debitor ita tradidit, assignatis et servis
" culturæ necessariis : quæritur : an et Stichus villicus, et cæteri
" servi ad culturam missi, et Stichi vicarii obligati essent ?
" Respondi : eos duntaxat, qui hoc animo a domino inducti
" essent, *ut ibi perpetuo essent, non temporis causâ* accom-
" modarentur, obligatos." (f)

DLXXI. Scotland, in this as in other respects, resembles
both as to phraseology and in fact the law of foreign countries
more than England. Property in Scotland is divided into
heritable and *moveable ;* "things which are heritable" (Mr.
Bell says) "go by succession to the heir; are not assigned by
marriage ; they go with land to the buyer ; remain for the
landlord at the end of a lease ; they are affected by inhibition,
and carried by adjudication ; and they are regulated by the
territorial law, not by that of the owner's domicil. On the
other hand, moveables fall to the executor in succession ; are
assigned by marriage ; remain with the seller of land or of
houses ; are removeable by a tenant on leaving his farm ; are
attached by arrestment ; carried by poinding ; and in bankruptcy and succession they are regulated by the law of the
owner's domicil. The character of any corporeal subject, as
in these important respects, heritable or moveable, may be
either by its nature as being immoveable, like lands or houses ;
or as moveable, like furniture or cattle ; or by connection or

---

(e) *Dig.* xix. t. i. s. 17.
f) *Dig.* xx. t. i. s. 32.

accession to some subject which has by nature the character of immoveable or moveable ; or by destination of the owner, either as in connection with something else, or in regard to succession."(g)

DLXXII. Under the French term *biens*, as under the Latin term *bona*, all property was comprised.

Merlin thus distinguishes the different kinds of *biens :*

" *Biens.*   Nous entendons ici par ce mot tout ce qui peut " composer les richesses et la fortune de quelqu'un." (h)

" § 1. *Biens meubles.*

" Ce sont ceux qui peuvent se mouvoir ou être transportés d'un lieu à un autre, lorsqu'ils ne sont point destinés à faire perpetuellement partie d'un fonds. d'un héritage ou d'un bâtiment.   Ainsi, les meubles meublans d'un hotel, les ahimaux domestiques, l'or, l'argent, en un mot, tout ce qui peut se déplacer sans être détérioré, et sans donner essentiellement attéinte au fonds dont il dépend, est dans la classe des choses mobilières, sans considérer si l'objet est d'un grand ou d'un petit volume ; et c'est à raison de sa mobilité qu'on lui donne le nom de *meuble.*

" Mais outre la mobilité de l'objet, il faut encore considérer son inhérence plus ou moins grande avec le fonds auquel il est attaché, savoir si l'on peut l'en séparer sans alteration, et si ce n'est que pour un temps ou ci c'est pour toujours qu'il est destiné à la place qu'il occupe.   S'il parait qu'on puisse le transporter sans fracture ni détérioration, s'il ne fait point partie d'un fonds, ou s'il n'est point destiné à y demeurer perpétuellement attaché, il est purement mobilier, conformément à l'art. 90 de la coutume de Paris, qui, en cette partie, fait le droit commun du royaume ; si, au contraire, l'une de ces trois conditions lui manque, il entre dans la classe des immeubles, et en suit toutes les regles. (i)

(g) *Bell's Comm. on the Laws of Scotland* (*Shaw's edit.* 1858), vol. ii. b. 3, c. ii. pp. 709-10.

(h) *Merlin, Rep. de Jur.* vol. ii. p. 114.

(i) *Ib.* p. 115.

" *Meubles incorporels.* Les biens de cette espéce sont les
" droits qui tendent à nous procurer des objets mobiliers en
" vertu de contrats, de promesses ou d'obligations ; les actions
" auxquelles ces droits donnent lieu, sont aussi de le même
" nature, suivant la maxime, *omnis actio ad consequendum*
" *mobile, est mobilis.*" (*k*)

" § 2. *Biens immeubles.*

" Ces sortes de biens sont de deux espèces ; les uns sont
" *corporels*, comme nous l'avons dit des meubles, et les autres
" *incorporels*.

" Les immeubles corporels sont les fonds de terres, comme
" prés, vignes, étangs, bois, édifices, &c. Tout ce qui en dé-
" pend essentiellement, comme les fruits pendans par racines,
" les arbres, les clótures, est de la même qualité ; en un mot,
" tout ce qui n'est point susceptible de mobilité, et qui n'entre
" point dans la classe des choses mobilières dont nous venons
" de parler, est immeuble.

" Les immeubles incorporels sont ceux dont l'immobilité
" n'est pas sensible, et qui, par cette raison, demandent un
" certain détail." (*l*)

" Les actions qui tendent à nous procurer un immeuble, sont
" de la même qualité que cet immeuble." (*m*).

" Dans les pays contumiers en général, les rentes constituées
" à prix d'argent sont sans difficulté au rang des immeubles.
" Dans celles qui ne s'expliquent point à cet égard, on suit
" l'art. 94 de la coutume de Paris, qui les immobolise." (*n*)

" Aujourd'hui, les rentes perpétuelles et viagères sont
" reputées meubles dans toute la France." (*o*)

" Les immeubles corporels ne suivent d'autre loi que celle
" du lieu où ils sont situés." (*p*)

DLXXIII. Pressed by the manifest absurdity of applying

(*k*) *Merlin, Rep.* p. 117 ; *Code Civil*, art. 529.
(*l*) *Ib. de Jur.* p. 119.
(*m*) *Ib.* p. 119.
(*n*) *Ib.* p. 120.
(*o*) *Ib.* p. 120 ; *Code Civil*, art. 529.
(*p*) *Ib.* p. 121.

the doctrine *mobilia sequuntur personam* to the foreign possessor of English personal property, Story (*q*) endeavours to
escape from it by saying, "When, however, we speak of
" *moveables* as following the person of the owner, and as go-
" verned by the law of his domicil, we are to limit the doc-
" trine to the cases in which they may properly be said to
" retain their *original* and *natural* character ;" and again (*r*),
" not only lands and houses, but servitudes and easements, and
" other charges on lands, as mortgages and rents, and trust
" estates, are deemed to be in *the sense of law* immoveables by
" the *lex rei sitæ.*"

But of what *law* is Story here speaking, as causing chattels
real, such as rents, which are treated as *personal property* by
English Law, to be governed by the law of the *situs ?* And
what law does Story rely upon for his statement, that only
such moveables as retain their original and natural character
follow the person ? Not the Law of England or of his own
country (which in an *international* treatise he persists in
calling the *common law*), but on the law to be derived from the
reasoning of jurists, to whom he refers in a note, for no decision of an English or N. A. United States Court can be cited
in support of his opinion.

There is in fact no judicial authority for the position, that
if an English or American citizen died *intestate,* and *domiciled in a foreign country,* the law of that country would not
govern *the whole* distribution of *all* his *personal* property in
England or in the United States, including, therefore, arrears
of rents due, leases for an indefinite term of years, and other
chattels real and *natural* immoveables.

The person in possession of the Foreign Letters of Administration would obtain, as a matter of course, Administration in England to such property as part of the *personalty*
of the deceased.

(*q*) S. 382.
(*r*) S. 447.

CHAPTER XXVII.

JURA INCORPORALIA.

We have considered the nature of Moveable and Immoveable Property of *jura in re ;* there remains a class of property which jurists make a third class, *jura ad rem,* that is, *incorporeal rights,* " quæ bona neque dicuntur *mobilia* " neque *immobilia* sed *tertiam* speciem componunt et di-" cuntur *incorporalia.*" (a)

These are considered subjects of property. They are perhaps more strictly the means of obtaining property ; (b) thus, rights of action, and of succession (*jus hereditatis*) debts, which are holden by the better authorities to be attached to the person of the creditor. (c)

These incorporeal chattels form part of what is happily termed, in the Roman Law, the *universitas juris* of the successor to a deceased person, or of the assignees of a bankrupt.

Thus Donellus says, " hereditas enim res est incorporalis in " jure consistens et quamvis in hereditate contineantur res " corporales ipsum tamen jus hæreditatis incorporale est. Quæ " incorporalia " (he adds) " nusquam sunt ; " and having no place, he shows that the *lex rei sitæ,* which he generally adopts, as has been said, cannot govern in their case, but that " relinquitur omnino locus is unus in quo controversia hære-

---

(a) *Casaregis in Rubr. Stat. Gen. de Success. ab Intestat.* n. 64, 65, t. iv, pp. 52–3, cited by *Story,* s. 399, n. 1, from *Livermore's Dissertations,* p. 162, s. 251.

(b) I am not speaking of *servitutes,* or the *jus emphyteuseos,* which are of the nature of immoveable property. It is perhaps difficult correctly to classify mortgages.—*Story,* s. 523.

(c) *Story,* s. 399.

" ditatis tractanda sit, ubi scilicet qui convenitur habet domi-
" cilium." (d)

This subject is further treated of hereafter in the consideration of *obligations* and of *succession testamento et ab
intestato.*

DLXXIV. There are two classes of *incorporeal chattels*
which have obtained particular consideration in the Law of
England.

       I. *Patent Rights.*

       II. *Copyrights.*

The latter of these has, as will be seen, been clothed with an
International character.   Both are regulated by Statute Law.

DLXXV. The grant of (I.) a Patent Right (e) is an act
of royal power, not *ex debito justitiæ.*   A Patent Right is
assignable by a writing under hand and seal; it is also competent to the patentee, without an entire alienation of his
interest, to grant deeds of license to any one or more persons
to manufacture the article. (f)

No decision has been given in England upon the subject of
the foreigner's capacity to be an assignee of such a right; but
there seems no reason to doubt that he, or at least an *alien
anni* has such capacity.

DLXXVI. It is clear, however, that according to the general principles of International Law, (g) such Patent Rights

---

(d) *Comm. de J. C.* l. xvii. cf. *actiones*—si actiones interpretamur jura
persequendi dicimus actiones quæ sint res incorporales."—Lib. xix.

Cf. *Story,* ss. 322—399.

Stephen's Comment. vol. ii. c. iii.

(e) As to patent rights, see

5 & 6 Will. IV. c. 83.

2 & 3 Vict. c. 67.

7 & 8 Vict. c. 67, ss. 2, 7.

15 & 16 Vict. c. 83.

16 & 17 Vict. c. 5, c. 115.

(f) *Stephen, ubi sup.*

(g) *Fælix,* l. ii. t. ix. c. vi.

M. *Renouard, des brevets d'invention; Code internationale de la pro-*

(*brevets d'invention*) do not extend beyond the territorial limits of the sovereign who grants them, and are not recognized by foreign states.

DLXXVII. In France two questions—one directly, the other indirectly, relating to these subjects—have undergone judicial examination.

1. Is it lawful for a Frenchman to make or counterfeit the subjects of a patent granted by a Foreign State?

To this question the answer has been without hesitation in the affirmative. Such patents are considered exclusively as creatures of the municipal law of each state. " We have " not yet advanced " (says Fælix, (*h*) with evident regret) " to " the stage which would apply to them the principle of the " *comitas gentium.*"

The second question is

2. Is it lawful for a Frenchman to stamp upon *his* merchandize the stamp or mark of a *foreign* manufacturer ?

It is melancholy to record that the *Cour de Cassation* (*i*) has decided the affirmative to this question. " It is " (Fælix says) (*k*) " one more misfortune to add to those which a narrowminded " legislation and jurisprudence have already drawn down upon " France, by provoking measures of *retorsion* in Foreign " States."

There is something ludicrous in the attempt of the *Cour de Paris* (*l*) to atone, as it were, for this injustice, by deciding that a foreigner cannot be *criminally* proceeded against in France for fraudulently using the stamp of a French manu-

---

priété *industrielle artistique et littéraire,* par *M. M. Pataille et Huguet* (Paris, 1855).

(*h*) *Ubi sup.*

(*i*) See decision of 12th July, 1848, *Dev. Car.* 48, 1, 416, cited in *Demangeat's* note to *Fælix.*

(*k*) *Ubi sup.*

(*l*) 19th and 20th November, 1850, *Dev. Car.* 52, 2, 345, *Demangeat's* note to *Fælix.*

facturer in a Foreign State. M. Demangeat, moreover, thinks that he would be liable to civil damages.

DLXXVIII. (II.) Copyright is the exclusive right which the law allows an author of reprinting and republishing his own original work.

It is a right of which no traces are to be found in the Roman Law. In England it was of a most uncertain character till the reign of Queen Anne, (m) when it became the subject of Statute Law, from which (n) it has received considerable protection and favour.

DLXXIX. But all States were unanimous in their opinion that they were under no obligation to recognize the exclusive right of this intellectual property of foreigners within their territories. The arguments, bad and good, are well known upon this subject. At the same time the German Confederation (o) seized the opportunity of the Congress of Vienna to

---

(m) 8 Anne, c. 19.

(n) See, also, 15 Geo. III. c. 53 ; 41 Geo. III. c. 107.

(o) " Nous devons dire un mot de la disposition relative à *la contre-faction.* Il n'y a pas de pays où cette espèce d'industrie soit poussée plus loin qu'en Allemagne. Le partage de ce pays en plusieurs souverainetés la favorise, et elle trouve de la protection dans les principes de gouvernement de quelques états. La monarchie Autrichienne, le royaume de Würtemberg, et le grand-duché de Bade sont les principaux foyers de cette espèce de brigandage littéraire, qui est la principale cause de la cher té des livresen Allemagne. La contrefaction est illicite, dans chaque état, à l'égard des auteurs ou éditeurs sujets du même état ; mais la réimpression d'ouvrages imprimés dans un pays étranger n'a jamais été regardée contrefaction ; c'est un droit que les Allemands, les Français, les Suisses, les Anglais, et les Hollandais ont de tout temps librement exercé les uns envers les autres. Ce principe, vrai dans sa généralité, entraîne de graves inconvénients dans une nation partagée, comme la nation Allemande, en un grand nombre de souverainetés, si, au lieu de se regarder comme parties du même, tout, chacune, de ses souverainetés veut jouir des droits d'un état particulier. Telle a cependant été, et est encore dans ce moment, la pretention de quelques souverains allemands, de manière que les ouvrages publiés dans les états

propose that copyright should be as much respected throughout the different States which composed the confederation, as through the different provinces of a single State.

The reasoning was applicable to the whole civilized world; the different States of which ought, in all matters of Comity, to consider themselves as members of one family; and the great States of Europe—not as yet of America—have incorporated by treaty the doctrine of International Copyright into the system of International Law.

Thus the German Diet introduced a convention upon this subject between the different members of the Confederation in 1837. Austria and Prussia gave in their adherence on behalf of those portions of their territories which did not belong to the Confederation. Austria and Sardinia had a convention in 1840, to which the other States of Italy, and one of the Cantons, adhered.

In 1837 Prussia passed a law of reciprocity in this matter with all Foreign States. In 1838 the English parliament passed a yet more liberal statute presently to be mentioned. At first, France held back, but in 1852 she promulgated a decree subjecting literary piracy to the punishment of her penal Code.

In 1846 England entered into a treaty with Prussia; in 1847 with Hanover; in 1851 with France; in 1854 with Belgium.

---

des rois de Prusse et de Saxe peuvent être contrefaits dans le grand duché de Bade. On a vu en Allemagne un autre abus d'un principe juste par lui-même : il y est arrivé que des ouvrages originaux, publiés dans une partie de l'Allemagne, ayant été contrefaits dans une autre, les éditions illégitimes, qui avaient paru sous la protection des lois de ce dernier pays, se trouvèrent favorisées au détriment des originaux qu'on regardait comme production étrangère. La Prusse avait depuis longs temps donné un exemple de justice qui avait trouvé peu d'imitateurs, en prohibant, la vente de toute édition contrefaite dans quelque partie de l'Allemagne que ce fût, quand même les auteurs ou l'éditeurs de l'original n'étaient pas régnicoles."

Koch (ed. *Schoell*), *Hist. des Traités de Paix*, c. xli. s. 5.

The substance of these conventions is—

1. That the authors and artists of both countries are entitled to enjoy the same rights as those which the legislation of each State has granted to its own subjects.

2. That the advantage of the treaty extends to all works of literature and art, including translations; to dramatic works not printed, and to articles in newspapers and periodicals, which are not of a political character. But these concessions are accompanied with certain restrictions and obligations : thus, it must be notified by the author on the title-page, that he reserves to himself the right of translation ; and with respect to other works of literature and art, they must be duly registered within three months of their first publication, at Paris, at the office of the Minister of the Interior ; and in England at Stationers' Hall, with or without the deposit of a copy or of a print, according to the nature of the work, and the law of the State.

3. That the reciprocity applies only to works of literature and art published or edited after the 17th January, 1852, in France ; and the 28th January, 1852, in England. As to works published or produced previously to that period, they are to be governed, so far as they affect foreign authors and artists, by the Common Law of each State. (p)

DLXXX. The provisions of the English Law on this subject are thus more fully stated by Mr. Serjeant Stephen :—

" Protection, also," (he says) " under certain conditions, is " afforded to literary and other productions, though first pub- " lished in a *foreign* country.   And this subject of *interna-* " *tional* copyright is now regulated by 7 & 8 Vict. c. 12, " (repealing a former statute of 1 & 2 Vict. c. 59,) (q) and by

---

(p) *Code Intern. de la Propr. Industr.* &c. par *Pataille* et *Huguet*, p. 123.

(q) Until the passing of this act of 1 & 2 Vict. c. 59, foreigners first publishing a work abroad, had neither at Common Law, nor by virtue of the statute of 8 Ann. c. 19, or 54 Geo. 3, c. 136, any copyright in England.   See *Chappell* v. *Purday*, 14 *Meeson and Welsby's Rep.* 303 ;

15 & 16 Vict. c. 12, whereby, among other regulations, it is provided, that by order in council her majesty may, as respects *books, prints, articles of sculpture, and other works of art,* which shall be, after a future time specified in such order, first published in any foreign country to be named in such order, allow the respective authors, inventors, designers, engravers, or makers, and their personal representatives, privilege of copyright therein for any period not exceeding the term to which like productions would be protected if first published in the United Kingdom ; and may, as respects *dramatic pieces* and *musical compositions,* which shall be, after a future time specified in such order, first publicly represented or performed in any foreign country named in such order, allow the authors to have the sole liberty of representing and performing them within the British dominions during any period, not exceeding the term during which they would be entitled by law to such sole liberty, if the first representation or performance had been in the United Kingdom. And also that, by order in council, her majesty may, as regards *translations* of books first published—or of dramatic pieces first publicly represented—in any foreign country, direct that the authors of such books or dramatic pieces shall be empowered to prevent the publication in the British dominions of any translation of such books, or the representation of any translations of such dramatic pieces not authorized by them, for such time as shall be specified in her majesty's order, not extending beyond five years from the time at which authorized translations shall be first published or represented respectively. Provision is, however, made, that no such order shall have effect, unless, on the face of it, it be grounded on a due reciprocal protection secured by the foreign power therein named, for the benefit of parties, interested in works

---

Jeffreys v. *Boosey,* 24 *Law Journal (Exch.),* 81 ; *S. C.* 4 *House of Lords Rep.* 815. See note at the end of this chapter.

first published in the dominions of her majesty; nor unless, within a limited time, the work sought to be protected be duly registered, and a copy thereof, (if it be a book, a print, (*r*) or a printed dramatic piece, or musical composition,) deposited at Stationers' Hall; nor (in the case of translations) unless the original work be registered, and a copy deposited in the United Kingdom, in the manner required for original works, as above mentioned; nor unless the author notifies on the title-page his intention to reserve the right of translation; nor unless a translation, sanctioned by the author, be published within certain limited periods; nor unless such translation be registered, and a copy thereot deposited, as in the case of original works." (*s*)

(*r*) If it be a *print* first published in a foreign country, it must also, by 8 Geo. 2, c. 13, have the name of the proprietor on each copy as well as on the plate.   See *Avanzo* v. *Mudie*, 10 *Exch.* 203.

(*s*) *Stephen's Commentaries* (edit. 1858), vol. 2. p. 41-2.

APPENDIX TO CHAPTER XXVII.

CASE OF JEFFREYS *v.* BOOSEY.

By the judgment in this case it was decided as follows, viz. :—The object of 8 Anne, c. 19, was to encourage literature among British subjects, which description includes such foreigners as, by residence here, owe the Crown a temporary allegiance ; and any such foreigner, first publishing his work here, is an " author " within the meaning of the statute, no matter where his work was composed, or whether he came here solely with a view to its publication.

Copyright commences by publication ; if at that time the foreign author is not in this country, he is not a person whom the statute meant to protect.

An Englishman, though resident abroad, will have copyright in a work of his own first published in this country.

B., a foreign musical composer, resident at that time in his own country, assigned to R., another foreigner, also resident there, according to the law of their country, his right in a musical composition of which he was the author, and which was then unpublished.   The assignee brought the composition to this country, and before publication, assigned it, according to the forms required by the law of this country, to an Englishman.   The first publication took place in this country.

It was held, reversing the judgment of the Court of Exchequer Chamber, that the foreign assignee had not, by the law of this country, any assignable copyright here in this musical composition.

Per *Lords Brougham and St. Leonards.*   Copyright did not exist at Common Law ; it is the creature of Statute.

Per *Lord St. Leonards.*   No assignment of copyright under 8 Anne, c. 19, the benefit of which is claimed by the assignee, although from a foreigner, can be good in this country, unless it is attested by two witnesses.

Per *Lord St. Leonards.*   There cannot be a partial assignment of copyright.*

---

* *Jeffreys* v. *Boosey* (A.D. 1854), 4 *House of Lords Reports*, p. 815.

In favour of Foreigners' foreign assignees' right to an assignable copyright.

Mr. Justice Crompton.
  „   „   Williams.
  „   „   Erle.

Mr. Justice Wightman.
  „   „   Maule.
  „   „   Coleridge.

Against.

Mr. Baron Alderson.
  „   „   Parke.
Lord C. J. Pollock.
  „   „   Jervis.

Lord Chancellor Cranworth.
Lord Brougham.
  „   St. Leonards.

CHAPTER XXVIII.

ACQUISITION AND ALIENATION OF MOVEABLE AND IMMOVEABLE PROPERTY.

CAPACITY TO ACQUIRE OR TO ALIENATE.

DLXXXI. Having considered in what the nature of moveable and immoveable property consists, and by what laws it is determined, we now approach the consideration of the rules of Private International Law with respect to the acquisition and the alienation of Property by Foreigners.

DLXXXII. As it is an incident to the Sovereign Power of every Independent State to have authority over all *persons* residing or being within its borders, so it is an incident to the same power to have authority over all *things* or *property* of every description within its borders.

The Laws of each State, therefore, govern the whole property of individuals, whether they be Natives or Foreigners.

But the same Comity which, in the application of the Law, distinguishes for some purposes between the persons of Natives and Foreigners, makes a distinction both as to their *capacity to acquire property*, and also as to the *form* and *manner* of its *acquisition or alienation*.

DLXXXIII. The following summary of the opinions of jurists upon this important point is, it is believed, correct :—

1. There are those beginning with Huber (*a*), and ending with Savigny (*b*), who hold that this *capacity to acquire* or *alienate* is governed by the Law of the Domicil of the acquirer or alienator.

(*a*) S. 12.
(*b*) VIII. s. 357, 11.

2. There are those who hold that this *capacity* does not belong to the qualities of the person, as such, but to the legal working or effect of these qualities, and, therefore, that the *lex fori*, before which the matter is adjudicated upon, and not the Law of the Domicil, should be applied.

3. Those who hold, with Story for their principal exponent, that, generally speaking, the Law of the Domicil should be applied, but not in the case of *immoveables*. In this case, the *lex rei sitæ, or* the *Statutum reale*, must govern—a position emphatically condemned by Savigny.

But those who maintain the first opinion admit the following exceptions (c):

a. Where the capacity to acquire or alienate is forbidden by the Law in which the property is situated.

β. Where it is doubtful whether the property be or be not among the *res quorum commercium non est*, the *lex rei sitæ* is to prevail.

γ. Where a question arises as to property without an owner, *bona vacantia*, as to whether the particular property can be acquired by *occupatio*.

For instance, *jura regalia*—rights of the Crown and Government—such as mines, minerals, treasure trove, or amber, in the kingdom of Prussia. In such cases it is admitted that not only ought the *lex rei sitæ* to prevail, but that the property acquired under such a title ought to be recognized by all other States.

DLXXXIV. Having considered what Law governs the *capacity* to acquire and to alienate property, we ought, perhaps, to inquire in the next place what Law governs the *form* and *manner* of acquisition and alienation. And this inquiry would lead us to an examination—

1. Of the opinions of jurists.

2. Of the domestic jurisprudence of States expressed either

(c) *Savigny,* viii. s. 367, 11.

in their written Codes or in their practice, manifested by public acts of the State or by judicial decisions.

The subject is, however, discussed at length in that portion of this volume which relates to *obligations:* and it is only intended in this place to give the outlines of a sketch, the filling up of which the reader will find in the later part of this work.

DLXXXV. The opinions of jurists on this subject may be ranged, as on the subject of *capacity*, under three classes :—

1. Those who maintain that the *lex domicilii* alone ought to govern both kinds of property.

2. Those who maintain that the *lex rei sitæ* alone ought to govern both kinds of property.

3. Those who maintain that the *lex domicilii* governs the moveable or personal, and the *lex rei sitæ* the immoveable or real property.

DLXXXVI. Those who hold the *first* of these opinions do so chiefly in relation to the property of à deceased foreigner, considering that this, of whatsoever character and wheresover situated, forms an *"universitas juris,"* to be governed by the Law of the Domicil. This opinion, however, founded on an exaggeration of the doctrine of Personal Statutes, has certainly no root in the system of Private International Law (*d*), and it has a manifest tendency to interfere with the sovereignty which is vital to every independent State.

DLXXXVII. Those who hold the *second* of these opinions are not numerous (*e*); they belong to the present age, and are, I believe, confined to Germany. They have lately added a host to their numbers in the adhesion of *Savigny* (*f*), who, in his recent work, expresses a very strong opinion upon this point. It may be expedient to state the substance of his reasoning,

---

(*d*) "Mais c'est exagérer évidement la portée du statut personel que de prétendre lui soumettre des immeubles par le motif, qu'ils font partie d'une succession."—*Fælix*.

(*e*) *Tittmann, Mühlenbruch, Eichhorn, Wächter, Savigny.*

(*f*) VIII. s. 366, 367, 11.

as it embraces the arguments of his predecessors, especially of *Wächter* (*g*), who is entitled to the chief place among the promulgators and maintainers of the doctrine that the *lex rei sitæ* ought equally to govern the moveable and immoveable property of foreigners.

DLXXXVIII. It is refreshing and instructive to turn from the absence of theory and system which the decisions and dicta of English and North American lawyers too frequently exhibit to the philosophical and luminous statement of Savigny (*g*) upon this subject. After stating the arguments of those who maintain that the *lex domicilii*, and of those who maintain the *lex rei sitæ* is alone applicable to *moveable* property, he expounds his own opinion to the following effect :—

DLXXXIX. In considering the Rights of *Things*, we enter immediately upon the question of the dominion in which these *Things* are. *Things* are sensible and tangible ; they occupy a definite *place*, and that place is the seat of the Legal Relation (*Rechtsverhältniss*) of which they are the object.

Whosoever wishes to acquire, enjoy, and exercise a right over a *Thing* betakes himself for that purpose to the *place* in which it is situate, and subjects himself willingly, so far as his Legal Relation to that particular *Thing* is concerned, to the law in force within that *place* wherein the *Thing* is.

When, therefore, it is asserted that his Rights relating to this *Thing* are governed by the *lex rei sitæ*, this position rests upon the same principle as that which applies the *lex domicilii* to govern a question of Personal *Status*—the authority of both laws, in fact, springing from the voluntary subjection of the individual to the law of a particular place.

The old Roman Law, indeed, knew nothing of the *forum rei sitæ ;* but this doctrine was early introduced in relation to actions or suits respecting the recovery of property, and was afterwards applied to other actions *in rem.* It is true, however, that even in these instances that law did not exclusively

---

(*g*) I. 292—298 ; ii. 199, 200, 383—389.

prescribe the *forum rei sitæ*, but left to the plaintiff the option between the *special* remedy, the *forum rei sitæ*, and the *general* remedy, the *forum domicilii* (*h*).

But this optional arrangement is too vacillating and uncertain to be adopted in modern jurisprudence. Therefore, one of the two rules must be fixed upon, and that one must be the *lex rei sitæ* (*i*) ; first, because that is the Law to which the individual has by his own will in this particular matter submitted and subjected himself; secondly, because the greatest confusion would follow from adopting the *lex domicilii*, for it is to be remembered that there may be more persons than one interested in the Right to the particular Thing, each of which Persons may have a different Domicil, and a question full of doubt and perplexity actually arises as to which Domicil is to furnish the Law. This doubt and perplexity is obviated by adopting the *lex rei sitæ*.

Therefore all States have adopted this rule of Private International Law with respect to immoveable or real property : but a distinction has been drawn between this kind of property, and that which is of a moveable or personal character.

It must be admitted that this distinction has been relied upon by almost all the jurists of an earlier date than the pre-

---

(*h*) *Savigny, ib.* n. *b, c, d,* citing *Vatic. Frag.* s. 326 : the contrary is not to be inferred from l. 24 s. 2 (s. 1), *de Judic.,* which passage refers, not to the *forum rei sita,* but to the *forum originis,* which every Roman citizen had in the city of Rome, in addition to his own home, but from which *Legates* had the privilege (see Chapter on Ambassadors in the Second Volume of this Work) of withdrawing themselves.—L. 3, c. (3, 19) *ubi in rem. Nov.* 69.

(*i*) *Donelli, Comment. de Jure Civili,* lib. xvii. He says, " There are but three exceptions to the *lex rei sitæ*.

" 1. If with the consent of the owner the action has been brought elsewhere, ' est enim in consentientem cujusvis judicis jurisdictio.'

" 2. If the *possessor* has *dolo malo* removed the *res* from the place where it was, to the injury of the *petitor*.

" 3. If the action has been begun where the *res* was, and *pendente judicio* it has been removed elsewhere by the *possessor*."

sent times, and incorporated into many Codes ; nevertheless, it has no foundation in reason or principle—it has arisen from a misapplication of the Law of Inheritance and Succession, [and which, according to our author, is rightly governed by the Law of the Domicil (*k*),] to the Rights (*l*) respecting Things or Property in general, which is governed by the law of the place, and so it was declared to be by the Bavarian legislation of the middle of the eighteenth century (*m*).

Those who maintain the opposite opinion evade or gloss over the difficulties attendant on it. It is easy to say " the Law of the Domicil shall decide ;" but of *whose* Domicil ? of the Person legally entitled to the Thing ; but who is that Person ?—the Proprietor. But which Proprietor, if two persons, claims that designation ; or if the thing has passed from one person to another, which Proprietor—the old or the new one ? Suppose, however, that the answer be " the Domicil of actual Possession"—then it must be recollected that there are various rights growing out of and connected with the Thing itself, which may have been the subject of transfer between individuals, all of whom may have *different* domicils.

" The principal question," he continues, (*hauptfrage*) " still " remains, namely, whether the nature and reason of the " thing furnish any ground for the position that the rights to " moveables should be subjected to a local law different from " that which governs immoveables. It must be absolutely

---

(*k*) *Ib*. s. 366 (172) ; s. 375 (295).

(*l*) In this, as generally, *Savigny* closely follows *Donellus*, cf. *Comment. de Jure Civ.* l. xvii., who explains that the " bæreditas res est *incorporalis* in jure consistens," and that the " res singulæ hæreditariæ" are included in the " nniversitas" of the succession, and that the only " hæreditatis locus is in quo controversia hæreditatis tractanda est ubi scilicet, qui convenitur, habet domicilium."

(*m*) *Ib*. note *g*. (173) *Schäffner*, s. 55, *Codex Bavar. Maximil*. p. i. c. 2, s. 17 :—" Es soll endlich *in realibus vel mixtis* auf die Rechten *in loco rei sitæ* ohne Unterschied der Sachen, ob sie beweglich oder unbeweglich, cörperlich oder uncörperlich seynd, gesehen und erkannt wird."

denied that any such is furnished. The difference of opinion upon this subject has probably originated from too abstracted a consideration of it. I will endeavour to make it clear that in the business of practical life the subject assumes a very different form.

" The examination will have the double result of disclosing the origin of the opinion which I combat as erroneous, and of bringing into daylight that element of truth which it does contain.

" When we examine the place which moveables occupy in space, we find two extreme cases diametrically opposed to each other, the intermediate ground between which is occupied by many other cases with manifold gradations.

" First, The space which moveables occupy in space may be so indeterminate and uncertain as to render it impossible to know precisely what that place is, or what the territory is, of which the local law is to be applied, so that the notion of a voluntary submission to this local law is entirely excluded.

" The following instances fall under this category :—

" A traveller who with his luggage is transported by coach or railway passes in one day through several territories without bestowing even so much as a thought on the one in which he happens for the moment to be. A similar instance occurs when a merchant sends wares into a distant territory during the whole time that these wares are on their passage ; more especially when these are sent by seas to different ports, and, perhaps, to different parts of the world in search of the best market. In all such cases the *lex loci rei sitæ* is evidently inapplicable ; we are obliged to search for some resting-place (*Ruhepunkt*), in which such wares are destined to remain for a longer or for an indefinite time. It may happen that such a place is pointed out in a manner not to be mistaken by the clearly demonstrated intention of the proprietor, or it may happen that this place coincides with his domicil. Take as an example the travelling trunk, which the traveller usually brings home when his journey is over ; or the wares which their owner has sent abroad, but which have not found a market, and which, he, therefore, brings home again, there to await the occurrence of a more favourable season.

" It is, doubtless, the one-sided consideration of such cases which has led to the promulgation or the support of the doctrine that the local Law of the Domicil was universally application to moveables.

" Secondly. We have to consider the case which is the opposite of the one just discussed, namely, the case of moveables, the destination of which binds them to remain fixtures in a particular place.

" Such is the case of the furniture of a house, its library, its collection of objects of art, and the moveables included in the *inventarium* (n) of a landed estate, such as corn, cattle, agricultural implements. It is true that the destination of even such things may be changed—they may be taken into another place or another country ; but these changes are accidental, and are not within the actual intentions and present will of their owner.

" The relation between these moveables and the person is like that which subsists between the person and the domicil, which is considered at the present moment as permanent, though it remains susceptible of continual change for the future.

" There is not, in fact, a plausible reason for considering these things in any other light than that of immoveables. On the contrary, they ought, like immoveables, to be subject to the law of the place—that is, the law of their actual position, and not according to the domicil of their owner or possessor. This is indeed the opinion of the majority of writers,

---

(n) *Inventar* is the expression of *Savigny,* cf. v. " *Inventarium,*" in *Adelung's Dictionary.*—" Bewegliche Dinge, welche zu einem grundstücke gehören, bey demselben verbleiben, mit dem Besitzer nicht verändert werden ; besonders in der Landwirthschaft, wo die auf solche art zu eimem Gute gehörigen sämmtlichen Geräthschaften, Stücke, Vieh Getreide u. s. f."

even of those who otherwise stoutly maintain the distinction on principle between moveables and immoveables, but who make for this particular class of moveables an exception to their general rule, and form them into an intermediate class.

" Between the two classes of moveables which have been discussed are to found many others with the greatest variety of differences between them. For instance, the merchandize which the owner keeps in deposit at a particular place which is not that of his Domicil, for an indefinite period ; so, too, the baggage which the owner brings with him during his sojourn in a strange country, and the like. The particular circumstances of each case must determine whether these moveables belong to the first or the second class. This determination will not be affected by the shortness or length of the period during which these things remain at a particular place, but by the nature of the rule of law about the application of which the question arises. Thus, for instance, if the dispute arose as to the form of the alienation (tradition or simple contract), a much briefer sojourn at a determinate place would suffice to warrant the application of the law of the place where the thing was situate, whereas a question of possessing title (*usucapio*) might be subject to different considerations.

" Speaking generally, however, we ought to hold fast to the application of the law of the place where the thing is situate (*lex rei sitæ*), as a general rule, and regard as a comparatively rare exception the case of moveables belonging to the first of the classes which have been treated of in the foregoing remarks."

DXC. While Savigny is contending that there ought to be in principle no difference between the application of the law to moveable and immoveable property, he is obliged to make an admission which, in reality, is fatal to his position, viz., that where the Law of Succession to immoveable property is connected with the public and constitutional policy of the State, that in this case his maxim does not apply.

Thus, in England, the succession of the eldest son to all the realty of his father is closely connected with the support of that aristocracy which, whether within or without the House of Peers, is an essential branch of the British constitution.

In France, on the other hand, the compulsory partition of landed property is not less an essential part of that constitution, which has a Democracy and an absolute Sovereign, but no intermediate aristocracy. (o)

DXCI. The Courts of Louisiana, notwithstanding the protests of Story and Livermore, agree with the doctrine of Savigny. By the Common Law of England and North America, a sale of goods between the parties is complete without delivery ; by the Roman Law (p), delivery is requisite. That law prevails in Louisiana. The Supreme Court of that State has decided in the most solemn manner that the transfer of personal property in that State is not complete, so as to pass the title against creditors, without delivery ; though it would be complete by the Law of the Domicil of the owner who transfers it (q).

DXCII. (3.) With respect to the *third* opinion—viz., that the *lex domicilii* governs the *moveable* or *personal*, and the *lex loci rei sitæ* the *immoveable* or *real* property—that is certainly the abstract opinion which the greatest number of accredited authors and jurists conspire to recommend. But,

---

(o) Thus *M. Demangeat,* "Cette opinion intermédiaire qui consiste à distinguer entre les meubles et les immeubles pour determiner la loi qui doit régir la succession nous paroit en définitive préférable aux deux autres. La considération qui, suivant nous, est c'est que dans chaque état la loi sur les successions n'est qu'un corollaire de l'organisation politique : il y a dès lors un intérêt d'ordre public à ce que les immeubles laissées en France par un étranger, aussi bien que les immeubles, laisseés en France par un Français soient devoter et réportir conformément à notre loi démocratique."—*Du Statut Personel, Rev. Pratique,* p. 634.

(p) *Cod.* l. ii. t. iii. 20.

(q) *Olivier* v. *Townes,* 14 *Martin's (American) Rep.* 93 ; *Story, s.* 386.

then, in practice, and especially in recent practice, a great approach has been made to Savigny's doctrine of the *lex situs*. Story says, " The general rule is that a transfer of personal " property, good by the law of the owner's Domicil, is valid " wherever else the property may be situate. But it does not " follow that a transfer made by the owner according to the " law of the place of its actual *situs*, would not as completely " divest his title, nor even that a transfer by him in any *other* " foreign country would not be equally effectual, although he " might not have his domicil there." And again :—" In the " ordinary course of trade with foreign countries no one thinks " of transferring personal property according to the forms of " his own Domicil ; but it is transferred according to the form " prescribed by the law of the place where the sale takes " place." (*r*)

It is manifest, and admitted by the foreign civilians, as well as by English authorities, that personal property, consisting of *jura incorporalia*, such as local stocks, public funds, regulated by local laws, can only be transferred according to the *lex situs*. (*s*) The peculiar case of the transfer of ships is dealt with in a subsequent part of this volume.

DXCIII. The cases decided in the English Court on the subject of the piracy of foreign trade-marks, show a greater regard for Comity than the decisions of the French tribunals.

In a very recent case an *alien ami* manufactured, in his own country, goods, which he distinguished by a peculiar trade-mark. The goods obtained considerable reputation both in his own country and in various other foreign countries, and also in some British colonies ; but it was not shown that any of such goods had ever been even introduced or imported into England. The defendant was in the habit of manufacturing in and selling in this country, goods similar in appearance, and with an exact copy of the plaintiff's peculiar trade-mark.

(*r*) *Story*, s. 384.
(*s*) *Robinson* v. *Bland*, 2 *Burrows' Rep.* 1079 ; *et vide post,*

Some of these imitative articles were sold and used abroad in countries where the *alien ami's* goods had obtained a reputation. (*t*) It was holden by the Court, that he was entitled to an injunction restraining the defendant from copying or imitating the trade-mark. The doctrine seems to have been laid down in this case, that a man has no property in a trade-mark, but he has a right to prevent anybody else from using it, so as to attract custom which otherwise would flow to himself. Also that a person on whom an injury is fraudulently committed may have a remedy in the Court of any country where the fraud occurs, and even although he be at the time an alien enemy. (*u*)

DXCIV. In the last case on this subject a bill was filed by an American trading company, incorporated by the Law of the State of Connecticut, in the United States of America, for an injunction to restrain a manufacturer of Birmingham from continuing the fraudulent use of the trade-marks of the company, and for an account of the profits made by him from such use. He, by his answer, admitted the use of the trade-marks complained of; but, by way of rebuttal of the charge of fraud, stated, that in so using the trade-marks, he had only followed a custom prevalent at Birmingham for manufacturers of goods of the kind sold by the company, to affix on the goods ordered by merchants a particular trade-mark, relying on the respectability of the merchant, when known to them, for the fact that those merchants had authority to act as agents of, or by way of license from, the person entitled to the exclusive use of the trade-marks; and that he had been informed that the company themselves had ordered goods to be manufactured at Birmingham, with their own trade-mark upon them, for the purpose of sale in foreign countries. These statements were left uncontradicted by the company. The Court, upon motion for decree, ordered that an *interim in-*

(*t*) *Collins Company* v. *Brown; Same* v. *Cohen* (1857), 3 *Kay and Johnson's Rep.* 423.

junction, which the defendant had previously submitted to, should be continued for a year, with liberty to the company to bring an action within that time, to try their right at law ; and in case of their not proceeding at law and to trial within that time, then that their bill should thereupon stand dismissed, with costs. (*u*)

(*u*) *Collins Company* v. *Reeves* (V.-C. Stuart, 1859), 28 *Law Journal, Chanc.* 56.

CHAPTER XXIX.

OBLIGATIONS—GENERAL REMARKS UPON.

DXCV. In every society persons must not only exist, but
act.(a) "*Vox actus* (according to the Roman Law) est generale
" verbum, sive *verbis* sive *re* quid agatur." (b)

Each person has his own sphere of rights limited and cir-
cumscribed by the rights of others. Within this sphere he
enjoys the full liberty of acting, but he lies under an *obligation* (c) not to encroach, without permission, upon the sphere
of his neighbour. If he does so, he lies under an *obligation*
to make *reparation* to him; therefore the Roman jurists said
rightly, "*obligationes ex maleficio nascuntur.*" Nevertheless
it is ordained by the Author of man's nature that he should
interchange his rights with his fellow-man, (d) and should
continually pass beyond the sphere of his own legal action,
and change and abandon his own private rights. As a matter
of fact, all men do so; the consequence of this is, another
class of *obligations*, arising not *ex maleficio*, but *ex facto*.

(a) *Warnkönig, Doctrinæ Juris Philosophiæ,* cap. viii. *De Factis et
Obligationibus.*

(b) *Dig. de Verb. Sign.* l. xix.

(c) Though *this* idea is not conveyed by the term *obligatio*, in the
Roman Law, (*vide post*)—*Hobbes* says, with his usual perspicuity,
" Where liberty ceaseth, there obligation beginneth."

(d) " La vie et les buts des hommes s'entre-croisent : personne ne
suffit à soi-même ; pour vivre et se developper chacun doit compter
sur un grand nombre de conditions placés dans la volonté de ses sem-
blables. C'est pour s'assurer ces conditions de la part d'une personne,
qu'on entre dans un contrat avec elle ; et la fidélité dans les engagements est une condition et partant un droit de la vie sociale."—*Ahrens,
Phil. du Droit*, p. 396 (Brux. 1844).

If a man enjoy or use the right of another with his consent, no *obligation* arises; but if this enjoyment or use be granted for a limited period, or under a condition, and the enjoyment or use be continued beyond the period, or without the fulfilment of the condition—if a man promise to *give* or *do* a certain thing, and the promisee in consequence acts in a manner which he would not otherwise have acted with respect to his own rights or property, and the promisor does not fulfil his promise—in these cases, also, an *obligation* to make *restitution* or *reparation* arises, or, as the Roman jurists say, an *obligatio ex contractu,* or *ex quasi contractu.*

DXCVI. There may be obligations springing from promise or contract which the civil law of a country does not enforce, (e) for which it allows no *action* to be brought in its Courts of Municipal Law. The Civil Law of all countries has prescribed that certain contracts on which an action may be brought, shall be attended with certain formalities or solemnities in the execution. The *stipulatio* of the Romans, the English *Statute of Frauds*, illustrate this position. But there are other obligations which spring up amid the daily necessities of society, and which, wanting these formalities and solemnities, nevertheless found an action in Courts of Municipal Law. These latter are not the growth of the peculiar character of any nation, but are common to all nations— a part of the necessary development of social life wherever it exists. In other words, there are two classes of obligations, namely, *obligationes juris civilis,* and *obligationes juris gentium.* By this latter term, *juris gentium,* is not meant the *natural obligations* of rational affections, such as gratitude, love, or obedience, but those obligations which the common necessities of a common humanity have everywhere introduced into social life, such as are expressed in the following passages of the Institutes:—" Ex hoc *jure gentium* omnes penè contractus in-

---

(e) Though it does not deny that they are contracts: *vide post,* decisions upon the English Statute of Frauds.

" troducti sunt, ut emtio, venditio locatio conductio . . . .
" mutuum et alii innumerabiles." (*f*)   And of the Digest:
" Ex hoc jure Gentium . . . .   obligationes institutæ
" exceptis quibusdam quæ a jure civili introductæ sunt." (*g*)

The Roman lawyers, therefore, were wanting neither in
philosophical truth nor practical sagacity, when they distinguished, as we shall presently see, the various *causes* of *Obligation*, and divided *contracts*, the principal source of obligations, into those which were executed—

    1. Re.
    2. Verbis.
    3. Literis.
    4. Consensu.

DXCVII. (*h*) All institutes of law are connected, or appear
to be connected, with each other. The philosophical investigation of the character of each institute requires an investigation
into the reality or unreality of this connection.

The Rights which flow from Obligations may seem, at first
sight, to be connected rather with the Rights of Family, than
of Things. The ties of Obligation, like the ties of Family,
subsist between two definite persons. On the other hand, the
essence of the relation of Obligation consists in the subjection
of the acts of an individual to the will of a stranger. The
essence of the relation of Family consists in the moral and
natural bond which is formed, continuously and insensibly, by
the free co-operation of the different members of a family.

The Right to Things does not indeed require, as its basis,
the two definite persons who are indispensable to the right
called *obligation ;* but the two Rights agree in this—that they
both consist in the dominion of a definite person over a portion of the external world. Taken together, they make up

---

(*f*) *Inst.* l. i. t. ii. s. 2.

(*g*) *Dig.* l. i. t. i. s. 5.

(*h*) *Savigny, Obligationenrecht,* i. s, 54, is the author whom I have
closely followed in the observations in this paragraph.

the whole Right of Property of which they are co-ordinate portions, (i) though their operation be very different.

For in the Rights to Things, the operation of the principle of Property is to sever—in the Right of Obligations, to bind together.

Moreover, there is this further affinity between the two Rights—the acts which the Obligor is bound to do for the Obligee, are capable of being estimated in money; and the most frequent and most important Obligations have no other object than the use or acquisition of Property.

DXCVIII. The affinity of the Rights of Obligation to the Rights of Family has been pointed out. Nevertheless, in the general system of jurisprudence, the Rights relating to Family, to Inheritance, and Testamentary disposition, the Rights relating to Things or to Corporeal Property, are discriminated (k) from the Rights relating to Obligations, by some striking characteristics. The former are necessarily confined within a narrow range of positive law. The liberty of individuals as to these Rights is hemmed in within certain fixed limitations of instituted rules, the general features of which are the same in all civilized States.

The Rights relating to Obligations are of different kinds. With respect to them, individual liberty has far wider scope; and the rules of instituted law concerning them are of greater number and variety. Moreover, though many and various laws have been gradually and slowly built up to meet particular exigencies of society, which have generated particular Obligations; the Obligations by which men may be bound are not limited in number or character. Their category is not exhausted by past legislation or judicial decision. Obligations are of necessity continually increasing and assuming new forms, as the state of society becomes more complicated and

---

(i) *Savigny, System R. R.* b. i. s. 56-7-8.
(k) *Savigny, Obligationenrecht,* i. *Einleitung* (15).

artificial ; (*l*) and when direct precedent is wanting, the *principles* of instituted law must be, from time to time, flexibly applied for their adjustment. (*m*) "Obligationes" (*Gaius* says) "aut ex contractu nascuntur, aut ex maleficio, *aut pro-* " *prio quodam jure, ex variis causarum figuris.*" (*n*)

The principles of this *proprium jus* must be derived from the philosophical investigation of the nature of the Right of Obligation.

DXCIX. There is also another marked and peculiar feature in the history of the development of the Law of Obligations. It is this, that with respect to it, the doctrines of the Roman Law have been more largely copied than those of any other portion of this jurisprudence into the Municipal Law and Codes of Europe.

Even England has not wholly denied herself this great advantage ; for, though her Common Law has, for the most part, either not applied or misunderstood and misapplied the Roman Law on this subject, many of its principles have found their way—owing partly, no doubt, to the fact of the Lord Chancellors having, before the Reformation, been ecclesiastics versed in the Civil and Canon Law—into the English prætorian or equity jurisprudence.

An intimate acquaintance, therefore, with the provisions of the Roman Law upon Obligation, is indispensable both to those who would thoroughly master the subject, and also to those who have to expound or to administer Private International Law. (*o*)

(*l*) " Während die dinglichen Rechte einen ziemlich fest begrenzten Kreis von rechtlichen Beziehungen zur Sache nicht leicht überschreiten, bietet das Obligationenrecht eine unendliche Fälle der mannichfaltigsten Varietäten dar : sein Gebiet ist unermesslich wie alle Formen das geselligen Verkehrs unter dem Menschen."—*Blume, Deutsches Privatrecht*, s. 252.

(*m*) *Savigny, Obl.* l. s. 4 (17).

(*n*) F. i. pr. *De Oblig. et Act.* viii. 44—7.

(*o*) " Ferner haben sich in dem Obligationenrecht die Rechtsbegriffe

The authority of the Roman Law upon Obligations in the Codes of France may be estimated from the remarks of one of the most recent French commentators, (*p*) that from the article 1,100 to the article 1,384 of the French Code, there is scarcely a rule upon the subject which is not borrowed more or less directly from this source. Zachariæ observes, in his excellent work on the French Code, that the compilers of that Code drew not only the general principles of Obligation, but those of each particular contract (*q*) from the Roman Law, which presented a model difficult to equal, and it may be said almost impossible to excel. (*r*)

The examination of the treasures bequeathed to us by the Roman jurisprudence, will form the subject of the following chapter.

---

und Grundsätze der Römer, Vorzugsweise der anderen Rechtstheilen, in anerkanter Wirksamkeit erhalten."—*Savigny, Obl.* i. s. 4—17.

(*p*) *Traité Elémentaire de Droit Romain,* t. ii. p. 58, par *R. de Frisquet.*

(*q*) This does not, as will be seen, extend to the forms of *action* by which obligations may be enforced.

(*r*) *Droit Civil Français,* par *K. S. Zachariæ, traduit de l'Allemand sur la cinquième edition,* &c., par *G. Massé* et *C. Vergé,* 1857, tom. iii. p. 342.

CHAPTER XXX.

OBLIGATION—ITS MEANING IN ROMAN LAW.

DC. *Obligatio* is thus defined in the Roman Law :—

" Obligatio est *juris vinculum* quo necessitate *adstringi-*
" *mur* alicujus solvendæ rei (*a*) secundum nostræ civitatis
" jura."

These *jura*, it is well observed by Donellus, embraced both
the *jus civile* and the *jus gentium*. (*b*)

Again :—

" Obligationum substantia—in eo consistit —— ut *alium*
" *nobis obstringat* ad dandum aliquid, vel faciendum vel præ-
" standum." (*c*)

The use of the expression *obligatio*, in the Roman Law, is
very commonly misunderstood, it is construed without regard
to its subject or its origin.   It has been used in its popular
sense in the foregoing volumes of this work, which relate to

(*a*) *Inst*. l. iii. t. xiv. pr.

(*b*) *Donellus* explains (lib. xii. c. 1) admirably every part of this
question.

" *Vinculum*—Translatione ductâ a vinculis corporalibus : et rectê
ductâ : quia quod efficit vinculum corporale in his qui vincti sunt id
efficit jure obligatio in his qui sunt obligati.

" *Solvendæ*—Solvere est præstare non quidvis, sed quod debetur—
præstatio rei debitæ.

" *Rei*—Non solum *res* sed etiam *facta*—ut sive quid ex obligatione
dandum est, datur—sive quid *faciendum* ita præstatur et fiat.   Hoc
exigit verbum *rei*, quod, cum per se ponitur, generale est.

" *Secundum nostræ civitatis jura*—Aliam enim necessitatis præstati-
onem habet *jure gentium naturalis obligatio*, aliam *jure civili, civilis*.
Atque hæc sunt jura duo civitatis nostræ."

(*c*) *Dig*. l. xliv. t. vii. 3.

Public International Law, (*d*) namely, as the mere correlative of *jus;* or, as it might be said in ordinary English, if one man has a right, another man lies under an obligation to respect it. The German jurists, Hugo and Savigny, (*e*) following Donellus, are careful to demonstrate the error of this opinion, when applied to civil or municipal law.

In the first place, it unduly narrows the force of the expression *obligatio*, confining its force to the *Status* of the obligor, and excluding that of the obligee.

In the second place, it unduly widens the expression *obligatio*, by making it applicable to every part of the law which relates to individuals—as, for instance, to the law of property, and even carrying it beyond the limits of Private into those of Public Law—as, for instance, the obligations of the subject to his Government. (*f*)

The technical expression *obligatio*, in its true meaning, embraces two different and opposite matters. It is correctly applied to signify either the diminished rights of the Obligor, or the extended rights of the Obligee.

The following passage from the *Institutes* illustrates this position :—

" In utrâque tamen obligatione una res vertitur, et vel " alter debitum accipiendo, vel alter solvendo, omnium peri· " mit obligationem, et omnes liberat." (*g*)

The image which the expression *obligatio* presents is that of a *bond*. It was chosen to represent a *bound* and un-free will. It is nearly allied to other technical expressions of Roman Jurisprudence, *nectere* and *nexum contrahere, contractûs solvere* and *solutio.* (*h*)

(*d*) Vol. iii. p. 1.

(*e*) *Savigny, Oblig.* i. s. 3.

(*f*) See *Donellus,* lib. xii. c. 4.

(*g*) *Inst.* l. iii. t. xvii. s. 1, *de duobus reis.*

(*h*) The true technical sense of *obligatio* has been pointed out, but it should be observed that this expression sometimes denotes *the groundwork or origin* of any legal relation, as in this passage, " in tutelâ *ex*

DCI. Every *convention* is, the Roman lawyers said, of two kinds. Both, indeed, proceed from the *free-will* of individuals; but having regard to its *origin* it appears that one is sanctioned by the general usage of civilized nations (*conventio jure gentium*); (*i*) the other is confirmed by a particular municipal law (*legitima conventio*). (*k*) Having regard to the *operation* and *effect* of a convention, the same proposition (*l*) may be thus stated : a convention may generate a *naturalis, i. e., a juris gentium obligatio*, or a *civilis obligatio*.

Thus, though both have the same origin, (*m*) they were not always attended with the same result.

The civil obligation was also enforceable by a civil *action* (*parit actionem*); the natural obligation was not so enforceable (*non parit actionem sed exceptionem*); as will be seen when the particular species of *obligatio* called *contractus* is discussed; in which this distinction of obligations into those enforceable and those not enforceable by action, receives its fullest and clearest illustration. (*n*)

---

unâ obligatione duas esse actiones constat." *Dig.* l. xxvii. t. iii. 1—21 (*de tut. et rat. distr.*) ; *Savigny, Obl.* i. s. iii. 14, n. *k*, for this and other instances. Sometimes also the *pawning* or *pledging* of a thing, because thereby a legal relation arises with respect to the thing, similar to that of the *debitor*, in the case of an *obligatio*. Thus we find the expressions *obligatio prædiorum* and *nectere pignori*. *Savigny, Obl.* i. s. iii. 14, n. *l*. ; *Dig.* l. t. xiv. 52, 2 (*de pactis*) ; l. xiii. t. vii. 27 (*de pign. act.*).

(*i*) " Non quæ inducitur jure gentium, sed quæ inducta ab hominibus, jure gentium probatur, valetque ad agendum."—*Donellus*, l. xii. c. ix.

(*k*) " Non quæ inducta sit lege, sed quæ lege aliquâ confirmetur."—*Ib.*

See note (*b*), p. 432, on the distinction between the use of "legitima conventio," by *Paulus* and *Ulpian*.

(*l*) *Savigny, Obl.* xi. 196.

(*m*) " Non enim jus inducit, ut quid homines conveniant aut pasciscantur inter se, quæ cuivis libera sunt : sed quæ ab illis sunt pacta aut conventa, ea jus probat aut improbat, ex illis actionem dando, ubi res actionem desiderat, hic denegando."—*Ib. Donellus, ubi supr.*

(*n*) *Savigny, Obl.* ii. p. 196.

DCII. It is, as we have seen, from some *act* of a person that the obligatio arises. An *obligatio* is incurred by an act of the obligor either (1) with or (2) without his consent.

If, *with his consent*, he has bound himself to another to do or abstain from doing something, he must keep his faith. He has made a *contract*—" Is consensus de re aliquâ prestandâ contractus est." (*o*)   He may also be bound *without his consent* (*p*), in two instances—(1) by intermeddling in the affairs of another, constituting himself his agent; or (2) by an act of injury done to another.

In the former case he is bound by the obligation of what the Roman Law called a *quasi contract*, so called because this intermeddling is neither a *maleficium* nor a *contractus*, but more nearly allied to the latter. (*q*)

In the latter case, the obligor has either committed a crime or done an accidental injury (more or less venial) to another. He is thereby bound *ex delicto* or *maleficio*, or *ex quasi delicto* or *maleficio*. Hence, the famous fourfold division of the *facta* which founded a *civilis obligatio* (*r*) in Roman Law. Of these the *contract* is of the greatest importance.

DCIII. The particular relation in which two persons, between whom an *obligatio* subsists, stand towards one another, is designated in the Roman Law by the technical expressions of *creditor* and *debitor*, *creditum* and *debitum*. These expressions are used without any reference to the origin of the *obligatio*, though in the earlier period of the Roman Law they were restricted to the case of a loan. But Gaius observes, " Creditorum appellatione non hi tantum accipiuntur

---

(*o*) *Donellus*, lib. xii. c. v.

(*p*) " Extra consensum duo sunt in facto nostro quæ nos aliis eo facto ipso jure obligent *rerum alienarum administratio suscepta*, et *delictum*."—*Ib*.

(*q*) To the English lawyer an illustration is offered by the doctrine that a man by intermeddling without title with the effects of a deceased person, becomes *Executor de son tort*.

(*r*) *Donellus*, lib. xii. c. v.

" qui pecuniam crediderunt : sed omnes, quibus ex quâlibet
" causâ debetur." (s)

DCIV. Apart from the advantage incident to a thorough
and philosophical knowledge of the subject of Obligations,
some acquaintance with the nomenclature and reasoning of
the Roman Law is necessary to the student of Private International Law, upon two grounds—First, as has been already
mentioned, in order that he may understand the true meaning
of the language of the commentators upon this law, who take
for granted (as *Grotius* in his treatise on Public International Law does), in their readers, a knowledge of the Roman
Law.

Secondly, because the Roman Law not only forms the basis
of the Continental Law upon this subject, but also is used to
supply the deficiencies and silence of their positive law or
written codes.

This latter advantage is forcibly pointed out in Savigny's
last work. (t)

(s) *Dig.* l. l. t. xvi. 11, *de V. S. et Eod.* 10.
(t) I. *Savigny, Obl.* s. 14, 123.
II. *ib.* s. 76, 231.

NOTE TO THE FOREGOING CHAPTER.

DICTIONARY OF GREEK AND ROMAN ANTIQUITIES.

(*Obligationes*, p. 819.)

"There is no special name in the Roman Law for a right against a determinate person or determinate persons. The name for ownership is *Dominium*, to which is opposed the name *Obligationes*, as descriptive of rights against determinate persons.

" It is correctly remarked (*Austin, an Outline of a Course of Lectures on General Jurisprudence*) :—' That in the writings of the Roman lawyers, the term *obligatio* is never applied to a duty which answers to a right *in rem*," that is, a right which is good against all the world. But, as the duty answering to a right *in rem* is only the duty of forbearance, that is, of not doing anything to interfere with the right, there is no inconvenience in the want of a name : the right to the exclusive enjoyment of anything (*corpus*) is ownership ; all other people are not owners ; as soon as an act is done which is an infringement of an owner's right, or, in other words, a *delictum* (in one sense in which the Romans use this word), an obligation arises by force of such act (*obligatio ex delicto*), and gives the injured person a right of action against the wrong-doer.' "

CHAPTER XXXI.

CONTRACTUS IN ROMAN LAW.

DCV. We have now to consider that source of Obligation called Contract.

The first division of (*a*) *Conventiones* by the Roman lawyers relates to their

I. *Historical Origin ; viz.,*

      1. *Légitimæ Conventiones* (*b*).

      2. *Juris Gentium Conventiones.*

The explanation of this division is the same as has been given with respect to *obligations,* of which, in fact, it is only an application to that particular source of obligation called *Contracts.*

It is to be observed, however, that the *jus civile* recognized and gave effect to—that is, rendered actionable, supplied with a

---

(*a*) *Dig.* l. ii. t. xiv.

Ib. l. xliv. t. vii.

Inst. l. iii. t. xiv. xv. xvi.

Cod. l. iv. t. x.

Savigny, Obligationenrecht, ii. s. 52.

(*b*) *Dig.* ii. t. xiv. 5—7, *pr.* I, *de pactis.* *Ulpian's* expression of "*legitima conventio,*" referred to the ancient solemn contracts. The expression as used by *Paulus* (6 *ib.*), "*Legitima conventio est quæ lege* aliquâ confirmatur," is wholly different—referring to a *convention* not properly belonging to the category of *contract,* but accidentally clothed with that character by a particular *lex.*

Savigny (*ubi supra*) fully explains this and the error of supposing that this passage in *Paulus* warranted the notion that *pactum legitimum* meant a *pactum* on which an action might be brought by virtue of an Imperial Constitution.

causa—all the more important contracts of the *Jus Gentium*, as the contracts of Sale, Loan, Hiring, and the like.

The *Legitima Conventio*, (c) strictly so called, disappeared in the Justinian compilations.

II. The next division relates to the character of the contract, whether it be *unilateral* or *bilateral;* though, as Savigny remarks, the Roman Law had no strictly technical expressions of this kind. (d)

The unilateral contract presented the simplest form of obligation ; according to it one party was creditor, another debtor.

The contracts arising from Loan, from Promise of a Gift, from the *stipulatio*, belonged to this division.

The bilateral contract is illustrated by Sale, Hiring, Partnership.

Between these two kinds, and partaking of the nature of both, the Romans placed the *Commodatum, Depositum, Mandatum.*

III. Another division relates not to the legal form of the contract, but to the object of the contracting parties—viz.,

The division into contracts,—

(1.) Which had for their object the exclusive advantage of one party, which must, of course be also unilateral ; as in the instance of the *Promise of a Gift*, by which the condition of one party was directly bettered, or of a *Depositum*, by which the condition of neither party was directly bettered, but one obtained through the other the advantage of security for his property.

(2.) A contract which had for its object the advantage of both parties, but which might be *unilateral,* as in the case of a Loan for Interest ; *bilateral,* as in the case of a Sale or Hiring.

This division is called by modern writers *conventio lucrativa* or *gratuita* and *conventio onerosa;* but these are not technical expressions of Roman Law. (e)

(c) *E. g.*, the *nexus—dotis dictio—literarum obligatio.*

(d) II. *Oblig.* s. lii. 2, 12.

(e) *Savigny, ubi supr.*, " Des dispositions à titre gratuit," is a well-known branch of French Law.

IV. Another division relates to the particular form of action by which certain contracts are protected.

1. *Contractus stricti Juris*, which were protected by *Actiones stricti juris* or *conditiones*.

2. *Contractus bonæ fidei*, which were protected by *actiones bonæ fidei*. (*f*)

It is to be observed that this division is not identical with the division into *legitimæ* and *juris gentium conventiones*, though sometimes erroneously supposed to be so. (*g*)

DCVI. The true signification of the word " obligatio " has been explained.

It is also of importance to the student of this branch of Private International Law to understand accurately the senses (*h*) in which the Roman Law used the words *reus, correus, conventio, contractus, pactum, causa,* which so frequently occur, both in the compilations of that law and in the commentaries upon it.

The term *rei* (*i*) comprise all the parties, whether two or more, whether *creditores* or *debitores*, to an *obligatio*. Sometimes persons under the same obligations are called *correi*.

Properly and technically speaking *conventio* is, according to the Roman Law, the *genus*, of which *contractus* and *pactum* are two *species*. (*k*)

Contractus is the convention which generated a *civilis obligatio*, and, therefore, founded an *actio* or action at

---

(*f*) II. *Savigny, Obl.* s, 52, 15.

(*g*) *Ib.* s. 72, 196.

(*h*) *Ib.* s. 72, 196.

(*i*) "Reos autem appello non eos modo qui arguuntur sed omnes " quorum de re disceptatur : sic enim olim loquebantur."—*Cic. de Or.* l. ii. 43.

"Conventionis verbum generale est, ad omnia pertinens de quibus negotii contrahendi transigendique causâ consentiunt qui inter se agunt." —*Dig.* ii. t. xiv.

(*k*) *Pactum— conventum—pactio—conventio* are often used, however, as the general names for any agreements.

law. Pactum, or *nudum pactum,* (*l*) generated a *naturalis obligatio* (*m*) only, and, therefore, did not found an action at law, but only the defensive rights of Equity or Prætorian Law, called *exceptio* (*n*) and *retentio.*

This form of the civil action was technically called the *oausa* of the contract. (*o*) The word *causa* is, indeed, sometimes used in the material and untechnical sense of the motive cause, (*p*) but the former is the proper sense ; and it is a mistake of Blackstone (*q*) and Kent, (*r*) indicating a most superficial acquaintance with the Roman Law, to consider the English *consideration* as identical with the Roman *causa.*

DCVII. The principal division of the subject of obligation in the Roman Law related to its *effect* and *operation ;* and with reference to this, conventions were divided into those upon which an action might or might not be brought.

It may be convenient to place before the reader in this place the celebrated language of Ulpian incorporated in the Digest (*s*) :—" Juris gentium *conventiones*" (he says) " quæ-" dam *actiones* pariunt quædam *exceptiones.* Quæ pariunt " actiones in suo nomine non stant, sed" (What can be more " happily expressed ?) " *transeunt in nomen contractûs,* " ut emtio venditio. Sed et si in alium contractum res non " transeat, subsit tamen *causa :* eleganter Aristo Celso respon-" dit esse obligationem. Sed *cum nulla sub est causa præter* " *conventionem,* hic constat non posse constitui obligationem,

---

(*l*) *Vide post,* further observations as to *pactum* generally.

(*m*) This distinction of *naturalis* and *civilis obligatio* corresponds with the division of *legitimæ* and *juris gentium conventiones,* mentioned before.

(*n*) *Dig.* l. ii. t. xiv. 4, 1, 7 ; *Mackeldey, Lehrbuch,* ii. s. 363.

(*o*) *Savigny,* II. *Oblig.* s. 72.

(*p*) *Puchta Pandekt.* s. 257 :—" Si quis sine *causâ* ab aliquo fuerit stipulatus deinde ex eâ stipulatione experiatur."—*Dig.* l. xliv. t. iv. 3.

(*q*) *Comment.* vol. ii. 444.

(*r*) *Comment.* vol. ii. 463. The error is corrected in a uote to the edition of 1851.

(*s*) *Savigny,* II. *Obl.* viii. 214.

" igitur *nuda pactio* obligationem non parit, sed parit excep-
" tionem." (*t*)

Originally, therefore, *contractus* denoted an actionable convention, and *pactum* one not actionable.

In course of time, however, the stern Civil Law yielded, and conventions, which were not *contractus*, became actionable ; and though the distinction remained, so to speak, in the books, practically many *pacta* become actionable, though without a technical name, which the glossators endeavoured, not very happily, to supply, by speaking of *vestita*, as opposed to *nuda pacta.* (*u*)   *Pactum*, therefore, cannot be *always* considered as a convention which did not found an action.

DCVIII. Upon this division of contracts into *actionable* and *not actionable*, the Roman Law founded the four species of *actionable contracts*, already adverted to :—" Obligationes" (both Gaius and Justinian said)" quæ sunt ex contractu aut " *consensu* contrahuntur aut *re* aut *verbis* aut *literis.*" (*x*)

DCIX. Of these four species, the two former (*consensu, re,*) are distinguished in principle from the two latter (*verbis, literis*). (*y*)

The *causa* by which a convention passes from the category of *pacta* and enters that of *contractus*, and becomes

---

(*t*) *Dig. de pactis*, l. ii. t. xiv. 7. cf. *cod.* 15,—*Hermogenianus* :— "Divisionis placitum, nisi traditione vel stipulatione sumat effectum, ad actionem, ut nudum pactum, nulli prodesse poterit." And again, *Ulpian*, speaking of an *action* founded on a promise of reward for discovering a fugitive slave, says, " Et quidem *conventio*, ista non est *nuda* ut quis dicet, ex pacto *actionem* non oriri, sed habet in se *negotium* aliquod : ergo *civilis actio* oriri potest, id est præscriptis verbis."

Dig. l. xix. t. v. 15 (*De prescriptis verbis et in factum actionibus*).
Cod. l. ii. t. iii. 21—28 (*De pactis*).
Savigny, ubi supr. n. e.
See also *Warkönig's Instit.* p. 287.
(*u*) *Donellus, Savigny*, II. *Obl.* s. lxxiii. 214.
(*x*) *Gaius*, iii. 89.
Inst. l. iii. t. xiv.
Dig. l. xliv. t. vii. 52.
(*y*) *Savigny, Obl.* ii. s. 72.

protected by a *civilis obligatio* or *actio*, is either *res* or *consensus*.

a. Re contracta obligatio is the title of a contract which was originally concluded by the delivery of a thing, and which the donee bound himself to restore to the donor. And under this particular aspect, this contract embraced the four species of—

1. Mutui datio.
2. Commodatum.
3. Depositum.
4. Pignus.

β. Consensu contracta obligatio was the title of a contract which, on the ground of its substance and contents, was *actionable*, and did not require the aid of any technical or external *causa*.

Under this contract were ranged the four species of—

1. Emtio, venditio.
2. Locatio, conductio.
3. Societas.
4. Mandatum.

DCX. The two remaining kinds of contract relate to the forms of the particular convention; but there is a more (*a*) general aspect under which this contract of consent must be regarded: according to the Roman jurist, it had for its *object* not only the *giving of a thing*, but also the *doing of an act ;* and hence arose the famous decision, which has found its way into modern continental jurisprudence, and has been even eulogized by the English Blackstone. (*b*)

1. Do ut des.
2. Do ut facias.
3. Facio ut des.
4. Facio ut facias. (*c*)

(*a*) *Savigny, Obl.* ii. s. 73.

(*b*) *Commentaries*, vol. 2. 444-5.

(*c*) Sometimes (*Warkönig, Inst. Jur. Civ.* 321) called *contractus innominati*, or *incerti*, but improperly according to *Savigny*.

This contract, under this general aspect, did not produce the particular *actio commodati* or *depositi*, but an *actio* which comprehended all cases under the name of *actio præscriptis verbis* or *actio civilis*.

γ *Verborum obligatio* is the title of a contract which was entered into through the medium of the *spoken* question of the Creditor and the answer of the Debtor, both conducted according to a set form of words : (*d*) hence arose the unilateral contract which, under the name of *Stipulatio*, was, until the time of Justinian, the peculiar and favourite form of Roman convention, and under which title some of the most important doctrines relating to Obligation and Contract are, even in the Justinian compilations, discussed. (*e*)

δ *Literarum obligatio* (*f*) was the title of a contract, which, before the time of Justinian, was concluded through a particular form of *written* words, and founded on the domestic manners of the old Roman citizens with respect to money transactions.

(*d*) *Dare spondes? Spondeo of Plaut.* cap. iv. 2, 117.

(*e*) *Warkönig, Instit. Jur. Civ.* 296.

(*f*) *Mackeldey, Lehrbuch,* ii. s. 414.   See his very learned note.

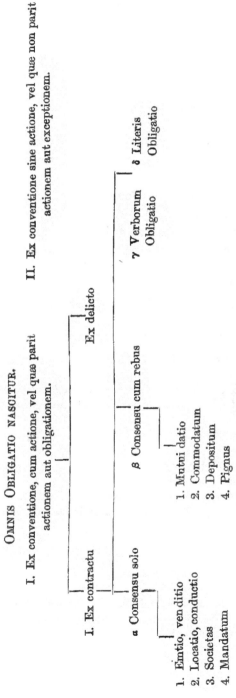

OMNIS OBLIGATIO NASCITUR.

I. Ex conventione, cum actione, vel quæ parit actionem aut obligationem.

II. Ex conventione sine actione, vel quæ non parit actionem aut exceptionem.

I. Ex contractu

Ex delicto

α Consensu solo

1. Emtio, venditio
2. Locatio, conductio
3. Societas
4. Mandatum

β Consensu cum rebus

1. Mutui datio
2. Commodatum
3. Depositum
4. Pignus

Sometimes called by modern writers *con-tractus nominati*; while other *obligationes ex re*, for which the Roman Law had no particular name, have been called *contractus innominati*.

γ Verborum Obligatio

δ Literis Obligatio

CHAPTER XXXII.

OBLIGATIONS—ENGLISH LAW.

DCXI. The law of England and of the United States of North America upon the subject of Obligation (*a*) is principally derived from the following sources :—

1. The judgments of Courts of Common Law.
2. The Statute of Frauds. (*aa*)
3. The judgments of the Courts of Equity.

And to these may be added, with respect to some of the States which constitute the great North American Republic,

4. The Roman Law. (*b*)

DCXII. The Common Law (*c*) of England considers *obliga-*

(*a*) I. English authorities referred to : *Blackstone's Commentaries*, vol. 2, c. 30, ix.

The Law of Vendors and Purchasers of Estates, by E. Sugden, Lord St. Leonards, præsertim, c. 4, Of Parol Agreement, general construction of statute.

Smith's Law of Contracts (ed. *Malcolm*).

Addison's Law of Contracts and Rights and Liabilities ex contractu.

II. North American United States :

Kent's Comm. vol. 2, lecture 39, ed. 1851.

(*aa*) This Statute is generally adopted throughout the United States of North America—*Kent*, iv. p. 316—with the exception of Louisiana, *ib.* 637.

(*b*) *Kent*, ii. p. 616.

(*c*) Blackstone remarks (vol. ii. t. 2, c. 30, ix.) that "almost all the rights of personal property (when not in actual possession) do in great measure depend upon contracts of one kind or other, or, at least, might be reduced under some of them, which, indeed, is the method taken by the Civil Law ; it having referred the greater part of the duties and rights which it treats of to the head of Obligations *ex contractu* and *quasi ex contractu*."

tions only under the category of contracts, which it technically divides into three classes—

1. Contracts by matter of record.
2. Contracts under seal or by deed, called covenants.
3. Contracts not under seal nor by deed, called simple contracts, or by parol.

Practically, however, the two latter classes are alone of importance.

DCXIII. This Law defines a Contract as an agreement of two or more persons, upon sufficient consideration to do or not to do a particular thing. The agreement may convey an interest in possession ; as when goods are delivered and the price paid, that is a *contract executed.* Or it may convey an interest *in futuro* or in action ; as where a vendor agrees to sell and deliver goods, and a vendee agrees to accept and pay for them at a future time, that is an *executory contract.* It also considers Contracts as *express* or *implied,*—the former when the parties express their meaning, the latter when the law presumes a contract for some value given or service rendered.

The term *Consideration* is of great importance in English Law ; it means, speaking generally, a compensation, a *quid pro quo* of an adequate character, moving from the promisee, promised by him, not by a third party, (*d*) to the promisor, an inducement not of morality, affection, or honour, but of a kind which municipal law can estimate ; or, as it has been perhaps best defined, "any benefit to the person making the promise, or " any loss, trouble, or inconvenience to or charge upon the " person to whom it is made." (*e*) The consideration must not be contrary to law, public policy, or good morals.

Such a consideration is essential to the validity of a Contract *not under seal,* except in the instance of bills of exchange and negotiable notes which have passed into the

---

(*d*) *Smith*, 91.
(*e*) *Smith*, 90.
Kent, ii. 585.

hands of third parties without notice of the original defect,—
that is, of innocent indorsees. (*f*)

The mistake which English lawyers and writers on law
make in supposing that they are following the Roman Law
when they apply the maxim *ex nudo pacto non oritur actio*,
and imagine that the English technical word *consideration*
and the Roman technical word *causa* are convertible terms,
has been already remarked upon.

This necessity of showing or proving a consideration is also
of importance, because it is the mark of distinction between
what are called Simple Contracts and Contracts by Deed.   In
the case of this latter, the law presumes, on account of the
solemnity of its form, that it has been made upon a good and
sufficient consideration.

The presumption, however, may be rebutted by showing
that it was founded on an illegal and immoral consideration.

By proving this, a man may defend himself from his
liability to a contract expressed in deed, but not by showing
that there was no consideration.

DCXIV. The English Law about written contracts not expressed in *deeds*, involves some very subtle considerations,
especially as to their proof. On the one hand, it is an inflexible
rule that a contract reduced into writing shall be proved by
that writing only, and shall not be *contradicted* or *altered*
by *contemporaneous* verbal expressions. On the other hand,
though it is not lawful to show that the meaning of a written
contract has varied by words *at the time of making it*, it is
sometimes lawful to show that it was *subsequently so varied*,
that, in fact, a *new agreement* was made.

But, though this may be done where the contract is one
which the Law does not require to be in writing, yet, where
a writing is necessary, it cannot be allowed ; for, if it were, the
effect of the verbal evidence would be to turn a contract which

---

(*f*) The settled rule in England and North American United States.
Kent, ii. 584, and cases there cited.

the Law requires to be in writing into one partly in writing and partly in words. (*g*)

Where, indeed, parties have contracted with reference to some known and established usage, in such cases the usage is sometimes allowed to be engrafted on the contract, in addition to the express written terms. Yet even in such cases the English Courts never admit evidence of an *usage* inconsistent with the written contract. (*h*)

DCXV. (2.) The foregoing observations relate to Contracts at *Common Law*—that is, to Contracts not governed by any Act of Parliament. We have now to consider them as affected by the Statute of Frauds. This Statute was passed in the twenty-ninth year of the reign of Charles II., and is the third chapter of the Statute-book of that year. " It is said " (as Mr. Smith observes) " to have been the joint production of Sir " Matthew Hale, Lord Keeper Guilford, and Sir Leoline " Jenkins, an eminent Civilian. (*i*)   The great Lord Notting- " ham used to say of it, '*that every line was worth a subsidy;*' " and it might now be said with truth that every line has *cost* " a subsidy, for it is universally admitted that no enactment " of any legislature ever became the subject of so much litiga- " tion.   Every line, and almost every word of it, has been the " subject of anxious discussion, resulting from the circumstance " that the matters which its provisions regulate are those " which are of every day occurrence in the course of our " transactions with one another." (*k*)

" The two sections which mainly affect *Contracts*, are the 4th and the 17th.   The 4th section enacts," " That *no action* " *shall be brought* (*l*) to charge any Executor or Adminis- " trator upon any special promise to answer damages out of " his own estate ; or whereby to charge the defendant upon

---

(*g*) *Smith*, p. 29.

(*h*) *Ib.* p. 34.

(*i*) *Vide ante*, vol. i. Introd.

(*k*) *Smith*, *ib.* p. 37.

(*l*) See following notes as to meaning of these words.

any special promise to answer for the debt, default, or mis-
carriage of another person; or to charge any person upon
any Agreement made upon consideration of marriage; or
upon any Contract or sale of lands, tenements, or hereditaments, or any interest in or concerning them ; or upon any
agreement that is not to be performed within the space of
one year from the making thereof; unless the agreement
upon which such action shall be brought, or some memorandum or note thereof, shall be in writing, and signed by the
party to be charged therewith, or some other person there-
" unto by him lawfully authorized." (m) The words *no action
shall be brought* in this Statute, have received an important
construction in their bearing upon that class of Contracts
which belong to Private International Law. The English
Courts have holden that this enactment does not affect the
solemnities of the Contract, but only the rules of *procedure*.
And, therefore, though a parol Contract, within the fourth section of the Statute of Frauds, be made in France, and be valid
there, yet that an action on it will not lie in England. (n)

The 17th section provides, that " *no contract* for the sale
" of any goods, wares, or merchandizes for the price of £10
" or upwards *shall be good,* (o) except the buyer shall accept
" part of the goods so sold, and actually receive the same; or
" give something in earnest to bind the bargain, or in part
" payment; or that some note or memorandum in writing of
" the said bargain be made and signed by the parties to be
" charged by such Contract, or their Agents thereunto law-
" fully authorized." (p)

(m) *Smith,* p. 39.

(n) *Leroux* v. *Browne,* 12 *Common Bench Rep.* 801. It is parcel of
the procedure, and not of the formalities of the contract, Mr. J.
Maule observes in this case.

(o) *Reade* v. *Lamb,* 6 *Exchequer Reports,* 130, for effect of the words,
" *no contract shall be good,"* in 17th section, as contrasted with " *no
action shall be brought,"* in 4th section. This case is at variance with
the prior one of *Carrington* v. *Roots,* 9 *Meeson and Welsby's Rep.* 248.

(p) *Smith, ib.* p. 73.

The intention of the legislature was to comprehend within the 4th and 17th sections, the subject matter of every *parol* Contract, an uncertainty in the terms of which was likely to produce perjury. (*q*)

DCXVI. There is another Statute which, as it had for one of its objects to prevent the evasion of the Statute of Frauds, ought to be mentioned in this place ; it cannot be better introduced than in the words of Mr. Smith : " After the 4th section " of the Statute of Frauds had rendered verbal guarantees un- " available, it became the fashion in such cases to bring actions " upon the case for *false* representations, under circumstances in " which, before the Act, the transaction would have been looked " on as one of guaranty.   For instance, if A. went to a trades- " man to persuade him to supply goods to B., by assuring him " that he should be paid for them, the tradesman, in case of B.'s " default, could not, it is true, bring an action of assumpsit as " upon a warranty, because there was no written memorandum " of what passed ; but he brought an action on the case, in " which he accused A. of having knowingly deceived him as " to B.'s ability to pay ; and if the jury thought this case made " out (as a jury composed of tradesmen were very apt to do), " he succeeded in his action, and received pretty nearly the same " sum as he would have done if there had been a guaranty." However, as this was a palpable evasion of the Statute of Frauds, the legislature put an end to it by enacting, in Statute 9 Geo. 4, c. 19, commonly called Lord Tenterden's Act, " that " no action shall be brought whereby to charge any person " upon or by reason of any representation or assurance made " or given concerning or relating to the character, conduct, " credit, ability, trade, or dealings of any other person, to the " intent or purpose that such other person may obtain credit, " money, or goods upon, unless such representation or assurance " be made in writing, signed by the party to be charged there- " with." (*r*)

(*q*) *Kent,* iv. 638.

(*r*) *Smith,* p. 57.   For leading cases on the construction of this

DCXVII. (3.) The English Courts of Equity (s) exercise a *divisum imperium* upon some subjects with the Courts of Common Law; thus the subject of *agreements* belongs, in some respects, to either forum ; but while the Common Law Courts can at present only award *damages* for the nonperformance of a Contract, the Court of Equity can decree the *specific performance of it.* So over *accounts, partnerships,* and that large branch of fiduciary jurisprudence known in England by the name of *trusts,* the Courts of Equity are supreme.

The Equitable powers of the Courts of Common Law have been theoretically much increased by a recent Statute; (t) practically, however, the exercise of these powers has been hitherto confined within very narrow limits. (u)

DCXVIII. (4.) The High Court (x) of Admiralty (y) takes cognizance of certain maritime Contracts relating to Bottomry Bonds, which are Contracts made in a Foreign port, founded upon *sea risks,* for which the *ship* is pledged (z).

Bottomry Bonds are Contracts in the nature of Mortgages of a ship on which the owner borrows money to enable him to fit out the ship, or to purchase a cargo for a voyage proposed, and pledges the keel or bottom of the ship, *pars pro toto,* as

---

Statute, see *Lyde* v. *Barnard,* 1 *Meeson and Welsby,* 99 ; *Swan* v. *Phillips,* 8 *Adolphus and Ellis,* 457 ; *Devaux* v. *Steinkeller,* 6 *Bingham, New Cases,* 84.

(s) See *Kent,* iv. p. 167, an important note on the variety of customs in the different States of the Union as to the establishment of separate Courts of Equity and Common Law, or blending the powers of both in one tribunal. *See* also *Story's Comment. on Equity Jurisprudence,* vol. i, ch. 1.

(t) 17 *Vic.* c. 125, ss. 68—77, 83—86.

(u) *Teede* v. *Johnson,* 11 *Exchequer Reports,* 840.

(x) *Edwards's Admiralty Jurisdiction, London,* 1849.

(y) And the Admiralty of the *Cinque Ports* within its limited jurisdiction.

(z) *Treatise of the Law relative to Merchant Ships and Seamen, by Chief Justice Abbott (Lord Tenterden), London ; Pritchard's Admiralty Digest, London,* 1847.

a security for repayment. It is, moreover, stipulated that if the ship is lost in the course of the voyage by any of the perils enumerated in the contract, the lender also shall lose his money ; but if the ship shall arrive safe, then he shall be paid back his principal, and also the interest agreed upon, called marine interest, however this may exceed the legal rate of interest (a).

The High Court of Admiralty (b) has also jurisdiction over Contracts, express or implied, arising from causes of possession, from repairs done or necessaries furnished to ships, and from seamen's wages ; also over that implied obligation arising from *salvage*, which in its simple character is the service which those who recover property from loss or damage at Sea (c) render to the owners with the responsibility of making restitution, and with a lien for a compensation or reward.

To this jurisdiction over *obligationes ex contractu*, must be added a jurisdiction over those *obligationes ex delicto*, which arise from the *collision* (d) of " ships or sea-going vessels " either at sea or in English rivers (e).

The nature of the obligation is well stated by Dr. Lushington, in a case in which he distinguishes (speaking of the duty of the Registrar and Merchants, as referees of the High Court of Admiralty,) between cases of Collision and cases of *Insurance :* " One" (the learned Judge says) " of the prin-" cipal and most important objections to the report under " consideration is this, that the Registrar and Merchants, in " fixing the amount to be paid for repairs and the supply of " new articles in lieu of those which have been damaged or de-

---

(a) *The Atlas*, 2 *Haggard's Admiralty Reports*, p. 48.

(b) Its jurisdiction is of very high antiquity. See vol. iii, p. 547, for its authority in time of war ; but its powers in time of peace have been increased by the recent Statutes of 3 & 4 Vic. c. 65, and 3 & 4 Vic. s. 66 (1840).

(c) Or *who save life*, according to modern administration of the law.

(d) Words of s. vi of Statute.

(e) *Vide ante*, vol. i, p. 210, as to the jurisdiction of all States within cannon-shot of their own shores.

stroyed, have deducted one third from the full amount which such repairs and new articles would cost. This deduction, it is said, has been made in consideration of new materials being substituted for old, and is justified upon the principle of a rule which is alleged to be invariably adopted in cases of insurance. The first question then which I have to consider, is the applicability of the rule in question to a case of the present description ; and this question, it is obvious, involves a principle of considerable importance, not only as regards the decision in this particular case, but as establishing a rule for assessing the damages in all other similar cases. Now, in my apprehension a material destinction exists between cases of insurance and cases of damage by collision, and for the following reasons :— With respect to all policies of insurance, I apprehend that the cases are cases of Contract. In the construction and regulation of such Contracts, all the customs of Merchants founded in equity are always considered as forming a part of the Contracts themselves ; and the presumption is that all Merchants are cognizant of the customs existing in their own particular vocations, and have them in contemplation in all Contracts which they may enter into in their several transactions of business.

" In the immediate case, for instance, of a policy of insurance upon a ship, the Shipowner who insures his vessel is aware of the custom in question, and at the time the insurance is effected he knows that he pays a smaller premium for the insurance, in consideration of the deduction to be made in case of loss or damage to his ship. If such loss or damage ensued thereupon, he cannot claim to receive more than the custom sanctions and allows; and in recovering the amount of his loss, minus the deduction of the one-third, he in point of fact receives all that he agreed to receive in pursuance of the Contract which he entered into with the underwriter.

" With regard to cases of collision, it is to be observed that they stand upon a totally different footing. The claim of the suffering party who has sustained the damage arises not *ex contractu*, but *ex delicto* of the party by whom the damage

" has been done ; and the measure of the indemnification is not
" limited by the terms of any Contract, but is co-extehsive with
" the amount of the damage. The right against the wrong-doer
" is for a *restitutio in integrum*, and this restitution he is bound
" to make without calling upon the party injured to assist him
" in any way whatever. If the settlement of the indemnification
" be attended with any difficulty (and in those cases difficulties
" must and will frequently occur,) the party in fault must bear
" the inconvenience. He has no right to fix this inconvenience
" upon the injured party, and if that party derives incidentally
" a greater benefit than mere indemnification, it arises only
" from the impossibility of otherwise effecting such indemnifi-
" cation without exposing him to some loss or burthen, which
" the Law will not place upon him." (*f*)

DCXIX. Whatever practical advantage the French Code
may derive from its arrangement of this subject, it cannot be
denied that it is open to grave theoretical objections. It
reverses the philosophical and natural order of things, by treating, first, of Contract, a particular source of Obligation ; and,
secondly, of Obligation generally. The third title of the
third book of the Code is " *Des Contrats ou des Obliga-*
" *tions conventionelles en général.*" The fourth title of the
same book is " *Des Engagemens qui se forment sans conven-*
" *tion.*" Under the former title the French Code lays down the
general principles which govern all conventions, whether they
have a specific legal title or not ; and refers the particular
rules of Law which govern particular Contracts to the titles
under which they are treated, such as Marriage, Sale, Lease,
Partnership, Agency ; and allots to Contracts belonging to
commerce, technically so called, a particular Law with particular rules. (*g*)

(*f*) *The Gazelle*, 2 *W. Robinson's Admiralty Rep.* p. 280-1.

(*g*) *Code Civil*, l. iii. t. iii. 1107 :—" Les contrats, soit qu'ils aient une
" denomination propre, soit qu'ils n'en aient pas, sont soumis à des règles
" générales, les règles particulières à certains contrats sont établies sous
" les titres relatifs à chacun d'eux, et les règles particulières aux trans-

DCXX. These *Contrats* or *Obligations conventionelles* assume the following legal designations :

1. *Synallagmatique* or *bilateral* when the two Contracting parties reciprocally bind themselves to each other.

2. *Commutatif* when each Contracting party engages himself to give or do something which is considered as an equivalent for what has been given to or done for it.   When the equivalent is contingent upon the uncertain event of gain or loss to the party, the Contract is called *aléatoire*. (*h*)

3. *De bienfaisance* is the name of a Contract in which one of the parties procures from the other a purely gratuitous advantage. (*i*)

4. *À titre onéreux* is the name of a Contract which obliges each of the parties to give or to do something.

DCXXI. Under the title "*Des engagemens qui se forment* "*sans convention*" are comprehended the following *obligations:*

I. Those which are imposed by the *Law, and altogether without the consent* of the individual ; such are the obligations which arise from the fact of vicinage between neighbours ; such too, according to this Law, is the obligation of accepting the office of tutor.

This class of obligations is distinguished in principle from those which arise,

II. From the *personal act of the individual,* as these acts may be of two kinds, *lawful* or *unlawful :* from the *personal lawful act* flow the obligations (*engagemens*) called *quasi Contrats ;* from the *unlawful intentional act* termed *délit*, and the *unlawful unintentional* act termed *quasi délit,* flows the obligation of *repairing the injury* to the individuals, and with or without the punishment of the wrongdoer by the State.

" actions commerciales sont établies par les lois relatives au commerce." —See *Rogron, Code Napoleon expliqué,* for a clear and concise commentary on these heads (*Paris,* 1853).

(*h*) See *F.* tit. xii. 1964.

(*i*) *Rogron* says, " Par exemple, la donation faite sans charges ; si elle " en était grevée, elle serait *mixte,* c'est-a-dire *a titre onéreux,* jusqu'à " concurrence de la valeur des charges, et de *bienfaisance* pour le reste."

APPENDIX TO CHAPTER XXXII.

"The term '*Obligation*' is used by the Roman Jurists, and by Pothier, in the preliminary article to his treatise on Obligations, as denoting, in its proper and confined sense, *every legal tie* which imposes the necessity of doing or abstaining from doing any act; and as distinguished from *imperfect* obligations, such as charity and gratitude, which impose a general duty, but do not confer any particular right; as well as from *natural* obligations, which, although they have a definite object, and are binding in conscience, cannot be enforced by legal remedy. English lawyers, however, generally use the word *obligation* in a more strict and technical sense, namely, as importing only one particular species of contracts, that is, *Bonds;* and they adopt the term "Contract" when they wish to convey the more extensive idea of the responsibility which results from the voluntary engagement of one individual to another, as distinguished from that class of liabilities which originates in torts or wrongs unconnected with agreement. In the language of our Law, therefore, the term *Contract* comprises, in its full and more liberal signification, every description of agreement, obligation, or legal tie, whereby one party binds himself, or becomes bound, expressly or impliedly, to another, to pay a sum of money, or to do or omit to do a certain act; but in its more familiar sense it is most frequently applied to agreements not under seal. The term *agreement*, on the contrary, is rarely used amongst us, except in relation to contracts not under seal; and this is evidently its proper use; for, if considered in its strict and more critical meaning, it clearly imports a reciprocity of obligation; and in that point of view it does not include specialties, which in general require no mutuality of stipulation. The word *promise*, again, is used to denote the mere engagement of a person, without regard to the consideration for it, or the corresponding duty of the party to whom it is made.

" It is now, however, very material to consider what particular meaning is generally attached to these various terms. The essential distinctions between the different kinds of contracts constitute a much more important subject of inquiry. These distinctions are clearly ascertained; and, as they assign to each class of contracts attributes and consequences of the most marked character, they demand a cursory notice before we discuss in detail the proper subject-matter of this work, viz., *contracts not under seal.* *

" Contracts, or obligations *ex-contractu,* are of three descriptions, and they may be classed, with reference to their respective orders or degrees of superiority, as follows : 1. Contracts of Record ; 2. Specialties ; 3. Simple Contracts."

---

* *Chitty (Jun.) on Contracts (by Russell), ed.* 1857, p. 1.

CHAPTER XXXIII.

OBLIGATIONS—CONFLICT OF LAWS.

DCXXII. The foregoing sketch of the leading principles of the Law governing Obligations adopted by the chief countries of the civilized world has shown, that amid much general similarity there are not unimportant points of difference between them.

We are now led to consider what rules International Comity requires to be adopted, in those cases in which one and the same Obligation is, in some of the stages from its inception to its fulfilment, subjected to the jurisdiction of different countries possessing different *municipal* Laws upon the subject.

It is proposed to examine this question, first, with respect to (A) THE FORM, and, secondly, with respect to (B) THE SUBSTANCE of an obligation.

DCXXIII. First, then, we have to consider which Law, in an apparent or real conflict of Laws, should govern THE FORM, and the prosecution of this enquiry will perhaps be best conducted by observing the following order :

1. To consider what are the true principles derived from the Reason of the Thing, having especial regard to the expression of that Reason in the general usage of civilized states (*droit coutumier general—allgemeines Gewohnheitsrecht*).

2. What is the doctrine relating to this subject of the *conflict* of Laws in the jurisprudence of ancient Rome.

3. What are the express provisions of Modern Codes.

4. What are the rules to be deduced from the decisions of the tribunals in England and the United States of North America.

DCXXIV. The following general observations appear equally applicable to all the foregoing categories :

a. The distinction between the Law applicable to the *form* and the *substance* of the Obligation is recognized in all these catagories.

β. The distinction between obligations *juris gentium* and *juris privati* is recognized in all these categories.

γ. The conflict of Laws may ensue from two causes, either from a collision between different Laws on the same subject in the *same* territory, or from the collision of different Laws in *different* territories on the same subject.(*a*)   In the first instance, the conflict arises from the change of the Law itself, as where a later abrogates or repeals an earlier Law.   In the second instance, the conflict arises from a change in the condition of the facts or the person, by which they fall under the dominion of different Laws.

DCXXV. First, then, what are the true principles derived from the Reason of the Thing, and how has that reason been expressed in the usage of civilized states ? (*b*)

The true theory of the subject would seem to require that *the form* of the contract should be regulated by the Law of the place of its fulfilment or execution.

But as in practice it often happens that the place of fulfilment is far removed from the place of the origin of the Contract,—as it may be difficult to know and even impossible (*c*) to follow the forms prescribed by the Law of the place of fulfilment in the place of the origin,—the general usage of states in-

---

(*a*) *Savigny*, R. R. viii. (5), s. 344.

Örtliche Gränzen der Herrschaft der Rechtsregeln-Zeitliche Gränzen der Herrschaft.

(*b*) *Savigny*, VIII. s. 381.

(*c*) *E. g.* The Prussian Law requires a testament to be made through the intervention of a Court of Justice.   A Prussian dying in France or England, therefore, must die intestate, if he happen *not* to have made his will before he entered into either of these states.

creasing in force ever since the sixteenth century, has almost universally adopted the rule which is expressed by the phrase *locus regit actum. (d)*

DCXXVI. There are, however, important exceptions to the recognition of this rule.

1. Foreign jurists (*e*) hold that where the *status* of the Person is concerned the rule is inapplicable. The person who is a minor by his domestic Law cannot become a major by the operation of foreign Law, or a person declared infamous by the former, become rehabilitated by the latter.

The rule applies only to the legal form in which the expression or declaration of the will of the party interested shall be couched.

The question of *Status* is not under the control of the will of the person interested, but is under the authority of the State of which he is a member.

2. The legal acts of a person are of a twofold character, and there is an important difference between them.

a. There are legal acts which can be done anywhere and are wholly unconnected with any particular place.

β. There are legal acts which are necessarily connected with a particular place.

To the former class belong the usual class of Contracts, and, in the opinion of Foreign jurists, the making of a testament.

To the latter class belong perhaps the most numerous and most important of those *acts* which relate to the Right to Things. Acts which are so intimately connected with the Things themselves, upon which they operate, as to be necessarily done in the place in which the Things are situated.

(*d*) *Story,* s. 260, 261, and the authorities there cited.

Savigny, VIII. s. 381, and note *c.*

Fœlix, l. 2, t. 1, c. 1, s. 17, &c., and the authorities there cited.

P. Voet, De Stat. sect. 9, c. 2, s. 9.

J. Voet, s. 13—15.

(*e*) *Savigny, ib.*

Pre-eminent among such acts is that of Tradition; among them also are many transactions of mere form, such as the act connected with Bankruptcy or Insolvency, termed the Judicial Cession (*cession judiciaire, gerichtliche Auflassung*), Enrolment or Registration of mortgages or deeds, and others of a like character, which can only be duly executed before a particular public functionary and at a particular place.

In these instances, according to the general jurisprudence of States, the *lex rei sitæ* prevails ; and it is to be observed that this rule cannot be confined to Immoveable Things, but must be extended sometimes to such as are Moveable, as, for instance, in those cases in which the Tradition of the Thing itself is necessary. " In every disposition or Contract," Lord Mansfield said, " where the subject-matter relates *locally* to England, " the Law of England must govern and must have been in-" tended to govern. Thus, a conveyance or will of land, a " mortgage, a Contract concerning stocks, must all be sued " upon in England ; and the *local nature of the thing* requires " them to be carried into execution according to the law " there." (*f*)

DCXXVII. The Roman Law contained no special provisions with respect to Contracts affecting Immoveable Property ; but the legislations of many countries require that in these cases the *lex rei sitæ* shall be observed. The Prussian Code does so in express terms ; (*g*) and according to that Law, inasmuch as all Contracts for a value of above 50 Thalers must be in writing, it follows by almost necessary implication that all immoveable property in that country can only be transferred by a written instrument.(*gg*)

The English Law contains, a like provision.(*h*)

(*f*) *Robinson* v. *Bland*, 2 *Burrows, Rep.* 1079 ; 1 W. Blackst.Rep. 259. Cf. *Donelli*, Comm. lib. xvii. c. 17.

(*g*) *Savigny*, VIII. s. 381 (354).

Pr. Algem. Landrecht, I. 5, s. 115.

(*gg*) *Savigny, ib.* n. (*e*).

(*h*) *Vide post*, notice of the *Statute of Frauds.*

DCXXVIII. The foregoing observations as to the stringency of the Rule *locus regit actum* are subject to an important limitation. It frequently happens that the *form* prescribed by the place in which the act is done is not absolutely *necessary*, but simply what jurists call *facultative*—that is, at the option of the party to adopt or not, leaving him still the power of adopting the form of the place to which the act really has reference.

The true test whereby to decide whether the character of the *lex loci* be or be not *facultative*, is to examine whether the object of it be to favour and assist the parties and to facilitate their acts; if so, it is very generally admitted that it is *facultative*, and leaves it competent to the parties to adopt the form of the place in which the act is to take effect.(*i*)

DCXXIX. The proper bearing of this limitation of the rule *locus regit actum* upon *Testaments* will be considered hereafter: it has been already considered in its relation to *Marriages*.(*k*)

DCXXX. Savigny agrees with those jurists who reject any limitation of the rule *locus regit actum* arising from the circumstance that the act has been done in a foreign country, for the purpose of evading the Law of the domicil of the parties, *in fraudem legis;* for instance, for the purpose of avoiding an expensive form, stamped paper, or the like. If this evasion deserve punishment, it should be punished by fine or some penalty of the kind, and not by invalidating the act itself; at all events, it would require a positive Law of the State to produce this effect.

The recent policy of England on this point, with respect to

(*i*) *Savigny*, VIII. s. 382 (358), and n. (*o*) (*p*).

Rodenburg, t. 2. l. 3. s. 2-3.

Fœlix, p. 107.

Wächter, II. 377—380.

Hertius, s. 10—23.

Schäffner, s. 83, more doubtful.

(*k*) *Vide supra.*

stamps upon Bills of Exchange, made out of the country, but meant to take effect in it, will be considered hereafter.

DCXXXI. Secondly—

We have next to consider whether the rule *locus regit actum* has its root in the Roman Law, and what are the passages therein which appear to relate to this question of jurisprudence.

An examination of these passages will show that the rule, however wise and expedient, is in reality not to be found in the Roman Law. "It is," (Wächter (*l*) says), "incomprehensible "how it could ever have been attempted to ground such a "proposition upon the Roman Law." Savigny (*m*) is of the same opinion.

DCXXXII. The passage usually relied upon as proof that the Roman Law contains the rule *locus regit actum* is taken from an opinion of Gaius, in the Digest, upon Evictions, " Si fundus venierit, ex consuetudine ejus regionis, in quâ nego-" tium gestum est, pro evictione caveri, oportet ;" (*n*) but in this passage Gaius says nothing about the external form of any Contract, least of all is he speaking of any compulsory Law of the State upon the subject. (*o*)

He is speaking not of rules of law, but of certain customs as of facts, and of their consequences in a matter left to the free will of the contracting parties and not restrained by any imperative or necessary law.

The same remark applies to another sentence cited from an opinion of Ulpian in the book " *de diversis regulis juris* " *antiqui*" in the Digest : (*p*)   " Semper in stipulationibus et

---

(*l*) *Wächter*, Ueber die Collision der Privatrechtsgesetze verschiedener Staaten, 2467, to be found in the 44th volume of the *Archiv für die Civilistische Praxis.*

(*m*) VIII. s. 382 (360).

(*n*) *Dig.* l. xxi. t. 2, 6.

(*o*) *Fœlix*, s. 74.

Wächter, ubi sup. s. 5 (248).

Savigny, s. 372 (253), s. 356. i. k (81).

(*p*) *Dig.* lib. l. t. xvii. 34.

" in cæteris confractibus sequimur id quod actum est, aut si non
" pareat quid actum est, erit consequens ut id sequamur, quod
" in regione in quâ actum est frequentatur. Quid ergo si
" neque regionis mos appareat, quia varius fuit? ad id quod
" minimum est redigenda summa."

And also to another passage from an opinion of Papinian
cited in the book *De usuris* &c., on the Digest: (*q*) "Cum
" judicio bonæ fidei disceptatur arbitrio judicis usurarum modus
" ex more regionis ubi contractum sit, constituitur;" and here
the citation usually, but improperly, stops; for the opinion
continues, "*ita tamen ut legi non offendat.*" Here it is quite
clear that Papinian is not speaking of a Contract made in a
foreign country, or the words would have been to the effect,
that the *Law of the foreign country* should only be so far
applicable as they were not contrary to the *Roman Law*,
which was binding upon the judge.

DCXXXIII. Perhaps the most specious passage in favour
of the opinion that the maxim *locus regit actum* is to be
found in the Roman Law is the following:

" Si non speciali privilegio *patriæ tuæ* juris observatio re-
" laxata est, et testes non in conspectu testatoris testimoni-
" orum officio funeti sunt; nullo jure testamentum valet." (*r*)

This was the case of a *Testament* made without the observance of the well-known rule of Roman Law, that the witnesses should be in the immediate presence of the Testator,
" in conspectu testatoris." (*s*)

In answer to a question made by a lady called Patroclia,
probably the heiress nominated in the Testament, the Emperors Diocletian and Maximian *rescribed* that the Testament
was null, " si non speciali priviligeio (*t*) *patriæ tuæ* juris obser-
" vatio relaxata est."

(*q*) *Dig.* xxii. t. 1. pr. 1.

(*r*) *Cod.* lib. vi. t. xxiii. 9.

(*s*) So it is afterwards said in the same book of the Code, " testes
" ipsos audito nomine hæredis *sub præsentiâ ipsius testatoris* nomen
" hæredis suis subscriptionibus declarare.—*Cod.* lib. vi. t. 23—30.

(*t*) *Privilegium* here means a particular right granted by an Imperial
constitution to the town.

The words *patriæ tuæ* appear at first sight to indicate a collision between different local rights, but on further reflection it is evident that the *patria* of the Heiress could not be a circumstance decisive of the case. *It is not said where the Testament was made.* It is not improbable that the Testator made his testament at his own home, where the Heiress was also domiciled. The Rescript therefore does not enforce the application of the *locus regit actum* rule : it simply asserts that in the case of a collision between a particular and a general Law the former must prevail, which, Savigny (*u*) remarks, is an unquestionable proposition.

DCXXXIV. The next passage also relates to a *Testament* " Impp. Val. et Gallien, A. A. Alexandro :"

" Testamenti tabulas ad hoc tibi a patre datas, ut in " patriam perferentur, affirmans, potes illuc perferre, ut secun- " dum leges moresque locorum insinuentur ; ita scilicet ut, " testibus non præsentibus, adire prius vel pro tribunali, vel per " libellum Rectorem provinciæ procures, ac permittente eo, " honestos viros adesse facias, quibus præsentibus aperiantur, " et ab his rursum obsignentur." (*x*)

In this case a father, absent from his domicil, remits before his death his Testament to his son, desiring him to take it to the place of that domicil. The Emperors decide by a Rescript that, with respect to the opening of the Testament before the Court of the place, that the Laws and customs of that place shall be observed. Here is no mention of any collision of Laws, but only of the true rule that judicial procedure shall be governed by the *lex loci*.

DCXXXV. The next passage relates to a case of *Emancipation*. The Emperors Diocletian and Maximian *rescribed* to one Herennius, " Si lex municipii, in quo te pater emanci- " parit, potestatem Duumviris dedit, ut etiam, alienigenæ " suos emancipare possint ; id quod a patre factum est suam " obtinet firmitatem." (*y*)

(*u*) VIII. s. 382 (361).
(*x*) *Cod.* lib. vi. t. xxxii. 2.
(*y*) *Cod.* l. viii. t. xlix. 1.

A father having emancipated his son before the Ducemvirs of a city, in which he was a stranger, the validity of the emancipation was disputed.

As a general rule the municipal magistrates did not possess the *legis actio* but only by way of special privilege, (z) and hence the doubt in this case.

The Emperors laid down the Law that the validity of the act depended upon the provisions of the Law of the city. If that conferred on the Duumvirs the *legis actio* with power to exercise it even with regard to strangers, the transaction was valid. Most truly does Savigny say there is not the faintest trace in this case of any collision of local Laws.

DCXXXVI. It remains to notice a passage sometimes cited for the same purpose from the Canon Law.

" De Franciâ quidam nobilem mulierem de Saxoniâ, lege
" Saxonum duxit in uxorem, verùm quia non eisdem utuntur
" legibus Saxones et Francigenæ, causatus est, quòd eam non
" suâ, id est, Francorum lege desponsaverat, (vel acceperat,
" vel donaverat,) dimissâque illâ, aliam superduxit. Diffinivit
" super hoc sancta Synodus, ut ille transgressor Evangelicæ
" legis subjiciatur pœnitentiæ, et à secundâ conjuge separetur,
" et ad priorem redire cogatur."(a)

From this passage it would appear that a Saxon had married a French woman, and in so doing had followed not the Saxon but the French Law. Having lived with her many years and had children by her, he had recourse to the flaw in the mode of contracting the marriage, repudiated her, and married another wife. An assembly of the church pronounced this proceeding culpable, annulled the second and declared valid the first marriage.

Here again, Savigny remarks, is no mention of the collision of local laws; indeed, the place in which the Contract was entered into is not mentioned. The decision is founded upon

---

(z) *Savigny, Gescheïhte des* R. R. *im Mittelalter,* b. i. s. 27.
(a) *Decret. Greg.* lib. iv. t. 1. c. 1 (*De Sponsalibus et Matrimoniis*).

the doctrine of the Canon Law, which held the first marriage to be binding and indissoluble, and that the observance of this or that custom of the Civil Law was a circumstance of no significance as far as the validity of the bond was concerned.

DCXXXVII. Whatever therefore may be the soundness and value of the rule *locus regit actum*, it derives no direct authority from any passage in the Roman or Canon Law, which are the foundations of all Christian Law.

How this rule came to be discussed by the *Glossatores*, and first adopted by Bartolus (*b*) in the matter of *Testaments*, will be considered hereafter.

DCXXXVIII. Thirdly—

We have to consider whether and to what extent the Modern Codes of Christian States have expressly incorporated, among their provisions, the rule *locus regit actum*. (*c*)

DCXXXIX. As to the French Law on this subject. It had been proposed by the French government to introduce into the code the following provision :   " La forme des actes " est réglée par les lois du lieu, dans lequel ils sont faits " on passés." But it was urged that this provision was unnecessary for acts done in France ; as, since the Revolution, there was one and the same form throughout the kingdom, and that if it were intended for acts done out of the kingdom it was *ultra vires* of the French legislation, that therefore it must be confined to acts done by Frenchmen in a foreign state, and that upon this hypothesis the proposed article was couched in too general terms ; for instance, it might be holden as operating to validate the marriage of a French minor, in a state governed by the Law of the Council of Trent, to which he had resorted for the express purpose of marrying without the paternal consent.

In consequence of these considerations the French govern-

(*b*) *Fœlix*, l. ii. t. i. s. 74.
(*c*) *Fœlix*, l. ii. t. i. c. 1, s. 85, &c.
Savigny, VIII. s. 382 (363).

ment omitted this article. Nevertheless, Merlin observes, (*d*)
the *Conseil d'Etat* considered the rule *locus regit actum* to
be one of those notorious rules which do not require the express sanction of the legislature. The recognition of the rule is
implied in the articles 47 and 999, (*e*) to which Fælix (*f*) adds
the conclusion of article 170. (*g*)

DCXL. The rule *locus regit actum* was the rule which
anciently, and previous to the compilation and promulgation
of codes, obtained throughout all the German States. (*h*)

DCXLI. The *Prussian* Code does not contain any recognition of *locus regit actum* as a general principle.

The 33rd (*i*) article might appear to derogate from it, but
Savigny (*k*) points out that this article does not say that it is
incompetent to strangers to use a form prescribed by a particular statute, or that an act adopting such a form would not
be valid, but only that native subjects and not foreigners are
bound to adopt this form.

In all matters of Contract (*l*) the Prussian Code expressly

(*d*) *Rep. de Jurispr.* v. *loi*, s. 6. n. 8.

(*e*) *Art.* " Tout acte de l'etat civil des Français et des étrangers, fait
" en pays étranger, fera foi, s'il a ête rédigé dans les formes usiteés dans
" le dit pays."

Art. 999. " Un Français qui se trouvera en pays étranger pourra
" faire ces dispositions testamentaires par acte sous signature privée
" ainsi qu'il est prescrit en l' article 970 ou par acte authentique, avec
" les formes usitées dans le lieu *ou cet acte sera passé.*"

Art. 1319. " L'acte authentique est celui, qui a été reçu par *officiers*
" *publics* ayant le droit d'*instrumenter dans le lieu* ou l'acte a été rédigé
" et avec les *solemnites* requises."

(*f*) Sect. 85.

(*g*) " S'il a été celebré dans les formes usitées dans le pays."

(*h*) " Die uralte in ganz Deutschland von jeher geltende Regel *locus
" regit actum*, die also dadurch von Seiten unserer Gesetzgebung die
" unzweifelhafteste Anerkennung erhält."

Savigny, viii. s. 382 (367).

(*i*) Cf. s. 34—*Einleitung*.

(*k*) VIII. s. 382 (364).

(*l*) I. t. 5, s. 111, 112, 113, 114.

recognizes the rule for *moveable* property, but for *immoveable* property it exclusively applies the *lex rei sitæ*.(*m*)

It may be observed here in passing that this code is silent as to the form of Testaments made abroad.

DCXLII. The *Austrian* code does not contain in its text any express recognition of the rule, in those articles (*n*) in which it speaks of engagements contracted and conventions entered into by strangers either in Austria or abroad, applying to them sometimes the Austrian and sometimes the Foreign Law; it does not clearly specify whether the application of these laws relates to the *substance* or the *form* of the act, but it is the opinion of competent judges that these articles relate to both.(*o*)

DCLXIII. *Bavaria*, (*p*) *Wurtemburg*, (*q*) *Baden*, (*r*) apply the rule; Wurtemburg with the qualification, however, that the *form* adopted be not specially prohibited, either by the law of the state in which the act is done, or by that of the state in which it is to be enforced.(*s*)

The code of the *Netherlands* contains a general recognition of the rule.(*t*)

DCXLIV. As to the *Italian* States, *Sardinia* (*u*) does not recognize absolutely the rule *locus regit actum*, but only under the condition of reciprocity in the law of the Foreign State, whose subject claims the application of the rule.(*x*)

The Code of the Two Sicilies contains no enunciation of a general principle on the subject, but it reproduces those articles

---

(*m*) *Ib.* s. 115.

(*n*) 35, 36, 37.

(*o*) *Fœlix*, s. 85, citing *Winiwarter's* Commentary.

(*p*) I. 2, s. 17.

(*q*) *Art.* 22.

(*r*) *Art.* 3.

(*s*) *Fœlix*, s. 85.

(*t*) *Art.* 10.

Fœlix, s. 85, citing *Hartogh*.

(*u*) *Art.* 14—18.

(*x*) *Art.* 64.

of the French Code which take for granted the existence of the Rule. (*y*)

DCXLV. As to the *Swiss Cantons*, the remark just made applies to the *Canton de Vaud*. (*z*) The *Cantons de Berne* and *de Fribourg* contain no express enactment on the subject, which, however, is to be found in the code of the *Canton de Lucerne*. (*a*)

DCXLVI. The Russian Digest of laws contains an enactment to the effect that acts done in a foreign state conformably to the Law of that state, although not conformable to the form prescribed by the Law of Russia, shall be admitted as evidence of the act having been rightly executed, until it be impugned by contrary proof. (*b*)

DCXLVII. The Code of *Louisiana* (*c*) enacts that *the form* and effect of public or private acts shall be governed by the laws and usages of the state in which the acts are done. But *the effect of acts which* being formally done in one state are to be carried into execution in another state, depends upon the Law of the latter. (*d*)

DCXLVIII. Fourthly—

It remains to consider the decisions of this subject in the tribunals of England and the United States of North America.

There is no doubt that the tribunals of both these states have promulgated, in the most decided and positive terms, the maxim *locus regit actum* as to all acts of Obligation or Contract.

(*y*) Articles 49, 180, 895, 925, of the *Code of the Two Sicilies* reproduce articles 47, 170, 979, 999 of the *French Code.*

Fœlix, s. 85.

(*z*) *Fœlix, ib.*

(*a*) Art. 6, " La forme des actes est réglé par la loi du pays où ils ont été faits."

Fœlix, ib.

(*b*) *Fœlix*, s. 85.

(*c*) *Art.* 10.

(*d*) *Fœlix*, s. 85.

No act of this kind executed in a foreign country is holden valid by the tribunals of either of these states unless executed according to the formalities prescribed by the Law of that foreign country. (*e*)

Indeed, the maxim is considered by these tribunals to apply, not only to the external form, but, as will be hereafter noticed, to the internal substance of the act of obligation. And this may be the reason why the distinction between the application of the rule to the form and to the substance is not very clearly taken in Story's elaborate work.

The application of the Rule to the Contract of marriage has already been noticed.

(*e*) *Story*, s. 242, 242 (*a*), 243.

The English leading cases are *Trimby* v. *Viquier*, 1 *Bingham's New Cases*, 151, 159.

Don v. *Lipman*, 5 *Clarke and Finnelley's Reports, House of Lords.*

De la Vega v. *Vianna*, 1 *Barnewell and Adolphus' Reports*, 284.

British Linen Company v. *Drummond*, 10 *Barnewell and Cresswell's Reports*, 903.

CHAPTER XXXIV.

OBLIGATIONS—SUBSTANCE—REASON OF THE THING.

DCXLIX. We have now to consider the Law which in a real or apparent conflict of laws should govern an obligation as to (B) THE SUBSTANCE. (*a*)

DCL. In the prosecution of this inquiry it is proposed to observe the same order as has already been observed with respect to THE FORM of an obligation.

First, then, What are the true principles derived from *the Reason of the Thing ?* Obligations, like other Rights to Things, must appertain to a definite place. With respect to that Right to Things, as we have seen, (*b*) the person is taken out of his abstract individuality and brought within the domain of a local Law governing his right.

What is this place? What is, to borrow the expression of Savigny, (*c*) *the seat of the obligation ?*

The answer as to the peculiar class of rights termed Obligations has a peculiar difficulty. The object of other Rights is material and sensible ; but the object of an obligation is, comparatively speaking, incorporeal and invisible, and we must begin by giving a body to it, in order to answer the question. We are enabled to give this visible body to the obligation by considering its nature and its outward appearance or development.

Now, every obligation (1) arises out of visible facts, and (2) must be fulfilled through the medium of visible facts : and both classes of these facts must happen in a particular place.

(*a*) *Savigny*, VIII. s. 369—370.
(*b*) *Vide ante*, c. xxviii. and xxxiii.
(*c*) *Savigny*, VIII. s. 360.

Is the former or the latter place—or, in other words, is (a) the place where the obligation is entered into, or (β) the place where it is to be executed—the true seat of the obligation ? (d)

DCLI. (a) The reasons against considering *the place of the origin of the obligation* to be *the seat* of it appear to be, that this place is accidental, of a transitory character, and unconnected with the actual development and practical working of the obligation.

β. The principal reasons for considering *the place of the fulfilment of the obligation* to be the seat of it appear to be, because this place is intimately connected with the essence of the obligation ; for the essence consists in this, that something which previously to the obligation was uncertain and was within the competence of the obligor to do or not to do, has since the obligation become certain and necessarily binding on him. (e)

Now, this certainty and necessity constitute the fulfilment of the obligation. The place in which this certainty and necessity can be reduced to practice is the place which the parties to the obligation have had in view, for it is the place of the fulfilment. (f) This place must be identical with the proper

---

(d) " *Factorum genera,* unde obligatio oritur sunt illa, quæ ante com-" memoravi, quatuor, contractus, quasi contractus, maleficium, quasi " maleficium."—*Donellus,* lib. XVII. c. 14, p. 60, 30.

Donellus, lib. XVII. c. xvii. to end of c. xvii., well deserves the most careful study on this subject.

(c) The obligations of *do ut des facio ut facias* &c., are, in truth, *double* obligations, and do not impugn the position in the text.

(f) *Donellus,* lib. XVII. c. 12. p. 51 :

" Jure communi omnino quatuor res sunt quæ eos, qui ex personâ " suâ conveniuntur* jurisdictione ejus apud quem agitur subjiciunt—— " Domicilium litigatoris in teritorio judicis constitutum—Obligatio, " quâ de agitur, ibi contracta—Res ita sitæ de cujus proprietate aut " possessione agitur. Judicium ibi apud cum cæptum". . . . " * est " autem *convenire* aliquem, coram appellare, cum præsente agere, de re " aliquâ qui nobis de eæ re respondeat : ut præsens quidem dicatur *con-* " *veniri,* absens autem per præsentem defendi." (Ch. xi. 49, 40.)

forum to the adjudication of which the obligation is *naturally* and *by the free will of both the parties* made subject. But though the seat of the obligation and this jurisdiction to which it is *naturally* subject are in truth one, this remark nevertheless does not apply to an accidental *forum*, or even to the *forum domicilii* of the defendant, which, according to the opinion of the best jurists, may be always resorted to by the plaintiff. (*g*)

Many of the earlier writers were of opinion that the place of jurisdiction was identical with the place of the origin of the obligation; an error which, as Savigny remarks, arose from confounding all obligations with contracts, and which led them to use the expression *forum contractûs*, which is unsatisfactory and unscientific, however generally adopted, and which arises from a misapprehension of a passage, which will presently be noticed, in the Roman Law.

It is to be observed, however, that even these writers admit so many exceptions to their rule as practically to destroy it. Modern writers, on the contrary, usually abandon this rule, and in lieu of it identify the place of jurisdiction with the place of the fulfilment: and rightly, if this latter be correctly determined.

It is to be always remembered that in obligations it is the will of the contracting parties and not the Law which fixes the place of the fulfilment—whether that place be fixed by *express words* or by *tacit implication*—as the place to the jurisdiction of which the contracting parties elected to submit themselves. This jurisdiction, again, is intimately connected with the particular Law which is to be applied to govern the obligation.

DCLII. The question, therefore, as to what is *the seat of an obligation* is one of theory only, but nevertheless the consideration of it assists the answer to the two practical questions—viz.,

---

(*g*) *Savigny*, viii. s. 355 (72), s. 370 (212), s. 372 (248).

I. To what jurisdiction is each obligation subject?

II. What local Law is applicable to it?

As, generally speaking, these two coincide, the same answer applies to both.

According to Savigny (*h*) that jurisdiction and that local Law are to be found—

1. In the place where the will of the parties has fixed the fulfilment of the obligation, whether this will be directly expressed, or be necessarily deducible from the nature of the acts which accompany the obligation.

2. In default of any place so fixed, then in the place where the obligor carries on the business which gave rise to the obligation.

3. In the place of the origin of the obligation, when it happens to be identical with the domicil of the obligor.

4. In the place of the origin of the obligation, though it be not the domicil of the obligor, if the circumstances show that this is the place of the fulfilment contemplated by the parties.

5. In all other cases in the domicil of the obligor.

DCLIII. Though the place of *special jurisdiction* and the *local Law* of the obligation thus generally coincide, there is one important difference between them.

The plaintiff or obligee may always elect at his pleasure the *forum* either of the *special* or of the *general jurisdiction;* viz., that of the domicil of the defendant or obligor. But the plaintiff or obligee alone cannot abandon at his pleasure the *local Law* applicable to the obligation, that being always exclusively determined either by a specified place of fulfilment, or in default of that by the place of the origin of the obligation, or by the domicil of the obligor, according to the circumstances of each case.

DCLIV. As all the foregoing rules rest upon the presumption that the obligor has voluntarily submitted himself to a particular

---

(*h*) VIII. s. 370 (226-7), 372 (247).

local Law, that presumption may be rebutted either by an express declaration to the contrary, or by the fact that the obligation is illegal by that particular Law, though legal by another. The parties cannot be presumed to have contemplated a Law which would defeat their engagements. Nor is it to be understood that these rules as to the seat and the local Law of obligations, though generally applicable, can be without exception applied to every possible question of legal right arising out of an obligation.

This is a subject which requires a profound and comprehensive study of the different kinds of obligation and of the different questions of legal right arising from them. (*i*)

DCLV. Secondly—

As to the doctrine relating to this subject to be collected from the Roman Law.

This question again subdivides itself into two inquiries :

1. What is the general doctrine of the Roman Law as to the true *place* or *seat of the obligation ?*

2. What is the doctrine of the Roman Law relative to a *conflict of Laws* of different states upon this matter?

(I.) With respect to the general doctrine of the Roman Law as to the true *place* or *seat* of the obligation. (*k*)

The true rule of the Roman Law appears to be, that, if the place of fulfilment be not determined by the express words of the Contract, the debtor must fulfil his obligation wheresoever he is sued, *ubi petitur ;* so that the place of fulfilment would depend, according to this Law, upon the option of the creditor. He might choose the *forum originis* or the *forum domicilii;* and the debtor might have various *domicilia*, each sufficient at least to found a jurisdiction for this purpose. According to the Roman Law, therefore, the *place of fulfilment* would not determine the *place of jurisdiction*, but would be determined

---

(*i*) *Savigny*, viii. s. 372, s. 374.
(*k*) *Savigny*, viii. s. 370.

by it (*l*). The leading passages which prove that such is the principle of the Roman Law are the following, taken

(*a*) From the title (*m*) " De annuis legatis et fideicommissis."

" Cum in annos singulos quid legatum sit, neque ascriptum,
" quo loco detur ; *quocunque loco petetur, dari debet ;* sicuti
" ex stipulatu, aut nomine facto petatur."

(*β*) From the title (*n*) " De judiciis et ubi quisque agere
" debet."

" Quod legatur, siquidem per personalem actionem exigetur,
" *ibi dari debet, ubi est :* nisi dolo malo hæredis subductum
" fuerit : tunc enim ibi dari debet, ubi petitur. Preterea quod
" pondere, aut numero, aut mensurâ continetur : ibi dari debet,
" ubi petitur ; nisi adjectum fuerit, *centum modios ex illo*
" *horreo*, aut *vini amphoras ex illo dolio*". The passage continues, with a limitation indeed, to be presently more fully noticed—" Si autem per in rem actionem legatum petitur,
" etiam ibi peti debet, ubi res est. Et, si mobilis sit res, ad
" exhibendum agi cum hærede poterit, ut exhibeat rem, sic
" enim vindicari a legatario poterit."

(*γ*) From the title (*o*) " De legatis et fideicommissis."

" Cum res legata est, si quidem propria fuit testatoris, et
" copiam ejus habeat heres, moram facere non debet, sed eam
" praestare. *Sed si res alibi sit, quam ubi petitur, primum*
" *quidem constat, ibi esse præstandam, ubi relicta est,* nisi
" alibi testator voluerit nam si alibi voluit, ibi praestanda est,
" ubi testator voluit, vel ubi verisimile est cum voluisse. Et
" ita Julianus scripsit tam in propriis, quam in alienis legatis.
" Sed si alibi relicta est, alibi autem ab herede translata est
" dolo malo ejus, nisi ibi præstetur, ubi petitur, heres con-

---

(*l*) Thereby, in Savigny's opinion, reversing the true order of things ;
" So wird also durch jene Lehre das wahre Sachverhaltniss geradezu
" umgekehrt". VIII. s. 370 (230).

(*m*) *Dig.* lib. xxxiii. t. i. 1.

(*n*) *Dig.* lib. v. t. i. 38.

(*o*) *Dig.* lib. xxx. t. i. 47.

" demnabitur doli sui nomine ; ceterum si sine dolo, ibi præ-
" stabitur, quo transtulit. (S. 1.) Sed si id petatur, quod pon-
" dere, numero, mensurâ continetur, si quidem certum corpus
" legatum est, veluti frumentum ex illo horreo, vel vinum ex
" apothecâ illâ, ibi præstabitur, ubi relictum est ; nisi alia
" mens fuerit testantis, sin vero non fuit certa species, ibi erit
" præstandum."

(δ) From the title " *De condictione triticariâ.*" (*p*)

" Si merx aliqua, quæ certo die dari debebat, petita sit,
" veluti vinum, oleum, frumentum, tanti litem æstimandam,
" Cassius ait, quanti fuisset eo die, quo dari debuit ; si de die
" nihil convenit, quanti tunc, quum judicium acciperetur. Idem-
" que juris in loco esse, ut primum æstimatio sumatur ejus
" loci, quo dari debuit *si de loco nihil convenit, is locus spec-*
" *tetur, quo peteretur. Quod et de ceteris rebus juris est.*"

(ε) From the title " De rebus *creditis.*" (*q*)

" Vinum quod mutuum datum erat, per judicem petitum
" est ; quæsitum est, cujus temporis æstimatio fieret, utrum
" quum datem esset an quum lis contestata fuisset, an quum
" res judicaretur? Sabinus respondit : si dictum esset, quo
" tempore redderetur, quanti tunc fuisset, si non quanti tunc,
" quum petitum esset. Interrogatus, cujus loci pretium sequi
" oporteat? Respondit : *si convenisset, ut certo loco reddere-*
" *tur, quanti eo loco esset, si dictum non esset, quanti, ubi*
" *esset petitum.*"

DCLVI. We have next to consider what is the doctrine of
the Roman Law, relative to the application of a particular
local Law in the event of a conflict of laws of different states,
upon the subject of the true place or seat of an obligation. (*r*)

And the consideration need not occupy us longer than Pon-

(*p*) *Dig.* xiii. t. iii. 4.
Cf. *ante*, vol. i. p. 65.
(*q*) *Dig.* xii. t. i. 22.
(*r*) " Certi juris est, neminem judicem mittere posse actorem in
" possessionem eorum bonorum quæ ejus territorio subjecta non sunt."
Donellus, xviii. c. 14, p. 65—20.

toppidan's celebrated chapter which is headed " On snakes in
" Norway :" " There are no snakes in Norway."

There are no direct and positive rules on this subject of the
conflict of Laws in the Roman Law (s), therefore the theory *of
the place of the jurisdiction of the obligation,* which has been
just considered, is of the more importance as supplying the
answer to the question, what *local Law* is to be applied to
govern the obligation ?

Savigny strongly insists upon this to prove that the intimate
connection between the *place of jurisdiction* and the application of the *local Law,* is not only well founded in theory, but
fruitful of practical advantages ; for he argues that the same
presumption as to the voluntary submission of the obligor,
when he incurs the obligation, which founds both the *seat* and
the *jurisdiction* of the obligation, ought equally to determine
what is the *local Law* applicable to the obligation, and thus,
that when you have fixed the place of fulfilment you have at
the same time fixed the *local Law.*

The rules therefore, as has been stated, which determine the
former, may be reproduced to determine the latter consideration. The *local Law* which is to govern the obligation, therefore, is to be found—

1. If there be a place fixed for the fulfilment of the obligation, in that place.

2. If the obligation be connected with a business continually carried on by obligors, then in the place where the carrying on of that business is permanently fixed.

3. If the obligation arise from a single act of the obligor
done at his own domicil, then in the place where that act has
been done, and no subsequent change of domicil at all effects
the question.

4. If the obligation arise from a single act of the obligor

(s) " Fur welche Frage es an quellenmässigen Bestimmungen des
" Römischen Reehts eigentlich ganz fehlt." *Savigny,* viii. s. 372 (246).

See some isolated instances collected by the usual industry and commented upon with the usual acumen of the same author, *ib.* s. 356.

done away from his domicil, but in a place which the circumstances show to have been intended as the place of fulfilment then in that place.

5. In the absence of all those predicaments, then in the domicil of the obligor.

DCLVII. It has been said that the Roman Law furnishes no direct and positive rules as to which Law, in the event of a conflict of laws, shall govern the obligation. (*t*)

It is proper, however, to notice in this place those passages from the Roman Law, which some writers have erroneously relied upon as furnishing such direct and positive rules, but which may be cited as indirectly bearing upon the subject.

" Semper in stipulationibus et in cæteris contractibus id " sequimur quod actum est. At si non pareat quid actum est, " erit consequens ut id sequamur, quod in regione in quâ " actum est, *frequentatur.*" (*u*)

" Si fundus venierit, ex *consuetudine* ejus regionis, in quâ " negotium gestum est pro evictione caveri oportet." (*x*)

In the first place, it is to be observed that these passages refer to local *customs*, and not to local Laws.

In the second place, their object is to furnish a rule of *interpretation* (*y*) for a Contract; for instance, that it shall be presumed, unless the contrary appear, that the parties to a contract intended to conform to the *usage* of the country in which it was made. With respect to the second citation, it may be also a presumption that the parties to the contract intended to submit themselves to the Law of a specific *place:* the words

---

(*t*) *Savigny,* viii. s. 356, s. 372.

Fœlix says that the passages hereafter referred to were rules adopted in case of conflict between different " *usages* " of the Roman Empire ; " ces decisions peuvent indubitablement être invoquées aujourd'hui " comme raison écrite." Sec. 96.

(*u*) *Dig.* l. t. xvii. s. 34, *De Reg. Jur.*

(*x*) *Dig.* xxi. t. ii. s. 6, *De Evict.*

(*y*) The same remark applies to this passage: " Quæ sunt moris et " consuetudinis in bonæ fidei judiciis debent venire."— *Dig.* xxi. t. i. " s. 31, s. 20, *De ædilitio Edicto.*

ejus regionis in quâ negotium gestum est exclude, Savigny observes, some other region or place. But what place? He concludes that both the parties to the Contract were domiciled in the *same* place—in that place there prevailed a particular usage different from the ordinary usage, with respect to *evictions*, and the jurisconsult decided that the price to be paid under the eviction must be estimated not according to the general usage, which is excluded, but according to the particular usage of the particular place.

This construction of the foregoing passage in the Digest, is to be borne in mind in considering two further passages usually cited upon this subject in the Digest :

"Venire bona ibi oportet, ubi quisque defendi debet, id "est—ubi domicilium habet—aut ubi quisque contraxit. "Contractum autem non utique eo loco intelligitur, quo nego- "tium gestum sit, sed quo solvenda est pecunia." (z)

"Contraxisse unusquisque in eo loco intelligitur, in quo, ut "solveret, se obligavit." (a)

The last of these passages speaks of the *jurisdiction*, not of the *local Law* : the former passage is so loosely worded that it may refer to either. It has been seen that Savigny maintains that the *jurisdiction* and the *local Law* are inseparably united.

DCLVIII. Thirdly—

We have to consider what are the express provisions of Modern Codes upon this subject.

The Prussian Code (b) contains provisions having for their object to ensure an equality of rights between Foreigners and Native subjects in their dealings with each other. This is the general principle of this code ; the exceptional departures (c) from it have, Savigny assures us, their origin in the benevolent

---

(z) *Dig.* xlii. t. v. 1, 2, 3, *De reb. auct. jud.*

(a) *Dig.* xliv. t. vii. 21, *De oblig. et act.*

(b) *Savigny*, viii. s. 372.

Wächter, ii. 1—9.

Pr. Allgem. Land Recht, Einleitung, s. 23—25 : compare s. 34 with 23.

(c) *A. L. R. Einleitung,* s. 27—35.

intention of protecting certain legal acts of foreigners from consequences of nullity, which might result from the collision of local Prussian laws; and not in the intention of subjecting foreigners to the exclusive authority of Prussian Law.

The same author remarks, that the doctrine respecting personal and real statutes which prevailed at the time of the compilation of the code, has exercised a great influence upon the provisions relating to foreigners, and that to the imperfections of this doctrine are chiefly to be ascribed certain doubts and difficulties in the application of the principle to the Law of succession and inheritance.

DCLIX. The Austrian Code (d) is very similar to the Prussian upon this subject. It recognizes the equality of rights between the foreigner and native subject; and contains, like the Prussian Code, certain provisions for the purpose of preventing Contracts and agreements between them from being invalidated by local ordinances.

DCLX. The French Code (e) contains but few provisions relative to the collision of domestic and foreign Laws. But the principle of an equality between foreigners and native subjects, as to the acquirement and enjoyment of civil rights, is distinctly asserted therein.

DCLXI. Though the French Code be silent on the subject, it has been expounded by French jurists, such as Merlin, Massé, and Fælix, in a manner worthy of a country to which the science of Law is so largely indebted. Fælix (f) thus lays down the general Law on this subject, in accordance with Merlin and with the decisions of the French tribunals: " Le " principe général en cette matière est que les parties contrac- " tantes ont eu l'intention de se conformer dans leurs conven- " ventions à la loi du lieu où celles ci ont été consenties et " sont devenues parfaites, et, par suite de les soumettre à cette

---

(d) Oesterreich. Gesetzbuch, s. 4, ss. 33—37.

(e) Code Civil, art. 11—13.

(f) L. 2, t. i. c. 2, s. 1.

Merlin, Rep. v. Etranger.

" loi ; en d'autres termes, que *la valeur intrinsèque, la sub-*
" *stance, le lien* (vinculum juris) des conventions depend de la
" loi du lieu où elles ont reçu leur perfection ; l'acte valable
" ou nul d'après cette loi le sera également partout." And he
adds—" La même loi est encore applicable lorsque la validité
" intrinsèque de la convention n'etant pas contesteé il y a sim-
" plement lieu de *l'interprêter.*"

But to this statement of a general rule he immediately sub-
joins five important exceptions.

The first, alone, is so considerable as to shake the foundations
of the rule : viz., when the act or Contract is to be *executed* in
a country different from that which it is *made.*

In the opinion of the writer of these pages, as will presently
be seen, this exception is the rule, and the exception and rule
should change places.

The *second* exception is one already referred to, and universally admitted when the Contract is contrary to the morality or public policy of the state.

The *third* exception is when the court has to decide, not on
the substance of the plaintiff's claim (*le fond de la demande*),
but on the defendant's particular replication to it (*des défenses*). (*g*)

It can scarcely be doubted, however, that whatever may be
said, and something is said in a later chapter as to the mode
of procedure and all that appertains to it being governed by
the *lex fori*, that Fælix errs in ranging under that Law what
foreign jurists call *défense* or *exception péremptoire, i. e.*, a
plea to the validity of the obligation itself, and not merely
the technical defence which is implied by the simple term
exception.

The *fourth* exception is when two or more fellow-citizens
enter into a Contract in a country equally foreign to both.

In this case Fælix follows John Voet (*h*) in pronouncing,
that if the Contract be in accordance with the Law of their

(*g*) *Fælix, ib.* s. 100.
(*h*) *Ad Dig.* tit. *De statutis,* n. 15.

common country it is valid everywhere, and at all events in their own country.

The *fifth* exception is when the Contract is entered into for the purpose of evading and defeating the Law of the country of one of the contracting parties. (*i*)

But this is an exception which Savigny rejects, and as to which M. Demangeat, the last editor of Fælix, thinks it open to the discretion of the judge to say whether the Contract shall be null and void or some other penalty be inflicted. (*k*)

DCLXII. To the foregoing exceptions, Fælix adds special considerations upon the following points:

1. Where the Contract or engagement has taken place or is connected with more places than one.

2. Where it has been effected by a mandatary or by correspondence.

3. With respect to the confirmation of Contracts.

4. With respect to changes in and modifications of Contracts.

5. With respect to conditional conventions or Contracts.

These special points will be considered in the following pages in which the doctrine of the English and N. A. U. States Courts, on the general subject of foreign contracts, is about to be discussed.

(*i*) *Fælix, ib.* s. 102.

k) *Fælix,* s. 82, *M. Demangeat's* note (*a*).

CHAPTER XXXV.

OBLIGATIONS—SUBSTANCE—DIVISION OF SUBJECT.

DCLXIII. We have next to consider what are the rules to be deduced from the writings of jurists and from the decisions of the tribunals in England and the United States of North America, upon a real or apparent conflict of laws with respect to the *substance* of obligations or contracts. But in prosecuting this inquiry it will be expedient to distinguish between—

1. The general Law relating to Obligations and Contracts.

2. The *lex mercatoria* or Law Merchant upon this subject, which again requires sub-division into—

a. The general Law Merchant.

β. The Law relating to Bills of Exchange.

DCLXIV. Story's eighth chapter in his Conflict of Laws, is rich in ample quotations from jurists of a date precedent to the present century, with the exception of the great civilian Donellus, to whom it is matter of surprise that he makes no reference, although this admirable commentator does not treat directly of the principles of obligations and contracts, and not directly of a conflict of the laws of different states.

Of the modern writers, such as Fælix, Massé, Demangeat, in France,—Rocco in Italy,—Wächter and Savigny in Germany,—Story refers, and but occasionally, to Fælix alone.

In the following pages the writings of these authors will be frequently referred to ; while for the later writers, with the exception of Donellus, Story will be very generally relied upon.

DCLXV. There are particular expressions of modern jurists upon the subject of obligations and contracts to the understanding of which the following observations may conduce. (b)

The *facts* which found a *legal right* are of two kinds, and, so to speak, perform two functions. (c)

1. They are either such as perform the general and necessary function of causing the *application* of an ascertained rule of Law.

2. Or they perform the particular and accidental function of necessitating the *making* a rule of Law, to meet the special case.

In the language of English jurisprudence, the former case would be governed by the application of the express words of a statute or the authority of a judicial precedent; the latter case would be governed by the new application of an old principle of Law.

Having regard to these two classes of facts, modern jurists have very generally adopted a division of the attributes of an obligation into—

1. *Essentialia;*
2. *Naturalia;*
3. *Accidentalia;*

A division which rightly implies that in an obligation there are inherent—

1. Attributes, without which the very notion of the obligation would be at an end; as, in a loan, the actual delivery of the thing lent.

2. Attributes which are inherent in the obligation, but which the will of the contracting parties may separate from it; as, the *diligentia*, which, as a matter of general Law, is acquired at the hands of the Vendor or Hirer.

(b) *Savigny, Oblig.* i. s. 4—18.

(c) These observations are applicable to other portions of Law, as well as to obligations: *ib.* 21.

3. Attributes, which are not, as a matter of general Law, inherent in the obligation, but which the will of the contracting parties may make so inherent (*pacta adjecta*).

DCLXVI. The Roman jurists recognised these distinctions: (*d*) but it is important to observe how they applied to them the technical terms of their legal vocabulary. They use two technical terms to express the *essentialia* of modern jurists.

1. *Substantia;*
2. *Natura;*

But they still more frequently use the term *natura* to express the *naturalia* of modern jurists.

In applying therefore the Roman Law, great care must be taken to ascertain in which sense the term *natura* is used in the passage cited.

DCLXVII. Many modern jurists also make use of the expression *autonomy*, as designating the case in which the *facts* founding the legal right are of the special character belonging to the latter of the two divisions just mentioned: but against this use of the term Savigny strongly protests. (*e*) It is a term borrowed from the Public Law of Germany, in which system it is used to designate a peculiar privilege of the nobles and of certain Corporations to govern themselves by a kind of domestic legislation. Having therefore a defined juridical meaning, the application of it, either to the case above mentioned or to the case in which persons voluntarily submit themselves to a particular local Law, is, in the opinion of this eminent man, to weaken its proper meaning, and to gain neither precision nor clearness by its novel use.

(*d*) " Quod si nihil convenit tunc ea præstabuntur quæ *naturaliter* " *insunt* hujus judicii potestate."—*Dig.* l. xix. t. 1, 11, 1.

" Potest mandatum ex pacto etiam *naturam suam* excedere."—*Dig.* l. xix. t. 5, 5, 4.

" Quotiens enim ad jus quod *lex naturæ ejus* tribuit de dote actio " redit."—*Dig.* l. ii. t. 14, 27, s. 3.

(*e*) *Oblig.* i. s. 4.

System des R. R. viii. s. 360, 113.

DCLXVIII. As this chapter will contain an investigation of the modern rules which govern the substance of foreign Contracts, or, according to the phrase to which in England we are most accustomed, the *conflict of laws* on this subject, it seems expedient to arrange the investigation so as to make it, in some degree at least, accord with what appears to be the best division adopted by continental jurists; that is, to consider the Law which governs—

I. The *validity, nature,* and *interpretation* (*f*) of the Foreign Contract.

II. The *immediate effects,* flowing *directly* from the nature of the Contract, and so bound up with it that without them there would be in fact no Contract. (*g*)   These are what French jurists designate as *les effets* as distinguished from *les suites.* So Fælix observes : " Les *effets* dérivent de la nature " même de l'acte ou de l'exercice du droit établi par l'acte."

III. The *mediate effects,* (*h*) flowing *indirectly* from the

---

(*f*) *Massé,* l. ii. t. ii. c. 1. s. 110, says, il faut distinguer entre—

1. *L'interpretation* (under which he includes the nature of the engagement).

2. *Les effets.*

3. *Les suites.*

Rocco, c. v. p. 319, 1 : Intrinseca validità dei contratti, natura e qualità d'essi, c. vi. p. 322.

Fælix, l. ii. t. i. c. ii. s. 96 : La valeur intrinsèque, la substance, le lien, l'interprétation.

Story, c. viii., in which the want of a preliminary notice of the heads under which the subject is distributed must be supplied, by referring the reader to s. 242, s. 263, s. 321, s. 322, s. 330. It will be seen from comparing s. 263 with s. 321, that Story confuses the distinct considerations of the *nature* and *effect* of Contracts.

(*g*) *Rocco,* c. vii. p. 328-9 : " Perciò le appelliamo *immediate* essendo " il risultamento diretto della convenzione è ad essa affatto inerenti."

Fælix, s. 109 : " Il ne faut pas confondre *les effets* des contrats avec *les* " *suites* accidentales qu'ils peuvent engendrer les effets, &c."

Massé, t. ii. s. 113 : Sometimes the division is, but less accurately, made into *suites immêdiatcs* and *suites accidentelles.*

(*h*) *Rocco, ib.:* " Queste si chiamano *mediate* perché per esistere vuolsi

nature of the Contract, and therefore requiring the happening of some previous event, as the condition of their existence, which is not required by the *immediate effect*. The *mediate effects* are not *inherent* in the Contract, which may exist without them. Indeed, the parties may stipulate for their absence. These are called *les suites* by French jurists: " Les suites," Fælix says, " n'ont pas une cause inhérente au Contrat même : " elles resultent d'événements postérieur au Contrat et qui " surviennent à l'occasion des circonstances dans lesquelles le " Contrat a placé les parties." (*i*)

Under the head of *mediate effects* Fælix includes the *accidental consequences ;* they are with perhaps more accuracy treated by Rocco as a distinct division, but it is proposed to consider them together in the following pages. (*k*)

These arise from some fact posterior to the making of the Contract, and neither directly nor indirectly flowing from it, but from the act of the parties subsequent to it, such as negligence, delay (*mora*), or any other fault in the fulfilment of the obligation, and the reparation of an error, defect, or fault by subsequent Ratification.

DCLXIX. First, according to the order which has been laid down, we have to consider the principles of comity applicable to the *validity, nature,* and *interpretation* of Obligations and Contracts. (*l*)

" una cosa di più che nelle immediate conseguenze non si chiede." He instances a *guarantee* for *eviction* in the event of the *dominium* of a thing sold not belonging to the seller.

(*i*) *Ib.* s. 109.

(*k*) " V'ha una terza specie di conseguenze, le quali nè *immediamente* " nè *mediammente* dal contratto ma *ex post facto* originano da un aveni- " mento posteriore ad esso come a dire dalla negligenza, dalla mora e " da *ogni colpa* incorsa in eseguendo l'obligazione, si sviluppano nella " esecuzione del contratto, sono un remoto risultamento delle relazione " in il contratto stesso ci metta ; ma necessarie non sono ad ottenére gli " effetti proprî di ciascuna obligazione, non hanno una causa inererite " alla convenzione."—*Rocco, ib.* 330-1.

(*l*) *Fælix,* liv. ii. t. i. c. ii. s. 1 : Valeur intrinsèque des engagemens bilateraux et unilateraux.

Story deals, as English and United States Lawyers generally do, with the whole question of *obligations* under the head of *contracts*, (*m*) and he remarks, that according to universally admitted principles every valid Contract requires—

α. That it should be made by parties capable of Contracting.

β. That it should be voluntary.

γ. That it should be on a sufficient consideration.

δ. That it should be lawful in its nature. (*n*)

We need not stop to inquire whether these positions are strictly accurate or the language sufficiently precise. Their general truth is apparent. He then lays down a canon, that if a Contract be valid in the place where it is made, it is valid everywhere. (*o*) There are, indeed, exceptions, such as have been already noticed on the general subject of the reception of Foreign Law. (*p*) He observes that the same rule applies, *vice versâ*, to the invalidity of Contracts. (*q*)

The next canon, relating to the substance of contracts, is that the *lex loci contractûs* (*r*) governs their (*s*)

1. Nature.
2. Obligation. (*t*)

(*m*) *Conflict of Laws*, chapter viii.

The Scotch Law may be said, theoretically at least, to preserve, as from the more philosophical structure of its jurisprudence might be expected, the distinction between the two. See *Bell's Comment.* (*ed. Shaw*, 1838), vol. ii. c. 2, " *Of Obligations and Contracts.*"

(*n*) S. 232, *ib.*

Kent makes a simpler division into—1, the obligation and construction of contracts; 2, the application of the remedy.

(*o*) S. 242.

(*p*) *Vide ante.*

(*q*) S. 243.

The next canon relates to the *form* and is that the formalities required by the *lex loci* for contracts are indispensable everywhere else : s. 260.

(*r*) *Vide ante*, for the impropriety of this phrase.

(*s*) S. 263.

(*t*) S. 263: " The *obligation* of a Contract is the duty to perform it, " whatever may be its *nature.*"

3. Interpretation.

4. Effects. (*u*)

DCLXX. This statement, however, respecting the paramount influence of the *lex loci contractûs*, though simple and clear enough at first sight, proves on further inspection to be, without an important qualification and limitation, a very unsafe guide in unravelling the jurisprudence on Foreign, or indeed English, contracts or obligations.

For much later in his chapter on "Foreign Contracts," Story is obliged to admit that "there is no doubt that the phrase *lex* " *loci contractûs* may have a *double meaning* or aspect, and " that it may indicate the place where the Contract is actually " made, or that where it is virtually made according to the " intent of the parties; that is, the *place of payment or per-* " *formance*." (*x*) Then he remarks that most of the foreign " jurists do expressly and directly recognise the rule, that where " the Contract is made in one place and is to be performed in " another, *not only may the Law of the latter be properly* " *called the locus contractûs*, but that it ought in all respects, " except as to the formalities, and solemnities, and modes of " execution, to be deemed the rule to govern such cases." (*y*) Nay, he goes further, and inclines to admit the validity of the reasoning which establishes the converse proposition, namely, that a Contract invalid by the Law of the place where it is made, is valid if good by the Law of the place of payment. (*z*)

DCLXXI. The reader of the foregoing pages will not fail to observe how far these admissions and qualifications go, to justify the remark of Savigny, as to the impropriety of the expression *lex loci contractûs*, and to establish the strength of his position that the true seat of an obligation is the place of its fulfilment.

(*u*) S. 321.

(*x*) S. 298.

(*y*) S. 301.

Vidol v. *Thompson*, II. *Martin's (Amer.) Rep.* 23.

(*z*) S. 305. Cf. ss. 278, 286, 287, 290, 296, 300, 301, 301 *a*, 305.

Any diligent reader of Story's learned and valuable chapter on "Foreign Contracts" cannot fail to be perplexed by the indistinct manner in which the general principle of their construction is, in spite of the mass of authorities cited, laid down. It seems to the writer of those pages that the language of Gothofredus, cited by Story himself, in a later part of this chapter, enunciates the true principle in the concisest manner: " Hac verba ' Ubi contractum est,' sic intellige, ubi actum est " ut solveret." (a)

DCLXXII. It must be always borne in mind that the object of the tribunal which has to decide upon a Contract, must be to ascertain what was the intention of the parties; that intention, unless a positive Law of the state interposes a bar, is the Law of the Contract.

If that intention be not clear, recourse must be had to presumptions, either those of facts arising from the particular circumstances of each case; or those of Law, in the absence of such particularity. The latter, which have been established partly by judicial decisions, partly by general acceptance from a respect paid to the jurists who have enunciated them, are in truth the subject of the present consideration. (b)

DCLXXIII. The cardinal principle of the English Law upon the obligations and relations of the foreigner in England, is thus laid down by Lord Ellenborough : " We always import," says this learned judge, " together with their persons, the ex- " isting relations of foreigners as between themselves according " to the Law of their own countries; except, indeed, where " those laws clash with the rights of our own subjects here, and " one or other of the laws must necessarily give way, in which

---

(a) *Gothofred*. N. 10, ad *Dig*. 1. xxii. t. i. 1.

(b) *Fœlix*, s. 96, says—" Lorsque les contractans n'ont pas expressé- " ment adopté la loi du lieu où le contrat a été passé alors commencent " les présomptions, toutes les législations sont d'accord pour établir " que lorsqu'il s'agit d'une convention le juge doit s'attacher principale- " ment à la commune intention expresse ou présumée des parties." He then cites the *Roman Law*, all the existing *Codes*, and *Kent*, xi. 554-5.

" case our own is entitled to the preference. This having been
" long settled in principle, and laid up among our acknow-
" ledged rules of jurisprudence, it is needless to discuss it
" further." (c)

There are obligations which must necessarily from their
nature be fulfilled or executed in a particular place : this original necessity furnishes a rule for the interpretation of the
obligation, for the Law of that particular place must have been
contemplated as the Law of the obligation by the parties to it.

This case is stated by Lord Mansfield, in one of those judgments which has made English Jurisprudence so largely indebted to him : " There is a distinction," this great jurist says,
" between local and personal statutes; local ones regard such
" things as are really upon the spot in England, as the statute
" of frauds, which respects bonds situate in this kingdom.   So
" stock-jobbing contracts and the statutes thereon have a refer-
" ence to our *local* funds ; and so the statutes for restraining
" insurances upon the exportation of wool, respect our own
" ports and shores.   Personal *statutes* respect *transitory* con-
" tracts, as common loans and insurances. (d)   In every dispo-
" sition or Contract, where the subject matter relates locally to
" England, the Law of England must govern and must have
" been intended to govern.   *Thus a conveyance or will of*
" *land, a mortgage, a Contract concerning stocks, must all*
" *be sued upon in England.*"   Lord Mansfield adds these
strong and clear expressions : " And the *local nature of the*
" *thing requires them to be carried into execution according*
" *to the Law here.*" (e)

DCLXXIV. And yet, as will be seen in the matter of testaments, "the local nature of the thing" bequeathed, does not,

---

(c) *Potter* v. *Brown*, 1 *East's Reports*, 124—130.

(d) *Robinson* v. *Bland* (leading English case), 1 *W. Blackstone's Reps.*
234—246.

(e) 1 *W. Blackstone's Rep.* 259 ; 2 *Burrow's Rep.* 1079, after second
argument on the case.

according to the English decisions, cause the English Law to govern the instrument, if the testator be domiciled abroad, and if the testament bequeath property, which the English Law considers as personal; *e. g.,* leasehold for any definite number of years, will be pronounced valid or invalid according to the Law of a foreign domicil by the English tribunals.   It should be remarked that Lord Mansfield, in the case just cited, uses the term *statute* in the sense affixed to it by civilians.

DCLXXV. As to the *validity* of the Contract, the presumption of Law is, in the absence of an express declaration or a strong counter-presumption, that the parties intended to observe the Law of the place in which the Contract was made. (*f*) " La valeur intrinsèque," Fælix says, " la substance, le lien (*g*) " (*vinculum juris*), depend de la loi du lieu où elles ont reçu " leur perfection ; l'acte valable ou nul d'après cette loi le sera " également partout." (*h*)

The same rule applies to what is termed *the nature* (*i*) of the Contract, but which is perhaps more properly included under the next category of *interpretation.*

DCLXXVI. The Court of Louisiana, in one of its latest decisions, expresses itself as follows : " The idea that the Law " of a man's domicil follows him through the world, and " attaches to all his contracts, is as novel as unfounded. " The proposition was not, indeed, maintained in general " terms ; but that offered to the court in relation to the " Contract is identical with it ; and it is impossible for us not

---

(*f*) *Trimby* v. *Vignier,* 1 *Bingham, New Cases,* 151-9 ;

De la Vega v. *Vianna,* 1 *Barnewell & Adolphus, Rep.* 284 ;

British Linen Company v. *Drummond,* 10 *Barn. & Cresswell,* 903,—are the leading English cases.

Bank of United States v. *Donally,* 8 *Peters' Rep.* 361—372 ;

Wilcox v. *Hunt,* 13 *Peters' Rep.* 378-9,—are the leading cases in the U. S. of North America.

(*g*) *Fælix,* s. 97, calls all these *solennités intrinsèques.*

(*h*) *Fælix,* s. 96.

(*i*) *Vide ante.*

to feel, that, if the defendant and appellant are to have the
Contract decided by the laws of Louisiana, it will be equivalent to a declaration of this amount, that an inhabitant of
this state carries its laws with him wherever he goes, and
they regulate and govern his contracts in foreign countries;
that, whether a man contracts with him in Paris or London,
our municipal regulations are the measure of the rights and
duties of both parties to the Contract. That the legislature
of Louisiana may have a right to regulate the contracts of
her own citizens in every country so long as they owe her
allegiance, may or may not be true. But where the citizen
contracts abroad, with a foreigner, it is evident the rule must
be limited in its operation. The legislature may refuse permission to enforce the agreement at home; but abroad, and
particularly where the agreement is entered into, it is valid.
*The general rule, however, is never to extend the prohibi-
tion to contracts made abroad unless there be an express
declaration of the legislative will.*" (k)

DCLXXVII. The following extract from a letter of Sir L.
Jenkins, to Charles II., contains a clear statement of what
were, in that very learned civilian's opinion, the true principles
of international Law respecting the execution of a bond of
foreign obligors.

" That whether the bond in question was sealed and de-
" livered in Scotland or in England, your majesty may please,
" if it be transmitted, or remaining in the registry of the
" Admiralty of Scotland, to order the register of that court
" (who by his office stands chargeable with it) to transmit
" hither the original bond; *That the petitioner may have the
" remedy which the Law affords upon a bond against the
" sureties living in England, it being usual in aid of justice,
" as in all other places of Christendom, so in these your
" majesty's two kingdoms, to have the benefit of Law, and*

(k) *Arago* v. *Currell*, 1 *Louisiana* (*Amer.*) *Rep.* 528. Mr. Justice
Martin delivers opinion of court, cited in *Story's Conflict of Laws.*
(4 *Amer. Edition*) pp. 447-8, note.

" *execution where the obligors in a bond do live, though the*
" *bond itself were not made in the same kingdom.*

"This is the constant usage in all parts where the Civil
" Law obtains, and I myself can, upon experience, witness the
" practice of it in Scotland ; for a merchant of Aberdeen,
" having become bound to me in a statute merchant of £3,000
" in the manner and form peculiar to England, I (being in-
" trusted for a stranger) have been lately forced to sue that
" statute merchant, and having transmitted the original bond
" into Scotland I have had very good justice before the lords
" of your majesty's sessions there, and execution against the
" party, though there be no such form of obligation as our Eng-
" glish statute merchant is, received or known in Scotland."(*l*)

DCLXXVIII. We have considered the principles of Law
applicable to the *validity* and *nature* of the Contract.

We next approach the question of the *interpretation* of the
Contract. (*m*)

The rule of the English and North American United States
lawyers upon this matter is, "that the interpretation of the
" Contract must be governed by the Law of the country where
" the Contract is made ; " (*l*) but Story, who lays down this
rule, immediately adds, " especially in interpreting ambiguous
" contracts ought the domicil of the parties, *the place of exe-*
" *cution*, the various provisions and expressions of the instru-
" ment, and other circumstances implying a *local reference*, to
" be taken into consideration." (*n*)

DCLXXIX. The foreign jurists (*o*) say that there are three

(*l*) *Life of Sir L. Jenkins*, vol. ii. p. 749.

(*m*) With respect to *Ships* there is a very peculiar provision in a
recent English Statute referring to the case of a conflict of laws—17 &
18 V. c. 104, s. 20 ; *vide post.*

(*n*) S. 272.

(*o*) "Lors donc que le lieu de l'execution, est celui du domicile des
" parties ou celui de la passation du contrat, on peut p er comme rè gle
" générale que c'est la loi du lieu de l'execution qui determine les effets
" solidaires de l'obligation. Mais lorsque l'obligation doit être exécutée
" dans un lieu qui n'est ni celui du domicile des obligés, ni celui du con-

sources from which, according to the circumstances of the case, the interpretation of a Contract may be derived :

1. The law of the state in which it is made.
2. The law of the state in which it is to be executed.
3. The law of the domicil of the parties. (*p*)

But it will be found on examination that the third is pretty much identical with the second, for the law of the domicil is resorted to because the presumption is' that the law was that which the parties intended should govern the execution of the Contract ; and it will also be found, though the matter is involved in the obscurity of redundant verbiage, that the *lex loci contractûs* practically means the Law of the place of execution, which, after all, is the Law which it is endeavoured to discover through the medium of legal presumption when the Contract is silent or ambiguous. (*q*)

DCLXXX. The Roman Law says, "Semper in stipulationi-
"bus et in cæteris contractibus id sequimur quod actum est ;
" aut si non pareat quod actum sit, erit consequens ut sequa-
" mur quod in regionie in quâ actum est frequentatur."(*r*) And
again, " Quæ sunt moris et consuetudinis in bonæ fidei judiciis
"debent venire." (*s*) Savigny shows, as has been seen, that the former passages applied to cases where both parties were domiciled at the place where the Contract was made ; but this distinction has not been observed by foreign codes or jurists.

The civil code of France, as we have seen, (*t*) reproduces the maxim (*u*) in these words : " Ce qui est ambigu s'interprète par

---

" trat j'inclinerais pour la loi du lieu du contrat quand les parties n'ont "pas la même nationalité ; et pour la loi du domicile, quand il s'agit " d'individus de la même nation contractant ensemble en pays êtranger." *Massé, Le Dr. Comm.* ii. 193.

(*p*) *Fœlix*, s. 94.

(*q*) *Merlin, Rep.* v. *Loi, add.* p. 690.

(*r*) *Dig.* l. t. xix. 34 (*De reg. jur.*).

(*s*) *Dig.* xxi. t. i. 31 (20) (*Ædilitio edicto*), *et vide Dig.* v. t. i. (*De judiciis*), *Dig.* xxi. t. ii. 6 (*De evict.*)

(*t*) *Vide ante.*

(*u*) *Art.* 1159.

" ce qui est d'usage dans le pays où le contrat est passé," though, according to Fælix, (x) this article of the French Code was not intended to refer to foreign contracts. But Delvincourt, (y) Toullier, (z) Merlin, (a) Massé, (b) are of the contrary opinion.

DCLXXXI. Merlin founds his opinion on the ground that those who contract in a state must be holden to submit themselves to the Law of that state. Massé, pronouncing this opinion of Merlin to be a resolution of one question by another, puts the adoption of the Law of the state on the ground that there is no other Law by which the will of the contracting parties can be interpreted.

But Massé does not apply this rule to parties domiciled in the same state, in which case he thinks that the place of execution, in the absence of contrary proof, furnishes the rule. Massé further agrees with Boullenois and Dumoulin that no rule of Law over-rides the intention of the parties when that can be discovered. Dumoulin therefore says, with truth as well as energy, " Quia putent ruditer et indistincté quod debent " ibi inspici locus et consuetudo ubi sit contractus ; quod est " falsum ; quin imo jus est in tacitâ et verisimili mente con- " trahentium."

DCLXXXII. In truth, to those who hold absolutely the doctrine of *locus regit actum* as applicable, not merely to the form (a subject discussed in the last chapter), but to the validity, nature, and interpretation of the obligation, a question of no mean difficulty presents itself for solution—namely, Is this rule applicable to foreigners temporarily commorant or *transient*, as well as to *domiciled* persons ? *Donellus* observes, with respect to the *mercator*, the *advena*, and the *maritus in causâ dotis*, that these persons constitute an exception

---

(x) *Fælix*, s. 120.

(y) *Ibid.*

(z) *Ibid.*

(a) *Rep.* v. *Loi, add.* p. 590.

(b) *Le Droit Comm.* ii. 153.

to the rule, that the defendant must defend himself *ubi contraxit*, because in these special cases there was a *tacit* agreement to the contrary in the original Contract. (*c*)

DCLXXXIII. It is well observed by Savigny, (*d*) that there are two senses in which the expression *interpretation* may be used, a *general* and a *restricted* sense. According to the former, the application of every rule of Law which supplies what is not literally stated in the Contract, falls under the category of interpretation. It is manifest, however, that this generalisation of the expression deprives it of any proper and peculiar signification. In order to give it this, a restricted sense must be imposed upon it; it must be confined to cases of doubt arising from the defective structure or ambiguous expressions of the Contract. It is a question of fact, like the interpretation of a Law. The object is in both cases to ascertain the true meaning which the oral or written words were intended to convey.

It is in this sense that the Roman Lawyers said, " Id sequi- " mur quod *actum est*," (*e*) "in obscuris inspici solere *quod* " *verisimilius est*, aut *quod plerumque fieri solet.*" (*f*)

DCLXXXIV. Interpretation is not therefore, according to Savigny, a question of the application of a *lex loci*, though the local language may serve to explain the mind of the contracting parties; but if the question be, what place furnishes the language which is the subject of doubt, Savigny denies that the answer can be either the place in which the Contract was entered into, or the place in which it is to be executed.

Savigny illustrates this position by the case of a Contract effected by correspondence. The language of the Contract in

---

(*c*) *Comm.* l. xvii. cap. xiv. p. 64, *ed. Francf.* 1595.

(*d*) *Savigny, R. R* .viii. s. 374. He selects as the principal authors on this point of interpretation, *Boullenois*, t. ii. *obs.* 46, 10 *règle*, p. 489—538 ;

Story, s. 272—280 ;

Wächter, Archio füt die Civil. Praxis, b. xix. s. 114—125.

(*e*) *Dig.* l. l. t. xix. 34, *De Reg. Juris.*

(*f*) *Ib.* 114.

this case is to be construed by the usage of the place in which the writer of the first letter dwelt, not by the usage of the place in which the letter was received and accepted, although this is the place in which the Contract was concluded, because the writer of the first letter must be presumed to have had the meaning of the language of the place in which he dwelt, and from which he was writing, present to his mind at the time.

Wächter furnishes another illustration in support of the same position. An Insurance Company (*g*) at Leipsic contained among its printed terms an exception in the case of a *disturbance* of the *public peace (Aufruhr, émeute)*. An insured property having been set fire to from without (*auswärts, dehors*) the question arose whether the company were protected by the exception, inasmuch as the legal construction of what constituted a disturbance of the public peace (*Aufruhr*) varied in different states. Wächter rules rightly, according to Savigny, that the Saxon Law, under the dominion of which the terms of the insurance were made, furnishes the true interpretation.

DCLXXXV. The domicil is, according to Savigny, an important element in the question of interpretation. If the Contract be made orally or in writing in the place in which both parties are domiciled, the language of that place is unquestionably applicable to the interpretation.

This is not necessarily the case when only one party has his domicil in that place. It is then a matter of inquiry whether it is probable that the non-domiciled party was acquainted with, and intended to use, the language according to its meaning at that place.

The position of the Roman Law, " Id sequamur quod in " regione *in quâ actum est*, frequentatur," (*h*) is not opposed to this doctrine ; for this text proceeds on the natural supposition that both parties are domiciled in the place of the Contract. The same remark applies to another passage : " Si fun-

---

(*g*) *Fire*, apparently.
(*h*) *Dig*. l. l. t. xix. 34.

" dus venierit ex consuetudine ejus regionis in quâ negotium
" gestum est pro evictione caveri oportet." (*i*)

DCLXXXVI. Upon the same principles Savigny contends
that you cannot consider the language of the place of the
execution of the Contract as furnishing the invariable guide
for its interpretation ; though there are certain portions of a
Contract to it may be so considered. For instance, if the
Contract stipulate for a particular sum of money, merchandize according to a particular weight or measure, a quantity
of land according to a particular measurement in a particular
country, and the terms of the Contract which express the
value and the weight, or the admeasurement, admit of more
than one interpretation, the interpretation supplied by the
language of the place of execution is to govern, both because
that was in all probability in the mind of the contracting
parties ; and because it would not unfrequently be impossible
to execute the Contract according to any other interpretation. (*k*) Such it may be observed is the express provision
upon the subject in the Prussian code. (*l*)   .

DCLXXXVII. Here again it is to be observed that there
are passages in the Roman Law which are apparently but not
really at variance with these principles.

For instance, in that system of jurisprudence it is said, that
in the case of a *stipulation* the interpretation is to be against
the person who stipulates ; (*m*) in the case of sale, against the
seller ; (*n*) in the case of letting, against the proprietor or lessor.

(*i*) *Dig.* l. xxi. t. ii. 6.

(*k*) *Savigny, ib.* ; *Boullenois,* p. 496-8.

(*l*) *A. L. R.* i. v. s. 256-7.

(*m*) *Dig.* xxxiv. t. v. 26 : " Cum quæritur in stipulatione quid acti sit
" ambiguitas contra stipulatorem est."

Ib. xxxv. t. i. 38 (18) : " In stipulationibus cum quæritur quid actum
" sit, verba contra stipulatorem interpretanda sunt."

(*n*) *Dig.* ii. t. xiv. 39 : " Veteribus placet pactionem obscuram vel
" ambiguam venditori et qui locavit nocere, in quorum fuit potestate
" legem apertius conscribere." *Ib.* xviii. t. i. 21 : " Labeo scripsit ob-
" scuritatem pacti nocere potius debere venditori, qui id dixerit quam

The reason assigned is, that, as it was in the power of these parties to have prevented by a clearer statement any doubt as to their meaning, the difficulty is, in fact, imputable either to their negligence or their bad faith.

But these passages expressly apply to terms or words which are *in themselves* obscure or equivocal ; whereas the principles and doctrine of interpretation which we have been just considering apply to expressions which are *not in themselves* obscure or equivocal, but have different meanings in different places, though in each place their meaning is clear and unambiguous.

DCLXXXVIII. Savigny complains that Story and a host of writers resolve the question of interpretation into a rule of local Law, whether it be the place of making or executing the obligation.

Boullenois, (o) Savigny, (p) Wächter, (q) and others hold that the true object is not to establish an inflexible rule of Law, but to ascertain in each case the real intention of the contracting parties by reference to the general rules of interpretation applicable to the construction of contracts.

DCLXXXIX. It is a matter of controversy whether a limitation to that maxim is or is not furnished by the fact, that the Contract is made *in transitu* by two foreigners belonging to the same country and not domiciled, but merely *commorant* in the place where the Contract is made.

Boullenois (r) and other jurists are of opinion that in this case the Law of the domicil governs the Contract. Story observes, " Without undertaking to say that the exception may " not be well founded in particular cases, as to persons merely

---

" emptori: quia potuit re integrâ rem apertius dicere." *Ib.* l. t. 17, 172 : " In contrahendâ venditione ambiguum pactum contra venditorem " interpretandum est."

(o) Pp. 494—498.

(p) VIII. s. 374.

(q) *Passim.*

(r) *Boullenois,* 2 *Observo.* lxvi. pp. 456, 489, 490; cited *Story,* s. 273.

" *in transitu*, it may unhesitatingly be said, that nothing but
" the clearest intention on the part of foreigners to act upon
" their own domestic Law, in exclusion of the Law of the place
" of the Contract, ought to change the application of the
" general rule.   And indeed, even there, if the performance of
" the Contract is to be in the same country where it is made,
" it seems difficult upon principle to sustain the exception." (*s*)

DCXC. Fælix decides that in this case the presumption of
Law is in favour of the place where the Contract is perfected—
that is, executed, as he puts it.

" Il arrive" (he says) " par fois que les parties négocient une
" convention pendant qu'elles parcourent ensemble divers lieux,
" quel sera alors le *locus contractûs ? Ce sera celui dans lequel*
" *le Contrat est devenu parfait.*   En effet, c'est là seulement
" que le *duorum pluriumve in unum placitum consensus* (*t*)
" est intervenu : la plupart des auteurs sont d'accord sur ce
" point."(*u*)

Titman and Wächter, however, think that the engagement
of each party should be decided by the Law of the domicil of
each.

Eichhorn is of opinion that each of the parties is limited to
such rights as the accidental place in which he happens to put
in force the Law may furnish.

" Mais" (continues Fælix) "alors il n'auroit pas de con-
" sentement mutuel des parties *in idem placitum* et par consé-
" quent pas de Contrat : donc ces deux systèmes sont inadmis-
" sible."

DCXCI. It should seem that proof, that the parties were
ignorant of the Law of the place of the Contract, would greatly
strengthen the reason for the exception in such a case.   If
the parties intended that the Contract should be performed
where it was made, the presumption would be very strong
that they intended the Law of the place to govern it.

(*s*) *Story*, s. 273.

(*t*) *Dig*. l. ii. t. xiv. 1, *De Pactis :* " Et est pactio duorum pluriumve
" in idem placitum consensus."

(*u*) *Fælix*, s. 104.

The case of a foreigner contracting with a native is materially different.

DCXCII. It is said, and as it should seem with perfect justice, that a Contract being, though valid in the place it is made, invalid if it be at variance with the Law of the place of its performance, the converse proposition is true; viz., that a Contract invalid where it is made is valid if in accordance with the Law of the place of its performance.

Upon this point the courts of England and the North American United States appear to be agreed. It is chiefly on questions of *interest*—a subject to be presently discussed—that this position of Law has been enunciated.(*x*)

DCXCIII. It will be observed that all the rules collected and laid down by Story respecting what he designates the *validity*, the *nature*, the *obligation*, the *interpretation* of contracts, presuppose or assume that the *place of performance* and the *place of the making of the Contract* are identical. But when they are not so—that is, neither by express statement nor by tacit implication—then these incidents of the Contract are, in conformity with the presumed intention of the parties, to be governed by the Law of the place of performance.(*y*)

In truth, this proposition was established by Lord Mansfield, the creator of our commercial Law, in one of the earliest cases which he decided: "The Law of the place" (he said) "can never " be the rule where the transaction is entered into with an " express view to the Law of another country, as the rule by " which it is to be governed."(*z*)

(*x*) *De Pace* v. *Humphreys*, 20 *Martin (American)*, p. 1, 30.
Connor v. *Bellamont*, 2 *Atk. R.* 381 *(Lord Hardwicke)*.
Stapleton v. *Conway*, 3 *Atk. R.* 727; 1 *Vesey's R.* 427.
Dewar v. *Span*, 3 *Durnford and East*, 425.
Story, s. 305.
2 *Kent's Comm.* (1851), p. 576, *lect.* 39.
(*y*) S. 280.
Andrews v. *Pond*, 13 *Peter's (American) Rep.* 65; leading case in the United States of North America.
(*z*) *Robinson* v. *Bland*, 2 *Burrows' Rep.* 1077-8.

DCXCIV. If no place of performance be specified in the Contract, or it be of such a character as to admit of being performed any where, then, according to the jurisprudence of England and the United States, it is governed by the Law of the place in which it is made.(*a*) So in a leading case decided by the House of Lords, Lord Brougham, speaking of a bill of exchange, drawn and accepted in Paris by a Scotchman domiciled in Scotland, said, " This therefore must be taken to " be a French debt, and then the general Law is, that, where " the acceptance is general, naming no place of payment, the " place of payment shall be taken to be the place of the con- " tracting of the debt."(*b*)

Acting on this principle the North American United States Courts have holden, that an antenuptial Contract made in reference to another country, as the future domicil of the parties, is governed by the Law of that domicil as to rights of personal property,(*c*) and also, that if a merchant in America orders goods from England and the English merchant executes the order, the Contract is governed by the Law of England on the ground that the Contract is there consummated.(*d*)

(*a*) *Story*, s. 282, 317, 345, 346.

(*b*) *Don* v. *Lippman*, 5 *Clarke & Finnelley's Rep.* 1, 12, 13 : *vide post*, in chapter on *lex mercatoria*, the leading case of *the Milburn*.

(*c*) *Le Breton* v. *Miles*, New York Court of Chancery, 8 *Paige*, 261. 11 *Kent Comm.* 575 (460), note.

(*d*) *Whiston* v. *Stodder*, 8 *Martin's Louis. Rep.* 93; 11 *Kent*, 575.

CHAPTER XXXVI.

CONTRACT — INTERPRETATION—MERCHANT ACCOUNTS.

DCXCV. We have now to consider the *second* division of this subject; viz., the *immediate effects* (*a*) of an obligation, those which are derived from the very nature of the obligation or the exercise of the rights directly flowing from it; *e. g.*, in a Contract of buying and selling, the delivery of the thing bought and the payment of the price for which it is bought are two immediate effects of the Contract. If the contracting parties have chosen to make a power of repurchase or redemption a part of the Contract, that, though not belonging abstractedly speaking to the obligation would by their act become one of the immediate effects of it. (*b*)

DCXCVI. In the event of doubt, such as must often arise in cases of a mixed nature, whether the parties had reference to the place of the making or the place of the performance of the Contract, the inclination of the judges in the United States of North America, which would probably be followed in England, has been to adopt the Law of the place of making.

DCXCVII. With respect to a class of immediate effects of Contract of great importance to the commercial code,—namely, the matter of *advances* and *sales*, and *mutual accounts of credit and debt* between merchants,—the courts of the North American United States have decided that advances are to be governed by the Law of the place where they are advanced; sales of goods by the Law of the place where they are re-

---

(*a*) *Vide ante*, p. 483.
(*b*) *Rocco*, p. 329.

ceived.(*c*) The rule has received practical illustration more frequently in the case of *balances of accounts.* For instance, a case arose in which goods had been consigned for sale in Trieste by a merchant of Boston, and advances were made by the *agent* of the consigners in Boston, to an amount exceeding the amount of the proceeds of the goods when sold. The consigners brought a suit to recover the balance, and the question was at what rate of exchange the balance should be allowed : this raised an earlier question—viz., where was the balance reimbursable ? at Boston, or Trieste ? The court held at Boston, where the advances had been made, and consequently allowed *the par of exchange* at Boston where it was payable ; but it held that if the advance had been made at Trieste the balance would have been reimbursible there. (*d*)

DCXCVIII. This case, it will be observed, introduces the question of *agency* in its effect upon the *interpretation* of foreign contracts.

The decision in it was delivered by Story from the judgment seat, and it is at variance with a later case decided in Louisiana. In that case an advance had been obtained in Louisiana from an agent of a foreign principal residing there, on merchandize to be shipped to and sold by the latter abroad ; the proceeds of the sale fell short of the advances. It was decided that the rate of interest, on a balance, due to the foreign principal, by reason of this deficiency, must be determined by the Law of the domicil of the principal, where the merchandize was sold.

The judges said, that, though this decision conflicted with that of Story, it was in accordance with the general mercantile

---

(*c*) *Story*, s. 282, 3, 4, 4*a.* Leading North American cases appear to be—

Corlidge v. *Poor*, 15 *Massachusets Rep.* 427.

Bradford v. *Harvey*, 13 *Mass.* 18.

Milne v. *Morton*, 6 *Binney's Rep.* 353, 359, 365,

Consequa v. *Fanning*, 3 *Johnson's Rep.* 587, 610.

(*d*) *Story*, s. 284*a.*

Grant v. *Hexley*, 3 *Sumner's* (*Amer.*) *Rep.* 523

opinion, which in a matter of this sort was entitled to great weight. (*e*)

DCXCIX. The Roman Law enumerates, with its usual perspicuity and conciseness, the categories of this class of conventions. " Labeo ait convenire posse vel re vel per epistolam, " vel per nuncium, inter absentes quoque." (*f*)

DCC. Savigny (*g*) considers the cases of a Contract concluded by correspondence, a Contract signed at different places, a Contract entered into by the oral declarations of an agent.

The more general opinion of continental and especially German jurists is, that a Contract by correspondence is made in that place in which the first letter was received and answered in the affirmative. The Law of this place, they say, governs the Contract. Savigny, however, rejects this opinion : he compares the writer of the letter to the traveller, who, for the purpose of making a Contract, pays a transient visit to the party, with whom he is about to contract ; and Savigny observes, that if their Contract be completed it would be governed as to its legal consequences, not by the Law of the place where the traveller sojourned for the moment, but by the Law of the place in which the Contract was to be executed. And so in the case of a Contract concluded by correspondence, the Law of the place of the intended execution, if any place be designated, governs the Contract ; and if no place of execution be specified, each of the contracting parties may invoke the Law of his domicil. (*h*)

According to the Prussian Code, when the Law of the respective domicils is different, that Law which is most favourable to the maintenance of the Contract is to be followed. (*i*)

If the Prussian Courts had to decide, not on the maintenance

(*e*) *Ballister* v. *Hamilton,* 3 *Louis. Ann. R.* (*Amer.*), 401.
Story (5th ed.), s. 284-6.
(*f*) *Dig.* l. ii. t. xiv. 2.
(*g*) VIII. s. 373, III A.
(*h*) " So gilt für jede Partei das Recht ihres Wohnsitzes." *Savigny, ib.*
(*i*) *A. L. R. i.* v. s. 113, 114.
Savigny, viii. s. 373.

but on the execution of the Contract, Savigny says the spirit of the Prussian Law would apply to each party the Law of his domicil.

Grotius says, that a Contract by correspondence (*per literas inter absentes*) ought to be governed *jure solo naturæ;* but what Law would be enforced by the *jus naturæ* in this instance he does not specify, though it would appear that it was not the Law of the place in which the Contract was actually entered into. (*k*)

DCCI. The Courts of the North American United States have established the following propositions, that—

1. Where a travelling agent to procure orders for goods, but without authority to sell, transmitted from one state to his principal in another state an order for goods to be sent to persons in the first-mentioned state, and the goods were so sent, it was held that the sale was made in the state where the principal was, and that its legality must be governed by the Law of that state. (*l*)

2. (*m*) A promissory note executed in Canada, and no place of payment mentioned, is to be treated as a note of that place, and the rights, duties, and obligations growing out of it, are to be determined by the laws of that province. (*n*)

3. Sureties, indorsers, and guarantees are liable according to the Law of the place of their Contract. (*o*)

4. The Laws of the state where a note is made payable

(*k*) " Quare etiam si peregrinus cum cive paciscatur tenebitur illis " legibus" (that is, the Law of the *civis*); " quia qui in loco aliquo con- " trahit, tanquam subditus temporarius legibus loci subjicitur. Planè " aliud erit si in mari pactio fiat aut in vacuâ insulâ, aut per literas " inter absentes; Talia enim pacta jure solo naturæ reguntur." Lib. xi. c. 9, 5, 3.

(*l*) *Woolsey* v. *Bailey,* 7 *Foster* (N. H.), 217.

Smith v. *Smith,* 7 *Foster* (N. H.), 244.

(*m*) *Vide post,* Chapter on Bills of Exchange.

(*n*) *Pech* v. *Hibbard,* 26 *Vt.* (3 *Deane*), 698.

(*o*) *Walker* v. *Forbes,* 25 *Ala.* 139.

govern the liabilities of the parties thereto; and such laws must be pleaded and proved as matters of fact. (*p*)

DCCII. (*q*) Casaregis, whose reasoning is adopted by Story, (*r*) points out that, when a merchant orders his correspondent to buy goods for him in a foreign country, and the correspondent executes the order by buying the goods of a third person, two contracts are created; " duo perficiuntur " contractus, Primus, *mandati,* inter mandantem et man- " datorium alter, *emptionis* et respectivè *venditionis* inter " eundem mandatorium, uti emptorem nomine mandantis, et " venditorem;" and he adds both these contracts—namely, that of mandate between principal (*mandans*) and agent (*mandatarius*), and that of purchase and sale between the vendor and the agent, as purchaser in the name of the principal, are completed or created in the place or residence of the agent or *mandatarius.*

The doctrine of Casaregis on this subject has been accepted both by England (*s*) and the North American United States. (*t*)

(*p*) *Pryor* v. *Wright,* 14 *Ark.* (1 *Barb.*), 189.

For notes of the above cases, see Putnam's United States Annual Digest, vol. ix. (1855), p. 378.

(*q*) *Discursus legales de Commercio,* 179, s. 1, 2.

(*r*) *Story,* s. 285.

(*s*) " If I residing in England send down my agent to Scotland, and " he makes contracts for me there, it is the same as if I myself went " there and made them," the Lord Chancellor observed, in *Pattison* v. *Mills,* 1 *Dow. & Clarke, Rep.* 342.

The same Law has been laid down with respect to an English corporation contracting by its agent in Scotland; the Contract is to be considered a Scotch Contract. *Albion F. & L. Insurance Company* v. *Mills,* 3 *Wilson & Shaw, Rep.* 218, 233.

(*t*) Story remarks (s. 286, note 2), on the difficulty of reconciling this doctrine with what appeared to be the opinion of the court and counsels in *Acebar* v. *Levi,* 10 *Bingham's Rep.* 376, 379, 381, the place of *payment* and *delivery* is in that case different from the place of *Contract:* no *decision,* however, hostile to the opinion in the text was given. Cf. *Story,* s. 262a. n. 1, s. 318, n.; *Vidal* v. *Thompson,* 11 *Martin (Amer.) Rep.* 23, 25.

DCCIII. A similar principle is applied by Casaregis and adopted by Story as to the *ratification*, (*u*) by a correspondent, of a purchase made by an agent without orders. The Contract is to be considered as governed by the Law of the place of purchase, and not by the Law of the place of ratification, because that refers back to the place and time of purchase. (*x*)

In accordance with this doctrine the acceptance by a person in one country of a bill drawn upon him by a person in another country, is, as will be seen, (*y*) a Contract in the place where the acceptance is made. (*z*)

(*a*) *Savigny* admits that this case affords a just exception to the rule, that the Law of the domicil of each subscriber or acceptor (*Unterzeichner*) should govern, and cites the Prussian Law, which is the general Law of Germany, on this point: by this Law, every engagement resulting from a bill of exchange is governed by the Law of the place in which the engagement is made; if, however, the bill be invalid by the law of the place in which it is made, but valid according to German Law, subsequent endorsements made in Germany are valid; and a bill drawn in a foreign land between two Germans, if conformable to the German Law, is valid in Germany. (*b*)

DCCIV. Hertius takes this view of a conflict of laws between the place of Contract and the place of ratification. If the ratification have for its object to supply additional proof or strength to the Contract (*ad conciliandam contractui majorem fidem*), then the Law of the place of the Contract is to prevail; but if the ratification gives validity to the Contract (*ut contractus sit validus*), then the Law of the place of the ratification is to prevail.

(*u*) *Ratification* is ranked by *Fœlix* among the *accidental consequences* of a Contract, s. 113; *vide post.*

(*x*) *Casaregis' Disc.* 179, s. 20, 64, 76, 80, 83; cited *Story*, s. 286, n.

(*y*) *Vide post*, separate chapter on this subject.

(*z*) *Story*, s. 286.

P. *Voet*, *De Stat.* s. 9, c. 2, s. 14.

(*a*) VIII. s. 373, 111.

(*b*) *Preussiche Gesetz: Sammlung* (1849), 68.

This view does not seem unreasonable, though Story appears to discountenance it. (c)

DCCV. A difficult question (d) upon the Law of agency (e) may arise out of mandatory or procuratorial instruments, called in England *letters of attorney* or *proxies*. It may be that a person resident in one state has authorized by a letter of attorney, duly executed in that state, his agent in another state to sell some moveable property in this second state. The principal dies, the agent sells the property in ignorance of but after the death. By the Law of some states—*e. g.*, Massachusetts—the death of the principal revokes the letter of attorney, and the act of the agent would be invalid; by the Law of other states—*e. g.*, France and Louisiana—the act of the agent done in *bonâ fide* ignorance of the death of the principal would be valid. (f)

If the principal reside in the state the Law of which revokes the letter of attorney, and the agent in the state the Law of which upholds it, which Law shall govern this Contract?

Though, as Story (g) remarks, there be no doubt that when an authority is given to an agent to transact business for a principal in a foreign state, the authority is, in the absence of proof to the contrary, to be construed and enforced according to the Law of that foreign state, yet Story cannot discover that this question has ever been decided " either at home or abroad."

(c) S. 286a.

Hertii opera de Collis. Legum, s. 4, n. 55.

The questions arising from the agency of the master of a ship will be considered in a separate chapter on Mercantile Law.

(d) *Story*, s. 286d.

(e) It is discussed here, though, strictly speaking, perhaps, it belongs to the category of *mediate* effects: *vide ante*, p. 483, *et post*.

(f) *Story, Conflict*, s. 286(d); *on Agency*, s. 488-9.

Code Civil of Louisiana, 300.

Code Civil (France), Art. 2008.

Pothier, Oblig. n. 81.

(g) S. 286d.

Owings v. *Hull*, 9 *Peter's (Amer.) Rep.* 607, 627-8.

It would seem, however, that his opinion rather inclines to
holding that the Law of the state in which the principal resided
should prevail. (*h*) But surely the first principle of Private
International Law—namely, the duty as well as the expedience
of upholding, wherever it is possible, *bonâ fide* transactions
with the subjects of foreign states—leads to a different conclusion, and is in accordance with the doctrine of France and
Louisiana.

DCCVI. This portion of the subject, relating to the law
applicable to contracts concluded by a correspondence, may be
not impertinently closed by the statement of Savigny's opinion.
He observes that—

" The greater number of contracts flow from the personal
" agreement of two parties. In this case the place in which
" the parties are both present, is also the place in which the
" obligation originates. This is the road which is most usually
" travelled, but it may be departed from by various ways.

" For instance, a particular Law or the will of the parties
" may render the observance of certain formalities necessary to
" the validity of the Contract; such as, that the Contract
" should be reduced into writing, or that there should be the
" intervention of a notary public or of a court of justice.

" In such cases the true place of the Contract is the place
" in which these formalities are executed, for previously to
" their execution neither party is obliged.

" A more difficult and a more frequent case is one in which
" the Contract is made, not by the parties in person, but by
" the intervention of an agent, or by deeds signed in different
" places, or, lastly, by the means of a simple correspondence
" by letter. As to this class of cases there is a great difference
" of opinion; such a case, in fact, embraces three distinct

(*h*) The analogies, moreover, to which Story refers as to the limited
authority of the master of a ship are questionable. *Vide post*, chapter in
which the Private International Law with respect to ships and shipping
is considered.

" questions, although the greater number of writers have not " discriminated them."

1. In what place was the Contract made?

2. What place furnishes the jurisdiction over it?

3. What place furnishes the local Law, to which it is subject?

" Upon the first question I do not hesitate to answer, that " the place of the Contract was the place in which the first " letter was received, and from which an affirmative answer " was sent; because there was expressed the agreement be- " tween the wills of the parties.

" The writer of the first letter is therefore to be considered " as having betaken himself to the residence of the other " party, and there to have received his consent.

" This doctrine has been adopted by various writers; others, " on the contrary, raise against it the following objections.

" The affirmative answer might have been, they urge, with- " drawn before it reached its destination; or have been an- " nulled by a revocatory declaration: the Contract, therefore, " is only complete in that place in which the writer of the " first letter received the answer, and became aware of the " consent of the other party.

" But it cannot be admitted that we may set aside the true " principles of Law on account of so exceptional a case. It " most frequently happens that the two declarations succeed " each other without the least difficulty of the kind suggested; " and if such difficulty should appear, the question could not " be decided without regard being had to a number of particu- " lar circumstances; so that for such a case the perfectly " arbitrary rule, which those who oppose my opinion lay " down, would be wholly insufficient.

" I pass on to the second question, in what place does " the jurisdiction over the obligation exist when the Contract " is affected through the medium of a correspondence by " letter?

" It might be answered, according to analogy, in that place " in which the first letter was received, and followed by an

" affirmative answer.   But this is absolutely inadmissible.   In
" truth, the sender of the first letter, can, at the utmost, be
" only likened to a traveller ; certainly not to one who has
" established a permanent residence at the domicil of the other
" party : he has not therefore submitted himself to the juris-
" diction of that place.

" A Contract made through the medium of a correspon-
" dence, can only, in its relation to each party, be considered
" as having been made at his own domicil, and as subjected to
" the special jurisdiction which appertains to every obligation
" considered in and by itself ; if, nevertheless, the Contract
" specified the place of its execution, this specification would
" determine the jurisdiction over the obligation.

" The particular nature and exigencies of a Contract affected
" by Promissory Notes or Bills of Exchange introduce impor-
" tant modifications of these principles.   Thus in that Law of
" Prussia which was the means of bringing about the new
" Law on Promissory Notes and Bills of Exchange throughout
" Germany—it was provided that not only did the place of
" payment and of domicil determine the jurisdiction, but
" that every party liable upon the Promissory Note or Bills
" of Exchange might be cited before that tribunal in which
" an action upon the note or bill had once been brought
" founded."

As to the third question, (i) Savigny is of opinion that the
local Law is that of the place of execution if any be specified ;
if none, then each party remains subject to the Law of his own
domicil.

DCCVII. The Prussian Code provides that, when a different
Law prevails at each domicil as to the *form* of the Contract, that
Law shall be followed which best maintains the Contract.   It
would be, Savigny thinks, in accordance with the spirit of this
Law to apply to the debt or obligation of each party the Law
of his own domicil.   He again excepts, on account of their

(i) VIII. s. 373.

peculiar character, notes and bills (*k*) from the application of this principle.

DCCVIII. It has been already observed (*l*) that Grotius, (*m*) speaking of a "pactio, inter absentes per literas," has said, "talia enim pacta solo *jure naturæ* reguntur." Savigny regrets that writers who maintain this opinion have not stated in what treatise of natural Law directions upon the subject are to be found.

DCCIX. Among the *immediate effects* of the Contract, Fælix includes the delivery of the thing sold, the payment of the price, the actions of buyer and seller, the rights of rescinding or dissolving the Contract for whatever legal cause.

DCCX. So also the obligation of the seller to bear the loss of the thing sold, occasioned by his *mora* of the seller, and, Demangeat adds, the obligation of the buyer to pay the price notwithstanding the loss of the thing sold, when that loss has not been caused by the act or fault of the seller, the obligation to pay interest and all incidents connected with it, but not of damage,—the question whether the obligation be real or personal—whether the obligors are singly or jointly responsible, the question of acquittal or discharge of the oblilation.

DCCXI. Of these *consequences* or *effects* of the Contract, the following have been the principal subject of discussion in the English and North American Courts.

DCCXII. The question as to what Law shall govern *the repayment of advances* made by a merchant in one state, at the request of a merchant resident in another.

The North American United States Courts have holden, that the undertaking of this Contract is to replace the advance at the place in which it is actually made, and therefore the merchant who makes the advance is entitled to have it replaced there, and to receive interest according to the Law

---

(*k*) *Vide post*, separate chapter on this subject.

(*l*) *Vide ante*, p. 504.

(*m*) *De J. B. et P.* l. ii. c. 11, v. 3.

See, too, *Hert. de commeatu literarum*, s. 16, 19 (*Comm.* vol. 1, p. 243).

of that place.   So the United States Courts have also decided, that where a proposal to purchase goods is made by letter sent from one state to another state, and is assented to in the latter state, that the Contract of sale is made in the latter state. (*n*)

It is of course competent to the contracting parties to stipulate that the advance shall be replaced and the interest paid in some other place, or according to the Law of some other place.

So if a security for a debt be given by a_ merchant in one state, at the request of a merchant in another, the Law of the place in which the security is given governs the contract. (*o*)

DCCXIII. On the same principle as that mentioned in the last paragraph, if a loan be made in one state and security given for its repayment in another, the Law of the place of the loan governs the Contract, for it is there that the money is covenanted to be repaid.

But again : it must be observed, that the express or implied will of the contracting parties may prevent the operation of this general rule.   For instance, if the security be a mortgage, and that mortgage is to be actually executed in a foreign state, and the money paid there, that is the place of the fulfilment of the Law, and the Law of that place must govern, though the money has been advanced elsewhere.(*p*)   " Indeed, Story truly remarks, " in all these cases we are to look to the " real intentions of the parties and their acts as expressive of " them."(*q*)

(*n*) *Story*, s. 286, *last ed.; M'Intyre* v. *Parks*, 3 *Metc.* 207.

(*o*) *Story*, s. 284, 287.

Lanusse v. *Barber*, 3 *Wheaten's (Amer.) R.* 101, 146.

Grant v. *Healey*, 2 *Chand. (Amer.) Law R.* 113.

Bayle v. *Eachorie*, 6 *Peter's (Amer.) R.* 635, 643, 644.

Story cites also *Hertii Opera*, t. i. ; *De Coll. leg.* s. 4, n. 55.

Story does not cite any English decision.

(*p*) *Story*, 287 (*a*), s. 293 (*b*) ; *De Wolf* v. *Johnson*, 10 *Wheaton's (Amer.) Rep.* 367, 383.

(*q*) S. 393 (*b*) ; *Bannatyne* v. *Barrington, Lord Chancellor Napier* (Ireland), 1859.

DCCXIV. As to *interest*, the jurists generally speak of three kinds of interest :

1. Interest naturally incident to the Contract, either by express or implied stipulation, not founded on any wrongful act of a party (*intérêt*).

2. Interest due for the non-performance of the Contract, which the English call *damages,* and the French *dommages-intérêts.*

3. Interest due from delay in the due performance of the Contract, founded therefore on the wrongful act of a party, which the French call *intérêts moratoires.* (*r*)

DCCXV. The interest due or accruing upon a Contract is to be paid according to the Law of the place of the performance of the Contract. (*s*)

This is a proposition upon which, where the contract for the interest is *express*, the Continental, the English, and the

---

(*r*) *Fœlix,* s. 109, p. 231, 2, 3, n. *a.* 234, *ed. Demangeat :* " Un des effets " ordinaires de tout acte renfermant l'engagement de payer une somme " d'argent est l'obligation d'en servir les intérêts : la question de servir " si ces intérêts sont dus, et à quel taux, se règle par la loi du lieu ou le " contrat a été passé, ou du lieu fixé pour le payment à moins que les " parties n'aient adopté une autre loi à ce sujet ;" but the *dommages-intérêts,* aud according to Demangeat the *intérêts moratoires,* are governed by the place of execution.

(*s*) Among English cases see *Montgomery* v. *Bridge,* 2 *Dow. & Clark, Rep.* 297.

Fergusson v. *Fyffe,* 8 *Clarke & Finn. Rep.* 121, 140.

Connor v. *Bellamont,* 2 *Atk. Rep.* 382.

Cash v. *Kennion,* 11 *Vesey, Rep.* 314.

Robinson v. *Bland,* 2 *Burr. Rep.* 1077.

Harvey v. *Archbold,* 3 *Barn. & C.* 626.

Stapleton v. *Conway,* 3 *Atk. Rep.* 382.

Dewar v. *Span,* 3 *Durnf. & East, R.* 425.

Arnott v. *Redfern,* 2 *Carr. & Payne, R.* 88, cannot be considered a correct exposition of the law.

Story, s. 291, 296, 293 (*c*) note 3, *cf. Story.*

2 *Kent's Comm.* Lect. 39, 460-1.

United States Lawyers, are very generally agreed. (*t*)   The unanimity is not so complete where the interest is to be *implied*, (*u*) the English and the United States Lawyers holding that the same rule governs this case, while some of the continental jurists hold that the domicil of the creditor in some cases, and the domicil of the debtor in others, should furnish the rule of Law.

The civil Law, if the place of Contract be identical with the place of performance of the Contract, (*x*) appears to be in favour of the English practice.   The chapter in the Digest, of which the title is " De usuris, et fructibus, et causis, et omni-" bus, accessionibus, et morâ," opens with this position.   " Cum " judicio bonæ fidei disceptatur, arbitrio judicis usurarum " modus *ex more regionis ubi contractum est* constituitur " ita tamen ut legem non offendat." (*y*)

The transaction upon which the interest is allowed, must be one bonæ fidei : if it be a desire for defeating the usury laws of a state, it will be justly treated as a fraud and a nullity. (*z*)

DCCXVI. It is proper to notice in this place a serious conflict in the decisions of the North American United States upon this question of interest directly, but indirectly on the whole question of Foreign Contract.

The supreme court of Louisiana (*a*) decided in a case of Foreign Contract, that there might be *two* places of a Contract, viz., (1) that in which it is made, *locus ubi contractus celebratus est ;* (2) that in which it is to be performed, or in which

---

(*t*) *Story*, s. 294.

(*u*) *Story*, s. 295.

(*x*) Thus *John Voet* (t. i. p. 938), *Ad Pand.* l. xxii. t i. s. 6, says, " Dummodo meminerimus illum propriè locum contractûs in jure non " intelligi, in quo negotium gestum est, sed in quo pecuniam ut solveret " se quis obligant." He refers to *Dig.* l. xlii. t. 5, s. 3.

(*y*) *Dig.* xxii. t. i. 1, et vide *ib.* 37 : " Usuras venire, *eas autem, quæ in* " *regione frequentantur, ut est in bonæ fidei judiciis constitutum.*"

(*z*) *Andrews* v. *Pond*, 13 Peters' (*American*) *Rep.* 65, 77-8. *Story*, s. 293 (*a*).

(*a*) *Story*, s. 298 to s. 301.   *Story*, s. 301 (*a, b, c*).

the money is to be paid, *locus ubi destinata solutio est ;* and the court therefore held, that if the Law of *both* places be not violated, with respect to the rate of interest, the Contract for interest would be valid. (*b*) The court supported this position by referring to the writings of several foreign jurists. *Story* impugns both the decision itself, and the authorities on which it is founded.

These authorities, he contends, no where assert: (*c*)

1. That the validity of the same Contract is not to be judged of throughout and in all its parts by one and the same Law.

2. That a Contract is valid notwithstanding that it neither complies with the Law of the place where it was made, nor the Law of the place where it is to be performed.

3. That the passages cited by the court from jurists, are either those in which they were considering the *form* of the Contract,

4. Or the *mode of execution*, when the places of making and performing happened to be identical,

5. Or the interpretation and extent of contracts generally,

6. Or the rule, where the Contract is made in one (the same) place.

7. That several of those jurists expressly admit that, where the Contract is made in one place, and is to be performed in another, the latter is the *locus contractûs*, and furnishes the rule in all respects except as to the *form* and *mode of execution.*

8. That they all agree, that as to payment or performance the place of performance is to govern, and that *interest* is but an incident or accessary to the *principal.*

(*b*) *Story*, s. 298.

Dupace v. Humphreys, 20 *Martin's (American) Rep.* 1, sustained in *Chapman* v. *Robertson,* 6 *Paige's (American) Rep.* 627, 634.

But see *Van Schaike* v. *Edwards,* 2 *John.* (*Amer.*) *Ch. cases,* 355.

(*c*) *Story*, 299 (*a*), 301 (*a, b*).

9. That the subject of interest is expresssly treated of by those jurists, and without any exception as to the application of the general rule, and the learned writer and judge examines the positions of Alexander, Burgundus, Everhardus, Christinæus, Gregorio, Lopez, Dumoulin or Molinæus, Boullenois, Paul Voet, John Voet, Huberus, and the famous passage in the great civilian Bartolus, which is in fact the parent of all commentaries upon the conflict of Laws, (d) and contends that the result of his examination justifies the positions which have been just mentioned.

The English Courts would probably extend the doctrine laid down by Lord Mansfield, (e) that the place of payment furnished the Law of the Contract, to interest as well as principal, and would therefore support Story's opinion, and not the judgment of the Court of Louisiana.

DCCXVII. The American Chancellor, Kent, agreeing with the decisions of Lord Hardwicke, (f) sums up the Law on this subject in these words:

" The Law of the place where the Contract is made, is to " determine the rate of interest, when the Contract specifically " gives interest; and this will be the case, though the loan be " secured by a mortgage or land, in another state, unless there " be circumstances to show that the parties had in view the " Law of the latter place with respect to interest. When that " is the case the rate of interest of the place of payment is to " govern." (g)

Another instance, if another were wanting, of the ambiguity and impropriety of the expression *lex loci contractûs* when used, without explanation, to convey the true rule upon this matter of Foreign contracts.

(d) *Story*, s. 299 to s. 304.

(e) *Vide supra*, p. 240 ; *Robinson* v. *Bland*, 2 *Burr. Rep.* 1077.

(f) *Connor* v. *Bellamont*, 2 *Atk. Rep.* 381.

Stapleton v. *Conway*, 3 *Atk. Rep.* 727; 1 *Vesey, Rep.* 429 ; *et vide* *Dewar* v. *Span*, 3 *Durnford & East, Rep.* 425.

(g) 2 *Kent's Comm. Lect.* 39, p. 576 (1851).

The language of Paul Voet (*h*) upon this matter is worthy of attention : " Ne tamen hic oriatur confusio—*locum con-* " *tractûs duplicem* facio, *alium, ubi fit,* de quo jam dictum, " *alium in quem destinata solutio.* Illum locum verum, " hunc fictum, appellat *Salicet* (in L. 1. C. de Summ. Trin. " n. 4). Uterque tamen rectè locus dicitur contractûs, etiam " secundum leges civiles, licet postremus aliquid fictionis conti- " neat. Hinc *ratione effectûs et complementi* ipsius contrac- " tûs, spectatur ille locus in quem destinata est soluti. Id " quod ad *modum, mensuram, usuras,* et *negligentiam,* et " moram post contractum initum, accedentem, referendum " est."

(*h*) *De Statut. eorumque concursu*, s. ix. c. 11, n. 11, 12, cited by Roccc p. 344.

CHAPTER XXXVII.

THIRD DIVISION—MEDIATE EFFECTS OR ACCIDENTAL CONSE-
QUENCES OF CONTRACTS—DAMAGES—CURRENCY—STORY'S
COLLATERAL INCIDENTS, ARISING BY (1) OPERATION OF
LAW, (2) ACT OF THE PARTIES—LIENS, PRIORITY OF—LIA-
BILITY OF PARTNERS.

DCCXVIII. We have now to consider the *third* division
of the subject; viz., The *mediate effects* and *accidental consequences* of contracts. (*a*) "We have called (Rocco (*b*) says), the
accidental consequences of contracts, those which neither medi-
ately nor immediately are derived from them, but which take
their origin from facts subsequent to the contracts themselves;
from circumstances which intervene and effect the status
and the relation in which the contracts have placed the parties."
Between these consequences and those discussed in the last
chapter, (*c*) there are grave distinctions. "The former, when the
Contract is made in our kingdom, are governed by our laws;
the latter are subject to the laws of the place in which the fact
which produced them happened." These *accidental consequences* are called *suites* by Fælix, (*cc*) as distinguished from
effets.

DCCXIX. One of the most important of these *accidental
consequences* of a Contract is the right to damages (*dommages,
intérêts,* and *intérêts moratoires*) arising out of delay, *dex
morâ* (*la demeure dans l'exécution*), in the fulfilment of it.

(*a*) *Vide ante,* p. 484.
(*b*) P. 340.
(*c*) Immediate and mediate.
(*cc*) S. 109, *ed. Dem.* p. 234.

Story (*d*) is of opinion that the rule, as to the Law which shall govern the assessment of damages, and determine their rate, is analogous to the rule of Law respecting interest which has been just discussed.

Thus the United States Courts have decided, that if a note be made in a foreign country, for the payment of a certain sum in sugar at a valuation, and there be a breach of the Contract, the Law of the place governs the assessment of the damages.(*e*)

The same principle is applied in fixing the rate of damages for dishonoured bills of exchange. (*f*)

DCCXX. The right to damages arises also from wrong done to property, that is, in this branch of Private International Law, to personal property, or *ex delicto*. Thus, if a ship in foreign or colonial waters be wrongfully seized or appropriated, the interest of that locality will be allowed by way of damages against the wrongdoer.(*g*)

DCCXXI. A question (*h*) often mooted, and not very satisfactorily or consistently settled either by the English or the United States Tribunals, arises with respect to the value of the *currency* by which the amount of a debt which has been contracted in one country and is sued for in another, is to be ascertained.

The following predicaments appear to embrace the cases which arise under this head :

1. Where the *par value* between the currencies of the two countries is nominal or established by Law.

2. Where there is no established par.

(*d*) S. 307.

(*e*) *Story*, s. 307.

Courtais v. *Carpentier*, 1 *Wash. Cin. (Amer.) Rep.* 376.

(*f*) *Slacum* v. *Pomeroy*, 6 *Cranch's (Amer.) Rep.* p. 22.

Hazlehurst v. *Kean*, 4 *Gate's (Amer.) Rep.* 19.

(*g*) *Ekins* v. *East India Company*, 1 *P. Williams, Rep.* 394, 6. *Story*, s. 307.

Consequa v. *Willing*, *Peters' Circuit Rep.* 225, 303.

(*h*) *Story*, s. 307 to 313.

3. Where the debt has been contracted to be paid in a particular specified coin.

4. Where the currency between the time when the debt was contracted or became due, and the time of actual payment, has suffered a depreciation in value.

DCCXXII. With respect to these four predicaments there are two general propositions, the latter being indeed a necessary conclusion from the former, which applies to them all.

First, the primary consideration in all cases is, in what place was the money, according to the original Contract, payable; for the creditor, in whatever place he may sue, is entitled to have an amount equal to what he must pay, in order to remit it to the place in which it is payable.(i)

This rule is well expressed by the two Voets.(k) *John Voet* says, "Quid si in specie de nummorum aut reddituum soluti-
" one difficultas incidat, si forte valor sit immutatus; an spec-
" tabitur loci valor, ubi contractus erat celebratus, an loci in
" quem destinata erat solutio? Respondeo, *ex generali regulâ*
" *spectandum esse loci statutum, in quem destinata erat*
" *solutio.*" (l)

Paul Voet says, "Si major, alibi minor, eorundem num-
" morum valor sit in solutione faciendâ, non tam spectanda
" potestas pecuniæ, quæ est in loco, in quo contractus celebratus
" est, quam potius quæ obtinet in regione illâ in quâ *contrac-*
" *tûs implementum* faciendum est."(m)

The second general proposition flows as a natural conclusion from that which has just been stated, viz., That the creditor is entitled to receive that sum in the currency of the state in which the suit is brought, to which he is entitled in the state in which the debt is payable, a sum calculated therefore by the *real* and not the *nominal* par of exchange.(n)

(i) *Story*, s. 310.

(k) *Story*, s. 309, 310, cites these authorities in the notes.

(l) *De Stat.* s. 9, c. 2, s. 15.

(m) *Ad Pandec.* 1. xii. t. i. 25.

(n) *Story*, s. 309. *Cash* v. *Kennison*, 11 *Vesey, Rep.* 314 (*Lord Eldon*).

This is the doctrine generally adopted by continental jurists. With respect to the third predicament, namely, where the Contract is to be paid in a particular specified *coin*, Story (*o*) is of opinion that the *mint value*, not the *mere bullion value*, of the coin in the state in which the coin is issued, furnishes the proper standard, because it is referred to by the parties by its descriptive name as coin.

DCCXXIII. It unfortunately happens, that the decisions of the tribunals in England and of the North American United States are by no means uniform; they are indeed inconsistent both in a national and an international point of view.

Story goes so far as to pronounce that " there is an irrecon- " cileable difference in some of the authorities on this sub- " ject." (*p*)   It is probable that the increased and happily in- creasing knowledge both of the civil and of foreign Law in both states, may lead to judgments settled on the sound prin- ciples of general jurisprudence. (*q*)

DCCXXIV. The fourth predicament relates to the deprecia- tion of money between the time when the debt was contracted or due, and the time when it is actually paid; *Nobilissima questio*, as it has been not improperly designated. (*r*)

(*o*) S. 309.

(*p*) S. 311 (*a*).

(*q*) The English cases are *Ekins* v. *East India Company*, 1 *Peere Williams' Rep.* 396 (Lord Chancellor Cowper, 1717).

Delegal v. *Naylor*, 7 *Bingham's Rep.* 460 (831).

Scott v. *Bevan*, 2 *B. & Adolphus, Rep.* 78 (1831, Q. B. Lord Tenterden C. J.).

Lee v. *Wilcocks*, 5 *Serge & Rawle's Rep.* 48.

Stapleton v. *Conway*, 1 *Vesey (Sen.), Rep.* 427 (1750, Lord Chancellor).

Rourke v. *Picketts*, 10 *Vesey (Jun.), Rep.* 332 (1804, Master of the Rolls).

Saunders v. *Drake*, 2 *Atk. Rep.* 466 (1742, Lord Chancellor).

Cash v. *Kennion*, 11 *Vesey, Rep.* 314 (1804-5, Lord Chancellor).

Cockerell v. *Barber*, 16 *Vesey, Rep.* 461 (1809-10, Lord Chancellor).

Dungannon v. *Hackett*, 1 *Eg. Cases Abridg.* 288-9.

r) *Vinnius ad instit.* l. iii. t. xv.

This question may present itself in two very different forms :

1. As a case of International Law arising *ex delicto* of a wrongdoer, whether a state or an individual.

2. As a case of International Law arising out of a Contract between individuals, the subjects of or domiciled in different states, or from the dispositions of a unilateral act, such as a will or deed executed by an individual who is a subject of or domiciled in one state, which affects the rights of an individual who is a member of or domiciled in another state.

DCCXXV. (s) As to the case of the wrongdoer it has no analogy, as Sir William Grant observed, to the case of creditor or debtor; the obligation on the wrongdoer, be he a government or an individual, is to undo the wrong act and put the party into the same situation as if he had never done it. So in the case reported by Sir John Davies: he says, " Two cases were put by the judges who were called to the " assistance of the Privy Council, although they were " not positively and formally resolved," he says, " it is said, if " a man upon marriage receive 1000*l.* as a portion with his " wife, paid in silver money, and the marriage is dissolved " *causâ precontractûs*, so that the portion is to be restored, it " must be restored in equal good silver money, though the " state shall have depreciated the currency in the meantime. " So, if a man recover 100*l.* damages, and he levies that in " good silver money, and that judgment is afterwards reversed, " by which the party is put to restore back all he has received, " the judgment-creditor cannot liberate himself by merely " restoring 100*l.* in the debased currency of the time, but he " must give the very same currency that he had received." And, as Sir W. Grant observes: " That proceeds upon the " principle, that if the act is to be undone, it must be com- " pletely undone, and the party is to be restored to the situa-

---

(s) *Pilkington* v. *Commissioner for Claims on France,* 2 *Knapp's Privy Council Reports,* p. 19. This is the leading case on this subject.

" tion in which he was at the time the act to be undone took
" place."(t)

2. In the case of the Contract or other civil act of individuals, the opinions of jurists of all states are much divided. Some, among whom are the great names of Doumoulin, Hotomannus and Donellus, fix upon the time of the making the Contract (*tempus contractûs*) as governing the question of the value. Others, among whom are Bartolus, Baldus, De Castro, and the favourite authority on this subject, Vinnius, fix upon the time of payment (*tempus solutionis*). Vinnius, however, sums up judicially the case as follows: " Siquidem neutri con-
" trahentium injuriam fieri volumus, ita definiendum videtur,
" ut si *bonitas monetæ intrinseca*, mutata sit, *tempus con-*
" *tractûs*, si *extrinseca*, id est valor imposititius, tempus solu-
" tionis in solutione faciendâ, spectari debeat."(u) Or as he is happily paraphrased by Sir W Grant in the leading case above referred to :

" He takes the distinction, that if, between the time of con-
" tracting the debt and the time of its payment, the currency
" of the country is depreciated by the state, that is to say,
" lowered in its intrinsic goodness, as if there were a greater
" portion of alloy put into a guinea or a shilling, the debtor
" should not liberate himself by paying the nominal amount
" of his debt in the debased money, that is, he may pay in the
" debased money, being the current coin, but he must pay so
" much more, as would make it equal to the sum he borrowed.
" But he says, if the nominal value of the currency, leaving it
" unadulterated, were to be increased, as if they were to make
" the guinea pass for 30s. the debtor may liberate himself from
" a debt of 1l. 10s. by paying a guinea, although he had bor-
" rowed the guinea, when it was but worth 21s."(x)

DCCXXVI. It is to be observed, however, that Vinnius

(t) 2 *Knapp's P. C. Reports*, pp. 20, 21.

(u) *Vinnius ad Instit.* lib. iii. tit. xv. *Textus de mutuo comm.* n. 12.

(x) 2 *Knapp's P. C Rep.* p. 19.

accompanies his statement of the Law on this subject with the caution, invariably applicable to all questions of foreign Contract, "intellige si nihil de eâ re *expressè dictum* sit, neque "*mora* intervenerit." (*y*)

DCCXXVII. Sir John Davies, in his report of "*Le case de* "*mixt monies*," reports the opinion of the judges upon the following point : (*z*) A bond was given in England for the payment of £100 sterling, current and lawful money " of England," to be paid in Dublin, Ireland ; and between the time of giving the bond, and its becoming due, Queen Elizabeth, by proclamation, recalled the existing currency in Ireland, and issued a new debased coinage, (called mixed money,) declaring it to be the lawful currency in Ireland. A tender was made in this debased coin, or mixed coin, in Dublin, in payment of the bond. The question before the Privy Council of Ireland, was, whether the tender was good, or ought to have been in currency or value equal to the current lawful money then current in England. The court held the tender good : first, because the mixed money was current lawful of England, Ireland being within the sovereignty of the British Crown, *before the day of payment* ; (*a*) and secondly, because the payment being to be in Dublin (*le lieu de payment*), it could be made in no other currency than the existing currency of Ireland, which was the mixed money.

Story (*c*) observes upon this statement, that " the court do " not seem to have considered, that the true value of the Eng- " lish current money might, if that was required by the bond, " have been paid in Irish currency, though debased, by add- " ing so much more as would bring it to the par. And it is " extremely difficult to conceive, how a payment of current

---

(*y*) *Knapp's P. C. Rep.* p. 19.

(*z*) *Story's Conflict of Laws*, ch. viii. s. 313, note 2, p. 502.

(*a*) *Sir John Davies' Reports*, p. 27, 6th *Resolution*.

(*b*) This is not noticed by Story in his abstract of the sentence, which I have generally followed.

(*c*) Ibid.

" lawful money of England could be interpreted to mean cur-
" rent or lawful money of Ireland, when the currency of each
" kingdom was different, and the royal proclamation made a
" distinction between them, the mixed money being declared
" the lawful currency of Ireland only."—This is a very fair observation : but it is not equally fair to say,—" that perhaps the
" desire to yield to the royal prerogative of the Queen a sub-
" missive obedience, as to all payments in Ireland, may ac-
" count for a decision so little consonant with the principles of
" Law in modern times."

DCCXXVIII. Story, however, with due submission to so
high an authority be it said, does not appear to me to have
stated this case with sufficient fulness ; he does not notice the
argument from the expression *current* (*d*) money, namely, that
these terms in a *Contract* referred to a *future* time, and that
" verba *currentis* monetæ tempus *solutionis* designant." The
term *current* in a *will*, the judges said, would convey a different sense, because the testator in a bequest of so much current
money would intend to refer *ad tempus conditi testamenti.*
Nor does there appear to be any ground for the assertion, that
the judges were influenced by a servile submission to the royal
prerogative. The decision turned in some measure upon the
locus solutionis being Dublin, though the *locus contractûs*
was London.

Story cites a passage from Pothier, and states that he differs
from Vinnius ; he might have added, that this great jurist
argues, however, unconsciously, in accordance with the decision
of the judges in the case of the mixed moneys.

DCCXXIX. Pothier, in his "*Traité du Contrat de Vente,*" (*e*)
deals with the question of a seller's reserved right to repurchase
(*rémére*), and thus expresses himself : "Il nous reste à observer à
" l'égard du prix, qu'il peut étre rendu en une monnoie diffé-
" rente de celle en laquelle il a été payé. S'il a été payé au

---

(*d*) *Davies' Rep.* p. 27.
(*e*) Partie v. c. ii. s. 5, n. 415.

vendeur en or, le vendeur peut le rendre en especes d'argent, et *vice versâ.* Pareillement, quoique depuis le paiement du prix qui a été fait au vendeur, les especes, dans lesquelles il a été payé soient augmentées ou diminuées ; quoiqu'elles aient été décriées, et qu'au temps du rémeré il y en ait de nouvelles qui soient de meilleur ou de plus mauvais aloi le vendeur qui exerce le rémeré, doit rendre en especes qui aient cours au temps auquel il exerce le rémeré la même somme ou quantité qu'il a reçue en paiement, et rien de plus ni de moins. La raison est que, dans la monnoie, ce ne sont pas les especes que l'on considere, mais seulement la somme ou valeur que le souverain a voulu qu'elles signifiassent. *Ea materia formâ publicâ percussa usum dominiumque non tam ex substantiâ præbet quàm ex quantitate; L.* 1. ff. *de contr. empt.* Ce ne sont pas tant les especes que le vendeur est censé avoir reçues, lorsquelle prix lui a été payé, que la somme ou valeur signifieé par ces especes ; et par conséquent il doit rendre, et il lui suffit de rendre la même somme ou valeur en des especes qui aient cours, et qui soient les signes autorises par le prince pour signifier cette valeur." And Pothier adds, "Ce principe étant certain dans notre pratique Françoise, il suffit de l'avoir exposé; *il retranche toutes les questions que les docteurs font sur les changemens de monnoie.*"

Under this head of *mediate effects* or accidental consequences, it may be permitted perhaps to range the following incidents of contracts, which are treated of by Story under the head of *collateral incidents. (f)*

They arise either by (*a*) operation of Law, or (*β*) by act of the parties ; viz.,

1. The liability of partners.

(*f*) S. 322, 322, *a.* 322, *b.* These would fall under *Rocco's* division of *mediate consequences*, sometimes called *natural* consequences by jurists, because Rocco says they do not touch the substance of the Contract, but are a natural appendage to it ; see Rocco, p. 329— 333.

2. The right of redemption—*e. g.*, of an assigned debt.

3. The right of warranty.

4. The right of discussion; that is, properly speaking, the obligation of the creditor to proceed against or *discuss* the principal solvent debtor, before he can attach the surety.

5. The liens incident to a Contract; *e. g.*,

a. The lien of a vendor upon lands or goods until the purchase money be paid.

β. The right of stoppage *in transitu* (*g*) in case of the insolvency of the purchaser.

γ. The lien of a bottomry bond.

δ. Of mariners on the ship for their wages.

ε. The lien for priority of payment in certain obligations. This question is partly considered in some subsequent observations on the *transfer* of obligations.

DCCXXX. Story pronounces his opinion, that with regard to these and the like cases the general Law is, that wherever the liability, the right, the lien, or the privilege is created by the Law of the place in which the Contract is made, it will be respected and enforced by the Law of the country in which the Contract is executed. (*h*)

It is also said by the same high authority, that the converse of this proposition is true, that if the lien or privilege does not exist in the place in which the Contract is made it will not be allowed in the place in which it is executed, or in which a suit is brought to enforce its execution, although the Law of that place would sustain it. (*i*)

Foreign jurists, however, though generally agreeing in this doctrine with respect to liens, not unfrequently distinguish between their effects upon moveable and immoveable pro-

---

(*g*) *Vide post,* chapter on *lex mercatoria.*

(*h*) *Story,* s. 322, *b.*

Carroll v. *Waters,* 9 *Martin* (*Amer.*), *Rep.* 500.

(*i*) *Whiston* v. *Stodder,* 8 *Martin* (*Amer.*), *Rep.* 95, 134-5.

perty; governing the liens on the latter *lege rei sitæ*, and the former *lege loci contractûs.* (*k*)

DCCXXXI. The recognition of the lien does not imply the recognition of its title to priority over other liens, because such right of priority attached to the lien in the place of its creation. The doctrine of the North American United States Courts is, that "the right of priority forms no part of the Con-" tract, it is extrinsic and rather a personal privilege depen-" dent on the Law of the place where the property lies, and " where the court sits which is to decide the cause." (*l*)

Some eminent foreign jurists hold this doctrine without qualification; others take distinctions as to the domicil of the obligor or debtor, some insisting that in the case of moveables the rule of the original domicil travels with the person, some, like Rodenburgh, maintaining that if the domicil be changed the Law of the new domicil operates upon the moveables in the old domicil. (*m*)

But, amidst this conflict of opinions as to liens upon *moveable* property, (*n*) there is a preponderance of authority in favour of the operation of the *lex rei sitæ* upon *immoveable* property; (*o*) though there are not wanting dissentients from this doctrine.

(*k*) *Story*, s. 322, *c.*

(*l*) Chief Justice Marshall, in *Harrison* v. *Sterry*, 5 *Cranch's* (*Amer.*) *Rep.* 289, 298.

See too *Ogden* v. *Saunders*, 12 *Wheaton's* (*Amer.*) *Rep.* 361-2.

Story, s. 323.

Thus *Hertius:* " Emnivero quia *antelatio* (priority) ex jure singulari " vel privilegio competit, non debet in præjudicium illius civitatis sub " quâ debitor degit et res ejus mobiles extendi censentur, extendi. Ad " jura igitur domicilii debitoris ubi fit concurcus creditorum, et quo " omnes cujuscumque generis lites adversus illum debitorem propter " connexitatem causâ traduntur." *De Collis, leg.* s. 4, n. 64; cited *Story*, s. 325 (*b*).

(*m*) *Rodenburgh, de div. stat.* t. ii. c. v. s. 16 ; cited *Story*, s. 325 (*g*).

(*n*) See the authorities collected, *Story*, s. 322, *d.* 325, *n.*

(*o*) *Story*, s. 325 (*o*).

It is a doctrine, however, firmly imbedded in the Law of England and the North American United States.

DCCXXXII. It is a maxim which applies to all the foregoing considerations, and which is pretty generally adopted by States, that in the case of an irreconcileable conflict between rights acquired *lege loci contractûs* and those acquired *lege fori,* the former yield to the latter; that is, comity between States gives place to the positive Law of the particular State which has judicial cognizance of the matter. (*p*) This maxim has indeed been already expressed in the early part of this volume.

DCCXXXIII. According to the jurisprudence of the North American United States, the Law of the place where the Contract is made will govern the Contract as to the liability of partners and part owners.

If by that Law they would be liable *in solido,* that liability will follow the Contract everywhere, although by the Law of the domicil of the partnership the partners might not be liable *in solido,* but only for a *proportionate share.* (*q*)

The Law of some countries, as will be seen hereafter, offers a remarkable illustration of this position in the case of bills of

---

(*p*) *Vide ante,* p. 487-8.

Potter v. *Brown,* 5 *East's Rep.* 124—130 (Lord Ellenborough: leading English case).

Saul v. *His Creditors,* 17 *Martin (Amer.) Rep.* 596, (leading case for the United States,) 2 *Kent's Comm. lect.* 39, p. 461.

Story, s. 326, 327, 327 *a.*

Huterus, 1, 3, 11 : " In tali *conflictu* magis est ut jus nostrum quam " jus alienum servemus." See also a very important case decided by Mr. Justice Porter (who also decided *Saul* v. *His Creditors*).

Ohio Insurance Company v. *Edmondson,* 5 *Louis. (American) Rep.* p. 295—305.

Story, s. 327*a.*

As to conflict between *maritime policies, vide post,* and *Story,* 327*b.*

(*q*) *Story,* s. 322.

Ferguson v. *Flower,* 16 *Martin (Amer.),* 312.

Carroll v. *Waters,* 9 *ib.* 500.

exchange ; for this Law holds, that if the drawer was bankrupt at the time when the acceptor accepted he is discharged from his acceptance, and this consequence travels with the bill everywhere as an inseparable incident. (*r*)

(*r*) *Pardessus, Droit Comm.* art. 1495 ; cited by Story, s. 322.

CHAPTER XXXVIII.

THE LEX LOCI CONTRACTÛS AND THE LEX REI SITÆ, CON-
SIDERED WITH REFERENCE (I.) TO THE TRANSFER OF REAL
PROPERTY, (II.) TO SECURITIES AND LIENS UPON REAL
PROPERTY.

DCCXXXIV. In this chapter some observations will be
made upon these two questions; viz.,

I. Does the *lex loci contractûs* or the *lex rei sitæ* govern
the transfer of real property?

II. Does the *lex loci contractûs* or the *lex rei sitæ* govern
as to liens, hypothecs, or mortgages, given in the place where
the Contract is entered into upon real property situated in
another state?

DCCXXXV. (I.) The case of a Contract respecting the transfer of *immoveable property* illustrates the variety of the rules
which the foreign writers upon Private International Law consider applicable to a Contract to which a foreigner is a
party: (*a*) they say that,

1. The capacity of the obligor to enter into the Contract is
determined by reference to the Law of his domicil. (*b*)

2. The like capacity of the obligee by the Law of his
domicil.

3. The mode of alienation or acquisition of the immoveable
property is to be governed by the Law of the situation of that
property. (*c*)

4. The external form of the Contract is to be governed by
the Law of the place in which the Contract is made.

(*a*) *Fœlix*, s. 67.
Story, s. 368, 372c.
(*b*) This, it is remembered, may involve the discussion of nice questions on the *change* of domicil.
(*c*) So *Rocco*, p. 337.

It is even suggested by Fælix, that sometimes the interpretation of the Contract may require the application of a *fifth* Law.

DCCXXXVI. The Law of England and the North American United States requires the application of the *lex rei sitæ* to all the four predicaments mentioned in the last section. (*d*)

DCCXXXVII. But a distinction is to be taken between contracts to transfer property, and the Contract by which it is transferred. The former are valid if executed according to the *lex loci contractûs;* the latter require for their validity a compliance with the forms prescribed by the *lex rei sitæ.* Without this compliance the *dominium* in the property will not pass. (*e*)

DCCXXXVIII. With respect to the *extent of interest* in immoveable property capable of being acquired or alienated, English and Foreign Law are pretty much in accordance. Both pronounce that the *lex rei sitæ* is alone to govern the question. (*f*)

DCCXXXIX. With respect to the subject, or what kind of property is to be considered immoveable, (*g*) that question is also to be decided by the *lex rei sitæ.* (*h*) It may or may not consider moveable identical with personal property. It may or may not consider things to constitute moveable or immoveable property according to their own nature, or according to an arbitrary rule of its own.

DCCXL. (II.) As to the operation of the *lex loci contractûs* and the *lex rei sitæ* upon securities and liens upon real property. The distinction between *moveable* and *immoveable property,* its important bearing upon questions of comity, and the difficulties arising from the peculiar character of *personal property* in England, have been made the subject of notice in an earlier

---

(*d*) *Story*, s. 424, s. 430, s. 435, s. 365.

(*e*) I. *Burge Comm.* p. 24, 844, 845.

(*f*) *Story*, s. 445, and authorities there cited.

(*g*) *Vide ante*, remarks on moveable and immoveable property.

(*h*) *Story*, s. 447.

part of this work. (*i*) But the reader is now referred to them on account of their connection with a possible incident to foreign contracts involving considerations of much nicety and difficulty. (*k*)

DCCXLI. A Contract may be made, as in the case of a loan, in one State, and a *security* given for it in the shape of an *hypotheca*, a *gage* or *mortgage*, upon *lands* lying in another State. The question arises whether the *lex loci contractûs* or the *lex rei sitæ* is to govern this incident of the Contract.

DCCXLII. It is expedient to consider this question, *first*, with reference to States the basis of whose jurisprudence is the Roman Law, and, *secondly*, with reference to the Law of England and the North American United States.

DCCXLIII. The jurisprudence of foreign states on this subject is founded, either upon the Roman or upon a distinct Municipal Law, or upon a recognition of certain principles of the Roman Law with certain more or less important additions and exceptions introduced by the policy of the state.

DCCXLIV. Savigny (*l*) remarks—1. That the hypothecation, gage, or pledge (*Hypotheca*, (*m*) *Pfundrecht, Droit de gage*), in the system of Roman jurisprudence, appertained to the class of rights called *real* (*jus in re*), good against third parties, acquired through the intervention of a simple Contract, and without delivery or act of taking possession. (*n*)

(*i*) *Vide ante*, Chapter xxvi.

Story, s. 287*a*, 372*d*, 435, 447, 523.

Savigny, viii. s. 368 (191-8), s. 374 (289), s. 390 (421).

Fælix, i. p. 135-6, n. *a*. (*ed. Dem.*).

3 *Burge, Comm.* chapter xii. *præsertim*, section vi.

Rocco, p. 337.

Williams on the Law of Real Property, p. 333-4.

(*k*) The principal interests of a *personal* nature derived from *landed* property in England, are *a term of years*, and a *mortgage debt*.

(*l*) VIII. (191-2), s. 103.

(*m*) Hypotheca, Pignoris jus, atque possessione rei pignori datæ, constitutum. *Dirksen's Manuale*, p. 424, v. *Hypotheca*.

(*n*) " The right," Mr. Burge observes, " which a creditor may acquire " in the property of another by its being pledged to him as a security

2. The Contract might be tacit or implied, because there are many acts connected with legal obligations which imply, according to a general principle of jurisprudence, that a gage or pledge has been given as a security for a claim. The expressions "... tacitam conventionem de invectis illatis ... " quasi id tacitè convenerit.... tacitè solet conventum accipi, " ut perinde teneantur invecta et illata, ac si specialiter con- " venisset ... tacitè intelliguntur pignori esse ... etiamsi nomi- " natim id non convenerit," are among those in the Digest which illustrate this position.

3. The Roman Law made no distinction between moveable and immoveable things, as the objects of such gage. (o)

4. The express as well as the tacit Contract might refer, not only to particular portions of property, but to the whole estate.

DCCXLV. Savigny further rémarks, that those European states which are governed, as a general rule, by the Roman Law, have, in the particular instance of gage or mortgage, made some important deviations from it. These deviations have been chiefly with reference to the extent to which the tacit or implied gage operates ; and the municipal laws of these states recognise, some a greater, some a less, number of obligations guaranteed by a fiction of a Contract of hypothecation or mortgage.

" for the satisfaction of a demand which he has against the owner of " that property is under the civil Law, and those systems which are " founded on it, perfectly distinct from the *dominium :* it is called *hypo-* " *theca* or *pignus ;* it is a Contract, ' quo jus in re constituitur credi- " 'tori in securitatem crediti.' " (*Huber. Prælect.* lib. xx. t. i. p. 1028) ; 3 *Burge,* 161.

(o) As to the difference between *pignus* and *hypotheca,* the Institutes say (l. iv. t. vi.),

"Inter *pignus* autem et *hypothecam* quantum ad actionem nihil interest : nam de quâ re inter creditorem et debitorem convenerit, ut sit pro debito obligata, utrâque hâc appellatione continetur. Sed in aliis diffe- rentia est, nam *pignoris* appellatione eam proprie contineri dicimus, quæ simul etiam traditur creditori, maximè si mobilis sit : et eam quæ sine traditione *nudâ conventione* tenetur propriè *hypotheca* appellatione contineri dicimus."

DCCXLVI. Take, for instance, the following case : Two states are governed generally speaking by the Roman Law. In the one the rule of the Roman Law prevails, that where a bridal portion (*dot*) has been promised, it is guaranteed by the implied hypothecation of the whole property of the promissor; in the other this rule has not been established. Two inhabitants of the former state enter into a dotal or marriage contract ; the promissor or obligor possesses landed property in the latter state ; the question arises, Is this property burdened with an implied or tacit hypothecation ? It may be answered negatively, on the ground that the *lex rei sitæ* must prevail. But, according to Savigny, the answer would be wrong, because the latter state acknowledges the possibility of an hypothecation through the medium of a contract alone, and even of a tacit contract alone. It is a question of fact whether, in the case suggested, there be or be not such a contract, which can only be decided by the *lex loci contractûs*. But, according to that law, the dotal contract is guaranteed by the tacit hypothecation of the whole property of the promissor; and this piece of land is a portion of that property ; it is therefore burdened by the tacit hypothecation. But if the dotal contract had been completed in the latter state, neither that piece of land nor the rest of the property of the promissor would have been so burdened.

DCCXLVII. There exists, however, a much greater discrepancy between the German States which have adopted in general the Roman Law of hypothecation, and those which have built this law upon an entirely new foundation. Prussia is the type of states of this latter class.

DCCXLVIII. The Law of Prussia does not admit that a simple contract can establish a right of hypothecation as a right affecting real property, which it calls a *real* right (*dingliches Recht, droit réel*). The Law of Prussia also makes a distinction between moveable and immoveable property. In the case of immoveables, a *real right* can only be created by an inscription in the register of hypothecations (*Hypothekenbuch*). A contract relating to the inscription of a particular piece or portion of land confers a title, by means of which this inscription can be demanded, but a general contract of hypothecation over the whole of a property does not support and demand for an inscription of particular portions of land. In the case of moveables, a right of hypothecation affecting realty arises only from the delivery or *tradition* of the thing : a contract relating to the hypothecation of definite particular things founds a claim for the tradition of those things.

But when a contract of hypothecation, tacit or express, takes place in a state which is governed by the Roman Law, it will not, *per se*, extend to the moveable property of a debtor in Prussia ; at the most it can only operate as a claim to have such property, through the medium of *inscription* or *tradition*, subjected, and these only under certain specified conditions, to the hypothecation. If, on the other hand, a contract of hypothecation takes place in Prussia, having for its object either individual things or a whole property, and the debtor possess property in a state governed by the Roman Law, there is no reason why this property should not be deemed validly hypothecated, inasmuch as the Roman Law does not make the validity of the hypothecation dependent either upon the *lex loci contractûs* or upon the *domicilium* of the hypothecator ; in this case, therefore, the *lex rei sitæ* may and ought to be unreservedly applied.

DCCXLIX. There remains the following case for consideration : In a state governed by the Roman Law a moveable is validly hypothecated by a contract, express or tacit ; afterwards this moveable is brought into Prussia. Does the lien of hypothecation continue to affect it so as to enable the pawnee or mortgagee to bring an action against its possessor, whether the pawner, or mortgagor, or a third person? Can the pawnee or mortgagee dispose of it if he becomes possessed of it by some accident and without tradition ? The plausible answer is in the affirmative, because it may be said that a right once acquired to a thing is not affected by the removal of that thing from one place to another. But the answer, Savigny says, would be wrong. It is not, in truth, a question whether one and the same right of hypothecation which may be acquired in different ways in different states, just as property acquired in one state by tradition, in another by contract, is universally recognised as property. The right of hypothecation acquired by simple contract is altogether a different institution or creature of law from that which can only be acquired by tradition; the two have nothing in common but their name and object. The pawnee or mortgagee, therefore, who, in the case suggested, sought to exercise his right of hypothecation in Prussia, would be calling upon that state to enforce an institution of law which it does not recognise, and this is a proceeding in principle inadmissible. (p) But, on the other hand, the pawnee or mortgagee in Prussia, who has become possessed by tradition of an hypothecated moveable, can enforce his right in a state governed by the Roman Law, inasmuch as he has united in himself all the conditions of hypothecation required for its validity by the law of that state. It may be here observed, the rank and priority of creditors having a right of hypothecation over one and the same thing is governed by the *lex rei sitæ.*

DCCL. The French jurisprudence upon the effect of foreign hypothecations is, as at present actually administered, unfavourable to their operation upon property in France; but the decisions of the French tribunals on this subject do not appear to be approved by the jurists of that state, whose influence upon the future decisions of the tribunals seems to be scarcely if at all less than that of mere judicial precedents. (q)

M. Fælix, in an essay written for the *Revue Étrangère et Française,* admitted the right of hypothecation of the wife and the minor over property in a foreign state, subject to

---

(p) *Vide ante,* remarks as to the erroneous doctrine that a state which does not recognise among its legal institutions a divorce *a mensâ et toro,* may be required to enforce it in the case of foreigners married in a state which does recognise it.

(q) *Vide ante.*

these conditions : 1. That the *lex sitûs* recognises this kind of hypothecation.   2. That the personal law of the wife or minor also recognises it.   3. That there exists a treaty between the two states to the effect that recognises this right of hypothecation in the case of a foreign wife or minor.   In his later and greater work, *Traité du Droit International privé*, Fælix makes no mention of the *third* condition, the necessity of which he has abandoned, according to the opinion of his latest editor, M. Demangeat.   This learned person observes that the French Law concedes to foreigners all the civil rights (*droits privés*) of Frenchmen, with certain exceptions formally specified in the text of the code, and he laments, as a deplorable interpretation of the eleventh article of that code, a judicial decision that the *hypothèque legale* is one of the *droits civils*, which appertain exclusively to Frenchmen.

As to the general question whether an hypothecation recognised by the personal law ought to be equally recognised by the *lex sitûs*, Fælix answers in the affirmative ; M. Demangeat refuses to go this length.   He is of opinion that the *lex sitûs* must be considered to some extent " c'est au statut réel à " determiner le mode de conservation et le rang du droit " d'hypothèque."   At the same time he agrees with Savigny, and thinks that a French wife ought to be allowed a right of hypothecation over the property of her husband in a foreign state, provided that this state recognises that species of *real rights* which is called hypothecation.(*r*)

DCCLI.   Secondly,—with reference to states in which the jurisprudence of England prevails as to the Law which governs liens on real property.

Little can be added to the authorities collected by Story and Burge on this subject.   And first, with respect to a contract for which a security on real property has been given. The English decisions, as Story points out, have been, that the Law of the place where the loan is made is to govern, for the

---

mere taking of a foreign security does not necessarily alter the locality of the contract. It by no means necessarily follows from the taking of such security, that where it is taken the contract is to be fulfiled. The legal fulfilment of a contract of loan on the part of the bondsman is repayment of the money; the security is but the means of ensuring what has been contracted for—that is, to pay where he borrows, unless another place of payment be expressly designated by the contract. But if the mortgage is actually to be executed in a foreign country, and the money is to be paid there, the loan will be deemed to be there completed, although the money may have been actually advanced elsewhere. (s)

DCCLII. Story also refers to the following case as, though somewhat different in its circumstances, being yet illustrative of the general principle—a case which occurred formerly in England : By a settlement made upon the marriage of A. in England, a term of 500 years was created upon estates in Ireland in trust to raise £12,000 for the portions of daughters. The parties to the settlement resided in England, and a question afterwards arose whether the £12,000, charged on the term of years, should be paid in England without any abatement or deduction for the exchange from Ireland to England. It was decided that the portion ought to be paid in England, where the contract was made and the parties resided, and not in Ireland, where the lands lay which were charged with the payment, for it was a sum in gross, and not a rent issuing out of the land.(t)

DCCLIII. In the case of *Waterhouse* v. *Stansfield*, the difficult question arising out of a debt secured by a mortage on foreign land underwent some discussion in that case: a mortgagor resident in this country mortgaged, by deed executed in England, to mortgagees also resident here, real estate in Demerara ; and before the mortgagees completed their title to the mortgaged property according to the laws of Demerara,

---

(s) *Story's Conflict of Laws*, ch. viii. s. 287 a.

(t) *Ib.* s. 288; *De Wolf* v. *Johnson*, 10 *Wheaton's (Amer.) R.* 367.

the mortgagor became bankrupt, and his assignees in this country sold the property and received the proceeds. The question was, whether the rights of the contracting parties have ceased to be governed by the Law of Demerara, *the lex loci rei sitæ*, and must be governed by the Law of this country, *the lex loci contractûs*. Lord Justice Turner made the following among other observations :

" Upon the argument of this claim several points were " made on the part of the plaintiffs. First, that the defendants, " the assignees, are bound by all the equities by which the " bankrupt was bound ; and that the court, finding them in " possession of the proceeds of an estate, which by Contract " with the bankrupt was bound in favour of the plaintiffs, " will give effect to the Contract against those proceeds.

   *   *   *   *   *   *   *

" The case of *Exparte Pollard* (*u*) was cited upon the first " point ; but in that case the Law of Scotland presented no " impediment to the mortgage being completed ; the Contract " bound the bankrupt, and therefore his assignees, and there " was no impediment to its completion. But in this case the " Contract indeed may bind the bankrupt and the assignees, " and yet, by the Law of Demerara, may not have been " capable of being fulfilled. The two cases, therefore, are " widely different ; and I cannot hold this case to be governed " by *Exparte Pollard.*

" If it can be decided in favour of the plaintiffs, without " some further inquiry, it must, I think, be upon the more " broad and general ground, that the property having been " sold, and the proceeds of the sale received by the defendants, " the assignees, the rights of the parties have ceased to be " governed by the Law of Demerara, the *lex loci rei sitæ*, " and must be governed by the Law of this country, the *lex*

(*u*) *Expate Pollard, re Courtney, Montague & Chitty's Rep.* 230, and 4 *Deacon's Rep.* 27 : reversing s. c. 3 *Montague & Ayrton's Rep.* 340 ; 2 *Deacon's Rep.* 367 ; 6 *Law J. Rep. N. S. Bankr.* 95.

Martin v. *Martin,* 2 *Russ. & Mylne,* 528.

" *loci contractûs*. No authority has been cited, nor have I
" been able to find any which touches this point; but I think
" it must depend upon the question, how far the *lex loci rei*
" *sitæ* extends. If it regulates, not merely the disposition of
" the estate itself, but also the disposition of the proceeds of
" the estate, it cannot, I think, be permitted that a different
" Law should intervene and defeat those regulations. The
" interest in the proceeds is in substance and effect an interest
" in the estate itself, and no rule is more universal than that
" the *lex loci rei sitæ* governs the disposition of the estate. If
" the *lex loci rei sitæ* only permits the alienation of the estate
" upon the terms of the proceeds being applied in a particular
" manner, this is a restraint upon the alienation; and there is
" no doubt that the restraints which may be put upon aliena-
" tion must in all cases be governed by the *lex loci rei sitæ*.
" Again, how could a Contract to dispose of the proceeds of an
" estate in a manner contrary to that prescribed by the *lex*
" *loci rei sitæ* be enforced? I cannot, therefore, adopt the
" broad position contended for on the part of the plaintiffs,
" but must send the matter to the master for further inquiry
" as to the Law of Demerara." (*x*)

DCCLIV. According to Mr. Burge, both the constitution
or acquisition of the whole *jus hypothecæ* in immoveable property, and the right and obligations of the mortgagor and
mortgagee, are wholly dependent on the *lex sitûs*. Therefore,
" whether the *hypotheca* be *conventional*, or *express*, or *tacit*,
" or *judicial*, or *general*, or *special*, it can effect immoveable
" property so far, only, as it is sanctioned by the Law of the
" place in which the property is situated."

He relies upon *Rodenburgh, Matthæus, P. Voet, J. Voet,*
for this doctrine, which seems to be well established both on
principle and authority. With respect to the possible conflict
between the *lex contractûs* and the *lex sitûs* as to privileges or

---

(*x*) *Waterhouse* v. *Stansfield* (*V. C. Turner*, 1852); *Law Journal*,
N. S., vol. 21, p. 882-3.

preferences arising out of the hypotheca or mortgage, Mr. Burge adopts the opinion of Rodenburgh, the two Voets, and Matthæus, that such privileges or preferences, even though conferred by the *lex domicilii* or the *lex contractûs*, must be governed as to their admissibility by the *lex sitûs*. So it may happen that instruments prepared in England as mortgages of property in her colonies may be ineffectual for that purpose, though the colonial court may collect the intention of the parties from these instruments, and endeavour to execute it according to the *lex sitûs*. (y)

DCCLV. On the other hand it may happen that the hypotheca or mortgage security may be valid according to the *lex sitûs* of the property, and yet the debt or contracts be invalid, because contrary to the *lex contractûs*. On this principle it has been well decided, both in England and the North American United States, that the taking foreign security does not necessarily entail as a consequence that the Contract is to be fulfilled where the security is taken. A loan of money in England with a mortgage security in a West Indian colony, was not allowed to have reserved for it the rate of interest allowed by the *lex sitûs* (*i. e.*, of the colony), because contrary to the *lex contractûs* (*i. e.*, of England). (z)

Upon the same principle the Common Law courts of England, (a) France, (b) and the North American United States, (c) agree with the majority of jurists, (d) in holding that no action can be entertained or a judgment *in rem* be pronounced as to immoveable property situated in another state.

(y) *Ib.* 394.

(z) *Wolf* v. *Johnson*, 10 *Wheaton's* (*Amer.*) *Rep.* 323.
Stapleton v. *Conway*, 3 *Atkin's Rep.* 727 ; 3 *Burge*, 395-6.

(a) *Mostyn* v. *Fabrigas, Cowper's Rep.* 180.
Doulson v. *Matthews*, 4 *Durnford & East's Rep.* 503.

(b) *Cod.* 463, t. xix. l. iii.

(c) *Story*, s. 467.

(d) 13 *Burge*, 396.

DCCLVI. The English court of chancery, however, entertains suits which have for their object to acquire a title and obtain possession of property situated out of its jurisdiction. It is difficult to defend this stretch of authority on sound principles of international jurisprudence.   Mr. Burge observes, (e) "that this court professes only '*agere in perso-* " *nam;* ' but, as it compels the defendant to divest himself of " the property or to subject it to a burthen, it indirectly acts " on the property." The exercise of this jurisdiction, when it is founded on some Contract made or some equity arising between persons in England, respecting lands in the colonies or in a foreign country, as in *Penn* v. *Lord Baltimore*, (f) or in *Cranstown* v. *Johnston*, (g) may be consistent with the principles laid down by jurists in the case of judgments which are both personal and real.   But the exercise of its jurisdiction in making decrees for the foreclosure or sale of mortgaged property in the colonies is not so easily understood; it cannot, he observes, carry its decree into execution without the aid of the *forum rei sitæ;* and Mr. Burge is of opinion that the decree of the court of chancery ought not to operate as a lien on property out of its jurisdiction to the prejudice of a third party, who had acquired legally a previous lien and had no notice of the decree. (h)

(e) 13 *Burge*, 398.
(f) 1 *Vesey's Rep.* 444.
(g) 3 *Vesey's Rep.* 170, 5 *ib.* 276.
(i) 3 *Burge*, 399.

CHAPTER XXXIX.

TRANSFER OR ASSIGNMENT OF OBLIGATIONS BY THE OBLIGEE,
(I.) BY ACT OF OBLIGEE, (II.) BY OPERATION OF LAW—
QUESTION AS TO PRIORITY OF LIENS BETWEEN ASSIGNEE
OF OBLIGEE, AND CREDITOR OR TRUSTEE OF OBLIGEE—
BANKRUPTCY—PRESCRIPTION.

DCCLVII. The obligation may be transferred in two
ways : (I.) By the voluntary act of the obligee ; (II.) By the
operation of the Law in the event of the obligee's insolvency or
bankruptcy.

DCCLVIII. (I.) The obligee may of course transfer his
obligation to another person, who would be called in English
Law his assignee.   If the subject of the obligation happen to
be in one State, and the assignment to be made in another,
some questions of importance and of difficulty may arise as to
the Law which is to govern the form of the assignment, the
manner of enforcing it, the possible conflict between the
rights and liens of the assignee and the creditor or trustee
of the assignor.

DCCLIX. What the English Law terms *choses in action,*
e. g., Debts and Rights or Causes of Action, are universally
treated by jurists as attached to the person of the creditor,
and governed by the Law of his Domicil. (*a*)   They may be
the subject of assignment either absolutely or conditionally,
with or without notice of intimation to the debtor, according
to that Law.   This position is, in fact, a part of the general

---

(*a*) *Story,* ss. 353, 355, 356, 395—400 ;
3 *Burge,* 777–8 ;
1 *Bell,* 556.

proposition that moveables are transferable according to the *lex domicilii* of the owner. It is well supported as an axiom of English, Scotch, and North American United States Law, by the authority of Lord Hardwicke, Lord Loughborough, Lord Kenyon, Lord Kames, and Mr. Justice Story. (*b*)

The English Judges, as will be seen, apply this doctrine not only to *voluntary assignment* by the party, but also to *assignment by operation of Law*, as in case of bankruptcy.

DCCLX. The *lex fori*, as will be seen, governs the form in which remedies are to be enforced. On this principle Mr. Burge is of opinion that even an obligation, assignable by the *lex domicilii* of the obligee, must be sued upon in England, where choses in action are by the common Law not assignable in the name of the original obligee ; an Irish case (*c*) to the contrary cannot, he thinks, counterbalance the English cases (*d*) which have decided this point.

It would seem to be reasonable, however, that a distinction should be taken between the case of an obligation which was assignable in its origin and inception, and the case of one not so assignable, (*e*) and to confine to the latter class the rule insisted upon by Mr. Burge.

DCCLXI. As to the form of the assignment itself, the *lex loci* of the transaction must govern : this question and others kindred to it are more fully discussed in a subsequent chapter on Bills of Exchange.

(*b*) *Sill* v. *Worswick*, 1 *H. Blackstone*, 131, 665, &c., and cases therein referred to.

Selkrig v. *Davis*, 2 *Rose's Bank. Cases*, 97.

Hunter v. *Potts*, 4 *Durnford & East's Rep.* 182—192.

Story, s. 397-8.

(*c*) *O'Callaghan* v. *Thomond*, 3 *Taunton's Rep.* 81.

(*d*) *Folliott* v. *Ogden*, 1 *H. Blackstone*, 131.

Innes v. *Dunlop*, 8 *Durnford & East's Rep.* 595.

Wolf v. *Oxholm*, 6 *Maule & Selwyn*, 99.

Jeffery v. *MacTaggart*, *ib.* 126.

(*e*). *Westlake*, s. 242.

DCCLXII. Questions of great nicety and difficulty may arise on the subject of priority of liens, in cases where the assignment is validly made in one state of an obligation or of any other personal property but the property happens to be locally in another state, by the Law of which it is liable to be attached by a creditor or trustee of the assignor. The true rule would seem to be, that if the creditor or trustee of the assignor had notice, at any time before judgment, of the prior lien of the assignees, such lien would be entitled to priority. The *lex fori* might certainly hold a different doctrine, and apply wrongly the maxim *qui prior est in tempore potior est in jure;* but then the property might be found afterwards in a third state, and the assignee might there sue for it, and the court of this third state decide that the assignee, and not the creditor or trustee of the assignor, was entitled to it.

DCCLXIII. On the other hand, where the attachment has been made by the creditor or trustee in the place where the property actually is, before the assignor has made the assignment, there is room for the application of the maxim *qui prior est in tempore potior est in jure;* and Story agrees, with the high authority of Casaregis, that it would be rightly applied by giving priority to the lien of the creditor or trustee over that of the assignee. (*f*)

DCCLXIV. In the last chapter we considered the transfer of an obligation by the voluntary act of the obligee. In this (*g*) chapter we have to consider the transfer of an

---

(*f*) *Story*, s. 399, 400, 400*α* (5th ed.), refers to recent decisions in *Louisiana.*

(*g*) *Savigny*, viii. s. 374 E.

J. Voet, s. 17.*Comm. ad Pand.* xx. 4, s. 12.

Puffendorf, t. i. obs. 217.

Merlin, Rep., Faillite et Banqueroute, s. 2, 11, art. x.

11 *Massé*, s. 61, 72, 314, 315, 328.

Story, s. 338—341 as to *discharge;* 403—423 as to *assignment.*

2 *Bell's Comm.* (ed. *Shaw*), 1294.

obligation by the operation of the law upon the property of the obligee; that is, the effect of his bankruptcy or insolvency. (*h*)

DCCLXV. The effect of the bankruptcy or insolvency (*concursus creditorum—Concurs. Faillite—Banqueroute*) of the obligor upon the obligation is most important; it has the double consequence of *transferring* and of *discharging* the obligation. (*i*)

DCCLXVI. Bankruptcy—as it is well put by Savigny—supposes this state of things: a debtor unable to pay more creditors than one (*k*) the full amount of his debt to them. In order to apportion this amount, his whole property must be collected into one mass or heap, be turned into money, and distributed according to certain principles amonsgt his creditors.

As the object to be attained by this process is to deal with the claims and rights of various creditors, this can only be successfully accomplished at one place; and that place, it is obvious, ought to be the Domicil of the debtor. This is a case, therefore, in which the *special* jurisdiction appertaining to the obligation itself must give place to the jurisdiction over the person of the obligor.

That this question should receive an uniform answer from

III. *Burge*, 886, ch. xxii.

Westlake, ch. ix.

(*h*) By the bill now introduced by the Attorney-General (Sir R. Bethell), this anomalous and discreditable distinction will be removed, " the two systems will be entirely blended together, and there will be " a common adjudication of bankruptcy affecting both traders and " non-traders."—*Speech of At.-Gen.* p. 8 (1860).

(*i*) This portion of the subject is considered in a later chapter, on the *discharge* of obligations.

(*k*) "Bankruptcy is nothing in the world more than taking the " whole of the debtor's property by one universal execution, or by one " universal surrender, for the benefit of his creditors."—*Speech of At.-Gen.* (1860), p. 1.

the various States which compose the great community of moral societies, is a matter of the last importance to the best interests of commerce ; and, perhaps, the practice of comity is more in accordance with reason and justice upon this point than upon any other.

DCCLXVII. The collection of the scattered property of the debtor into one mass, and its conversion into money, can be effected without difficulty where the property is situate within one state and one jurisdiction. The difficulty arises when the property is dispersed, situate in various states, and subject to various jurisdictions : what jurisdiction shall then obtain, what Law ought to govern the dealing with the bankrupt's estate, both as to its collection and distribution, and be binding on all the creditors ?

DCCLXVIII. It is clear that in all cases in which the property of the bankrupt is in various states, that one of two systems must be adopted : Either (I.) there must be as many adjudications in bankruptcy as there are places in which there happens to be a portion of the debtor's property ; or (II.) there must be one adjudication in bankruptcy at the Domicil of the debtor. The first is a barbarous system, fraught with inconvenience and injustice. It is also open to the objection of establishing the *forum rei sitæ* for personal actions. The second is in harmony with the soundest principles of comity. And if the foreign state allows the curator appointed by the state of the debtor's Domicil to bring actions according to the *lex fori* in its own tribunals, the national independence is preserved, while international and general justice is promoted.

DCCLXIX. The true principles of International Law are laid down by Gail in clear language : "Quoniam sæpe contingit, " hujusmodi decoctores et debitores fugitivos. et fraudulenter " latitantes, in *diversis locis* merces et alia bona habere, quis " erit judex competens, pro faciendà immissione vel venditione " quorumcumque bonorum in alieno territorio existentium ? " *Dicendum judicem domicilii debitoris adeundum esse,* " ad hoc ut cognoscat, et pronuntiet super faciendà immissione, " vel venditione quorumcumque bonorum existentium." He adds a sound limitation, or rather accessary proposition : " Ut " *executio* non potest fieri per eundem judicem sed *judex* " *territorii adiri, et pro faciendâ executione* requiri debit." (*l*)

DCCLXX. The decisions of the English, Scotch, and Irish have, after much debate and controversy, slowly but firmly incorporated the true principles of International Law upon this question into their domestic jurisprudence. The following propositions are now firmly established :—First, that the moveable or personal estate of the bankrupt must be taken to be situated in that state in which the bankrupt is domiciled. Secondly, that a proceeding by adjudication in bankruptcy in England or in Ireland, and the assignment following thereupon,—a sequestration in Scotland,—and, in fine, any assignment under the bankrupt Law of a foreign state in which the debtor was domiciled,—have the effect of transferring to the persons nominated by Law—whether assignees, trustees, syndics, or curators—the whole *moveable* estate of the bankrupt. England, therefore, recognises the operation of the foreign bankrupt Law upon English personalty ; and expects, and as far as she can enforces, the same recognition of Law, bankrupt Law, upon personalty in a foreign state. From these two principal propositions the following are corollaries which have been worked out on reason and principle : viz.,

1. That an attachment by an English creditor, not acquired by a specific lien *prior* to, but acquired *after*, the assignment of a foreign bankruptcy, with or without notice (*m*) to the bankrupt, is impotent to effect the assignment.

2. That, nevertheless, if the Law of the foreign state in which the property may be, should, in violation of comity, exercise jurisdiction over the property, and by express regulation prefer the claim of the attaching creditor to the

---

(*l*) Lib. ii. obs. 130 ; lib. i. obs. 113, n. 16 ; cited 3 *Burge*, 905.

(*m*) *Story*, s. 409.

Westlake, s. 279 (4).

previous assignment under the bankruptcy, the title so conveyed by the *lex rei sitæ* and *lex fori* would not be disregarded in England so as to compel the creditor, when within English jurisdiction, to refund the property so acquired. (*n*)

3. That such a creditor, however, will not be allowed to take advantage of the English Bankruptcy without first communicating the benefit derived from his proceedings in the foreign state.

4. That the last-mentioned axiom, however, does not apply where the creditor obtains by his diligence something which did not and could not form a part of the English fund, or pass to the assignees under the assignment, *e. g.*, foreign real estate. (*o*)

DCCLXXI. The case of *Le Feuvre* v. *Sullivan*, recently decided by the Privy Council, is one of great importance in its bearing upon the present question. In 1833, A., domiciled in Jersey, deposited with B., domiciled in England, a policy of insurance effected in Jersey upon A.'s life, for the sum of £499, as security for the sum of £210, advanced by B. to him. This transaction took place in England. No notice of the deposit was given to the Insurance Office, who afterwards, upon a false representation of the loss of the policy, delivered to A. a duplicate of the policy, which, in 1833, he by deed assigned to his wife (from whom he had obtained a judicial sentence of *separation de biens*), in consideration of the sum of £400, alleged to have been paid by her to him. Notice of this assignment was given to the

---

(*n*) *Sill* v. *Worswick*, 1 *H. Blackstone's Rep.* 693.

Cazenove v. *Prevost*, 5 *B. & Alderson*, 70.

(*o*) *Cockerel* v. *Diekens*, 2 *Moore's P. C. Reps.* 98.

Mr. Westlake remarks (s. 284), that in England and the North American United States a bonâ fide payment, made by bankrupt's *debtor* under process of foreign Law, protects him from a second payment at the suit of the assignees in the bankrupt's Domicil. (*Le Chevalier* v. *Lynch, Douglas, Rep.* 170.) The assignees can only recover from the *creditor*.

Insurance Office. A., or his wife, paid the premiums till A.'s death. In 1838, A. became insolvent, and made a *cessio bonorum* of his property, but no proof of B.'s debt was registered by him under A.'s insolvency. In an action brought in Jersey by A.'s wife against the Insurance Office to recover the amount of the policy, B. intervened, and claimed a lien under the deposit with him by A. of the original policy. Held, first, that as B.'s Domicil was English, and the contract made in England, B. had by the English Law a lien upon the policy : second, that the *cessio bonorum* made by A., in Jersey, did not affect such lien. (*p*)

DCCLXXII. In the same case it was decided that a debtor's *person*, and his general estate before and after his death, may, by bankruptcy, or judicial insolvency, or lapse of time, be effectually discharged or protected from a debt to which *property* specifically pledged for it, specifically charged for it, or specifically made a security for it, may yet remain liable. (*q*)

DCCLXXIII. The French Law is, in its general principle, liberal on this subject; it admits the syndic, nominated (*r*) by the state, which has cognizance of the bankruptcy, to take proceedings against the bankrupt's effects in France : nor, as it would appear, according to the latter opinion, does it inquire whether the bankruptcy has been declared with or contrary to the consent of the bankrupt ; in either case (*s*) the sentence operates in France as a *chose jugée* by a competent

---

(*p*) *Le Feuvre* v. *Sullivan, Executors* (1855), 10 *Moore's P. C. Rep.* p. 1 (marginal note).

(*q*) *Le Feuvre* v. *Sullivan*, 10 *Moore's P. C. Rep.* p. 13.

Clark v. *Mullick*, 3 *Moore's P. C. Rep.* 252, was the case of an *assumpsit* by the assignee of a bankrupt, under an English commission, against a native of India, resident within the jurisdiction of Calcutta. The English Bankruptcy Acts were holden not to affect the mode of taking evidence in India.

(*r*) *Fœlix*, s. 468, ed. *Demangeat,* p. 204, n. *a.*, editor reviews in a note the whole law.

(*s*) *Massé*, t. ii. s. 314, thinks only in the latter case.

tribunal.   But this proposition does not extend to the case of a bankrupt who has two trading establishments, (t) one of which is in France, the other foreign.   There seems to be a doubt, however, whether the sentence of the foreign bankruptcy can be pleaded in bar of proceedings taken by individuals against the effects or the property in France.   Fælix asserts that it cannot : M. Demangeat thinks it can, except against a French creditor : an exception in favour of native subjects, the principle of which pervades many of the judgments of the French courts in cases where the rights of a foreigner and a native come into collision.   Another question has been much discussed—whether a foreign sentence of bankruptcy affects the civil capacity of the bankrupt in France.   Fælix affirms that it does, the same as *un jugement d'interdiction.* (u) Massé thinks that the bankrupt would not be permitted to have an account at the Bank of France, or be allowed the entrée of the Bourse ; but that it would be competent to him to make payments and transfer property not forbidden by the sentence of bankruptcy ; that the sentence has the effect of a *real* and not a *personal* statute.

M. Demangeat agrees with this opinion, and it is founded on the high authority Casaregis.   And as to immoveable property, the law of the French *Code de Commerce* (x) respecting the *inscription* of the *realty* of a bankrupt renders the doctrine above stated indispensable.

The French tribunal also will pronounce a sentence of bankruptcy in the case of a foreigner,—an exception to its usual principle on the subject of foreigners, founded on the

---

(t) *Vide post.*

(u) S. 89 : " L'individu interdit dans son pays, l'est aussi en pays " étranger. Il en est le même du failli déclaré tel dans sa patrie ainsi " que de l'absent."

(x) " Les syndics sont tenus de prendre inscription au nom de la masse " des créanciers, sur les immeubles du failli dont ils connaissent " l'existence."—*Art.* 490,

doctrine, that such a sentence is only "*une mésure*
" *conservatoire.*" (*y*)

DCCLXXIV. The decisions of the courts of the United States
of North America, contrary to the opinions both of Story (*z*)
and Kent, (*a*) do not admit this extra-territorial operation of
foreign bankruptcy laws ; grounding their breach of comity in
this respect upon the plea that the admission of the foreign law
would in this case prejudice the right of their own citizens. (*b*)
Nevertheless, in most of the cases in which assignments under
foreign bankrupt laws have been denied to give a title against
attaching creditors, (*c*) it has been admitted that the assignees
might maintain, under such assignments, suits in the United
States courts for the property of the bankrupt; and Story
justly observes that this admission surrenders the principle,
inasmuch as the assignees could not sue unless they possessed
some title under the assignment.

DCCLXXV. In fact, as Story (*d*) says, the point in the
North American United States has hitherto been a struggle
for priority and preference between parties claiming against
the bankrupt under opposing titles ; the assignees claiming
for their general creditors, and the attaching creditors for their
separate rights.

These priorities and privileges are, in the case of *moveable*
property, as a general rule, governed (*e*) by the law of the

---

(*y*) So decided by *Trib. de Commerce de la Seine*, 7 Oct., 1846 ;
Gar. des Trib. 8 Oct.

(*z*) S. 409, &c.

(*a*) 2 *Comm.* 406.

(*b*) *Belton* v. *Valentine*, 1 *Curtis* (*Amer.*) *C. C. R.* 168.

Booth v. *Clark*, 17 *Howard* (*Amer.*), 322.

Remsen v. *Holmes*, 20 *Johnson's* (*Amer.*) *R.* 229 : this appears to be
the leading case.

(*c*) *Story*, s. 420.

(*d*) S. 420 ; *Ogden* v. *Saunders*, 12 *Wheaton's* (*Amer.*) *R.* 359—365.

(*e*) The *lex sitûs* may prescribe a different rule.

Andrewes v. *His Creditors*, 11 *Louisiana R.* (*Amer.*) 476.

debtor of the domicil, and in the case of *real* property by the *lex rei sitæ;* (*f*) the same principle ought to be applied both to the assignments of the debtor, voluntarily made, and to an assignment made under the operation of a law of bankruptcy.

DCCLXXVI. Upon this nice question of the *privilegia* or priority of liens, it is to be observed that the states which have adopted as their basis the Roman Law, (*g*) have, according to Savigny, (*h*) worked out the following system.

All the creditors are divided into five classes :—

1. Those who have absolute privileges or rights of priority.

2. Those who have privileged hypothecs.

3. Those who have ordinary hypothecs.

4. Those who have personal privileges.

5. All who are not included under the foregoing categories.

Of these five classes, the first, the fourth, and the fifth consist of pure obligations, and are clearly justiciable by the Law of the place in which the bankruptcy is declared, whatever may be the place in which the obligation had its origin, or in which it was to be fulfilled.

The second and the third classes relate to creditors who have a hypothec or mortgage. Every creditor of this description has in reality a right of a mixed character, composed partly of a simple creditor's right, and partly of a right appertaining to real property.

In Savigny's opinion, the tribunal of bankruptcy sitting in the domicil of the debtor, ought to include these hypothecs or mortgages ; but should preserve to each creditor the priority· and privilege conferred on him by the Law of the place in which the thing, which is the subject of the hypothec or mortgage, is situated. For he holds it to be clear Law that

---

(*f*) *Story*, 423.

(*g*) See the *cessio bonorum* of the Roman Law discussed in a later chapter on the *discharge* of obligation.

(*h*) *Savigny*, viii. s. 374.

this right of priority is governed by the *lex rei sitœ*. The proof that such a scheme is practicable, is to be found in the fact that it is the basis of various treaties which Prussia has entered into with her neighbours, and which is found in practice to work well.

DCCLXXVII. Mr. Bell, after speaking of the establishment in Scotland of the true principles of International Law on the subject of bankruptcy, in the case of individuals, observes, " Great difficulty still remained in the case of a *company* " having a Domicil in several countries. Admitting the " doctrine of *Strothers* v. *Reid,* as ruling the case of an " *individual—viz.,* that the Law of the Domicil regulates, in " bankruptcy, as in succession, the effect of the conveyance to " the creditors,—still it was doubtful what should be the effect " of a double Domicil with a double set of creditors, and " trusting to the laws of bankruptcy as established in the " Domicil of their debtor. This was the difficulty that occurred " in the case of the *Royal Bank of Scotland* v. *Stein;* but " the court disregarded the distinction, and held the proceed- " ings in bankruptcy, in either of the Domicils of the company, " to comprehend the whole personal estate of the entire " concern." (*i*)

But in England a different opinion appears to have obtained. Sir W. Grant has holden, that the bankruptcy of a partner, resident in England, could not affect the partners remaining in the West Indies, so as to divest them of the management of the partnership concerns, or of the disposition of the part- nership property; and that the British West Indian creditor of the firm, who had attached a debt due to the firm in the West Indies, and procured a judgment and satisfaction there, could not be compelled to refund the same upon a suit brought by the assignees against him in England. (*k*)   Story considers

---

(*i*) 2 *Bell* (ed. *Shaw*), 1296.
Rose's Cases, 462.
(*k*) *Brickwood* v. *Miller,* 3 *Merivale's Rep* 279.

this doctrine to be generally recognised by foreign states, in cases where partners reside in different states." (*l*)

DCCLXXVIII. In 1856 a very important case, involving the consideration of the rules of International Law, applicable to cases of double partnership, came before the Lords Justices. D. and Y. carried on business in Liverpool in partnership as " D., Y., & Co." D. & Y. and Y. also carried on business in Pernambuco in partnership, as " D., Y., & Co." The two firms were separate and distinct, and the third partner in the Pernambuco trade had not any interest in the Liverpool business. The Pernambuco house drew bills upon and they were accepted by the Liverpool house, bonâ fide, and in the ordinary course of business ; and two of such bills came into the hands of G. & K. honestly in the due course of trade.

The English firm became bankrupts, and afterwards the Pernambuco firm entered into a " concôrdata" with their creditors, under which they vested property in trustees for the benefit of their creditors. G. & K. received a dividend, under the " concordata," out of the assets vested in the trustees of the Pernambuco firm, as drawers of the bill. They subsequently attempted to prove against the Liverpool firm, as acceptors of the bills, but one of the Commissioners decided, upon the authority of Ex-parte Hinton, that there was no right to double proof, and, upon appeal, the same was affirmed, Lord Justice Turner agreeing with the Commissioner, Lord Justice Knight Bruce dissenting.

Such bills, it was holden, having been accepted in England, are to be dealt with by the rules of English Law.

In this case, Lord Justice Knight Bruce said, " I avow my opinion to be, that abstract justice and the principles of commercial law and of general jurisprudence are with the

---

(*l*) *Story*, s. 422.
Merlin Rep. Faillite, s. 2, art. 10.
Harrison v. *Cherry*, 5 *Cranch's* (*Amer.*) *Rep.* 289, 302.

petitioners, that the law of England is not opposed to them, and that our order should be accordingly." (*m*) The House of Lords, however, held, on appeal, that the double proof was not admissible, and affirmed the decision of the Court below. (*n*)

DCCLXXIX. The International effect of assignment under Bankruptcy Laws, is confined by the practice of states to *moveable* property. These laws therefore only transfer such *immoveable* property as lies within their jurisdiction. It follows that an assignee or curator, appointed by these Laws, cannot assume the possession or administration of immoveable property in a foreign state, unless his authority is enforced by the judicial tribunals of that State. (*o*) And yet Mr. Bell

---

(*m*) *Ex-parte Goldsmid*; In re *Dean and Youle* (1856), *Law Journal*, vol. 25 (N. S.), p. 25 ; *S. C. The Jurist*, vol. 2 (1856), p. 1106.

(*n*) *Same Case* (August, 1859), *The Jurist*, N. S., vol. 5, p. 1230.

Referring to this decision the City Article in *The Times* (August 18, 1859,) observes, " It must, therefore, in future, be understood that a bill " of exchange drawn abroad upon any establishment in London connected " by an identity of membership will, in the event of bankruptcy, involve "'a recourse as limited as if it were simply a promissory note. The result " will be to cause the bills of native firms abroad to be preferred to those " of English firms drawing upon their own connections. Indeed, this " has already been manifested, the Brazilian Government, upon whose " account the bills which formed the subject of the present trial were " purchased for remittance, having, it is said, since the question was " raised, ordered their financial agents to make no more purchases of " paper drawn upon Europe by houses thus constituted."

All the English cases on the subject will be found referred to in this case—but especially the cases of *Ex-parte Moult*, 1 *Montagu's Rep.* 321; and *Ex-parte Hinton*, 2 *De Gex's Rep.* 550—approved and affirmed.

A Joint English Commission of Bankruptcy has been holden not to be superseded on the ground of a previous separate Irish Commission. *Ex-parte Cridland*, 3 *Vesey & Beame's Rep.* 94.

(*o*) *Gaill.* l. ii. obs. 130.

Voet, lib. xlii. t. vii. n. 2.

Voet, lib. xx. t. iv. n. 12.

P. Voet, de Stat. s. 9, c. ii. n. 18 ; s. 4, c. ii. n. 6.

1 *Boullenois*, 129, 150 ; cited 3 *Burge*, 921.

justly observes, that the spirit and policy of the Laws, considered internationally, should open to the creditors of bankrupts the power of attaching real estates.

The provisions of a recent English Insolvent Debtors Act,(*p*) vest in an assignee all the bankrupt's real and personal estate, "both within this realm and abroad;" in Scotland effect has been given to this provision.(*q*)

(*p*) 1 & 2 V. c. 110.

(*q*) 2 *Bell* (ed. *Shaw*), 1297, n. c.

CHAPTER XL.

OBLIGATION—DISCHARGE—UNDER WHAT LAW.

DCCLXXX. It is proposed in this chapter to consider the question—

1. How an *obligatio* is discharged or becomes extinct.

2. By what Law the discharge or extinction is governed.

The latter question is, of course, the one which is more properly the subject of this treatise; but the former is not an uninteresting question of general jurisprudence.

DCCLXXXI. And first as to the Roman Law, the basis of European jurisprudence: " Ut obligandi," Donellus says, " certi modi sunt jure constituti, ita et liberandi." (*a*)

An *obligatio* ceases to be binding (*tollitur*) in various ways. The following are said to be discharges of an *obligatio ipso jure* :—

1. By actual payment of what was due—*solutione*. (*b*)

2. By a verbal acknowledgment in a particular form of words that payment has, though actually it has not, been received—*acceptilatione*. (*c*)

(*a*) *Comm. de J. C.* l. xvi. c. 1—" *De solutionibus et omnis generis* " *liberationibus.*" This is an admirable chapter, and deserves the most careful study.

(*b*) By whatever means the *obligatio* ceases, " solvitur obligatio " is the proper technical expression.

3 *Burge*, ch. xxi. p. 781.

Rocco, p. 347, c. 8.

Savigny, R. R. V. s. 248.

Puchta Pand. s. 286—292.

(*c*) *Dig.* xlvi. t. iv. ; xlviii. t. xi. s. 7.

At first only applied to debts contracted by *stipulatio*.

3. An *obligatio* contracted *per es et libram*, by which the debtor becomes *nexus*, might be dissolved by a similar symbolical process.

4. By being changed into another *obligatio*, for which the technical term was *novatio*. (*d*)

5. By the relations of obligor and obligee, or of debtor and creditor becoming united in one person, which is termed *confusio*.

DCCLXXXII. The following are said to be discharges of an *obligatio*—*ope exceptionis* or *per exceptionem.*

1. By a decision of a competent court of justice, *res judicata*, or *ex causâ judicatâ*. Indeed, strictly speaking, the *obligatio*, in its technical sense, ceased as soon as legal proceedings, *litis contestatio*, began ; but the *naturalis obligatio* is not destroyed by the *res judicata.*

2. By a treaty (*e*) or agreement known to the civil (*f*) and canon Law (*g*) by the term *transactio*, which is *species pacti*. Three conditions were necessary to found this mode of extinguishing an obligation : (*h*)

a. That the *transactio* should be *de re dubiâ ac lite incertâ*.

β. That something should be promised.

γ. Or something done as an equivalent for the right waived.

DCCLXXXIII. The modes of discharge or extinction, according to the English Law, vary in name, but scarcely in substance, from those of the Roman and Continental jurisprudence.

For instance, the direct fulfilment of the obligation, or the payment of the debt, is of course the *solutio* ; its extinction

---

(*d*) *Dig.* l. xlvi. t. ii.

(*e*) Called by the Germans *vergleich :* see *Puchta Pandekt.* s. 294 : different from *compromiss*, which answers to our *arbitration.*

(*f*) *Dig.* ii. 15.

Cod. l. ii. t. iv. *De transactionibus.*

(*g*) *Devoti Instit. Canon.* l. iii. t. xviii. *De pactis et transactionibus.*

(*h*) *Cod. ib.* 38.

or *merger*, (*i*) by the acceptance, on the part of the obligee, of another *and higher* security, (*k*) answers to the *novatio;* its extinction by the marriage of the obligor and obligee, or by the appointment of the obligor as executor, (*l*) answers to the *confusio;* the *set off* answers to the *compensatio;* the Statutes of Limitation answer to the *præscriptio.*

The same observations apply to the North American United States, with the exception of Louisiana, which is governed by the Roman Law.

DCCLXXXIV. The Civil Law required for the discharge of certain conventions, that the *transactio* should be effected through the medium of the *Aquiliana stipulatio.* But these technicalities were disregarded by the Canon Law, which greatly favoured this mode of adjusting disputes:

" Sed canones," Devoti says, " non laborant de istâ nimis " attenuatâ diligentiâ juris civilis et Aquilianâ etiam stipula- " tione neglectâ, obligationes quoquo modo contractas *trans- " actione* omnino perire volunt." (*m*)

DCCLXXXV. We have now to consider (II.) by what Law (*n*) the validity of the discharge or extinction of the obligation is governed. (*o*)

DCCLXXXVI. The general principle is thus enunciated by two distinguished jurists: " Ut ita," *J. Voet* says, " secundum " cujus loci jura implementum accipere debuit contractus " juxta ejus etiam leges resolvatur." (*p*) · *Burgundus* lays

---

(*i*) *Broom, Comm. on Common Law,* p. 283, &c., as to *merger.*
(*k*) 3 *Burge,* 793.
(*l*) *Ib.* 798.
(*m*) *Devoti, ib.* s. vii.
(*n*) *Rocco,* c. viii.
11 *Massé,* s. 127, &c.
3 *Burge,* 874.
Story, s. 330, &c.
2 *Bell, Comm.* 1294 (ed. *Shaw*).
Westlake, s. 246.
(*o*) *Vide ante,* p.
(*p*) Lib. iv. t. i. n. 29.

down the rule, perhaps, more accurately : " Ea qua ad com-
" plementum vel executionem contractûs spectant, vel abso-
" luto eo superveniunt, *solere a statuto loci dirigi, in quo*
" *peragenda est solutio.* Rationem mutuantur a juriscon-
" sulto, qui unumquemque vult, in eo loco comtraxîsse intel-
" ligi in quo ut solveret se obligavit." (*q*)

The result of all the best authorities, juridical and judicial,
is that the discharge of an obligation, in the state in which it
was contracted to be discharged, is everywhere recognised as
a valid discharge.   It is frequently said that the discharge
must be according to the Law of the place of the contract, but
this is, because that is assumed to be identical with the place
fixed for the payment of the debt (*r*) or discharge of the
obligation: and Burgundus, therefore, says accurately, "*locus*
" in quo peragenda est *solutio.*" (*s*)   This is in accordance
with the maxim taken from the Roman Law, " Contraxîsse
" unusquisque in eo loco intelligitur in quo ut solveret se
" obligavit." (*t*)

It is to be remembered that the place in which the contract
is made is always presumed to be the place in which it is to
be performed unless some other place is named. (*u*)

DCCLXXXVII. The decisions of the English and North
American United States are happily in accordance with the
opinions of foreign jurists. Lord Mansfield first laid down
with authority and firmness the rule, " that what is a dis-
" charge of a debt in the country where it was contracted is a
" discharge of it everywhere." (*x*)   And this judgment is one

---

(*q*) Tr. iv. ⅄. 29, of 2 *Boullenois*, p. 498 ; cited 3 *Burge*, 875.

(*r*) *Vide ante*, p.

(*s*) So *Paul Voet, de Stat.* s. ix. c. 11, n. 11, c. 12 ; cited *Rocco*, 344 :
" Ratione *effectus* et *complementi* ipsius contractûs, spectatur ille locus,
" in quem destinata est *solutio.*'

(*t*) *Vide ante*, p. 476.

(*u*) 3 *Burge*, 875.

(*x*) *Ballantine* v. *Golding*, 1 *Cooper's Bankr. Laws*, 347.
Hunter v. *Potts*, 4 *Durnford & East's Rep.* 182.
Potter v. *Brown*, 5 *East's Rep.* 130.

of the most important subjects of International Jurisprudence which has taken firm root in English Law.

And it is to be observed that the English authorities, as well as the continental, maintain the universality of the rule, and recognise in its application no distinction between a native subject and a foreigner as between foreigners. And on the whole the same doctrine may be said to be maintained by the North American United States. (*y*)

DCCLXXXVIII. The only limitation to this rule is that which has been before adverted to, (*z*) and which accompanies all questions of comity; viz., the discharge of the obligation must of course not contravene the plain principles of justice, or be manifestly injurious to the clear and fair rights of the native subject whose state is called upon to recognise the validity of the discharge. " If a state," says a great American judge, (*a*) " should enact that its citizens should be " discharged from all debts due to creditors living without " the state, such a provision would be so contrary to the " common principles of justice, that the most liberal spirit " of comity would not require its adoption in any other " state." (*b*)

DCCLXXXIX. It appears, too, that the rule *e converso* is applicable; namely, that a discharge of a contract by the Law of the place where the contract was not to be performed ought not to operate as a discharge in any other state.

This rule has been firmly established by judicial decisions of Great Britain and the North American United States. (*c*)

(*y*) *Story*, s. 340.

(*z*) *Vide ante*, p.

(*a*) Mr. Chief Justice Parker, in *Blanchard* v. *Russell*, 13 *Massachusets Rep.* 6.

Story, s. 349, 350, 351.

(*b*) To the same effect is the case of *Wolfe* v. *Oxholme*, 6 *Maule & Selwyn's Rep.* 92; though, in my judgment, as I have already ventured to observe, the principle of Law was wrongly applied to the act of a belligerent state. *Vide ante*, vol. iii. p. 133.

(*c*) *Smith* v. *Buchanan*, 1 *East's Rep.* 6, 11.

DCCXC. As to *the form* of the discharge or payment;
according to sound principles of International Jurisprudence,
a discharge in the form which is valid in the place where it
is given ought to be holden valid everywhere, although
another form would be required by the Law of the place in
which the obligation was contracted to be fulfilled. It is, as
Massé (*d*) says, "une *suite* de la convention," not one of its
mediate or *immediate effects;* it is an *ex post facto* act,
evidently governed by the local Law. Story (*e*) says, "the
" reasonable intrepretation of the general rule would seem to
" be, that while contracts made in one country are properly
" held to be dissoluble and extinguishable according to the
" Laws of that country, as natural incidents to the original
" concoction of such contracts, they are and may at the
" same time also be equally dissoluble and extinguishable by
" any other acts done or contracts made subsequently in
" another country by the parties, which acts or contracts,
" according to the Law of the latter country, are sufficient
" to work such a dissolution or extinguishment."

So in *Warrender* v. *Warrender*, (*f*) a case before referred
to in this treatise, Lord Brougham said : " If a contract for
" a sale of chattels is made, or an obligation of debt is
" incurred, or a chattel is pledged in one country, the sale
" may be annulled, the debt released, and the pledge re-
" deemed by the Law and by the forms of another country
" in which the parties happen to reside, and in whose courts
" their rights come in question, unless there was an express
" stipulation in the contract itself against such avoidance,
" release, or redemption." His Lordship continues—" But,

Lewis v. *Owen,* 4 *Barnewall & Alderson's Rep.* 654.
Phillips v. *Allan,* 8 *Barnewall & Cresswell's Rep.* 477.
2 *Bell's Comm.* s. 1267.
Story, s. 342 ; he says, " where the contract is *made* or performed."
(*d*) 2 *Massé,* s. 127.
(*e*) S. 351 *c.*
(*f*) 9 *Bligh's Rep.* 125.

" at any rate, this is certain, that if the Laws of one country,
" and its courts, recognise and give effect to those of another,
" in respect to the constitution of any contract, they must
".give the like recognition and effect to those same foreign
" Laws when they declare (*g*) the same kind of contract
" dissolved."

DCCXCI. On principle, therefore, the discharge of an
obligation, according to *the form* of the *lex loci* in which
it is discharged, ought to be treated as a discharge everywhere. Thus, in the case put by Story, (*h*) a bond executed
in England for the payment of money, if payment be made
in France, and a discharge given in that country under a
written but *unsealed* instrument, it would certainly be holden
valid in France, it ought to be holden valid in every third
country, and it ought also to be holden valid even in England.
" For " (Story argues) " if the contract derives its whole origi-
" nal obligatory force from the Law of the place where it is
" made, it is but following out the same principle to hold,
" that any act subsequently done, touching the same contract
" by the same parties, should have the same obligatory force
" and operation upon it, which the Law of the place, where it
" is done, attributes to it." Story does not see any reason
why, in this respect, there should be any difference between
those contracts which affect *personal* property only, and those
which impose a *charge* upon *real* property. This doctrine of
the *indirect* effect of a discharge according to the *lex loci* of
liens on immoveable property, is not inconsistent with the
proposition that *lex situs* governs *directly* the rights to such
property ; and he quotes with approbation the following
remarks of Lord Brougham in *Warrender* v. *Warrender* :—
" All personal obligations may, in their consequences, affect
" real rights in England; nor does a Scotch divorce, by

(*g*) This is according to the maxim, fully adopted by the English
Law, " Eodem modo quo quid constituitur, eodem modo dissolvitur."
(*h*) S. 351*a*.

" depriving a widow of dower or arrears of pin-money, charged
" on English property, more immediately affect real estate
" here than a bond or a judgment released in Scotland,
" according to Scotch forms, discharges real estates of a
" lien, or than a bond executed or, indeed, a simple contract
" debt incurred in Scotland, eventually and subsequently
" charges real estate." (*i*)

DCCXCII. It may be proper, however, to observe here,
that, with respect to what are termed, in English Law,
executory contracts, respecting real or immoveable property,
the English, Scotch, and North American United States
Courts pronounce, *uno ore*, (*k*) that they are governed exclusively by the *lex situs*. Considerable difference of opinion
upon the subject prevails among foreign jurists. (*l*)

On the other hand, the great majority of foreign jurists
agree with the English and Scotch authorities in holding that
contracts respecting personal property, debts, and the like,
have no fixed *situs*, but follow the person of their owner. (*m*)

DCCXCIII. The cases considered in the foregoing paragraphs relate to the actual, *substantial* discharge of the
obligation, according to its true intent and meaning, though
according to a form unknown to the *lex loci* in which the
obligation was contracted.

The obligation, however, may be otherwise discharged. The
obligor and obligee may consent that the obligation shall be
dissolved, or the obligee may freely release the obligor from
the bond, or the obligation may be discharged, as has been
stated, by the introduction of a new obligation between the
same obligor and obligee (*novatio*), or by the obligor and
obligee, or creditor and debtor, becoming the same person

(*i*) 2 *Bligh's Rep.* 125.

(*k*) *Story*, s. 363.

(*l*) *Ib.* s. 368.

(*m*) *Ib.* s. 362.

Vide ante as to *Savigny's* opinion.

(*confusio*). In these cases a new obligation, or a new contract, supersedes and dissolves the former.

This new obligation, or contract, is to be governed by the same rule as the former one, that is, by the Law of the place in which it is to be fulfilled.

DCCXCIV. We have been considering what Law shall govern with reference to cases in which the discharge of the obligation has been effected by the *acts of both the parties* to it. But there remains the difficult question as to what law shall govern the discharge of the obligation, without the consent of the obligee, *in invitum*, by the mere *operation of the law*.

It was mentioned in a former chapter, that the discharge of an obligation might be effected by the operation of law without the consent of the obligee in the case of an adjudication in bankruptcy. (*n*) In that chapter, the discussion of the principles by which such a discharge was effected was necessarily anticipated.

It remains to add a few remarks upon this mode of discharge.

DCCXCV. According to the old Roman Law, the debtor was liable to imprisonment and to the disgrace (*infamia*) consequent on the seizure and sale of all his property; in order to avoid the severity of this, a law was passed, or a practice arose, dating from the time of Sylla or Julius Cæsar, which protected the debtor whose insolvency had been caused by misfortune from the severity of the old Law, on the condition of his voluntarily surrendering all his property.

This act of surrender was called the *cessio bonorum;* (*o*) it would seem also to have been attended by this advantage, that if the debtor acquired property, subsequent to the *cessio,* his creditors could not seize upon the whole of it, but could only

---

(*n*) *Vide ante,*

(*o*) *Dig.* l. xlii. t. 3 ; *de cessione bonorum.*

Cod. vii. 71 ; *qui bonis cedere possunt.*

compel him to pay a portion : " In id quod facere potest,
" inhumanum enim erat spoliatum fortunis suis in solidum
" damnari." (*p*)

The *cessio* might be made judicially in court, or by a
declaration out of court, at the will of the debtor, communicated by a letter or messenger.

The creditors to whom the *cessio* was made, were not allowed
to retain and divide the property, but were compelled to sell it
to the highest bidder. After the sale, but not before, the debtor
was divested of the *dominium* over his property. As soon as
the *cessio* was announced, a *curator* (*q*) was appointed, who
undertook the care and administration of the property
previously to its sale, and by whom all actions competent to
the debtor were enforced.

The *cessio bonorum*, it should be always remembered,
properly speaking, operated as a discharge of the debtor; it
did not take away, but only suspended, the right of the
creditor to bring an action against his creditor. (*r*)

DCCXCVI. The doctrines of the Roman Law upon the
cessio bonorum have been introduced into the jurisprudence
of the continent, especially of Holland, Spain, and France; and
it is more or less blended in these countries with the modern
law of bankruptcy, which affords a permanent discharge to the
debtor from his obligations to his creditors.

DCCXCVII. The following principles upon this subject
appear to have obtained the approval of most civilised
states : (*s*)

(*p*) *Inst.* l. iv. t. 6.

Cf. Dig. l. xlii. t. 3, 4.

(*q*) *Dig.* l. xlii. t. 7, *De curatore bonis dando :*

" 2. De curatore constituendo hoc jure utimur, ut Prætor adeatur
" isque curatorem curatoresve constituet ex consensu majoris partis
" creditorum : vel Præses Provinciæ, si bona distrahenda in Provinciâ
" sunt."

(*r*) *Dig.* l. xlii. t. 3, 7.

(*s*) 3 *Burge*, 294.

1. If the proceedings consequent on the bankruptcy only release the *person* of the debtor, and not his *debt*, the debt may be satisfied by the seizure of his future property in a state other than that in which the bankruptcy took place.

2. If they discharge the *debt*, and if the state in which the bankruptcy took place be also the place of the obligation, then, but not otherwise, according to English, Scotch, French, and North American jurisprudence, the *discharge* is available against an action in any foreign state.

DCCXCVIII. The following case, decided by the Privy Council in England, illustrates the working both of the French and English Law on this question of comity. Quelin, the appellant, had been declared a bankrupt by a judgment of the Tribunal of Commerce at Nantes, on the 20th January, 1823. He obtained a protection from arrest (*sauf conduit*), but afterwards absconded to Jersey. In his absence he was prosecuted for a fraudulent bankruptcy, and was condemned *par contumace* to five years' imprisonment and hard labour (*travaux forcés*). Previously to his bankruptcy, he had given a note of hand for 7,000 francs (*billet à ordre*) to a widow of the name of Nau, in Nantes. She proved the amount of this note as a debt under the bankruptcy, but did not attend the meeting for the appointment of an assignee (*syndic definitif*) and banker, and afterwards indorsed the note over to a third person, who indorsed it to the respondent, the plaintiff in the court below, an inhabitant of Jersey. He sued the appellant for the amount of the note in the Royal Court there. The appellant pleaded his bankruptcy in France in bar of the action, and on his plea being overruled he appealed to the Privy Council. Their Lordships ordered the following questions to be referred to two French advocates, to be named by the British ambassador at Paris :—1st. Whether a person whose property had passed to Syndics under the Law "*de la faillite*" could afterwards be sued by any creditor, who had proved his debt before the Syndics? 2nd. If, generally, such person could not afterwards be sued by such a creditor, did he lose that protection by a sentence *par contumace*, and by competent judges, for not having been able to give a proper account of his receipts and disbursements, for having mis-applied several sums of money and other property to the pre-judice of his creditors, for having concealed his books, or not having kept them, and for having violated the *sauf conduit* granted him by the Tribunal of Commerce ?   The ambassador made choice of Messrs. Delagrange and Dupin ainé, and they having given their opinion upon the first point, "that the bankrupt could not be sued even by a creditor who had not proved his debts before the Syndics, and *a fortiori* could not be sued by one who had proved ; " and upon the second, "that the sentence, *par contumace,* would not have any effect so as to give a new right to sue to a creditor ; " their lordships, on the 23rd of February, 1828, reversed the judgment of the court below. (*t*)

DCCXCIX. The Privy Council have decreed that a certifi-cate obtained under an English bankruptcy is a bar to an action for debt contracted by the bankrupt at Calcutta pre-viously to his bankruptcy, although the creditor had no notice of the commission and was resident at Calcutta. (*u*)

DCCC. In accordance with the principle stated above, the Scotch courts held that where a debt had been contracted in Berbice, and a commission of bankruptcy had been issued in England against the debtor, under which he had been declared a bankrupt, and afterwards obtained his certificate, that such certificate was no bar to an action brought by the creditor against the heir of the debtor. (*x*)

DCCCI. *Prescription* is another mode by which obliga-tions are ended.   When the Law of prescription of the place in which the obligation is to be fulfilled differs from the Law of the place in which the action is brought to enforce the per-formance of it, which ought to prevail ?   There has been con-

---

(*t*) *Edwards* v. *Ronald* (1830), 1 *Knapp's P. C. Rep.* p. 266 (note).
(*u*) *Ibid.*
(*x*) *Rose* v. *Macleod,* 4 *S. & D.,* 311 ; cited 3 *Burge,* 926.

siderable difference of opinion on this subject; but the preponderance of reasoning and authority seems to be against the principle maintained by English Law. According to all true principles, Savigny says, the Law of the place of the performance shall prevail. (y) The reasons upon which the Law of prescription is founded are intimately connected with the nature of the obligation; and, apart from this ground of theoretical justice, the practical equity of the doctrine is obvious. It takes from each of the parties all power of making an arbitrary selection which may be injurious to the other. So in the case of a variety of jurisdictions to which recourse might be had, it prevents the injustice which the plaintiff might commit, by selecting that which recognises the longest term of limitation; and it will not allow the defendant, by transporting his Domicil within the jurisdiction which recognises the shortest term of limitation, to defraud the plaintiff. The time of prescription has been immutably fixed for both at the time of the contract by the Law of the place in which it is agreed that it shall be fulfilled. The opinion of Savigny is supported by many and weighty authorities, (z) and by the decision of the principal court of his own country. (a)

DCCCII. On the other hand, the doctrines that prescription is governed by the *lex fori*—that it is a question of *procedure*—that it relates to the *remedy*, not to the *nature* of the obligation—that it is among what jurists call the *ordinatoria* and not the *decisoria litis*, are propositions also maintained by jurists, and now firmly imbedded into the Law of England, Scotland, and the North American United States, (b) but upon reason-

---

(y) *Savigny, R. R.* v. s. 237, viii. 374.

(z) *Hertius,* s. 65.

Schäffner, s. 89.

Wächter, ii. 408—412, cites various authors.

(a) In 1843. *Seuffert, Archiv.* ii. num. 120.

(b) *Burge,* iii. 878, &c.

Story, s. 576, cites *Boullenois* and *Pothier, sed cf. Fælix,* s. 100, who shows that both Boullenois and Pardessus limit the application of this

ing which, as it would seem to the writer of these pages, Mr. Westlake(c) properly says, confounds the *interpretation* of the contract with the operation upon it of the *lex loci contractûs*, and which admits that the debt may be still supposed to be existent and owing, against which it nevertheless opposes the prescriptive bar of the *lex fori.*

DCCCIII. The foregoing decisions of the English courts, and those which agree with them, have at present only established this doctrine, that prescription is governed by the *lex fori*, with reference to cases in which the Prescription of the place of the contract *barred the remedy*, but did not *extinguish the claim.* Does not this latter kind of Prescription at least appertain to the "*decisoria*," and not to the "*ordinatoria* litis et causæ?" No decision, indeed, of the English or North American United States has established as yet this proposition in its full extent. The opinion and reasoning however, both of Story (*d*) and Burge, (*e*) and the judgment of the English Court of Common Pleas, (*f*) have sustained the

---

doctrine to a case in which the parties have not expressed any place for the execution of the contract.

Don v. *Lippmann, 5 Clk. & Fin. Rep.* 16 ; *Fergusson* v. *Fyffe, 8 Clk. & Fin.* 140 ; leading English and Scotch cases.

(*c*) P. 233, s. 250.

Fælix, s. 100, for himself says, " Lorsqu'il s'agit non pas de statuer " sur le fond de la demande mais d'apprecier des *defenses*, que y sont " opposées et que ont leur base dans la loi du lieu ou siege le tribunaļ " suivi de la cause on suivra cetté dernière loi." *Demangeat* shows that *Fælix* has made a mistake here, and predicted of *defenses* what was true of *exceptions.* Demangeat entirely agrees with Savigny.

(*d*) S. 483.

(*e*) III. 883, 4.

(*f*) *Huber* v. *Steiner,* 2 *Bingham's R.* (*N. S.*) 211.

Mr. Bell, in his *Commentaries on Scotch Law,* observes (*Shaw's Ed.* p. 76, s. 38), " In order correctly to mark the principle on which the " doctrine of extinction of obligations by Limitation proceeds, it is " necessary to distinguish between Limitations, properly speaking, and " what more correctly is called Prescription. Limitation is a denial of " action on an instrument or document of debt after the lapse of a cer-

proposition to this extent, viz., that if the statutes of limitation of the state in which the contract is to be performed extinguish the right, and declare it to be absolutely void after the lapse of a prescribed period, and the parties have been during that period resident within the jurisdiction of the state, that then even the Law of England will consider this prescription as extending both *ad valorem contractûs* and *ad decisionem litis*, and respect it accordingly.

DCCCIV. The larger proposition, however, mentioned above, may perhaps be deemed still open for discussion before tribunals which administer the law of England; and perhaps upon a fuller and further consideration it may be found that the residence of the parties *subsequent to the making of the contract* cannot really affect the true question, namely, whether an *extinctive prescription*, at least, incident to the Law of the place of the fulfilment of the obligation, be not a matter which concerns the nature and essence of the obligation itself, whether it was not a condition provisionally contemplated by the parties at the time when the obligation was incurred. The very learned and accomplished editor of the English "Leading Cases" (g) thus expresses himself on this point:—"Supposing the Law of " a foreign country to be, that a contract is, after a certain " time, to be deemed absolutely extinguished, it seems not " quite reasonable to say that the removal of the parties out " of the jurisdiction, while that time is running, should autho- " rise the courts of this country to consider it *in esse* after the " period prefixed. The authorities establish, that the Law of

---

" tain time, without regard to the actual subsistence of the debt. Pre- " scription is a legal presumption of payment or abandonment of the " debt. This distinction is grounded on a real difference of principle, " and it enters into all arguments on the more nice and difficult ques- " tions in this department. Limitation is either by convention or by " statute: the former being the condition in the obligation, the latter " established on grounds of public expediency."

(g) *Smith's Leading Cases*, i. 367-8.

Note on *Mostyn v. Fabrigas.*

" the country where the contract is made must govern it, and
" must be looked on as impliedly incorporated with it. Now,
" if the contract had contained a *proviso* that it should be
" absolutely void, if not enforced within a certain time, no
" doubt the English courts would hold it void after the expira-
" tion of that time. But what difference can it make that
" such proviso is implied from the Law of the country where
" the contract was made, instead of being expressed in terms?
" Is it not in both cases equally part of the contract? If,
" indeed, the rule of the foreign Law be, that the contract
" shall, after the lapse of a certain time, become void, provided
" that the parties to it continue to reside all that time in the
" same country, the arrival of the period prefixed or its avoid-
" ance will depend on the contingency of their abstaining
" from absenting themselves, and, if they leave the country,
" never will arrive at all; and this is, perhaps, what Judge
" Story intends by the words, 'that the parties are resident
" ' within the jurisdiction during all that period, *so that it has*
" ' *actually operated upon the case.*' For if the Law be so
" framed as to *operate upon the case* without such residence,
" the qualification appears to be inapplicable." (*h*)

DCCCV. The Supreme Court of the North American
United States has, however, certainly laid down the rule that
the statute of limitations of the country in which the suit is
brought may be pleaded to bar a recovery upon a contract
made out of its political jurisdiction, and that the limitation
of the *lex loci contractûs* cannot be so pleaded. It considers
that this has become a fixed rule of the *jus gentium privatum*,
unalterable in the opinion of that court either in the North
American United States or in England, except by legislative
enactment. (*i*)

But the same court recognised, as the inferior courts of the
same country had done before, the distinction between a Law

(*h*) *Mostyn* v. *Fabrigas, Smith's Leading Cases*, vol. i. p. 367.
(*i*) *Townsend* v. *Jenison*, xviii. *Curtis's* (*Amer.*) *Rep.* pp. 201-2.

of limitation which went directly to the extinguishment of the debt, claim, or right, and one which operated merely as a bar to the remedy. (*k*)

DCCCVI. A case was brought before Sir William Grant, arising under a possessory Law of Jamaica, which converted a possession of seven years under a deed, will, or other conveyance, into a positive absolute title against all the world, without exception, in favour of any one, or any right, however a party may have been situated during that time, or whatever the previous right of property may have been. The great English judge took in this case the distinction between statutes which barred the remedy, and statutes which prohibited the bringing a suit after a limited time. (*l*)

DCCCVII. The foreign jurisprudence upon this matter is perspicuously stated by *Massé.* (*m*)

There have been various systems :

1. That which governs the prescription by the Law of the Domicil of the creditor or obligee.

2. That which adopts the Law of the debtor or obligor.

3. That which adopts the Law of the place in which the demand for the fulfilment is made.

4. That which adopts the Law of the place where the contract is made.

5. That which adopts the Law of the place of payment or discharge.

DCCCVIII. Pothier (*n*) alone countenances the first system. Burgundus (*o*) and Merlin (*p*) expose the error on which his specious reasoning is founded.

(*k*) *Ib.* 206, *et vide Shelby* v. *Gay*, 11 *Wheaton's (Amer.) Rep.* 361;
Brent v. *Chapman*, 5 *Cranch's (Amer.) Rep.* 358 ;
Lincoln v. *Battelle*, 6 *Wend.* 475 ;
Story's Conflict, s. 582.
(*l*) *Beckford* v. *Wade*, 17 *Vesey's Rep.* 87.
(*m*) *Le Droit Commercial*, ii. s. 74.
(*n*) *Prescription*, n. 251.
(*o*) *Ad. consuet. Flandriæ*, 2*de traité*, n. 23.
(*p*) *Rep. v. Prescription*, s. 1—3, n. 7, t. xxvii. p. 404.

The second system is supported by Merlin (*q*) and Voet, (*r*) and by decisions of the superior courts of Cologne and Berlin; (*s*) but what if the debtor or obligor change his Domicil? of which Domicil is the law to be followed—that of the Domicil at the time of making the contract, or that of the subsequent Domicil?

The third system is supported by Huber, (*t*) on the ground that " præscriptio et executio non pertinent ad valorem con- " tractûs, sed ad tempus et modum actionis instituendæ, quæ " per se quasi contractum separatimque negotium constituit."

The fourth system is far preferable to the third, (*u*) for it avoids the deplorable consequence of allowing the creditor or obligee to vary, according to his pleasure, the length of time of the Prescription, which contradicts (by rendering Prescription uncertain) the very end of all Prescription ; for, as Hertius says, " si actioni non viri secundum leges ubi judicium instituitur, " prescribentur, interdum incertissima fuent præscriptionis " tempora, quoniam unus homo diversis locis non rarò potest " conveniri." (*x*)

Nevertheless, Massé rightly pronounces against this fourth system, for Prescription is really connected with the execution or fulfilment of the obligation to which it opposes itself as a bar.

The fifth system, therefore, is the right one; it causes the Law of the place of fulfilment to prevail when that place is indicated ; that of the Domicil of the debtor or obligor when it is not, for there the obligation is in that case to be fulfilled. Troplong, Demangeat, (*y*) and, as we have seen, Savigny, agree with Massé, as, it would seem, does also the reason of the thing.

(*q*) *Rep. v. Prescription*, t. ix. p. 498.

(*r*) *Pand.* l. 44, t. 3, n. 12.

(*s*) *Fœlix*, s. 100.

(*t*) *De confl. legum*, n. 7, *de jurispr. univers.* l. 3, ch. ii. s. 34.

(*u*) Supported by *Rocco*, 375.

(*x*) *De collis. leg.* s. 65.

(*y*) *Fœlix*, ed. *Dem.* s. 100, n. a.

DCCCIX. It is a maxim of universal jurisprudence that if the obligee or creditor refuse to receive his due when tendered to him, the debtor or obligor is not to suffer by his caprice, but is entitled to the discharge of his debt or obligation. According to the Roman Law, the debtor must make an offer (*oblatio*) of capital and interest at the place appointed for payment; this, if refused, was followed by a solemn act of depositing the sum, by a *sealing up* (*obsignatio*), either *apud œdem sacram* or *in tuto loco*, and by the discharge of the obligation. "Obsignatione " totius debitæ pecunia solenniter factâ, liberationem contingere " manifestum est;" then follows a condition of importance to the present subject, "sed ita demum oblatio debiti liberationem, " parit si *eo loco quo debetur solutio fuerit celebrata.*" (*z*)

Story (*a*) observes, that a defence or discharge good by the Law of the place where the contract is made, or is to be performed (he means the latter), is good everywhere; so he observes say John Voet, Casaregis, Huber, Burgundus, and Dumouslin. Thus infancy, if a valid defence by the *lex loci contractûs*, is valid everywhere. A tender and refusal good by the same Law, either as a full discharge, or as a present fulfilment of the contract, will be respected everywhere. (*b*)

(*z*) *Cod.* viii. 43, 9, *de solutionibus.*

(*a*) S. 331, 332.

(*b*) *Ib.* and *Male* v. *Roberts*, 3 *Espinasse's R.* 163. *Vide post* as to payment of Bills of Exchange.

CHAPTER XLI.

LEX MERCATORIA.

DCCCX. The *lex mercatoria* (*a*) is so important a branch of Private International Law, that it has seemed to the writer of these pages expedient to treat it apart from the general law on obligations which have been the subject of preceding chapters. It is proposed to consider it under the two following divisions, which, though they do not perhaps entirely exhaust the subject, supply principles applicable to every part of it.

1. The general maritime law ; which will include the right of stoppage *in transitu.*

2. The mode of carrying on traffic by bills of exchange.

DCCCXI. "The maritime law," Lord Mansfield justly observed, "is not the law of a particular country." Upon the same principle, Thöl, (*b*) the most learned of modern foreign writers upon mercantile laws, treats his subject as embracing " partly the commercial legal relations between individuals—

(*a*) " To this head may most properly be referred a particular system " of customs used only among one set of the king's subjects, called the " custom of merchants or *lex mercatoria ;* which, however different " from the general rules of the common law, is yet ingrafted into it and " made part of it ; being allowed for the benefit of trade to be of the " utmost validity in all commercial transactions ; for it is a maxim of " law that ' cuilibet in suâ arte credendum est."—*Blackstone's Comment.* i. Introd. s. 3.

(*b*) The Law Merchant is a system founded on the rules of equity and governed in all its parts by plain justice and good faith.

Master v. *Miller,* 4 *Durnf. & East, Rep.* 342.

Lennig v. *Ralston,* May 16, 1854, Supreme Court of Pennsylvania.

Das Handelsrecht von Dr. Heinrich Thöl, Gottingen, 1854.

Bell's Commentaries (ed. *Shaw*), book i. part 2, " *Of Maritime Law.*"

Story's Conflict of Laws, s. 286 (*b*), 384, 385, n. 1 ; 391—402 (*a*) ; see, too, s. 322 (*b*) *in fine—*Bottomry bond ; 323, note ; 401—403 ; 327, *a, b.*

" Private mercantile or commercial law (*Privathandelsrecht*) ;
" partly mercantile or commercial legal relations between
" government and subjects—Public commercial or mercantile
" law (*Offentliches Handelsrecht*) ; partly commercial or mer-
" cantile legal relations between different states—International
" mercantile or commercial law (*Handelsvolkesrecht*)." (c)

The recognition of this general maritime law is, as will be
seen, especially remarkable in the cases of tort or collision between ships, one or both of which belong to a foreign state,
upon the high seas.

DCCCXII. The sources of this *Lex Mercatoria*, (and the
observation applies to both divisions of the subject mentioned
in the last paragraph,) spring from the usage of maritime
states, founded on the necessities of commerce, upon the natural rights and obligations which, independently of municipal
law, grow out of commercial intercourse ; upon the reasonings
of accredited writers upon this branch of jurisprudence, which
reasonings have been built up, by judicial decisions in England,
into a fabric of municipal commercial law. In other countries
the same effect has been produced by the incorporation into
codes of the.leading principles previously established upon the
authority of jurists. In England also, during the last few
years, a commercial code has in fact been created, though it
has assumed the technical form of an Act of Parliament. (d)

DCCCXIII. So far as these codes and statutes incorporate
the general maritime jurisprudence, no injury is done to Private International Law ; but when they incorporate some
principle of domestic or municipal policy at variance with that
law, there is danger of a conflict and collision between the
interests of one state and those of the general community of
states, which may lead both to individual injustice, and to a
disturbance of the amicable relations of independent nations.

(c) Or, "*particulares gemeines allgemeines Handelsrecht*," ib. 1, 2.

(d) 17 & 18 Vict. c. 104, The Merchant Shipping Act.

See appendix to this chapter for the sections of this statute which
apply to foreigners.

DCCCXIV. Illustrations of this danger and inconvenience may be easily furnished. The English Merchant Shipping Act provides that under certain circumstances the property of a ship may be changed at home while she is navigating the ocean, and of course, therefore, without any papers on board evidencing the change of ownership. It may happen, however, that the ship which has undergone such change of ownership at home is subsequently sold abroad by the master as agent for the former proprietor. It is very probable that in such a case the foreign court would disregard the peculiar law of England, and adhere to the general maritime law of Europe. Such appears to have been the reasoning of the Civil Tribunal of Havre, in the case of the *Ann Martin*: (e) "Attendu que " la nature de ce contrat qu'on a qualifié de mortgage d'après " la loi anglaise, est peu importante au procès ; que, soit qu'il " constitue une vente réelle ou une simple vente apparente, ou " un nantissement accompagné de certains priviléges particu- " liers dérivant de la législation étrangère sous l'empire de la- " quelle il a été souscrit, la decision doit être la même ; qu'il " s'agit, en effet, de la propriété d'un navire navignant sous le " nom de *Clauss et Comp.*, qu'il est impossible d'admettre que " sous une legislation commerciale quelconque il soit reçu qu' " en cours de voyage cette propriété puisse être transmise à " un tiers ou lui être engagée a titre de nantissement, sous qu' " aucune trace de cette mutation ou de cette modification de " propriété soit imprimée aux papiers due bord ; que la bonne " foi qui est l'âme du commerce repugne à une semblable " idée." (f)

(e) 19th April, 1856, appealed to the Court of Appeal at Rouen, but *non constat* what became of the appeal. The extract is from a *note* published by the appellants. " *Castrique et Comp.* (appellants) contre *Protteux et Consorts* (intimés). *Vide post* in the chapter on Evidence and Foreign Judgment why the authority of this judgment, when it came before the English tribunals, was not recognised by them.

(f) This doctrine accords with that laid down by Mr. Justice Martin in *Arago* v. *Currell*, 1 *Louis.* (*Amer.*) *Rep.* 528. *Vide* post, authority of master as agent.

DCCCXV. On the other hand, the English High Court of Admiralty, supported by the judicial committee of the Privy Council, has been careful never to apply to a foreign vessel the rules of navigation prescribed by statute for British vessels. (*g*) In all cases of collision upon the high sea or in foreign waters, between a foreign and English vessel, (*h*) or between two foreign vessels, the wrongdoer, whether he be foreigner or English subject, is ascertained by a reference to the old rule of the sea, founded on the principle of general maritime law, and not to the rule prescribed by the English statute. Cases of *Collision*, like cases of *Salvage*, are considered as belonging to the *jus gentium*.

DCCCXVI. There seems, however, no reason why; if it should happen that the foreign law of the party to the collision agreed with the principles of the English statute, (*i*) these principles should not be applied to the adjudication of this case.

The parties in such a case would have a common law binding on themselves, distinct from the general maritime law, and neither party could complain if they were holden amenable to their own law.

DCCCXVII. The High Court of Admiralty has, in what are called *causes of possession*, jurisdiction to take a ship from a wrongdoer, and deliver her over to a person claiming as the right owner. It will exercise this jurisdiction in a suit

---

(*g*) 17 & 18 Vict. c. 104, s. 296.

(*h*) *Cope* v. *Doherty* (*ship Tuscarora*), decided by V. C. Page Wood, 1858, 4 *Jur. N. S.* 699 ; 27 *Law Journ. Chancery*, 600.

Affirmed on appeal before the Lords Justices. 4 *Kay & Jervis's Rep.* p. 367.

The Zollverein, Swaby's Ad. Rep. p. 96.

The Dumfries, ib. 63, 125, 567.

The Nostra Signora de los Dolores, 1 *Dodson's Ad. Rep.* 290.

The Vernon, 1 *W. Robinson's Rep.* 316.

The General Steam Navigation Co. v. *Guillon,* 11 *Meeson & Welsby's Rep.* 877.

(*i*) *Westlake,* s. 276.

between foreigners in this country, with the consent of parties, or when the case has been referred to its decision by the application of the representative, or even of the consent of the foreign state to which the parties belong. At first, it did so with reluctance, because these questions had ceased to be dependent on the *jus gentium*, and had become dependent on the municipal regulations of foreign states, with which it was but imperfectly acquainted. Of late years, however, this jurisdiction seems to have been exercised without scruple. (*k*)

DCCCXVIII. The fourteenth book of the Digest contains three very celebrated titles or chapters :

1. *De Exercitoriâ actione.*
2. *De Lege Rhodiâ de jactu.*
3. *De Institoriâ actione.*

These are, in fact, the bases of the doctrine of *agency* in European commercial jurisprudence, especially in its effect upon *third* parties. The *dominus navis* is properly the owner of a ship. The *exercitor*, the charterer, hirer, or employer of a ship for a whole voyage. The *magister navis* (*l*) is the modern master or captain. European law follows the Roman law, in allowing the master to appoint in case of need a deputy ; and the Roman law (*m*) held that the *utilitas navigantium* required that the owner should be bound by the act of substitution, though he had especially forbidden the master to appoint a deputy. The owner is said, *præponere*, to appoint the master, and the appointment is expressed by the word *præpositio.* (*n*)

(*k*) *The Martin of Norfolk*, 4 *Robinson's Rep.* 297.

The Johan and Sigmund, Edwards' Rep. 242.

The See Reuter, 1 *Dodson's Rep.* 23.

(*l*) "Magistrum navis accipere debemus cui totius navis cura mandata est. Magistrum autem accipimus non solum quem exercitor præposuit sed et eum quem magister."

(*m*) That is, the *Prætorian* law ; for the old strict Roman law did not generally speaking allow an action against the principal to grow out of an act of an agent.

(*n*) "Igitur *præpositio* certam legem dat contrahentibus."

The *Institor* was the clerk or shopman of a person in trade : "Appellatus est ab eo quod negotio gerendo *instat*," says the Digest. (*o*)

The relation of the *Institor* to his principal did not hold out to *third* parties the same presumption of unlimited authority as agent, which the relation of *Magister* to his principal did hold out to them.

The *institor* was at home, and reference could be easily made to his principal, *qui eum præposuit.*

DCCCXIX. The Roman law, moreover, held owners to be responsible *in solidum* (*p*) for the obligations of the master, whether they arose *ex contractu* or *ex delicto*. But by the general maritime law of Europe the liability of owners for the wrongful acts of masters is limited to the value of the vessel and freight, and by abandoning these to the creditor the owners may discharge themselves. (*q*) This limitation, however, did not form part of the *common law* of England, or of the N. A. United States, but has been introduced into them by special statute.

DCCCXX. "Omnia facta magistri debet præstare qui eum " præposuit alio quin contrahentes decipientur," (*r*) is the language of the Digest in the famous title, " De exercitoriâ ac- " tione," which is full of that written equity which so often

---

(*o*) L. xiv. t. 1, 1—4.

(*p*) *Dig.* l. xiv. t. 1, 20—25 : " Si plures navem exerceant cum quolibet " eorum in solidum agi potest."

And *Dig.* l. iv. t. 9, on the edict : "Nautæ caupones, &c., ut recepta " restituant," where it is said, "nautam accipere debemus cum qui " navem *exercet*."

(*q*) *Emerigon, Contrats à la Grosse*, c. 4, s. 11.

Boulay Patey, Cours de Droit Comm. t. 1, 263—298.

Kent's Comment. iii. 218.

Abbott on Shipping, pt. 3, c. 5.

The Rebecca, Ware's (Amer.) Rep. 188.

Malpico v. *McKnown*, 1 *Miller's Louis. Rep. (Amer.)* 259.

Arago v. *Currell*, ib. 528.

(*r*) *Dig.* l. xiv. t. i. 1—5.

renders the Roman law the fountain of international jurisprudence.

This maxim is stated in the Roman law without limitation or distinction as to the place in which the authority of the master is exercised. But the exigencies of modern commerce have introduced a wise and just distinction between the authority of the master exercised in a home or in a foreign port. The principle on which the distinction rests is that in a home port the authority of the owner is easily accessible, while in a port abroad the necessities of the ship may require instant succour, and, as Mr. Bell observes, " this is the great principle " of distinction between the *actio exercitoria* and the *actio* " *institoria* of the Roman law." (s)

DCCCXXI. The authority of the master of a ship, as agent of the owner in a foreign port, has however given rise to a difficult international question on the law of contract. (t)

By the English law, the master of a ship may, in a foreign port and under certain circumstances, borrow money for the *necessities* of his ship, and may give a security called a bottomry bond, which will render the ship and freight, and sometimes the *cargo*, (u) liable for repayment of the loan.

But according to the English law the validity of this bond depends, first, upon the money being borrowed, not for merely useful, but for absolutely necessary supplies ; secondly, upon the bond having been taken where the owner was known to have no credit, to be in a state of unprovided necessity. If the master takes up money from a person who knows that he has a general credit in the place, or an empowered assignee or

---

(s) *Story on Agency*, s. 33.
Bell's Commen. (ed. *Shaw*), bk. i. pt. ii. c. 13, 3.
(t) *Story's Conflict of Laws*, s. 286 b.
Story on Agency, s. 36.
" The contract with the master, in all questions between him and the " owners, is properly *locatio conductio operarum* ; in relation to stran- " gers it is the contract of *agency.*" *Bell's Commen.* (ed. *Shaw*), i. 382.
(u) *The Gratitudine*, 3 *Robinson's Rep.* 240.

agent willing to supply his wants, then the giving a bottomry bond is a void transaction. (x)

Moreover, the English decisions hold (y) that the master's authority to bind the ship or the owner in a *foreign* port is governed by the law of the domicil of the owner, and not by the law of the place in which the bond is given. So that a foreigner, who in his own country made a valid contract for supplying mere useful repairs to the master of an English ship, would find the bond given by the master worthless when it was attempted to enforce it in the country of the master.

In the United States of North America there is a conflict of decisions upon this subject. The Courts of Louisiana have twice pronounced in very elaborate judgments that the law of the place of the contract, and not the law of the owner's domicil, furnishes the rule by which his obligations in this matter are governed. (z)

" Where a general power is confined to an agent, the party " contracting with him is not bound by any limitation which " the principal may have affixed, at the time or since, by dis- " tinct instructions. Now, in the case before us, if instructions " be supposed to have been given to the master, not to bind " the owner beyond the value of the vessel and freight, or for " any act which the latter could not prevent, would parties " contracting with the former, in a foreign country, be bound " by them ? We think it is certain they would not. *Every* " *contract, which by the general maritime law the master* " *can make, is binding upon the owner.* By putting the " former in command, and sending him abroad, the latter in-

---

(x) *The Nelson,* 1 *Haggard's Ad. Rep.* 169, 175-6.

(y) At least, as *Story,* s. 286 *b,* correctly remarks, " such seems the " course of the adjudications." Though perhaps this question of con- flict between two laws, in the matter of the master's authority, has never been satisfactorily argued.

(z) *Malpica* v. *McKnown,* 1 *Miller's Louis. Rep.* 249—254.
Arago v. *Currell,* ib. 528.
Story, s. 286 *c,* and note.

" vests him with the general powers masters have as such, and
" those who contract with him have nothing to do with any
" private instructions by which the general power may have
" been limited. If the limitation arises not from the owner's
" instructions, but from the particular laws of the country
' from which the vessel has sailed, must not the consequences
" be the same ?   Can these laws limit the master's power
" more effectually than the owner could, or can they extend
" farther ? We think not. They have no force in a foreign
" country, where they are presumed to be equally unknown. (a)

In a more recent case a different law was laid down. The
case was this :—A vessel, owned in Massachusets, being on
a voyage from a port in Spain to a port in Pennsylvania, was
compelled by stress of weather to put into Bermuda, where
the master sold the vessel and the whole cargo. The shippers
brought an action against the owner to recover the amount of
their consignment. This put in issue the right of the master
to sell the whole cargo and bind the owners by his act. The
court determined that the liability of the owners was governed
by the law of Massachusets, their domicil, and not by the law
of Spain, where the contract of shipment was made, nor by the
law of Pennsylvania, where the goods were to be delivered. (b)

The Scotch lawyers agree with this exposition of the law by
the Circuit Court of the United States and by the English
tribunals.   Mr. Brodie enters into the question at length and
concludes, " The clear result is, that the transactions must be
" held to have reference to the master's implied mandate, ac-
" cording to the law of his own country—a mandate which it
" is the duty of those who deal with him as an agent to ascer-
" tain the extent of." (c)

(a) *Arago* v. *Currell*, 1 *Louis.* (*Amer.*) *Rep.* 528, Judgment by Mr.
Justice Martin; see *Story's Conflict of Laws* (*4th American edit.*) 447-8,
note, s. 286.

(b) *Pope* v. *Nickerson*, 3 *Story's Rep.* 465.

Story, s. 286 (ed. 1857).

(c) *Notes on Lord Stair's Institutes*, vol. ii. 995-6.

Story, s. 286 b, note.

The Court of Louisiana, however, argues, " What we do by
" another we do by ourselves; and we are unable to distin-
" guish between the responsibility created by the owner send-
" ing his agent to contract in another country, and that pro-
" duced by going there and contracting himself." (*d*)

And again, " If there be a principle better established than
" any other, on the subject of the conflict of laws, it is, that
" contracts are governed by the laws of the country in which
" they are entered into, unless they be so with a view to a
" performance in another. Every writer on that subject re-
" cognises it. Judicial decisions again and again, throughout
" the civilised world, have sanctioned it. Why, then, should
" this form an exception ?" (*e*)

DCCCXXII. It will not have escaped the reader of the former pages on the subject of *Obligations*, that the English and
North American United States Circuit Courts adopt in this
instance the principle of continental and civil law, viz., that
the law of the domicil regulates the capacity to contract, and
depart, under the supposed pressure of mercantile expediency,
from their doctrine that this capacity is governed by the law
of the place of contract.

DCCCXXIII. It certainly appears to the writer of these
pages that the general principles of International Law support
the decisions of the Louisiana Courts rather than the judgment
of the Circuit Courts of the United States. The Law of Nations requires good faith as much in commerce as in war.
The money *bona fide* advanced for the necessities of a foreign
ship in a foreign port to a person like the captain, *presum-
ably* authorised to bind his employers, ought to be repaid by
them in every case ; unless, indeed, the lender was affected
with the knowledge of the limited powers of the captain. In

(*d*) *Story,* s. 286 c.
Malpica v. *McKnown,* 1 *Louis. Rep.* 249—254.
(*e*) *Arago* v. *Currell,* 1 *Louis. Rep.* 528.
Story, s. 286 c.

that case the terms of the owner's authority to the captain
may govern the contract, or, as the Digest says, "*præpositio*
"*certam legem dat contrahentibus ;*" or, perhaps, unless the
lender was grossly wanting in the ordinary *diligentia* required
by the law of all persons of inquiry into the powers of the
person with whom he is contracting. This opinion derives
strength from the following language of Emerigon.

DCCCXXIV. The opinion of Emerigon upon the power
of the master to bind the owners by his contract must have
great weight in all questions of comity relating to this subject :

"Si la faculté," says this high authority, (*f*) "de prendre des
" deniers à la grosse pendant le cours du voyage, avait été
" expressément prohibée au capitaine, ceux qui lui ont fourni
" de l'argent, auront-ils action contre les Armateurs ?

" Il semble d'abord que dans ce cas, toute action devroit
" être déniée aux preteurs contre les propriétaires, au bénéfice
" de qui l'argent n'a pas ete employé : *qui cum alio contra-*
" *hit, vel est, vel debet esse, non ignarus conditionis ejus.*
" (*L.* 19, *ff. de reg. jur.*) Divers Textes paroissent de reunir
" pour etablir ce sentiment.

" *L.* 7, *ff. de exercit. act.* Sciat *ut in hoc se credere, cui*
" *rei magister quis sit præpositus.*

" *L.* 1, § 7, *ff. eod.* *Non autem ex omni causâ prætor*
" *dat in exercitorem actionem, sed ejus rei nomine cujus*
" *ibi præpositus fuerit.*

" *D. Lege, s.* 12.   *Præpositio certam legem dat contrahen-*
" *tibus, modum egressus non obligabit exercitorem.*

" *Si sic præposuit, ne alter sine altero quid gerat, qui*
" *contraxit cum uno, sibi imputabit, d. Leg.* 1, *s.* 14.

" Tout cela est vrai, si le préteur était instruit des défenses
" faites au capitaine ; mais s'il ignorait les défenses, l'action
" sera ouverte contre les propriétaires, attendu la foi publique.

(*f*) *Emerigon.   Traité des Assurances et des Contrats à la Grosse,* t. ii.
c. 4, s. 8, s. 3, 4.

" des pouvoirs que cette qualité lui défere.   Ceux qui con-
" tractent avec lui en pays étranger, ne sont pas obligés de lui
" faire exhiber ses titres, et il peut aisément les leur cacher.
" Tout capitaine est présumé *Maître*, et jouir du libre exercice
" Le s. 5 de la Loi ci-dessus citée, après avoir décidé que le
" contrat passé avec celui que le capitaine a subrogé en sa
" place, est obligatoire vis-à-vis des propriétaires, ajoute qu'il
" en serait de même, quoiqu'ils eussent nommément prohibé
" à leur capitaine d'en subroger un autre.   *Dicendum erit*
" *eo usque producendam utilitatem navigantium.*

" Je conviens qu'il y a une grand différence entre celui qui
" s'embarque dans un navire, on qui y charge des marchan-
" dises, et celui qui prête de l'argent au capitaine.   Mais le
" motif de la loi, fondè sur l'erreur commune, doit être admis
" dans tous les cas.

" Je crois donc que, malgré la prohibition fait au capitaine
" de prendre des deniers à la grosse en cours de voyage, ceux
" qui de bonne foi auront donné leur argent à ce capitaine
" infidele, n'auront pas moins action contre les propriétaires,
" et privilege sur le navire.   Il faudroit que la prohibition
" leur eût été auparavant intimée, ou que du moins elle eût été
" rendue publique dans le lieu du contrat. (*g*)

" Duarenus, ff. *de exercit. act.* page **1297**, expliquant la
" loi Lucius Titius, dit qu'il suffit que celui qui prête de l'argent
" au capitaine infidele, se soit comporté *avec quelque diligence,*
" de maniere à n'être soupçonné coupable d'aucune fraude,
" *satis est eum adhibere aliquam diligentiam,* ut non ap-
" pareat *eum malo animo mutuam pecuniam* dedisse.   D'où
" il suit, que si la négligence est extréme, et qu'il y ait fauté

(*g*) L. 11, s. 17, ff. de inst. act.   *Vide Stypmannus,* pt. 4, c. 15, n. 135,
p. 543.

Loccenius, l. 3, tit. 7, n. 9, p. 1033.

Peckius et Vinnius, p. 88, 103, 111.

Roccus, de Navib., n. 12.

Cassaregis, disc. 71, n. 8.

Pothier, des Obligations, n. 79, t. 1, p. 39.

" grave, on peut suivant les circonstances, lui refuser toute
" action contre les armateurs ; *gravis culpa dolo æquipa-*
" *ratur.*

" M. Valin, *art.* 19, *tit. du Capitaine*, page 417, rappelle
" la disposition de la même Loi *Lucius Titius.* 'Mais tout
" ' cela,' dit-il, 'comme trop subtil et trop pointilleux, a été re-
" ' jetté dans l'usage du commerce, et il suffit pour autoriser le
" ' créancier prêteur, à agir contre le propriétaire du navire,
" ' qu'il ait prêté le somme de bonne foi au capitaine, c'est-a-
" ' dire, qu'il n'y ait ni preuve, ni *présomption suffisants* de
" ' collusion entre le capitaine et lui.'

" Cet auteur n'exclut pas les présomptions suffisantes de
" collusion, lesquelles dépendent des circonstonces au fait, qui
" varient à l'infini. Celui qui vent s'embarquer ou charger
" des marchandises, n'a pas souvent le choix du vaisseau. Il
" est forcé, *propter navigandi necessitatem*, de se servir du
" premier navire qui se présente. Mais, celui qui prete son
" argent à un capitaine, le fait volontairement et sans y être
" contraint ; le motif de l'edit du preteur, cesse a son égard.
" Il est donc juste qu'il y apporte la prudence commune, *ali-*
" *quam diligentiam.* (h)

Emerigon then speaks of the manner in which the celebrated *Ordonnance* had curtailed the powers of the captain :

" Mais notre Ordonnance a réduit le pouvoir du capitaine
" en cours de voyage, ou *à prendre deniers sur le corps, ou*
" *à mettre des apparaux en gage,* ou *à vendre des marchan-*
" *dises de son chargement* pour les nécessités du navire. S'il
" tire des lettres de change sur ses Armateurs, cet engagement ;
" quoique conçu en nom qualifié, lui devient personnel, atten-
" du qu'il a excédé son mandat légal. Il ne doit contracter
" aucune obligation qui ne soit inhérente au navire meme, et
" qui ne dépende du succès de l'expédition maritime ; c'est

(h) *Vide Cujas, Vinnius, Faber, et autres Docteurs sur la dite Loi
Lucius Titius 7, ff. de exercit. act. Stypmannus*, pt. 4, c. 6, n. 124 ; c.
15, n. 154, p. 418 et 544.
Pothier, des Obligations, n. 448, t. i. p. 231.

" à quoi se borne l'autorité que sa qualité de *maître* lui défere,
" a moins qui son raccord, ou le droit commun, en certains cas,
" ne lui donnent un pouvoir plus étendu." (*i*)

DCCCXXV. "The general principle," Dr. Lushington says,
" sanctioned by maritime law is, that the master has not,
" as master, any authority to sell; that necessity only will jus-
" tify such a sale and render the transfer valid. The question
" then is, as to the existence of such an adequate necessity.
" This necessity is to be judged of by all the circumstances. I
" will mention some of them. 1. The state of the condition
" of the vessel. 2. Consequences of not proceeding to sell.
" 3. Facility of communication with the owner.. 4. The re-
" sources of the master, or the total absence of all resources.
" 5. In some degree, too, the power and means of the owner
" to avert a sale. I conceive that the law inclines against
" sales of this description, and throws the burden of strict
" proof upon the purchaser, for it is his duty to ascertain the
" authority under which the master acts, or the circumstances
" which render a sale imperatively necessary; and from this
" proof, save where there has been a decree by a competent
" court, no formality can release him. (*k*)

DCCCXXVI. According to the English law, the authority
of the master of a ship to pledge by bottomry for the purpose
of raising money for the absolute necessaries of the ship, only
arises when he cannot obtain the necessary advances upon the
personal credit of the owner; and such power to raise money
by bottomry is vested in the master, although the owner resides in the same country, provided there is no means of communication with the owner, and the exigency of the case
requires it.

(*i*) *Emerigon, Traités des Contrats*, t. ii. c. 4, s. 11, s. 5.

(*k*) *The Glascow*, otherwise *Y͞a Macrow*. Sale of English vessel by
the master at *Savannah*, sustained. *Swabey's Ad. Rep.* i. 146.

The cases of the *Bonita* and the *Charlotte* are now awaiting judgment
in the High Court of Admiralty on this point. December, 1860.

In a recent cáse, decided by the English Privy Council, a bottomry bond was granted in New York by the master of a ship, to obtain money for necessary repairs; the owner where-of was residing *at St. John's, New Brunswick.* A communication by electric telegraph existed between the two cities. The bondholder had previously acted as the general agent of the owner, and no intimation of the transaction was made by the master to the owner until after the execution of the bond.

It was holden upon appeal (reversing the sentence of the Admiralty Court) that the master having the means of communication with the owner, no such absolute necessity existed as to authorise him to pledge the ship without communication with the owner, and the bond was declared void. (*l*)

DCCCXXVII. The recent case of the *Milford* presents a remarkable, and perhaps questionable, application of the statute law (*m*) of England to an American ship:

A subject of the United States shipped at San Francisco, as second mate on an American ship, on a voyage to the United Kingdom. During the voyage he became master. On his arrival in this country he proceeded for his wages as master against the freight. An appearance was given for the owners, under protest, that by the American law the master had no lien on the freight for wages. It was holden that this was a question of remedy, and must be governed by the *lex fori,* and that as there was nothing to show any special contract, the master was entitled to all the remedies which the law of this country affords in a case of wages. The protest was overruled with costs. (*n*)

(*l*) *The Oriental* (1851), 7 *Moore's P. C. Rep.* 398.

See also *The Buonaparte,* 8 *Moore's P. C. Rep.* 459.

(*m*) See express provision in *Merchant Shipping Act* (17 & 18 Vic. c. 104, s. 290), as to *Conflict of Laws* in certain cases. See *Sect. at length in Appendix to this Chapter.*

(*n*) *The Milford* (1858), *Law Times,* v. 31, p. 42.

DCCCXXVIII. When the preservation of the ship has required the throwing overboard or sacrifice of a portion of the goods, equity demands that a general contribution be made by all towards a loss sustained by some for the benefit of all; and this is called in England by the name of *general average.* (*o*)

The law on this subject was transplanted from the maritime code of Rhodes into the Roman Law, as follows:—"Lege Rhodiâ cavetur, ut, si levandæ navis gratiâ jactus mercium factus sit, omnium contributioue sarciatur quod pro omnibus datum est." (*p*)

The principle of this rule has been adopted by all commercial nations, but with considerable variation in practice as to the kind of losses which demand its application, and as to the nature of the interests compellable to contribute. The question, therefore, may arise, and has arisen, what Law ought to bind the underwriters to reimburse a contribution exacted in a foreign port. (*q*) The English cases have established the following propositions:—

First, with respect to what Law shall govern the construction of the insurance covenant as to what is general average. It has been finally decided, after much doubt and consideration, that the insurer of goods to a foreign state is not liable to indemnify the assured, though a subject of that state, who has been obliged by a decree of a competent court of that state to pay a contribution as for general average, which by the law of England is not general average, unless it be proved as a fact in the case that the insured and insurer contemplated in their

---

(*o*) According to the English Law, "All loss which arises in conse-"quence of extraordinary sacrifices made, or expenses incurred, for the " preservation of the ship and cargo, come within *general average*, and " must be borne proportionably by all who arc interested." *Birkley* v. *Presgrove*, 1 *East's Rep.* 220.

(*p*) *Dig.* lxiv. t. 2.

(*q*) This point seems to have escaped the attention of Story in his *Conflict of Laws.*

contract the general usage amongst merchants, or the usage of the port in which the general average was struck. (*r*) The North American United States' cases are in accordance with this doctrine. (*s*)

Secondly, in cases of admitted general average, England, in conformity with the maritime laws and usages of all nations, holds (*t*) that the place of the ship's destination, or delivery of her cargo, is the place at which the average is to be adjusted.

This adjustment must be made conformably to the Law of that place.

When so made it will be conclusive as to the items, as well as to the apportionment thereof, upon the various interests, although it may be different from what the English Law would have made, if the adjustment had been settled in an English port. (*u*)

DCCCXXIX. The general Law of the North American United States upon the subject of the power of the master is clearly stated in the two following extracts from the judgments of their Supreme Court :

" It is true," it is said in one of these judgments, " the master " of a steamboat, like other agents, has not an unlimited

---

(*r*) *Park on Insurance*, 900.

Power v. *Whitmore* (leading case on this point), 1815, 4 *Maule & Sel. Rep.* 149.

Newman v. *Cazalet, Park, ib.*

(*s*) *Schmidt* v. *United Ins. Co.*, 1 *Johnson's Rep.* 249.

Lenox v. *United Ins. Co.* 3 *Johnson's Cases*, 178.

Stiff v. *Louisiana State Ins. Co.* 6 *Mad. N. S.* 629; cited by Westlake, p. 196.

(*t*) *Consolato del Mare*, s. 225. *Bynkershoek*, 2 *J. P.* l. iv. c. 24.

(*u*) *Simonds and Loder* v. *White*, 2 *Barnewall & C. Rep.* 805.

Park on Insurance, 298-9.

Dalgleish v. *Davidson* (1824), 5 *Dowling & R. Rep.* 6.

Tudor's Leading Maritime Cases, 96-7.

Notes on *Birkley* v. *Presgrove*, 1 *East's Rep.* 220 (leading English Common Law case on what is general average).

See *The Copenhagen*, 1 *Robinson's Rep.* 293 (Lord Stowell ; leading Admiralty case—distinction between *general* and *particular* average).

" authority. He is the agent of the owner, to do only what is
" usually done in the particular employment in which he is
" engaged. Such is the general result of the authorities. (x)
" But different employments may, and do, have different
" usages, and, consequently, confer on the master different
" powers. And when, as in this case, a usage appears to be
" general, not unreasonable in itself, and indirectly beneficial
" to the owner, we are of opinion the master has power to act
" under it and bind the owner." (y)

In the other case the judges of the Supreme Court say—

" Upon the first question, we have no doubt that there may
" be cases in which the contract of the captain in relation to
" the amount of salvage to be paid to the salvors, or his agree-
" ment to refer the question to arbitrators, would bind the
" owners. In times of disaster, it is always his duty to exer-
" cise his best judgment, and to use his best exertions for the
" benefit of the owners of both vessel and cargo ; and when,
" from his situation, he is unable to consult them or their
" agent, without an inconvenient and injurious delay, it is in
" his power to compromise a question of salvage, and he is not
" bound in all cases to wait for the decision of a Court of
" Admiralty. So, too, when the salvage service has not been
" important, and the compensation demanded is a small one,
" it may often be the interest of the owners that the amount
" should be settled at once by the captain, and the vessel pro-
" ceed on her voyage, without waiting even a day for the pur-
" pose of consulting them. *But in all such cases, unless the*
" *acts of the captain are ratified by the owners, his conduct*
" *will be carefully watched and scrutinized by the court,*
" *and his contracts will not be regarded as binding upon*

(x) *Smith on Mer. Law*, 559 ;
Grant v. *Norway*, 10 *Com. B.* 688 ; *S. C.* 2 *Eng. L. & Eq.* 337 ;
Pope v. *Nickerson*, 3 *Story*, 475 ;
Citizens' Bank v. *Nantucket Steamboat Co.* 2 *Story*, 32.

(y) *The Steamboat New World and others* v. *King, Curtis's* (*Amer.*)
Rep. vol. xxi. p. 261.

" *the parties concerned, unless they appear to have been*
" *bonâ fide, and such as a discreet owner, placed in the like*
" *circumstances, would probably have made.* If he settles
" the amount by agreement, those who claim under it must
" show that the salvage allowed was reasonable and just. If
" he refers it to arbitrators, those who claim the benefit of
" the award must show that the proceedings were fair, and
" the referees worthy of the trust." (z)

DCCCXXX. We have now to consider the right known to
English lawyers as the right of *stoppage in transitu*, in its
application to cases in which foreigners are concerned.
According to the Roman Law, a contract of sale worked a *jus
ad rem*, but did not, by the mere effect of consent, as in
England, (a) work a *jus in re*, a transference of the property
(*dominium*) in the thing sold : "qui rem nondum emptori
" tradidit adhuc ipse dominus est."(b) And again, "traditionibus
" et non nudis pactis dominia rerum transferuntur." It was a
necessary result of this maxim that either party might withhold performance of his obligation on the other becoming
unable to perform his part.

The Law of continental Europe adopted, pretty generally,
the rule that a seller was entitled, in all cases, and even after
actual delivery, to have restitution of his goods, if unchanged
in form, and capable of being distinguished from the stock of
the buyer. The Scotch Law allowed restitution to the seller,
on the ground of presumptive fraud, within three days of the
bankruptcy of the buyer. This right of the seller, according to continental Law, was called the right of Revendication.

DCCCXXXI. A right analogous to that of Revendication (c) was introduced, by the reason of the thing and the

---

(z) *Houseman* v. *The Schooner North Carolina, Curtis's (Amer.) Rep.*
vol. xiv. pp. 18, 19.

(a) Subject to lien, while undelivered, for the price. *Cf. Abbott on
Shipping*, 418.

(b) *Instit.* l. iii. t. xiv. 3.

(c) 3 *Burge*, 770.

exigencies of commerce, into the English Law at the end of the seventeenth century, and into Scotland at the end of the eighteenth century : it was called, and is now universally known as, the right of *stoppage in transitu*. It has been adopted by France in her Code de Commerce, in the place of the old *Revendication*. (*d*)

"The Law" (Lord Wensleydale observed, in a leading case on this subject) "is clearly settled, that the unpaid vendor has
" a right to retake the goods before they have arrived at the
" destination originally contemplated by the purchaser, unless
" in the meantime they have come to the actual or construc-
" tive possession of the vendee. If the vendee take them out
" of the possession of the carrier into his own before their
" arrival, with or without the consent of the carrier, there
" seems to be no doubt that the transit would be at an end ;
" though, in the case of the absence of the carrier's consent, it
" may be a wrong to him, for which he weuld have a right of
" action. This is a case of *actual possession*, which certainly
" did not occur in the present instance. A case of *construc-*

Story, s. 401-2.

1 *Bell's Com.* 119.

Merlin, Rep. Revendication.

Portula Dizionario di diritto e di economia, tit. Revendicazione.

Savigny (viii. s. 374 D) speaks of the right of the seller to resile from or retract (*das Recht des Rücktritts*) before delivery as contrary to the *Common Law* ; but, according to many Local Laws, in the case of immoveables, the right depends on the *lex rei sitæ*.

Thöl, Handelsrecht, i. p. 288, s. 69.

Bassevi, Annotazione al Codice Civile Austriaco, s. 366, 375, 824.

Code Nap. art. 1612, 1613.

2 *Rogron*, p. 2098.

Blume, Deutsches Privatrecht, 136, s. 174.

(*d*) *Code de Commerce*, l. iii. t. iii. *de la revendication*, contains, among other provisions, the following :—

576. Le vendeur pourra, en cas de faillite, revendiquer les marchandises par lui vendues et livrées, et dont le prix ne lui a pas été payé, dans les cas et aux conditions ci-après exprimés.

" *tive* possession is, where the carrier enters expressly, or by
" implication, into a new agreement, distinct from the original
" contract for carriage, to hold the goods for the consignee as
" his agent, not for the purpose of expediting them to the
" place of original destination, pursuant to that contract, but
" in a new character, for the purpose of custody on his account,
" and subject to some new or further order to be given to
" him." (*e*)

DCCCXXXII. The right of stoppage *in transitu* is, Lord
Stowell (*f*) observed, not only "the doctrine of the Law of
" England," but "the general expression of the mercantile
" Law on the subject." The consignor has what Lord Mans-
field called "a proprietary lien" upon goods *in transitu* for

---

577. La revendication ne pourra avoir lieu que pendant que les marchandises expédiées seront encore en route, soit par terre, soit par eau,
et avant qu 'elles soient entrées dans les magasins du failli ou dans les
magasins du commissionaire chargé de les vendre pour le compte du
failli.

578. Elles ne pourront être revendiquées si avant leur arivée, elles
ont été vendues sans fraude sur factures et connaissemens ou lettres des
voiture.

579. En cas de revendication, le revendiquant sera tenu de rendre
l'actif du failli indemne de toute avance faite pour fret ou voiture, commission, assurance, ou autres frais, et de payers les sommes dues pour
mêmes causes, si elles n'ont pas été acquittés.

580. La revendication ne pourra être exercée que sur les marchan-
dises qui seront reconnues être identiquement les mêmes, et que lorsqu'il sera reconnu que les balles, barriques ou enveloppes dans
lesquelles elles se trouvaient lors de la vente, n'ont pas été ouvertes
que les cordes ou marques n'ont été ni enlevées ni changées, et que les
marchandises n'ont subi en nature et quantité ni changement ni alteration.

(*e*) *Tudor's Leading Cases in Mercantile and Maritime Law, White-
head* v. *Anderson*, p. 547; *S. C.* 9 *Meeson and Welsby's Rep.* 518.

(*f*) "*The Constantia*," 6 *Robinson's Ad. Rep.* 325-6. *Lord Stowell*
referred to *Emerigon*, i. p. 318, 19, as showing that the *Vendeur primitif*
might protect himself against non-payment by seizure of the goods, but
this is perhaps not so much a right of stoppage *in transitu* as the right
of revendication : *vide ante*.

which payment has not been received. This doctrine was transplanted from the *lex mercatoria* into the Common Law of England. Great doubt and dispute have prevailed, and, perhaps, still do prevail, as to whether this right of stoppage amounts to a rescinding of the contract, or to a mere extension of the doctrine of the seller's lien upon the thing sold.

DCCCXXXIII. It may be well to state that the English decisions appear to have established the following propositions as incident to this right :

1. The Right of Stoppage (*g*) *in transitu* can only be exercised by a seller or person standing in the position of a seller of goods.

2. The Right is limited to cases (*h*) in which the *bankruptcy* or *insolvency* of the vendee has taken place. A *partial* payment by the vendee does not prevent the exercise of this right.

3. As a general rule the (*i*) *transitus* is not at an end until the goods arrive at the actual or constructive possession of the consignee; during this period, as well as while they are in the vendor's possession, the vendor's right of stoppage remains.

4. Notice on the part of the vendor (*k*) by himself or agent to the carrier not to deliver the goods, suffices to cause the right of stoppage to attach.

5. The better opinion seems to be that the effect of the exercise of the right is merely to replace the seller in the same position as if he had not parted with the possession of the goods, and not to rescind the contract; but the point cannot be said to have been decided. (*l*)

6. The Right of Stoppage is defeated when a bill of lading

(*g*) *Tudor's Leading Maritime Cases*, 551.

(*h*) *Ib.* 554.

(*i*) *Ib.* 555.

(*k*) *Ib.* 565.

(*l*) *Ib.* 567.

has been indorsed to a *bonâ fide* purchaser, without notice, for valuable consideration, and with the authority of the original seller. (*m*)

DCCCXXXIV. What Law is to decide as to whether this right of stoppage exists or not? The *lex loci contractûs*, Mr. Burge says, (*n*) relying on Casaregis, (*o*) and on English (*p*) and North American United States decisions. (*q*) It is a lien, (*r*) Story says, which has rightfully attached *in rem*, and ought not to be locally displaced by the mere change of the local situation of the property.

The reason of the thing seems to be in favour of these opinions.

(*m*) *Tudor's Leading Maritime Cases*, 568.

(*n*) 3 *Burge*, 770.

(*o*) *Disc.* 179, n. 53, 55.

(*p*) *Inglis* v. *Underwood*, 1 *East's Rep.* 514. In this case the right of stoppage *in transitu* was holden to be governed by Russian, materially different from English Law, and it was enforced against English creditors ; but the circumstances were peculiar, the lien was Russian, and enforced in Russia.

(*q*) *Whiston* v. *Stodder*, 8 *Martin's Rep.* 134-5.

(*r*) S. 402 ; see, too, 1 *Bell*, 129, *in fine*.

APPENDIX TO CHAPTER XLI.

It may be convenient to mention in this place those sections of the recent Commercial Statute of England (*The Merchant Shipping Act,* 17 & 18 *Vict.* c. 104) which bear in any degree upon questions of Maritime International Law.

Right of Detention of FOREIGN SHIP *for Damage.*

Sec. 527. "Whenever any injury has, in any part of the world, been caused to any property belonging to her Majesty, or to any of her Majesty's subjects by *any foreign ship*, if at any time thereafter such ship is *found in any port or river of the United Kingdom, or within three miles of the coast thereof,* it shall be lawful for the Judge of any Court of Record in the United Kingdom, or for the Judge of the High Court of Admiralty, or in Scotland the Court of Session, or the Sheriff of the County within whose jurisdiction such ship may be, upon its being shown to him by any person applying summarily that such injury was probably caused by the misconduct or want of skill of the master or mariners of such ship, to issue an order directed to any officer of customs or other officer named by such judge, requiring him to detain such ship until such time as the owner, master, or consignee thereof has made satisfaction in respect of such injury, or has given security, to be approved by the judge, to abide the event of any action, suit, or other legal proceeding that may be instituted in respect of such injury, and to pay all costs and damages that may be awarded thereon ; and any officer of customs or other officer to whom such order is directed, shall detain such ship accordingly."

Sec. 528. "In any case where it appears that before any application can be made under the foregoing section *such foreign ship* will have departed beyond the limits therein mentioned, it shall be lawful for any commissioned officer on full pay in the military or naval service of her Majesty, or any British officer of customs, or any British consular officer, to detain such ship until such time as will allow such application to be made and the result thereof to be communicated to him ; and no such officer shall be liable for any costs or damages in respect of such detention unless the same is proved to have been made without reasonable grounds."

Who to be Defendant in Suit for Damage.

Sec. 529. "In any action, suit, or other proceeding in relation to such injury, the person so giving security as aforesaid shall be made defendant or defender, and shall be stated to be the owner of the ship that has occasioned such damage ; and the production of the order of the judge made in relation to such security shall be conclusive evidence of the liability of such defendant or defender to such action, suit, or other proceeding."

Owner of damaging Vessel not answerable beyond Value of his Ship and Freight.

Sec. 504. "No owner of any sea-going ship, or share therein, shall, in cases where all or any of the following events occur without his actual fault or privity, (that is to say)

"1. Where any loss of life or personal injury is caused to any person being carried in such ship ;

"2. Where any damage or loss is caused to any goods, merchandize, or other things whatsoever on board any such ship ;

"3. Where any loss of life or personal injury is by reason of the improper navigation of such sea-going ship as aforesaid, caused to any person carried in any other ship or boat ;

"4. Where any loss or damage is by reason of any such improper navigation of such sea- going ship as aforesaid, caused to any other ship or boat, or to any goods, merchandize, or other things whatsoever, on board any other ship or boat ;

"be answerable in damages to an extent beyond the value of his ship and the freight due or to grow due in respect of such ship during the voyage which at the time of the happening of any such events as aforesaid is in prosecution or contracted for, subject to the following proviso, (that is to say) that in no case where any such liability as aforesaid is incurred in respect of loss of life or personal injury to any passenger, shall the value of any such ship and the freight thereof be taken to be less than 15l. per registered ton."

Sec. 17th enacts that, "The second part of this Act shall apply *to the whole of Her Majesty's dominions.*"

Description and Ownership of British Ships.

Sec. 18th enacts that, " *No ship shall be deemed to be a British ship unless she belongs wholly to owners of the following description*, (that is to say)

"1. Natural-born British subjects :

Provided that no natural-born subject, who has taken the oath of allegiance to any foreign sovereign or state, shall be entitled to be such owner as aforesaid, unless he has subsequently to taking such last-mentioned oath taken the oath of allegiance to Her Majesty, and is, and continues to be, during the whole period of his so being an owner, resident in some place within Her Majesty's dominions, or if not so resident, member of a British factory, or partner in a house actually carrying on business in the United Kingdom, or in some other place within Her Majesty's dominions :

" 2. Persons made denizens by letters of denization, or naturalized by or pursuant to any act of the imperial legislature, or by or pursuant to any act or ordinance of the proper legislative authority, in any British possession :

Provided that such persons are and continue to be, during the whole period of their so being owners, resident in some place within her Majesty's dominions, or if not so resident, members of a British factory, or partners in a house actually carrying on business in the United Kingdom, or in some other place within Her Majesty's dominions, and have taken the oath of allegiance to Her Majesty, subsequently to the period of their being so made denizens, or naturalized.

" 3. Bodies corporate established under, subject to the laws of, and having their principal place of business in the United Kingdom, or some British possession."

British Ships must be registered.

Sec. 19. " Every British ship must be registered in manner hereinafter mentioned, except,

" 1. Ships duly registered before the Act comes into operation :

" 2. Ships not exceeding fifteen tons burden, employed solely in navigation on the rivers or coasts of the United Kingdom, or on the rivers or coasts of some British possession, within which the managing owners of such ships are resident :

" 3. Ships not exceeding thirty tons burden, and not having a whole or fixed deck, and employed solely in fishing or trading coastwise, on the shores of Newfoundland or ports adjacent thereto, or in the Gulf of St. Lawrence, or on such portion of the coasts of Canada, Nova Scotia, or New Brunswick, as lie bordering on such gulf.

" And no ship hereby required to be registered shall, unless registered, be recognised as a British ship, and no officer of customs shall grant a clearance or transire to any ship hereby required to be registered for the purpose of enabling her to proceed to sea as a British ship, unless the master of such ship, upon being required so to do, produces to him such certificate of registry as is hereinafter mentioned, and if such ship attempts to proceed to sea as a British ship, without a clearance or transire, such officer may detain such ship until such certificate is produced to him."

Rule as to Ships meeting each other.

Sec. 296 enacts that "Whenever any ship, whether a steam or sailing ship, proceeding in one direction, meets another ship, whether a steam or sailing ship, proceeding in another direction, so that if both ships were to continue their respective courses they would pass so near as to involve any risk of a collision, the helms of both ships shall be put to port, so as to pass on the port side of each other ; and this rule shall be obeyed by all steam ships and by all sailing ships, whether on the port or starboard tack, and whether close-hauled or not, unless the circumstances of the case are such as to render a departure from the rule necessary in order to avoid immediate danger, and subject also to the proviso that due regard shall be had to the dangers of navigation, and, as regards sailing ships on the starboard tack close-hauled, to the keeping such ships under command."

The last-stated enactment does not apply to foreign vessels, or to a foreign and English vessel.*

Conflict of Laws.

Sec. 290. "If in any matter relating to any ship, or to any person belonging to any ship, there appears to be a conflict of laws, then, if there is in the third part of this act any provision on the subject which is hereby expressly made to extend to such ship, the case shall be governed by such provision, and if there is no such provision the case shall be governed by the law of the place in which such ship is registered."

---

* *The Zolverein,* 1 *Swabey, Ad. Rep.* 96 ; 2 *Jur. N. S.* 429, *Adm.*

"A British and foreign vessel had come into collision. By the general
" maritime law the foreign vessel was pronounced in fault, but by the Merchant
" Shipping Act, c. 104, s. 296, 298, 299, it was provided that if a ship did not
" port her helm when meeting another ship, and a collision occurred, such
" ship could not recover any recompense for any damage sustained. The
" British ship did not port her helm ; it was therefore urged that she could not
" recover, by reason of her own default :—Holden, that the 17th and 18th Vic.,
" c. 104, ss. 296, 298, 299, did not apply to cases in which foreign vessels were
" concerned, and that therefore the general maritime law must prevail, and the
" British vessel was entitled to be recompensed for the damage she had sus-
" tained."

CHAPTER XLII.

BILLS OF EXCHANGE AND LITERÆ CAMBII—LETTRES DE CHANGE—WECHSEL—WECHSELGESCHÄFTE.

DCCCXXXV. We have now to consider the rules of Comity with respect to that great instrument of commerce, Negotiable Paper—Promissory Notes, or Bills of Exchange. (a)

This subject was, on account of its importance and certain peculiarities incident to it, not included in the foregoing chapters on *Obligations*, but reserved for special consideration, though the general principles of the law relative to them are of course applicable to bills of exchange.

DCCCXXXVI. The contract of a bill of exchange, like other contracts, in this respect must be considered with reference to—

1. The *lex domicilii*, the law which governs the personal capacity to contract.

2. *The lex loci contractûs.*

3. The *lex loci solutionis.*

4. The *lex fori.*

DCCCXXXVII. First, as to the *lex domicilii*, or the personal capacity to enter into this contract.

A bill of exchange must be considered with reference to the different persons interested or concerned in it, such persons

---

(a) See generally *Byles on Bills of Exchange*, c. 32,—Of the effect of Foreign Law in England relating to Bills of Exchange and Promissory Notes.

Savigny, vol. viii. s. 364 (*Wechselrecht*).

1 *Fœlix* (ed. *Dem.*), pp. 76, 160, 177, 181, 224, 244, 238.

2 *Massé*, ss. 141—148.

being, according to the nomenclature of English law, the drawer, the payee, the acceptor, the endorser.

A bill is, in the technical phrase, said to be *honoured* when it is duly accepted ; when it becomes payable by lapse of time it is said to have *arrived at maturity ;* and, when acceptance or payment thereof is refused, it is said to be *dishonoured. (b)*

It has been established as a general principle in the English Courts that the liabilities of the drawer, the acceptor, and endorser, must be governed by the laws of the countries in which the drawing, acceptance, and endorsement respectively took place.

DCCCXXXVIII. The English law, which looks exclusively to the *lex loci contractûs* in contracts, and excludes all consideration of personal capacity by the law of the domicil, has some advantage over the foreign law in this particular instance. Savigny admits that there is no matter on which there exists such a variety of local and personal law as on the personal capacity of the drawer of a bill of exchange. Some foreign writers endeavour to get rid of the difficulty, and still adhere to the general doctrine respecting the personal statute following the person everywhere, by allowing in this instance a *special* capacity of the drawer derived from the place where the act is done, though in other respects his *general* capacity still remains governed by the law of the domicil. Savigny rejects this rather lame device, and maintains that upon true and sound principles the law of the domicil must decide the question of capacity : but such is the difficulty of the case that it demands, he thinks, positive legislation in each state upon the subject.

DCCCXXXIX. Since the 27th of November, 1848, a law has prevailed throughout the whole of Germany, which removes, so far as that country is concerned, all practical difficulty connected with the subject. By that law every subject

---

(b) *Story on Bills,* s. 126, p. 47.

capable of entering into any contract, is capable to be the drawer of a bill of exchange.

And with respect to foreigners, though the personal capacity is to be governed by the law of the domicil, yet, whosoever is concerned with the making of a bill of exchange in a foreign state, is to be treated as capable of doing so, if he is so treated by the law of the land in which it is made.

This law was accepted by Prussia on the 1st of February, 1849.

DCCCXL. There does not appear to be any direct authority in French (c) jurisprudence upon the subject of the capacity of the drawer being regulated by the law of his domicil : but according to general principles the capacity would in that state be regulated by that law.

DCCCXLI. In most of the states on the European continent the law has affixed an incapacity upon all but certain specified classes to be parties to bills of exchange. It may be doubted whether the English courts would recognise this incapacity, though, according to all sound principles of Comity, they ought to do so. It is a matter, however, which has not yet received any judicial decision (d) in England, or in the United States of North America. (e)

DCCCXLII. In England and the North American United States (f) the incapacity is the exception, and not the rule, and is confined to the following classes :

1. Minors.
2. Married women.

(c) The French law on the general subject will be found *Code de Commerce*, l. i. t. viii., *De la lettre de change, des billets à ordre, et de la prescription*. In the edition of this Code, 1836, by Dr. Sautayra, there is a perspicuous little preface to the above chapter. It will be found printed in a note to this chapter.

(d) See *Westlake*, ss, 348, 401.

(e) *Story, Bills of Exchange*, c. iv., *Competency and Capacity of Parties to Bills*.

(f) *Story on Bills of Exchange*, ss. 81, 82.

3. Alien enemies. (*g*)

4. Insane and imbecile persons. And in England also

5. Clergymen—so far as engaging in the traffic of bills of exchange for a livelihood is concerned—an incapacity which is in accordance with the general Canon Law.

Otherwise, these states adopt the general law laid down by Heineccius, " Nullum est dubium quin cambiare possint qui-" cumque possunt contrahere, nisi id leges cambiales, speciatim " prohibeant." (*h*)

DCCCXLIII. Secondly,(*i*) as to the *lex loci contractûs*. The general principles respecting conventions contrary to public morality or public policy, of course apply to the particular contract, which assumes the form of a *Bill of Exchange;* and the English courts apply to these instruments that questionable doctrine of refusing to take notice of the Revenue Laws (*k*) of a foreign state ; (*l*) so far, at least, as to hold, that a document which, by the Law of a foreign country, is not admissible in evidence for want of a stamp, may, nevertleless, be admitted in England. For it is *now* (*m*) clear that if by the

---

(*g*) This restriction does not apply to a *neutral* drawer or endorser, of an alien enemy, or to a bill drawn by one alien enemy upon another in favour of a neutral, so far as the latter is concerned. So as to an endorsement. See *Story on Bills of Exchange*, s. 104.

(*h*) *De jure camb.*, c. v. ss. 1, 2, 13, 14 ; cited in *Story on Bills of Exchange*, s. 71.

(*i*) *Story on Bills of Exchange (Amer.)* ; see *Allen* v. *Kemble*, 1 *Moore's P. C. Rep.* 323, for the high authority of this work in England.

Byles on Bills of Exchange, c. xxxi., *Of foreign bills and notes*, ed. 1857, London. There appear to have been no less than three American editions of this most useful little work.

Ross's Leading Cases of Commercial Law, i. 792, 804, 812, 841, 858, 859, 860, 861, 877.

(*k*) *Vide ante*, vol. ii. p. 37, and App. ii. p. 483.

(*l*) *James* v. *Catherwood*, 3 *Dowling & Ryland's Rep.* 190.

Wynne v. *Jackson*, 2 *Russell's Rep.* 351.

Holman v. *Johnson (Lord Mansfield)*, *Cowper's Rep.* 343.

(*m*) *Bristow* v. *Sequeville* (1850), 5 *Exchequer Rep.* 275, disposes of the former cases, which are confused and contradictory ; see *Alves* v.

foreign Law the want of a stamp renders the contract void, it cannot be enforced in this country.

The English government has, however, taken care of its own revenue in this matter, and by a recent statute has imposed a stamp duty on bills drawn out of the United Kingdom, but paid, indorsed, transferred, or otherwise negotiated within it. (n)

DCCCXLIV. It may be well to observe that the English Law presumes that a bill purporting to be drawn abroad was really so drawn, though evidence to show the contrary is admissible. (o)

The courts of the United States of North America have rightly holden that if the protest of a bill of exchange, made in another state, is required by the Laws of that state to be under

---

Hodgson, 7 *Durnford & East's Rep.* 237; *Clegg* v. *Levy*, 3 *Campbell's Rep.* 166; with *Wynn* v. *Jackson*, 2 *Russell's Rep.* 351; *James* v. *Catherwood*, 3 *Dowling & Ryland's Rep.* 190, in contradiction of it; *Boucher* v. *Lawson, Cases temp. Hardwicke*, 83—94, decides that a contract in England, between Englishmen, to smuggle against the laws of Portugal was valid; not, however, that a contract in Portugal, by persons domiciled there, would be valid. See the conflict of these cases on this subject, well analyzed in *Story on Bills*, 160, note *n*, which is *identical* with the note of the learned reporter to the case of *Leroux* v. *Brown*, 12 *Exch. Rep.* 809. I do not know to which author the note properly belongs; but the case of *Bristow* v. *Sequeville*, mentioned above, makes the English law at least clear on this point.

(n) 17 & 18 *Vic.* c. 83, ss. 3, 4, 5, 6. There has been an important recent decision on this statute in the Court of Exchequer; it is reported in *The Weekly Reporter* of Saturday, May 23rd, 1857: "The statute 17 & 18 *Vic.* c. 83, s. 3, imposing a duty on foreign bills which are 'paid, indorsed, transferred, or otherwise negotiated within the United Kingdom,' does not render a stamp necessary where a bill drawn abroad has been indorsed abroad to a person in England and presented by him for acceptance in England, and therefore that the bill was admissible in evidence without a stamp." (*Sharples and others* v. *Rickards.*)

(o) *Abraham* v. *Dubois*, 4 *Campbell's Rep.* 269.

Bire v. *Moreau*, 2 *Carrington & Payne's Rep.* 376.

Byles, 353.

seal, a protest, not under seal, will not be regarded as evidence of the dishonour of the bill. (*p*)

DCCCXLV. Under this head of the *lex loci contractûs* the decisions of the English courts have established the following maxim :—

That an *acceptance* void or avoided by the Law of the country where it is given is not binding in England.

This maxim England has enforced through her courts of equity. It is illustrated by a case, in which it appeared that by the Law of Leghorn, if a bill be accepted, and the drawer then fail, and the acceptor have not sufficient effects of the drawer in his hands at the time of acceptance, the acceptance becomes void. An acceptor at Leghorn, under these circumstances, instituted a suit at Leghorn, and his acceptance was thereupon vacated. Afterwards he was sued in England as acceptor ; by way of defence he filed his bill for an injunction and relief, and Lord Chancellor King granted a perpetual injunction, enjoining the plaintiff from suing on the bill. (*q*)

Upon the same principle a written agreement, of the kind called in England an I O U, given for money lent for the purpose of playing at games of chance, being an unlawful agreement in England, but a lawful agreement in the country where it was given, has been holden valid in England. (*r*) So the payment of part in discharge of the whole of a debt, though ineffectual by the law of England, has, nevertheless, been holden effectual to bar the whole debt in England, it having been shown to be effectual for that purpose, according to the law of the country in which the bill was negotiated, and the payment having been made, the bill being then due and payable, and in the hands of the true holder. (*s*)

(*p*) *Story on Bills*, s. 138 ; *on Conflict*, s. 260.
(*q*) *Burrows* v. *Jemimo*, 2 *Strange's Rep.* 733 ;
Wynne v. *Calendar*, 1 *Russell's Rep.* 295 ;
Byles on Bills of Exchange, 349.
(*r*) *Quarrier* v. *Colston*, 12 *Law J.*, *Chancery*, 57.
(*s*) *Ralli* v. *Dennistoun*, 6 *Exch. Rep.* 493-4 (1851).

DCCCXLVI. The two following cases relate to the important question of *indorsement* as governed by the *lex loci contractûs.*

A bill of exchange was made, and indorsed in blank by the payee, in a country in which each of the parties, the maker and the payee, were, at the respective times of making and indorsing, domiciled, and in which the indorsement in blank did not operate as a transfer of the note; this indorsement was holden void in England, although in England an indorsement in blank operates as a complete transfer, because the foreign Law in this case, and not the domestic Law which regulated the mode of suing, (*t*) was the law by which the contract was governed.

DCCCXLVII. In the United States of North America the question of the different obligations created by indorsements in different states often arises. Story (*u*) observes, that " by the general Commercial Law, in order to entitle the " indorsee to recover against any antecedent indorser upon a " negotiable note, it is only necessary that due demand should " be made upon the maker of the note at its maturity, and " due notice of the dishonour given to the indorser. But, by " the laws of some of the American states, it is required, in " order to charge an antecedent indorser, not only that due " demand should be made, and due notice given, but that a " suit should be previously commenced against the maker, and " prosecuted with effect in the country where he resides; and, " then, if payment cannot be obtained from him under the " judgment, the indorsee may have recourse to the indorser. " In such a case, it is clear, upon principle, that the indorse- " ment, as to its legal effect and obligation, and the duties of " the holder, must be governed by the law of the place where

---

(*t*) *Trimby* v. *Vignier*, 1 *Ross*, 8, 10, 11 (A. D. 1834). The decision in this leading case, by C. J. Tindal, overrules that of Vice Chancellor Leach (A. D. 1826) in *Wynne* v. *Jackson*, 2 *Russell's Rep.* 352-3.

(*u*) *On Bills*, s. 156.

" the indorsement is made. (x) And it appears that a decision
" to this effect was given in the case of a note made and
" indorsed in the state of Illinois. In that case, Mr. Chief
" Justice Shaw, in delivering the opinion of the court, said,
" ' The note declared on being made in Illinois, both parties
" ' residing there at the time, and it also being indorsed in
" ' Illinois, we think, that the contract created by that in-
" ' dorsement must be governed by the law of that state.
" ' The law in question does not effect the remedy, but goes to
" ' create, limit, and modify the contract effected by the fact
" ' of indorsement. In that, which gives force and effect to
" ' the contract, and imposes restrictions and modifications
" ' upon it, the law of the place of contract must prevail, when
" ' another is not looked to, as a place of performance.' " (y)

DCCCXLVIII. In England a bill of exchange or promissory
note is not transferable by indorsement unless it be payable
" to the bearer " or " to order ; " but in Scotland without these
conditions such an instrument is transferable by indorsement.
In a case which came before the Scotch courts in 1843, the
following promissory note had been granted :—

" £412 sterling.   " *Edinburgh*, 19th July, 1840.

" Six months after date, I promise to pay to Frederick
" Boucher, Esq., manager of the British and Australasian
" Bank, 55 Moorgate Street, *London*, the sum of four hundred
" and twelve pounds sterling, value received.

(Signed)   " MURD. ROBERTSON."

This note was indorsed in *England* by Boucher; when the
note became due Robertson refused to pay it. The question
for the Scotch court was whether the note was to be considered as English or Scotch. The court held that it was

_____

(x) *Story on Bills*, s. 157.
(y) *Ibid.*

Scotch in all its incidents ; that it was not, as contended, made payable *at* London ; that " 55, Moorgate Street, London," were words of designation as to the payee, not words relating to the *lex loci solutionis ;* that being Scotch it was transmissible by indorsement in England. (*z*)

In this case Lord Medwyn made some valuable observations on the nature and effect of indorsement. (*a*) " It is often " (he observed) " said, and truly, that by indorsation a new contract " is created ; and I was puzzled at one time with the circum- " stance that the indorsation in the present case was by an " Englishman to an Englishman, and executed in England ; " and it appeared difficult for me to conceive how such a con- " tract could be validly entered into in a country where such " an indorsation was not valid, so as not to constitute a right " in favour of the one, or an obligation against the other. " But although it might be consistent with principle to allow " the law of the place where the indorsement was made to " regulate its effect between indorser and indorsee, as between " the indorsee and the maker no new contract is created, the " contract between them remaining the same original con- " tract, regulated by the *lex loci contractûs ;* the indorsee is " merely substituted in the place of the original payee, and " the maker remains under the same liability he contracted at " the time he made the note, which was to pay to the payee " or to the holder by indorsement ; and he cannot object to the " form of the transfer, if it be made according to the law which " gives its character, and regulates the quality of the note ; " that is, in the present case, according to the law of Scotland."

DCCCXLIX. In the matter of bills of exchange, as of other contracts, the *lex loci contractûs* governs the *construction* of the instrument, where the contract is not express, while, . if it be special the construction must be in accordance with the express terms in which it is made. (*b*)

(*z*) *Robertson* v. *Burdekin,* 1 *Ross's Leading Cases,* 812.

(*a*) *Ross's Leading Cases in Commercial Law,* vol. i. p. 831.

(*b*) See an important judgment of the Supreme Court of Pennsylvania, May 16, 1854, *Lennig* v. *Ralston et al.* in a note to this Chapter.

A bill (c) drawn upon a third person in discharge of a present debt is, in truth, an offer by the *drawer* that, if the *payee* will give time for payment, he, the drawer, will give an order on his debtor (the *acceptor*) to pay a given sum at a given time and place. The payee agrees to accept this order, and to give the time, with a proviso, that if the acceptor do not pay, and he the payee (or the holder of the bill) give notice to the drawer of that default, the drawer shall pay him the amount specified in the bill, with lawful interest; but the question still remains as to whether the drawer incurs any obligation that the bill shall be paid at any, and, if at any, at what particular place. The answer of the English law, in conformity with the reason of the thing, and with the doctrine of general jurisprudence on this point, is as follows:—The drawer, by his contract, undertakes that the drawee shall accept and shall afterwards pay the bill, according to its tenor, at the place and domicil of the drawee if it be drawn and accepted generally; at the place appointed for payment, if it be drawn and accepted payable at a different place from the place of domicil of the *drawee*. If this contract of the drawer be broken by the drawee, either by non-acceptance or non-payment, the drawer is liable for payment of the bill, not where the bill was to be paid by the drawee, but where he, the drawer, made his contract, and with his interest, damages, and costs, as the law of the country where he contracted may allow. In every case of a bill drawn in one country upon a drawee in another, the intention and the agreement are, that the bill shall be paid in the country upon which it is drawn. If this payment be not so made, the drawer is liable, according to the laws of the country where the bill was drawn, and not of the country upon which the bill was drawn.

(c) In the following part of this paragraph I have adopted, with little alteration, the very words of our distinguished judges, the late Baron Alderson (*Gibbs* v. *Fremont*, 9 *Exch. Rep.* 30) and Mr. Pemberton Leigh (Lord Kingsdown) (*Allen* v. *Kemble*, 6 *Moore's P. C. Rep.* 321-2).

DCCCL. Thirdly, as to the *lex loci solutionis*. The first case about to be mentioned may appear to be at variance with the Scotch case to which attention has just been drawn, but in reality it is not so. An English court, in the case of *De la Chaumette* v. *Bank of England*, (*d*) decided that a promissory note payable to bearer, *made and payable in England*, was transferable by delivery abroad, although by the law of the country where the delivery took place mere delivery was inoperative. In this case the *lex loci solutionis* was admitted to govern the contract. The substance of the case itself, and the distinction between it and the Scotch case is thus stated by Lord Justice Clerk Hope : (*e*)

" A party brought an action, as the correspondent or agent
" of a foreign house, against the Bank of England, for recovery
" of a note of the Bank for £500, which that foreign house
" said they had bought abroad, but which was detained by the
" Bank, on the ground that it was stolen. The case was tried
" before Lord Tenterden, and a rule for a new trial made abso-
" lute on two grounds ; first, that the foreign house might
" prove, in point of fact, that 'they gave such value for the
" ' note as to exempt them from any reasonable ground of
" ' suspicion of any knowledge that it had been improperly
" ' obtained.' That point has nothing to do with this case,
" and was of itself necessary for the ends of justice ; secondly,
" Lord Tenderden said it might be raised as a point at the
" second trial, whether an English bank-note—a promissory
" note, transferable in England only by statute, could be trans-
" ferred at all abroad. Lord Tenterden says, 'The court gives
" ' no opinion on the point, but merely gives the party the
" ' opportunity to raise it on the record, which was not done
" ' before.' From this it is clear that that point is left open ;
" but the suspender does not appear to see that the court there
" thought the legal character of the note, as made in England,

---

(*d*) *Barne. & Adol. Rep.* 385 ; *Byles*, 350.
(*e*) *Ross's Leading Cases*, vol. i. 826-7.

" was so peculiarly the important fact to look to that, though
" indorsable in England, yet being so by statute alone, it might
" be a question whether its character at common law in Eng-
" land must not follow it everywhere, and decide its quality
" elsewhere, and not the character impressed on it by statute.
" Probably there could be no difficulty in deciding that point,
" but the case only proves how much the Court of King's
" Bench looked to the character and qualities of the contract
" as an English contract."

DCCCLI. According to the English and North American
law, a contract to pay *generally*, without any specification of
place, is governed by the law of the place where it is made. (*f*)
This doctrine is consistent with holding that such a contract is
payable *anywhere*. (*g*)

DCCCLII. **3.** We have now to consider the *lex fori* in its
application to this subject.

The English courts had at one time holden that *protest* and
notice of dishonour are parcel of the contract formed by a bill
of exchange, and that they are not incidents of the remedy
belonging to the breach of the contract, (*h*) and that therefore
both *protest* and *notice of dishonour* must be regulated by
the law of the country where the bill was payable. But
this (*i*) doctrine may be said to have been greatly shaken, if

---

(*f*) *Donn* v. *Lippmann*, 5 *Clark & Fin.* 1, 12, 13.
Story's Conflict, s. 317.
(*g*) *Story, ib.*
(*h*) *Byles*, 350—354.
(*i*) In the case of *Allen* v. *Kemble* (6 *Moore's P. C. Rep.* 322), Mr.
Pemberton Leigh observed that " the case, however, mainly relied upon
by the respondents, was *Rothschild* v. *Currie* (1 *Q. B. Rep.* 45, A.D. 1841).
In that case, a bill was drawn in *England* on a party resident in
Paris, and made payable in *Paris*, in favour of a payee resident in
England. It was indorsed over in *England*, by the payee, to a party
also resident in *England*. The bill having been dishonoured by the
acceptor, in *Paris*, it was held that protest and notice of dishonour,
regular according to the law of *France*, though alleged to be insufficient
according to the law of *England*, were sufficient to charge the indorser.

not entirely overthrown, by later decisions, which have established, contrary to former decisions, that the drawer is liable according to the law of the country where the bill is drawn; and that the liabilities of the indorser are governed by the law of the country of the indorsement. (*k*)

The better opinion seems to be that the protest and notice of dishonour must be regulated by the law of the country where the bill was drawn, but not where the bill is payable. (*l*)

DCCCLIII. A promissory note may be made and dated in a particular country and made payable in a *currency* which obtains in several countries, under the same denomination but with a different value. In which currency is the note to be paid?

The answer of the English courts is—In the currency of that country in which the note is payable; that will be, as has been seen, either in a place specified in the instrument itself, or, in default of such specification, in the place in which the note is made—that being, according to the presumption of

---

It may be observed, that since the cases above referred to were decided the whole law upon this subject has been most carefully, elaborately, and learnedly examined by Mr. Justice Story in his treatise on Bills of Exchange, and he disapproves of the decision in the case of *Rothschild* v. *Currie* (*Story on Bills*, note, p. 352); but, without expressing any opinion upon that decision, it is enough for us to observe that the court did not profess to depart from any principles of law acted upon in previous cases, and whether those principles were, or not, accurately applied to the particular case, is not for the present purpose material."

In *Gibbs* v. *Fremont*, as reported in the *Law Journal*, vol. 22, p. 304, it is said, "*Alderson*, B., referred to *Rothschild* v. *Currie* as of questionable authority." In this case occurs one of those misapplications of the Roman law, consequent on a partial and imperfect knowledge of the whole system, which is but too common with English lawyers and judges. 1 *Ad. & Ellis's N. Rep.* 49.

(*k*) *Cooper* v. *Lord Waldegrave*, 2 *Beavan's Rep.* 282.

Allen v. *Kemble*, 6 *Moore's P. C. Rep.* 321.

(*l*) *Byles*, 350, *cf.* with 354.

Story's Conflict, s. 360.

law, the place in which the parties intended it to be payable. (*m*)

DCCCLIV. The English courts have holden that if a bill be drawn in a country where the *interest* is twenty-five per cent. on a drawee in a country where the interest is only six per cent., that the higher rate of interest is recoverable against the drawer, but the lower rate against the acceptor, who accepted the bill in the country in which the lower rate prevailed. (*n*)

DCCCLV. It may be useful to observe, with reference to the administration of law in England, that in cases of this description the *rate* of interest is a question of law for the judge to decide, and is not left, as English lawyers speak, to the jury : but the amount of the interest in each place is to be so left, and so also is the question whether any damage has been sustained requiring the payment of interest at all, for those are questions of fact. (*o*)

DCCCLVI. The English courts consider that if the interest be expressly or by necessary implication specified on the face of the instrument, there the interest is governed by the terms of the contract itself. But if not, it seems to follow the rate of interest of the place where the contract is made. (*p*)

DCCCLVII. The time when the payment of the bill is to accrue is governed by the *lex loci solutionis*. This law therefore governs the question as to whether *days of grace* are to be allowed and their number. (*q*)

(*m*) *Kearney* v. *King*, 2 *Barn. & Alderson's Rep.* 301.

Sprowle v. *Legge*, 1 *Barn. & Cresswell's Rep.* 16 (A.D. 1822).

See other cases cited note *y*, p. 372, *Byles on Bills; Story*, s. 272.

(*n*) *Allen* v. *Kemble*, 6 *Moore's P. C. Rep.* 314 (A.D. 1848), and *Gibbs* v. *Fremont* (A.D. 1853), (*Baron Alderson's Judgment*), 9 *Exchequer Rep.* 31, are the leading English cases. When Lord Langdale decided the case of *Cooper* v. *Lord Waldegrave*, 2 *Beavan's Rep.* 282 (A.D. 1840), he remarked how little there was to be found in English decisions upon the subject.

(*o*) *Gibbs* v. *Fremont*, 9 *Exchequer Rep.* 31.   (*p*) *Ib.* p. 30.

(*q*) *Story on Bills*, s. 155.

NOTE TO THE FOREGOING CHAPTER.

CODE DE COMMERCE, LIV. I. TIT. VIII. S. I.

"DE LA LETTRE DE CHANGE.

" Les lettres de change étaient inconnues chez les Grecs et chez les Romains. Les historiens ne s'accordent point sur l'époque où elles ont commencé à être en usage. Les uns prétendent que nous en devons l'invention aux Juifs, qui, chassés de France et établis en Lombardie, avaient trouvé le moyen de retirer leurs fonds, confiés par eux entre les mains de leurs amis, en se servant de lettres secrètes, et conçues en peu de mots. D'autres l'attribuent aux Florentins de la faction Guelphe, lorsque, chassés par les Gibeling, ils se retirèrent en France et dans d'autres lieux de l'Europe. Mais, sans s'arrêter à toutes ces conjectures, ne vaut-il pas mieux, avec l'orateur du gouvernement, chercher l'origine de la lettre de change dans les progrès du commerce, dans l'extension des relations commerciales, qui en a été la suite, et qui a produit la nécessité de balancer les valeurs réciproquement acquises, ou déposées par les négocians éloignés les uns des autres, et mutuellement créanciers et débiteurs. Cependant, une loi de Venise, rapportée par *Nicolas de Passeribus* dans son livre Script. Privat., livre 3, prouve que les lettres de change étaient en usage dès le 14e siècle. Le monument le plus ancien de notre législation où il soit question de lettres de change, est une ordonnance de Louis XI de 1462. Le mot *change* a deux acceptions : dans l'une, il exprime le profit qu'on tire de l'opération ; dans l'autre, l'opération elle-même. On distingue deux sortes d'opérations de change : l'une, que les docteurs appellent *cambium reale vel manuale*, qui n'est que le change d'une espèce de monnaie. On nomme *changeurs* ceux qui exploitent cette espèce de change. L'autre opération de change, que l'on nomme *cambium locale, mercantile, trajectitium*, est le contrat de change proprement dit. Ce contrat n'est autre chose qu'une convention par laquelle une personne, moyennant une somme d'argent qui lui est remise ou promise dans un lieu, s'oblige à faire payer à la personne qui la lui remet une même somme dans un autre lieu et dans un temps convenu. On appelle *banquiers* les commerçans qui se livrent à cette seconde branche d'opérations de change. Ce contrat s'exécute au moyen de la lettre de change. On définit généralement la lettre de change une lettre revêtue des formes prescrites par la loi, par laquelle une personne mande à son correspondant dans un certain lieu de payer à un tiers ou à son ordre une certaine somme d'argent en échange d'une autre somme, ou de la valeur qu'elle a reçue de ce tiers dans l'endroit où la lettre est tirée. Ainsi, il ne faut pas confondre la lettre de change avec le contrat de change. En effet, cette dernière prouve l'existence du contrat ; elle fournit le moyen d'arriver à son exécution ; mais elle n'est point le contrat même. Mais qu'est-ce que le *change* proprement dit, c'est-à-dire l'operation qui s'exécute au moyen d'une lettre de change ? Est-ce une vente d'argent, un intérêt que l'on retient sur les lettres de change ? Non ; le change est le bénéfice résultant d'un échange d'argent, dans lequel les contractans se distribuent le prix des frais qu'il en coûterait pour faire transporter une somme d'un lieu à un autre. En affet, comme il y a du danger de faire voiturer de l'argent, et qu'il y en a aussi à prendre des lettres de change, puisqu'elles peuvent quelquefois n'être pas payées avec exactitude, il en résulte une balance en parfait équilibre, ou a l'avantage de l'un des contractans, qui rend la condition meilleure que celle de l'autre. Ajoutez que l'abondance ou la rareté de l'argente, conséquemment la rareté ou l'abondance des lettres de change, et l'opinion de solvabilité du preneur et de celui qui doit la payer est une considération qui fait transiger avec plus ou moins de facilité. Ainsi, le droit de change ne sera donc qu'une espèce de retour de ce qu'au temps où la lettre de change est négociée, suivant le course de la place, l'argent a plus de valeur que cette lettre de change sur le lieu où elle est payable. Si, par exemple, les négocians de Bordeaux ont beaucoup d'argent à faire payer à des negocians de Marseille, et qu'il y ait peu de lettres de change sur Marseille ; les lettres de change gagneront sur l'argent ; le négociant de Marseille qui recevra une lettre de change sur Bordeaux, retirant un avantage de cette négociation, devra donc payer une différence. Dans ce cas, on dit que le change de Marseille sur Bordeaux est *bas*, ou bien qu'il est *pour Bordeaux*. Au cas contraire, on dit qu'il est *haut*, ou qu'il est *pour Marseille*. Le change est *au pair* lorsqu'entre deux villes on donne, par exemple, 1000 fr. dans l'une pour recevoir 1000 dans l'autre. Trois personnes concourent à la formation de la lettre de change : 1—Le *tireur*, qui crée la lettre, en mandant à un tiers, domicilié dans un autre ville, d'en payer le montant ; 2—Le *preneur*, au profit de qui elle est créée, et qui en a donné la valeur au tireur ; 3—L'*accepteur*, sur qui la lettre est tirée, et qui s'engage à la payer. Lorsqu'il n'a point accepté, on le nomme *tire;* et *accepteur*, lorsqu'il l'a accepté. Lorsqu'il y a négociation de la lettre de change, le preneur prend le nom d'*endosseur*, pour désigner que, par son ordre écrit au dos de la lettre de change, il donne à un autre, qui prend le nom de *porteur*, le droit d'en exiger le paiement. Voyons maintenant quelle espèce de contrat la lettre de change a formé entre ces diverses personnes. Entre le tireur et le preneur, la lettre de change forme le contrat de change ; en effet, le preneur échauge ce qu'il donne en un lieu, ou ce qu'il s'oblige à donner au tireur, contre l'argent que le tireur s'oblige de lui faire compter dans un autre lieu au moyen de la lettre de change. Entre le tireur et l'accepteur, c'est un mandat. L'accepteur n'est que le mandataire du tireur. Entre l'endosseur et le porteur il y a deux espèces de contrats : 1—Cession et transport de droits de l'endosseur opérés au moyen de l'endossement ; 2—Contrat de change, par lequel celui à qui l'ordre est passé, c'est-à-dire le porteur, échange l'argent qu'il donne à l'endosseur dans le lieu où se fait l'endossement contre l'argent que l'endosseur s'oblige de son côté de lui faire recevoir dans le lieu où la lettre de change qu'il lui remet a été tirée. Ce contrat produit les mêmes engagemens entre l'endosseur et le porteur que ceux que le tireur avait contractée vis-à-vis du preneur. L'accepteur est solidairement obligé avec le tireur envers le preneur, les endosseurs et le porteur. Lorsqu'une négociation se fait au moyen d'un billet, on nomme cet effet, *billet a ordre* ; *souscripteur*, celui qui le crée et qui doit le payer ; *bénéficiare*, celui au profit duquel il est souscrit. On appelle *traite*, la lettre de change tirée par un banquier sur son correspondant ; *remise*, celle que le banquier envoie à son correspondant pour en faire le recouvrement, ce que l'on nomme, dans le langage du commerce, *encaisser*. On dit qu'un billet ou une lettre de change est *négocié*, pour indiquer qu'il a été vendu ; quand il est échangé contre un autre ou contre de l'argent, on dit qu'il est escompté ; lorsqu'il été donné pour solde, on dit qu'il a été *passé à ordre pour solde.*"

From the *Daily News* of Wednesday, June 7, 1854 :

" BILLS OF EXCHANGE.—IMPORTANT AMERICAN OPINION.

"*Supreme Court of Pennsylvania, May* 16, 1854.

" The following opinion in the matter of bills of exchange, delivered by Judge Lewis, is of interest to the mercantile community :

"*Lennig* v. *Ralston et al.*—Error to the District Court of Philadelphia.—Lewis, J.—This suit is brought for the benefit of the Commercial Bank of London, upon an instrument which bears upon its face every mark of a foreign bill of exchange, drawn in Philadelphia, upon a house in London, and accepted by the latter. It is true that the bill was not actually negntiated in this State, so that it is not, within the letter of the statute of 1821, a bill 'drawn in Pennsylvania.' The drawers had a mercantile house in Philadelphia, and they placed 'Philadelphia' at the head of the bill as the place at which it was to bear date, leaving blanks for the day of the month, and the year. They fixed the amount of it and signed it, leaving blanks also for the period which the bill had to run before maturity, and for the names of the payee and acceptors.

All this was done by the defendants here. The instrument was then sent, in this imperfect condition, to their partner in London. This authorised him to fill the blanks and negotiate it in London, and he did so. It was purchased by the Bank without any notice of the manner in which it originated, or of the fact that it was issued in that city and not in Philadelphia. When that institution became the holder it bore the dress of a bill of exchange drawn in Pennsylvania; and, upon the principle that every one is presumed to intend to produce all the consequences to which his acts naturally and necessarily lead, the presumption is that the defendants intended that the purchasers of it should receive it under the belief that it was a bill drawn in Philadelphia in the usual course of business. *The question is whether they shall be compelled to perform their contract in the sense in which they intended the opposite party to understand it, or in a sense contemplated only by themselves, and entirely excluded by the terms of the instrument itself.* It is very material to the parties that this question should be properly decided. The bill was drawn on July 3, 1850. The act of May 13, 1850, reducing the damages on dishonoured foreign bills of exchange to 10 per cent., contains a provision limiting its operation to bills drawn after the 1st of August, 1850. So that, if the bill in question is to be enforced according to its terms, the act of 30th March, 1821, giving 20 per cent. damages for its dishonour, furnishes the rule of decision.

"All writers of authority on questions of morals agree that promises are binding in the sense in which the promissors intended at the time that the promissees should receive them. *Paley*, chap. 5; *Wayland*, chap. 2; *Adams*, pt. 3, chap. 5. Upon this principle, it was deemed a gross violation of contract when Mahomet, after promising to 'spare a man's head,' ordered his body to be cut through the middle. When Tamerlane, at the capitulation of Sabasta, promised to 'spill no blood,' it was an infraction of the treaty to 'bury the inhabitants alive.' These monstrous constructions of contracts were condemned by the civilized world as gross violations of the established rule of construction already indicated (*Vattel*, b. 2, chap. 17, s. 274). There can be no plainer principle of equity than that which requires every one to speak the truth, if he chooses to speak at all, in matters which affect the interests of others. He that knowingly misrepresents a fact for the purpose of inducing another to part with his money or goods, is held to his representation in favour of the party who confided in it. It is upon this principle that the maker of a negotiable instrument is not allowed to impair its value in the hands of a *bonâ fide* holder, by denying the existence of a consideration, or by otherwise showing that it is not what it purports to be. *Chitty on Bills*, 9; 7 *C. & P.* 633; *Byles on Bills*, 65. On the same principle, a man who procures credit for an insolvent person, by knowingly misrepresenting him to be a man of ability, is bound to answer in damages for the injury thereby produced. In truth, the law merchant is a system founded on the rules of equity, and governed in all its parts by plain justice and good faith. *Master* v. *Miller*, 4 *T. R.* 342.

" *When this bill was dressed in the costume of a Pennsylvania bill, it thereby gained a credit in the foreign market which it would not otherwise have received. The act of* 1821, *providing ample damages in case of the dishonour of bills drawn in Pennsylvania, contributed to give it that credit. That act must be considered as operating on the minds of those who purchased it.* In *Ripka* v. *Gaddis*, it was declared by this court, after a careful examination of the authorities, that 'it had been long established in the case of negotiable paper of every kind, that it is construed and governed, as to the obligation of the drawer or maker, by the law of the country where it was drawn or made; as to that of the acceptor, by the law of the country where he accepts; and as to that of the indorser, by the law of the country where he indorsed.' In *Hazelhurst* v. *Kean* (4 *Dal.* 20), it was affirmed that 'the parties in the purchase of a bill of exchange must be supposed to have in contemplation the law of the place where the contract was made, and it (that is, the law of the place where the bill was drawn) necessarily forms part of the contract.' In *Allen* v. *the Bank, Wh.* 4-5, the same principle was re-asserted. From this rule, thus repeatedly recognised and well established, it follows that the Bank in the purchase of this bill must be supposed to have had in contemplation the law of Pennsylvania, providing indemnity for its dishonour. The law of this State was therefore a part of the contract of purchase, and we have no right to impair its obligation.

"There is no reason why the statute of 1821 should not receive a liberal construction. It has been held that it is not a penal, but, on the contrary, it is a remedial act; that the damages given are not for punishment, but are intended as compensation; that its provisions are just and equitable, and highly necessary in a commercial community, to guard the interests of innocent inuividuals, and to secure good faith in commercial transactions. 5 *Wharton*, 425. No one can foresee the extent of the injury which the holder of a foreign bill of exchange may suffer from its dishonour. It is not like a domestic obligation, the breach of which can, in general, be repaired by the presence and credit of the holder. But the dishonour of foreign bills may occur, and usually does occur, at points where the holders cannot supervise the result, and where they have neither means nor credit to provide against the injury. These instruments are generally procured at a premium by the holders for the purpose of making their purchases in the country where they are payable, or as the means of pursuing their travels, or maintaining their credit abroad. The great distance between the residence of the drawers and that of the acceptors, must necessarily cause great delay in procuring indemnity from the former.   In the meantime the loss to the holders, if they rely exclusively upon the bills to maintain their credit, and carry on their business, might be irreparable.   Under such circumstances the recovery of the face of the bill only, with the usual interest, re-exchange, and costs, would be but a cold and inadequate remedy for so great an injury.   The act of 1821 was deemed necessary, in order to do justice in such cases, and for the purpose of maintaining our commercial credit in other countries.   It should receive such a construction as will best promote the intentions of the legislature in these respects. Upon the whole, we are of opinion that the bill should be met by the drawers in the same sense in which they manifestly intended that it should be received by the holder, and we think that the District Court was in error in adopting a different rule.

" Judgment reversed, and judgment for the plaintiff in error for 1,453 dols. 31c., with interest from the 18th May, 1852, and costs of suit."

CHAPTER XLIII.

RIGHTS RELATING TO SUCCESSION.

DCCCLVIII. We now approach the consideration of the Third Division or branch of the subject of this volume, (a) namely, the consideration of what law ought to govern *the rights relating to succession to property.*

These rights grow out of a rule which is in truth highly artificial, though so generally incorporated into the law of all civilized states as to appear natural—the rule that it is competent to a person to extend his power and will beyond the limits of his own existence, and to transfer after his death property to living persons. This will may be either express—that is, by being recorded in a testament (*testatio mentis*) ; (b) and then there is a *testamentary succession*—the heir *succeeds* to the deceased ; or it may be tacit—then the law presumes what the intentions of the deceased were ; and there is a succession *ab intestato.* The Roman law was philosophical in its conception and precise in its language on this subject : " Nihil aliud est hæreditas quam *successio in universum jus* quod testator habuit." (c)

By a remarkable fiction it treated the *hæreditas* as a moral person—"Hæreditas non hæredis personam sed defuncti sustinet." (d) And the countries which have adopted this law as the basis of their jurisprudence have the adage, *hæres sustinet personam defuncti.* (e)

(a) *Vide ante,* pp. 23, 389.

Savigny, viii. s. 366 (172), s. 375 (295).

Merlin, Rep., Heritier.

(b) "Testamentum ex eo appellatur quod testatio mentis sit." *Inst.* l. ii. t. x.

(c) *Dig.* lib. l. t. xvi. 24.

(d) *Dig.* l. xli. t. i. 34, 61 ; *et cf. Dig.* l. v. t. iii. 50 ; *et.* l. xxvii. t. v. 31.

(e) 3 *Massé,* p. 392.

DCCCLIX. The first question of importance is, What *forum* has jurisdiction over the *whole question of the succession ?*—that of the *situs ?* or that of the domicil ?

Donellus examines this question, and concludes, "relinquitur omnino locus is unus, in quo *controversia hæreditatis* tractanda sit, ubi scilicet qui convenitur, habet domicilium." (*f*) And again : "nunquam alibi de hæreditate agi posse quam ubi possessor domicilium habeat." That is, the *petitio hæreditatis* should be in the *forum*,—where the heir or representative of the deceased is ; though the *petitio rerum singularum*—*e.g.*, as to legacies of particular things—may be, perhaps, necessarily preferred before another *forum*.

DCCCLX. The next question is—By what law shall the *forum*, so seized of the general subject, decide the question which arises, *mutatis mutandis*, in the matter of *testamentary succession*, as in the matter of obligation ; namely, as to

1. The legal capacity of the testator ?
2. The form of the testamentary instrument ?
3. The dispositions contained in it ?
4. The construction or interpretation of it ?

Next, in the case of succession *ab intestato*, what law ought to govern the rights of parties to the property of the intestate ?

Or, in the language of continental jurisprudence, are the *statutes* which govern the matter of succession *personal* or *real ?* (*g*)

DCCCLXI. Upon the question of the Law generally, applicable both to testamentary succession and to succession *ab intestato*, the jurisprudence of states admits of a threefold division.

1. The jurisprudence which submits the *universitas juris* (both moveable and immoveable property) of the succession to the Law of the last domicil of the deceased. This is in accordance with the opinion of Savigny and with the decisions of superior tribunals of Germany.

(*f*) *Comm.* 1. xvii. c. xvii. p. 76.
(*g*) *Vide ante*, chapter xvi. 235.

2. The directly opposite jurisprudence, which submits the property to the Law of the place where it happens to be : which admits the possibility therefore of different Laws being applied to different portions of the property, and which lays down no principle as to debts and credits, leaving them to be practically dealt with in each case, according to the best expedient which can be devised. This jurisprudence is founded upon the strict feudal law of territorial sovereignty.

3. The intermediate system of jurisprudence which subjects the personalty to the Law of the domicil of the deceased—the realty to the Law of the *situs.* This is the jurisprudence of England, France, (*h*) and the United States of North America.

DCCCLXII. Such is the outline of the jurisprudence of the principal States upon the general question of succession. We have next to consider the separate questions which have been just mentioned, as arising out of testamentary succession.

DCCCLXIII. (1.) As to the legal capacity of the testator. Upon this matter the reader is referred to what has been already said upon the general question of the capacity of the foreigner, both as to the capacity to contract a marriage (*i*) and to acquire or alienate property, (*k*) and to the chapter on personal and real statutes. (*l*)

But the answer to this question may be generally stated thus : The Law of the actual domicil of the testator at the time of making his testament governs the question of his legal capacity to do the act. (*m*)

DCCCLXIV. (2.) As to the form (*n*) of the testament. The

(*h*) *Foelix,* s. 61, and the authors there cited.

(*i*) P. 260.

(*k*) P. 407.

(*l*) P. 233.

(*m*) *Story,* s. 464.

(*n*) " The domestic judge," Vattel says, " ought to decide on the validity of the form, and his sentence ought to be everywhere acknowledged ; but as to the validity of bequests, the judge of the place in which they are situated may decide." *Vattel,* l. ii. c. vii. 167.

jurisprudence of the continent wisely, justly, and philosophi-
cally allows an option (*n*) to the testator to adopt either

(*a*) The form required by the *lex loci actûs ;* or,

(*β*) The form required by the *lex domicilii.* The adoption
of either form is, as jurists say, *facultative,* not *imperative,*
though the general maxim be *locus regit actum.*

England (*o*) and the North American United States (*p*) un-
wisely, arbitrarily, and unphilosophically compel the testator to
adopt the form prescribed by the *lex domicilii.*

DCCCLXV. But a further question on the same point may
arise. A testator makes his testament according to the Law of
his actual domicil, but before he dies he changes his domicil.
Must he make a new testament if the old one be not according
to the form of the new domicil?

The jurisprudence of those states which consider the adoption of the form of the instrument as *facultative,* not *imperative,* ought, in consistency, to maintain that a will made
according to the form of the *lex loci,* at the time of its making,
ought to be valid. Such is accordingly the doctrine laid down
by Fælix. (*q*)

(*n*) "The object of the Law,"·Savigny truly says, "is to favour and
facilitate, not to thwart, the act of the party. There can be no doubt,"
he adds, "that it is facultative, and so it is generally holden. ' Dieses
ist denn auch meist anerkannt worden.' " *Savigny,* viii. s. 381, *in fine.*

(*o*) *Rocco,* p. 306 : " Ond'é che possiamo dirittamente giudicare *quanto
erronea* sia la sentenza di quegli autori, i quali come essenziale alla validità d'ogni atto chiedono l'adempimento *esclusivo* delle forme del luogo
ove esso è celebrato," &c.

Fælix, s. 83: "Nous tenons pour valable l'acte passé â l'étranger
suivant les formes prescrites dans la patrie." *Cf. Code Civil,* arts. 999
and 1317. Yet the Court of Cassation held that it could not pronounce
for the validity of a will made in France, but not according to French
Law, on the ground that comity required the strict application of the
maxim, *locus regit actum.* 1 *Fælix,* p. 166, ed. *Dem.*

(*p*) *Vide ante,* p. 207.

Croker v. *Marquis of Hertford,* 4 *Moore's P. C. Rep.* 339.

Bremer v. *Freeman,* 10 *Moore,* 361.

(*q*) Sec. 77 : "L'acte fait dans un pays étranger suivant les formes

Upon this point, Savigny (r) has the following passage :—
"A modern author (s) adds the following restriction :—The
"testament, he says, is valid if the testator die in the foreign
"state.   But if he return to his own country the testa-
"ment becomes void, unless the municipal law of it happens
"to recognise testaments so made.   I do not think that this
"restriction is justifiable on principle, and it seems to have ob-
"tained no approbation from other jurists.   Nevertheless, a
"prudent father of a family would do well to make a new will
"on his return home in order to be secure against every possi-
"ble attack."

Story (t) considered it to be an undecided point, whether
the *construction* of a will made under these circumstances
would be governed by the law of the old or the new domicil.
Yet he cites with approbation John Voet, as maintaining the
invalidity of a will made before the change of domicil, and
agrees with him in this opinion. (u)

Since the death of Story a Missouri court has decided that
this opinion is the law. (x)

But this doctrine is surely fraught with obvious and many
inconveniencies, and with the great evil of rendering difficult
and uncertain that which it is one great object of civilization to

---

qui y sont prescrites, ne perd pas sa force, quant à sa forme, par le retour de l'individu au lieu de son domicile : aucune raison de droit ne
milite en faveur de l'opinion contraire.

"Il en est de même en cas de changement de domicile des parties ou de
l'une d'elles, parce que la forme dépend de la loi du lieu de la confection
de l'acte."

Sec. 117 : "Le testament conserve sa validité quant á la forme, non
obstant le changement de domicile du testateur, parce que cette forme
dépend de la loi du lieu de la confection de l'acte."

(r) VIII. s. 381 (356).

(s) *Eichhorn, Deutsches Recht, s.* 37.

(t) Sec. 479 g.

(u) *Story,* s. 473.

J. *Voet, ad Pand.* l. xxxviii. t. iii. ; t. ii. s. 12. p. 292.

(x) *Nat* v. *Coon,* 10 *Missouri Rep.* 543.

render easy and certain—the validity of testaments. It is to be lamented, therefore, that this doctrine has been in some degree countenanced, though not judicially adopted, by the Judicial Committee of the Privy Council. (y)

DCCCLXVI. (2.) As to the dispositions contained in the testament, where no prohibitory laws of the state in which the moveable property is situate interfere, both by English Law, and by what may be fairly termed the general consent of jurists, the Law of the domicil of the testator governs the question of testamentary disposition, as that of the donor or transferer governs the question of transfers *inter vivos* (z.) Immoveable property, as a general rule, is governed by the *lex rei sitæ*. (a)

DCCCLXVII. It would seem that even in the case of immoveable property, the Law of the domicil governs the construction of the testamentary instrument, unless it clearly appears that the testator in the expressions which he used had in view the *lex sitûs*. (b)

DCCCLXVIII. The opinions of foreign jurists (c) are generally in accordance with these decisions of the English Courts of justice,

DCCCLXIX. Quite consistently with these decisions the English Law holds, nevertheless, that a testament duly executed

---

(y) *Bremer* v. *Freeman*, 10 *Moore's P. C. Rep.* 359.

(z) *Story*, s. 472.

(a) *Story*, s. 479 e.

Harrison v. *Nixon*, 9 *Peter's* (*Amer.*) *Rep.* 483, 504. So as to the *currency* in which legacies are payable.

Wallis v. *Brightwell*, 2 *Peere's W. R.* 88.

Saunders v. *Drake*, 2 *Atkins*, 465 (1742).

Pierson v. *Garnet*, 2 *Brown's Ch. C.* 38.

Malcolm v. *Martin*, 3 *Brown's Ch. C.* 50.

(b) 2 *Burge*, p. 858.

Story, 469 h.

Westlake, ss. 329—332.

Trotter v. *Trotter*, 3 *Wilson & Sh. R.* 407 (1829); *cf.* with *Bernal* v. *Bernal*, 3 *Mylne & Cr. R.* 559 (1838).

(c) See them collected by *Story*, s. 478-479 h.

in a foreign state, according to the Law of that state, by a testator domiciled therein, must be clothed with the authority of an English Court of Probate before it can affect moveable property in England : (d) though the English court will adopt the Foreign law as conclusive on the subject of the validity of the testament.

DCCCLXX. (3.) With respect to the construction and interpretation of testaments, testamentary declarations, and the like, the English Law distinctly rules that the interpretation shall be governed by the law of the domicil of the deceased person.   The Law upon this point was settled and expounded, and the distinction between this rule and the rule relating to the admissibility of evidence very clearly laid down, by Lord Brougham in a recent judgment of the House of Lords.

DCCCLXXI. "It is on all hands," he said, "admitted that the whole distribution of Mr. Yates's personal estate must be governed by the Law of England, where he had his domicil through life, and at the time of his decease, and at the dates of all the instruments executed by him.   Had he died intestate, the English statute of distributions, and not the Scotch Law of succession in moveables, would have regulated the whole course of the administration.   *His written declarations must therefore be taken with respect to the English Law.   I think it follows from hence that those declarations of intention touching that property must be construed as we should construe them here by our principles of legal interpretation.*   Great embarrassment may, no doubt, arise from calling upon a Scotch court to apply the principles of English Law to such questions, many of those principles being among the most nice and difficult known in our jurisprudence.   The Court of Session may, for example, be required to decide whether an executory devise is void, as being too remote ; and to apply, for the purpose of ascertaining that question, the criterion of the gift passing or not passing, what would be an estate in realty, although in

---

(d) *Price* v. *Dewhurst,* 4 *M. & Craig's R.* 76, 80.

the language of the Scotch Law there is no such expression as executory devise, and within the knowledge of Scotch lawyers no such thing as an executory estate tail.   Nevertheless, this is a difficulty which must of necessity be grappled with, because in no other way can the English law be applied to personal property situated locally within the jurisdiction of the Scottish forum, and the rule which requires the Law of the domicil to govern succession to such property could in no other way be applied and followed out.   Nor am I aware that any distinction in this respect has ever been taken between testamentary succession and succession *ab intestato*, or that it has been held either here or in Scotland that the court's right to regard the foreign Law was excluded wherever a foreign instrument had been executed.   *It is therefore my opinion that in this, as in other cases of the like description, the Scotch court must enquire of the foreign Law as a mattter of fact, and examine such evidence as will show how in England such instruments would be dealt with as to construction.   I give this as my opinion upon principle, for I am not aware of the question ever having received judicial determination in either country.*

"But here I think the importing of the foreign code (sometimes incorrectly called the *Comitas*) must stop; what evidence the courts of another country would receive, and what reject, is a question into which I cannot at all see the necessity of the courts of any one country entering.   Those principles which regulate the admission of evidence are the rules by which the courts of every country guide themselves in all their enquiries.   The truth, with respect to men's actions, which form the subject matter of their enquiry, is to be ascertained according to a certain definite course of proceeding, and certain rules have established, that in pursuing this investigation some things shall be heard from witnesses—others not listened to; some instruments shall be inspected by the judge —others kept from his eye.   This must evidently be the same course, and governed by the same rules, whatever be the subject matter of investigation; nor can it make any difference whether the facts, concerning which the discussion arises, happened at home or abroad; whether they related to a foreigner domiciled abroad or a native living and dying at home. As well might it be contended that another mode of trial should be adapted as that another law of evidence should be admitted in such cases. Who would argue that, in a question like the present, the Court of Session should try the point of fact by a jury, according to the English procedure, or should follow the course of our dispositions or interrogatories in courts of equity, because the testator was a domiciled Englishman, and because those methods of trial would be applied to his case were the question raised here? The answer is, that the question arises in the Court of Session, and must be dealt with by the rules which regulate enquiry there. Now, the law of evidence is among the chief of these rules; nor let it be said that there is any inconsistency in applying the English rules of construction and the Scotch ones of evidence to the same matter, in investigating facts by one Law and intention by another. The difference is manifest between the two enquiries; for a person's meaning can only be gathered from assuming that he intended to use words in the sense affixed to them by the Law of the country he belonged to at the time of framing his instrument. Accordingly, where the question is what a person intended by an instrument relating to the conveyance of a real estate situated in a foreign country, and where the *lex loci rei sitæ* must govern, we decide upon his meaning by that law, and not by the Law of his country where the deed was executed, because we consider him to have had that foreign law in his contemplation." (e)

DCCCLXXII. In accordance with the principle of this judgment, though long before it was delivered, the English courts have holden that a devise bad by the law of the

---

(e) *Yates* v. *Thomson & others*, 3 *Clark & Finnelly's Rep.* pp. 585—588 (1835).

testator's domicil, though good by the Law of the state in which it is to be executed, is an invalid devise. (*f*)

DCCCLXXIII. So, as to ascertaining the particular class or description of persons entitled to take under a particular denomination or *designatio personarum*, the law of the domicil is to govern.

DCCCLXXIV. (II.) As to successions *ab intestato* in the case of moveable property. (*g*) The questions which may arise under this head are chiefly the following (some of which, it will be seen, apply also to testamentary succession) :—

What Law ought to decide—

1. What persons are entitled to distribution ?

2. What portions of the estate of the deceased ought to be primarily chargeable with the payment of the debts of the deceased ?

3. What Law ought to regulate the currency in which legacies and shares are to be paid, and the amount of interest payable on legacies and shares of property ?

4. What Law ought to decide as to the duties or taxes payable to the Government upon testaments and successions *ab intestato* ?

DCCCLXXV. The answer to the first question is, that the succession to moveable property is governed by the Law of the actual domicil of the intestate at the time of his death ; and that this Law decides who are the persons entitled in distribution ; and in what degree of preference, if any, they are so entitled. This answer is now given decidedly by the Law of England and of the North American United States. (*h*) The same answer is given pretty generally by foreign jurists ; it is, as they say, the *personal statute* which governs the case.

(*f*) *Curtis* v. *Hutton,* 14 *Vesey's R.* 537—541 (*Sir W. Grant*)—a case of the Mortmain act.

See also 3 *Peter's (Amer.) R. App.* 501—503.

Story, s. 479 *d.*

(*g*) *Story,* chapter xii.

(*h*) *Story,* ss. 480, 484, 484 *a.*

Savigny, viii. s. 375.

DCCCLXXVI. As to the second question, the law of the domicil of the intestate ought also to decide whether particular debts are payable out of the personal or real estates, (*i*) and what fund is primarily liable, and matters of the like kind. But it cannot be said that there is any uniformity of opinion among foreign jurists upon this point. (*k*)

DCCCLXXVII. With respect, however, to immoveable property, the *lex sitûs* prevails : it governs both the *succession ab intestato* itself, and the description of persons who are to take under it. This is certainly the Law of England, and is in accordance with the opinion of some eminent foreign jurists. (*l*) It is remarkable, however, that with respect to *testaments* of immoveable property, the description of persons who are to take under some general designation is ascertained, according to English Law, by the *lex domicilii*, (*m*) unless the context clearly furnishes a different interpretation.

DCCCLXXVIII. (3.) With respect to the Law which ought to regulate the *currency* in which legacies and shares are to be paid and the amount of interest payable thereon. In England it has been holden that legacies and shares themselves are payable according to the Law of the country, and in the currency of the country in which the testator is domiciled, unless, indeed, the testament affords clear evidence that the

---

(*i*) 4 *Burge*, 722—734.

Story, ss. 489, c. 6. 528-9.

Anon. 9 *Modern R.* 66.

Winchelsea v. *Garretty*, 2 *Keen's R.* 293 (1837).

As to the *conflictus* on this point of Scotch and English Law, see *Brodie* v. *Barry*, 2 *Vesey & Beame's R.* 130, and *Drummond* v. *Drummond*, therein referred to ; *Yates* v. *Thomson and others*, 3 *Clk. & Finnelly's R.* 544 ; *Anstruther* v. *Chalmers*, 2 *Simons R.* 1.

As to English and North American Law—*Gordon* v. *Brown*, or *Brown* v. *Brown*, 3 *Haggard's Ecc. R.* 455, note ; 4 *Wilson & Shaw's R.* 28.

(*k*) *Story*, s. 489 *b*, *c*.

(*l*) *Story*, s. 484, 484 *a*.

J. Voet, ad Pand. l. xxxviii. t. xvii. *n.* 35.

(*m*) *Story*, s. 484. See also *Rittson* v. *Stordy, The Jurist*, vol. i. (N. S.) 771, *Equity* (1855).

testator contemplated another currency. (*n*)   Nor is this rule varied by the circumstance that such legacy is to be paid out of real property situate where the currency differs from that which prevails in the testator's domicil.(*o*)   As to the *interest*, the English rule appears to be, that shares and legacies carry the interest of the state in which the assets have been placed by the executors or administrators since they became payable ; the Law presumes that such interest has been made. (*p*)

DCCCLXXIX. (4.) With respect to the Law which ought to regulate the payment of duties to Government on testaments and successions, England imposes duties on probate or administration, and duties on legacies or shares.   The former are payable according to the *lex loci* of the assets at the death of the testator or intestate ; the latter are payable according to the *lex domicilii* and to the country of the deceased person, wherever the legatees or successors reside. (*q*)

(*n*) *Burge*, iv. 594.
Story, s. 479 *b*.
(*o*) See cases collected, 4 *Burge*, 595, 6.
(*p*) *Raymond* v. *Brodbelt*, 5 *Vesey's Rep*. 199.
Bourke v. *Ricketts*, 10 *Vesey*, 330 (1804).
Westlake, s. 321.
(*q*) See this very clearly stated by *Mr. Westlake*, s. 320.
Thomson v. *Advocate Gen*. 12 *Clk. & Finnelly's Rep*. 29 (1845).

CHAPTER XLIV.

ADMINISTRATION OF JUSTICE IN THE CASE OF FOREIGNERS
—CIVIL AND CRIMINAL LAW—CIVIL LAW: 1. VOLUNTARY
JURISDICTION—NOTARIES—COMMISSIONS —LITTERÆ REQUI-
SITORIÆ — 2. CONTENTIOUS JURISDICTION — FOREIGNER
PLAINTIFF— DEFENDANT — TWO FOREIGNERS—FOREIGN —
ENGLISH LAW — COMMON LAW — CHANCERY LAW—IMMOVE-
ABLE PROPERTY.

DCCCLXXX. We have now to consider the Fourth Division of this volume, which concerns the administration of justice in cases in which a foreigner is concerned. This administration may require, in the case of the foreigner, as of the subject, the application of the civil or the criminal law. It seems most convenient to treat of the former category in the first instance.

DCCCLXXXI. The civil jurisdiction to which a foreigner may have recourse or be amenable, is either (1) Voluntary or (2) Contentious.

The chief organ of the *voluntary* jurisdiction is the Notary Public, who is in fact a kind of international officer, to the testimony of whose acts all civilized states give credit—an officer less known and more restricted in his powers in England (a) than on the continent, (b) but in England also a well-recognised and important functionary. Recent English statutes have

---

(a) See effect of notary's certificate in evidence, 11 *Exchequer Rep.* 482, *Cole* v. *Sherard*. See also " *In the matter of Elizabeth Hurst,* 15 *Com. B. Rep.* 410 (1854) ; and *Re Clericetti, ib.* 726 (1855).

Burn's Eccles. Law (ed. *Phill.*) vol. iii. title *Notary*.

Brooks on Notaries.

18 & 19 *Vict.* c. 42, s. 1.

(b) *Code Civil*, art. 971—979, confers on notaries the exclusive power of making testaments.

See, too, *Fœlix*, i. s. 227.

conferred upon the English consul much of the authority of the notary.

DCCCLXXXII. Under this head of voluntary jurisdiction, also, should be considered those requests which the tribunals or authorities of one state are, in the execution of justice, obliged to make to the tribunals or authorities of a foreign state, to permit or enforce the investigation of facts or the acquisition of evidence in the territory of that foreign state. A commission generally issues for this purpose, which the French call *Commission Rogatoire,* (c) a proceeding familiar to all acquainted with the proceedings of the civil and especially the canon law. The ordinary who required the testimony of a witness in the diocese of another ordinary, issued letters of request (*litteræ requisitoriales*) for that purpose.

DCCCLXXXIII. These commissions are almost invariably respected by foreign tribunals; the formula given by Denisart expresses the foundation of pure comity on which they rest: "Nous vous prions de . . .   comme nous ferions le sem- " blable pour vous, si par vous nous étions priés et requis." (d) Till lately, England and the United States of North America, instead of directing the commission to the foreign tribunals, have been in the habit of entrusting their execution to certain of their own citizens, lawyers, magistrates, or consuls, (e) as the case may be—a mode of proceeding which rendered it optional on the part of witnesses whether they would give or withhold their testimony; but by later statutes (f) English judges are empowered to issue commissions to the judges of a foreign

---

(c) *Fœlix,* i. titre iv.

(d) *Nouveau Denisart* v. *Commission,* s. 3, n. 3.

(e) See 18 & 19 *Victoria,* c. 42, as to powers conferred on ambassadors, British ministers, and consuls abroad, to administer oaths, &c.

Also ss. 13 & 23 of 15 & 16 *Victoria,* c. 76.

(f) 1 *William IV.* c. 22.

3 & 4 *Victoria,* c. 105.

Clay v. *Stephenson,* 3 *Adolphus & E. Rep.* 807 (1835).

Ponsford v. *O'Connor,* 5 *Meeson & W.'s Rep.* 673 (1839).

Taylor on Evidence, s. 366.

court; and by a more recent statute English tribunals are empowered to order the examination of witnesses in England in relation to a civil or commercial matter pending before any foreign tribunal. (g)

DCCCLXXXIV. But the English court has ruled that a commission may issue to the judges of foreign courts as individuals to take the examination of witnesses, notwithstanding the examination may not be conducted according to the Law of England. Yet it would seem that if illegal evidence be returned, or if it appear either on the face of the return or by extrinsic evidence that the examination has been so conducted as to render it inadmissible, the whole or part may be rejected at Nisi Prius.

In a recent case a former commission issued by the same party having proved abortive, in consequence of the witnesses refusing to be examined by an English commissioner according to the English Law, the court, on granting a new commission to the foreign judges, imposed the payment of the costs of the former commission. (h)

In a case of *Pischer* v. *Sztaray*, (i) (heard before the Court of Queen's Bench, May, 1858,) a commission to examine witnesses, which had issued to the judges of a Hungarian court as individuals, was returned unexecuted, and an affidavit of the defendant's attorney stated that he was told by a secretary of the Austrian Legation in London that the commission ought to have been addressed to the court as a court, and not to individual judges.

Thereupon, the Queen's Bench ordered the commission to issue to the court as a court—the usual clause prescribing the form of oath to be omitted—the plaintiff having the opportunity on the return of the commission to object to the admissibility of the evidence taken under it; the costs of the abortive

---

(g) 19 & 20 *Victoria*, c. 113.

(h) *Lumley* v. *Gye*, 2 *Common Law Rep.* 936.

(i) *Law Times*, xxxi. 130.

commission to be the plaintiff's costs in the cause, at all events.

DCCCLXXXV. It has been considered to be no answer to an application for a commission to examine witnesses abroad (supported by the ordinary affidavit), that the opposite party deposes that there are persons in this country, and documents accessible to the applicant, which would supply him with any information he could obtain from the witnesses he proposes to examine. And after a judge has exercised his discretion on such an application, the court will not disturb his decision unless it is manifestly wrong. (k)

The court has ruled that it will not permit a writ of subpœna *ad testificandum* to issue, to compel the attendance of a witness resident out of the jurisdiction, unless it be shewn that the evidence cannot be had under a commission, or otherwise than by the personal attendance of the witness. (l)

As to the mode of executing a commission under the recent statute the following decision is important: A commission having issued to be executed at New York, returnable in a month, with leave to defendant to cross-examine, there was, some weeks afterwards, a consent by him " that no objection to the admissibility of the evidence taken should be made by reason of the time of taking or returning such evidence, saving all just exceptions to the evidence." The commission was returned executed two or three days after such consent, having been executed without any notice to the defendant of the time at which he might attend its execution. It was holden by the court, that, nevertheless, the evidence taken under it was admissible at the trial. (m)

DCCCLXXXVI. The first question which arises respecting the exercise of *Contentious* jurisdiction in a suit to which one of the parties is a foreigner, seems to be—What is the *forum*

(k) *Adams* v. *Corfield*, 28 *Law Journal* (*Exch.*), 31.

(l) *Dunne* v. *Lewis*, 8 *Irish Common Law Reports, Append*. liv.

(m) *Whyte* v. *Hallett*, 28 *Law Journal* (*Exch.*), 208.

competens (*n*) in the particular case? First, the answer may depend, in some degree, upon the position in the suit, so to speak, taken up by the foreigner.

He may be (1) plaintiff (*demandeur*), or (2) defendant (*defendeur*); and again, he may be (3) plaintiff or defendant in a suit in which the other party is a (*a*) native (*reguicole*) or (*β*) a fellow-countryman, or (*γ*) a foreigner, and not his fellow-countryman.

Secondly, the answer may depend upon the nature or subject of the suit, whether it be an action *in rem* or *in personam*, real or personal—the latter being by the English Law identical with *transitory* (*o*) actions; and, therefore, according to that law, capable of being brought wherever the defendant can be found.

Thirdly, the answer may depend upon the accident of *place*, or, in other words, upon the place in which the obligation sought to be enforced was originally incurred, or in which it was agreed that it should be executed — a consideration necessarily in some degree forestalled in the preceding chapter. Thus jurists have said that the competence of a tribunal is to be determined:

1. Ratione domicilii.
2. Ratione contractûs.
3. Ratione destinatæ solutionis.
4. Ratione dominationis.

In the following paragraphs the effect of these different categories will be considered.

DCCCLXXXVII. In every civilized state the plaintiff foreigner is allowed to bring his suit against the native. (*p*)

(*n*) The preface to the Brazilian Code (xxiv. note 1) well observes, that *actiones* are, in their true and primary sense, *jus persequendi*; in their derived and secondary sense, *medium persequendi*.

(*o*) *Robinson* v. *Bland*, 1 *W. Blackstone's Rep.* 234—246. *Story*, s. 554.

(*p*) *Fœlix*, l. ii. t. ii. c. i. s. 128, &c.

This permission, which rests upon the clearest principle of national justice, may be and is more or less hampered, in certain states, with difficulties in its practical working; (q) but in the abstract it is universally recognised.

The Code Civil of France expressly incorporates this principle into its provisions, and it also extends the permission by making the naturalized foreigner amenable in the same manner as the *native;* (r) and judicial interpretation has carried the principle a step further by placing also the stranger who has been admitted to *establish his domicil* in France in the same category, for this purpose, as the native. (s)

This is the Law of France in cases where there is no reciprocity in the Law of the state of the foreigner. Those states which have modelled their codes upon that of France, have adopted this provision.

DCCCLXXXVIII. The Law of the United States of North America confers on particular tribunals (t) the cognizance of cases between an alien and a citizen, or citizens of different states. These tribunals are the *Federal Courts.* It is the character of the parties (*ratio personarum*) and not the nature of the suit, which founds the jurisdiction of these tribunals. The jurisdiction is confined to cases between citizens and foreigners, or citizens of different states, and does not extend to suits between alien and alien.

DCCCLXXXIX. The tendency of modern European jurisprudence is to open to the foreigner the ordinary courts of

---

(q) See *M Demangeat's* note to *Fœlix*, s. 127.

(r) Even where the obligation has been contracted abroad and previously to his naturalization. *Fœlix*, s. 129; *Cour de Cassation*, March 27, 1833 ; *Gaz. des Trib.* April 10, 1833.

(s) So decided by the *Cour de Cassation* in a case of *separation de corps*, July 25, 1855. *Dev. Cor.* lvi. i. 148 : *Demangeat's* note to *Fœlix*, s. 129.

(t) 1 *Kent's Com.* 343.

Cf. the institution of the *Recuperatoires*, vol. i. p. 18.

justice of the country. The consular jurisdictions, in unchristian states, form a partial exception to this otherwise general rule. (*u*)

DCCCXC. Though the plaintiff foreigner be thus allowed to bring his suit, he is, by the Laws of all states, compelled to give bail (*fournir caution*) (*x*) for costs and damages. The French Law admits two exceptions to the general rule; viz.,

1. Cases in which matters of commerce or trade are concerned.

2. Cases in which the plaintiff foreigner possesses, in France, immoveable property, of value sufficient to cover the costs and damages. (*y*)

3. To these must, of course, be added cases in which, by the specific provisions of a treaty, foreigners are exempted from the necessity of finding bail.

4. An exception must also be made in the case of a stranger who acts as a plaintiff ministerially under the authority of a court of justice. (*z*) With some modification, the principle above mentioned is incorporated into all codes founded upon the Code Civil of France. (*a*)

DCCCXCI. We have next to consider the case of the foreigner as *defendant* (*défendeur*) (*b*) in a suit. Here, again, the Roman Law furnishes the maxim which lies at the root of all international and of most domestic jurisprudence on this matter; that maxim is *actor sequitur forum rei.* The

---

(*u*) *Massé.*

(*x*) The Novell, cxii. c. ii., of Justinian probably furnishes the origin of this practice and policy; it is entitled "*De cautione quæ ante reorum citationem præstari debet ab actore.*" It may, however, as M. Demangeat thinks, have sprung, independently of the Roman Law, from old Teutonic usages.

(*y*) *Code Civile*, art. 16.

Code de Procedure Civile, arts. 166, 425.

(*z*) *Id est*, if he be "porteur d'un titre *paré.*" *Fœlix*, s. 140.

(*a*) *Fœlix*, l. t. xi. c. ii. s. 1.

(*b*) *Cf. Fœlix*, i. t. ii. ch. ii. s. 3.

English Law allows, in personal actions, no exception from this rule : wherever the defendant is, there the plaintiff may sue him.   It is true, that to this proposition is generally added by writers the qualification, that the *defendant* be domiciled in order to found the competency of the tribunal, but not domiciled in the strict sense of the term, *animo et facto*, with intention of *personal* residence ; domiciled in the sense of *commorant* appears to be all that the English Law requires.

DCCCXCII. We have considered generally the principles of Law applicable to the foreigner as plaintiff and defendant. In this consideration it has, however, been assumed that the other party to the suit was a native subject, or a person entitled to be holden as such for the purposes of the suit.   But what are the principles of Law applicable to a suit in which *both parties* are *foreigners?* The answer would not appear to be difficult— namely, the same principles which are applicable to two subjects.   Foreigners who are admitted to reside or be commorant within the limits of a state, and permitted to contract obligations, *juris gentium,* with each other, cannot be denied the right, equally *juris gentium,* of resorting to the courts of justice of the country for the purpose of enforcing the fulfilment of such obligations.   It is but a half measure of justice, as Mr. Massé (c) observes, to permit the foreigner to sue a subject, and to refuse him justice, in the case of another foreigner.

In the existing state of societies, all obligations *juris gentium* borrow something from the Municipal Law : " Ex hoc jure gentium . . commercium, emptiones, venditiones, locationes, conductiones, obligationes institutæ, exceptis quibusdam quæ a jure civile introductæ sunt," (d) is the language of the Digest. All civilized nations but France act toward foreigners upon the principles contained in this passage.   Even those

---

(c) *Droit Commercial,* t. ii. s. 171.

(d) *Dig.* l. i t. i. 5.

who maintain that foreigners *inter se* are confined in a foreign state to the power of entering into obligations or making contracts *juris gentium* only, must admit that there must be some means of compelling their execution, or of affording redress for their non-fulfilment; for to permit such obligations to be entered into is tacitly at least to treat them as legal, and, if legal, capable of enforcement; or otherwise the foreigner must be permitted to do justice for himself, and to seek as he best can in natural law that redress which the civil law denies to him. (*e*) He cannot be altogether *ex-lex*.

DCCCXCIII. The doctrine stated in the preceding paragraph is adopted by the jurisprudence of every civilized state but one, that one, most strange to say, which in its general jurisprudence may fairly claim pre-eminence over other modern nations, France. That state, acting upon a caricature of the true principle of national independence, holds that it has no civil jurisdiction over foreigners, and that to exercise it would be an infringement on the rights of independent states.

The French tribunals, therefore, at present hold themselves *incompetent* to entertain suits between undomiciled foreigners relating to *personalty*, except, indeed, in matters of commerce. (*f*)

This extraordinary departure, no less from the duty of a state towards all who are commorant within its boundaries than from the principles of international comity, has provoked, not unnaturally perhaps, measures of *retorsion* (*g*) in various states —as in Austria, Prussia, Bavaria, and Wurtemberg.

(*e*) *Massé, ib.*
Fœlix, s. 146.
(*f*) *Massé,* s. 167. " Quant aux actions personelles et mobilières la tendance générale de la jurisprudence actuelle est de n'admettre la compétence des tribunaux français entre étrangers d'une manière absolue qu'en matière commerciale. En matière civile et même pour les engagements passés en France, on exige que les tribunaux français soient competents, que l'un des étrangers soit domicilié en France on y jouisse des droits civils."
(*g*) See vol. iii. p. 8, of this work,

The best accredited French jurists (*h*) regret and condemn this Law, which has been made by the decisions of courts, and, as these jurists contend, on a misapplication or misinterpretation of the true principles of jurisprudence.

It is, perhaps, in consequence of these opinions that the more recent decisions in France have shewn a tendency to distinguish between contracts made abroad and contracts made in France between two foreigners, and an inclination in the latter case to maintain the competency (*i*) of the French tribunals.

The exception, founded on article 420 of the Code de Procedure, in favour of commercial matters, and the decisions establishing this exception, do, in fact, condemn the rule. The language of the *Cour de Cassation* establishing this exception is remarkable: " Qu'il s'agit d'un acte de commerce, consé- "quemment d'un *contrat du droit des gens*, soumis, dans son "exécution, aux lois et aux tribunaux du pays où il a en "lieu." As if the "droit des gens" was not equally applicable to all contracts entered into between strangers within the territory of the state. How much more liberal and just is the opinion of Pothier, who, speaking of the community of goods between married persons, observes: "Lorsque des étrangers, quoique non naturalisés, mais domiciliés en France sous une coutume qui admet la communauté de biens sans qu'il soit besoin de la stipuler, y contractent mariage saus passer aucun contrat de mariage, la communauté légale a lieu entre ces personnes. Il est vrai que ces personnes ne sont pas capables du droit civil, qui n'a été établi que pour les citoyens, tel que le droit des testamens, des successions, du retrait lignager;

(*h*) *Massé*, s. 167.

Fœlix, s. 146. : " Quant aux réclamations qu'un étranger peut avoir à exercer contre un autre étranger la loi Française diffère de celui du presque tous les autres pays civilisés. . . . . Cette jurisprudence . . . . . nous semble contraire au droit des gens Européen."

See also s. 157.

(*i*) See note (*u*) by *M. Demangeat* to *Fœlix*, s. 151, p. 293, t. i.

mais elles sont capables de ce que appartient au droit des gens, tel que sont toutes les conventions. Ou la communauté légale n'est fondée que sur une convention que les personnes qui contractent mariage sont présumées avoir eue d'etablir entre elles une communauté, telle que la loi de leur domicile l'etablit ; *supra*, n. 10 ; de laquelle convention, de même que de toutes les autres conventions, les étrangers sont capables. La communauté légale peut donc avoir lieu entre ces personnes ; à plus forte raison la conventionnelle. (*k*)

Questions of *status* (*d'état*) between foreigners, the French courts decline to entertain also, on the ground that they relate to matters of public order of a foreign country. (*l*) The French courts have also considered themselves incompetent to entertain a suit for separation on behalf of a foreign wife ; but, according to later decisions, it would seem that such a suit on the part of the wife will be entertained by them when the defendant is a foreigner *authorized* to establish his domicil in France, and the defendant can only avoid their jurisdiction by proving *in limine litis* that he is domiciled in a foreign state. M. Demangeat observes, that the court ought to go further and entertain suits of this kind between foreigners merely resident (*simplement résident*) in France, inasmuch as these cases concern the public order of the state in which they reside. (*m*)

The French courts also consider themselves incompetent to adjudicate upon questions of nullity of marriages between two foreigners, (*n*) and upon other matters of the like kind. They have also refused to adjudicate on succession to the moveable property (*purement mobilière*) of an undomiciled foreigner dying in France. (*o*)

(*k*) *Pothier Oeuvres—de Traité de la Communauté*, première partie, chapitre première, article première.

(*l*) *Fœlix*, s. 158.

See the recent English statute 21 & 22 *Victoria*, c. 93 (1858).

(*m*) *Fœlix*, s. 158 ; note by *M. Demangeat*.

(*n*) *Ibid*.

(*o*) *Vide ante* (chap. xxvi.) as to what constitutes *moveable* property.

DCCCXCIV. The kingdoms of Belgium and the Two Sicilies have adopted the French practices upon this point. Holland, Prussia, and some other German states are more liberal, and open the tribunals of justice to two foreigners as to two natives.

DCCCXCV. England exactly reverses the practice of France in this matter; and in admitting one foreigner to sue another for the breach of an obligation contracted *abroad*, it goes beyond the most liberal aspirations of the French jurists. The practice of England must be stated at some length.

DCCCXCVI. And, first, with respect to the Common Law. "Actions," Mr. Serjeant Stephen observes, "are either *local* or *transitory*; the former being founded on such causes of action as necessarily refer to some particular locality, as in the case of trespasses to land; the latter on such causes of action as may be supposed to take place anywhere, as in the case of trespasses to goods, batteries, and the like. Real actions are always in their nature local—personal are for the most part transitory. Between local and transitory actions there is this important distinction—that the former are, as the general rule, tried in the proper county where the cause of action arose and by a jury of that county; the latter may be tried in any county, at the discretion (in general) of the plaintiff. It follows from this, that when an injury is committed out of England, and its nature is such as to make the action local, no action at all will lie for its redress in any English court. On the other hand, where the nature of the injury is such that the action is transitory, such action will lie in the English courts, whether the injury was committed in England or elsewhere." (*p*)

DCCCXCVII. Secondly, with respect to the form of writ of summons against a defendant, resident out of the jurisdiction, and not being a British subject. The Common Law Procedure Act (*q*) gives a form of writ in this case; and the proceedings

---

(*p*) *Stephen's Comm.* vol. iii. 451.

(*q*) S. 19 of 15 & 16 *Victoria*, c. 76 (1852).

under it are the same as those against a British subject who is out of the jurisdiction, except that a notice of the writ is required to be served on the defendant, instead of a copy of the same ; but the notice gives the same information as the copy. After service of this notice, or leave to proceed without personal service, the same proceedings may be taken as in the case of a British subject out of the jurisdiction. (r)

DCCCXCVIII. Thirdly, with respect to security for costs in the case of a foreigner, the Common Law courts have holden that they will not require security for costs to be given by a plaintiff who is a foreigner and usually resident abroad, if at the time he is actually in this country, (s) and that it is not sufficient ground for requiring security for costs, that the plaintiff, a foreigner, lately came to England, having no family connections or permanent abode in it, and likely soon to leave it ; if it be not sworn that he has a permanent residence abroad. (t)

DCCCXCIX. The courts of Equity have laid down a general rule (u) that all persons not lying under certain disabilities, are entitled to maintain a suit as plaintiffs in the Court of Chancery. This rule is not affected by the circumstance of their being resident out of the jurisdiction of the court, unless they be alien enemies, or are resident in the territory of an enemy without a license or authority from the Government here.

In order, however, to prevent the defendant from being defeated of his right to costs, it is a rule, that if the plaintiff in a suit is resident abroad, the court will, on the application of the defendant, order him to give security for the costs

---

(r) Smith's Action at Law, by Prentice (ed. 1857), p. 66.

(s) Tambisco v. Pacifico, 7 Exch. Rep. 816 ; 21 Law Journ. (Exch.) 276. The principle of this judgment was acted on by the judge of the Probate Court in the case of Crispin v. Bell & Bell in the year 1860.

(t) Drummond v. Tillinghist, 16 Q. B. Rep. 740 ; 15 Jurist, 384 (1851).

(u) Daniell's Chancery Practice, ed. Headlam, vol. i. p. 31, sect. 6 ; " Persons residing out of the jurisdiction."

of the suit and, in the meantime, direct all proceedings to be stayed. (x)

DCCCC. From analogy to the course adopted where the plaintiff is resident out of the jurisdiction, the Courts of Equity

---

(x) Barker v. Lidwell, 1 Jones & Lat. 703.

See further, as to giving security for costs, the following cases :

Player v. Anderson, 15 Sim. 104 ;

Sibbering v. Earl of Balcarras, 1 De G. & Sm. 683 ;

Fox v. Blew, 5 Maddocks, 148 ;

Cliffe v. Wilkinson, 4 Sim. 124 ;

Lautour v. Holcombe, 1 Ph. 264 ;

Maloney v. Smith, 1 M'Clel. & Y. 213 ;

Mullett v. Christmas, 2 Ball & Beatty's (Irish) Rep. 422; vide etiam, Stackpole v. Callaghan, 1 Ball & B. 566 ;

Hill v. Reardon, Mad. & Geld. 46 ;

Ker v. Duchess of Munster, Bunbury's Rep. 35 (1718) ;

Winthorp v. Royal Exch. Ass. Comp. 1 Dick. 282 ;

Walker v. Easterby, 6 Ves. 612;

Evelyn v. Chippendale, 9 Sim. 497 ;

Colebrook v. Jones, 1 Dick. 164 ;

Lord Aldborough v. Burton, 2 M. & K. 401;

Lillie v. Lillie, 2 M. & K. 404;

Vincent v. Hunter, 5 Hare, 320 ;

M'Gregor v. Shaw, 2 De Gex & Sm. 360 ;

Watteeu v. Billam, 3 De Gex & Sm. 516;

Green v. Charnock, 2 Brown's C. C. 371; S. C. 2 Cox, 284; S. C. 1 Vesey, jun. 396 ;

Hoby v. Hitchcock, 5 Ves. 699;

Blakeney v. Dufaur, 2 De Gex, Macn. & Gor. 771 ;

Migliorucci v. Migliorucci, 1 Dicken's Rep. 147 ;

Craig v. Bolton, 2 Brown's C. C. 609; Anon. 10 Vesey, 287.   But filing a demurrer before moving for security has been deemed no waiver of the right : Watteeu v. Billam, 3 De Gex & Sm. 516 ;

Mason v. Gardner, 2 Brown's C. C. edit. Belt, 609, notis ;

Dyott v. Dyott, 1 Mad. 187 ; and see Wythe v. Ellice, 11 Beav. 99;

Exparte Seidler, 12 Sim. 106;

Adams v. Colethurst, 2 Anstruther, 552 ;

Seilaz v. Hanson, 5 Ves. 261 ;

Harvey v. Jacob, 1 Barn. & Ald. 159; and see Baddeley v. Harding, Mad. & Gal. 214.

will, upon application, restrain an ambassador's servant, whose person is privileged from arrest by the 7 Ann. c. 12, from proceeding with his suit until he has given security for costs. (*y*)

DCCCCI. All states are agreed, France inclusive, that it is competent to them to exercise jurisdiction over foreigners in the matter of immoveable property (*immovables purement réelles ou mixtes*) situated within the territory. (*z*)   According to French Law, the question as to the immoveable property must be the principal question, and not an accessory. (*a*)

Judgment obtained in the state of the domicil of two foreigners may be put in force by aid of the French courts to affect moveable property in France. (*b*)

Provisional measures, (*c*) (*mesures conservatrices ou provisoires*) having for their object to secure the safety of person or property of foreigners, are within the competence of the French courts. (*d*)

So if the necessity of adjudicating upon a civil matter between foreigners arises out of a *criminal* matter (*matière criminelle, correctionelle de police*), it is within the competence of the French tribunal. (*e*)

DCCCCII. These peculiarities of French jurisprudence have been more especially dwelt upon, because the French code and the French practice have influenced and influence many continental states.

(*y*) *Anon. Mos.* 175.

Goodwin v. *Archer*, 2 *J. Williams*, 452.

Adderley v. *Smith*, 1 *Dick.* 355.

(*z*) *Fœlix*, s. 160.

(*a*) *Ib.*

(*b*) *Ib.* s. 161.

(*c*) The absence of any such general power in the English courts is much to be lamented, though, to a certain extent, it will be seen that the end is attained by the process of injunction.

(*d*) *Fœlix*, 162.

(*e*) *Ib. s.* 165.

DCCCCIII. The peculiar *status* of ambassadors, their exterritorial privileges and immunities from the civil and criminal law of the state in which they represent the person of a foreign sovereign, have been fully discussed in a former volume of this work. (*f*)

(*f*) 2 vol. ch. vii. viii.

CHAPTER XLV.

LAW OF PROCEDURE—LEX FORI—EVIDENCE, DIFFERENT KINDS OF—PROOF OF FOREIGN ACTS—OF FOREIGN LAW.

DCCCCIV. It ought to be a canon of International Law that, wherever a foreign tribunal is rightly seised of a cause, and is in the exercise of a lawful jurisdiction, the mode of proof and the rules of evidence which that tribunal adopts should not be questionable before any other forum. It is a consequence of the well-established rule of comity, " de his quæ " pertinent *ad litis ordinationem* inspicitur locus judicii."(*a*) An exception to this canon might, no doubt, be furnished by a case in which the plain rules of natural justice have been violated; but such an exception it is hardly safe to contemplate, and no practical rule can be built upon it. (*b*)

DCCCCV. But when the jurisdiction of a tribunal is duly founded, a question may arise as to what proof it ought to receive as sufficient with respect to an act done in a foreign state. Is it the proof which the foreign state would deem sufficient? or that which the technical rules of the *forum* which has cognizance of the cause require?

It may be worth while to consider some principles generally admitted by jurists upon this subject.

DCCCCVI. Every code of Laws, ancient and modern, the Roman Law, the Canon Law, the Codes of modern states, have admitted the following various classes of proof. (*c*)

1. The proof by a written instrument (*preuve littérale*).
2. The proof by witnesses (*preuve testimoniale*).

(*a*) *Vide ante*, citation from *Bartolus*, p. 242.

(*b*) *Fœlix*, ii, s. 369.

(*c*) *Fœlix*, l. ii. t. iii.

3. The proof by the oath of the party to the suit.

4. The proof by presumption (*par presomption*).

5. The particular kind of proof afforded in matters of commerce by the account books of persons engaged in trade (*livres des commerçants*), which is perhaps, strictly speaking, a branch of the first division, which has been mentioned.

DCCCCVII. With respect to the proof by a written instrument (*preuve littérale*), this species of proof is generally admitted by all civilized states. If therefore a question arises before the tribunal of one state, in which an instrument written in another state is produced as evidence, it is never rejected because such a kind of evidence is inadmissible, though the external form of the instrument and the solemnities relating to it may be made the subject of examination. But before this examination can be instituted, or the written instrument received as evidence, a burden lies upon the party producing it to show that the instrument has been executed, or is in comformity with the Law of the place in which it was written.

By what means this burden of proof shall be discharged is a question for the *lex fori* to decide.

" The peculiar rules of evidence," Mr. Taylor observes, " adopted in one country, whether established by the practice " of its courts, or enacted by the legislature for the govern- " ment of those courts, cannot be extended to regulate the " proceedings of courts in another country, when transac- " tions, which took place in the former country, become the " subject of investigation in the latter. (*d*) For instance, if " the assignees of a bankrupt under an English fiat were to " bring an action in Calcutta against a debtor of the bankrupt, " and the pleas were to put in issue the bankruptcy and the " assignment, the affirmative of these issues could not be " proved by producing copies of the proceedings in the Bank- " ruptcy Court, purporting to bear the seal of that court,

---

(*d*) *Clark* v. *Mullick*, 1 *Moore's Privy Council Rep.* 279, per Lord Brougham.

" and to be signed by the clerk of enrolments ; for, although,
" by the statutes relating to bankruptcy, such evidence would
" be sufficient in English courts of justice, it would not even
" be admissible in India, as the acts do not extend to that
" country. (e)   Again, although, by the Scotch Law, all instru-
" ments prepared and witnessed according to the provisions of
" the act of 1681, are probative writs, and may be given in
" evidence without any proof, yet still, if it were required to
" prove one of these Scotch instruments in an English court,
" its mere production would not suffice, but it would be
" necessary to call one or other of the attesting witnesses.(f)

    " The case of *Brown* v. *Thornton*, (g) is another illustration
" of this rule.   There, a charterparty had been entered into
" at Batavia, and, in accordance with the Dutch Law, which
" prevails in that colony, the contract had been written in the
" book of a notary, and a copy sealed by the notary and
" countersigned by the Governor of Java, had been delivered
" to each of the parties.   In the courts of Java, the contract is
" proved by producing the notary's book ; but in all other
" Dutch courts, the copies are received as due evidence of the
" original.   Under these circumstances, the plaintiff in an
" English court tendered his copy of the charterparty as
" evidence of the contract, but the court held that it was
" inadmissible, on the ground that English judges could not
" adopt a rule of evidence from foreign courts.

    " Several other cases could be cited to the same effect ; (h)
" and in all, the distinction is recognized between the *cause of*
" *action*, which must be judged of according to the Law of
" the country where it originated, and the *mode of proceeding*,
" including, of course, the rules of evidence, which must be

(e) *Clark* v. *Mullick*, 3 *Moore's Privy Council Rep.* 252, 280.

(f) *Yates* v. *Thomson*, 3 *Clark & Fin.* 577, 580, *et seq.*, per Lord
Brougham.

(g) 6 *Adolphus & Ellis*, 185.

(h) *Don* v. *Lipmann*, 5 *Clark & Fin.* 1, 13—17.

" adopted as it happens to exist in the country where the
" action is brought." (*i*)

DCCCCVIII. A recent English statute has greatly facili-
tated the proof of foreign judgments and acts of state by
enacting, that " all proclamations, treaties, and other acts of
" state of any foreign state, or of any British colony, and all
" judgments, decrees, orders, and other judicial proceedings of
" any court of justice in any foreign state, or in any British
" colony, and all affidavits, pleadings, and other legal docu-
" ments filed or deposited in any such court, may be proved
" in any court of justice, or before any person having by law
" or by consent of parties authority to hear, receive, and
" examine evidence, either by examined copies or by copies
" authenticated as hereinafter mentioned : that is to say, if the
" document sought to be proved be a proclamation, treaty, or
" other act of state, the authenticated copy to be admissible
" in evidence must purport to be sealed with the seal of the
" foreign state or British colony to which the original docu-
" ment belongs ; and if the document sought to be proved be a
" judgment, decree, order, or other judicial proceeding of any
" foreign or colonial court, or an affidavit, pleading, or other
" legal document filed or deposited in any such court, the
" authenticated copy to be admissible in evidence must pur-
" port either to be sealed with the seal of the foreign or
" colonial court to which the original document belongs, or, in
" the event of such court having no seal, to be signed by the
" judge, or if there be more than one judge, by any one of the
" judges of the said court, and such judge shall attach to his
" signature a statement in writing on the said copy that the
" court whereof he is a judge has no seal ; but if any of the
" aforesaid authenticated copies shall purport to be sealed or
" signed as hereinbefore respectively directed, the same shall
" respectively be admitted in evidence in every case in which

---

(*i*) *Smith's Leading Cases*, 167 ; see also, *Story*, ss. 629, 636.
Taylor's Law of Evidence, vol. i. p. 46.

" the original document could have been received in evidence,
" without any proof of the seal where a seal is necessary, or of
" the signature, or of the truth of the statement attached
" thereto, where such signature and statement are necessary,
" or of the judicial character of the person appearing to have
" made such signature and statement." (k)

DCCCCIX. Upon the principle contained in the preceding
sections, the *lex fori* must always decide what kind of proof it
will require of the existence and the meaning of a foreign law.
The English rule upon this subject, stated generally, (l) is that
it must be proved by calling as a witness a foreign advocate or
jurist, or one who is *peritus virtute officii* in the knowledge
of that foreign Law, and that in each case, because it is
possible that the *lex fori* may have changed since it was
proved in a former case, however recent. (m)

In the case of *Dalrymple* v. *Dalrymple*, nevertheless,
Lord Stowell said, " The authorities to which I shall have
" occasion to refer are of three classes : first, the opinions of
" learned professors given in the present or similar cases;
" secondly, the opinions of eminent writers as delivered in
" books of great legal credit and weight ; and thirdly, the
" certified adjudication of the tribunals of Scotland upon these
" subjects. I need not say that the last class stands highest
" in point of authority, where private opinions, whether in
" books or writing, incline on one side, and public decisions
" on the other, it will be the undoubted duty of the court,
" which has to weigh them, *stare decisis.*" (n)

And in *Bremer* v. *Freeman* (1857), the Judicial Committee
of the Privy Council held itself at liberty to form an opinion
on the articles cited from the Code Napoleon. (o)

(k) 14 & 15 *Victoria*, c. 99, s. 7.

(l) *Taylor on Evidence*, s. 1042.

(m) *M'Cormick* v. *Garnett* (1854), *De Gex & Mc Naghten & Gordon's
Rep.* 278.

(n) *Dalrymple* v. *Dalrymple, Consistory Rep.* vol. ii. p. 81.

(o) *Moore's P. C. Rep.* vol. x. p. 306; see also *Sussex Peerage Case*, 11
Clk. & Fin. Rep. 114– 117; *Nelson* v. *Lord Bridport*, 8 *Beav. Rep.* 527.

DCCCCX. The English *lex fori* requires that the witness who is to prove foreign law shall be either a legal person or in an official situation, which requires for the due execution of its duties a competent knowledge of that Law; but with respect to a foreign *usage* or *custom*, any witness acquainted with the fact would probably be considered competent. (*p*)

DCCCCXI. With respect to the effect of books kept by commercial persons as furnishing evidence, Savigny (*q*) adopts the opinion of the Supreme Court of Appeal of Cassel, namely, that the Law of the place where the books are kept should decide as to their admissibility and credibility as evidence. He admits that, inasmuch as this kind of proof belongs to the Law of procedure, it ought, properly speaking, to be governed by the Law of the forum, which exercises jurisdiction over the matter; but in this case the proof is inseparably bound up with the form and efficacy of the transaction itself. The foreigner who deals with a trader whose establishment is in a state, the law of which admits the books of the trader as evidence, subjects himself voluntarily to that law.

DCCCCXII. The proposition, that a written instrument cannot be impugned upon grounds which are not authorised by the *lex loci* where it was made, is followed, according to Fælix, by the necessary consequence that no proof can be admitted in a foreign state relative to the validity of that instrument, other than that which would have been admitted by the *lex loci* of the State in which it was made. Thus, in France it is not permitted to adduce proof by witnesses to impugn the contents of a written instrument, or to prove what was said before or after its execution; and, therefore, if an instrument executed in France were to be the subject of litigation in another State—Prussia, for instance—where a contrary rule prevails, and where such oral testimony is

---

(*p*) *Sussex Peerage Case*, 11 *Clk. & Fin. Rep.* 124.
Taylor on Evidence, ss. 10, 43.
(*q*) *R. R.* viii. s. 381, iii.

admissible, it ought, nevertheless, not to be admitted in the case of an instrument executed in France. (*r*) This point will presently be further considered in the discussion on *oral evidence.*

DCCCCXIII. When the place of execution is once determined, the law of that place ought to govern both the question of the external formalities, and the question of the authenticity of the act or instrument: "il est du droit des gens," the authors of the *Nouveau Denisart* say, "que ce qui est au-"thentique dans un pays le soit chez toutes les nations." (*s*) The importance of this proposition derives illustration from the great difference which exists in the laws of States, both relatively to the persons charged, as public officers, such as notaries or tabellions, with the execution of contracts, testaments, and the like instruments, and also relatively to the degree of faith which shall be given to their acts. (*t*)

DCCCCXIV. In accordance with the principle which has been stated, an English court has holden, that an erasure in a foreign affidavit in the recital of a death, the certificate of which was proved as an exhibit, was immaterial, notwithstanding the notary, before whom the affidavit was sworn, had not affixed his initials to the erasure ; and, in a case in which it was proved that the practice of verifying the mark of a marksman in an affidavit sworn abroad did not require, as in this country, the notary to insert in the *jurat* that "the witness saw the deponent make his mark,"—it was holden that the omission of these words was immaterial. (*u*)

DCCCCXV. Secondly, with respect to *oral proof by witnesses* (*u*) (*preuve testimoniale*), very material differences exist

---

(*r*) *Fœlix*, s. 227.

(*s*) *Ibid*, s. 226.

(*t*) *Ibid*, s. 228.

(*u*) *Savage* v. *Hutchinson* (*V. C. Wood*, 1853), *Equity Reports*, vol. iii. p. 368.

(*x*) For the Roman law on documentary evidence see *Dig.* xxii. 4.

in the practice and laws of different States upon this subject. It may frequently happen that a party to a suit loses his cause in one State on account of the inadmissibility of evidence before the tribunals of that State which would have been admitted, and by its admission have secured his success before the tribunals of another State.   Upon the hypothesis that each forum must exclusively enforce its own rules of evidence, it requires but a slight acquaintance with the laws and practice relative to evidence in England, France, Germany, and Spain, to be aware how often it must be of vital consequence to the suitor to ascertain before what tribunal his suit will be instituted.   It is, in truth, of the utmost importance that a general rule of comity should prevail with respect to what law should govern the admissibility of evidence relative to an act done abroad.   There are two well-established categories under which jurists rank all matters relating to forensic proceedings, namely, *ea quæ litis formam concermunt ac ordinationem,* and *ea quæ spectunt decisoria causæ et litis decisionem.*   Under which of these two categories the admissibility of evidence should be placed, is perhaps the most embarrassing question which can be found within the range of Private International Law.

DCCCCXVI. The reasoning of Rocco (*y*) on this subject

Cod. iv. 21, " *de fide instrumentorum et amissione eorum.*"   *Instrumenta* in its general sense included every kind of proof—oral as well as documentary ; but in its more usual sense documentary proof only.   It would appear from a curious passage in *Aulus Gellius* that the Roman judge did not confine the party to any particular kind of proof, or insist in any case upon documentary proof alone.   A. Gellius sat as a judge in an action for money had and received, but the plaintiff, "neque *tabulis* neque *testibus* id factum docebat," the defendant insisted, and it would appear legally, that evidence on the character of the parties would not be taken, " clamitabat probari apud me debere pecuniam datam *consuetis modis, expensi latione, mensæ rationibus, chirographi exhibitione, tabularum obsignatione testium intercessione, ex quibus si nullâ re probaretur,* dimitti jam se oportere, et adversarium de calumniâ damnari."—*A. Gellius,* lib. xiv. c. 2.

(*y*) Cap. xi. p. 363.

deserves more attention than it appears to have received. He adopts the division into the *ordinatoria* and the *decisoria litis*, and argues that the admissibility or inadmissibility of a certain mode of proof, the consideration whether that should or should not be allowed to be established by oral testimony, are matters which have no small effect upon the *decision* of a cause, inasmuch as it often happens that a fact or proposition can only be judicially established by the species of proof which is refused. On the other hand, the ascertainment of the particular manner and form in which the testimony should be given—for instance, whether it should be given in the presence of one party or of both, whether openly or secretly—relates entirely to the order of procedure.

It is, he afterwards observes, a firm and settled principle of international jurisprudence that rights duly acquired in one State should not be subject to defeasance in another State. But if the foreign magistrate, whose aid is sought for the enforcement of an obligation, may reject the species of proof, which the parties had before their eyes at the time when they contracted the obligation, rights duly acquired in one State may not only be altered but may be annihilated in another State. A party to the obligation naturally contemplated, at the time of its being entered into, the mode of proof allowed by the *lex loci contractûs* as capable of being adduced to elucidate any obscurity in the terms of the obligation itself. He provided himself with no other proof: if that should turn out to be the only proof by which the obligation can be sustained, and that be rejected by the foreign tribunals, the obligation itself is particularly overthrown. Therefore, Rocco says, the foreign tribunal, which has to enforce the contract, ought not to reject a species of evidence which the law of the place of the contract would have admitted.

DCCCCXVII. Fælix is clearly of opinion, and is supported by the highest French judicial authorities, that the *lex loci contractûs*, and not the *lex fori*, ought to decide the question of the admissibility of oral evidence to sustain or impeach the obligation; inasmuch as the question relates to the

"*fond* de la contestation," and not to the "*forme de pro-*
" *céder.*" (*z*)

Fælix cites Story (*a*) and Burge (*b*) as exponents of the
English practice, and as agreeing with him in this position—
with what justice we will now proceed to consider.

DCCCCXVIII. The English tribunals, and those of the
North American United States, have been much embar-
rassed (*c*) by the extreme practical difficulty of distinguishing between cases in which the admission of evidence affects
the substance and merits of the cause, and those in which it
can be considered as solely a matter of procedure.

Thus, for the construction and interpretation of written
foreign instruments, it seems to be established that the evidence *legis loci contractûs* must be received : what *such*
evidence is must be proved, like all foreign law, as a matter of
fact : but the questions as to the competency of witnesses—as
to whether a certain matter can be proved by written or
oral testimony—as to what is the force of certain evidence,
whether it proves or not a certain fact—are questions belonging to the *lex fori;* and the usual formulary is, that the
admission and the rules of evidence belong to the *ordinatoria
litis* and are governed *lege fori*, and not *lege domicilii* or *lege
loci contractûs.*

DCCCCXIX. " The cases," Lord Justice Clerk Hope (*d*)
observed, " must be rare indeed in which the court of one
country can be called upon to administer justice according to
the law of evidence or prescriptions obtaining in another
country, when no question is raised as to the forms (*e*) and
requisites of the written instruments or the exemplification of

---

(*z*) *Fælix*, s. 233.

(*a*) *Ibid.* s. 629.

(*b*) *Ibid.* i, p. 29.

(*c*) *Story*, s. 636 : " This most embarrassing and as yet (in a great
measure) unsettled class of questions."

(*d*) *Robertson* v. *Burdekin*, 1 *Ross's Comm. Ca.* 818 (A. D. 1843).

(*e*) *Cf. Story*, s. 260 *d*, and note.

them in another country. No case certainly is to be found in the English or Scotch courts in which they have admitted the proposition that they ought to govern their enquiries into a *matter of fact* by the law of evidence of another country."

DCCCCXX. In the following extracts from three successive judgments of the House of Lords, it will be seen how the vigorous mind of Lord Brougham applied itself to this difficult question, and the steps by which the formulary or maxim above mentioned became incorporated into English jurisprudence.

In *Yates* v. *Thomson*, (*f*) a case in which a question arose in Scotland upon the *interpretation* of a will made in England, Lord Brougham, as we have seen, (*g*) held that the testator's written declarations must be taken with respect to the English law ; and that it followed from this proposition that those declarations of intention touching that property were to be construed as they would be construed by English principles of interpretation. But that the importing of the foreign code must stop. " What evidence," he added, " the courts of another country would receive, and what reject, is a question into which I cannot at all see the necessity of the courts of any one country entering. Those principles, which regulate the admission of evidence, are the rules by which the courts of every country guide themselves in all their enquiries. The truth with respect to men's actions, which form the subject-matter of their enquiry, is to be ascertained according to a certain definite course of proceeding ; and certain rules have established, that in pursuing this investigation some things shall be heard from witnesses, others not listened to ; some instruments shall be inspected by the judge, others kept from his eye. This must evidently be the same course, and governed by the same rules, whatever be the subject-matter of investigation. Nor can it make any difference, whether the

---

(*f*) 3 *Clk. & Finnelly's R.* 577-8.
(*g*) *Vide ante*, p. 631.

facts concerning which the discussion arises happened at
home or abroad; whether they related to a foreigner domiciled
abroad, or a native living and dying at home. As well it
might be contended that another mode of trial should be
adopted, as that another law of evidence should be admitted
in such cases. Who would argue, that, in a question like the
present, the Court of Sessions should try the point of fact by
a jury according to the English procedure, or should follow the
course of our dispositions or interrogations in courts of equity,
because the testator was a domiciled Englishman, and because
those methods of trial would be applied to his case, were the
question raised here? The answer is, that the question
arises in the Court of Session, and must be dealt with by
the rules which regulate enquiry there. Now, the law of
evidence is among the chief of these rules; nor let it be
said, that there is any inconsistency in applying the English
rules of construction and the Scotch ones of evidence
to the same matter, in investigating facts by one law and
intention by another. The difference is manifest between the
two enquiries; for a person's meaning can only be gathered
from assuming that he intended to use words in the sense
affixed to them by the law of the country he belonged to at
the time of framing his instrument. Accordingly, where the
question is, what a person intended by an instrument relating
to the conveyance of real estate situated in a foreign country,
and where the *lex loci rei sitæ* must govern, we decide upon
his meaning by that law, and not by the law of the country
where the deed was executed, because we consider him to have
had that foreign law in his contemplation. The will of April,
1828, has not been admitted to Probate here; it has not even
been offered for proof, so that there is no sentence of any competent jurisdiction upon it either way. But in England it
would never be received in evidence, nor seen by any court;
neither would it have been seen if it had been proved ever so
formally. Our law holds the probate as the only evidence of a
will of personalty, or of the appointment of executors; in
short, of any disposition which a testator may make, unless it

regards his real estate. Can it be said, that the Scotch Court is bound by this rule of evidence, which, though founded upon views of convenience, and, for anything I know, well devised, is yet one which must be allowed to be exceedingly technical, and which would exclude from the view of the court a subsequent will, clearly revoking the one admitted to probate? The English courts would never look at this will, although proof might be tendered that it had come to the knowledge of the party on the eve of the trial. A delay might be granted to enable him to obtain a revocation of the probate of the former will. It is absurd to contend that the Court of Session shall admit all this technicality of procedure into its course of judicature as often as a question arises upon the succession of a person domiciled in England. Again, there are certain rules just as strict, and many of them not less technical, governing the admission of parol evidence with us. Can it be contended that, as often as an English succession comes in question before the Scotch Court, witnesses are to be admitted or rejected upon the practice of the English Courts? nay, that examination and cross-examination are to proceed upon those rules of our practice, supposing them to be (as they may possibly be) quite different from the Scotch rules? This would be manifestly a source of such inconvenience as no court ever could get over. Among other embarrassments equally inextricable there would be this; that a host of English lawyers must always be in attendance on the Scotch courts, ready to give evidence, at a moment's notice, of what the English rules of practice are, touching the reception or refusal of testimony, and the manner of obtaining it; for those questions which, by the supposition, are questions of mere fact in the Scotch Courts, must arise unexpectedly during each trial, and must be disposed of on the spot, in order that the trial may proceed. The case which I should, however, put, as quite decisive of this matter, comes nearer than any other to the one at bar; and it may, with equal advantage to the elucidation of the argument, be put as arising both in an English and in a Scotch

Court. By our English rules of evidence no instrument proves itself, unless it be thirty years old, or is an office copy, authorised by law to be given by the proper officer, or is the 'London Gazette,' or is by some special act made evidence, or is an original record of a court under its seal, or an exemplification under seal, which is a quasi record. By the Scotch law all instruments prepared aud witnessed according to the provisions of the act of 1681, are probative writs, and may be given in evidence without any proof. Now, suppose a will of personalty or any other instrument relating to personal property, attested by two witnesses, and executed in England, according to the provisions of the Scotch act, is tendered in evidence before the Court of Session ; it surely never will be contended that the learned judges, on being satisfied that the question relates to English personal succession, ought straightway to examine what is the English law of evidence, and to require the attendance of one or other of the subscribing witnesses, where the instrument is admissible by the Scotch law as probative? Of this I can have no doubt. But suppose the question to arise in England, and that a deed is executed in Scotland according to the act of 1681, by one domiciled here, would any court here receive it as proving itself, being only a year old, without calling the attesting witnesses ? It would have a strange effect to hear the circumstance of there being two subscribing witnesses to the instrument, which makes it prove itself in the Parliament House of Edinburgh, urged in Westminster Hall as the ground of its admission without any parol testimony. The court would inevitably answer, 'Two witnesses; then, because there are witnesses, it cannot be admitted but they must, one or other of them, be called to prove it.' The very thing that makes the instrument prove itself in Scotland, makes it in England necessary to be proved by witnesses. I have, therefore, no doubt whatever, that the rules of evidence form no part of the foreign law, according to which you are to proceed in disposing of English questions arising in Scotch Courts."

DCCCCXXI. In the leading case of Don *v.* Lipmann, (*g*) Lord Brougham said :—

"No one will contend, in terms, that the foreign rules of evidence should guide us in such cases; and yet it is not so easy to avoid that principle in practice, if you once admit, that, though the remedy is to be enforced in one country, it is to be enforced according to the laws which govern another country. Look to the rules of evidence, for example. In Scotland, some instruments are probative ; in England, until after the lapse of thirty years, they do not prove themselves. In some countries forty years are required for such a purpose; in others thirty are sufficient. How, then, is the law to be ascertained which is to govern the particular case ? In one court there must be a previous issue of fact; in another, there need be no such issue. In the latter, then, the case must be given up as a question of evidence. Then come to the law. The question, whether a parol agreement is to be given up, or can be enforced, must be tried by the law of the country in which the law is set in motion to enforce the agreement. Again, whether payment is to be presumed or not, must depend on the law of that country, and so must all questions of the admissibility of evidence ; and that clearly brings us home to the question on the Statute of Limitations. Until the act of Lord Tenterden, a parol agreement or promise was sufficient to take the case out of the Statute of Limitations; but that has never been the case in Scotland. It is not contended here, that the practice of England is applicable to Scotland ; but these are illustrations of the inconvenience of applying one set of rules of law to an instrument which is to be enforced by a law of a different kind." (*h*)

DCCCCXXII. In the latest judgment on this subject, the same high authority judicially pronounces that, as to the stipulations of a contract made abroad, our courts are bound

---

(*g*) 5 *Clark & Finnelly's Rep.* 15.

(*h*) *Story, ib.* 893.

by foreign law, which must be to them a matter of fact. But it is a totally different thing as to the law of evidence. The law of evidence is the *lex fori* which governs the courts. Whether a witness is competent or not; whether a certain matter requires to be proved by writing or not; whether certain evidence proves a certain fact or not; that is to be determined by the law of the country where the question arises, and where the remedy is sought to be enforced, and where the court sits to enforce it. (*i*)

DCCCCXXIII. Nevertheless, with respect to the title to real property, it has been holden that if an enrolled and recorded copy has, *lege sitûs*, the same force as the original, such copy is itself a conveyance, and that an examined copy is receivable in England, without evidence of search for the original, because it is not regarded as a copy of a copy, but as being made from a duplicate original. (*k*) It is, perhaps, difficult to reconcile the principle of this decision with that of Lord Brougham in the matter of personal property above mentioned.

DCCCCXXIV. Story says, that with regard to *Wills* of Personal Property made in a foreign state, it seems to be almost a matter of necessity to admit the same evidence to establish their validity abroad as would suffice for this purpose in the domicil of the testator; otherwise the favourite doctrine *mobilia sequuntur personam* would be practically overthrown; and therefore parol evidence has been admitted to prove the manner in which the testament is made and proved in the place of the testator's domicil, in order to lay a foundation for the establishment of the testament elsewhere. (*l*) Still the reader must bear in mind the observations of Lord Brougham in *Yates* v. *Thomson*.

(*i*) *Bain* v. *Whitehaven, &c.*, 3 *House of Lords Cases*, 1—19.

(*k*) *Tulloch* v. *Hartley*, 1 *Younge & Coll. Rep. in Chancery*, 114.

(*l*) § 636.—*De Sobry* v. *De Laistre*, 2 *Harris & Johnson's (Amer.) Maryland Rep.* 191—195.

DCCCCXXV. Upon the important question whether the *lex fori* or the *lex loci contractûs* ought to govern in cases where Prescription or a Statute of Limitation is pleaded or relied upon, the reader is referred to what has been said in a former chapter on the Discharge of Obligations. (*m*) But it may be well to notice in this place, that with respect to English Statutes of Limitation the English courts have ruled—

1. That the Statute of Limitations (21 Jac. 1, c. xvi. s. 7) is no bar to a party, whether he be a subject of the realm or a *foreigner*, who was not in England at the time the cause of action occurred, and who continues resident abroad. (*n*)

2. That the proviso in the 7th section of the 21 Jac. 1, c. xvi., which allows a person who is beyond the seas when the cause of action accrued to bring his action within six years "after his being returned from beyond the seas," includes a *foreigner* who, after the cause of action accrued, comes to England for the first time. (*o*)

DCCCCXXVI. The *priorities* and *privileges* of creditors, in the marshalling and distribution of assets, are considered by Story,(*p*) who founds his opinion on a passage from Rodenburgh, as matters relating to the forms and order of proceedings, and as therefore ruled by the *lex fori*. This operation appears, however, to be subject to some qualifications. (*q*)

(*m*) P. 571.

(*n*) *Le Veux* v. *Berkeley*, 2 *Dan. & L.* 31 ; 5 *Q. B.* 836 ; 8 *Jurist*, 666 ; 13 *Law Journ. Q. B.* 213.

(*o*) *Lafond* v. *Ruddock*, 13 *C. B.* 813; 17 *Jurist*, 624 ; 22 *Law Journ. C. P.* 217.

See also, respecting the Statute of Limitations where party is beyond the seas, the cases of *Fannin* v. *Anderson*, 7 *Q. B.* 811 ; 9 *Jurist*, 969 ; 14 *Law Journ. Q. B.* 282;

Townsend and another v. *Deacon*, 6 *Dan. & L.* 659 ; 3 *Exch.* 706 ;

Story v. *Fry*, 1 *Younge & Coll. N. C. C.* 603;

Re Friston, 1 *Prac. Rep.* 74.

(*p*) S. 423 (*b*); *cf. Cook* v. *Gregson*, 2 *Drury's Rep.* 286.

(*q*) As to *liens* on property depending on the *lex situs*, *vide ante*, p. 546 ; as to cases of *Bankruptcy*, p. 546 ; and as to *Stoppage in transitu*, p. 596.

DCCCCXXVII. The question as to the time within which an *appeal* must be instituted is clearly among the *ordinatoria litis,* and determinable by the *lex fori.* (*r*)

(*r*) *Tulloch* v. *Hartley,* 1 *Grange & Coll. C. C.* 114.

CHAPTER XLVI.

FOREIGN JUDGMENTS.

DCCCCXXVIII. In these chapters it is proposed to consider the effect, both which ought to be and which is, given by the tribunals of one state to judgments delivered by the tribunals of another state ; (a) that is, the practice of comity respecting *Foreign Judgments.* The subject regarded from an English point of view would have been properly treated in the former chapter, under the category of evidence ; but regarded more generally, and with reference to foreign jurisprudence, it seems to require a separate and distinct consideration.

DCCCCXXIX. The authority of a judgment in time of peace is derived exclusively from the civil law of the territory in which it is given ; it cannot, therefore, according to strict principles of international *law*, have effect or operation in a foreign territory. But International *Comity*, "*usu exigente et humanis necessitatibus*," speaks another language, and a

---

(a) *Donelli, Comm.* lib. xxii. c. v., *de exceptione rei judicatæ, quibus, adversus quos, quâ de re competit.*

Fœlix, ii. s. 319.

Klüber, Europäisches Völkerrecht, 59, considers a foreign judgment ought to be executed by other States on the ground of its being a convention between the parties, or an arbitration submitted to by them.

Pinheiro Ferreira treats it as the result of a tacit contract on the part of the foreigner, to be found by the law of the State in which he resides. *Notes sur Vattel*, p. 304.

Massé, ii. s. 305, is also of this opinion—*quasi contrahitur in judicio.*

Generally on the *exceptio rei judicatæ, cf. Savigny*, v. 84, 209, 253, 376, 378 ; vi. 267, 271, 413.

Merlin, Qu. de Droit v. *Jugement*, s. 14, No. 1.

Pothier, Tr. des Obl. p. iv. c. iii. s. 3.

foreign judgment is generally in some shape or other, and with more or less restriction, upholden and executed by all States.

DCCCCXXX. Both from the jurisprudence and the positive enactments of States upon this subject, the general axiom may be deduced—that no State allows a foreign judgment to be executed within its territory, except under the authority and by the order of its own tribunal. But the practice of States is various upon this subordinate point—namely, whether the foreign judgment shall be executed at the simple request of a party (*simple demande ou requête*) or the formal requisition (*commission rogatoire*) of the foreign tribunal; or whether the permission to execute it shall be delayed until the domestic tribunal has examined, more or less, the grounds upon which the foreign tribunal founded its decision. (*b*)

DCCCCXXXI. It follows, from the principles laid down in the early part of this volume, that no State will recognise or allow to be executed a foreign judgment, (*c*) which contains any provisions or order contrary to the public morals or public policy of the realm in which execution of it is sought. The French tribunals have lately furnished a strong illustration of this principle ; the *Cour de Paris* having decided that it was unlawful to permit the execution in France of a Swiss judgment of divorce between Swiss parties, although the execution was only requested to enforce the payment of costs awarded against one of the parties, and although by a treaty between (*d*) France and Switzerland it was expressly provided that definitive judgments in civil causes should, after they had been legalized by the competent authority, be executed in France. (*e*)

(*b*) *Pardessus*, t. vi. No. 1486.
Revue étrangère, t. iii. p. 127, &c. (*Aubry.*)
Fœlix, ii. s. 320.
(*c*) *Vide ante*, pp. 11, 12.
(*d*) 18th July, 1828.
(*e*) *Fœlix*, ii. p. 43 (ed. *Demangeat*), n. a.—*Dev. Car.* xlix. 211.

DCCCCXXXII. It seems a clear proposition of reason and law that the foreign judgment when recognised must be interpreted and considered, as to its effects, according to the law of the State in which it was pronounced; Savigny and Fœlix are in complete accordance upon this not unimportant point. (*f*)

DCCCCXXXIII. In order to understand the reasoning of foreign jurists on this subject, it is necessary to bear in mind the distinction between two effects ascribable to a foreign judgment.

1. It may be pleaded as an *exceptio rei judicatœ*, or, as it is said in England, a plea in bar.

2. It may be given effect to and *executed* in the same manner as a domestic judgment. (*g*)

DCCCCXXXIV. The great majority of states (*h*) give effect to a foreign judgment in all cases in which the following conditions have been fulfilled.

1. The tribunal which pronounced the judgment must have been competent, according to the law of the state to which it belonged, (*i*) to decide upon the matter adjudicated upon.

(*f*) *Savigny*, viii. s. 373 *b*.

Fœlix, ii. s. 324.

(*g*) " De tout ce qui précède, il resulte que les jugemens étrangers " alors même qu'ils se 'ont pas été déclarés exécutoires par un tribunal " français, font foi, jusqu'à preuve contraire et qu'ils out l'autorité de " la chose jugée." *Massé*, ii. s. 305 *in fine*.

See, too, *Martens*, l. 3, c. 83, s. 94: he says, when—1, the tribunal is competent ; 2, the foreigner has been duly heard ; 3, the cause duly and *dejinitively* decided—"il se peut point appartenir à une puissance " étrangère d'admettre chez elle un second procès sur là même cause, " et celui que l'intenterait peut dans tous les pays être repoussé par " *exceptio rei judicatœ* que la sentence dit porté contre un sujet né " dans le pays ou contre un domicilié."

(*h*) *Fœlix*, ii. s. 327.

Merlin, *Qu. de Droit* v. *Jugement*, s. 14, No. 1, 3e ed. p. 20.

Bynkershoek de Foro Leg. c. l. ; *Forum Competens, origo et natura, Subjectio duplex*—1, i. *rei* ; 2, *personœ*.

(*i*) *Ib.* ss. 321, 327.

2. The tribunal must be duly seised or possessed of the subject of its decision. The jurisdiction of it must be properly founded. It is not competent to a tribunal to cite before it a person who belongs neither by birth, nor domicil, nor temporary residence, to the State from which it derives its jurisdiction, unless he have property, or has incurred some obligation within the limits of the State, concerning which there is a litigation before this tribunal. (*k*)

3. The foreigner who was a party to the suit must have been fairly heard before the tribunal according to laws of the State, and on an equality in every respect, including the right of appeal, with a native subject.

The tribunal must have decided upon the very subject-matter which it is attempted to litigate again. It must have decided definitively and either in the last resort (*en dernier resort*), or, which is the same thing, without any appeal prosecuted from its decision to the superior courts of the state in which it was pronounced.

When these conditions are united, the *exceptio rei judicatæ* ought to be in all, and is in most states, admitted as a complete bar to a second litigation upon the subject so adjudicated upon.

DCCCCXXXV. To these three conditions some States add another, namely, that of *reciprocity*. It is absolutely necessary for the validity of the plea *exceptio rei judicatæ*, in the case of a foreign judgment, that the State, whose tribunal has pronounced it, should itself admit the validity of the like plea in its own tribunals.

Austria, Prussia, and most of the German States govern by the *common law ;* Denmark, Switzerland, Rome, Sardinia, adopt this rule.

DCCCCXXXVI. France, Spain, Portugal, Russia, Sweden, Norway, Belgium, the Two Sicilies, and Tuscany, before and of course since its annexation to Sardinia, Greece, the canton

---

(*k*) *Vide post, Vallée* v. *Dumergue*, 4 *Exchequer R.* 290.

of Geneva, do not require or admit the principle of reciprocity as necessary for the plea of *exceptio rei judicatæ*. England, Scotland, and the United States of North America, go a step further and practically execute (*l*) a foreign judgment delivered by the tribunal of a State, which does not itself give effect to a foreign judgment as constituting an *exceptio rei judicatæ*.

DCCCCXXXVII. It has been said, that in some way or other all civilised States uphold foreign judgments; but they do not therefore allow them to take effect as if they were domestic judgments; they do not concede to them what the French call *l'execution parée* (*executio parata*). Generally speaking, such an examination into a foreign judgment is instituted as suffices to show that it does not contravene the public policy of the State in which it is to be executed, and that it is clothed with the proper authority of the tribunal from which it emanates.

DCCCCXXXVIII. That the form and manner of its execution are exclusively governed by the law of the State which recognises and executes the judgment is a clear proposition of public as well as International Law, and does not appear to have been ever controverted.

DCCCCXXXIX. The jurisprudence and practice of States may be divided under three heads:

1. Of those which act upon the principle of reciprocity in recognising foreign judgments.

2. Of France, and other States which follow its example; these refuse altogether to recognise the authority of the foreign judgments (*l'autorité de la chose jugée*).

3. Of England and the United States of North America, which recognise, without regard to the principle of reciprocity, the authority of the judgment of a competent foreign tribunal.

DCCCCXL. With respect to the practice and jurisprudence of France upon this subject, it is most emphatically condemned by Fælix, as contrary both to the true interpretation of the

---

(*l*) *Vide post.*

municipal law of France, (m) and to the just demand of comity, as, in fact, deserving of unmitigated condemnation. (n) It would appear, however, upon the authority of M. Massé, (o) that practically France gives almost as much effect to foreign judgments as England ; France does not admit the authority of the foreign judgment sa ssuch ; they must be rendered capable of execution (exécutoires) by the decision of a French tribunal ; but before this has taken place they are received as *evidence*, only to be rebutted by the strongest counter evidence of the *facts* on which they are founded, and which they verify.   Whether they ought to be clothed with the authority of a domestic judgment, without being revised and the facts re-examined, or whether they ought to be simply and without examination clothed with the authority of the *pareatis* of a French judgment, is a question which has, more than any other, divided the opinions of French jurists. M. Massé's opinion is, that the French tribunal ought to satisfy itself, that the foreign judgment contains affirmatively and negatively the requisitions which have been mentioned above, (p) and then to grant its *exequatur* (q) for the execution of the judgment.

DCCCCXLI. No country has been more liberal than England in giving effect to the decisions of foreign courts.   This will be found the just conclusion from the decisions which have taken place in British courts, from the time of the decision of

---

m) The solution of this question depends upon the true construction of *Art.* 2123 of the *Code Civile*, and *Art.* 546 of the *Code de procédure*, as compared with the ancient law of France.

(*n*) " Suivant nous cette interpretation est contraire au sens littéral de la loi, à son esprit, aux rapports de bon voisinage qui existent ou doivent exister entre les diverses nations pour leur utilité réciproque, et enfin aux usages, suivis ans la majeure partie des Etats de l'Europe." *Fœlix*, i. s. 347.

(*o*) II. *Massé*, s. 305.

(*p*) *Vide ante*

(*q*) II. *Masse*, s. 306

Weir's Case, in the reign of James I., to the decision in *Vallée* v. *Dumergue*, (*r*) in the English Court of Exchequer, in the year 1849, and *Barber* v. *Lamb*, in the Court of Common Pleas, in 1860.

DCCCCXLII. Great doubts, indeed, long existed, and perhaps are not now wholly removed, as to the *degree of effect* which should be given to foreign sentences in England ; whether they should be wholly conclusive, or be considered as *primâ facie* evidence only, and liable to be rebutted.

It will be found, I think, upon examination of all the cases, that the doubt has arisen, partly from a want of discrimination of the principle applicable to judgments *in rem, in personam,* and *inter partes ;* and partly from not sufficiently distinguishing between the propriety of questioning a foreign judgment upon the facts and *merits ;* and of questioning it upon the ground of *want of jurisdiction,* either intrinsically, (*s*) or over the parties ; (*t*) or upon the ground of its misunderstanding the English Law ; or upon the ground of the absence of the common

---

(*r*) *Story's Conflict of Laws*, c. xv.

Kent's Commentaries, &c. vol. ii. part iv. s. 27.

Starkie on Evidence, vol. i. p. 270.

Taylor on Evidence, vol. ii. ss. 1242—1261.

Burge's Commentaries on Foreign and Colonial Law, vol. iii. p. 1044.

Smith's Leading Cases, vol. i. note on the *Duchess of Kingston's Case.*

(*s*) *Havelock* v. *Rockwood*, 8 *Durnford & East*, p. 268.

Bowles v. *Orr*, 1 *Younge & Col. R.* 464.

(*t*) *General Steam Navigation Company* v. *Guillon*, 11 *Mer. & W.* 894 : " It becomes, therefore, unnecessary to give any opinion whether the pleas are bad in substance ; but it is not to be understood that we feel much doubt on that question. They do not state that the plaintiffs were French subjects, or resiant, or even present in France, when the suit began, so as to be bound by reason of allegiance, or domicile, or temporary presence, by a decision of a French Court ; and they did not select the tribunal and sue as plaintiffs ; in any of which cases the determination might have possibly bound them. They were mere strangers, who put forward the negligence of the defendant as an answer, in an adverse suit in a foreign country, whose laws they were under no obligation to obey."

requisites of justice, such as a litigating party being judge; (*u*) or the defendant not being cited; (*x*) for manifest error as to Law; (*x*) for not being conclusive in the country where it has been pronounced; (*y*) that the matters in issue before the foreign tribunal were not the same; (*z*) that the proceedings in the foreign court were not taken for the same *purpose* as the suit in which its judgment is sought to be made conclusive, though the issue were the same; (*a*) for being between different parties; or on the ground of fraud; (*b*) or that it

---

(*u*) *Price* v. *Dewhurst*, 8 *Simon's R*. 279.

(*x*) *Buchanan* v. *Rucker*, 1 *Campbell*, *R*. 67.

Wilkinson v. *Johnston*, 3 *Barn. & C. R*. 428.

But especially *Novelli* v. *Rossi*, 2 *Barn. & Adol. R*. 757. *Cf*. note to this case for error of French Court as to English Law.

Becquet v. *Macarthy*, 3 *Barnwell & Adolphus*, 957.

Alison v. *Furnival*, 4 *Tyrwhitt*, *R*. 751, shows that an error as to its own law by a foreign tribunal must be very manifest indeed to induce the English Court to set aside the judgment on this ground.

(*y*) *Plummer* v. *Woodburne*, 4 *Barnwell & Cress. R*. 625.

(*z*) *Ricardo* v. *Garcias*, 12 *Clark & F. R*. 368.

(*a*) In this case it would seem not to be conclusive : *Behrens* v. *Sieveking*, 2 *Myl. & Cr*. 602.

(*b*) But in *Douglas* v. *Forrest*, 4 *Bing. R*. 686, proceedings were carried on against a party without any personal notice of the suit, and in his absence, where there had been only a Scotch warning, the judgment was enforced ; but Chief Justice Best said (p. 703), " To be sure, if attachments issued against persons who never were within the jurisdiction of the Court issuing them, could be supported and enforced in the country in which the person attached resided, the legislature of any country might authorise their courts to decide on the rights of parties who owed no allegiance to the government of such country, and were under no obligation to attend its courts, or obey its laws. We confine our judgment to a case where the party owed allegiance to the country in which the judgment was so given against him, from being born in it, and by the laws of which country his property was, at the time those judgments were given, protected. The debts were contracted in the country in which the judgments were given, whilst the debtor resided in it." So if the party were subject to the jurisdiction when the suit commenced, *Cowan* v. *Braidwood*, 1 *M. & G*. 892, or where the party

were so grossly defective as to leave in doubt what had been decided. (c)

DCCCCXLIII. With respect to impeaching foreign judgments upon the *merits*, the state of the English law appears to be this : That where all the conditions above mentioned have been complied with, the foreign judgment *inter partes* would be considered as conclusive and unimpeachable, (d) and as following under the maxim of the Roman law, "res judicate pro veritate accipitur. (e) This opinion is supported not only by principle and analogy, but by the preponderating authority of the actually decided cases, and especially of those which have been adjudicated upon since the year 1840. The reasoning of Mr. Starkie—and it would not be easy to cite a higher authority on this point—is as follows :

"The principle upon which a judgment is admissible at all is, that the point has already been decided in a suit between parties or their privies by some competent authority, which renders future litigation useless and vexatious. If this principle extends to foreign as well as domestic judgments, as it plainly does, why is it to be less operative in the former than in the latter case ? If it does not embrace foreign judgments, how can they be evidence at all ? By admitting that such judgments are evidence at all, the application of the principle is conceded : why, then, is its operation to be limited as if the foreign tribunal had heard nothing more than an *ex parte* statement and proof ?" (f)

---

agreed to receive a particular notification, *Vallée* v. *Dumergue*, 4 *Exchequer R.* 303.

(c) *Obicini* v. *Bligh*, 8 *Bingham's R.* 335.

(d) *Walker* v. *Witter*, 1 *Douglas*, 1 (Lord Mansfield) ; *Houlditch* v. *Marquis of Donegal*, 8 *Bligh*, *N. S.* 470 ; *Don* v. *Lipmann*, 5 *Cl. & Fin.* 1—20, are the cases which carry with them the most weight the other way, but less, however, upon a careful examination, than is usually ascribed to them.

(e) *Dig.* l. i. t. v. s. 25 : "Ingenuum accipere debemus etiam eum, de quo sententia lata est quamvis fuerit libertinus, quia res judicata pro veritate accipitur."

(f) *Starkie's Law of Evidence*, vol. i. p. 273-4.

Most unquestionably, however, such judgments would be considered, according to *all* the cases, as constituting the strongest *primâ facie* evidence of the right that could be produced, and as throwing a very heavy burthen of disproof upon the party opposing it. It is, moreover, a general rule of English Courts to regard the substance rather than the form of foreign judgments. (*g*) And it seems clear that where a foreign judgment was offered to prove the same fact, but for a different or collateral purpose, then, if the judgment had been delivered by a court of exclusive jurisdiction, it would be conclusive evidence upon the question so incidentally arising. (*h*)

DCCCCXLIV. A case decided by the Court of Common Pleas during the present year (1860) shows very clearly the different aspects under which a foreign judgment *in rem*, and one *in personam*, are judicially considered in England. (*i*) "In 1853, and until November, 1854, C., a British subject, was sole and registered owner of the British ship A. In December, 1853, the ship sailed for Australia, and thence to Madras. At Australia the master drew a bill of exchange on C., in favour of L., residing in Australia. C. never accepted the bill, and it was dishonoured at maturity. In November, 1854, while C. was still owner and registered as owner C., C. mortgaged the ship to H., who was registered as mortgagee. In February, 1855, H. transferred his interest in the ship to E., who was registered as mortgagee. E., in April, 1855, transferred such interest to the plaintiff, but the transfer of the plaintiff was not registered till April, 1857. On 11th May, 1855, C. was adjudged a bankrupt. On 4th May, 1855, the ship arrived at Havre, in France, and B., who resided in England, and was holder of the said bill of exchange, indorsed to T., a French subject domiciled in France, who commenced a suit on the bill in France, against the master, who appeared

---

(*g*) *Henley* v. *Soper*, 8 *Barn. & Cresswell R.* 20 (Lord Tenterden).

(*h*) *Starkie's Law of Evidence*, vol. i. p. 277*b*.

(*i*) *Castrique* v. *Imrie and another*, *Court of Common Pleas*, 1860 (*Weekly Rep.*, vol. viii. p. 344).

and allowed judgment to go against him by consent, and was condemned to pay the amount of the bill ; and in consequence the ship was seized and detained in the custody of the French court. Neither C., nor H., nor E., nor plaintiff, was, before the judgment, served with any summons or process, nor had they any opportunity of appearing in the suit, or objecting to the judgment. By the French law, the ship could not be sold until the judgment was confirmed, and the sale of the ship ordered. T. caused C., who appeared by the ship's papers and certificate of registry to be the sole owner, to be summoned, as also C.'s official assignee. · Judgment by default was given, by which the ship was to be sold. The plaintiff commenced a suit in France to replevy the ship from custody, which was decided against him, and the ship was sold and the defendants bought her, and refused to give her up to the plaintiff on demand. The ship was afterwards lost. The plaintiff brought trover, in England, for the ship. The judgment of the Court was delivered by Willes, J. " The first question in this case is, whether the proceedings of the court of Havre can be examined into here, if those proceedings are *in rem*, or not. If a judgment of that character determined that the ship was charged with a privilege or lien for advances, and was liable to be sold to defray them, then, unless it appears on the face of such proceedings that the judgment was void, it could not be questioned even by persons who, like the plaintiff, were not before the court that pronounced it. *If, on the other hand, the proceedings were in personam, and the liability of the ship was only brought incidentally in question, such proceedings would not be binding upon persons who were not parties to them.* The question of property must be decided as between such parties, without regard to the judgment, if shown to be erroneous. It appears to us that the proceeding must be considered as of the latter class, namely, *in personam*. They were originally instituted against the master personally, and so far as they related to the vessel it was proceeded against as a security for the judgment of Trotteux against the master. This we hold to have been a suit *in personam*, upon the

authority of the judgment of Jervis, C. J., in the case of *Bold*
v. *Buccleuch*, 7 M. P. C. Ca. 267, especially in that part of
the judgment which is in page 286. *It is clear that the judg-*
ment of the Court of Havre, if examinable, cannot be sus-
tained; for it proceeds on the erroneous assumption that
article 191 of the Code de Commerce created a mercantile lien
on the ship, though English, in respect of advances made to
the master in an English port, by persons carrying on business
there on a bill drawn by him upon his English owner in England, merely because the bill happened to be one fallen into
French hands, and the vessel had touched in the ordinary
course of navigation at a French port. This proposition of
French law is not sustained by anything stated in the case,
though we have the satisfaction of knowing that the opinion of
the court of Rouen on this point, when the matter was brought
forward there, was in accordance with our own, that that article
of the Code de Commerce is not applicable to the present case.
The question as to the effect of the French proceedings is,
therefore, reduced to this, whether the sale of A.'s vessel in
execution for B.'s debt under the process of a foreign court,
not proceeding *in rem*, is binding on A. in England.   It is
clear such a sale in this country would be wholly void as
against A., and we are not informed that the law of France
differs in this respect from our own.   This is in our minds
decisive of the present case ; and we are relieved from considering whether in the present case, if it had appeared by the
French law the title of a purchaser in a judicial sale is valid,
notwithstanding the invalidity or illegality of the preliminary
proceedings, such law would be recognised in this country
as giving such title to a purchaser according to the maxim
locus actum. We pronounce no opinion upon this latter point,
which we mention only lest it might be supposed we had overlooked it. For these reasons the proceedings in France did
not defeat the title which, by the law of England, the plaintiff
acquired unencumbered by any lien or privilege for advances
on the bill drawn in respect of them."

DCCCCXLV. In the event of the foreign judgment being

in favour of the plaintiff and made the foundation of his suit in England, as he cannot issue, as has been seen, execution upon it here, he must enforce it by bringing a fresh action, technically called an *action of assumpsit*, (*k*) for the recovery of what is due to him under the judgment. In that action the judgment forms evidence, or is in the nature of evidence, of a contract between the parties. It is important to observe, however, that the foreign judgment does not operate as a *merger of the original ground of action* : but if the plaintiff sue on the original ground, it may possibly be competent to the defendant to controvert it, notwithstanding the judgment ; though even then it would be *primâ facie* evidence for the plaintiff. (*l*)

DCCCCXLVI. If the foreign judgment be set up by way of *defence* to a suit in an English court, such a judgment pronounced *adversely* to the party who brings the suit for the second time in England will, if properly pleaded, be conclusive against him. If it be not pleaded, but put in evidence, it will be cogent but not conclusive evidence on behalf of the defendant. (*m*) And it is probable, though the point has not been expressly decided, that if a foreign judgment had been recovered against the defendant, but had also been satisfied, the fact might be pleaded as a bar to a second suit in this country.

DCCCCXLVII. The distinction commented upon in the last two paragraphs between an original ground of action being merged in a foreign judgment, and such judgment being set up

---

(*k*) The English Court of Chancery will entertain a bill founded on a decree of a Foreign Court of Equity, for the purpose of giving effect to it, in regard of English property.

Houlditch v. *M. of Donegal*, 8 *Bligh N. S.* 301.

Henderson v. *Henderson*, 6 *Queen's Bench*, 297.

Paul v. *Roy*, 15 *Beavan's R.* 439.

(*l*) *Smith* v. *Nicholls*, 5 *Bingham*, 208.

Mr. Smith's note, Leading Cases, vol. i. *ubi supra*.

(*m*) *Smith* v. *Nicholls*, *ubi supra*.

Taylor on Evidence, vol. ii. p. 1254, 1255.

in defence, is clearly shown in the following very recent decision. (n) The plea to a declaration for money had and received was, that the plaintiff had impleaded the defendant for the identical causes of action as then sued for, and recovered from and been paid by the defendant the sum of £45 and costs, in the Supreme Court of Constantinople, established under 6 & 7 Vict. c. 94. The plea was demurred to ; but it was holden that a good answer to the action was disclosed by it.

Chief Justice Erle (with whom the other judges agreed) said :—" I am of opinion that this plea is good, and that the judgment, therefore, should be for the defendant. It was objected, that it was not stated sufficiently clearly that the Court had jurisdiction. We hold that it was sufficiently stated, and in the case of *Robertson* v. *Struth*, 5 Q. B. 941, it was decided that the declaration for debt on the judgment of a foreign court need not state that the judge had jurisdiction over that court ; and if any objection as to its not having been clearly stated, the case referred to is a sufficient authority to show that such objection would not be valid. Here is the judgment of a foreign court upon the issue between the parties and payment of the sum recovered, which appears to me to be a satisfaction of the debt ; and as to the court having authority to adjudicate, the plaintiff has chosen his court, and has had the judgment of that court, and the other party has paid what was awarded. In *Henderson* v. *Henderson*, 11 Q. B. 1015, the judgment turned upon the point that it must be presumed that a foreign court had authority over the matter. The great distinction between that case and the present one is, that *the defence does not rest on the principle of the cause of action being merged in the judgment ; but on the principle of there having been judgment by the court to which the plaintiff himself resorted,* and the sum recovered under that judgment having been paid by the defendant. This seems to me to be analogous to a case where the parties have resorted

---

(n) *Barber* v. *Lamb, Court of Common Pleas,* 1860 (*Weekly Rep.* vol. viii. p. 461).

to an arbitration, and the arbitrator has made his award, and the sum has been paid, which is binding upon both parties ; and it is contrary to any principle of law, that a party who has chosen his own tribunal, and has got what was awarded to him, should be allowed, if he is dissatisfied with the decision, to go to another tribunal for the purpose of trying to get another award, which would be more satisfactory to him."

DCCCCXLVIII. In the case of *Alison* v. *Furnival* an action was brought in the English court of Exchequer by the provisional syndics of a bankrupt named Beuvain against a person named Furnival, founded upon the award of French *arbitrators*, who alone, according to the French law, were capable of deciding certain differences growing out of the partnership of the bankrupt and the defendant. The decision of the court is so important and so clear upon the principles of English jurisprudence, respecting questions of foreign evidence, and foreign judgments, that it is here given at length :—

" Many objections were taken in this case to the right of the plaintiff, to recover. It was contended, first, that the agreement was not proved. Secondly, that this was considered as an action on the award only, and that the arbitrators were not duly appointed. Thirdly, that the award was not made pursuant to the submission, and was therefore void. Fourthly, that the plaintiffs had no right to maintain the action. Fifthly, that the declaration was not proved. We have considered these objections, and are of opinion that they are not well founded, and that the rule must be absolute to enter a verdict for the plaintiffs.

" The first objection is, that the agreement was not properly proved. This divides itself into two branches ; one, that even if there were no evidence of a duplicate original in existence, this proof would not have been sufficient, because the original, deposited with the notary, ought to have been produced, or clear proof given that by the written law of France it could not be removed. Another branch of this objection is, that it was proved that there was another original of this agreement in existence, and that the copy was only secondary evidence and not admissible until the original was accounted for, and that no such notice was given.

"It seems to be clear that this document was not acknowledged before a notary, and is therefore not to be deemed a notarial act. It was simply deposited for safe custody ; but there was sufficient evidence on the testimony of M. Colin that it is the established usage in France, though without any provision of the written law, not to allow the removal of documents so deposited, and consequently to let in secondary evidence of the contents, for such evidence is admissible where it is in effect out of the power of a party to produce the original, and that was sufficiently proved in this case to the satisfaction of the learned judge whose province it was to decide upon this question, and we cannot say that his decision was wrong.

"The second branch of this objection is, that there was evidence of the existence of a duplicate original, and that there is an established rule, that all originals must be accounted for before secondary evidence can be given of any one. There is no doubt as to this rule, but we are not satisfied that there was any such duplicate original in this case, which had the same binding force and effect on the *defendant* as the one deposited and proved ; the only evidence of its existence is the expression *fait double* at the foot of the agreement ; but what is the precise meaning of these terms, or what was the nature of the duplicate executed in this case, if there was one, was not made out by the evidence, and neither in the numerous cross interrogatories (63) exhibited to the witness *Albert*, nor his depositions, which were read on the trial, is there one which hints at the existence of any other obligatory documents than the one deposited with the notary. It is very true that the 1325th Article of the *Code Civile* requires duplicates where there are two interests; but I do not see how we can properly take notice of their laws, as it was not proved on the trial. The objection is one strictissimi juris, and beside the justice of this case ; and we think that it ought not to succeed, unless the existence of the duplicate original, in the proper sense of that word, was more distinctly made out than it was in this case.

" I now come to the objections on the merits ; and first, as to the appointment of the arbitrators. It is contended, in the first place, that by the express agreement of the parties in article 12, merchants must be appointed. and that the *Tribunal de Commerce* had power to appoint others. This depends upon the construction of that article (12 of the agreement). We do not think that the *Tribunal de Commerce* is restricted by this clause from appointing arbitrators not merchants. The parties are ; but the court has a general power, and it is to be remarked that in none of the proceedings in the French courts is the objection taken, that the *Tribunal de Commerce* exceeded its powers in this respect. It is then said that the *Tribunal de Commerce* has no power to annul the appointment made by the defendant himself, which they have done by their act of 15th November, 1827. Now, by this act it appears that the appointment of a foreigner as arbitrator was not a due exercise of the power received by the twelfth article, and void, and was the same as if no arbitrator at all had been named by the defendant; and we must assume the judgment of the court to be according to the French law, at least until the contrary was distinctly proved, according to the principle laid down in *Becquet* v. *MacArthy*.

"Next, it is contended, that the Tribunal ought to have appointed two arbitrators and not one ; but is there any substantial difference in allowing the former appointment to stand, naming another, and expressly appointing the arbitrators already named and the other jointly, de novo ? Certainly there is not, and in this respect also we must assume that the *Tribunal de Commerce* acted according to law, unless the contrary be proved.

" The third head of objection is to the award itself, which it is suggested is not warranted by the submission. The award has proceeded upon the principle that Beuvain, instead of being merely placed in statu quo, and reimbursed the expenses incurred upon the faith of the contract (which could have been done by awarding to him as damages the expense of constructing the new works, deducting the value of the materials) has, moreover, under all the circumstances of the case, a right to be placed in the same situation as if the defendant had fulfilled his contract; and it is impossible for me to say that this principle of adjudging the damages is wrong, as being contrary to natural justice, nor is there evidence that it is not conformable to the law of France ; indeed, it appears to follow the rule laid down in the 1149th Article of the *Code Civile*.

" The fourth head of objection is, that the plaintiffs cannot sue ; and this objection subdivides itself into several : Firstly, that by the terms of the appointment two out of three cannot sue. The answer to this objection is, that by the law of France, in such a case, two out of three may do an act as well as one separately, and that is distinctly proved by M. Colin. Secondly, it is said he ought to have the previous authority of the *Juge Commissaire*. They are directed by the appointment to act under the *surveillance* of the *Juge Commissaire* by article 492 of the *Code de Commerce;* but M. Colin proves that they may bring an action without his authority, for that is the effect of his testimony ; and though the defendant's witness Gérard gave evidence to the contrary, it seems to amount only to this, that a syndic would not act properly in doing so, not that the want of previous directions would avoid the act and constitute a defence to the action ; and this is in conformity with the principle in which the cases cited for the plaintiff relating to actions brought by assignees of insolvents in this country were decided. Thirdly, it is insisted that by the law of France two cannot maintain an action for the debt due to the bankrupt, and this also depends upon the evidence. That all may sue appears by articles 492 and 499 of the *Code de Commerce,* both given in evidence ; that the bankrupt is deprived of the administration of his effects, appears by article 442, also read at the trial, and M. Colin deposes that two have the same power to act under this appointment as three, and there is no evidence to the contrary. Fourthly, it is insisted that if two can bring an action, it is a condition precedent upon the construction of the instrument of appointment, that the third should be absent, or should have objected to the act done, and that there was no proof of either circumstance in this case ; but we are of opinion that this would be to put a very strict construction upon the term of the appointment. It seems to us that the act of two only sufficiently implies the absence or want of consent of the third, and that the effect of the authority given by the appointment is, in substance, to authorise two to do valid acts as to third persons without the other ; and it was in fact proved that by the law of France one of the arbitrators might act if the other two were absent or not consenting, but that they should not so act without the absence of or want of consent of that other. Lastly, it is said that though two may act and bring an action, yet they must sue in the name of all. Now, the effect of the testimony of M. Colin is, that two may sue in France without a third, and the witness for the defendant does not prove the contrary, and there seems no reason why it should not be so. The property in the effects of the bankrupt does not appear to be absolutely transferred to these syndics in the way that those of a bankrupt are in this country to assignees ; but it should seem that the syndics act as mandatories or agents for the creditors, the whole three or any two or one of them having the power to sue for and recover the debts in their own names. This is a peculiar right of action created by the law of that country, and we think it may, by the comity of nations, be enforced in this as much as the right of foreign assignees or foreign corporations appointed or created in a different way from that which the law of this country requires ; *Dutch West India Company* v. *Moses;* (o) *National Bank of St. Charles* v. *De Bernales ;* (p) *Soloman* v. *Ross.* (q) We do not pronounce an opinion whether this objection is available on the plea of nil debet, or ought to have been pleaded in abatement, though we were much struck with the argument of the learned counsel

---

(o) 1 *Strange's R.* 612.

(p) 1 *Hen. Blackstone's R.* 131.

(q) 1 *Ryan* v. *Moody's R.* 190.

for the plaintiffs on that point, for we think it is not available at all upon the evidence in this case.

"The fifth head of objection is that of variance—that the award is said to be registered in the Tribunal de Commerce instead of the *Cour de premier instance;* but the answer is, that this is clearly a surplusage.

"The sixth, that there is a variance, because Beuvain is averred to be a bankrupt, whereas he is only an insolvent in ' *en etat défaillite ;*' but this depends entirely upon the argument that the *English* term bankrupt necessarily means the same as the *French banqueroute,* which it does not; and it is to be observed, that in the *English* copy of the appointment of Syndics the word *faillite* is translated bankruptcy. These are all the objections to the plaintiff's right to recover; we think that they are not well founded, and that the action is maintainable without attributing to the acts of any of the French courts the same force as if they had been judgments between the litigating parties." (*r*)

DCCCCXLIX. As to the decision of the North American United States :

" The general doctrine," Story observes, (*s*) "maintained in the Courts of the United States in relation to foreign judgments certainly is, that they are *primâ facie* evidence, but that they are impeachable." But how far and to what extent this doctrine is to be carried, does not seem to be definitely settled. It has been declared, that the jurisdiction of the court, and its power over the parties and the things in controversy, may be enquired into ; and that the judgment may be impeached for fraud. Beyond this no definite lines appear to have as yet been drawn.

DCCCCL. *Judgments in rem* are adjudications upon the *status* of some particular subject-matter by a competent

---

(*r*) *Alivon and another* v. *Furnival* (A. D. 1834).

4 *Tyrwhitt's Rep.* 766, 772.

(*s*) S. 608 ; *cf.* cases collected in Digest to *Curtis* (*Amer.*) *R.* 264-5.

tribunal. These occur principally in the Probate and Admiralty Courts ; but they occur also in the Court of Exchequer.

It is justly observed by Mr. Smith, (t) that the universal effect of a judgment *in rem* depends upon the principle, that it is a solemn declaration, proceeding from an accredited quarter, concerning the *status* of the thing adjudicated upon ; which very declaration operates accordingly upon the *status* of the thing adjudicated upon, and *ipso facto* renders it such as it is thereby declared to be. A condemnation in the Prize Court not merely declares the vessel prize, but vests it in the captors. Thereupon the *status* of the thing is thus altered, and the sentence altering it, whether from a court of exclusive jurisdiction or not, ought to conclude the whole world.

DCCCCLI. Since the case of *Bernardi* v. *Motteux*, (u) it has been the clearly recognised law of England, that the sentences of Courts of competent jurisdiction to decide questions of prize, are received in England as conclusive evidence in actions upon policies of insurance, and upon every subject immediately and properly within the jurisdiction of such Foreign Courts. The question in later cases has not been with reference to the conclusive nature of the sentence, but whether it was given upon the point in controversy.

"The general law" (Chief Justice Tindal says) "is well known,—that the sentence of a foreign court of competent jurisdiction is binding upon all parties and in all countries, as to the fact on which such condemnation proceeds, where such fact appears on the face of the sentence free from doubt and ambiguity. But it is at the same time as well established

---

(t) 2 *Smith's Leading Cases, Duchess of Kingston's Case* ; *vide passim* the note upon it.

Geyer v. *Acquilar*, 7 *Durnford & East Rep.* 696.

Scott v. *Shearman*, 2 *W. Blackstone*, 977.

(u) 2 *Douglas Rep.* 526.

Lothian v. *Henderson*, 3 *Bosanquet & Puller's Rep.* 526.

Bolton v. *Gladstone*, 5 *East's Rep.* 160.

that, in order to conclude the parties from contesting the
ground of condemnation in an English court of law, such
ground must appear clearly on the sentence ; it must not be
collected from inference only." (x)

DCCCCLII. It need hardly be stated that unless the
foreign court be one of competent jurisdiction, its sentence
has no effect at all. Accordingly Lord Stowell designated the
adjudication of the prize court of a *belligerent* power sitting in
a *neutral* country, as "a licentious attempt to exercise the
rights of war within the bosom of a neutral country. (y)

DCCCCLIII. The courts of the United States in North
America hold the doctrine of the conclusiveness of judgment
in rem when the proceedings have been regular, quite as
strongly upon the general principle, as the courts in Great
Britain ; but it would appear that the latter hold such judgment conclusive not only as to the actual *res* decided, (z) but as

---

(x) *Dalgleish* v. *Hodson*, 7 *Bingham Rep.* 504.

See too Lord Alvanley's summary of the decisions in *Baring* v.
Clagett, 3 *Bosanquet & Puller's Rep.* 215.

Lord Ellenborough, however, said, in *Fisher* v. *Ogle* (1 *Campbell*,
418), "It is by an *overstrained comity* that these sentences are received
as conclusive evidence of facts which they positively aver, and on which
they specifically profess to be founded." But this remark appears to
have been extorted by the decisions of the French tribunals during
the last war, which he designated "the piratical way in which they
proceed." This remark he well reconciled with Lord Mansfield's judgment in *Saloucci* v. *Woodmass*.

Park on Insurance, 362.

Arnould on Insurance, i. 645.

(y) *Flad Oyen*, 1 *Robinson Rep.* 336.

See too *Haveloch* v. *Rockwood*, 8 *Durnford & East Rep.* 276.

Donaldson v. *Thompson*, 1 *Camp.* 429.

Oddy v. *Rovil*, 7 *Durnford & East Rep.* 523.

(z) *Bud* v. *Bamfield*, 3 *Swanston's Reports*. Lord Nottingham accorded a perpetual injunction to restrain certain suits of trespass and
trover for seizing the goods of the defendant (Bamfield) for trading in
Ireland contrary to certain privileges granted to the plaintiff and
others. The property was seized and condemned in the Danish Courts.

to all facts and matters incidentally decided. The decisions of the American courts are not harmonious on the subject.

DCCCCLIV. *Foreign judgments upon matters in their nature local* would be treated as conclusive in England. The difficulties necessarily incident to a re-examination of such matters in another country render this rule one of common justice as well as common sense.

The case of landed property affords an obvious illustration of this position. But the effect ascribed to foreign sentences in England will not be greater than that which they possess in the country in which they were given. A foreign judgment therefore *in rem* between two parties will not be conclusive against a third party, unless such an effect would be ascribed to it in the country of the judgment.

DCCCCLV. Not merely, however, in the case of landed property, but where the *res*, be it personalty or realty, is within the limits of the territory of the court (*a*) which gave the sentence —that sentence would be holden probably both in England and the North American United States as binding upon the property within the territory. But it would probably be considered as confined within those limits, and as having no exterritorial effect, especially where the parties affected by the sentence were not at the time subject to the jurisdiction of the court by domicil, residence, or origin, and had never appeared or contested the suit. (*b*)

Cases upon this point of law may probably arise when proceedings are attempted to be taken by creditors against personal property of a debtor in the hands of third persons, or against debts due by him to third persons—a proceeding sometimes technically styled the process of *foreign attachment*, or *foreign garnishment*, or in American law *trustee*

Lord Nottingham held the sentence conclusive against the suits, and awarded the injunction accordingly.

(*a*) As to the operation of a foreign judgment in the case of chattels in a foreign State, see *Koster* v. *Sapte*, 1 *Curteis' Rep.* 701.

(*b*) *Story*, s. 549, 592*a*, 607.

process. Many cases of this description as yet undecided will probably arise, to the decision of which the application of the principles above stated may furnish a safe guide.

DCCCCLVI. It must be borne in mind that there is an essential difference between foreign sentences of contentious and of voluntary jurisdiction. The latter contains in reality the act of the parties to the suit, to which the formalities of a court of justice are added as witnessing this act and consent. The former is the act of the judge himself; and it is the effect of sentences emanating from contentious jurisdiction that has been considered in the preceding pages.

NOTE TO THE FOREGOING CHAPTER.

I. List of the principal decisions, since 1830, on the effect of Foreign Judgments in England :

1830. *Martin* v. *Nicholls* (Vice Chancellor's Court—Shadwell), 3 *Simons*, 458. Apparently reversed, 1834, *Houlditch* v. *Donegal.*

1831. *Novelli* v. *Rossi* (Q. B.—Lord Tenterden), 2 *Barn. & Adol.* 764.

—— *Recquet* v. *MacCarthy*, *ib. et eod*, 957.

1834. *Alivon and another* v. *Furnival* (Exchequer), 4 *Tyrwhitt*, 768. Parke, B.

1834. *Houlditch* v. *Donegal* (House of Lords), 8 *Bligh*, 342—345 ; reversing apparently *Martin* v. *Nicholls*, 1830.

1838. *Koster* v. *Säpte* (Prerogative Court—Sir H. J. Fust), 1 *Curteis*, 701.

1839. *Smith* v. *Nicholls* (Common Pleas—Tindall, C. J.), 5 *Bingham*, 208.

—— *Ferguson* v. *Mahon* (Q. B.—Lord Denman), 11 *Adol. & Ellis*, 179.

1842. *Callender* v. *Dittrich*, 4 *Manning & Granger*, 68.

1844. *Robertson* v. *Struth*, 5 *Queen's Bench R.* 941.

—— *Henderson* v. *Henderson*, 6 *Queen's Bench R.* 274.

1845. *Ricardo* v. *Garcias*, 12 *Clark & Finnelly's Rep.* 368, (House of Lords—Lords Cottenham, Brougham, and Campbell) ; difficult to reconcile with *Houlditch* v. *Donegal.*

1846. *Reynolds* v. *Fenton*, 3 *Manning, Granger, & Scott's R.* 187.

1849. *Vallée* v. *Dumergue*, 4 *Exchequer Reports*, 290. English shareholders in French company. Assumpsit on the French judgment sustained (Baron Alderson).

1851. *Bank of Australia* v. *Nias*, 16 *Queen's Bench R.* 717, as to Colonial judgments.

1852. *Frith* v. *Wollaston*, 7 *Exchequer R.* 194.

—— *Paul* v. *Roy*, (Rolls Court—Sir J. Romilly), 15 *Beavan's R.* 433. English court will enforce a final judgment, but not an interlocutory order of a foreign court.

1853. *Meeus* v. *Thelluson*, 8 *Exchequer Reports*, 638. Foreign judgment upon a bill of exchange. Replication holden bad for not stating what the foreign law was at the time of the acceptance of the bill.

1856. *Kelsell* v. *Marshall* (Court of Common Pleas), 2 *Jurist* (N. S.), 1142, as to Colonial judgment.

1856. *Reiners* v. *Druce*, 23 *Beavan's Reports*, 145. Master of Rolls reviews former cases. Error on the face of a foreign judgment, apparent without the help of extrinsic evidence, invalidates it.

1860. February. *Castrique* v. *Imrie and another* (Court of Common Pleas).

—— April. *Barber* v. *Lamb*. *Vide ante.*

II. On the authority of *Res Judicata* in England—

1. As to courts generally.

2. As to courts of ultimate appeal.

Upon the first point, Lord St. Leonard observes (*Vendors and Purchasers*, p. 9, ed. 1857).

" Yet, whilst the seller's right is firmly established to this extent in equity, at law the rule has been laid down otherwise by Lord Mansfield in *Bexwell* v. *Christie,* (*a*) by Lord Kenyon in *Howard* v. *Castle,* (*b*) by Lord Tenderden at *nisi prius* in *Wheeler* v. *Collier ;* (*c*) and their view has been adopted by other judges. (*d*) *It would require a decision of the House of Lords to overrule the cases in equity,* and it is highly desirable that the Courts of law should adopt the equitable rule, restricted as it now is."

The same opinion as to the authority of the judgment of *inferior tribunals* is expressed by the same learned Lord in *Wilson* v. *Wilson.* (*e*) But as to the *second point*, viz., sentence of the ultimate appellant tribunal, he said (*f*) "The difficulty that I should have felt, as I have pointed out particularly, is with regard to the injunction that is actually to be found on the face of the decree ; but this House has now not the slightest power to touch that question ; *at all events not in this cause.* It has been doubted by a noble and learned lord, who is not now present, whether this House can correct any error which it has committed. (*g*) I confess, my lords, I have always entertained the opinion, that in the paticular case, you cannot correct the error ; it is settled ;

(*a*) *Cowper*, 395.

(*b*) 6 *Durn. and E.* 642, *m.* ; 3 *ib.* 93, 95.

(*c*) 1 *Ca.* 123.

(*d*) *Rex* v. *Marsh*, 3 *Yo. & Jer.* 331; *Crowder* v. *Austin,* 9 *Bin.* 368 ; *Thornet* v. *Haines,* 15 *Mee. & Wel.* 367.

(*e*) 5 *House of Lords Cases*, p. 59.

(*f*) *Ib.* 62.

(*g*) *Tommey* v. *White,* 3 *H. of L. Cases,* 68.

nothing but an act of Parliament can reverse it.   But I certainly hold, that this House has the same power that every other judicial tribunal has to correct an error (if it has fallen into one), in subsequently applying the law to other cases."   And Lord Brougham, in the same case, observed, (h) "My lords, I agree entirely with what my noble and learned friend has said as to the impossibility of anything but an act of Parliament altering any judgment of this House that has once been pronounced in a cause.   It is a totally different thing, and it is a *questio vexata*, how far we may or may not disregard any one of our own judgments, when applied to another cause."

The distinction between the repect paid to judgments in France and England has been noticed, p. 211-12.

(h) P. 71.

CHAPTER XLVII.

LEX FORI—PROVISIONAL MEASURES—INTERDICTA.

DCCCCLVII. It often happens that before the regular institution of a suit, justice and the interest of parties may require the aid and intervention of a court :

(I.) To prevent the apprehended or the actual infringement of rights. This intervention may take the shape of a measure affecting either the property or the person about to infringe such rights.

(II.) Or it may happen that an obligor or debtor is about to escape from the jurisdiction to which by virtue of his debt or obligation he is amenable, and the obligee or creditor may desire to prevent this escape by arrest of his person.

DCCCCLVIII. (I.) The former class of cases is provided for in all States which have founded their jurisprudence upon the Roman Law, (a) by the adoption of measures analogous in their effect to the Prætorian Interdicts. These were, properly and originally speaking, of a *prohibitory* character (*prohibitoria*), though in the time of Justinian they embraced measures having for their object the *restitution* of property (*restitutoria*), and the compelling the production of a particular person, subject, as a slave or child, to the control and within the power of another (*exhibitoria*).

(a) *Inst.* l. iv. t. xv.: " Erant autem interdicta formæ, atque conceptiones verborum, quibus prætor aut jubebat, aliquid fieri, aut fieri prohibebat, quod tunc maximè fiebat, cum de possessione aut quasi possessione inter aliquos contendebatur. Sec. 1: Summa autem divisio interdictorum hæc est : quod aut prohibitoria sunt aut restitutoria, aut restitutoria, aut exhibitoria. " Sunt tamen, qui putent propriè interdicta ea vocari quæ prohibitoria sunt, quia interdicere sit denunciare et prohibere : restitutoria autem et exhibitoria, propria decreta vocari. Sed tamen obtinuit, omnia interdicta appellari : quia inter duos dicuntur."

DCCCCLIX. These proceedings, which the French Law calls conservative and provisional measures (*a*) (*mesures conservatoires, conservatoires provisoires*), are admitted by that law in exception to its general principle; for even in the case of two foreigners the French Law applies this provisional remedy, while it refuses to entertain the question of the merit (*le fond*) of their dispute.

The president of a tribunal may empower a foreigner to seize money or effects in the possession of a Frenchman belonging to a foreign debtor.

(II.) It is competent also to the French tribunals to order an inventory of goods situated in France, and appertaining to a deceased stranger, although the proceedings necessary to secure by probate or administration a representative to the deceased have been taken, or, in the language of French Law, although *the succession has been opened* in a foreign State; and also, perhaps, to order a deposit of security for the value of the effects. It is also competent to the French tribunals to order such provisional measures as may be necessary to secure the personal safety and means of existence of a foreign wife or husband, or of their children. But it is only at the instance of a *commission rogatoire* that the French tribunal will nominate an administrator of the goods of a stranger physically or morally incapable to act for himself. The strange and melancholy state of the French Law, which permits a Frenchman to counterfeit the subject of a patent granted by a foreign state, and even to impress upon his merchandize the stamp of a foreign manufacturer, has been already adverted upon.

DCCCCLX. The English Law does not set itself in motion, as the foreign Law often does, to preserve by a provisional measure the goods of a deceased foreigner. The English Courts of Equity will, however, on their aid being invoked, extend their *injunction* (a provisional measure analogous to

---

(*b*) *Fœlix*, ss. 162, 250.

and founded upon the Roman *interdictum*) to the Foreigner as well as to the Englishman. Some striking instances of the exercise of this jurisdiction, in accordance with the soundest principles of Comity, will be found in the following sections.

DCCCCLXI. In the case of *Caldwell* v. *Vanvlissengen*, an injunction was granted against subjects of the kingdom of Holland, to restrain them from using on board their ships within the dominions of England, without the license of the plaintiffs, an invention, to the benefit of which the plaintiffs were exclusively entitled under the Queen's Patent.

Vice-Chancellor Turner in giving judgment said,—" I take the rule to be universal, that foreigners are in all cases subject to the laws of the country in which they may happen to be ; and if in any case, when they are out of their own country, their rights are regulated and governed by their own laws, I take it to be not by force of those laws themselves, but by the law of the country in which they may be adopting those laws as part of their own law for the purpose of determining such rights." He then refers to the opinions of Mr. Justice Story, in his treatise on the 'Conflict of laws;' (c) of Huberus, Boullenois, and Vattel, upon this subject ; and continues,— " In this country indeed the position of foreigners is not left to rest upon this general law, but is provided for by Statute : for by the 32 Henry 8, c. 16, s. 9, it is enacted, 'that every alien and stranger born out of the King's obeisance, not being denizen, which now or hereafter shall come in or to this realm or otherwise within the King's dominions, shall, after the 1st of September next coming, be bounded by and unto the laws and statutes of this realm, and to all and singular the contents of the same.' Natural justice, indeed, seems to require that this should be the case : when countries extend to foreigners the protection of their laws, they may well require obedience to those laws, as the price of that protection. These defendants, therefore, whilst in this country, must, I think, be subject to its laws." (d)

DCCCCLXII. An *alien ami* manufactured in his own country goods, which he distinguished by a peculiar trade mark ; the goods obtained considerable reputation, both in his own country and in various other foreign countries, and also in some British colonies, but it was not shewn at the trial that any of such goods had ever been even introduced or imported into England. The defendant, it appeared, was in the habit of manufacturing in and selling in this country goods similar in appearance, and with an exact copy of the plaintiff's peculiar trade mark. Some of these imitative articles were sold and used abroad in countries where the *alien ami's* goods had obtained a reputation. It was holden upon this state of facts that he was entitled to an injunction restraining the defendant from copying or imitating the trademark. (e)

It has been ruled, therefore, that a foreign manufacturer has a remedy by suit, in this country, for an injunction and account of profits against a manufacturer here who has committed a fraud upon him by using his trade-mark, for the purpose of inducing the public to believe that the goods so marked are manufactured by the foreigner. (f)

This relief, it has been said, is founded upon the personal injury caused to the foreigner by the defendant's fraud, and exists, although he resides and carries on his business in another country, and has no establishment here, and does not even sell his goods in this country. (g)

(d) *Caldwell* v. *Vanvlissengen, &c.*, 9 *Hare's R.* 415.

(e) *Collins Company* v. *Brown ; Same* v. *Cohen*, 3 *Kay & Johnson's Rep.* 423 ; 3 *Jurist (N. S.)*, 929.

(f) *Collins Company* v. *Brown*, 3 *Kay & Johnson's Rep.* 423 ; 3 *Jurist (N. S.)*, 929.

(g) *Ib.* It would appear that a person on whom an injury is frau-

DCCCCLXIII. It has also been decided that an alien can in the courts of this country sue to restrain the fraudulent appropriation of his trade-mark, although the goods on which such trade-mark is affixed are not usually sold by him in this country. (*h*)

DCCCCLXIV. (II.) With respect to the second class of cases, (*i*) viz., those relating to the arrest of a foreign debtor who is about to escape from the jurisdiction. (*k*)   The law upon this subject, both as to its substance and the form of procedure, is, of course, local; it is strictly the *lex fori* ; the *lex loci contractûs* has no influence upon its matter.

In England the provisional arrest before judgment, applicable equally to subject and foreigner, has been the subject of a recent statute. (*l*)   It is also competent to a Court of Equity to issue against a foreign debtor a writ of *ne exeat regno.*

DCCCCLXV. It would seem, however, that there must be a very strong case indeed to induce a Court of Equity to restrain a foreigner, domiciled in another country, from proceeding to obtain payment of debts according to the law of the country in which he is domiciled. (*m*)

DCCCCLXVI. An English Court of Equity will not lend its aid to compel a discovery in aid of the prosecution or defence of an action in a foreign Court. (*n*)

DCCCCLXVII. An English Court of Equity will enforce,

---

duleutly committed may have a remedy in the Courts of any country where the fraud occurs, and even although he is at the time an alien enemy.

(*h*) *Collins Company* v. *Reeves*, 4 *Jurist* (N. S.), 865 (V. C. Stuart).

(*i*) *Vide ante*, p. 698.

(*k*) *Cf. Fælix*, l. ii. t. v., *Des mesures conservatoires ou provisoires, &c.*

(*l*) 1 & 2 V. c. 110.

(*m*) *Maclaren* v. *Stainton, Maclaren* v. *Carron Company*, 26 *Law J. Chan.* 332.

(*n*) *Rent* v. *Young*, 9 *Simon's R.* 192.

Paul v. *Roy*, 15 *Beavan's R.* 433.

for the benefit of the crown, a trust of real estate created in favour of an alien. The devise being valid, and there being a *cestui que* trust, who can take, but not hold, the crown becomes entitled beneficially, and not the trustee or heir-at-law. (o)

(o) *Barrow* v. *Wadkin,* 24 *Beavan,* 1; 3 *Jurist* (*N. S.*), 679.

CHAPTER XLVIII.

PRIVATE INJURIES—WHERE TO BE REDRESSED.

DCCCCLXVIII. With respect to the class of *quasi obligationes* arising from the infliction of an injury (*maleficium*) upon a private individual, it is to be remembered that the prosecution of the injurer may have two objects—

1. Pecuniary reparation to the injured party, to obtain which a *civil* action may suffice. In this case, as Donellus says, " Civiliter agitur, id est de privato damno, et pecuniâ, quam inde debitam acta prosequatur." (*a*)

2. Or, secondly, the object may be the vindication of the authority of the law ; the punishment of the offender ; the deterring others from the commission of the like offence. To obtain one or all of these ends the *criminal* action is necessary : " Quatenus " (to use again the words of Donellus) " de his agitur criminaliter ad pœnam et vindictam criminis."

The Penal or Criminal Law of a State appertains, therefore, partly to its Private, partly to its Public Law.

DCCCCLXIX. That portion of it which relates to Public Law, so far as its administration affects the welfare of other States, so far as it partakes of an International character, has been already treated of in the first volume of this work. For instance, whether a State, apart from treaty, is bound by the obligation of *extradition*—how far, and between what States treaties upon this subject have affected the general law—exterritorial jurisdiction in the cases of crimes committed on board national ships on the high seas—mixed jurisdiction in the case of crimes committed on board foreign ships on the high seas—the crime of piracy on the high seas—the peculiar jurisdiction

---

(*a*) *Donellus, Com. de Jure Civili,* lib. xvii. c. xvi. . " *Ubi de maleficiis et criminibus agi oportet.*"

allowed by sufferance or treaty in Mahometan and heathen countries—are matters which concern directly the State in its collective capacity, and not individuals; or which, indirectly concerning individuals, and appertaining to Comity, have been treated of in the former volumes of this work.

DCCCCLXX. But Comity or Private International Law may be properly said to be (c) concerned with injuries committed against the property or person of some one resident or commorant within the limits of its jurisdiction, for which injuries a civil reparation is demanded; and it is proposed to offer a very few observations on the jurisdiction which is or ought to be exercised by the ordinary domestic tribunals of States upon this subject.

DCCCCLXXI. There are some questions which are improperly classed under this head, but which clearly belong to the category of Public Law. (d)

For instance, whether a State will take cognizance of an offence committed by one of its subjects within the jurisdiction of a foreign State, and if so what law and what forms of procedure it will apply to his trial, (e) are clearly questions of Public, and not of International Law. "The lex loci" (Lord Brougham observes) "must needs govern all criminal jurisdiction from the nature of the thing and the purpose of the jurisdiction." (f)

DCCCCLXXII. A State, however, lies under no obligation, and it is not within its moral competence, to punish a person happening to be resident within its limits, but who is not its subject, and who is charged with having committed a

---

(b) Fœlix, ii. titre ix.

Story, chapter xvi., on Penal Laws and Offences.

Essay on Foreign Jurisdiction and the Extradition of Criminals, by the Right Hon. Sir G. C. Lewis, 1859.

(c) Savigny, viii., is, however, of a contrary opinion.

(d) Vide ante, vol i.

(e) Fœlix, t. ix. ch. ii. and ch. iv., treats of both these questions.

(f) Warrender v. Warrender, 9 Bligh, 125; 2 Clark & Fin. 520—557.

crime, out of its jurisdiction, against the subject of a third State.   Jurists, however, are not agreed upon this point; and many contend that a *delictum*, an offence against Natural Law, is, wherever it has been committed, punishable everywhere.   Some are of opinion that the State in which the criminal is, ought to punish him if the State in which he committed the crime made a request to this effect, but not if it be made by the injured person.   Others think that the criminal ought to be surrendered ; others, that he ought to be expelled from the State.

DCCCCLXXIII. It is, however, within the moral competence, and, indeed, obligatory upon a State, to punish all crimes committed within its limits, not only upon one of its own subjects, but upon any person commorant within its dominions. Nor can it make any difference in principle whether the injured person happen to be or not to be within the dominions at the time when the injury is inflicted.   For instance, if a forgery be committed within the realm to the injury of an absent stranger, he is not the less on account of his absence entitled to insist upon criminal proceedings being taken against the forger. These principles are generally maintained by international jurists and writers on Public and Criminal Law, and are incorporated into the texts of many modern codes.   It is a subject of legitimate surprise to find writers of this class maintaining the proposition (*g*) that a State is not obliged to cause or allow a criminal to be prosecuted, if both the offender and the offended are merely commorant within its limits, and are not subjects. Such commorant persons, however, certainly owe a temporary allegiance to the State, and are, therefore, independently of any question of maintaining public order, entitled to a temporary protection, both in civil and criminal matters, or in those which partake of the character of both, such as cases of civil damages demanded for criminal offences.

(*g*) *Fœlix*, s. 573.

DCCCCLXXIV. The general rule, Fælix remarks, adopted by the positive legislation of States on this subject, which is one of Public Law, is to permit the criminal prosecution of a foreigner on account of crimes committed in another State only in those cases in which either the State in which the prosecution is to be carried on has been in its collective capacity injured by the crime, or in which the crime has been of the gravest kind (*de la plus haute gravité*). (*h*) The effect of this rule is to make the Criminal Law of a State a *personal* (*i*) *statute* to its subjects, travelling with them, and inseparably attached to them, wherever they happen to be: and such is the doctrine of Paul Voet (*k*) and others. It was the opinion of Bartolus (*l*) that *if*, and *when*, a State did take cognizance of crimes committed by foreigners in a foreign State, it must proceed according to the Criminal Law of that State—"Ut possit contra eum procedi et puniri *secundum statuta suæ civitatis;*" a proposition sufficiently impracticable, it should seem, to prove the wisdom and justice of abstaining altogether from such experiments.

DCCCCLXXV. According to the French Law (*m*) contained in the 5th, 6th, and 7th articles of their Criminal Code, *every Frenchman* guilty of a crime against the safety of the State, of forging the public seal of the State, national papers or bank notes, may be punished by the Criminal Law of France in France; so may foreigners, authors of or accomplices in their offences, if they are arrested in France, or if the French government has got possession of them by *extradition.* So much for offences against the State; as to offences against the individual, every Frenchman who has been guilty of a crime *against another Frenchman,* in a foreign State, is

---

(*h*) Sec. 574.

(*i*) *Vide ante,* p. 236.

(*k*) *De Stat.* s. 4, ch. ii. n. 6.

Story, s. 625.

(*l*) *Vide ante,* p. 241, n. 47.

(*m*) *Fælix,* s. 550.

punishable in France, if he has not been punished abroad, at the instance of the injured person. In Belgium this law prevails, with the sensible addition that the family of the injured party, who may of course be murdered, may prosecute.

DCCCCLXXVI. It is almost a necessary corollary, from what has been said, that the effect of a criminal sentence does not extend beyond the limits of the State in which it has been pronounced. Such is the better, if not the unanimous, opinion of jurists. (*n*)

Thus a person declared infamous in his own country, is infamous *de facto*, but not *de jure*, in another State. The banished man has a refuge in a State which takes no note of the sentence of exile. The confiscation of his goods in that State does not affect his property in another. To recognize this sentence as affecting either his honour or his fortune would be to inflict, as Martens observes, a second penal sentence on him. (*o*)

DCCCCLXXVII. The three preceding paragraphs have been a digression into Public from International Law; for to the former category belongs the jurisprudence and practice of States with respect to their own subjects abroad.

DCCCCLXXVIII. The general principle of English Criminal Law is strictly territorial and local ; even in the case

---

(*n*) See vol. ii. p. 483, Appendix ii., for remarks and cases on the refusal of Great Britain and the United States of North America to take cognizance of frauds upon foreign revenue laws.

(*o*) " Par une suite de ces mêmes principes, l'effet d'une sentence criminelle ne s'étend pas, hors des limites du territoire, sur la personne ou sur les biens de celui qui a été condamné ; tellement que celui qui a été déclaré infâme chez nous n'encourt chez l'étranger qu'une infamie de fait, non de droit ; que le bannissement décrété dans un pays n'empêche aucun autre pays de tolérer le banni, et que la confiscation des biens prononcée dans un pays n'emporte pas celle des biens situés dans un autre : ce serait donc punir de nouveau le coupable que de le priver dans un autre pays de son honneur ou de ses biens, ou de la bannir après lui avoir accordé le séjour ; ce qui toutefois exigerait une nouvelle procédure." *Martens*, s. 104.

of its own subjects English Common Law takes no cognizance of crimes abroad ; there are, however, certain very important exceptions introduced by Statute Law.

In very few instances, however, does the English Criminal Law (*p*) extend its jurisdiction generally over every class of British subjects in every part of the world, (*q*) viz., the offences of bigamy, treason, domicile, (*r*) and slave-holding. (*s*)

As to crimes committed by a particular class of her subjects abroad, England has recently enacted as follows : (*t*)

"All offences against property or person committed in or at any place either ashore or afloat out of Her Majesty's dominions by any master, seaman, or apprentice, who at the time when the offence is committed is or within three months previously has been employed in any British ship, shall be deemed to be offences of the same nature respectively, and be liable to the same punishments respectively, and be enquired

---

(*p*) The cases have been very few ; and Sir G. Lewis, p. 22, infers therefrom that the preventive effect of the statutes, certainly of H. 8, has been inconsiderable.

Under 33 H. 8, c. 23 (1541):

Governor Wall's case (1802), 28 *State Trials*, 51.

Rex v. *Depardo* (1807), *Russell & Ryan's Rep.* 134.

Rex v. *Sawyer* (1815), *ib.* 294.

Under 9 G. 4, c. 31 (1829):

Rex v. *Helsham*, 4 *Carrington & Payne's Rep.* 394 (1830).

Rex v. *Mattos* (1836), 7 *Carrington & Payne's Rep.* 458.

Regina v. *Azzopardi* (1843), 2 *Moody's Crown Cases*, 288.

Bernard's Case (April, 1858).

Under 18 & 19 Vict. c. 91, s. 21 :

Regina v. *Lopez, Regina* v. *Christian Sattler*, 7 *Cox's Criminal Cases*, 31.

(*q*) See Appendix for these Statutes.

(*r*) 9 G. 4, c. 31, s. 22.

(*s*) 33 H. 8. 20 ; 9 G. 4, c. 31, ss. 7, 8 ; and 6 & 7 Vict. c. 98.

(*t*) See also 6 & 7 Vict. c. 94, "*An Act to remove doubts as to the exercise of power and jurisdiction of Her Majesty within divers countries and places out of Her Majesty's dominions, and to render the same more effectual.*"

of, heard, tried, determined, and adjudged in the same manner, and by the same Courts, and in the same places, as if such offences had been committed within the jurisdiction of the Admiralty of England; and the costs and expences of the prosecution of any such offence may be directed to be paid as in the case of costs and expences of prosecutions for offences committed within the jurisdiction." (*u*)

And with respect to crimes committed by a British subject in a foreign port, or by a foreign subject on board a British ship on the high seas, England has recently enacted as follows :

" If any person, being a British subject, charged with having committed any crime or offence on board any British ship on the high seas, or in any foreign port or harbour, or of any person, not being a British subject, charged with having committed any crime or offence on board any British ship on the high seas, is found within the jurisdiction of any court of justice in Her Majesty's dominions, which would have had cognizance of such crime or offence if committed within the limits of its ordinary jurisdiction, such court shall have jurisdiction to hear and try the case as if such crime or offence had been committed within such limits." (*x*)

CCCCCLXXIX. The doctrine of the English Law as to foreign penal Law has been often and most distinctly laid down by English Courts of Justice. The opinion of Lord C. J. De Grey (*y*) that " crimes are in their nature local, and the jurisdiction of crimes is local," has been in substance repeated by most eminent judges; (*z*) by none with greater authority and clearness than Lord Brougham in the passage already cited—" the *lex loci* must needs govern all criminal jurisdiction from the nature of the theory and the purpose of the jurisdiction."

(*u*) 17 & 18 Vict. c. 104, s. 267 (*Merchant Shipping Act*).

(*x*) 18 & 19 Vict. c. 91, s. 21 (*Merchant Shipping Act Amendment*).

(*y*) *Verest* v. *Verest*, 2 *W. Blackstone's Rep.* 1058.

(*z*) *Folliott* v. *Ogden*, 1 *H. Blackstone's Rep.* 135, Lord Loughborough.

DCCCCLXXX. To return to the proper subject of this chapter, with respect to the criminal prosecution of foreigners in England, it is remarkable that England, conducting all trials of this kind through the intervention of a jury, has endeavoured to secure the foreigner from suffering injustice from this peculiar institution.

DCCCCLXXXI. England has, for a very long time, allowed to aliens the privilege in civil as well as criminal cases, of challenging the array, on the ground that the sheriff has not returned a jury *de medietate linguæ*, (a) that is, a jury one half of which consisted of aliens, supposing so many to be found in the place ; and this privilege is still preserved by the express enactment of a recent statute, (b) in favour of persons indicted for felony or misdemeanor ; which provides that, on the prayer of every alien so indicted or impeached, the sheriff or other proper minister shall, by command of the court, return for one half of the jury a competent number of aliens, if so many there be in the town or place where the trial is had ; and if not, then so many aliens as shall be found in the same town or place, if any ; and that no such alien juror shall be liable to be challenged for want of freehold or other qualification required by that act ; but that every such alien may be challenged for any other cause. (c)

DCCCCLXXXII. In England it has been decided that a foreigner charged in England with a crime committed there cannot successfully urge in his defence that he did not know he was doing wrong, though it may be a matter to be considered in mitigation of punishment. (d)

Ogden v. *Folliott*, 3 *Durnford & East's Rep.*733, 4, Mr. Justice Buller.

Wolff v. *Oxholm*, 6 *Maule & Selwyn's Rep.* 99, Lord Ellenborough.

(a) Cf. Meyer, *Institutions Judiciares*, t. ii. ch. 13—*Du Jury de medietate linguæ*.

Ib. t. iii. ch. 16, *Juge's consuls.*

(b) 6 G. 4, c. 50, s. 47.

(c) *Stephen's Comm.* vol. iv. p. 423.

(d) *Rex.* v. *Esop*, 7 *Carrington & Payne's Rep.* 456.

DCCCCLXXXIII. It has been also ruled by an English Court that a foreigner sojourning in England cannot decline to produce documents, or to give evidence in an English Court of Justice on the ground that he would by so doing (e) expose himself to a criminal prosecution in his own country, though in England no such consequence would follow. This decision, therefore, was founded on the principle that the English Courts paid no regard to the penal laws of a foreign state.

DCCCCLXXXIV. The law and practice of England are in accordance with the law of the United States of North America upon this subject. (f) "It is conceded" (C. J. Marshall says) "that the legislation of every country is territorial, that beyond its own territory it can only affect its own subjects or citizens. It is not easy to conceive a power to execute a municipal law, or to enforce obedience to that law, without the circle in which that law operates. A power to seize for the infraction of a law is derived from the sovereign, and must be exercised, it would seem, within those limits which circum-scribe the sovereign power. The rights of war, may be exercised on the high seas, because war is carried on upon the high seas; but the pacific rights of sovereignty must be exercised within the territory of the sovereign.

"If these propositions be true, a seizure of a person not a subject, or of a vessel not belonging to a subject, made on the high seas for the breach of a municipal regulation, is an act which the sovereign cannot authorize. The person who makes this seizure, then, makes it on a pretext which, if true, will not justify the act, and is a marine trespasser. To a majority of the court it seems to follow, that such a seizure is totally invalid; that the possession, acquired by this unlawful act, is his own possession, not that of the sovereign; and that such

---

(e) *The King of the Two Sicilies* v. *Willcox*, 1 *Simons N. R.* 329; V. C. Cranworth. *Cf. the North American Judgment Scovilla* v. *Caufield*, 14 *Johnson's Rep.* 338; cited *Story*, s. 621.

(f) *Story*, c. xvi. *Penal Laws and Offences.*

possession confers no jurisdiction on the court of the country to which the captor belongs." (*g*)

The same learned judge laid down concisely the proposition of law in another case in these words : " The courts of no country execute the penal laws of another." (*h*)

DCCCCLXXXV. This principle of confining criminal law within local and territorial limits, though on the whole sound and wise, is not free from many disadvantages. They have been and are principally conspicuous in the cases of border (*i*) population, and of crimes committed on board of foreign merchant vessels on the high seas.

It has often happened of late years that foreign vessels, on board of which, while on the high seas, some of the crew have been maimed or killed, have come into English ports. The author of the crime, perhaps the victim of it also, are on board the vessel when she arrives in the English port ; in many cases the victim is placed in an English hospital ; (*k*) witnesses of the crime are there : the criminal law is probably in most of these cases the same ; but even if this were otherwise it would be for the interest of every member of the commonwealth of states to assent to a modification, in such instances as these, of the principles of International Law, and to concede by special conventions a jurisdiction over the criminal to the state in whose port the vessel arrived.

It would be in most cases not a substitution of a foreign for a domestic jurisdiction, but the adoption of a foreign juris-

---

(*g*) *Rose* v. *Himely*, 4 *Cranch's* (*Amer.*) *Rep.* 279.

(*h*) *The Antelope*, 10 *Wheaton's Rep.* 66, 123.

(*i*) See this point among others forcibly put by Sir G. Lewis, pp. 30—35, and a striking illustration cited from *Villefort des Crimes et des Delits commis l'Etranger.*

(*k*) " Between the 1st of June, 1857, and the 1st of June, 1858, there were admitted into the Northern Hospital at Liverpool upwards of 150 patients, whose sufferings, in every single case, were owing to maltreatment at the hands of their officers." *The Times*, March 21, 1859, which contains a well-written article on the subject.

diction in lieu of none—in lieu of allowing an atrocious criminal to escape altogether the punishment due to his barbarity.

At present there is a practical impunity accorded to savage and brutal men, which encourages them in the commission of acts of cruelty upon the high seas at which human nature shudders ; and the true end of International law—the welfare and safety of individuals as members of states—is sacrificed to an over-scrupulous respect for a general principle, which has ceased in this particular instance to be a means of maintaining that end.

GENERAL APPENDIX.

GENERAL APPENDIX I.

In this Appendix the following Statutes to which reference has been made in the course of this volume, are printed at length:—

No. 1. An Act to amend the laws relating to aliens,—7 & 8 Vict. c. 66.

No. 2. An Act for the more effectual suppressing of the slave trade,—6 & 7 Vict. c. 98.

No. 3. An Act to remove doubts as to the exercise of power and jurisdiction by her Majesty, within divers countries and places out of her Majesty's dominions, and to render the same more effectual,—6 & 7 Vict. c. 94.

No. 4. An Act to provide for taking evidence in her Majesty's dominions in relation to civil and commercial matters pending before foreign tribunals,—19 & 20 Vict. c. 93.

No. 5. An Act to enable persons to establish legitimacy and the validity of marriages, and the right to be deemed natural-born subjects,—21 & 22 Vict. c. 93.

7 & 8 VICTORIA, Cap. 66.

An Act to amend the laws relating to Aliens.

WHEREAS it is expedient that the laws now in force affecting aliens should be amended, and that her Majesty should be enabled to grant to aliens the rights and capacities of British subjects, under such regulations and with such restrictions and exceptions as are herein-after provided. And whereas an Act of Parliament was made and passed in the twelfth year of the reign of his late Majesty king William the Third, intituled an Act for the further limitation of the Crown, and better securing of the rights and liberties of the subject; and another Act of Parliament was made and passed in the first year of the reign of his late Majesty king George the First, intituled an Act to explain an Act made in the twelfth year of the reign of king William the Third, intituled an Act for the further limitation of the Crown, and better securing the rights and liberties of the subject; and another Act of Parliament was made and passed in the fourteenth year of the reign of his late Majesty king George the Third, intituled an Act to prevent certain inconveniences that may happen by bills of naturalization. Be it therefore euacted by the Queen's most Excellent Majesty, by and with the advice and consent of the Lords Spiritual and Temporal, and Commons, in this present Parliament assembled, and by the authority of the same, that such parts of the said recited Acts of Parliament as are inconsistent with the provisions of this Act shall be repealed.

II. And be it enacted, That so much of the said Act of the first year of the reign of king George the First as provides, that no person shall hereafter be naturalised unless in the bill exhibited for that purpose there shall be a clause or particular words inserted to declare that such person shall not thereby be enabled to be of the Privy Council, or a member of either House of Parliament, or to take any office either civil or military, or to have any grant of lands, tenements, or hereditaments from the Crown to himself or any other person in trust for him, and that no bill of naturalisation shall hereafter be received in either House of Parliament unless such clause or words be first inserted, be repealed.

III. And be it enacted, That every person now born, or here-after to be born, out of her Majesty's dominions, of a mother being a natural-born subject of the United Kingdom, shall be capable of taking to him, his heirs, executors, or administrators, any estate, real or personal, by devise or purchase, or inheritance of succession.

IV. And be it enacted, That from and after the passing of this Act every alien, being the subject of a friendly state, shall and may take and hold, by purchase, gift, bequest, representation, or otherwise, every species of personal property, except chattels real, as fully and effectually to all intents and purposes, and with the same rights, remedies, exemptions, privileges, and capacities, as if he were a natural-born subject of the United Kingdom.

V. And be it enacted, That every alien now residing in, or who shall hereafter come to reside in, any part of the United Kingdom, and being the subject of a friendly state, may, by grant, lease, demise, assignment, bequest, representation, or otherwise, take and hold any lands, houses, or other tenements, for the purpose of residence or of occupation by him or her, or his or her servants, or for the purpose of any business, trade, or manufacture, for any term of years not exceeding twenty-one years, as fully and effec-tually to all intents and purposes, and with the same rights, remedies, exemptions, and privileges, except the right to vote at elections for Members of Parliament, as if he were a natural-born subject of the United Kingdom.

VI. And be it enacted, That upon obtaining the certificate and taking the oath herein-after prescribed every alien now residing in, or who shall hereafter come to reside in, any part of Great Britain or Ireland with intent to settle therein, shall enjoy all the rights and capacities which a natural-born subject of the United Kingdom can enjoy or transmit, except that such alien shall not be capable of becoming of her Majesty's Privy Council, nor a Member of either House of Parliament, nor of enjoying such other rights and capacities, if any, as shall be specially excepted in and by the certificate to be granted in manner herein-after mentioned.

VII. And be it enacted, That it shall be lawful for any such alien as aforesaid to present to one of her Majesty's principal Secretaries of State a memorial, stating the age, profession, trade, or other occupation of the memorialist, and the duration of his residence in Great Britain or Ireland, and all other the grounds on which he seeks to obtain any of the rights and capacities of a natural-born British subject, and praying the said Secretary of State to grant to the memorialist the certificate herein-after mentioned.

VIII. And be it enacted, That every such memorial shall be considered by the said Secretary of State, who shall inquire into the circumstances of each case, and receive all such evidence as shall be offered, by affidavit or otherwise, as he may deem necessary or proper for proving the truth of the allegations contained in such memorial ; and that the said Secretary of State, if he shall so think fit, may issue a certificate, reciting such of the contents of the memorial as he shall consider to be true and material, and granting to the memorialist (upon his taking the oath herein-after prescribed) all the rights and capacities of a natural-born British subject, except the capacity of being a Member of the Privy Council or a Member of either House of Parliament, and except the rights and capacities (if any) specially excepted in and by such certificate.

IX. And be it enacted, That such certificate shall be enrolled for safe custody as of record in her Majesty's High Court of Chancery, and may be inspected, and copies thereof taken, under such regulations as the Lord High Chancellor shall direct.

X. And be it enacted, That, within sixty days from the day of the date of such certificate, every memorialist to whom rights and capacities shall be granted by such certificate shall take and subscribe the following oath ; (that is to say,)

" I A.B. do sincerely promise and swear, that I will be faithful and bear true allegiance to her Majesty Queen Victoria, and will defend her to the utmost of my power against all conspiracies and attempts whatever which may be made against her person, crown, or dignity; and I will do my utmost endeavour to disclose and make known to her Majesty, her heirs and successors, all treasons and traitorous conspiracies which may be formed against her or them; and I do faithfully promise to maintain, support, and defend to the utmost of my power the succession of the Crown, which succession, by an Act intituled ' An Act for the further

Limitation of the Crown, and better securing the Rights and
Liberties of the Subject,' is and stands limited to the Princess
Sophia Electress of Hanover, and the heirs of her body, being
Protestants, hereby utterly renouncing and abjuring any obe-
dience or allegiance unto any other person claiming or pretending
a right to the Crown of this realm.   So help me GOD."
Which oath shall be taken and subscribed by such memorialist,
and shall be duly administered to him or her, before any of her
Majesty's judges of the Court of Queen's Bench or Court of
Common Pleas or Court of Exchequer, or before any master or
master extraordinary in Chancery ; and that the judge or master
or master extraordinary in Chancery, whether in England or in
Ireland, before whom such oath may be administered, shall grant
to the memorialist a certificate of his or her having taken and
subscribed such oath accordingly ; and such certificate shall be
signed by the judge, master or master extraordinary in Chancery,
before whom such oath shall be administered.

XI. And be it enacted, That the several proceedings hereby
authorised to be taken for obtaining such certificate as aforesaid
shall be regulated in such manner as the Secretary of State shall
from time to time direct.

XII. And be it enacted, That the fees payable in respect of the
several proceedings hereby authorised shall be fixed and regulated
by the commissioners of her Majesty's Treasury.

XIII. And be it enacted, That all persons who shall have been
naturalized before the passing of this Act, and who shall have
resided in the United Kingdom during five successive years, shall
be deemed entitled to and shall enjoy all such rights and capacities
of British subjects as may be conferred on aliens by the provisions
of this Act.

XIV. Provided always, and be it enacted, That nothing in this
Act shall prejudice, or be construed to prejudice, any rights or
interests in law or in equity, whether vested or contingent, under
any will, deed, or settlement executed by any natural-born subject
of Great Britain or Ireland before the passing of this Act, or
under any descent or representation from or under any such
natural-born subject who shall have died before the passing of
this Act.

XV. And be it enacted, That nothing herein contained shall
be construed so as to take away or diminish any right, privilege,
or capacity heretofore lawfully possessed by or belonging to aliens
residing in Great Britain or Ireland, so far as relates to the possession or enjoyment of any real or personal property, but that all
such rights shall continue to be enjoyed by such aliens in as full
and ample a manner as such rights were enjoyed before the
passing of this Act.

XVI. And be it enacted, That any woman married or who
shall be married to a natural-born subject or person naturalised

shall be deemed and taken to be herself naturalized, and have all the rights and privileges of a natural-born subject.

XVII. And be it enacted, That this Act may be amended or repealed by any Act to be passed in the present session of Parliament.

---

6 & 7 VICTORIA, Cap. 98.

An Act for the more effectual Suppression of the Slave Trade.

WHEREAS an Act was passed in the fifth year of the reign of King George the Fourth, intituled " An Act to amend and consolidate the Laws relating to the Abolition of the Slave Trade," whereby it is enacted (among other things), that it shall not be lawful (except in such special cases as are herein-after mentioned) for any persons to deal or trade in, purchase, sell, barter, or transfer, or to contract for the dealing or trading in, purchase, sale, barter, or transfer of slaves or persons intended to be dealt with as slaves ; or to carry away or remove, or to contract for the carrying away or removing of slaves or other persons as or in order to their being dealt with as slaves ; or to import or bring, or to contract for the importing or bringing, into any place whatsoever, slaves or other persons as or in order to their being dealt with as slaves ; or to ship, tranship, embark, receive, detain, or confine on board, or to contract for the shipping, transhipping, embarking, receiving, detaining, or confining on board of any ship, vessel, or boat, slaves or other persons for the purpose of their being carried away or removed as or in order to their being dealt with as slaves ; or to ship, tranship, embark, receive, detain, or confine on board, or to contract for the shipping, transhipping, embarking, receiving, detaining, or confining on board of any ship, vessel, or boat, slaves or other persons for the purpose of their being imported or brought into any place whatsoever as or in order to their being dealt with as slaves ; or to fit out, man, navigate, equip, despatch, use, employ, let, or take to freight or on hire, or to contract for the fitting out, manning, navigating, equipping, despatching, using, employing, letting, or taking to freight or on hire, any ship, vessel, or boat, in order to accomplish any of the objects or the contracts in relation to the objects which objects and contracts have herein-before been declared unlawful ; or to lend or advance, or become security for the loan or advance, or to contract for the lending or advancing, or becoming security for the loan or advance of money, goods, or effects employed or to be employed in accomplishing any of the objects or the contracts in relation to the objects which objects and contracts have herein-before been declared unlawful ; or to become guarantee or security, or to contract for the becoming guarantee or security, for agents employed or to be employed in accomplishing any of the

A A A

objects or the contracts in relation to the objects which objects and
contracts have herein-before been declared unlawful; or in any
other manner to engage or to contract to engage, directly or
indirectly, therein as a partner, agent, or otherwise; or to ship,
tranship, lade, receive, or put on board, or to contract for the
shipping, transhipping, lading, receiving, or putting on board of any
ship, vessel, or boat, money, goods, or effects to be employed in
accomplishing any of the objects or the contracts in relation to
the objects which objects and contracts have herein-before been
declared unlawful; or to take the charge or command, or to
navigate or enter and embark on board, or to contract for the
taking the charge or command or for the navigating or entering
and embarking on board, of any ship, vessel, or boat, as captain,
master, mate, petty officer, surgeon, supercargo, seaman, marine,
or servant, or in any other capacity, knowing that such ship,
vessel, or boat is actually employed, or is in the same voyage, or
upon the same occasion, in respect of which they shall so take the
charge or command, or navigate or enter and embark, or contract
so to do as aforesaid, intended to be employed in accomplishing
any of the objects or the contracts in relation to the objects which
objects and contracts have herein-before been declared unlawful;
or to insure or to contract for the insuring of any slaves, or any
property, or other subject matter engaged or employed or intended
to be engaged or employed in accomplishing any of the objects
or the contracts in relation to the objects which objects and
contracts have herein-before been declared unlawful: And
whereas it is expedient that from and after the commencement
of this Act the provisions of the said Act herein-before recited
shall be deemed to apply to, and extend to render unlawful,
and to prohibit the several acts, matters, and things therein
mentioned when committed by British subjects in foreign countries
and settlements not belonging to the British Crown, in like manner and to all intents and purposes as if the same were done
or committed by such persons within the British dominions,
colonies, or settlements; and it is expedient that further provisions should be made for the more effectual suppression of the
Slave Trade, and of certain practices tending to promote and
encourage it: Be it therefore enacted by the Queen's most
Excellent Majesty, by and with the advice and consent of the
Lords Spiritual and Temporal, and Commons, in this present
Parliament assembled, and by the authority of the same, That all
the provisions of the said consolidated Slave Trade Act herein-
before recited and' of this present Act shall, from and after the
coming into operation of this Act, be deemed to extend and apply
to British subjects wheresoever residing or being, and whether
within the dominions of the British Crown or of any foreign
country; and all the several matters and things prohibited by
the said consolidated Slave Trade Act or by this present Act,

when committed by British subjects, whether within the dominions of the British Crown, or in any foreign country, except only as herein-after excepted, shall be deemed and taken to be offences committed against the said several Acts respectively, and shall be dealt with and punished accordingly : Provided, nevertheless, that nothing herein contained shall repeal or alter any of the provisons of the said Act.

II. And be it declared and enacted, That all persons holden in servitude as pledges for debt, and commonly called " Pawns," or by whatsoever other name they may be called or known, shall, for the purposes of the said consolidated Slave Trade Act, and of an Act passed in the third and fourth years of the reign of King William the Fourth, intituled " An Act for the Abolition of Slavery throughout the British Colonies, for promoting the Industry of the manumitted Slaves, and for compensating the Persons hitherto entitled to the services of such Slaves," and of this present Act, be deemed and construed to be slaves or persons intended to be dealt with as slaves.

III. And whereas it is expedient to make further provision for the trial and punishment of offenders : Be it enacted, That all offences against the consolidated Slave Trade Act or against this present Act, which shall be committed by British subjects out of this United Kingdom, whether within the dominions of the British Crown or in any foreign country, or by foreigners within the British dominions, except in places where the British admiral has jurisdiction, may be taken cognizance of, inquired into, tried, and determined according to the provisions of an Act passed in the ninth year of King George the Fourth, intituled " An Act for consolidating and amending the Statutes in England relative to Offences against the Person."

IV. And whereas the provisions heretofore made for the hearing and determining in England of offences committed against the Acts for the abolition of the slave trade in places out of this United Kingdom have been found ineffectual, by reason of the difficulty of proving in this kingdom matters and things done elsewhere : Be it enacted, That in all cases of indictment or information laid or exhibited in the Court of Queen's Bench for misdemeanors or offences committed against the said Acts or against this present Act in any places out of the United Kingdom, and within any British colony, settlement, plantation, or territory, it shall and may be lawful for her Majesty's said court, upon motion to be made on behalf of the prosecutor or defendant, to award a writ or writs of Mandamus requiring the Chief Justice or other chief judicial officer in such colony, settlement, plantation, or territory, who are hereby respectively authorised and required accordingly to hold a court, with all convenient speed, for the examination of witnesses and receiving other proofs concerning the matters charged in such indictments or informations respectively, and in the meantime to cause public notice to be given of the holding of such courts, and summonses to be issued for the attendances of witnesses and of agents and counsel of the parties; and such examination as aforesaid shall be then and there openly and publicly taken in the said court *viva voce*, upon the respective oaths of the persons examined, and be reduced to writing, and be sent to her Majesty in her Court of Queen's Bench (in manner set forth and prescribed in an Act passed in the thirteenth year of George the Third, Chapter Sixty-three, intituled "An Act for establishing certain Regulations for the better Management of the affairs of the East India Company as well in India as in Europe); and such depositions, being duly taken and returned according to the true intent and meaning of this Act, shall be allowed and read, and shall be deemed as good and competent evidence as if such witnesses had been present and sworn, and examined *viva voce* at any trial for such misdemeanors and offences as aforesaid in her Majesty's said Court of Queen's Bench, any law or usage to the contrary thereof notwithstanding.

V. Provided always, and be it enacted, That in all the cases in which the holding or taking of slaves shall not be prohibited by this or any other Act of Parliament, it shall be lawful to sell or transfer such slaves, anything in this or any other Act contained notwithstanding.

VI. Provided always, and be it enacted, That nothing in this Act contained shall be taken to subject to any forfeiture, punishment or penalty, any person for transferring or receiving any share in any Joint Stock Company established before the passing of this Act in respect of any slave or slaves in the possession of such Company before such time, or for selling any slave or slaves which were lawfully in his possession at the time of passing this Act, or which such person shall or may have become possessed of or entitled unto *bona fide* prior to such sale, by inheritance, devise, bequest, marriage, or otherwise by operation of law.

VII. And be it enacted, That this Act shall be deemed and taken to be in force and to have effect from and after the first day of November in the year One thousand eight hundred and forty-three, and not before.

---

6 & 7 VICTORIA, Cap. 94.

An Act to remove Doubts as to the Exercise of Power and Jurisdiction by her Majesty within divers Countries and Places out of her Majesty's dominions, and to render the same more effectual.

WHEREAS by treaty, capitulation, grant, usage, sufferance, and other lawful means her Majesty hath power and jurisdiction within divers countries and places out of her Majesty's dominions: And whereas doubts have arisen how far the exercise of such power and jurisdiction is controlled by and dependent on the laws and customs of this realm, and it is expedient that such doubts should be removed: Be it therefore enacted by the Queen's most Excellent Majesty, by and with the advice and consent of the Lords Spiritual and Temporal, and Commons, in this present Parliament assembled, and by the authority of the same, That it is and shall be lawful for her Majesty to hold, exercise, and enjoy any power or jurisdiction which her Majesty now hath or may at any time hereafter have within any country or place out of her Majesty's dominions, in the same and as ample a manner as if her Majesty had acquired such power or jurisdiction by the cession or conquest of territory.

II. And be it enacted, That every act, matter, and thing which may at any time be done, in pursuance of any such power or jurisdiction of her Majesty, in any country or place out of her Majesty's dominions, shall, in all courts ecclesiastical and temporal and elsewhere within her Majesty's dominions, be and be deemed and adjudged to be, in all cases and to all intents and purposes whatsoever, as valid and effectual as though the same had been done according to the local law then in force within such country or place.

III. And be it enacted, That if in any suit or other proceedings, whether civil or criminal, in any court ecclesiastical or temporal within her Majesty's dominions, any issue or question of law or of fact shall arise for the due determination whereof it shall, in the opinion of the judge or judges of such court, be necessary to produce evidence of the existence of any such power or jurisdiction as aforesaid, or of the extent thereof, it shall be lawful for the judge or judges of any such court, and he or they are hereby authorised, to transmit, under his or their hand and seal or hands and seals, to one of her Majesty's principal Secretaries of State, questions by him or them properly framed respecting such of the matters aforesaid as it may be necessary to ascertain in order to the due determination of any such question as aforesaid; and such Secretary of State is hereby empowered and required, within a reasonable time in that behalf, to cause proper and sufficient answers to be returned to all such questions, and to be directed to the said judge or judges, or their successors; and such answers shall, upon production thereof, be final and conclusive evidence, in such suit or other proceedings, of the several matters therein contained and required to be ascertained thereby.(a)

(a) See, on the construction of this Section and Statute, the case of *Hervey* v. *Fitzpatrick* (1854), *Kay's Rep.* 421, before *V. C. Wood.*

IV. And whereas it may in certain cases be expedient that crimes and offences committed within such countries or places as aforesaid should be inquired of, tried, determined, and punished within her Majesty's dominions; be it enacted, That it shall and may be lawful for any person having authority derived from her Majesty in that behalf, by warrant under his hand and seal, to cause any person charged with the commission of any crime or offence the cognizance whereof may at any time appertain to any judge, magistrate, or other officer of her Majesty within any such country or place as aforesaid, to be sent for trial to any British colony which her Majesty may by any order or orders in council from time to time appoint in that behalf; and upon the arrival of such person within such colony it shall and may be lawful for the Supreme Court exercising criminal jurisdiction within the same to cause such person to be kept in safe and proper custody, and, so soon as conveniently may be, to inquire of, try, and determine such crime or offence, and upon conviction of the person so charged as aforesaid to correct and punish him according to the laws in force in that behalf within such colony, in the same manner as if the said crime or offence had been committed within the jurisdiction of such Supreme Court: Provided always, that before any such person shall be sent for trial to any such colony as aforesaid it shall be lawful for him to tender for examination to the judge, magistrate, or other officer of her Majesty to whom the cognizance of the crime or offence with which he is charged may appertain, within the country or place where the same may be alleged to have been committed, any competent witness or witnesses, the evidence of whom he may deem material for his defence, and whom he may allege himself to be unable to produce at his trial in the said colony; and the said judge, magistrate, or other officer, shall thereupon proceed in the examination and cross-examination of such witness or witnesses in the same manner as though the same had been tendered at a trial before such judge, magistrate, or other officer, and shall cause the evidence so taken to be reduced into writing, and shall transmit a copy of such evidence to the Supreme Court before which the trial of such person is to take place, together with a certificate under his hand and seal of the correctness of such copy; and thereupon it shall be lawful for the said Supreme Court, and it is hereby required, to allow so much of the evidence so taken as aforesaid as would have been admissible according to the law and practice of the said Supreme Court, had the said witness or witnesses been produced and examined at the trial before the said court, to be read and received as legal evidence at such trial: Provided also, that if it shall be made to appear at such trial that the laws by which the person charged with any criminal act would have been tried had his trial taken place before a judge, magistrate, or other officer of her Majesty in the country or place in which such act may be alleged to have been committed, vary from or are inconsistent with the laws in force within such colony, in respect either of the criminality of the act charged, or of the nature or degree of the alleged crime or offence, or of the punishment to be awarded for the same, such Supreme Court is hereby empowered and required to admit and give effect to the laws by which such person would have been so tried as aforesaid, so far as but not further or otherwise than the same relate to the criminality of such act, or to the nature or degree of such crime or offence, or to the punishment thereof: Provided also, that nothing herein contained shall be construed to alter or repeal any law, statute, or usage by virtue of which any crime or offence committed out of her Majesty's dominions might, at the time of the passing of this Act, be inquired of, tried, determined, and punished within her Majesty's dominions, or any part thereof, but the same shall remain in full force and effect, any thing herein contained to the contrary notwithstanding.

V. And whereas it may likewise in certain cases be expedient that the sentences passed within such countries and places as aforesaid at the trial of crimes and offences within the same should be carried into effect within her Majesty's dominions; be it enacted, That if any offender shall have been sentenced to suffer death or imprisonment for or in respect of any crime or offence of which such offender shall have been lawfully convicted before any judge, magistrate, or other officer of her Majesty within any such country or place as aforesaid, it shall be lawful for any person having authority derived from her Majesty in that behalf, by warrant under his hand and seal, to cause such offender to be sent to any British colony which her Majesty may by any order or orders in council from time to time appoint in that behalf, in order that the sentence so passed upon such offender may be carried into effect within the same; and the magistrates, gaolers, and other officers to whom it may appertain to give effect to any sentence passed by the Supreme Court exercising criminal jurisdiction within such colony are hereby empowered and required to do all acts and things necessary to carry into effect the sentence so passed upon such offender, in the same manner as though the same had been passed by such Supreme Court.

VI. And be it enacted, That if any offender shall have been ordered or sentenced to be transported beyond the seas by any judge, magistrate, or other officer of her Majesty within any such country or place as aforesaid, or, having been adjudged to suffer death, shall have received her Majesty's most gracious pardon upon condition of transportation beyond the seas, it shall be lawful for any person having authority derived from her Majesty in that behalf to cause such offender to be sent to any place beyond seas to which convicts may at any time be lawfully transported from any part of her Majesty's dominions, and, if there shall be no convenient means of transporting such offender without bringing him to England, to cause such offender to be brought to England in order to be transported, and to be imprisoned in any place of confinement provided under the authority of any law or statute relating to the transportation of offenders convicted in England, until such offender shall be transported or shall become entitled to his liberty; and as soon as any such offender shall have arrived at the place to which he may be transported, or, if brought to England, shall have been there imprisoned as aforesaid, all the provisions, rules, regulations, authorities. powers, penalties, matters, and things concerning the safe custody, confinement, treatment, and transportation of any offender convicted in Great Britain shall extend and be construed to extend to such offender as fully and effectually, to all intents and purposes, as if such offender had been convicted and sentenced at any session of gaol delivery holden for any county in England.

VII. And be it enacted, That if any suit or action shall be brought in any court within her Majesty's dominions against any person or persons for any thing done in pursuance of any such power or jurisdiction of her Majesty as aforesaid or of this Act, then and in every such case such action or suit shall be commenced or prosecuted within six months after the fact committed, and not afterwards, except where the cause of action shall have arisen out of her Majesty's dominions, and then within six months after the plaintiff or plaintiffs and defendant or defendants shall have been within the jurisdiction of the court in which the same may be brought ; and the same and every such action or suit shall be brought in the county or place where the cause of action shall have arisen, and not elsewhere, except where the cause of action shall have arisen out of her Majesty's dominions ; and the defendant or defendants shall be entitled to the like notice, and shall have the like privilege of tendering amends to the plaintiff or plaintiffs, or their agent or attorney, as is provided in actions brought against any Justice of the Peace for acts done in the execution of his office by an Act passed in the twenty-fourth year of the reign of King George the Second, intituled "An Act for the rendering Justices of the Peace more safe in the Execution of their Office, and for indemnifying Constables and others acting in obedience to their Warrants ; " and the defendant or defendants in every such action or suit may plead the general issue, and give the special matter in evidence ; and if the matter or thing complained of shall appear to have been done under the authority and in execution of any such power or jurisdiction of her Majesty as aforesaid or of this Act, or if any such action or suit shall be brought after the time limited for bringing the same, or be brought and laid in any other county or place than the same ought to have been brought or laid in as aforesaid, then the jury shall find for the defendant or defendants; and if the plaintiff or plaintiffs shall become nonsuit, or discontinue any action after the defendant or defendants shall have appeared, or if a verdict shall pass against the plaintiff or plaintiffs, or if upon demurrer judgment shall be taken against the plaintiff or plaintiffs, the defendant or defendants shall and may recover treble costs, and have the like remedy for recovery thereof as any defendant or defendants hath or have in any cases of law.

VIII. And be it enacted, That from and after the First day of October in the year One thousand eight hundred and forty-four so much of an Act passed in the Sixth year of his late Majesty king George the Fourth, intituled "An Act to repeal certain Acts relating to the Governor and Company of Merchants of England trading to the Levant Seas, and the Duties payable to them; and to authorise the Transfer and Disposal of the Possessions and Property of the said Governor and Company for the Public Service," as provides, "that from and immediately after the Enrolment of any such Deed or Instrument as therein mentioned all such Rights and Duties of Jurisdiction and Authority over his Majesty's Subjects resorting to the Ports of the Levant, for the Purposes of Trade or otherwise, as were lawfully exercised and performed, or which the Letters Patent or Acts by the said Act recited, or any of them, authorised to be exercised and performed, by any Consul or other Officers appointed by the said Company, or which such Consuls or other Officers lawfully exercised and performed under and by virtue of any Power or Authority whatever, should, from and after the Enrolment of such Deed or Instrument as aforesaid, be and become vested in and should be exercised and performed by such Consuls and other Officers respectively as his Majesty might be pleased to appoint for the Protection of the Trade of His Majesty's Subjects in the Ports and Places respectively mentioned in the said Letters Patent and Acts, or any or either of them;" and also that from and after the passing of this Act an Act passed in the Parliament holden in the Sixth and Seventh years of his said late Majesty King William the Fourth, intituled "An Act to enable his Majesty to make Regulations for the better defining and establishing the Powers and Jurisdiction of His Majesty's Consuls in the Ottoman Empire," shall be and the same are hereby repealed, save as to any matter or thing theretofore done under the authority of the same respectively.

IX. And be it enacted, That this Act may be amended or repealed by any Act to be passed during this Session of Parliament.

19 & 20 VICTORIA, Cap. 113.

An Act to provide for taking Evidence in her Majesty's Dominions in relation to Civil and Commercial Matters pending before Foreign Tribunals.

WHEREAS it is expedient that facilities be afforded for taking evidence in her Majesty's dominions in relation to civil and commercial matters pending before foreign tribunals : Be it enacted by the Queen's most excellent Majesty, by and with the advice and consent of the Lords spiritual and temporal, and Commons, in this present Parliament assembled, and by the authority of the same, as follows :

I. Where, upon an application for this purpose, it is made to appear to any court or judge having authority under this Act that any court or tribunal of competent jurisdiction in a foreign country, before which any civil or commercial matter is pending, is desirous of obtaining the testimony in relation to such matter of any witness or witnesses within the jurisdiction of such first-mentioned court, or of the court to which such judge belongs, or of such judge, it shall be lawful for such court or judge to order the examination upon oath, upon interrogatories or otherwise, before any person or persons named in such order, of such witness or witnesses accordingly ; and it shall be lawful for the said court or judge, by the same order, or for such court or judge or any other judge having authority under this Act, by any subsequent order, to command the attendance of any person to be named in such order, for the purpose of being examined, or the production of any writings or other documents to be mentioned in such order, and to give all such directions as to the time, place, and manner of such examination, and all other matters connected therewith, as may appear reasonable and just ; and any such order may be enforced in like manner as an order made by such court or judge in a cause depending in such court or before such judge.

II. A certificate under the hand of the ambassador, minister, or other diplomatic agent of any foreign power, received as such by her Majesty, or in case there be no such diplomatic agent, then of the consul general or consul of any such foreign power at London, received and admitted as such by her Majesty, that any matter in relation to which an application is made under this Act is a civil or commercial matter pending before a court or tribunal in the country of which he is the diplomatic agent or consul having jurisdiction in the matter so pending, and that such court or tribunal is desirous of obtaining the testimony of the witness or witnesses to whom the application relates, shall be evidence of the matters so certified ; but where no such certificate is produced other evidence to that effect shall be admissible.

III. It shall be lawful for every person authorised to take the examination of witnesses by any order made in pursuance of this Act to take all such examinations upon the oath of the witnesses, or affirmation in cases where affirmation is allowed by law instead of oath, to be administered by the person so authorised; and if upon such oath or affirmation any person making the same wilfully and corruptly give any false evidence, every person so offending shall be deemed and taken to be guilty of perjury.

IV. Provided always, That every person whose attendance shall be so required shall be entitled to the like conduct money and payment for expenses and loss of time as upon attendance at a trial.

V. Provided also, That every person examined under any order made under this Act shall have the like right to refuse to answer questions tending to criminate himself, and other questions, which a witness in any cause pending in the court by which or by a judge whereof or before the judge by whom the order for examination was made would be entitled to; and that no person shall be compelled to produce under any such order as aforesaid any writing or other document that he would not be compellable to produce at a trial of such a cause.

VI. Her Majesty's superior courts of common law at Westminster and in Dublin respectively, the court of session in Scotland, and any supreme court in any of her Majesty's colonies or possessions abroad, and any judge of any such court, and every judge in any such colony or possession who by any order of her Majesty in council may be appointed for this purpose, shall respectively be courts and judges having authority under this Act: Provided, that the Lord Chancellor, with the assistance of two of the judges of the courts of common law at Westminster, shall frame such rules and orders as shall be necessary or proper for giving effect to the provisions of this Act, and regulating the procedure under the same.

---

21 & 22 VICTORIA, Cap. 93.

An Act to enable persons to establish Legitimacy and the Validity of Marriages, and the Right to be deemed Natural-born Subjects.

WHEREAS it is expedient to enable persons to establish their legitimacy, and the marriage of their parents and others from whom they may be descended, and also to enable persons to establish their right to be deemed natural-born subjects: Be it therefore enacted by the Queen's most excellent Majesty, by and with the advice and consent of the Lords spiritual and temporal, and Commons, in this present Parliament assembled, and by the authority of the same, as follows:

I. Any natural-born subject of the Queen, or any person whose right to be deemed a natural-born subject depends wholly or in part on his legitimacy or on the validity of a marriage, being domiciled in England or Ireland, or claiming any real or personal estate situate in England, may apply by petition to the court for divorce and matrimonial causes, praying the court for a decree declaring that the petitioner is the legitimate child of his parents, and that the marriage of his father and mother, or of his grandfather and grandmother, was a valid marriage, or for a decree declaring either of the matters aforesaid; and any such subject or person, being so domiciled or claiming as aforesaid, may in like manner apply to such court for a decree declaring that his marriage was or is a valid marriage, and such court shall have jurisdiction to hear and determine such application and to make such decree declaratory of the legitimacy or illegitimacy of such person, or of the validity or invalidity of such marriage, as to the court may seem just; and such decree, except as herein-after mentioned, shall be binding to all intents and purposes on her Majesty and on all persons whomsoever.

II. Any person, being so domiciled or claiming as aforesaid, may apply by petition to the said court for a decree declaratory of his right to be deemed a natural-born subject of her Majesty, and the said court shall have jurisdiction to hear and determine such application, and to make such decree thereon as to the court may seem just, and where such application as last aforesaid is made by the person making such application as herein mentioned for a decree declaring his legitimacy or the validity of a marriage, both applications may be included in the same petition ; and every decree made by the said court shall, except as hereinafter mentioned, be valid and binding to all intents and purposes upon her Majesty and all persons whomsoever.

III. Every petition under this Act shall be accompanied by such affidavit verifying the same, and of the absence of collusion, as the court may by any general rule direct.

IV. All the provisions of the Act of the last session, chapter 85, so far as the same may be applicable, and the powers and provisions therein contained in relation to the making and laying before Parliament of rules and regulations concerning the practice and procedure under that Act, and fixing the fees payable upon proceedings before the court, shall extend to applications and proceedings in the said court under this Act, as if the same had been authorised by the said Act of the last session.

V. In all proceedings under this Act the court shall have full power to award and enforce payment of costs to any persons cited, whether such persons shall or shall not oppose the declaration applied for, in case the said court shall deem it reasonable that such costs shall be paid.

VI. A copy of every petition under this Act, and of the affidavit accompanying the same, shall, one month at least previously to the presentation or filing of such petition, be delivered to her

Majesty's Attorney General, who shall be a respondent upon the hearing of such petition and upon every subsequent proceeding relating thereto.

VII. Where any application is made under this Act to the said court such person or persons (if any) besides the said Attorney General as the court shall think fit shall, subject to the rules made under this Act, *be cited to see proceedings* or otherwise summoned in such manner as the court shall direct, and may be permitted to become parties to the proceedings, and oppose the application.

VIII. The decree of the said court shall not in any case prejudice any person, unless such person has been cited or made a party to the proceedings or is the heir-at-law or next of kin, or other real or personal representative of or derives title under or through a person so cited or made a party ; nor shall such sentence or decree of the court prejudice any person if subsequently proved to have been obtained by fraud or collusion.

IX. Any person domiciled in Scotland, or claiming any heritable or moveable property situate in Scotland, may raise and insist, in an action of declarator before the court of session, for the purpose of having it found and declared that he is entitled to be deemed a natural-born subject of her Majesty ; and the said court shall have jurisdiction to hear and determine such action of declarator, in the same manner and to the same effect, and with the same power to award expenses, as they have in declarators of legitimacy and declarators of bastardy.

X. No proceeding to be had under this Act shall affect any final judgment or decree already pronounced or made by any court of competent jurisdiction.

XI. The said Act of the last session and this Act shall be construed together as one Act ; and this Act may be cited for all purposes as "The Legitimacy Declaration Act, 1858."

GENERAL APPENDIX II.

BELOW is printed at length the leading American decision upon the application of Personal and Real Statutes.

Saul v. *His Creditors.* (a)

APPEAL FROM THE COURT OF THE FIRST DISTRICT.

Marginal Note of Reporter.

Subsequent statutes do not repeal previous ones by containing different provisions. They must be contrary.

The jurisprudence of Spain makes a part of the law of Louisiana.

The rules in relation to real and personal statutes, apply also to unwritten laws or customs.

Where the personal statute of the domicil is in opposition to a real statute of situation, the real statute will prevail.

Contracts are governed by the laws of the country where they are made, but they cannot be enforced to the injury of a State whose aid is required to carry them into effect.

Nor where they are in opposition to the positive laws of that State.

In the conflict of laws where it is doubtful which should prevail, the court that decides should prefer the law of its own country to that of the stranger.

Personal statutes of the country where a contract is sought to be enforced, may sometimes control the personal statutes of the country where the contract was made.

The law relating to acquests and gains made during marriage, is a real, not a personal statute, and governs marriages made in other countries, where the parties reside in this, as to all property acquired after their removal.

But they yield to an express agreement made on entering into marriage in another country.

The contract of pledge of incorporeal things will not give a preference unless evidenced by an authentic act, or one duly

---

(a) 5 *Martin's Rep.* N. S. 569—608.

recorded at a time not suspicious. And this contract *sous seing prive*, though made long before insolvency, cannot be recorded at a time when the debtor would be incapable of giving a preference by any act of his.

Porter, J., delivered the judgment of the Court. The tableau of distribution filed by the syndics of the insolvent, was opposed in the court of the first instance ; and the opposition being sustained, an appeal has been taken to this court by the syndics, by the bank of the United States, the Bank of Orleans, and the Bank of Louisiana.

The claims admitted by the judge, *a quo*, and which are now contested there, are :—

1st. That of the children of the insolvent, who claim as privileged creditors, for the amount inherited by them from their deceased mother.

2nd. That of John Jacob Astor, of New York, who avers that he is a creditor of the insolvent for the sum of $64,000, and that he has a privilege on 751 shares of stock of the Bank of Orleans, which were pledged to him, and now make a part of the estate surrendered.

3rd. That of Alexander Brown and Sons, of Baltimore, who also assert a privilege on bank-stock, which they state was pledged to them by the insolvent for the security of a loan of $9,000 and upwards.

The different questions of law arising on these claims, have been argued with an ability worthy of their importance. Some of these questions are now presented for the first time for decision ; and those which have been already before the Court and acted on, on other occasions have been examined with so much care by the counsel, and have received such additional light from the laborious investigation bestowed on them, that they come upon our consideration with as much freshness, as if this was the only time our attention had been drawn to them.

We shall take them up in the order in which they have been already stated ; and first as to the claim of the insolvents' children.

From the facts admitted by the parties, which admission makes the statement on this appeal, it appears, that Saül and his wife intermarried in the State of Virginia, on the 6th of February, 1794, their domicil being then in that State ; that they remained there until the year 1804, when they removed to the now State of Louisiana ; that they fixed their residence here, and continued this residence up to the year 1819, when the wife died ; that after their removal from Virginia, and while living and having their domicil in this State, a large quantity of property was acquired, which at the death of the wife remained in the possession of her husband, the insolvent.

The children claim the one half of the property, as acquests and gains, made by their father and mother in this State. The appellants contend, that as the marriage took place in the State of Virginia, by whose laws no community of acquests and gains was permitted, the whole of the property acquired here belonged to the husband.

This statement of the matter at issue shows that the only question presented for our decision is one of laws; but it is one which grows out of the conflict of laws of different states. Our former experience had taught us, that questions of this kind are the most embarrassing and difficult of decision, that can occupy the attention of those who preside in courts of justice. The argument of this case has shown us, that the vast mass of learning which the research of counsel has furnished, leaves the subject as much enveloped in obscurity and doubt, as it would have appeared to our own understandings, had we been called on to decide, without the knowledge of what others had thought and written upon it.

Until the discussion of this cause, it was generally understood by the bar and the bench in this state, that the question now agitated was well understood in our jurisprudence; and that from the period married persons from other states moved into this, the property acquired became common, and was to be equally divided between them at the dissolution of the marriage. We have not, therefore, been insensible to the argument so strongly pressed on us, that the question being already settled by the decisions of the tribunal of last resort in the state, the subject ought not to be opened again, and that the most important interests of society require there should be a time when contested points of jurisprudence may be considered as at rest. But these considerations are not in *this* case of sufficient weight, to preclude a re-examination of the principles on which the doctrine already stated has been established. A sufficient period has not elapsed to enable it to derive much authority from the acquiescence of others. The decision of the court cannot be supposed to have influenced parties entering into the marriage contract, or greatly to have affected any important interests in society. It applied only to married persons emigrating from other states, whose exertions or industry cannot be supposed to have been much changed, by the anticipation of the property going in one direction or the other; whose habits were formed before they came here, and no doubt remained the same after their migration, as before. We shall, therefore, proceed to the examination of the question, as if the case was now presented for the first time, and, we trust, without any bias that might be supposed to exist on our minds, from the opinions we have already expressed.

The investigation we are about to make will be best conducted by first examining our own statutes.

The old civil code provided that every marriage contracted within this state superinduces of right partnership, or community of acquests and gains. (Civil Code, 336, art. 63.)

Our revised code repeats this provision and adds another : that a marriage contracted out of this state between persons who afterwards come to live here is also subject to the community of acquests, with respect to such property as is acquired after their arrival. (Code, 2370.)

If the acquests and gains, in respect to which the present suit exists, had been made under the dominion of the law last cited, there would be an end to any dispute about their distribution ; but the marriage of the insolvent and his wife was dissolved by the death of the latter, before that law was enacted.

It has been contended, that as the article first cited provides for a community of acquests and gains on all marriages contracted within the territory, it is an evidence the legislature did not intend there should be a community on marriages made *without ; inclusio unius, est exclusio alterius.*

It would be giving too much weight to the argument *contrario sensu,* to adopt this construction. If the subject were one on which there had existed no previous legislation, it would certainly be fair to contend, that as the law maker has affirmatively declared, particular cases not enumerated should produce certain effects, this affirmative included the negative, that other cases not enumerated should not produce these effects ; though even then, this reasoning, which is founded on presumption, might yield to other circumstances, by which that presumption could be repelled. But when there already exists positive legislation on the same subject matter, providing for the very case which it is presumed is excluded, the argument loses almost entirely its weight. The law must then be interpreted by a well-known rule of jurisprudence, that an intention to repeal laws can never be supposed ; that subsequent statutes do not abrogate former ones by containing *different* provisions on the same subject ; they must be *contrary* to produce such effect. This rule, which is true in relation to all laws, is more particularly applicable to our codes, which were only intended to lay down general principles, and provide for cases of the most common occurrence. If, then, the provisions in our code cannot be considered to have repealed the former law, no argument can be drawn from them as to the intention of the legislature to do so, or their opinion on this subject. It is more than probable their thoughts were not turned to a case which is not of frequent occurrence. If they had intended to act on it, as the matter was, to say the least, doubtful, they certainly would not have increased these doubts by leaving their will to be inferred from an affirmative regulation on the same subject, but in relation to a different state of things. We are bound to believe they would have legislated directly on it, and have positively declared, as they have since done, what the rule should be, when people married in another country, and removed into this.

It being clear, then, that our own statutes furnish no guide for the decision of this question, recourse must be had to the former laws of the country.

The positive regulations of Spain on this subject, are contained in two laws; one of the *Fuero Real*, and the other of the *Partidas.*

That part of the law of the *Partidas* which directly applies to the case before the Court, is in the following words :—" E dezimos, que el pleyto que ellos pusieron entre si, deve valer en la manera que se avinieron ante que casassen, o quando casaron ; e non deve ser embargado por la costumbre contraria de aquella tierra do fuesen a morar. Esso mismo seria, maguer ellos non pusiessen, pleyto entre si; ca la costumbre de aquella tierra do fizieron el casamiento, deve valer, quanto en las dotes, e en las arras, e en las ganancias que fizieron, e non la de aquel lugar do se cambiaron." Pt. 4, tit. ii. ley. 23.

" And we say, that the agreement they had made before or at the time of their marriage, ought to have its effect in the manner they may have stipulated, and that it will not be avoided by the custom of the place to which they may have removed. And so we say it would be, if they had not entered into any agreement; for the custom of the country where they contracted the marriage, ought to have its effect as it regards the dowry, the *arras,* and the gains they may have made; and not that of the place to which they may have removed."

Some verbal criticism has been exercised on this law. It is contended by one of the parties, that it only intended to provide for the gains made before the removal of the married couple; or, at all events, that the words used leave the sense doubtful. By the other, that it regulates all, whether made before or after they left the country in which the marriage took place. The expressions used, though not free from all ambiguity, as the appellants have argued, we think ought to receive the construction for which they contend. The law was so understood by the commentators of that day, and the preceding parts of it, compared with the clause in which the obscurity is said to exist, serve to support this interpretation.

If these provisions in the *Partidas* stood alone, they would admit of a more favourable construction in support of the ground assumed by the counsel for the syndics, than they can receive, when taken in connection with the law of the *Fuero Real,* which is in the following words :—

" Toda cosa que el marido y muger ganaren o compraren, estando de consuno, hayanlo ambos por medio, &c."—*Novissima Recop.* lib. 10, tit. 4, ley. 1.

" Every thing which the husband and wife may acquire while together, shall be equally divided between them."

The codes in which these laws are found, were composed under the authority of Ferdinand the Third, and his son Alphonso the wise, nearly about the same time. The *Fuero Real* was published in the year 1255. The *Partidas*, although completed in 1260, was not promulgated until nearly a century afterwards.

By the Spanish writers, the former is considered, with respect to the latter, what the Institutes of Justinian are to the Pandects; and it has been admitted, that they may mutually aid in the interpretation of each other.

We have then two statutes presented for construction, one of which, not in terms the most clear, directs that the custom of the country where parties contract marriage should regulate their rights, in respect to acquests and gains; and another which declares, that every thing that husband and wife may gain or purchase, shall be equally divided between them.

If the question, as to the true interpretation of these laws now arose for the first time, we should hesitate what construction to put on them. Either, taken singly, and according to the letter, goes the whole length for which each of the parties before us contends; but before examining them to ascertain what conclusion we should come to, if left to our judgment unaided by the opinions of others, it is proper we should endeavour to learn what construction was put on them in the country where they were made. On whatever side the weight of authority should be found to preponderate, we may certainly adopt it. They who have had these laws for nearly five hundred years before they passed to us, must, we feel, have more knowledge of the intention and meaning of their own legislation, than we, at this remote period of time, who have come to a knowledge of them but, as it were, of yesterday, can possibly possess.

Nothing can be more satisfactorily shown, than the opinion of the commentators on the statutes of Spain, in relation to this particular subject. From the time Gregorio Lopez published his work on the Partidas, in the year 1555, down to Febrero, in the year 1781, the writings of no jurist of that country have been produced to us, who treats of this matter, that does not declare that the law of the Partidas, already cited, must be limited to property acquired in the place where the marriage is contracted, and that it does not extend to acquisitions made in another country, to which the parties may have removed, where a different rule should prevail. In the long list of writers, who have been cited in support of this doctrine, are to be found some of the most illustrious of whom the middle ages could boast, James of Arena, Gulielmus de Cuneo, Dynus, Raynaldus, Jean Favre, Baldus, Alciat, and Ancharanus, Gregorio Lopez on the four

Partidas, tit. 11, law 24.; Matienzo Commentaria, lib. 5, tit. 9, nos. 73 & 74; Febrero, pt. 2, lib. 1, cap. 4, s. 2, no. 62.

Trying the question, therefore, by authority, no doubt can exist on which side it preponderates, in the country where the statute was passed. Admitting, therefore, for a moment, that the letter of the law of the Partidas was violated, by the construction given to it by the commentators; that violation acquiesced in for centuries, by lawyers, courts, and the sovereign authority of the country, makes as much a part of the law of Spain at this day, as if the statute had been modified by the power in the state, in whom the right of legislation was vested. In looking into the laws of any country, we stop at the threshold if we look no further than their statutes; and what we should see there would in most instances only tend to mislead. In every nation that has advanced a few steps beyond the first organization of political society, and that has made any progress in civilisation, a more extensive and equally important part of the rules which govern men, is derived from what is called, in certain countries, common law, and here, jurisprudence.

This jurisprudence, or common law, in some nations, is found in the decrees of their courts; in others, it is furnished by private individuals, eminent for their learning and integrity, whose superior wisdom has enabled them to gain the proud distinction of legislating, as it were, for their country, and enforcing their legislation by the most noble of all means: that of reason alone. After a long series of years, it is sometimes difficult to say, whether these opinions and judgments were originally the *effect* of principles, previously existing in society, or whether they were the *cause* of the doctrines, which all men at last recognize. But whether the one or the other, when acquiesced in for ages, their force and effect cannot be distinguished from statutory law. No civilised nation has been without such a system. None, it is believed, can do without it; and every attempt to expel it only causes it to return with increased strength on those, who are so sanguine as to think it may be dispensed with.—*Duponceau on Jurisdiction*, 105.

Spain, who was among the first of the European nations that reduced her laws into codes, and who carried that mode of legislation further than any other people, early felt the necessity of a jurisprudence, which would supply the defects, and soften the asperities of her statutes. The opinions of her jurisconsults seem to have obtained an authority with her, of which the history of no other country offers an example. So early as the fifteenth century, a law was passed regulating the authority which belonged to the opinions of Bartolus, Baldus, Juan Andrea, and Abad. That law was, it is true, afterwards repealed by the first of *Toro*, and directions given that in case of doubt as to the true interpretation of the statutes, recourse should be had to the sovereign himself. What was the practical operation of this last statute, our researches do not enable us positively to state. It does not, however, seem to have made much change in the practice of their courts, for in the year 1713 we find an *auto accordado* in respect to the laws that should be followed in the decision of causes ; in which it is stated, as a great inconvenience, that the tribunals of justice *had resorted to foreign books and authors*, to the depreciation of *their own jurists ;* who, with great knowledge, had explained and interpreted their laws, ordinances, and customs. But admitting that after the promulgation of the law of Toro, the opinions of these jurists had not the weight they before received, and that in all unsettled cases recourse was had to the sovereign himself; when we find that nearly four hundred years after, the writers on the laws of Spain refer to no decision of their king and council on this point, express no doubt about it, and quote the opinions of jurists who wrote nearly the same length of time before them, what conclusion can we come to, but that *no doubt did exist on the subject in Spain.* That the whole nation acquiesced in the opinions of those who had early interpreted their statutes, and that the tacit consent of the sovereign himself must be presumed given to a construction which he had the power to change, but in which it is not shown he made any alteration.—*Novissima Recop.* l. 3, tit. 2 *leyes.* 3 & 11.

It is most clear, then, that this interpretation, which limits the law of the *Partidas* to the gains made in the country where the marriage was contracted, and excludes from its operation property acquired after a change of residence, comes to us recommended and fortified by every sanction that can give it value in the minds of those who sit in judgment; and whose duty it is to pronounce what the law is, and not what it ought to be.

The appellants, however, contend, that, although such may be the construction given to the statute in Spain, that construction is not binding on the Court, because this is a question of jurisprudence not peculiar to any distinct nation, but one touching the comity of nations, and embracing doctrines of international law, on which the opinions of writers not living in Spain are entitled to equal weight with those who professedly treat of her laws.

The strength of the plaintiffs' case rests mainly on this proposition, and it is proper to examine it with the attention which its importance in the cause requires.

But though of importance, it is not of any difficulty. By the comity of nations, a rule does certainly exist, that contracts made in other countries shall be enforced according to the principles of law which govern the contract in the place where it is made. But it also makes a part of the rule, that these contracts should not be enforced to the injury of the state whose aid is required to carry them into effect. It is a corollary flowing from the principle last stated, that where the positive laws of any state prohibit particular contracts from having effect, according to the rules of the country where they are made, the former should control; because that prohibition is supposed to be founded on some reason of utility or policy, advantageous to the country that passes it; which utility or policy would be defeated, if foreign laws were permitted to have a superior effect. On the very subject matter now before us, the writers who treat of it, although disputing about almost every thing else, agree in stating that a *real statute*, that is, one which regulates property within the limits of the state where it is in force, controls *personal* ones, which follow a man wherever he goes; indeed, it has been expressly, and with great propriety, admitted in argument, that where the personal statute of the domicil is in opposition to a real statute of situation, the real statute will prevail.—*Boullenois, Disc. Prelim.* p. 21, *ib. Demis. quest.* 6. 163; *Bouhier sur la Coutume du Duche du Bourgoyne, cap.* 23, 461; *Rodenburgh de Statutor. diversit. tit.* 2, *cap.* 5, *no.* 6.

If this be true, the question whether the opinions of foreign jurists shall control those of the country where the statute is passed, is at once settled. If the right of a nation to pass the statute which will affect a contract made in another country, be admitted, the right cannot be contested to her to say, whether she has done so or not. She is surely the best and safest expounder of her own laws. And we repeat here, what we said a few days since, on nearly the highest authority to which we could refer—"That no court on earth, that professed to be governed by principle, would, we presume, undertake to say, that the Courts of Great Britain, or France, or any other nation, had misunderstood their own statutes, and therefore erect itself into a tribunal by which that misunderstanding was to be corrected."—10 *Wheaton*, 159.

And if we did recur to the jurists of France and Holland for information, what would we get in place of the well-established rules in Spain? Much to confuse, and little to enlighten us. We should find great learning and ingenuity exercised by some to show, that the law which regulates the rights of property among married persons, is a *personal one*, which follows the parties wherever they go. By others, that it is *real*, and limited to the country by which it is made. But not one of them denies the power in a nation to pass a law, such as has been lately enacted by the State of Louisiana, that a married couple moving into it from another state, shall be governed by her laws as to their future acquisitions. None of them professes to comment on the laws of Spain, which her jurists say have the same effect with our late statute. They are not even mentioned by them. How wholly unsatisfactory, therefore, any general reasoning must be on different customs and usages, to prove that the law of the *Fuero* is a *personal* and not a *real* statute, we need not say.

With this view of the subject, we might conclude; but as it is always satisfactory for this court to feel, that the authority which governs it is founded in truth, we shall proceed to examine the grounds on which the opinions of the Spanish jurists have been so strongly assailed. In doing so, we are led into an examination of the doctrine of real and personal statutes, as it is called by the continental writers of Europe; a subject the most intricate and perplexed of any that has occupied the attention of lawyers and courts; one on which scarcely any two writers are found to entirely agree, and on which it is rare to find one consistent with himself throughout. We know of no matter in jurisprudence so unsettled, or none that should more teach men distrust for their own opinions, and charity for those of others.

Holland and France appear to be the countries where the greatest number of these questions have arisen, and where the subject has excited most attention. The doctrine which they denominate that of real and personal statutes, is not, as it might, from the terms used, be supposed, confined to written and positive law; but is applied also, to unwritten laws or customs; by which the state or condition of man is regulated—his contracts governed, or his property distributed at his death. It professes to furnish the rules which are to govern men in civil matters, when they pass from one country to another, and to distinguish and decide in all cases where the law of domicil and that of origin differ; where the rules of the place of contract and its execution conflict; where the countries in which a marriage is contracted and dissolved, have different regulations; or where, on the decease of the owner, his property is situated in several places, having different rules as to its distribution.

According to the jurists of those countries, a personal statute is that which follows and governs the party subject to it wherever he goes.

The real statute controls things, and does not extend beyond the limits of the country from which it derives its authority.

The personal statute of one country controls the personal statute of another country, into which a party once governed by the former, or who may contract under it, should remove.

But it is subject to a real statute of the place, where the person subject to the personal should fix himself, or where the property on which the contest arises may be situated.

So far the rules are plain and intelligible; but the moment we attempt to discover from these writers what statutes are real, and what are personal, the most extraordinary confusion is presented. Their definitions often differ, and when they agree on their definitions, they dispute as to their application.

Bartolus, who was one of the first by whom this subject was

examined, and the most distinguished jurist of his day, established as a rule, that whenever the statute commenced by treating of persons, it was a personal one; but if it began by disposing of things, it was real. So that if a law, as the counsel for the appellants has stated, was written thus: "The estate of the deceased shall be inherited by the eldest son," the statute was real; but if it said, "the eldest son shall inherit the estate," it was personal.

This distinction, though purely verbal, and most unsatisfactory, was followed for a long time, and sanctioned by many whose names are illustrious in the annals of jurisprudence; but it was ultimately discarded by all. D'Argentre, who rejected this rule to real and personal statutes, added a third, which he called mixed. The real statute, according to this writer, is that which treats of immovables—*In quo de rebus soli, id est immobilibus agitur;* and the personal, that which concerns the person abstracted from things—*Statutum personale est illud quod afficit personam universaliter, abstracte ab omni materia reali.* The mixed he states to be one which concerns both persons and things.

This definition of D'Argentre of a personal statute has been adopted by every writer who has treated of this matter. A long list of them, amounting to twenty-five, is given by Froland, in his *memoires concernans la qualites des statuts,* among which are found *Burgundus, Rodenburgh, Stockmans, Voet, and Dumoulin. Froland, Memoires concernans la qualite de Statuts, chap.* 5, *no.* 1.

But the definition which he has given of a real statute, does not seem to have been so generally adopted; it was, however, followed by *Burgundus, Rodenburgh, and Stockmans.*

Boullenois, who is one of the latest writers, attacks the definitions given by D'Argentre, and, as he supposes, refutes them; he adds others, which appear to be as little satisfactory as those he rejects. He divides personal statutes into personal particular and personal universal; and personal particular he subdivides again into pure personal and personal real.—*Boullenois, Traite de la Personalite et de la Realite des Lois, tit.* 1, *cap.* 2, *Obs.* 4.

Voet has two definitions: one, that a real statute is that which affects principally things, though it also relates to persons; and the other, that a personal statute is that which affects principally persons, although it treats also of things.

It would be a painful and a useless task, to follow these authors through all their refinements. President Bouhier, who wrote about the same time as Boullenois, and who has treated the subject as extensively as any other writer, after quoting the definitions just given, and others, says that they are all defective, and that he cannot venture on any, until the world are more agreed what statutes are real and what are personal. While they remain so uncertain, he thinks the best way is to follow the second definition of Voet, which is—"That a real statute is that which does not extend beyond the territory within which it is passed; and a personal is that which does."—*Bouhier sur les Coutumes de Bourgogne, chap.* 23, *no.* 59.

This last mode of distinguishing statutes, which teaches us what effect a statute should have by directing us to inquire what effect it has, is quite as unsatisfactory as the rule given by Bartolus, who judged of it by the words with which it commenced.

The rules given by Chancellor D'Agasseau, are perhaps preferable to any other. "That," says he, "which truly characterises a real statute, and essentially distinguishes it from a personal one, is not that it should be relative to certain personal circumstances, or certain personal events; otherwise we should be obliged to say, that the statutes which relate to the *paternal power, the right of wardship, the tenancy by courtesy* (droit de viduite), *the prohibition of married persons to confer advantages on each other*, are personal statutes; and yet it is clear in our jurisprudence, that they are considered as real statutes, the execution of which is regulated, not by the place of domicil, but by that where the property is situated.

"The true principle in this matter is, to examine if the statute has property directly for its object, *or its destination to certain persons, or its preservation in families*, so that it is not the interest of the person whose rights or acts are examined, but the interest of others to whom it is intended to assure the property, or the real rights which were the cause of the law. Or if, on the contrary, all the attention of the law is directed towards the person, to provide in general for his qualifications or his general and absolute capacity, as when it relates to the qualities of major or minor, of father or of son, legitimate or illegitimate, ability or inability to contract, by reason of personal causes.

"In the first hypothesis the statute is real, in the second it is personal, as is well explained in these words of D'Argentre:—
' Cum statutum non simpliciter inhabilitat, sed ratione fundi aut juris realis alterum respicientus extra personas contrahentes, totas hanc inhabilitatem non egredi locum statuti.' "—*Œuvres D'Agasseau, vol.* 4, 669, *cinquante, quartrieme plaidoyer.*

This definition is, we think, better than any of the rest; though even in the application of it to some cases difficulty would exist. If the subject had been susceptible of clear and positive rules, we may safely believe this illustrious man would not have left it in doubt, for if anything be more remarkable in him than his genius and his knowledge, it is the extraordinary fullness and clearness with which he expresses himself on all questions of jurisprudence. When he, therefore, and so many other men of great talents and learning, are thus found to fail in fixing certain principles, we are forced to conclude that they have failed, not from want of ability, but because the matter was not susceptible of being settled on certain principles. They have attempted to go too far: To define and fix that which cannot in the nature of things be defined and fixed. They seem to have forgotten that they wrote on a question which touched the comity of nations, and that, that comity is, and ever must be, uncertain : That it must necessarily depend on a variety of circumstances, which cannot be reduced within any certain rule : That no nation will suffer the laws of another to interfere with her own, to the injury of her citizens ; that whether they do or not, must depend on the condition of the country in which the foreign law is sought to be enforced—the particular nature of her legislation—her policy—and the character of her institutions : That in the conflict of laws, it must be often a matter of doubt which should prevail, and that whenever that doubt does exist, the court which decides will prefer the law of its own country to that of the stranger.

These principles may be in part illustrated by one or two examples, that we presume will receive general assent.

The writers on this subject, with scarcely any exception, agree that the laws or statutes which regulate minority and majority, and those which fix the state and condition of man, are personal statutes, and follow and govern him in every country.

Now, supposing the case of our law, fixing the age of majority at twenty-five, and the country in which a man was born and lived previous to his coming here, placing it at twenty-one, no objection could be perhaps made to the rule just stated, and it may be, and we believe, would be true, that a contract made here at any time between the two periods already mentioned, would bind him.

But reverse the fact of this case, and suppose, as is the truth, that our law placed the age of majority at twenty-one ; that twenty-five was the period at which a man ceased to be a minor in the country where he resided ; and that at the age of twenty-four he came into this state, and entered into contracts ; would it be permitted that he should in our courts, and to the demand of one of our citizens, plead as a protection against his engagements, the laws of a foreign country, of which the people of Louisiana had no knowledge ; and would we tell them that ignorance of foreign laws in relation to a contract made here, was to prevent them enforcing it, though the agreement was binding by those of their own state ? Most assuredly we would not.—4 *Martin*, 193.

Take another case. By the laws of this country, slavery is permitted, and the rights of the master can be enforced. Suppose the individual subject to it is carried to England or Massachusetts ; would their courts sustain the argument that this state or condition was fixed by the laws of his domicil of origin ? We know they would not.

These examples might be multiplied ; but they are sufficient to explain the ideas of this court, that it is almost impossible to lay down any general rule on the subject ; and that even the personal statutes of one country may be controlled by those of another.

From the various definitions already cited, it may be easily supposed that a vast diversity of opinion existed in their application to the contract of marriage. Both in France and Holland, it has been a subject of great contention; the courts and parliaments of different provinces deciding it differently; some of them considering the law which regulates the rights of parties in the country where the marriage takes place as real, some as personal.

An examination of the different treatises on this subject has convinced us that the greater number of the lawyers of those countries are of opinion, that in settling the rights of husband and wife, on the dissolution of the marriage, to the property acquired, the law of the place where it was contracted, and not that where it was dissolved, must be the guide. Such was the jurisprudence of the parliament of Paris. It was the opinion of Dumoulin, of Boullenois, of Rodenburgh, of Le Brun, of Froland, of Bouhier, of Stockmans, of Pothier, and it is that of Merlin. On the other side are found, D'Argentre, Cravette, Everard, Vandermulen, the Parliament of Rouen, the supreme Court of Brabant, and that of Metz.

But it is evident, the opinions of the greater number of those who think that on the dissolution of the marriage, the law of the place where it was contracted should regulate the rights of the spouses to the property possessed by them, is founded on an idea which first originated with Dumoulin, that where the parties marry without an express contract, they must be presumed to contract in relation to the law of the country where the marriage took place, and that this tacit contract follows them wherever they go.

It is particularly worthy of remark, that Dumoulin, the founder of this system, was of opinion, that the statute regulating the community was real, and that it was to escape from the consequences of this opinion he supposed a tacit contract, which, like an express one, followed the parties wherever they went. Such, at least, was the opinion which Boullenois entertained of Dumoulin's sentiments; and it appears supported by quotations which he makes from his works.—*Boullenois, Traite de personalite et de realite des lois*, Obs. 29, pp. 740, 757, 758.

Some of those who have adopted the conclusions of Dumoulin in regard to the marriage contract, treat the idea of a tacit agreement as one which exists in the imagination alone. But the greater number seem to have embraced it; and we are satisfied it is the main ground on which the doctrine now rests in France. So far, therefore, as great names can give weight to any opinion, it comes to us in a most imposing shape; but to our judgment it is quite unsatisfactory.

Admitting it for a moment to be true, that when parties married there was a tacit contract between them, their rights to property subsequently acquired should be governed by the laws of the country where the marriage took place; that tacit agreement would still be controlled by the positive laws of any country into which they might remove. This is admitted by Dumoulin himself, who, after treating of the tacit agreement, and stating that the statute is not legal but conventional—*Statutarium proprie non este nec legale, sed conventitium*—adds, such tacit convention cannot have this effect in another place where there exists a contrary statute, which is absolute and prohibitive—*alias si statutum csset absolutum et prohibitorium, non obstantibus pactis factis in contrarium; tunc non haberet locum ultra fines sui territorii.*—*Dumoulin on the first book of the Code, verbo conc. de stat. et consuet, loc. Froland, Memoires sur les Statuts, chap.* 4, 63.

If such be the consequence where the statute is prohibitive, we do not see why the same result should not follow from a *real statute,* which regulates things within the limits of the country where it is in force. The reason for both is the same, namely, that the laws of the country where the contract is sought to be enforced, are opposed to it. Why the one should have effect and the other should not, we profess to be unable to distinguish. It may be a question whether the statute is real or not; but the moment it is admitted to be so, it regulates all property acquired within its authority; then, according to the principles of Dumoulin the tacit agreement can no more control it, than it could the law which positively forbade such tacit agreement from having effect. So that even admitting this tacit agreement, we are brought back to the point from which we started; that is, whether the law regulating the right of husband and wife, be real or personal?

But, without agreeing with those who have treated the idea of Dumoulin, as one purely of the imagination, we think that he gives to this tacit consent a much more extended effect than it is entitled to. That in supposing when parties marry, they intend the laws of the place where the contract is made should govern them wherever they go, *he begs the question;* and that the first thing to be settled is, whether these laws do govern them wherever they go.

We are now treating, let it be remembered, of a case such as that before us, where there is no express contract; and the argument is, that the parties not having entered into an express agreement, the presumption must be, they intended their rights to property should be governed by the laws of the country where they married. This is admitted. But then this presumption as to their agreement, cannot be extended so as to give a greater effect to those laws than they really had. If it be true those laws had no effect beyond the limits of the state where they were passed;—then it cannot be true to suppose the parties intended they should have effect beyond them. The extent of the tacit agreement depends on the extent of the law. If it had no force beyond the jurisdiction of the power by which it was enacted; if it was real and not personal, the tacit consent of the parties cannot turn it into a personal statute. They have not said so; and they are presumed to have contracted in relation to the law, such as it was, to *have known its limitations*, as well *as its nature*, and to have had the one as much in view as the other. If the law of Virginia should have been, that for twenty years the acquisitions made by the parties belonged to one of them, and they married without an express stipulation to the contrary, they would be presumed to have contracted in reference to this *limitation of time*. If, on the contrary, the law is *limited as to place*, the tacit agreement which is founded on a supposed consent that the law should govern them, must be considered to have that limitation in view. In one word, the parties are presumed to have agreed that the law should bind them as far as that law extended, but no further. So that this doctrine brings us back again to the inquiry, was the statute real or personal? Did it extend beyond the limits of the country where the marriage took place, or did it not? which ever it may be found to be, the parties must be supposed to have contracted. In the absence of any thing *expressed* to the contrary, we cannot *presume* they intended to enlarge or restrain the operation of the law.

The most familiar way of treating this idea of tacit contracts, being made in relation to the laws of the country where they are entered into, is to say, that the agreement is to be construed the same way as if those laws were inserted in the contract. Now, supposing parties to marry in Louisiana, and that our statute, providing for the community of acquests and gains is real and not personal; that it divides the property acquired while in this state equally between the husband and wife, but does not regulate that which they gain in another country to which they remove; the insertion of this law in a contract would be nothing more than a declaration, that while residing *within this state* there should be a community of acquests and gains. An agreement such as this, could not have the same force as an express one, by which the parties declared there should be a community of acquests and gains *wherever they went;* for the one has no limitation as to place, and the other has. The maxim, therefore, which was so much pressed on us in argument, *taciti et expressi eadem vis*, is only true where the law to which the tacit agreement refers contains the same provisions as the written contract.

It was evidently on this distinction the cases of *Murphy* v. *Murphy*, and *Gales* v. *Davis's heirs*, were differently decided in this court. In the former there was an express contract, that there should be a community of acquests and gains between the parties, *even though they should reside in countries where different laws might prevail.* In the latter there was no express agreement; and the parties were not presumed to have made a tacit one, contrary to the law of the place where they married. They were not supposed to have agreed, that a real statute, which governed them only while there, was to follow them as a personal one, and regulate their property in another state. If principles so plain, required any authority, we would find it in the very author on whom the appellants principally rely. Dumoulin, after stating that the tacit contract will be controlled by a law that is contrary to it, in the country where the marriage is dissolved, adds—that it will be different where the agreement is express : " Nisi expresse de tali lucro conventium fuisset, quia pactio bene extenditur ubique, sed non statutum mere."—*Froland, Memoires sur les statuts, cap.* 4, *p.* 63.

Having thus stated the reasons why this doctrine of a tacit contract cannot be admitted by us to the extent pressed by the counsel, it only remains for us to examine whether the law of the *Fuero* was a real or personal statute. We consider it real. It appears to us to relate to things more than to persons; to have, in the language of D'Aguesseau, the destination of property to certain persons, and its preservation in families, in view. It gives to the wife and her heirs, the one half of that which would otherwise belong to the husband. Boullenois, who rejects Dumoulin's idea of a tacit agreement, says the statute which regulates the community is a personal one, because it fixes the state and condition of the spouses ; and he goes so far as to declare, that if his adversaries will not allow this doctrine to be correct, then the statute is real, for on no other ground can it be considered personal. We think the state and condition of both husband and wife are fixed by the marriage, in relation to everything but property, independent of this law ; and as it regulates property alone, it is not a personal statute.—*Boullenois, Traites des statuts, cap.* 5, *obs.* 29, *p.* 751; *cap.* 2, *obs.* 5, 80.

Upon reason, therefore, but still more clearly on authority, we think the appellants have failed to make out their case. We know of no question better settled in Spanish jurisprudence ; and what is settled there, cannot be considered as unsettled here. The jurisprudence of Spain came to us with her laws. We have no more power to reject the one than the other. The people of Louisiana have the same right to have their cases decided by that jurisprudence, as the subjects of Spain have, except so far as the genius of our government, or our positive legislation, has changed it. How the question would be decided in that country, if an attempt were made there on the authority of French and Dutch courts and lawyers, to make them abandon a road in which they have been travelling for nearly three hundred years, we need not say. The question is sufficiently answered by the *auto*, already cited; in which the adoption of the opinions of foreign jurists, in opposition to those of Spain, is reprobated and forbidden.

We conclude, therefore, that a community of acquests and gains did exist between the insolvent and the mother of the appellees, from the time of their removal into this state; and that the court below committed no error, in placing them on the bilan as privileged creditors, for the amount of those acquests which remained in their father's possession at the dissolution of the marriage.

INDEX.

A.

Acceptance. *See* Bill of Exchange.

Acquisition of Property by Foreigners, 407. *See* Property.

Admiralty (High Court of), Jurisdiction over Maritime Contracts, &c., 446. In Causes of Possession between Foreigners, 580.

Adoption, *status* and rights flowing from, 356.

Æneas Macdonald, Case of, referred to, 23.

Agent, Contracts entered into by means of, effects of, 502. (*See* Obligation.) Ratification of Contracts made by, 506. Opinion of Savigny on Contracts by, 508. Rights and powers of Master of Ship as Agent of Owners, 582.

Agreements (written), proof of, 442. *See* Contracts.

Alienation of Property by or to Foreigners, 407. (*See* Property.)

Alien, application of English Law to, with respect to Marriage and Wife's Dowry, 306. (*See* Settlement) That he has the rights of an English Patentee. (*See* Addenda.) When domiciled and naturalized in England, he is under same disabilities as a Native-born subject. (*See* Addenda.)

Ambassador, Necessary *domicil* of, 119. Privileges of, imparted to his *family and suite*, 120. Not to *strangers, ib.* Domicil of *origin* not changed by residence in *house* of, 126.

Ambassadors, Peculiar status and privileges of, from Civil and Criminal Law of Foreign Country, 652.

America (United States of North), Doctrine adopted by, respecting *Personal Status* of Foreigner, 244, 250. (*See* Status.) Difference between Laws of, and those of France, respecting Foreign Marriages, 277. (*See* Marriage.) Law of, as to effect of Marriage on *property* of parties, 299. (*See* Property.) Law of, respecting Divorce, 326. (*See* Divorce.) Propositions of, as to Law governing Contracts, 504. (*See* Contracts, Obligations.) Maritime Law of (*See* Maritime Law). Law of, on the subject of Foreign Bankruptcy, 553. Effect given by, to sentences and judgments of Foreign Tribunals, 690.

Ancillary Guardians, Appointment of, 383. *See* Guardian.

Anglo-Indian Officer, Domicil of, 100. (*See* Officer.)

Anjou (Duchess of), Claim of, to the Goods of the Dowager Queen Henrietta Maria, 38. 61.

Annandale (Lord), Case of, 93. 113. 172.

Appeal, limitation of time within which it must be instituted, 670.

Appendix—

To Chapter on Domicil. List of *Writers,* and French *decisions* on the subject, 215.

To Chapter on Statutes. Chapter from *Bartolus,* " De Summa Trinitate— Babrica lex Prima," 240.

To Chapter on International Copyright. Case of *Jeffreys* v. *Boosey,* 405.

To Chapter xxx., on *Obligations.* Extract from Dictionary of Greek and Roman Antiquities, 431.

To Chapter xxxii., on *Obligations.* Extract from " Chitty on Contracts," 451.

To Chapter xli., " Lex Mercatoriâ." Extract from " Merchant Shipping Act," (17 & 18 Vict. c. 104), 601.

To Chapter xlii., " Bills of Exchange," &c.—1. Extract from French Code du Commerce, 619. 2. Judgment of the Supreme Court of Pennsylvania, 621.

To Chapter on " Foreign Judgments."

Foreign Courts (*continued*).
  Procedure, when adjudicating on matters connected with or between subjects of another State, 653. Rules of Evidence to be adopted by, *ib.* Proof of Foreign Judgments, Decrees, &c. before, *ib.* Effect of Judgment and Sentences of, in Tribunals of other States, 671.
Foreign Divorce. (*See* Divorce.)
—— Domicil, effect of, wi'h respect to Privileges of Divorce (*See* Divorce.)
Foreign Guardian. (*See* Guardian.)
—— Laws, Application of, to Foreigners resident in another State. (*See* Comity, &c.) Proof of, 657. What kind of Evidence necessary, *ib.*
Foreign Marriage. (*See* Marriage.)
—— Nobleman, Privileges and Rights of, in Foreign State, 257.
Foreign Sentence (or Judgment). (*See* Sentence, Divorce, &c)
Foreign Ships, Rules of English Maritime Law as to Navigation not applicable to, 581.
Foreign State, Military or Naval Officer stationed in, Domicil of, 115. Citizenship in, a criterion of Domicil, 177. Property of Bankrupt in, 557. Right of Assignees over ditto, *ib.* (*See* Bankruptcy); Competency of Tribunals of, to adjudicate over matters between Subjects of another State, 644, &c.
Forum Competens over Matters or Suits between *Foreigners*, &c., 641.
France, Doctrines of, respecting application of Law of Domicil and Origin, 29. Cases decided in, upon the Domicil of Foreigners, 215. 228. *Doctrine* of, as to *Status* of Foreigners, 246. Law of, respecting Marriage (*See* Marriage). As to effect of Marriage on Property of Parties, 298 (*See* Property, &c.). Code of, respecting Divorce, 325. Law of, prohibiting Divorce, 329 (*See* Divorce). Law of, as to *Rights of Property moveable* and *immoveable*, 390. 394. Provisions of *French Code* on the subject of *Contracts* and *Obligations*, 449. On the Conflict of Laws in relation to them, 462, 477. On the Validity, Nature, and Interpretation of Obligations, 483. Law of, on the subject of Bankruptcy, 551. Exception of, from other States, as regards the administration of Justice to Foreigners, 645. Competency of Tribunals of, to adjudicate over Foreigners, 645. 651. Effect given by, to Judgments of Foreign Tribunals, 675.

G.

Gage. (*See* Mortgage or Hypothecation.)
Gassion (*Marquis* de), Case of the, 115.
General Average (*See* Maritime Law). Loss of Goods, Apportionment of Loss among all Owners of Cargo, &c., 593. What Law governs the Liability of Underwriters, *ib.*
Germany, Law of, respecting Mortgage or Hypothecation of Real Property, 535. Law of, respecting Bills of Exchange, 607.
Gifts (between *Husband and Wife*), Prohibitory Laws as to, 318. (*See* Marriage.)
Gipsies, have they a Domicil? 55.
Guardian of Minor, Power of, to change Domicil of Minor, 73. Of Lunatic, 91. (*See* Lunatic.) Foreign, 374. Choice and Constitution of, *ib.* Jurisprudence of Kingdom of Two Sicilies, respecting Foreign Guardian, 376. Guardian duly constituted should be recognized by all Countries, 377. Power of Guardian over the *Person* of the Ward, *ib.* Jurisprudence of England and North American United States, *ib.* Guardianship by Nature, 378 ; by Socage, *ib.*; for Nurture, 379. Power of, over *Property* of Ward, 380. Distinction between *moveable* and *immoveable* Property in Foreign Land, *ib.* Foreign Guardian and *moveable* Property in another Country, 381. Power of, over *immoveable* Property of Ward, 383. Opinion of *Savigny* and *Law of Prussia* respecting *immoveable* Property in Foreign Land, 384. Appointment of auxiliary or subordinate Curators or Guardians, 380. Obligation to undertake Office of, &c., 385. Guardian or Committee of *Lunatic*, 386. Guardianship of Prodigal, *ib.* Effect of *Commission of Lunacy* in Foreign Country, 386, 387.
Guise (Duke of), Case of the, 115.

H.

Hanover, Law of, respecting Marriages, 283. (*See* Marriage.)
Hardwicke (Lord Chancellor), Decision of, on the question of Domicil, 39.
Hautefort (Marquis de), Case of, referred to, 184.
Henry, Judgment in *Odwin* v. *Forbes*, 20. 47. 253.
Heresy, Incapacity arising from, by Do-

sent of Obligee, but by operation of Law, 567; effect of, *Cessio bonorum*, under old Roman Law, 567. By *Certificate of Bankruptcy, ib.*; effect of Bankruptcy as a *bar* to action for debt brought in a Foreign Country, 569. Discharge by *Prescription*, 570. Discharge by *tender* and *refusal*, 577 ; upon Bills of Exchange, &c. (*See Bills of Exchange.*) Between Owner and Master of Ship, 578.

Obligee, Transfer of Obligation by, 544. Assignee of, his right to priority of Lien, 546. Creditor or Trustee of, Priority of Lien of, 546.

Origo or Origin. (*See* Origin.)

Origin. Definition of, 24. Its application respecting Status of Individuals, *ib.* Different effect of, in Roman and Modern Jurisprudence, *ib.* As applied by the *Roman Law*, 26. Savigny's Opinion respecting, not exactly correct, *ib.* Obligations and Ties on Individuals arising from, *ib.* Indelible Incapacity imposed on Individuals by Country of, to do certain acts, 23. What personal law to which individual subject, *origin* or *domicil*, 29. Doctrines of France and England respecting, *ib.* Not changed by residence in *house* of Ambassador *abroad*, or within lines of an Army quartered *abroad*, 126. (*See* Domicil.) Domicil of, 141. Change of Domicil of, *ib.* (*See* Domicil.) Place of, a criterion of *Domicil*, 143. Whether law of, governs *personal Status* of Individual, 244.

Officer (Public). *Necessary Domicil of*, 98. *Military* and *Naval*, 100. In East India Company's Service, *ib.* In Foreign Service, 111. In Service of his own Country, but stationed in *Foreign Country*, 115. On half pay, 118.

Owners (of Ship), Liability of, in cases of Collision, and for *Acts and Contracts* of Master, 583. (*See* Maritime Law, &c.)

P.

Papers, Depository of, Place of, a criterion of Domicil, 175. (*See* Domicil.)

Parents, Rights and Powers of, over the person of the Child, 351. When in Foreign Country, by what Law governed, *ib.* Practice of Continental States, *ib.* ; of England respecting Authority of *Foreign* Parent over Child while in England, 352. Rights and Powers of, over *Property* of Child, *ib.* As affecting *moveable* and *immoveable* Property, 354. Opinions of Continental Jurists as to, *ib.* ; of English Courts, *ib.* Power of contracting to legitimatize Children born out of Wedlock, 364.

Partnership. Liability of Partners, 529. *Double*—Rights of Creditors to *double* proof, 556. (*See* Bankruptcy.)

Patent Rights. Granted by Sovereign, 398. May be assigned, *ib.* Grant of *licenses* to use, *ib.* Right of Foreigner to be Assignee of Patent, *ib.* Do not extend beyond territorial limits of *State* granting them, 399. Not recognized by Foreign State, *ib.* Frenchmen making or counterfeiting subjects of a Patent granted by a Foreign State, *ib.* Frenchmen using *stamp* or *goods mark* of Foreign Manufacturer, *ib.* *Provisional* measures of Law for preventing Infringement of, 699.

Paternal Rights. (*See* Parents.)

Personal Statutes, 233. 236. (*See* Statutes.)
—— Status, What Law shall govern, 244; How determinable, 245.

Personal Property of Wife. (*See* Property.)

Phillimore (Dr. R.), Letter to Lord Ashburton, as to the case of *the Creole*, 14.

Piracy of Foreign *Trade marks*, 417.

Plan of the Work described, 21.

Positive Laws of States. When *Legal Relation of Foreigner* in contact with *divers*, which Law should be applied, 22. How ascertained, *ib.* By reference to origin of Individual, *ib.* To domicil of, *ib.* To Acts of, *ib.* To Property of, *ib.* (*See* Origin, Domicil, Property.) The *jus personarum* or status of Foreigner, 229. Statutes, and their effects, 233.

Prescription (*See* Obligations). Laws of different Countries relating to, 570. *Discharge* of *Obligations* by, *ib.* Law of which Country governs the operation of, when Obligation created in one Country, but sought to be enforced in *another*, 570. Various systems adopted, 575. When pleaded in *bar* to action before Foreign Tribunal, 669.

Prisoner (The), Necessary Domicil of, 128.

Private Injuries. (*See* Injuries.)

Private International Law. (*See* Comity, &c.) References to Writers, and Decisions upon, 18.

Procedure (Law of). In Foreign Courts : where Foreign Court adjudicating in matters connected with or between Sub-

Russia, Law of, as to the *status* of Foreigners, &c., 249. Respecting Marriages, 283. (*See* Marriage.)

S.

Sailors, Domicil of, 146.

Saint Pater (*Marquis de*), Case of, referred to, 173, 174.

Sardinia, Law of, respecting Marriages, 284. See Marriage. Code of, respecting *Obligations* and *Contracts*, and a Conflict of Laws in reference thereto, 464.

Sautereau (Nicholas), Case of, 95.

Savigny, Opinion of, as to what Laws govern the *acquisition* and *alienation* of Property, 409.

Saxony, Law of, respecting *Marriages* of Foreigners and Subjects, 282. (*See* Marriage.)

Schleswig, Law of, respecting *Marriages*, 283. (*See* Marriage.)

Scotland, Law of, respecting Divorce, 325. of English Marriages, 325. 342. Law of, as to Property and Succession, 393. Law of, as to *form* of Testaments, in accordance with European Laws, and at variance with English Law. (*See* Addenda.)

Seafaring Men. (*See* Sailors.)

Sentence (or Judgment).

Foreign Sentence of Divorce, 322. Effect of, 322. By what Tribunal should be pronounced, *ib.* What Law Foreign State should apply, 327. Recognition of, by other States, 336. (*See* Divorce, &c.) Proof of Foreign Judgment or Decree before Foreign Tribunal, 653. 671. English Statute as to the proof of, in English Courts, 656; Chapter on, 671. Practice of *Comity* as to the reception of, *ib.* Effect given to, by

Statute of Frauds, Operation of, as to Contracts and Obligations, 443. (*See* Contracts.)

Statute of Limitations, Effect of, as Discharge of Obligation. (*See* Obligation, Prescription.)

Story on the subject of the personal Status of Foreigners, 251. On Foreign Marriages, 285. On English Marriages abroad, 288.

Student (the), Necessary Domicil of, 90.

Succession, *Rights relating to*, 625.

What *forum* has jurisdiction over whole question of,—that of the *situs* or that of the *Domicil*, 626. What Law shall govern? *ib*. As to *testamentary succession* and *succession ab intestato* generally, 627. As to *capacity* of Testator, *ib*.

Form of Testament, *ib*. Change of Domicil after execution of Testament, 628. As to the *dispositions* contained in the Testament, 630. *Moveable* and immoveable Property, *ib*. Foreign Will and *English moveable* Property, 631. Construction and interpretation of Testaments and Testamentary Papers, *ib*. Adoption of *Foreign Law* by Courts of Judicature, *ib*. But *not* of Foreign rules of Evidence, 632. As to what *class* or *description* of Persons shall take under some particular denomination, 634.

Successions ab intestato. How affected by Statutes, 236. (*See* Statutes.) In the case of *moveable Property*, 634. What Law shall govern as to, *ib*. Persons entitled to distribution, *ib*. What portion of estate primarily chargeable with debt, 635. Distribution, &c., immoveable Property, *ib*. *Currency* in which Legacies payable, *ib*. *Interest* payable on Legacies, *ib*. Interpretation of Testaments, *ib*. As to *duties* payable on Successions, *ib*.

Sweden, Marriage Laws of, 283. (*See* Marriage.)

T.

Taxes, Payment of, a criterion of Domicil, 175. (*See* Domicil.)

Tender, Effect of, as *Discharge* of Obligation, 577. (*See* Obligation.)

Tenterden's (Lord) Act (9 Geo. 4, c. 19), preventing evasion of Statute of Frauds, respecting Contracts, 445.

Testaments, How effected by Statute Law, 235. (*See* Statutes.) Capacity to make, 627. Form of, &c. (*See* Succession, Will, &c.)

Testamentary Papers, Construction of, 631. By Foreign Courts, *ib*. (*See* Succession, Will, &c.) Scotch Law, as to the form of, in accordance with European, but at variance with English law. (*See* Addenda.)

Testamentary Succession. (*See* Succession.)

Testator. (*See* Succession, Will, &c.)

Thurlow (Lord Chancellor), Decision of, on the question of Domicil, 39.

Time, *Length of, as a Resident*, a criterion of Domicil, 185.

Trade, House of, the place of, a criterion of Domicil, 165.